Acclaim for EDMUND WHITE*'s*

The Farewell Symphony

"White's prose style is at its best . . . filled with perfectly pitched descriptions. . . . *The Farewell Symphony* is about the page-by-page brilliance of White's elegant and honest voice."
　　　　　　　　　　　　　　　　　　　　　—*Boston Globe*

"Ambitious and elegiac . . . vivid and variegated . . . [White's] voice . . . is textured and rich, an ever-replenishing reservoir of fresh images and elegant phrasing."
　　　　　　　　　　　　　　　—*Los Angeles Times Book Review*

"A jolting novel. Mr. White writes about love as sex, sex as love, with candor that eventuates in often alarming honesty. Yet sympathy and compassion are his vital resources, and his novel . . . leaves you not sad or bitter, but actually quite wondrous of life."
　　　　　　　　　　　　　　　　　　　　　—Richard Ford

"Engagingly bittersweet. . . . White's writing modulates from rich lyricism . . . to the flat factuality of the cruiser's life."
　　　　　　　　　　　　　　—*The New York Times Book Review*

"Rife with brilliance. . . . No one writing in English today may turn out more striking metaphors as consistently as White."
　　　　　　　　　　　　　　　　　　—*Cleveland Plain Dealer*

EDMUND WHITE

The Farewell Symphony

Edmund White was born in Cincinnati in 1940. He has taught literature and creative writing at Yale, Johns Hopkins, New York University, and Columbia; was a full professor of English at Brown; and served as executive director of the New York Institute for the Humanities. In 1983 he received a Guggenheim Fellowship and the Award for Literature from the National Academy of Arts and Letters. In 1993 he was made a Chevalier de l'Ordre des Arts et Lettres. For his last book, *Genet: A Biography* (1993), he was awarded the National Book Critics Circle Award and the Lambda Literary Award. His other books include *Forgetting Elena, Nocturnes for the King of Naples, States of Desire: Travels in Gay America, A Boy's Own Story, Caracole,* and *The Beautiful Room Is Empty*. He lives in Paris.

Also by EDMUND WHITE

FICTION

Skinned Alive

The Beautiful Room Is Empty

The Darker Proof: Stories from a Crisis
(with Adam Mars-Jones)

Caracole

A Boy's Own Story

Nocturnes for the King of Naples

Forgetting Elena

NONFICTION

Our Paris: Sketches from Memory
(with Hubert Sorin)

The Burning Library

Genet: A Biography

The Joy of Gay Sex
(with Dr. Charles Silverstein)

States of Desire: Travels in Gay America

The
Farewell
Symphony

The
Farewell
Symphony

EDMUND WHITE

VINTAGE INTERNATIONAL

Vintage Books A Division of Random House, Inc. New York

FIRST VINTAGE INTERNATIONAL EDITION, SEPTEMBER 1998

Copyright © 1997 by Edmund White

All rights reserved under International and Pan-American
Copyright Conventions. Published in the United States by Vintage
Books, a division of Random House, Inc., New York, and in Canada by
Random House of Canada Limited, Toronto. Originally published
in Great Britain by Chatto & Windus Ltd., London, in 1997.
First published in hardcover in the United States by
Alfred A. Knopf, Inc., New York, in 1997.

Parts of this book have appeared in a different form
in *The New Yorker* and *Ploughshares*.

The Library of Congress has cataloged
the Knopf edition as follows:

White, Edmund, 1940–
The farewell symphony : a novel / Edmund White.
p. cm.
ISBN 0-679-43477-1 (hc).
I. Gay men—United States—Fiction.
II. Autobiographical fiction.
PS3573.H463F37   1997
813'.54—dc21   97-73825

Vintage ISBN 0-679-75476-8

Author photograph © Jerry Bauer

Random House Web address: www.randomhouse.com

Printed in the United States of America
10 9 8 7 6 5 4

To Michael Carroll

The Farewell Symphony is an autobiographical novel. Although its action parallels many of the events in my life, it is not a literal transcription of my experience. The characters are stylized versions, often composites, of people I knew in those years. Sometimes I have used Proust's method of merging or mitosis, i.e. condensing two people into one or distributing the traits of one person over two or more characters. These changes have been made to protect the privacy of people living—and of the numerous dead—but also to give a coherent shape to so many destinies.

Only those who are sad
or else have been sad at some time
need bother with my works.
Qui no és trist, de mos dictats no cur
(o en algun temps que sia trist estat).

—AUSIÀS MARCH,
fifteenth-century Catalan poet

The author thanks The Rockefeller Institute at Bellagio, where many pages of this book were written. He also expresses his gratitude to Jonathan Burnham at Chatto and George Andreou at Knopf for their sensitive, detailed and useful responses to this work, and to Alex Jeffers for typing it. He specially thanks Holly Ely for a close reading.

The

Farewell

Symphony

ONE

I'm beginning this book on All Saints' Day in Paris, six months after Brice's death. This morning I went with Brice's brother and his brother's lover to the Père Lachaise cemetery to leave some flowers before the white marble plaque that marks the niche where Brice's ashes are stored in an urn. At first there wasn't a receptacle for the flowers and we'd just leave them on the cold floor, where they'd quickly wilt. But then someone—the Spanish woman who cleaned for us once a week, perhaps—attached a little brass vase to the plaque, and that's where we put the flowers now. Today I left yellow freesias. Someone had Scotchtaped the photo of a young man to Brice's plaque and I wondered if it was a secret admirer who'd left his own portrait; retrospectively I was jealous. Maybe it was a photo of one of the other dead young men that had been taped to our plaque by mistake.

The ashes are in the columbarium, a fancy word for "dovecote." We wanted to be buried together, but since technically I'm not a Parisian, there was no way I could buy a plot or a niche at Père Lachaise, which is reserved for citizens of the capital. Brice thought of everything in his methodical way; he bought the niche for his urn but in my name. Now, legally, I can't be refused entrance when I die.

I've never liked to feel things in the appropriate way at the right moment. I know that Brice's brother is slightly puzzled that I don't visit the long, subterranean corridors of the columbarium more often. Even today I was dry-eyed, bored, more curious about the new plaques than anguished about Brice's. The day Brice was interred, there were only four other niches occupied along this whole wall. Now it's filling up quickly—at least two hundred newcomers have arrived in the last six months. Some are Vietnamese and their inscriptions are in both French and in Chinese characters. A few are young men in their twenties—I imagine they died of AIDS, too. There are Jews and Protestants as well as Catholics; Poles and Italians as well as French. There's even an American writer shelved just above Brice; he's had inscribed the words "Writer-Ecrivain" just below his name.

It's not that Brice's brother Laurent doubts my grief. He saw me six months ago, sitting on the curb just outside the funeral home, sobbing. We'd just made all the arrangements for the cremation and now I was crying like a Sicilian widow.

I'd been afraid I wouldn't feel anything when Brice finally died—but my body did all the feeling for me. It took over. My knees buckled, I lost my balance, tears spurted from my eyes. I staggered in the sunlight and nearly fell and had to be held up by Laurent and his lover.

Everything I'd lived through in the last five years had changed me—whitened my hair, made me a fat, sleepy old man, matured me, finally, but also emptied me out. I met Brice five years before he died—but I wonder whether I'll have the courage to tell his story in this book. The French call a love affair a "story," *une histoire,* and I see getting to it, putting it down, exploring it, *narrating* it as a challenge I may well fail. If I do fail, don't blame me. Understand that even writers, those professional exhibitionists, have their moments of reticence.

STRANGE THAT I should be living here, in Paris. Ever since I'd been a child, an imaginary Paris had been the bright planet pulsing at the heart of my mental star map, but the one time I'd gone to Paris I had been dressed in a horrible shiny blazer and everyone in the cafés had laughed at me. I said to a French acquaintance as we left the Flore, "I know I'm being paranoid," but he said matter-of-factly, "No, they *are* laughing at you."

A sign in the tailor shop window off the Boulevard St.-Germain warned that customers would not be allowed more than three fittings after the purchase of a suit and my mind winced at this proof of shame-less male vanity, so exotic to an American since Americans equated male vanity with effeminacy or Mafia creepiness. The year was 1968 and styl-ish young American men back home were wearing fringe and puffy-sleeved pirate shirts, headbands, mirrored vests and winklepicker boots, but the materials were synthetic, the colors garish, the fit very approxi-mate and the mood one of dressing up. Orange and black were popular colors. The long Mardi Gras of that decade in the States was a mockery of traditional good taste, a send-up of adult propriety, the recklessness of a generation that would never settle down long enough to study the fine gradations with which quality, and especially beauty, begin. And if the mood was festive, the festivity seemed more a gesture defying parental drabness than an assertion of a new-born hedonism. A true search for pleasure is an exacting science and is born from a profound interest in raglan versus fitted sleeves and in the precise arc a weighted hem on the bias will describe.

In 1968, Paris, despite Malraux's clean-up efforts, had not yet been converted into the triumphant, international capital it was to become in the eighties, a city gleaming with spotlit, steam-cleaned façades and newly built monuments (arch, pyramid, circular opera house). Back then it seemed a dim anthill. The Marais, which is now the chic gay ghetto, was then a dilapidated quarter of garment workers surging through the cold rain, a populous slum swarming over seventeenth-century aristo-cratic houses, a neon-lit sweatshop glimpsed through soot-streaked shut-ters, the old carved wood doors replaced by undulating tin barricades, a pitiful line of laundry strung across a *cour d'honneur* spouting crabgrass.

I was traveling with Jamie, a New York blueblood who shared an office with me. Although we'd talked about love and Wallace Stevens and T.S. Eliot and even Keats for hours back in New York in our Midtown office on the thirty-second floor, in Paris Jamie was irritatingly brittle and philis-tine and I began to despise him until we visited the Sainte Chapelle one morning. As we stood there beneath the soaring stained-glass windows, our feet dappled by the reds and yellows, I noticed that his face was glassy with tears at so much beauty and I liked him all over again. Somehow he had come by an introduction to another American, an American baron in Paris, gay like us, though Jamie had yet to tell me in so many words that he really was himself homosexual. This expatriate, Mr. Boulton, had cre-ated such a successful public relations campaign for Liechtenstein that he'd been made a papal baron, his fondest wish, and now he'd inscribed his coat of arms on his calling cards, his black velvet slippers and the chauffeur's door of his portly old Rolls.

Jamie, always in search of a bargain, had found us a smelly little Latin Quarter hotel that had nothing English about it except its name, the At Home. The proprietors were a minuscule, slippered couple who smoked Gauloises, drank red wine in the morning and, by all olfactory evidence, seldom bathed. They were Communists and looked at us with genuine class hatred the afternoon Mr. Boulton's chauffeur dropped a card on us, inviting us to dinner two days hence. Nothing could have been less in keeping with the times. A month later would be May, 1968, the moment when French students and workers would revolt and transform their society. Already the signs were everywhere, including the anti-American slogans scrawled in spray paint along the embankments of the Seine.

Mr. Boulton's nine other dinner guests were all French and all male. They switched seamlessly into perfect English whenever the two black servants, an old couple from the Antilles, entered to clear, but otherwise they crackled away in the lightest, most luxurious and incomprehensible French. The fifty-year-old man next to me, owner of a cosmetics firm, starved exquisitely thin, who left early before even the cheese was served (as he explained, in order to keep his figure and ensure his beauty sleep), thrilled his friends with his account of his weekend with an American Marine hitchhiker he'd picked up as he was driving back up to Paris from his château near Sancerre. Not that I knew what he was saying at the time; over dinner I'd merely tilted my mouth into and out of a variety of knowing or approving smiles and raised and lowered my eyebrows in a perfect hydraulics of feigned sympathy as his hands and voice expressed so much to everyone but me and won him gasps, laughter and quick, excited intakes of breath. Even Jamie understood more than I did.

After dinner, as everyone was standing around sipping bad brandy that came from the American baron's own vineyard, Jamie filled me in. I felt all the more crestfallen. Not only could I not contribute to or even follow the conversation, I wasn't masculine or handsome enough to provoke the sort of interest the Marine had awakened. The French, apparently, liked their Americans big, butch and dumb. I had read Proust but in English, which left me with the longing but not the language needed to shine in a Paris salon. Now I saw I'd have had better luck if I'd shaved my head and worn fatigues to dinner, anything rather than the shabby blazer I was still paying for on-time, with its buttons already shedding their gilt to reveal the tin underneath. I hated my shaggy haircut, my bad shoes, my limping tongue. A dashing young Parisian whose jacket sleeves were unbuttoned and rolled up like Cocteau's found himself trapped beside me for a moment on a small couch covered with pink velvet. In a characteristic American rush of confession, I said to him, "You know, it's so embarrassing not being able to speak French. I've never felt such an idiot. And the worst of it is I can read French perfectly well."

"Unfortunately we're not reading anything tonight," he said coldly.

An immense silence installed itself as I felt my smile dry and harden on my lips like spilled wax. I'd learned the day before that the French ascribe social silence to the unseen passage of angels; now I said, "*Un ange passe,*" and he said, "Very witty," and fled to an amusing group of friends he'd finally spotted.

I stood up and dropped my drained glass on the marble floor and awoke the next morning in my hotel room to discover I was terribly ill. I had a high fever and was so nauseous that even the smell of the café au lait the maid brought to our room sickened me. Jamie, who was being psychoanalyzed, decided I was "resisting" Paris.

I swooned into deep, uncomfortable sleeps, soaked my sheets through, pushed away the croissant that marked yet another morning. The sympathetic but sharp eyes of the maid frightened me because I feared she would deduce I had an incurable and highly infectious disease. She kept up a sprightly monologue as she made the bed and plumped the pillows; I sat on the only chair, smiled weakly, too feeble to care about much except returning to sleep, afraid she might denounce me to the Stalinist proprietors downstairs. Once she was gone I turned fitfully on a spit of dreams basted by the sounds of Paris—the bells, the passing conversations, always about money, the click of heels, the rain dripping from a choked gutter like a hypnotist's patter. . . . Somewhere, far from here, near the Arc de Triomphe, Odette was presiding over a salon beside a winter garden filled with white orchids that glowed palely under snow just beginning to fall and to stencil in ermine the iron casements holding the immense clear, cold panes.

Or so I thought, not knowing that the month was April, not February, and that the coming revolution of students and workers would eradicate the last traces of the Belle Epoque. I had a rare capacity for sleeping through history. In my infrequent moments of lucidity I'd contemplate, then achieve, a transit to the foul-smelling toilet in the hall. Since I'd stopped eating, nothing much was coming out of my body, except one day I noticed—despite the feeble light in the water closet that was turned on automatically only when the lock slid shut—that I'd produced a single rabbit pellet, shockingly white.

Jamie was intent on not humoring me, a policy that happened to fit in nicely with an affair he was apparently having with a Parisian, since he came back to the At Home now only to shave, give himself a maid's bath from the sink in our room and change his shirt, stockings and underwear. He was tinnily cheerful, as though afraid he might take pity on me. I asked him to get me a hard-boiled egg from the bar downstairs, given that was the only thing I could imagine eating. We were on the third floor and I didn't think I could negotiate so many stairs or even dress myself. With a shrug he agreed to indulge my hypochondria just this once.

One day, I don't know which, I did dress and go down to a Vietnamese restaurant in the street. I felt old and refined in my shabby clothes that hung loosely on me. I ordered something that turned out to be a lovely soup strangely perfumed, perhaps with citronelle and coriander. Paris seemed dangerously foreign; I knew that if I collapsed in a foaming fit I'd just be nudged out to the curb by an expensive little boot.

As soon as I was back in my room I plunged down through warm, brackish tides to wrest one small yellow pearl from the depths but it was poison, the sea heavy, my oxygen supply compromised. For a long time I was dragged across the shingle, my battered body wound and unwound on a bobbin of white water.

Then I woke up, perhaps it was midnight, my fever was in remission. I was clear-headed and in a panic. I knew that if I didn't do something now I might never emerge from sea-racked dreams. I showered, dressed and descended into the empty streets. Somehow I'd just assumed cabs would be cruising here as in any New York neighborhood. Finally I saw a de- serted taxi stand and three people in line ahead of me. Half an hour later I told the driver to take me to the American Hospital—far away in Neuilly, as it turned out. No one but a nurse was awake, but finally an English doctor was aroused. He examined and informed me I had "glandular fever"; had I known what this meant, I would have told him I had already had mononucleosis, the kissing disease. I said I suspected I had hepatitis.

"Oh, nonsense," he yawned. "The shellfish is perfectly good in France."

"But you can get it from sex, too," I said, "and lots of people in New York are coming down with it."

He said he seriously doubted my diagnosis, but a day later I jaundiced. When I went back to Neuilly with my yellow face he said, "But hepatitis isn't a serious disease. Just don't visit more than one museum a day. No reason to cut short your holiday."

In fact there was one museum I wanted to visit before flying home, the Musée Guimet of Oriental art. In college my favorite course had been Buddhist Art and half the things we'd studied had been slides of sculptures from the Guimet. As I struggled up the endless marble staircase I couldn't help but remember Bergotte, the novelist in Proust, who pays a dying visit to a Vermeer exhibit and collapses after seeing a little patch of yellow wall, presumably in the *View of Delft*. My goal was a Bodhisattva of the Sui dynasty, a slender figure in hesitant *contrapposto*, the tenderly modeled body girdled by a low chain over a pleatless gown, a long pearl necklace dangling like a flapper's to a point below the knees. The face was undeniably worldly (after all, the stretched-out ears revealed that the saintly Gautama had once been Siddhartha, a prince who'd worn heavily jeweled earrings), but it was sacred, if to be sacred meant to be Nothing at all. Of course the sculpture wasn't there or was in storage and I wandered, jaundiced, through acres of bad blue and white Ching pottery.

⟶ WHEN I FLEW back to New York, I was the color of old teeth and so thin and indifferent that everyone at the airport spoke to me in French. My doctor in New York hospitalized me. After eleven days he released me and I went home. He prescribed two months of bed rest, six months of sexual abstinence, a year without drink.

At that time I was living alone in the West Village in a ground-floor apartment. Before my illness I'd regarded it as just a pit stop where I'd shower, eat and change before rushing out again into the night to one of the nearby bars. If I came home at two or three in the morning without a trick my heart would pound. I was that afraid of being alone.

But now hepatitis restored me to my adolescence. My gym-built body dwindled back into boyish slimness, my ears stood out from my head. Forbidden sex and drink, I spent whole days and nights alone. I shuffled from the Pullman kitchen to the kidney-shaped couch, took several naps a day, received friends who arrived with groceries or laundry, let a book fall from my hands, contemplated walking to the corner store, listened to the radio. The couch and two armchairs my mother had given me from our old apartment; the bed I'd bought for fifty dollars from the warehouse. Until now I'd never felt at home here. The floor had seemed raked to tip the action up at an angle so as to be readily visible to the audience. As the subway rattled I felt the walls might tumble, leaving me naked in a spotlit shower or asleep in the shadowy arms of yet another lover. I read everything, surrounded by the mildly bleak coziness of my couch, comforter, tea and toast. The walls began to thicken, the place to seem authentic. Until now the volumes of Proust had always been like an invitation to a party I was about to attend, but now that I'd gone to Paris and suffered social disgrace, I read *Remembrance of Things Past* as a history of past lives rather than as a map leading to my future.

I was depressed, no doubt mainly because my liver was functioning badly but also partially because my curtailed and disastrous holiday and the long stay at home had broken my usual pace. As my face slowly whitened and my feces slowly darkened, I stood back and evaluated what I'd accomplished in almost thirty years of life.

I'd written five novels, but no one wanted to publish them, and four full-length plays, but no one wanted to perform them. I kept on writing almost every night in my office. I'd leave with the other employees at the end of the work day, eat a solitary dinner, then come back to the deserted thirty-second floor and write while looking out on the glittering city of empty skyscrapers. (Now that I make my living as a writer I'm glad those novels were never published.)

I'd been to two psychiatrists for several years each but I'd neither gone straight, as I'd hoped, nor accepted my homosexuality, as I'd feared. My job I despised. I had dozens of friends whom I cultivated with tireless assiduity as though they were temperamental home appliances, essential for a civilized existence but always in danger of going on the blink. I listened for hours to their problems, which I begged them to confide, but never mentioned my own, an omission they seldom recognized. I kept thinking I was storing up credit to draw on later.

I'd had sex with my first thousand men but that was a statistic that might sound like an achievement more to someone else than to me. Sex is an appetite that must be fed every day; even a thousand past banquets cannot nourish the body tomorrow. I was longing for the thousand and first knight whom at last I would marry and with whom I'd live ever after in the strictest fidelity. If marriage was my conscious but still deferred goal, I was less ready to admit I was always on the lookout for adventure.

Yet when I'd been healthy there had been nothing more exciting than to go to the gym after work on the nights I didn't stay late at the office. At the gym I'd perform movements in machines designed to stretch and swell muscles someone's hands would later smooth and relax. I'd shower, then hurry home to change into a pair of beltless tight black jeans, the fly half unbuttoned, a loose grey T-shirt and an old leather bomber jacket. Around ten I'd head out into the winter night. I could feel something young and vital pulsing in me, an unfocused exhilaration, as I walked through the slanting snow, my bare hands shoved into my pockets, for if the leather jacket was a concession to the cold, I was ready at a moment's notice to shed it to reveal my summer body—my ridged stomach beating a slow tam-tam against the T-shirt. If at an intersection I'd see someone similarly dressed and mustachioed accelerating his pace as he came down a side street, I'd stare at him in the most impenitent way. Whether I might want him was a secondary question. For the moment all I needed to do was to attract him. That was what mattered.

Sometimes I'd heard people refer to the pleasures of the chase; they eluded me. The idea of playing hard to get struck me as inexplicably perverse in a world where gestures misfired, voices gave out and everyone was shy. Heterosexuals, who revolved in a closed circle of friends under the brilliant scrutiny of their parents, who turned like the gleaming horses in an indoors training stable, could be sure their slightest signal would be observed. They could afford the luxury of elusiveness. They were accompanied by a reputation—for money, charm, intelligence, achievement, heritage or for poverty, boorishness, idiocy, idleness and obscurity (even the obscurity, paradoxically, was sure to be registered, even pedigreed). But all of my anonymous males—easily spooked, at once pursuer and pursued, stripped of their histories and reduced to the cruel materialism of a face and body and the harsh verity of a first impression—could not risk feigning rejection. Everyone had to be unambiguous, as glowing as a peacock's tail and as towering as a stag's antlers, secondary sexual characteristics evolved on the principle that more is more, even if the lyrebird's seductive tail so encumbers him he can no longer escape a predator.

Our immense bodies, nourished at such expense and pumped up so laboriously, were difficult to clothe and awkward to maneuver. In coat and tie we looked either fat or menacing, like Bar Mitzvah boys or nightclub bouncers rather than promising young executives. I became so muscle-bound I could no longer scratch my back or peel off a T-shirt. Gay boys who just ten years earlier had hissed together over cocktails, skinny in black pegged pants and cologne-soaked pale blue angora sweaters, and had disputed Callas vs. Tebaldi now lumbered like innocent kindergartners in snowsuits of rosy, inflated flesh from a solitary workout to a lonely hour of feeding before toddling off to an athlete's chaste sleep in a narrow bed.

One guy at our gym had become so huge from downing quarts of milk and dozens of rotisserie chickens that he had to be handed up the stairs by his brother, who would lift one leg after another for him as he came back up for yet another four-hour workout. The brother was as self-effacing and solicitous as the boy who leads the blind Samson into the temple. We all raised eyebrows and whispered that Samson had gone too far this time, while inquiring later in private about the exact details of his routine.

For we all knew that discipline and effort paid off, that after a week of strict training we could park a huge ripped body under a spotlight at a bar and if the shoulders were bigger than car fenders, the forearms the girth of horse's withers, the waist as slender as a napkin ring, the butt as imposing as a diva's bosom, then no one would notice a lisp, a biscuit-colored false tooth, a balding head or a disquieting personality flaw. We could have the pick of the lot at the bar. Friends and parents could say we'd gone too far, that we were in danger of becoming grotesque, that all this muscle would someday turn to fat, but for mating purposes the lyre could never be too large.

Living alone meant that I could receive anyone or be anyone I liked at any hour of the day. A complex metal grille outside my windows stenciled on my curtain its circles transected by a bass clef, security posing as decoration. As the curtain billowed, the outline of the bass clef moved out of focus. This pale fabric filled like a lung. It breathed or gasped for me or went tragically inert. While I slept it did my dreaming for me. When someone lay in my arms after sex it became a huge spinnaker propelling us across a moon-scrubbed sea. If I joked and gossiped on the phone with a friend it continued to lead a parallel life that was narrowly romantic, sighing and gesturing. Passersby cast their shadows—foreshortened or elongated according to the hour, full face or in profile according to their orientation—on my puppet screen, which democratically eliminated race, age, sometimes even gender and left nothing but moving forms that still managed to excite me. At night the blue vapor street light outside found a silk spider web stitched into my curtain.

One after another men came home with me, usually just once. I suppose most of them are dead now, all those young bodies I touched and undressed and tucked in when they fell asleep, the man with just one ball, the undertaker's son with the pale body who smelled of horse manure when I plowed him, he so brave and strong as he clenched the mattress and took his punishment like a man, the sociology professor who wished I was a bit smaller and dumber so he could cherish me, the blond salesman who lived next door and called me whenever it was raining and he didn't have the courage to go out stalking someone new, the famous kept boy who once pulled me into his apartment for thirty minutes of off-the-meter pleasure, the small and big penises, sheathed and circumcised, the hairy Italian and hairless Puerto Rican chests, the ardor, the kisses, the whispered secrets.

When the first personal ads for hustlers were printed in the *East Village Other* I ordered up a "former football player" who promised an "oatmeal massage." I persuaded him to skip the oatmeal and move right on to sex. A few days later I was in a local bar, Danny's. My date, the sociology professor, was drinking too much and becoming belligerent. Confident in my twenty-eight-year-old beauty, I said to him, "If you buy one more beer, I'm going to turn to the first person on my right and go home with him if he'll have me." He ordered another beer, I acted on my threat, and when I was out on the street with my prey, I recognized him and said, "But don't you remember me? The oatmeal rub? Last Wednesday?" I explained to him where I lived, what we'd said and done. At last, round-eyed, he said, "But you were *old* then."

Old eyes in a young body, with mine I looked at them all, memorized the intricate fittings of their knee bones, felt the burning ears and cold hands, burning scrotum and cold buttocks, kissed their feet and the crease where smooth bum joined hairy leg, dug with my fingers into their intricate ringed anuses too tight, then too loose, and listened there with my touch as one might listen to a pink-lipped shell for the sound of a distant sea, each shell different. The smooth cheeks at night were bristling and rasping at dawn, and button-shiny eyes were lined in the first light with what Cavafy so glamorously called the tell-tale signs of dissipation.

Politely scribbled first names and phone numbers, handed over at parting, were later found crumpled in the gutter just outside the door. These exchanges were required by etiquette and anyone who refused them would have been considered barbarous. All over the world new acquaintances promise to see each other very, very soon and don't, but only in America do they sincerely believe they will, at least at the moment of leave-taking.

Tricking, however, was so conventional, so hidebound, that its very form streamlined new people into and right out of each other's arms. There was the street cruise with its accelerating rhythm of exchanged glances, the seemingly aimless passing eye contact giving way to prolonged scrutiny, the unvarying choreography bringing the dancers together in a hesitation waltz of longing and fear. There was the embrace just inside the door and the apparently random caresses that lingered longer on cock or ass to express intention and the softer or louder moans when touched here rather than there to indicate compliance and desire. After sex there were the shower, the drink and the avowal, which began with admitting where one was from and ended with an account of the first time one had ever made love. Anthological and sociological, every account of gay life lists the numbers, notes the nuances, and that enumeration replaces all those tedious genealogies in the Old Testament, that string that begins and ends with "And X begat Y, who in turn begat Z." If poetry requires endless variations on a very few themes, then no existence could have been more poetic than ours. The days were drudgery and I sleepwalked through them, tired and hungover. But the nights were heart quickening—the hunt, the fierce grappling, desultory pillow talk.

I can remember a New Year's Eve, after my year of abstinence following my bout of hepatitis, when a blizzard turned New York into an arctic village. I didn't have a date and felt sorry for myself. I was trudging home through waist-high drifts that the winds built, then blew away. Booted and hooded partygoers shrieked as they slipped, or they delicately picked their way over the mountains that snowplows had already turned back. The words they muttered softly to themselves were carried across the snow with surprising fidelity.

On New Year's Eve the bars never close and at every intersection the dull throb of muted jukeboxes and a muffled chorus of voices inside were carried across the wastes. On my corner the windows of the local straight bar were frosted over and glowing with Christmas lights and beer-ad neon. A bare-headed man in a camel's hair coat emerged, saw me, smiled and wordlessly hooked his arm in mine. As snow devils pirouetted around us, snow chains noisily rattled far away, and the stuck traffic light burned a demented red beneath an old man's heavy white eyebrow, we kissed and kissed, bare hands frustrated by layers of clothing, our young faces flushed with drink under hair that was rapidly whitening, aging us alarmingly.

His name was Jim, he was from Virginia, I never saw him again, but as the first dawn of the new year turned the snowbanks outside my window a radioactive blue and the radiator knocked three times as though to an-

nounce my pale curtain was about to go soaring up, we lay in extravagant
ease on the tropical beach of my huge bed, every inch of our bodies
licked clean. The great romantics always live alone since a long run can
only dull the perfection of the opening night.

I don't use this theatrical language lightly. One young man, silent and
bored with my pre-sex chatter, stood, pulled me into his arms wearily, patted my ass and said, "Okay, boys, on stage," as he led me into the bedroom, where indeed he knew all his lines ("Yeah, baby, suck that big dick,
talk to it, treat it good"). His dialogue, like mine, like everyone's, had been
written by Erskine Caldwell, since in bed we would never have tolerated
the grammatical correctness ("treat it *well*") or precision ("that fair-to-
middling penis") we insisted on elsewhere. The middle-class manner we
considered indispensable in this anonymous city where everyone wore
jeans after hours we rigorously put aside when making love. Only ten
years later did we begin to see the charm of "executive sex," of reaching
up under a starched shirt and caressing a nipple or reaching into the fly of
grey flannel trousers, or unknotting and tossing a silk rep tie around the
neck of a Greek marble bust. . . .

IN COLLEGE I'd known a dandified, spinsterish black
woman named Janet who'd idolized me in a manner by turns mocking
and motherly. She was emaciated, lightly bearded, and she had an imperious way of keeping in line the big black men who shared her off-campus
house. They were rowdy football players, she an intellectual and artist, but
they were afraid of her frail discipline. She cooked for them and convoked
them to table with stern authority, although they could fluster her by flirting with her. Like me she was an aspiring writer and we'd work together
all night long on our manuscripts in her room, which had once been the
dining room in a ramshackle Victorian mansion and was still separated
from the rest of the house by a set of double doors that retracted on run-
ners into the walls.

Janet lived on cold chicken curry soup into which she would slice cold
apples. Cactuses lined the windowsills and Indian prints were thrown over
the broken-down armchairs out of a sense of respect for the wounded
and dying. We would work together all night and I'd fall asleep on her
daybed, which now I realize must also have been her night bed. In any
event she made a cult out of sleeplessness and seemed offended by the
suggestion that she needed anything more than five minutes' meditation

in an armchair. She would wake me with an old seventy-eight recording of *La Bohème* sung by Georges Thill in his light, silvery voice. The smell of freshly concocted curry and stale smoke and the penetrating sound of Georges Thill's French version of *O soave fanciulla* surrounded me those winter mornings or afternoons when I awoke and began almost instantly to correct the hand-written pages scattered across the floor, to down coffee, smoke cigarettes, talk, scribble, pace, read Janet's latest lines, watch the newly risen Michigan sun set.

Now, eight years later, Janet was teaching in a private Chicago school for disturbed children. She phoned me one evening as I was sitting in despair before an expensive, uneaten dinner I'd prepared for a handsome model I'd met on the train and invited to my place for my idea of a real French meal. He was due at eight o'clock. He'd still not arrived at nine-thirty when Janet called to say her favorite student, Craig, was just a block away from my apartment and in need of a place to stay.

"Has he eaten?" I asked.

"What?"

"Has he eaten? If he hasn't eaten he can come."

"You see, he's transferred to a school in upstate New York. He was staying with Maria's friend Beth, but Beth's girlfriend Bunny threw him out because—"

"I don't care about any of that so long as he's not eaten."

"I don't understand anything. Okay, I'll call him back. Poor boy. . . ."

When Craig arrived I seated him almost instantly in the seduction chair I had destined for the French model and fed him the coquilles St.-Jacques in a white wine and mushroom cream sauce, the cognac-soaked sweetbreads and the baba au rhum I'd been laboring over for a day and a half—a boozy menu only a young, fit body such as Craig's could possibly have digested. After my recent bout of hepatitis rich food made me sick.

For months now Janet had been writing me letters about Craig, whom she was in love with, although she was twenty-eight and he sixteen and her student, dyslexic and presumably half-mad. He had shoulder-length straight hair the color of tarnished bronze and a fine gold hoop in his left ear. He trembled so violently that the hoop was constantly spinning. He had very black, thick eyebrows and a stubby, masculine nose at odds with his lean body and his shy way of lowering his face toward the candlelight. The wavering flame danced on the hanging curtain of hair and the trembling earring.

Janet had warned me on the phone to keep my mitts off her property.

"He's a het-ero-sex-ual boy," she emphasized, "and you mustn't initiate him into your filthy vices." She spoke to me with the same tone of teasing reprimand she'd used to intimidate her burly roommates back in college.

Janet knew perfectly well that I had only one bed. She'd been up to her old subtle sadism by pushing a trembling heterosexual teen into my bed, one who if I touched would no doubt require extra years of very expensive psychotherapy.

By pouring out plenty of wine and playing the *Sgt. Pepper* album I had managed to relax Craig and excite myself. As bedtime approached, I rushed into the bathroom and swallowed a big sleeping pill. Just to be polite I asked him about his girlfriend and he spoke of several. The pill produced its effect; I yawned cavernously. But once the lights were out and we were in bed this shy, trembling boy became a masterful man planted firmly on top of me, the head of his basalt-hard penis digging into my navel, his hands shackling my wrists to the mattress above my head, then the tent of his hair grazing my forehead, shoulder, stomach, knee as he made a pilgrimage to all the stations of my surprised and grateful body before he laid his head on my chest and I felt the cold gold earring isolating my right nipple and smelled the rum from his baba. He slept while I watched the dawn whiten my nonplused curtain.

I wanted him to stay with me on every weekend away from his new boarding school and I felt sure he'd come back only if I insisted on his freedom. I gave him his own keys and told him to come and go as he liked. But he was in no rush to get away. The daylight metamorphosed him back into a bridle-shy adolescent. He told me he'd discovered two years earlier, when he was fourteen, that he liked men (Oh, I thought, Janet made up all that about his being heterosexual, her own desires crowding out the unwelcome truth). He had run away from home and hitchhiked to San Francisco, where he'd crashed at the pad of a really cool bearded cat in his forties who lived in the Haight and smoked a powerful lot of dope and built harpsichords and just hung loose. Craig's parents tracked him down and one night at three in the morning two hired guns broke the door in, trampled blindly, resonantly, over a harpsichord still without legs, and spirited off the groggy, barefoot boy to a waiting private plane.

"Your parents must be loaded," I said in hushed tones.

Craig said his father owned one of the biggest school textbook publishing houses in the country and admitted that his own inability to read was no doubt an unconscious slap in his father's face.

"Your dad probably would flip if he knew you were here," I said.

Craig took me by the hand and led me to the window. He pulled back the curtain. "See that guy in the corny trench coat over there? That's the private eye who follows me everywhere. Hi, George!" Craig gave the man a tiny salute. "That's what I call him, George. He's the world's worst gumshoe."

"Do you think armed dicks will come crashing through my door?" I asked, trying to sound coolly bemused, mentally cursing Janet.

"I'm sure my dad would approve—*does* approve of you," Craig said, a bit too condescendingly for my taste. "He likes white-collar types. And you're not going to kidnap me and hold me for ransom or drag his name through the papers and embarrass him by butt-fucking me during a front-page drug raid." For the first time I had a glimpse of how the rich are different from you and me—they accommodate our poor little morals without themselves subscribing to anything more stringent than dynastic loyalty.

Craig went off shopping, dutifully tailed by George. In three hours he came back carrying four pairs of shoes with platform heels and multicolored leather facings, buskins worthy of an ugly-customer rock star on speed or an ancient Greek comic on stage.

That night, as we lay in each other's arms, he told me of his dream, to buy a big house in Pacific Heights above San Francisco and live there with all his friends of both sexes. They would discuss life, make love, get high— his friends would be both students in Plato's academy and houris in a psychedelic harem.

We passed a joint back and forth in the dark and I felt my chest and arms light up with jukebox bubbles and my solar plexus swing yet another disc of volatile body music under the waiting needle of my heart, but my words seemed stranded, shunted off on a siding, waiting to be engaged.

Being high meant being in danger. I who'd never trusted my organs to function or my words and gestures to signify, I who feared the mechanical world and considered even crossing the street perilous, obviously I couldn't "go with the flow," as people were saying then. I knew the perfidious flow was nothing but white water buffeting the boat unerringly toward rocks that would splinter it. I feared being unworthy of this young man beside me—my cock too small, my breath corrupt, my skin clammy with too much experience.

But the minute he touched it, warm showers of sparks trailed his hand, as though my flesh were the phosphorescing sea in August. Our bodies were immense, geographical, ideal as those elemental gods, dispersed to the flowing elements except where touch quarried out a rich, juicy intricacy of shape and feelings—shame, bliss, sluttishness, awe.

I discovered that when stoned I skipped transitions and suddenly found myself already doing what I longed to do, as though the film had been badly edited and nothing differentiated the dream sequences from reality. It was enough for me to flash on a mental picture of myself as Craig's slave to discover I was already licking his feet. As soon as I saw his head on the pillow, fine straight hair fanning out to expose his jug ears and the powerful architecture of his jaw and skull, I was already straddling his chest and force-feeding his mouth. Fear of disgusting him surfaced for a moment only to be submerged by my own instantly realized fantasies, so powerful I assumed he must share them. Every action was saying something, at least to me, and saying it indelibly, as a brand sears. The tragedy of sex is that one can never know what this most intimate and moving form of communication has actually said to the other person and whether the message, if received, was welcome.

Now no one ever touches my body, which I neglect and let bulge, bloat and sag, although I dress it with more and more care, not yet reconciled to the shabbiness of age. No one ever looks at me on the street and my dreams become more and more erotic. Last night I dreamed that an old friend, a writer who's never done more than peck my cheek, caressed me obscenely and tenderly, promised to take me to his house after the theater, but I couldn't find him in the crowd and when I did I was at the wrong entrance and he was angry with me for having disobeyed his instructions.

Since I've already made physical comebacks several times in my life, I keep regarding my present disarray as a temporary disgrace. Every day I think at last I'll start my diet, go back to the gym, order new contact lenses, dye my grey hair, but every night I've still not begun to initiate these improvements and I go out to another long rich dinner. I'm living in Paris where everyone is slim but me. Superstitiously, I think that it's the extra bulk that's staved off AIDS all these years (I've been seropositive for a decade). Or perhaps being overweight ensures my fidelity to the dead Brice.

I've always been someone who masturbated while thinking not of ideal, imaginary partners but of actual people I've known in the past. My fantasies are memories as accurate as I can make them of past lovers and what they did to me. These days I find myself fucking the dead most of the time. Once when I asked the ninety-year-old Boris Kochno, Diaghilev's last secretary, if I could interview him, he said, "You must understand I don't want to meet new people. I prefer the company of my dead." And although I'm not quite there yet, I know what he means. When I was young I lived a far from satisfactory life thinking it was only a dry run for a better future, but those rehearsals turned out to be the only performances I would know and now I embrace the memories, which I'm afraid of touching up as I write them down, although I long for sleep and dreams. If in a dream I feel a melting tenderness toward one of my dead that I never experienced while he was alive and if I awaken bathed in grateful tears, it doesn't matter. I have no control over my dreams and I can't be held responsible for the improvements they make.

AFTER OUR TRIP to Paris, Jamie became still friendlier to me. Our office door would be closed, which permitted us to talk for hours on end without being observed or disturbed. We had so little work to do—just a few picture captions to turn out every week for our glossy national magazine—that we'd invariably panic on Friday morning and work feverishly all day in hushed concentration, trying to make up for a week we'd wasted on long lunches, coffee breaks, phone conversations with friends and social calls on other offices down the hall. Otherwise we were free to talk even if we were chained to our desks.

As a Midwesterner I was used to wide-eyed candor, but Jamie was tricky, reserved, both shy and disdainful. For the longest time I hadn't known if he was gay or straight. In Paris he'd introduced me to all those gay men but still looked blank when I'd mentioned their homosexuality. He had a metallic, upper-class New York voice and, snob that I was, I imitated his Tory pronunciations ("ennuhway" for *anyway*, "*thee*-uh-tuh" for what I had pronounced as "thee-*yay*-terr"); I learned to say "Beth is very social" rather than "Beth is a member of high society," as we had put it, cap in hand, back in Michigan. If I'd bear down on him with what he labeled a "personal question" (in the Midwest, *all* questions had been personal), he'd shake his head as though pulling himself out of a bad dream, call me by my last name with a thumping, head-prefect's gruffness and tell me, half-seriously, half-affectionately, that I was "impossible."

Today he'd be called a young fogey, but in the sixties nothing could have been less likely than a young journalist who wore garters to hold up his black lisle stockings and whose one concession to jauntiness was a polka-dot bow tie. He wasn't reviving the fifties, as people do now; he'd never abandoned the style of his adolescence. At twenty-nine he already had silver hairs scattered becomingly among the black. His eyes were grey-blue and one wasn't quite aligned with the other, especially when he was tired. Jamie played racquetball and always had funny stories to tell about antediluvian members of the Athletic Club, but the stories worked both ways, as a dismissal of outworn standards and as a reminder that those standards were still in full force.

He bit his nails. He lovingly inventoried the mementos on his desk. He slid down the corridors with tense shoulders hunched up around his ears. He flinched if someone called out his name. When the editor just above us summoned him, Jamie would go pale. I couldn't help but picture the lonely, self-sufficient twelve-year-old first-former at a strict prep school famous for its cold showers and rough sports. He had that precocious old-mannishness of the underloved preppie whose mother is nothing but a scented letter that arrives once a month, who ducks whenever addressed because he expects a blow or an insult, who goes through his stamp collection with the meticulousness of a miser, who panics if the school schedule varies by an hour, and is ashamed to admit he has nowhere to go over Thanksgiving break. By the time he's a sixth-former he's picked up a loud, irritating voice, a stock of snappy come-backs and a silver medal in the hundred-yard dash. Secretly he writes sonnets and reads Tennyson, whose *In Memoriam* is for him the perfect blend of technical polish and homoerotic Victorian pathos. And, despite his heartiness, there's a flaw in his regard.

Even Jamie's way of finally coming out to me was indirect. One evening, a year after our trip to Paris, there was a company party. We both got drunk on vodka and tonic and suddenly at seven we found ourselves only half-fed on pretzels and avocado dip. I myself had downed vast quantities of plump shrimp, loudly declaring that all my years of psychoanalysis had taught me just one thing, to eat my fill of expensive hors d'oeuvres without apologizing—a declaration that was itself an apology, of course. But we were still hungry. "I know an amusing place," Jamie said with a wink exactly as his grandfather might have done, with the same hint at naughtiness. We sped downtown in a taxi and there we entered the oldest gay bar in the Village, the ceiling picturesquely hung with cobwebs, sporting pictures in dark wood frames on the walls, brass fixtures on the bar and sawdust on the floor—all providing the right virile alibi. Jamie exaggerated his drunkenness, as though to explain how he'd confusedly ended up in such a *louche* place, it's all a lark, I'll never remember it tomorrow.

After that, at the office, I'd catch him looking at me with a combination of desire and complicity. He'd slouch down in his revolving chair, facing me, until I could see the outline of his crotch, and then he'd slowly wag his legs together. A lock of his hair fell over his brow, his voice deepened and his left eye became lazier than usual. Yet when I got up my nerve to tell him I found him attractive, he looked startled and laughed cruelly. Sharing an office is like being in a Beckett play, however, and after everything has been said you still must go on talking.

Jamie told me about a young man from an old Huguenot family whom he was obsessively in love with. With reverent discretion, Jamie was careful not to mention his name. His obsession was so pure, so abstract, that it made him speak constantly and colorlessly about the beloved, who was not a person with quirks but a paragon with neutral virtues, although I recognized the virtues were listed to justify a passion that had preceded them.

In those days I used to dance late every night at the Stonewall, where I'd developed a crush on an occasional customer, a high school principal. He was trapped in a loveless marriage with an unhappy Shakespearean actor who was completing his third year as the villainous tycoon in an execrable but well paying daytime soap opera. The principal, the one I liked, was Yugoslav, six foot four inches, and he laughed maniacally over anything. He had just three hairs on his chest, which was as hard and articulated as a cuirass. I'd toss back the vodka and tonic, which glowed blue when the black light was snapped on, and wait for the principal to arrive. He liked me, he took me home twice out of friendliness, but he was himself bewitched by Puerto Ricans, as who was not. Most of his inner-city students were Puerto Rican; when he tricked with stand-ins, in his fantasies they were the ones to administer the discipline to Teach. There was nothing profoundly democratic about New York, no one was ready to surrender an inch (of penthouse terrace surface, of office window exposure, of limo length) but *having* certainly looked feasible to the have-nots during those years when Puerto Rican pizza delivery boys got sucked off by lonely millionaires ordering in for the third time in an afternoon, hoping to get lucky, or when the white store manager of a supermarket elbowed off his panting assistant so as to be the one to service the Puerto Rican check-out boy during the city-wide black-out, the first friendly one that occurred on a winter's night in the mid-sixties. In our cold grey city Puerto Ricans were the summer, the color; white boys from the Midwest who'd first jerked off at age thirteen while looking at bare-chested Indians in Westerns on TV now could hold in their arms a three-dimensional tropical Indian from the Bronx who melted into smiles and shouted a muted "Ay!" when pinched.

The Stonewall was black and Puerto Rican. Into that hot house drifted a cool white camellia, a lovely pale white face belonging to a lean young man in black tie, Chesterfield, grey gloves, even shiny opera pumps, someone who pulled me wordlessly into his arms and waltzed me through that sweating throng as though the nineteenth century had just hurried through the room and recognized itself in a mirror.

He stared at me unsmilingly and unscrolled a long tongue into my mouth like the angel's words in a medieval Annunciation. I invited him home and found him to be complicated in ways that bored me. I learned he belonged to a group of elegant fags who attended the opera in black tie on Mondays, the "social" night, who dated interlocking sets of debs but fucked each other after hurrying the girls home, who belonged to the Racquet Club, who went fox-hunting together at My Lady's Manor in Monkton, Maryland, who crewed together in the Bermuda Cup. They called themselves the "White Russians," but all seemed to be named Reginald or Colin. They could sing satirical songs about life at Yale while nimbly accompanying themselves at the piano. They were active in an amateur Gilbert and Sullivan club that staged an operetta every spring, all proceeds going to a good Protestant cause such as senility or alcoholism. Two White Russians, in love with each other, had just married a pair of deaf sisters, extremely rich; they'd had the cheek to celebrate a double wedding. They camped it up wickedly with other White Russians on their yacht whenever Antonia and Olympia turned their backs.

My own White Russian was named Richard Smith, had big blue eyes that lingered a full musical beat behind the conversation, a compact, lean blond's body, no longer boyish and somehow indecent, *scalded* hairless, it seemed. He had an ironically social regard at odds with the endless clean tongue he would suddenly unroll into my mouth, as though his tongue had a will of its own. He'd be chatting away about his upcoming membership in the Century Club when suddenly, between sips of gin, I'd find his tongue lodged between my open jaws. The cool impertinence in his eyes, especially when they were seen up close, was nearly lunatic. He was fascinated by me, perhaps because I was indifferent to him, or probably because he was intrigued by my lack of social ambition. I didn't want to marry a rich woman who would know nothing of my "pranks on the side" (his phrase). The deb parties I'd attended as a teenager in the 1950s had seemed to me then manifestations of an enviable but unobtainable world; in New York in the 1960s they seemed preposterously irrelevant. Even the White Russians, apparently, treated them as nostalgic kitsch. In a provincial town such as Cincinnati or Baltimore, society was small, its rules coherent, its power undeniable, and the annihilating word *hip* had not yet been pronounced. In New York, however, that three-letter word so intimidated and intoxicated everyone under thirty that it had dismantled the old social machinery; the only people who still picked their way through the debris were the dowdy and the dull—and the duplicitous White Russians, who saw the situation as just another occasion for displaying their theatrical powers of mockery and dissimulation. These powers, of course, were about to be rendered meaningless by gay liberation, which represented as much a loss in aesthetic duplicity as a gain in styleless integrity.

One evening, on the way to a cocktail party being given by a colleague, I was walking alongside Jamie. I was recounting to him all my thoughts about Richard Smith. "He's driving me crazy. He keeps calling me. I can't bear him, though he *is* a pretty good fuck. But you must have met him," I said, suddenly putting the pieces together, "somewhere during your social peregrinations." Then I was conscious of the stifled sob at my side. Although he turned his face away I could see he was crying.

"Oh, Jamie," I said, "Richard is the guy—that guy—the one you . . ."

The hours and hours of Jamie's tormented, spiritually twilit descriptions of his paragon, even his report that his love had recently developed for the first time an infatuation with a ridiculously unsuitable man, a West Village clone, an idiotic bodybuilder who spurned him—all these details came flying back to settle on my shoulders. My callous words ("though he *is* a pretty good fuck") hung in the air. Here was I, each day listening to Jamie's morose and labyrinthine speculations, while hoping he would eventually find comfort in my arms, whereas the very person he so hopelessly loved was this creepy Richard I was fending off. I longed to comfort Jamie, unsay my words. I hoped he'd find me attractive now that he knew his beloved was pursuing me.

Suddenly Richard seemed much more interesting to me. The becoming aura of unobtainability he'd been lacking until now because he kept hurling himself at me stepped up behind him like the blue shadow a spotlight throws. Now he was haloed, three-dimensional, desirable. The next thing I knew he'd moved to Hong Kong to manage a branch of the family business and I never heard of him again.

Jamie, embarrassed, dried his tears and honked his nose. A few days later (so great was his capacity for secrecy) I discovered yet another aspect of his life he'd not yet mentioned in a year and a half of our sharing an office and daily confessions: he had a lover, whom he'd already been with for five years.

Jamie gave a cocktail party for the White Russians one night while his mother was out of town. There they all were in their Harris tweeds, Church shoes, Brooks Brothers shirts and Porcellin ties mixing martinis and tinkling the ivories, talking about next summer in the Hamptons and next Monday at the opera. The house was a stately ruin in the East Fifties, wedged between massage and pizza parlors. The neon sign from the massage parlor blinked shifting pink and white light through the dusty velvet curtains. Inside, everything was shabbily genteel—worn Oriental carpet, Ming figurine lamps with torn silk shades and an upholstered couch with sprung springs.

The nicest man there was named Gerry. He was blond, tall, with a wiry body, a ski-jump nose, clear glasses perched on the end of his nose and a way of investing more energy into the story than the person who was speaking had put there. He leaned into the conversation and tapped at it energetically, like a bird sharpening its beak on suet. He laughed and nodded with sympathy, understood everything, touched people, made them drinks, found echoes and instances of what they were saying in his own life and affirmed their tentative notions with well documented enthusiasm. He was quick to say, "But you know more than I do about that," or "That's exactly like you to say that." Although he was usually immersed in what people were saying, once in a while he'd draw back, observe, shake his head as though in amazed disapproval and then relieve his interlocutor by saying, "You're simply fabulous." If he'd been filmed while responding to someone and if later the film had been sped up, his head would have ticked as rapidly as a metronome from side to side during the conversation, never held steady or upright. Although he was working hard to charm everyone, the White Russians didn't like him, especially because Gerry, it seemed, was from humble origins but pretended his father was a retired naval officer. "He calls him the *Commodore*," someone named Furlong hissed, "but there is no rank of Commodore in the Navy. And look at him now, the little slut." Jamie—my Jamie, the timid prep-schooler who'd wept in the Sainte Chapelle—was carrying Gerry upstairs in his arms. "Did they just meet?" I asked Furlong.

"What? Just meet? But of course not, my good man, Jamie's been cornholing that little slut the past five years. They're what pederasts call lovers, vile term."

◯ I SCRATCH AWAY at these memoirs at midnight as my hound sighs and turns on the couch beside me.

Brice always liked the idea we'd both be cremated and our ashes mingled and put into a jar and stored in the dovecote at Père Lachaise. I worry about the practical details. Will his family mind the mingling? If I die several years later in America, will it be a big bore for someone to bring my ashes back on a plane? Will I feel far from home if I'm buried in Paris?

But where's home? A French woman friend spoke the other day about the pain of selling her senile grandmother's house and letting this part of the "patrimony" slip out of the family's hands. But I cast a wintry look on her attachment to mere property. I've lived in furnished sublets for the last ten years and have given my books away with each move, though I've also felt a clandestine urge to own land and a house but dismissed the longing as old-fashioned materialism designed to create the illusion of permanence just when we must be getting in training for transience, then extinction.

For me the sublet has been a spiritual exercise. Until a year before Brice died, when we finally rented in our own names a big five-room apartment next to the Tour St.-Jacques, as though we needed to step firmly on a block of melting ice just as we were approaching the rapids. I kept feeling he was trying to fix up a place for me to live in after he'd be gone, and I received each nail he drove into a wall as a gift he was making me with his frail body. At least our new neighborhood has all the trappings of earthly permanence. It's the oldest extant part of Paris and its narrow medieval streets were filled even back then with whores and writers (public scribes were given space to work under the arches of the Eglise St.-Martin). But if it seems permanent, it's also a place of evanescence, even dematerialization. The Tour St.-Jacques is all that's left of the leveled church, which in turn was built by the rich alchemist Nicolas Flamel, who one day invited his maid to precede him down the steps into his underground laboratory. On the way down she heard a loud whoosh, like the angry snapping-shut of a fan. When she turned around, the alchemist was vanishing. A month ago, when I heard that story, I sighed, thinking, Lucky man, to be spared the humiliation of decomposition. Real connoisseurs, my lover and I used to talk about what would constitute "*une belle mort*," "a fine death." More than once, on being told a supposedly tragic tale of a sudden demise (heart attack, car crash), we'd shock our mourning interlocutor by beaming and rubbing our hands together and murmuring, "*Quelle belle mort.*"

AFTER A MORNING of bad coffee and compulsive chatter with Jamie, I would spend melancholy lunch hours thumbing through new novels in book stores, trying to figure out why they had been published and my books rejected. In college I'd received several literary prizes and been published in the campus literary magazine. I'd been considered by my friends the writer most likely to succeed and thousands of cigarettes, drinks and hours had been consumed in discussing my "art." I didn't want to be very famous or even famous; I just wanted to be published. In fact no accolade seemed higher to me than that of "a minor writer," because it exempted its bearer from the obligation to treat the great themes (birth, marriage, adultery, divorce), which in any event were closed to me as a homosexual. I liked reading minor writers more than major ones—Henry Green more than George Eliot, Ronald Firbank more than Hemingway, Ivy Compton-Burnett more than Tolstoy.

But for the moment even the status of the minor writer seemed unattainable. My oldest friend, Maria, was surprised that I was so driven by the desire to publish; she was a painter who seldom painted and seemed just as happy "putzing around" her apartment, redecorating the bathroom or tending to her minuscule garden as she was standing in front of a canvas and brooding. Because painting was, as a genre, more resolutely avant-garde than fiction and directed to a much smaller audience, the freedom demanded of her was even more worrying than the combination of entertainment and art required of me. Yet even this "easy assignment" I'd failed to fulfill. Somehow I'd bungled the proportions. I loved to read my manuscripts out loud to Maria or my first lover, Lou, over the phone by the hour; perhaps my urge to please or the emotion I injected into my recitals with my voice made up for the blanks or faults on the page. But editors—all these people I didn't know—rejected those same manuscripts, often jotting a note, saying they found my writing "cold."

And yet my longest and most recent unpublished manuscript was a blow-by-blow description of the most passionate moments I'd ever known, my one-sided love for Sean, whom I'd pined after for the last four years. How could this book be "cold" when it was about my most tormented feelings? Had the people in my group therapy been right when they said I "over-intellectualized" things and consequently felt nothing? For one time in my life I, who thought of myself as ugly or, worse, corrupt, like a piece of meat that has gone off but still looks edible, had been briefly desired by a tall swimmer with a hairless body, dirty-blond hair, small blue eyes that looked too fragile for sunlight or direct address, a man who knew Latin and Greek, who'd made love to me before a candle and a mirror.

In those first few months together, four years previously, our faces had swum toward the mirror like those of the shepherds gaping down at the Christ child. We'd gone to a sentimental movie that had moved us because we had an excess of strong feelings longing for an occasion. Lightning looking for a rod—and after the movie let out, we'd run over a metal footbridge across the East Side Highway to the quay. Beside us the East River flowed quickly, half-industrial, half-wild, as though a mountain lion had wandered through city streets. It was a spring night and the superficial warmth of the previous day glided on the cold depths of winter air. Mist hung in the air before the street lamps. We ran and ran past late-night strollers. There we were, two fine young men, one dark, one blond, Sean's face drained pale except for a dark red rose in each cheek just above the beard line, small dark roses the color of life.

If I was fine it was because I was with him. Ordinarily everything seemed to me so drab, so arbitrary, as dry and yellow as sun-faded schoolroom blinds, and walking out into the world, away from a book or conversation, seemed a venture into dissolution. Entropy was my enemy, and as the world collapsed its music slurred and went sickeningly sour, Victrola running down.

But not tonight as we showered out into space with our own explosive force. We sang the song from the movie, we turned the searchlights of our faces toward each other as we ran and the beams crossed at a point in space where the doubled light was neither his nor mine but an intensity that constituted us.

As a teenager at my father's Michigan summer house I'd looked longingly, shamefully, at all those sharp-toothed scions standing up in their speedboats as they pulled into the dock, their torsos twisting as they fiddled with the line, or as they laughed and looked back to see how badly they'd splashed their passengers. Sean had been my scion, my high school swimmer, my head prefect. He was athletic, he smelled of leather and grass, his hairless blond torso rose up out of his lower body like that of a Burmese Buddha, shoulders gleaming and rounded, chest long and flat, waist dramatically slender, as though only such physical perfection could be the vehicle for the enlightened spirit.

Back then, in the fifties and sixties, I knew very few gay men and many of those I met were tormented or effeminate, yearning after cops or marines or moving men. Sean was gay—and he was as strong as a mover. He could size up another athletic man without yearning or innuendo, and if he liked me it was because he admired my mind. He also liked my body, sort of. He was the first man I'd met after I'd lost thirty pounds and started working out, but I didn't realize that I'd become a "number." I thought I was still the doughy-bellied guy I'd been, and Sean's interest in me struck me as miraculous.

He'd liked me, he'd slept with me fifteen times—and then he'd moved on. Maybe I wasn't exotic enough, too much the fellow Midwesterner. Or maybe he didn't like my weird combination of intellectual bullying and sexual enthrallment, as though Voltaire had taken the form of a masochistic girl. Maybe he saw me as too openly gay—yes, that was what he disliked. He wanted to drink German beer with another guy and dis-cuss Pythagoras with him and rugby before, almost accidentally, deciding to stay over; once in bed they'd jerk each other off in the dark, wipe up, yawn and fall asleep, the only sign of affection being a muted, playful sock in the jaw and a whispered, "Tiger . . ."

I was too histrionic with my big, pleading eyes, my oleograph fantasies of living with Sean as man and wife, my certainty that he alone could redeem me and confer humanity on me. Before knowing Sean I'd been what was called a "john queen," someone who haunted the public toilets in the subway and sucked off other men coming home from work. I'd felt I was a worm, a sex fiend, someone too ugly and effeminate and fat ever to know love. Then, surprisingly, Sean had fancied me for a moment, without realizing that he wasn't just dating me but rather raising me from one species to another.

I suppose those hopeless love affairs were a specialty of my generation, the one that came of age before gay liberation began in 1969. It may seem strange that a three-day riot could affect something so subjective as love, but of course what the Stonewell uprising changed was not love so much as self-esteem, on which mutual love depends.

My status as a human being depended on Sean's love. When he drew away from me I started writing my novel about him. As I'd go along, I'd show him the pages, one after another, and I hoped to mold him through my descriptions.

Back then I was anything but an objective observer. I was a moralist, if that meant I wanted to suggest new ways of acting through examples and adjectives that were subtly praising or censorious. I knew as well as anyone else that homosexuality was an aberration, a disease, but in my fiction I pretended otherwise. I gave my characters problems, minor problems that struck me as human, decorous, rather than the one irrevocable sin of being blasted from the start. I showed my homosexual characters living their lives openly and parallel to those of their heterosexual friends: pure fiction. I pretended the homosexuals had homes, loves, careers if not exactly the same at least of a similar weight and dignity. But my greatest invention was that I let my queers think about everything except the one subject that obsessed them: how they came to be this way, how they could elicit the world's compassion rather than hate and how they could be cured of their malady. I knew I didn't have the equilibrium or self-acceptance of my characters, but I thought by pretending *as if* (hadn't a whole German moral philosophy been based on the words *as if*?) this utopia already existed, I could authenticate my gay readers if not myself. Of course I had no such readers. I was an unpublished writer.

Now my strategy was being directed against Sean. He didn't think he was queer and he hated the idea that he might *end up* in the arms of a man; I was trying to convince him that human contact is flexible, more a dance partner's quick hoist or slipknot than the Stone Guest's funereal embrace. (Today of course I see that all these youthful fears of how one *ends up* are wide of the mark since the only end, as the Buddha foresaw, is old age, sickness and death, and on that compost heap strange, unexpected new flowers breed.)

Nothing in all the world—not even old age, sickness and death—is as painful as one-sided love, which is a foreglimpse of the other three. Love was the great bitter school for me, since it gave me something the minute it took it away. It seemed to give me the man I'd longed for over so many years. Back in boarding school I'd stared through the steam at raucous carefree jocks laughing and snapping towels at each other in the locker room (I was the face on the towel). Hugging my books to my chest I would scuttle drily across the quadrangle and watch them clown and hit and hug each other. In a dorm room one cute little guy would bounce on his big friend's lap and call out at the top of his lungs for the benefit of the other guys standing around, smiling, "Hey, this feels great, we should get married, how about dropping Sally, Rich, how about it? Drop the bitch and marry *me*"—a huge laugh, all that warm young flesh with the peach fuzz, the smells of sperm and Clearasil and cheap cologne and tuna fish for lunch and fresh sweat in hairless armpits, a tenderly veined and muscled hand, modeled by Michelangelo not in marble this time but terra cotta, red from the eternal cold of a Spartan, unheated school, this big, elegant hand emerging out of a sleeve of white linen and good tweed—all those powerful legs and soccer-playing butts in unpressed khakis, cuffless because they'd been let out as the boy grew, those perfect white teeth, sun-bleached eyebrows, small ears, baggy but secretly tumescent crotches, high-arched feet in thick white socks pulled halfway out of penny loafers under a scuffed wood desk, the ragged nails, the bobbing Adam's apples, and in the shower the hairless chest and twin oak-brown aureoles, one round as the earth, the other (because the hand is stretched high) elliptical as Saturn, the boy's lips a gash of garnet in a face drained dangerously pale by rugby practice, the knees black with a mud that under the flowing water snakes across the tile floor in the absinthe-green winter sunlight, cast by high windows on shoulders too wide for a torso all ribs and flat muscles, applied by the painter with just a few deft dabs of the palette knife. . . . Now a young man like one of my locker-room gods had been given to me but this one I was free to kneel before and worship. With all those earlier deities I had had to pretend I didn't see through their disguise, I had been forced to act as though I believed they were human beings like me (I worshipped them alone, in secret, and with just one hand, the other molding the air into the divine form), but now the thick, knobby godhead itself was plunged into my mouth, not just some tasteless wafer of the imagination.

I never lived on familiar terms with Sean, doubtless the reason I can still refer to him as a god even though I watched him crack up before my very eyes. He wept, producing long gleaming sheets of spit and snot that clung to his face and hands like a placenta or a pupa's chrysalis, except his metamorphosis was not toward something lighter and more beautiful, but heavier, bloated with medicine, stunned with grief. He spent six weeks on the psycho ward at St. Vincent's Hospital in New York, then was shipped home, fat and bewildered, to relatives in Minnesota. In my mind he'd been the powerful young man who'd rejected me and I'd wept many times a day over his defection, but to him my love had been just one more intolerable demand, on the same level as the need for good grades or the fear of ending up penniless—or gay.

If I remember Sean so well it's because he made me suffer so much. I lay on my bed for hours and hours writhing in pain, thinking about him. I'd picture his holding me and kissing me by candlelight before the mirror; I'd masturbate; then, as the sperm dried on my hand and the candlewax in the memory congealed, I'd start to cry. Without the piston of my fist driving it, the whole vast locomotive of my imagination stalled. I cried until I was exhausted, then I'd start to fall asleep. I'd awaken with a start, sitting up, unable to catch my breath. I was stifling. The blood pounded in my ear so loud that I couldn't sleep on my side. I found that the pulse was louder in my left ear than in the right, so I trained myself to sleep on my right. I'd cry so long I'd become exhausted; my esophagus ached; I felt as warm and snotty as a baby—would a psychiatrist say that I cried in order to feel like a baby, that my reaction to Sean's departure was a search for infantile comfort?

Or was that too ingenious? Perhaps I should have just accepted my loathsome dependence on him and recognized that nothing could be done with it. It couldn't be psychologized in some redeeming or even interesting way, nor was it the cornerstone of a philosophy—or even of my own brand of folk wisdom.

I suppose all of my life has been led in the aftermath of this love; I wish he'd burned his initials into my ass, at least I'd have something to show for all that pain. I'd entered into this passion for him half-jokingly, quite aware I was playing a love-sick role. What I hadn't bargained on was that my little self-conscious smile didn't immunize me from the deep infection that was inexorably changing me from inside, molecule by molecule. By the time the smile began to fade my bones and ribs and inner organs had all been thoroughly invaded and reconstructed.

Love—real, violent love—makes other people impatient. Heterosexuals didn't want to learn about the intricate domestic topography of Sodom; they preferred to draw a big X over the entire land. Anyway, all the world hates a lover. Friends are jealous, adults irritated, children unengaged, readers bored (the few I could round up to listen to my bulky manuscript). I'd trick friends into listening, not to my novel, but once again to my obsessive chatter by claiming I'd just had a startling new insight; only halfway through the same old circular story did their attentiveness surrender to frustration as they realized not one detail had been changed. With the long shot of indifference they'd say, "It just takes time, you'll soon be over it and off and running after some new piece of trouser." What they didn't realize was that I felt that if my thoughts of

Sean faded at all I'd be guilty of sacrilege; he was the Israel I'd promised never to forget. Memory and the repetition of our story was a way of defeating their cure-all, time.

When Sean left New York the whole city began to fade. Each skyscraper lost three floors, the taxis slowed down, the disconsolate vagrants stopped panhandling, the Hudson ran backwards, salty with tides of tears. The only thing that increased was the steam issuing from the manholes, since it was an endless exhalation of lonely desire.

My trip to Paris and the bout of hepatitis set a term to the first agony over Sean. He refused to communicate with me; it was as though he'd become a silent Cistercian. Now that I no longer had any contact with him (his grandparents, polite but firm, murmured, "He's not allowed to speak to his New York friends," and hung up), I began to elaborate his life, *our* life, in my novel. His blood turned into ink, his pale face became my blank page, the first three lines his deep frown. The power of this disease of love to devastate a spirit surprised me, materialist that I was. I who understood how Troy could be lost because Helen's nose was a centimeter longer than other women's, had a hard time comprehending this rotting away of a soul from within just because of something that wasn't there: a lack, a refusal, a departure, silence.

Of course I had lots of explanations, all suitably self-derogatory. I had chosen Sean precisely because he was unavailable. I apparently was unable to accept homosexuality into my intimate life; if I dreamed of a man every night but awakened every morning alone in my single bed, then I was still somehow indeterminate, neutral, available for a still undecided future.

(Another part of my mind objected, "But I thought he *would* love me. If I'd known in advance that he wouldn't, then I would never have suffered so much. A miracle, yes, if he'd loved me, but it was a miracle I was counting on.")

Or I said he was like my father, a cold, unfeeling man I longed to seduce. At night when I was thirteen I would sit outside my father's bedroom door in the darkened house, hugging my knees, and imagine entering and taking my stepmother's place beside him, a desire I pictured so clearly that I was afraid I might find myself actually doing it. What if at last I could seduce this sleeping, snoring man, who would wake up to find my legs, not his wife's, wrapped around his waist, his hard sex deep in my butt, the sharp dilation of surprise in his eyes quickly clouding over with pure pleasure?

(But another part of my mind objected that I didn't want Sean to be my father—nor did I long to be his child bride but his mate, two nearly identical pairs of jeans tossed on the floor, the trouser legs intertwined.)

Or I said that as a writer I would find a live-in lover too close for comfort. Didn't writers prefer to suffer alone and conjure up the cruelly absent beloved? Writers needed time out to work up their stories. Certainly I needed room and time to elaborate all the ways in which I was not loved, all the happy days together we'd missed out on due to that time I'd pressured him to say what he really felt, or that time I'd taken his hand on the Staten Island ferry deck, embarrassed him and lost all the ground I'd gained by my week of calculated indifference. Love and childhood are the writer's two great themes because they are the only seasons during which every object takes on a glow throbbing with meaning. A song can evoke tears; a balding teddy bear, with its curious woody smell (could it be stuffed with pine chips?), recalls solitary hours with such poignancy that the whole mental stage is plunged into a new, queer light. I was almost thirty but I was marinated in suffering as acrid as that I'd distilled during my lonely, desperate childhood. Sex and love with Sean had seemed a way out of that isolation; when he'd abandoned me I was left holding the dirty bag of my own unworthiness.

But it was all much simpler than that: ever since I was a kid I'd wanted someone beautiful to belong to me, a man who had beautiful hair, teeth, hands, skin, loins, bones, a beautiful way of walking pigeon-toed, of lifting a spoon seriously, simply to his lips, of scratching his neck, of pissing a full, hard stream, of plunging off a diving board forthright, without fear, of sleeping, one hand cast back, someone with full, plush lips, who had a fine dusting of gold hairs on his stomach and longer, darker, silkier hairs around his scrotum, whose leg muscles were flat and suggested even in repose the power to hold, to clasp, whose skin was warm to the touch as a clay pot left out in the sun, someone so beautiful he'd never had anything but romantic sex, someone who'd never made the first move, whose palms were callused and neck burned from manual labor, someone whose breath was sweet and so warm it fogged up the window on his side of the car, while the other passengers sat beside shamefully clear glass, someone who knew instinctively how to turn up the collar of his blue cashmere coat or to leave his white cotton pajamas unbuttoned to show his scabbard-flat chest, someone blessed with a driving intellectual curiosity so that he'd never had much interest in his own beauty, whose hair was as heavy, thick and straight as a cord that separates a masterpiece from the public.

⎯⎯⎯⎯⎯⎯⎯⎯⎯

⟶ TODAY when I came back to our apartment (I must learn to say "my" apartment, now that Brice is dead), I had a message on my machine to call James Assatly, a former student of mine who lives in Boston. He was high on morphine, he said the CMV had made him blind and now was in his spinal cord and was slowly paralyzing him.

"I've stopped eating or taking Acyclovir," he said. "It's my way of bowing out without committing suicide. I've met a priest, Father Phil, who's going to bury me. I was feeling terribly isolated until I met Father Phil, who told me it's my church, I must not forget it belongs to me, too, and that I have a right to be buried beside my family."

He thanked me for making his last two years such a whirlwind, though I felt bad I'd not been able to convince an editor to publish his book. I told him we all admired him for showing such courage and stoicism and gaiety. "Really?" he asked, surprised. "Well, that's what I tried to do."

Then we said good-bye and we assured each other that we loved each other. Just two years ago we'd gotten stoned one afternoon in his apartment and I'd put the make on him but he'd turned me down.

Now he said, "I do love you. I've always felt bad about that time." I told him it wasn't important. Anyway, last spring, when his nose was swollen and black with Kaposi's sarcoma he'd already said to me, "Now I know what it's like to be turned down. I'm so sorry I did that to you." He always had a tough, cool air about him; perhaps because he'd grown up poor, half-Irish, half-Syrian, he'd learned not to ask anyone for anything. Yet he asked me just now to write something to be read beside his grave.

TWO

I met a guy named—well, I'll call him Rod, though I'm tempted to use his real name since he might be dead now and his ghost would appreciate a "mention" (as they say in gossip columns).

Rod lived on Bleecker Street with a girl and a dog. He had been a psychology graduate student at Columbia who'd been pushed out of the program after he said in a group therapy practice session that he was homosexual. They'd all been encouraged to be as frank as possible, but homosexuality was considered a perversion, oral aggressive, possibly sadomasochistic, definitely infantile, that would necessarily occlude the objectivity of a future psychotherapist. He had to go, though the program director never admitted that homosexuality as such had been the disabling cause. No, he was told, it was more a matter of a general lack of seriousness, of professionalism. . . . Now Rod was making light boxes, which he assured me would become the art form of the future, entirely replacing painting. Back then people were always insisting that the novel was dead, the theater outmoded, easel painting washed up, human nature about to be radically revamped. We read William Burroughs' collage novels, eyes dutifully scanning page after page of repetitious, broken sentences. We saw group gropes of naked youngsters re-enacting Bacchic rites based on Greek tragedies, though denuded of the exalted language. Language was suspect, protest imperative, the tribe tyrannical, the author dying. Warhol had made the transition from canvas to screen. We watched hours and hours of his home movies, certain that the boredom was functioning to break down our conscious resistance, considered a bad thing. Of course the real fun was the audiences, the bits of mirror and velvet, the leg-of-mutton sleeves and bellbottoms, the flowing hair and curling cannabis smoke, for we were only slowly becoming aware that we constituted a new generation unlike any other before us in history.

After I had sex with Rod on the fold-out couch bed, his dog came bounding in and licked our milky stomachs clean. Today even a drop of sperm is rich with death, a mortal culture, but then porno magazines referred to it as a "soothing cream" and we liked to taste it, swallow it, smell it, rub it over our cheeks and murmur with a smile, "The fountain of youth." If someone had a big cock we called it "The Dick of Death," an expression no one would dare use today.

Adult men—all those aggressive, out-of-shape, heavy-breathing heterosexuals—might carry syphilis or at least gonorrhea in their bodies, we thought, contracted through their drunken, half-hard thrusting, the toil of making money, war, babies. But we were big, bucolic gay boys, and our brief transactions were redolent of summer camp, irresponsible as a groan heard in a shadowy forest or as transfiguring as the mystery of light glowing on a lake glimpsed through a rood-screen of leaves. We were engaged in a game of touch-tag far removed from the possibility of giving— or taking—a life.

Rod had a party at the end of every month, to which he invited the tricks he'd turned during the preceding thirty days. He threw all their numbers in a fishbowl and plucked them out and rang them up every fourth Saturday. Often they didn't remember him or he them. It was his benevolent idea of society, which, as so often happens in America, was mixed up with an inclination toward charity. All thirty guys would stand around his small apartment and scowl at each other, appalled to observe the range of Rod's erotic taste: black and white, short and tall, smooth-skinned and hairy, young and not quite so young, butch and twinky.

People kept entering. The front door led directly into the kitchen with its ratty linoleum floor and the tub in the center of the room covered for the moment with a board that served as a table to hold all the bottles of rot-gut wine the guests had brought. I'd offered a straw-covered quart of Chianti; my year of post-hepatitis sobriety had recently come to a reeling, jubilatory end.

Just beyond was the small living room, nearly filled by the bed when it was opened out though now it had contracted back into itself, a couch on which were seated a handsome young man and woman murmuring to each other in French. He had a red scarf tied around his left biceps, a romantic touch at odds with his glinting granny glasses. She wore nylons sparkling with silver chips. She was Black: her features small as an Ethiopian's.

The only other woman present was Penelope, Rod's roommate, a dainty little thing tottering by on very high heels and swaddled in a tight miniskirt. Her top had trailing lace sleeves. She was consoling Rod for some slight he'd suffered. Her tone was tinged with irony but the words were sympathetic, the compromise of a woman embarrassed to baby her lover in front of strangers and who tries to suggest this humiliating necessity may be just a game.

I swayed, bemused and a bit drunk, before the French couple. "Excuse me, do you speak English?"

"Of course," the young man said, "we're Americans. We just speak French to each other because that's what we're studying." He had a thin, Errol Flynn mustache, not the bottle brush popular then, and a long, rangy body, intelligent eyes, a languid manner and a studied smile. Everything about him was studied, the work of someone who'd been friendless and unloved as a child and who now, with the zeal of a good student, has set about mastering all the social skills. I recognized the game; I was playing it, though I suspected I'd started my lessons at an earlier age.

"Are you a Southerner?" I asked.

"A Southerner?" he repeated, as though examining something dubious at the end of a fork.

His wife was nodding vigorously and saying in a barely audible aside, "He certainly seems to have diagnosed the case. . . ."

We introduced ourselves. He was Butler, she Lynne. The word "brilliant" kept igniting the light box of my head—her brilliant smile, his brilliant glasses, her brilliant stockings, their intellectual brilliance. Lynne had the long neck and strong calves of a dancer, and the slightly obscene turnout; Butler folded back like the couch into himself, calm, poised, even elegant. His manner was lordly but intended to be accessible, like that of an Oriental despot vacationing at Saint-Tropez with just one wife. But if he appeared as though he were about to extend his beautiful large hand to be kissed, his facial expressions alternated complacence with a nervous critique of everything going on around him.

He seemed to have acquired his expectations and standards from nineteenth-century novels; he was repeatedly shocked by the impertinence or unseemliness of the Village gay guys milling around us, who'd had a few drinks and were now talking loudly, at once members of rival gangs and potential lovers. They weren't writers or even readers—they were just guys hoping to get laid on a Saturday night. Two fellows were even groping each other in the doorway and a small freckled hand had lifted a T-shirt to stroke a well turned brown waist. Was Butler really shocked by this tipsy, amorous rough-housing, or was he anticipating Lynne's reaction in order to defuse it? Why had he brought his wife to a gay party?

Our dainty hostess kept casting bemused glances our way as an adorably sulky Rod stretched out on the floor and buried his unkempt head in her lap. He'd drunk too much wine and was apparently wounded that two of the days, or dates, in last month's very rich calendar were merging in the bedroom, which Rod pretended was a violation of house rules, although the only rule it broke was his heart—or vanity. The dog was pulling on his shoe laces. Penelope crooned and whispered reassuring things to him—and soon enough was free to slip out from under the burden of his sleeping, smiling head.

She made her way over to us. "You're certainly the most fascinating group here," she said with a smile that projected good will and conveyed curiosity. Her articulation was perfect, like that of a school librarian, but I had the impression she wouldn't have blurred her speech even if she'd known it was grating since everything about her—her cool, ironic regard, her high heels and hair, her somewhat Victorian fashion sense crossed with the reigning look of the bug-eyed, bedraggled moppet—everything seemed born out of a complex fantasy of her own devising rather than out of a desire to please or follow fads. Her self-presentation was as entranced and impregnable as someone else's erotic scenario.

We were all bookish, as it turned out, and we talked about Proust, Isherwood, Stendhal, with the zest of true readers, excited into appreciation not analysis, endlessly eager to evoke favorite scenes and to judge characters as though they were real people. "Oh, *God*, remember when they realize they're in love just because the word *love* is pronounced—"

"Is she his aunt or his mother? I forget."

Lynne kept mentioning James Baldwin, and I wondered if it was because they were both Black. If we'd been Europeans, snobbism might have slipped into our talk, but since reading bore no cachet at all in America we were reduced to a pleasure as inconsequential as that of the stamp collector or armchair traveler.

What I liked most of all was that all three of my new acquaintances were not only bookish but also beautiful.

"Do you write?" I asked Penelope.

"Yes," she said, "though I shouldn't talk about it since I've never published anything."

"Join the crowd," I said. "What are you working on?"

She smiled a dodgy little smile, as though I might be mocking or stalking her, but she overcame her fear—*and* her vanity—to say with great firmness, "No one, not even Rod, has ever read anything I've written, though you'll all be encouraged to buy my first novel as soon as it comes out."

"Come on, tell," I said.

She straightened her skirt around her knees and said, "That would be against my principles. But surely you've introduced the subject because you're dying to tell us about your own belletristic efforts."

Butler, Lynne and I all froze, looked at each other, drew a breath and rocked with laughter. Penelope laughed too, delighted by the effect she'd produced. I speculated that she was one of those people who prefer being admired for their eccentricities than liked for their common fund of humanity, if they have such a fund. Soon we were eagerly talking about our belletristic efforts. Butler was a short story writer who favored the "avant-garde" and who had translated several of Raymond Roussel's obscure "texts" into a stiff-jointed English. Lynne was writing a thesis on Max Jacob and his influence on Picasso. I said, "My novel is purely autobiographical. Everything in it is exactly as it happened, moment by moment—sometimes even written down moments after the event. The main character bears my name. I'm writing it in order to persuade the love of my life to come back to me; I'm afraid it's going to be a very long book. That's the avant-garde technique I've invented: it's called realism."

Penelope asked, "Isn't that what most people call a diary?"

The truth was, I'd long since finished and typed my four-hundred-page novel and it was slowly making the rounds of all the New York publishers. It had already been rejected by a dozen. My agent sent me the editors' comments, if there were any. What shocked me most were how personal and arbitrary they were. Whereas I saw publication as a medal conferred on merit, the notes suggested how haphazard and capricious acceptance must be.

Butler said, "But everything written is a *version* of reality, even a betrayal of it—*tant mieux*, since a betrayal is already a choice, which is a conscious, imaginative act."

I protested that since "reality," at least the psychic reality that is the subject of books, takes place in our heads and nowhere else, a fictional account of reality is in no way a translation or "betrayal" of that material into another medium. Lynne murmured, "*Tradurre, tradire*," exactly as I knew she would.

Butler's eyebrows shot up to indicate his alarm at my heresy, whereas his beautiful hands lazily calmed the waters I'd riled. For if he was both a benevolent despot and a shockable miss, it was his hands that were benevolent and the eyes that were permanently alarmed. He pointed out that language is a closed system in no way connected to reality and that books can only be about other books; I pictured shelves in a dim library where all the books were gabbling contentedly amongst themselves like old people in bed.

"And yet realism is the great challenge," I said, "not the School of Realism with its sordid kitchens and tough streets, much less Social Realism, but rather the burning desire to render the exact shade of sadness, the sadness you feel when you finally get what you want." I spoke facilely, my commas eliminated by drink, and now I was looking into Lynne's merry eyes that were astonished by my recklessness. Suddenly I realized I was talking too much, a temptation I surrendered to only when the subject turned to books, and I dutifully returned to interviewing my new friends. My father had taught me that I need never feel ill at ease socially since all people love to talk about themselves at the slightest provocation—a lesson he, the world's most boring conversationalist, never observed except during business dinners.

While the gay boys around us were slow dancing, a romantic excuse for bumps and grinds and bodily examinations of a nearly medical thoroughness, I was trying to ingratiate myself with Lynne and Butler. I took them more seriously than the boys because they were a heterosexual couple or at least ambiguous sexually.

Couples fascinated me. All my life I'd been dancing attendance on them. I worked harder than they did to keep them together and often failed to see that their spats were just the fleeting coquetry of sex antagonism, the natural play in a joust that was more exciting because it was half-hostile. When I was with my couples I was never happy. In fact I was constantly anxious, afraid they'd separate, fearful I might unwittingly be the cause of their separation. Yet I could imagine becoming happy soon if only some movable part (I never figured out which) would tumble into place. I would resolve every morning not to become too involved with my couple of the moment, but by midafternoon I'd already been on the phone with each partner half a dozen times and had invited them to a peace-conference dinner that very evening. I would do everything to bring a smile to their lips, as though my survival depended upon their caprices. I invariably took the side of the man and counseled the woman to give in, concede everything, since to my mind it was clear that it was a buyer's market and she was selling. I had no doubt that he, no matter how unappealing, would find another woman right away, whereas I thought it was only a polite fiction that she was a full and equal partner in any marriage with a man. After all, I'd grown up with a woman—a frustrated, heavy-drinking, headstrong woman—who writhed with loneliness and impatience beside the silent phone. A woman took on importance only if a man desired her, but male desire itself was illusory or at best brief, and women desirable only by convention, not conviction.

Suddenly everyone was whispering, "Brandy," and the next thing I knew I was being introduced to a tall, slender drag queen in a sequined ball gown. She was young but had a mature, expertly painted face designed to appear—I won't say "natural," since nature had nothing to do with it—but plausible only if seen at a distance, on the stage, say. She took my big mitt in her tiny, slightly feverish hand. "I'm so upset," she said in a thrillingly low voice. "Jorge has just taken off with all my jewels. He threatened to kill me if I called the cops." Her eyes were tragic but a ghost of a smile alighted with a delicate "ping!" on her glossy scarlet lips outlined in black. Penelope said, "You poor girl," and pressed a whiskey into her hands. I tried to imagine Brandy's penis.

"Who's Jorge?" I asked, feeling as though I, too, were on stage, the embarrassed volunteer dragged up out of the audience.

"My husband," Brandy said solemnly. "He's the bouncer at the Club 86, a big Puerto Rican bruiser who beats me though I love him, God help me."

Like an idiot I didn't respond with another Billie Holiday or Helen Morgan song tag but with some irrelevant psychoanalytic twaddle. Brandy was too good an actress to let me spoil her scene; just as the audience was getting restless, she suddenly lifted my hand to her lips (though she was careful not to allow me actually to touch that gooey pot of strawberry jam) and whispered huskily, "Look, all these guys and dolls around us are all licking their chops over you, so slim and muscly in your grey T-shirt. You know what you are? You're the Universal Ball." It took me a moment to register what she meant.

As a former fatty and stoop-shouldered bookworm I had a hard time believing my amphetamine-powered diet, my years of working out, my painful hair-relaxing, and my newly acquired contact lenses, always attracting cinder specks and provoking tears, had actually paid off. Or perhaps the previous year's bout of hepatitis had made my face gaunt to just the right degree. So everyone desired me?

More likely, Brandy knew how to flatter me into the blushing silence she required. Once my pop-psychology remedies were disposed of (those were the years when we would have told Medea, had we encountered her still steaming in her sons' blood, "You must not like yourself very much"), she took the spotlight. She told us of Jorge's jealous rages, his epic drunks, his violence and, like a ballad singer, concluded each verse with a whispered chorus, "But I love him, he's my man."

Brandy was young like us but a throwback to an earlier era of butch-femme role-playing raised to the intensity of Greek drama; her high heels were her *cothurni*. She expressed our feminine longings to be beat and betrayed by a real man, half-buried wishes we could never have unearthed, wishes that in any event had been superseded by our desire to be wolves running with the pack, men among men, two hard cocks held together in one hand. Unlike us she didn't flash on an imagined glimpse of a raised hand or an angry snarl; instead she articulated those desires in well chosen words through expertly rendered lips, addressing us in an alto voice that fell within a female register but packed a virile wallop. We were Village kids with hippie hair, we were sporting tight jeans, no underwear, cheap deodorant, loose T-shirts and scuffed dirty bucks worn down at the heel; she was a Gallé bud vase, her green fishtail gown molded to her lightly padded hips, her blondined hair, interwoven with various falls and pieces, as full and fragrant as a blown rose. Important hair, as people say now. She was seductive, not sexual. Like rubes at the fair we were gawking at the bearded lady, or rather the beardless *gentleman* (do the rubes sometimes long to become the beautiful freak?).

Most of us gay guys had last dated a woman when we were eighteen; Brandy reminded us of our senior prom and brought out in us a throwback to gallantry, the deference paid to something deemed universally desirable that we just didn't happen to desire. At the same time it was all a trick, her act, something done with mirrors, as her sad smile and irony-drenched voice revealed.

BUTLER AND LYNNE were graduate students at Columbia. They invited me to dinner at their apartment in one of the teeming, shadowy side streets near the university. Lynne looked exhausted when I arrived. Very quickly I understood why. Everything in her dinner came out of an elaborate cookbook popular at that time; I recognized the very recipes I myself had devoted five and six hours to realizing. Butler looked cool and languid, and received me with alternating bouts of nerveless elegance and prim surprise.

I had adopted after six years in New York a certain saucy directness that shocked the recently arrived Butler. I'd learned to flatter people shamelessly, an excessiveness that took them by surprise but that they found to be shamefully gratifying. My theory was that, afraid of sounding insincere, no one dared to compliment his or her friends on quite obvious virtues; I was going to eliminate all half-hearted reticence. Then I'd also acquired the related knack of asking personal, even embarrassing, questions; I'd spring my question, "Do you really like sex?," without any advance warning or a plausible transition. I was careful to avoid painful subjects ("Are you still sleeping with your husband?"), because I wasn't a sadist, just a provocateur. I wanted to render conversations entertaining even to the participants; whereas few people had ideas to develop, they all had secrets to reveal. My impertinence was just another form of flattery.

Butler didn't take to it. He and Lynne were too Europeanized for it and preferred decorous vacuity, if need be, to premature confidences that might later be regretted. They didn't know me well enough to have heard I was "famous" for the question direct; what my friends considered an adorable eccentricity they regarded as rude. What they were particularly eager to ward off were any questions about their marriage. Was it a real marriage? How much did Lynne know about Butler's homosexual encounters? Did she resent them? Did she plan on having children? Would the children be told about Daddy's cock sucking? Did she like France because she felt more accepted there as a Black woman?

Nothing vulgar touched them. A record of Gérard Souzay singing Duparc was playing; for once I understood the French words and when the baritone suddenly exclaimed, "Like a dog love bit me," I burst out laughing, but Butler simply raised an eyebrow and I subsided back into silence.

Soon we were dipping into the crusty Lobster Thermidor. Outside, Negro neighbors were sitting on the stoop eating hot dogs from the Nathan's on the corner and listening to Aretha Franklin; they'd placed loudspeakers in the open ground-floor windows. Smiling with curatorial pride, Butler silenced Souzay and opened wide his windows so we could better enjoy Aretha; nothing escaped his connoisseurship. Or were they proving that Lynne had not rejected Black American culture?

As the good Burgundy flowed, our ideas became more heated, our smiles more lingering, our faces hotter. I was so fascinated by Butler that I thought I must be attracted to him—his long, smoothly muscled body, the muscles laid on like furled sail; his Smilin' Sam good looks, as I labeled them in deference to a mustachioed, brilliantined comic-strip hero of my youth; his beautiful dark eyes that winced with real pain when forced to look at the world's wickedness.

We discussed ideas for hours and hours, for in those days we did not yet see a dinner party with friends as a social ritual that must end no later than midnight, and that, in any case, would be repeated over and over, year after year, week in and week out, the tiniest variations on a few choice themes and a mildly pleasant way to feed in company. No, we saw each occasion as the unique opportunity to get to the bottom—of our minds, our hearts, of universal problems. The night set no limits on our fancy, fueled by wine. Dawn would sometimes creep up on us, unbuttoned and still garrulous, curled up on the carpet half-listening to *Das Knaben Wunderhorn*, our eyelids heavy, our veins pumping music and Muscadet instead of blood.

With Butler and a good bottle I found I had plenty of ideas, although they were all reactions to something he said, points where my barbed sensibility resisted his smooth assertions. He was convinced that all values including truth were arbitrary functions of a self-sustained cultural code, a floating web of relationships not attached to anything, mapping nothing. Worse, he imagined we were locked inside a cage of language and couldn't even look out through the verbal bars. Next to him I felt I truly was the thorough realist I'd half-jokingly presented myself as being the first time we met.

Butler was vexed with me because I wouldn't agree with everything he said and in truth my feistiness was more an effort to oppose him—a sort of intellectual arm-wrestling—than a defense of a solid position. My argumentativeness proved that what I felt for him was friendship. I might have been willing to submit to the idiocies of a beautiful lover, knowing all the while that what I really thought was hidden and sacrosanct some-where within me. But with Butler I was facing someone more deliberate than I, perhaps, but also more cultured. When I would phone him and ask him what he was doing he'd say, "Oh, just sitting in the sun and prac-ticing Italian verbs" (a subject he wasn't even studying at the university). His very application I took as a reproach to my disorder, although of course I made fun of what I called his "bluestocking" perseverance. Around him I wanted to seem frivolous and Wildean, but in fact I was as thick-thighed and self-improving as he.

We liked each other. He surprised me with his precise opinions expertly expressed and I liked his interest in me, the way he courted me. I even feared he might fall in love with me and leave Lynne for me—an eventu-ality that my vanity may have sought but that my conscience feared because of my exaggerated respect for heterosexual couples. I myself wanted to go straight some vague day very soon and marry a woman. For my twenty-eighth birthday Butler and Lynne invited me to an expensive French restaurant in Midtown where Butler translated the *carte* for me, consulted the *sommelier* at length and even paid the bill during a mock visit to the toilet—a discreet bit of European elegance opposed in spirit to everything my father enjoyed, since for him his solemn, conspicuous verification of the waiter's addition and his slow, deliberate stacking up of one twenty-dollar bill after another was the ceremonial bride-price weighed in before his awed guest, the clear measure of his cold esteem.

Butler and I spent long hours together walking through Central Park. I kept quoting the Logical Positivists to him, philosophers such as Rudolf Carnap or A.J. Ayer, whereas he spoke of Saussure and Roland Barthes; he'd never heard of my men nor I of his, nor was either of us eager to learn anything about the other. We each wanted to convince, something we'd always been able to do with friends up till now. I accused him of being uncritical, not sufficiently skeptical (I meant original), a slave to French fads, although in 1968 Structuralism and semiotics had not yet tri-umphed in America and he was ahead of the fad. He accused me of em-bracing a stony-hearted Austrian Positivism that went against my own artistic ambitions. I saw my Positivism as parallel to my Socialism; I could believe in them both precisely because they worked against the cultural and social elitism my natural allegiances might favor.

"Anyway," I said, "your Mr. Barthes or Bartleby, you say, believes in the death of the author whereas my ideas merely assign the writer a useful if highly limited role in the ideal society of the future."

We had but one article of faith in common. We were both Socialists although of the anguished puritanical sort who waste more time on wondering whether to give alms, translate Mallarmé or kill our rich parents than on discussing concrete steps toward social justice or taking power. Butler's parents weren't even rich and his imaginary sacrifice of them to the revolutionary firing squad was a form of social climbing. We wanted to imagine personal sacrifices worthy of a saint and cruelty worthy of Saint-Just. China's great Cultural Revolution, begun in 1965, thrilled us as we dimly heard echoes of it, because we liked the idea that intellectuals must endlessly examine their conscience and submit to work in the fields beside the "people," that entity we idealized in the abstract and despised in the particular, especially the funny-smelling, hard-drinking, unsmiling, racist members of the proletariat we were meeting in New York.

WE MAY HAVE discussed the faraway Cultural Revolution; what we didn't see was that a gay revolution was happening under our very noses. More and more gay men were telling me their stories, as though the main pressure behind cruising were narrative rather than sexual. "So many stories, so little time to tell them," might have been a T-shirt slogan back then. The silence that had been imposed for so many centuries on homosexuals had finally been broken, and now we were all talking at once. Sometimes we'd rather talk than fuck; perhaps we fucked so that we could indulge in the pillow talk afterwards. We talked and talked about our lives and even very young men could sound as though they were ancient as they recounted their stories. "Oh, that was years and years ago," they'd say, launching into tales about home, church, school.

Not all the stories inspired me with sympathy. One night after I left Butler's and Lynne's apartment I cruised a guy my age on Broadway who invited me home with him. He was tall, thick, hairy, his chest operatically wide under a straining white T-shirt, his hair wiry and long, pushed back behind his ears. He had a three-day beard. His dodgy green eyes protruded from his pale boxer's face, itself unhealthily attractive as though he'd just nursed a bruise with a piece of raw steak.

He spoke grammatical English with a thug's slur and in a low, resonant voice, a voice from the balls. He said, without a smile, "Warm come to my place and get furk?"

"Sure," I said, getting hard, frightened he might be dangerous. We walked side by side, block after block, heading down toward Riverside as an old Chevy with a broken exhaust pipe and good radio putt-putted past, swirling us in richest Motown, a falling gospel wail sustained by a sudden updraft of doo-dahing. In the darkened canyons of buildings only one window on the twentieth floor released a sulfurous yellow glow, and for some reason I thought of the words "half-life," something I imagined that rotting carbon emits. The Hudson, beyond the strip of park and the West Side Highway, exhaled a colder, damper breath into the hot night, like a trace of sweat perceived as the black stain through a blue shirt. Neither of us spoke, as though afraid to cut the sexual tension with mindless chitchat. He looked straight ahead but must have been aware I was side-swiping him at every step with another glance, calculating the flab at his waist, the heft of his hands, the girth of his calves. Was he clean? Was he a cold man who could express tenderness only in bed, or would there be no bed, just him backed up against a wall, cock jutting out of his jeans in the darkened hall, eyes squeezed shut, his mouth clamped shut when I would try to kiss him?

His apartment was in a 1920s building on Riverside overlooking the park. The rooms were all one step up and two down. There was a sitting room in a round tower lined with small beveled glass panes. The furniture was heavy and dark, heat-cracked leather club chairs, a roll-top oak desk, a frayed Oriental rug, a brass reading lamp with a green glass shade and, as soon as he'd poured us a whiskey each in a crystal tumbler, there was a contralto voice over all the hidden speakers in the six or seven rooms, a voice as ambiguous as a countertenor's but its opposite, for if a countertenor was neutered she was as fully gendered as an angel, consolation and authority joined in one voice.

At first I thought he must be a guest in the apartment of a much older professor, this place with its thousands of serious shelved books, the volume of Aristotle on the work table open to the *Nicomachean Ethics*, the voice on the sound system singing Handel with a pathos that seemed more noble because not quite human. I pictured the pained open mouths and tearful closed eyes of angels in a Bellini entombment as small hands lower into the ground the cadaver with its old, dark wounds in the hands and skinny side.

But then he started to tell me everything about his life. He'd been the last child in a poor family of nine. He'd grown up in western Pennsylvania, where his father worked in a filling station repairing cars. "I was intelligent," he said, "but I couldn't think because I didn't know any words. Middle-class people like you have no idea, but with a minuscule vocabulary it's as though you're trying to pick up blobs of mercury with tweezers." That he knew I was middle class seemed either dismissive or clinical; that one had a class identity at all seemed to me, an American, novel and threatening, for though I was a Socialist my principles could be applied only to other people. I myself was a pulsing, energized vacuum, I was an Artist, all potential, a capability entirely negative, a field of dangerously unattached and whirling neutrons.

He'd moved to New York, lived in the streets, turned tricks and one day hustled a guy who turned out to be a Columbia professor. "He seemed to recognize I was bright. Anyway he moved me in and started to teach me everything he knew at a breakneck pace—German, history, Hegel, Freud, Marx. Into two years I was able to compress ten years' worth of study."

He said that those two years had been the most exalted of his life. He'd been the wolf child, his teacher the Enlightenment philosopher, and I pictured the bedroom light gleaming on the student's fangs, the professor's well kept hands tangled in the facial fur as he whispered wisdom into one cocked ear.

Throughout those two years, recordings of this contralto singer had played night and day. "I came to think of her as my guardian angel, this singer, entering me with that penetrating voice. There is something sorrowful about that voice, not the Virgin Mary's lachrymose compassion but the tragic realism of . . ." He smiled. "Of Brünnhilde. Doesn't she sound like a warrior?" He told me he became obsessed by her. "I read a little book of tributes by various conductors and soloists and friends that had been put together after her early death—she'd died of throat cancer." He found out that she had a twin sister whom she'd always lived with. "They were inseparable and she was serene all her life, almost saintly, except for one brief period of six months when she was married. Then she was a bitch. She cried all the time, seemed always to be on the rag. Finally she left her husband and went back to her sister and resumed a sort of unearthly gentleness, even during her horrible last illness, a gentleness so unassailable that as I lay here night after night smoking joints I started to dream up certain things about her. I realized that she and her sister must have been lovers."

"How do you figure that?" I asked.

His powerful hand and thick legs were under the warm light shed by the lamp beside him but his face was eerie in the green halo cast by the glass shade. I felt a delicate unspoken decision was being taken: the more he told me about his life the less likely it was I was going to get fucked. We might end up cuddling like brothers but the mystery that goaded his sexual nastiness was being dissipated word by every word. "Figure? Well, I figure," he said, swiveling the floor lamp away from him so that now his entire body was subaqueous, "I figure that the only way somebody can be so *saintly* is if she has no needs, no emotional needs, no needs for anyone outside the closed circuit she and her twin, her *identical* twin, make up. Just think: if you loved and were loved by someone you'd known all your life, from whom you had no secrets, *could* have none, someone who had the same mole on the same place on the left hip, who laughed before you finished the joke, became ill *with* you after the same meal, whom even your parents couldn't tell apart after they'd not seen you for a few months— hell," he said, sitting forward, dangling one hand into the pink light under the green lamp, and I saw that hand (which he pulled back until it became vernal again) as my last vanished bid for sex that night, "I learned that her twin was living down in Philadelphia and I began to correspond with her, I even took the train down for tea, she was this nice old English *lady* who put a tea cozy in the shape of a Beatrix Potter *rabbit* over the pot. We talked about tessitura and the Danish broadcast during the war and she had me pegged for just another opera queen but I had to know if they'd been lovers so I invited her to New York last year, remember that's when Bergman's film about the lesbian sisters was playing, so I took her to that, she didn't know what to expect, and I could feel her tensing up beside me in the theater and when we got outside I pushed her up against the wall and I said, 'That's the way it was between your sister and you, wasn't it?' and she said, 'Yes, yes,' but of course I already knew I was right and I left her sobbing there in Times Square, boy, was I pleased with myself." It never occurred to him (or to me) to feel any *solidarity* with this woman as a fellow homosexual. No, she was an "old dyke" whom he'd gleefully tricked into revealing her secrets.

That night back home I went to sleep alone curled up beside an imaginary Sean. In my dream he couldn't stop fucking me, he bent me into dozens of different shapes but he had to stay inside me, otherwise he wasn't happy, he apologized if he was hurting me, but I understood, didn't I, and I did. In my sleep my asshole felt sore, it ached way inside and burned near the lips but when I woke up there was nothing wrong with it.

———————

AT WORK I was assigned a new researcher named Christa von Bernsdorff. In my office all the journalists were men and all their researchers women. The man was encouraged to take bold stands, exaggerate to the point of parody, besmirch or exalt reputations and simplify the truth until it took on the lineaments of narrative. The woman was enjoined to clip his wings and hold him to the facts, a prudent Athena, daughter to a headstrong Zeus. She had to find a "primary source" for each of his assertions, write its name in the margins and then put red dots over the words she'd verified and initialed. This system, though never described as such, was probably meant to be the perfect marriage between male creativity and feminine practicality. If it worked at all it did so for very different reasons. Since journalists enjoyed a fairly low status, the male writers were as haphazardly educated and as quick as most of their readers to caricature other people and over-simplify world events, whereas the women, who'd be working only until they made brilliant marriages, were debutantes with top grades from the best schools. They'd been beautifully trained for sixteen years to locate information, analyze facts and weigh arguments. Men on the same social and intellectual level as these women were all off getting rich as brokers or corporation lawyers and were certainly not wasting their time as hack writers.

The system, whatever its faults, suited my personality since a *writer* was neither a *reporter* nor a *researcher* and was never expected to step out of the building but rather to style the information culled and transported by one person that would later be assayed and corrected by another. This detachment and irresponsibility accommodated my slothful nature, unpredictably fearful or aggressive.

If I was as disorderly as Bacchus—arriving late to the office hung over, staring out the window and chain-smoking, talking to everyone for hours on the phone with my automatic concern, rehearsed gaiety, factitious charm—then Christa was as tall, beautiful and composed as, if not Athena, then Artemis. I rang hollow, she solid. I could easily imagine her suddenly appearing, grey-eyed and helmeted, beside a fallen warrior and arming him with supernatural strength. She was four inches taller than I, her nose was so long and pointy that the tip turned bright red on winter days and she had a natural beauty disdainful of all artifice. She didn't wear any makeup beyond a faint pink lipstick. Her cheekbones were dusted with a blonde down visible only in a cross light. Her shoulder-length blonde hair was held back with a cloth barrette that spanned her head except on the days when she wore her hair up off her long neck. On those days she suspended old, heavy Baroque pearl drops from lobes velvety with blonde baby's down. She was determinedly cheerful despite an underlying melancholy, and though she was obviously superior to us all, she made a conscious effort to schmooze with everyone during coffee break. She seemed lonely.

Because of our work we'd spend hours in a huddle, talking and talking, until slowly I'd pieced together her story. She didn't especially want to tell it. Or perhaps she had no gift for storytelling. She told it so badly that I knew she'd never served it up before. Her father had been a Russian aristocrat of the Baltic nobility with an estate in Estonia. *His* mother had been a lady-in-waiting to the last Czarina. After the Revolution he had studied at Cambridge, then eked out a miserable living in Paris translating things for the émigré press. There he'd met Christa's mother, a nineteen-year-old Providence Brahmin who'd been so tall and awkward and terrified of society that she'd warned her parents she'd make her debut only if they would promise to send her to Europe immediately afterwards for a year abroad. In Paris she'd met her Russian prince and bought him a *Schloss* just east of Potsdam.

I didn't respond with confidences of my own. I wanted her to like me; I was afraid she'd be repelled if I told her I was gay. Jamie was my only colleague who knew the truth about me.

One night while we were eating a catered dinner together in the office, our reward for working late, she blushed like a child before she could stammer, "I brought you some of my baby pictures to see." I couldn't understand her reluctance about showing them until I'd looked at them. She extracted out of a heat-curled envelope black-and-white snapshots of an unfamiliarly small and nearly square format, though shot with Hasselblad clarity.

Christa and her four blond brothers and sisters, all naked and golden, were crawling over the lap of a man in a Nazi officer's uniform. "The war came along and my father, as an aristocrat, was expected to serve as an officer," she said in a rush and I understood that depending on how I responded she was prepared to gather up these cards and flee the casino or stay and place her bets. I didn't say anything but hoped to radiate a neutral acceptance through a slight increase in body warmth.

"He was killed in battle in 1940. When the war came to an end my mother was really up the creek." A bitter little smile underscored the irony of this Americanism. "The Polish servants hated her because she was the wife of a Russian, the Soviet soldiers hated her because she was a Russian baroness, the Germans hated her because she was American and the Americans hated her because she was the widow of a Nazi officer *and* a traitor. *And* she'd forgotten to teach us kids English. We were all rounded up and put in an American detention camp where we stayed for a year and a half despite all the efforts of her family back in the States to pull strings to get us out. I can remember at last arriving in New York and eating in this vast dining room in my aunt's apartment on Park Avenue and I was in a threadbare dress and I couldn't speak English and my aunt, who's never had children, stared at us all with horror. We even held our forks in the left hand instead of switching it back and forth to the right. Our poor mother had had ten years of happiness with our father and now that was over and she didn't want to live in the world ever again. As soon as she could put her hands on some of her money she moved us all to a Vermont farm where I grew up a complete tomboy, always on horseback, never in a dress, and our mother built a good imitation of a Russian Orthodox chapel and was constantly kneeling before candles and icons thinking about her husband."

"Is she still there?"

"Yes." Christa smiled when she saw the frown dawning on my forehead. "Now, don't even *think* of suggesting she start a new life. Please, none of your bromides."

I laughed, caught in the act.

"I didn't even know I was a baroness until I read it on the invitation to my debutante party, which was also virtually the first time I'd ever put on a dress. I went to Columbia and twice I had Jewish roommates who made a stink and asked to be moved out when they—well, I never found out if they knew my father had served in the German army or whether it was just because I had a German name. No one, of course, ever stopped to ask me about my own political opinions, which veer to the extreme left and are resolutely opposed to racism."

One day I told another young woman who worked with us, "Christa is so great, so beautiful and so fascinating, but she's got one tic that drives me batty, she's always breaking off in mid-sentence and sighing."

The other woman laughed. "That's not a tic. She's sighing because she's in love with you." I see from an old diary that that occurred on February 9th, 1969.

I reported this development to Jamie. I think he was so unused to direct statements of an intimate nature that he paused for a full five or even six beats, like a hammy actor determined to milk his next line, before responding to my remarks. I guess I left him nonplused most of the time, an effect I registered as wickedly amusing but also tawdry.

"Congratulations, old man, I think that's positively ripping." Well, he didn't say *that*, but the words suggest the spirit of his reaction. He did thump me woodenly on the back and kept looking at me in a new way, as though I weren't just a vulgar, friendly clown but a possible contender, as though I, too, might be up to the snobbish, duplicitous bisexuality of the White Russians. He might have offered me a cigar.

For me Christa was at once her glowing legend (double-headed eagle) and a sweet, unintimidating person I liked to be with. She was slightly dull, just as Jamie was dull and for the same reason; neither wanted to serve up an anecdote, illustrate a point, stay in character, rise to the occasion. For them there was no occasion to celebrate, no wisdom to be garnered, no roles to play. They cultivated a tedious dailiness; anything more dramatic or even focused would have embarrassed them.

I liked to walk down the street with this heroic Sieglinde to whom I was a smaller, darker Siegfried and when I realized other men envied me, my response wavered between fearing the competition and wishing it'd been I, not she, who had widened their eyes.

We were best when we were alone. I started spending more and more time at her place.

She'd lived the last two years in Italy. She might be a Baltic baroness but she'd traded in that title for simpler fare, the hot daily pleasure and vexation of being a big blonde in Rome. From her time in Italy she'd learned a sexier, more robust way of eating, laughing, joking and thinking about her body. She claimed she found the constant male harassment in the street "funny," even "flattering." Even now, back in New York, if she didn't know the answer to a question, she'd respond with that explosive, rising monosyllable, "*Boh*," the Italian verbal shrug to indicate unapologetic ignorance, a sound halfway between a burp and the bubble exploding from the mouth of a surfacing deep-sea diver. She'd stroke her cheek with the back of her hand, to dramatize the beard of boredom, press her finger to her nose to enjoin caution and when our taxi got stuck once in a traffic jam, she mumbled, "*Menaggia*," with all the Job-like weariness of a Roman matron climbing the Capitoline steps.

All lovers tell each other their stories (La Rochefoucauld says people fall in love in order to have a captive audience), but the way they recount the past is never entirely candid, since the story of past lovers is necessarily a form of instruction to the new one. We complain of injustices endured in past affairs in order to convince our new partner to treat us better—or, perhaps, to re-create the same old débâcle. Christa told me of a man she'd known in Rome, an older Italian who was a Joseph Conrad scholar, was married but living apart from his wife, as so many Italians did in those days before divorce. He loved Christa's beauty and called her "my Viking," but when she declared her passion he simply pressed a finger to her lips and kissed her on the forehead, though he had to stand on tiptoe to do so. He wrote a column on books for the *Corriere della Sera*, yet she never saw him reading or writing; he gave lectures on Conrad and had even concocted an imitation of *Under Western Eyes*, but she'd never seen the book in a store or figured out when or where the lectures took place. He had a son Christa's age whom he adored, a Marxist economic historian, but she never met the guy or even saw his picture. Even Marco's Trastevere pied-à-terre turned out not to be his main residence, since he apparently had an old princely apartment, now dilapidated, on the Via Madama she was never allowed to visit.

After all this ambiguity Christa longed for honesty (she used the French word *transparence*) in her friendships; she wouldn't make a distinction between friendship and love and I wondered if this semantic confusion was meant to create a no-man's-land in which we could glide unnoticed from one dimension to the other—and back again if necessary, for she was so kind, so delicate, that she wouldn't have wanted to hurt me or make things awkward. American frankness, courtly refinement, Italian playfulness all came together in this marvelous woman, who also had something soldierly about her. As a gay man I wouldn't have dared to say that, but a straight guy at the office said, "Good old Christa, she's a regular guy," and this description stuck in my mind. She'd help me into my coat, she'd lend me ten bucks the day before payday, and in her unveiled eyes, her strong jaw, her upright posture and general "transparence," as well as in her complete lack of humid, ensnaring coquetry, I felt an absence of everything I hated about women, the deviousness, the emotional blackmail, the musky, layered mystery. At this time I read Gauguin's Tahitian journals, *Noa-Noa*, in which he said that in the Pacific he learned to love women again since the Polynesians were friendly, brown, naked, embraceable creatures unlike European women with their stays, their virtue, odors and schemes, and for a moment I convinced myself things might be just that simple. I, too, might love my Viking, my trooper, my giant blonde Tahitian.

And I was tired of men, as tired of their bulky, bristling bodies as I was weary of the despair they inspired in me. When I showed friends the novel I had written about Sean, I read it to them out loud to instruct them, through the coloration of my voice, as to exactly how they were to respond, but despite all my coaching they still found so much suffering lugubrious and exasperating. I needed to propagate the golden legend of my love in order to turn sentimental defeat into spiritual victory. I needed to demonstrate to other people that in the gay world in which men danced an allemande left and right with interchangeable partners I had chosen one man around whom to revolve in an endless do-si-do of devotion.

"But he's maddening, this character of yours," Jamie said, knowing the character was based on me. "He has no pride. It's sickening!"

I said, "But what of the medieval knight who kept one eye shut the rest of his life after he'd seen his lady for the last time? Isn't there something beautiful about that?"

"Beautiful?! A jerk."

"Or what of this Colombian poet I heard of," I persisted, "who was in love with a lesbian and had a sex change just to please her."

"*And?*"

"And she rejected him because he was just one more ugly dyke. But the gesture—"

"Loser. Grotesque loser. Anyway, there are so many other people in the world."

No, there aren't, I thought. The true lover is monotheistic.

In this remnant of a life I have left, I thought, I might as well find comfort with Christa. One long spring we spent together, shopping for food and cooking together, reading and reminiscing and listening to re-recordings of old Italian café songs from the turn of the century ("It was raining and I was crying," Christa translated). That spring was cold and bleak and raining but we were happy together inside her studio with the vast skylight sloping on an angle, wet gingko leaves pressed to the glass. I thought to myself that she was more beautiful than Sean, that if she were a man she'd be the handsomest man I'd ever known. Women liked me more than men did; at least the women I attracted were a cut above even those men who thought they were too good for me. I wavered between saying women had lower standards or insisting they were more interested in character and charm than in beauty and might.

Christa's whole interest in me seemed to be to make me feel good about myself, which she accomplished without resorting to flattery. We'd lie naked in bed, she tall and lean and adorned in nothing but a big summer hat heavy with cloth cabbage roses. She'd make a mushroom risotto when the skylight would dim and Sunday night would depress us with the thought of a return to work Monday morning. We played at being depressed because it was a different mode of coziness. I was so—not happy but peaceful with her that I thought, How ironic, just as I've finally managed to finish my gay novel I'm ending up in a woman's arms.

One day at breakfast she said, "I keep talking about *transparence* but I haven't told you about Gunther." She said that until recently she'd lived with him, a chemist from Hamburg, but that things hadn't gone all that well with him and besides, "I wanted to be unencumbered in case there was a chance of you and me getting together." She spoke in a high, soft voice with her head lowered and her eyes closed and I saw how embarrassed she was, especially since she must have known that if I spoke so often of the distant past it was to avoid talking about the recent past or the future and if I dwelled on childhood fears it was because I didn't want to tell her about my adult anxieties.

"I have something to confess, too," I said. "I've had quite a few affairs with men."

I let a long silence hang in the air and looked out the window.

"I never would have guessed it," she said. Then, in a firmer tone, she added, "It doesn't make the slightest difference."

But it did. I didn't dare tell her that many of these "affairs" had not been the twilit, star-crossed romances she might imagine but had rather been conducted kneeling on the floor of a public toilet, my vows exchanged only with the red unsheathed fury of the third penis of the afternoon. I had no tattoos or piercings but my nipples had a history, they were enlarged and they stiffened when brushed by a callused hand, just as my ass arched and filled out in my skintight jeans under a man's admiring scrutiny and my cock stiffened after the third glance back, a heliotrope trained to follow the light emanating from male eyes only.

When I was alone with Christa, as when I'd been alone with Maria years before, I could imagine myself at ease, the two of us happy. But one cold wet night after work, Christa and I took in a movie in the Village, then ducked into the Riviera Café on Sheridan Square for a bowl of chili. It was an island of boisterous heterosexuality in the flood of gay male life that flowed around it and I'd chosen it precisely because there, stupidly, I thought I wouldn't be tempted. And yet as we sat on the glassed-in terrace I saw wave after wave of handsome young guys go past, their voices ringing out above the rumble of subways passing under the sidewalk, their powerful young bodies, pale faces and black, slicked-back hair materializing in the mist rising from the grate, only to vanish into the dark of West Fourth Street, one man's hand around another's waist, a star of complicity glancing off a smile or eye, and I wanted to be with them, I felt I was trapped with my mother. Poor Christa suddenly looked much too adult and dowdy and her conversation sounded fatally innocuous.

When we were alone again in her apartment I sank into the eiderdown comforter of her love, but I felt something shameful about it. I wasn't a real man, I could barely keep it up, usually not at all, but despite my inadequacy Christa looked at me with such affection and admiration that I feared growing accustomed to it. Male indifference was bracing, Spartan, whereas female indulgence was corrupting, Persian. When I was with a woman I felt good, but was that realistic, advisable? I dreamed I was a coyote looking from a mesa down on a cheerful fire. I was cold and lonely, but if I approached the campsite it would be to kill or be killed.

I thought of Butler and Lynne; although they seemed happy enough, I imagined Lynne must always be afraid of losing Butler to another man. There was something hectic about her vivacity that seemed a continuously chanted spell to ward off just such a defection. Not that I wanted to deny the possibility of bisexuality, which suited my conflicting feelings for Christa as well as a novelistic craving for complexity. Everyone had been talking about "androgyny" for the last seven years and even the dimmest suburban barbershop had hoped to improve its clientele by advertising in bold letters on a prominent placard, "Unisex." And yet the long, straightened hair, the necklaces and finery and the newly fashionable skinniness affected by straight guys had only been new window dressing for the same old actions and attitudes. Gay men who dated women struck me as even less innovative. My stepmother's best friend was married to a gay man who'd always been a tyrant with her and their three daughters, one of whom had repeatedly attempted suicide. Once a year he'd gone on a "hunting trip" with his "best friend," but the other fifty weeks a year he was an angry force locked up in his study at the top of their huge house (he'd married his wife for her money).

The only two choices, it appeared, were marriage, cruel to the wife, stifling to the husband, and gay promiscuity, by definition transitory, sexy and sad for the young, frustrating and sad for the old.

What haunted me most now, however, was the idea of Gunther, a straight man as tall and blond as Christa, according to the description I forced out of her. She told me nothing of his character, but I fancied him too gruff to be pleasing during courtship but firm and loyal in wedlock. Christa was rejecting him because I was amusing, *une âme sœur*, but in the long run more *sœur* than soulful, perhaps, at least more than she bargained for. Of course I was sure Gunther could make her happy as I never could. Gunther was a real man, one I'd fashioned to be good enough for her.

I didn't want to be just a friend to my wife; she deserved love as much as I did. I certainly didn't want to be her rival, not even once for a fraction of a mental second; there were a few ways in which I wouldn't disgrace myself. Nor would I enter a marriage with the idea I could always divorce if it didn't work out; for me marriage remained a sacred institution because until now I'd seldom thought about it. It remained a pure form contemplated from without rather than a familiar interior requiring radical modifications.

I knew I was going to ruin Christa's life. If I left her now she'd go back to Gunther and be happy forever after.

Our project at work came to an end. I stopped seeing her for two weeks. One day Jamie told me she'd gone to Italy for a month. I timed my vacation to start when hers ended. When I came back to New York I found a heavy, embossed cream envelope in my mailbox. An inner envelope contained a coroneted invitation announcing Christa's wedding.

I let a month go by, then invited the new couple to dinner. He was indeed tall and blond, but tortured, balding, with a rictus for a smile and hand-rubbing courtliness. He was stern with Christa, given to bouts of nervous irritation.

A year later they had a child. Christa found a better job with a different company. Maria ran into her from time to time over the years. She never lost her hushed, precise, sometimes pained way of speaking, of shyly biting into her words as though they were stale bread. Her husband was too ill to work—something indeterminate or at least unpronounceable, a malady of the nerves, or was it something like Crohn's disease, a slow rusting of the intestines. The daughter, Maria reported, was superb, less stately than Christa, more awakened. She must now be just three or four years younger than we were when we first met.

Just last year Maria told me that Gunther was now well and back at work. Christa seemed happier than Maria had ever seen her.

〜〜〜〜〜〜◯ ROD HAD his monthly party, this time a *vernissage* for his latest tricks and light boxes. There I met Jimmy, a famous eighteen-year-old ballet dancer. His fame, I suppose, was roughly equivalent to Christa's title for me, a proof that these people (and my association with them) were esteemed by convention. Not that I thought in those terms. I was too intoxicated by their glamor since in the Midwest, where I'd grown up, celebrities had been as rare as aristocrats.

Jimmy was not the usual *jeune premier*, "all thighs and rose petals" as someone (Nabokov? James Merrill?) once said. I'm not quite sure what *thews* are, but he didn't appear to have them. He was just a tiny kid dressed in a jacket that swallowed him, its sleeves covering his delicate bluish hands. He had a big, thin-lipped mouth ripe with a disabused sadness that condescended once in a while to be flirtatious, just to keep the whole game rolling along, no matter how wearily. He had an appealing way of touching (not tugging or holding) my lapel when he spoke to me. Like most young dancers he was painfully ignorant, though in his case he was just as painfully sophisticated. He seemed to have suffered an early defeat that had drained him of all hope—perhaps the defeat was his talent.

Certainly after a short time I discovered how he was merely an inconspicuous acolyte serving at the big, flashy altar of his talent. Whereas no two people, not even any two directors, can agree about an actor's value, everyone, even the dopiest member of the audience, knows whether a dancer is good, better or best. Jimmy was the best. He could leap the highest and turn the most times without "traveling," that is, drifting unwittingly downstage or to one side or the other. He was faster and cleaner than the other men. He could turn as easily to the left as to the right. He could turn and leap, turn and leap, following a perfect giant circle of *grands jetés* inscribed within the square of the stage. He could leap up and beat his legs together faster than a barber's shears. His *port de bras* was elegant but not mannered, at once noble and unfussily American. He was too short to partner ballerinas convincingly, but he could do things no other man would attempt, such as kick the back of his head as he went flying offstage in an absurd rock adaptation of Vivaldi that had been especially concocted to show him off, a role so rapid and demanding that backstage assistants would clamp an oxygen mask over his nose and mouth before pushing him back in front of the audience.

On stage he was a demonstration of nuclear fission, neutrinos flying, energy melting down in a frightening implosion, but in my arms he was just a frail boy laboring under a curse of melancholy. I couldn't forget that his legs were insured for a million dollars as he wrapped them around my back. I was afraid of crushing his body, so full of longing was I or perhaps so celebratory in this exuberant return to my own sex.

I was proud to ride beside him in the company bus as it brought the dancers back from Brooklyn into Manhattan. I remember sitting beside him and holding his tiny hand as the bus went around Washington Square. "Oh, look at the neat arch!" one dancer called out. "Didn't we see an arch like that last week? Was it in Paris?" "Maybe Zurich." "Oh, Zurich, I *love* Sweden!"

To claim Jimmy as a member of my sex seemed presumptuous since on stage he was so agile, so strong, so lovely, his extensions so improbable and lawless that he seemed as isolated and sacred as a hermaphrodite. Just as a great painting looks strangely small when you look at the wrong side and you can scarcely reconcile this unimpressive square yard of canvas and crossed stretchers with the complexity of the young woman standing at the window looking out into a blaze of light, her hand resting on the half-open shutter, in the same way his sleeping body with its child-like arms, a waist I could encircle with both hands and his pale glabrous chest seemed unrelated to the bristling sting ray he opened out into as he soared through the lateral shafts of colored light.

He told me how painful the dancer's life was, both physically and emotionally. "You're always in pain and you have to dance your way right through a strain or pulled ligament. Even the so-called moment of glory," he said, "when you're taking a bow, you can hear the other dancers behind the curtain hissing to each other about all the stupid mistakes you made."

Jimmy lived with his sister, who was two years older than he. Back in Cleveland she'd begun ballet lessons when she was eight, as well brought up little girls did in those days, and Jimmy had been dragooned into the class, since there were ten girls and only one other boy. Their father, disturbed that little Jimmy was so uninterested in sports, was at first pleased when he saw how high his son could jump and how fast he could turn. His pleasure turned into horror when he realized what a sissy the boy was becoming, begging to wear his sister's tutu, crossing the living room on point with a frozen smile and weaving arms to greet him when he came from the office with a colleague.

But he and his wife were balletomanes, generally cultured, more than liberal, and he made a lot of money; when Madame Dolinskaya told them six years into their children's training that their kids were exceptionally gifted and ambitious and should be sent to New York, he and Jimmy's mother bowed before the curse some previously unnoticed Carabosse must have whispered over the cradle. For the first two years a housekeeper was hired to look after Jimmy and Sara when they came home from a long day at the Manhattan High School of Performing Arts and three ballet classes. But then Sara decided that though she had a certain small talent she was nothing next to Jimmy. She quit dancing, enrolled in a business administration course and started keeping house for her brother.

On days when he was performing Jimmy attended just one class, in the morning, but on off days he took so many that he crawled home. I was present once when he arrived pale, speechless, and just stretched out on the floor. His sister took off his clothes, unbandaged his poor feet and washed them, then rewrapped those permanent wounds. Finally she propped him up in front of the television and fed him. Within seconds he'd slumped into sleep.

He was always angry with the chief choreographer and his lover, the manager of the company. They didn't schedule him often enough, they didn't assign him the best roles nor create enough new ones. The same nerviness that made him so dazzling on stage rendered him impossible, sometimes nearly insane, in his dealings with his bosses. He did nothing but plot revenge on them, though they seemed harmless enough to me.

Jimmy's real enemy, whom he never talked about, was the leading New York dance critic. This ass, who had the common failing of making up for his ignorance by the vigor of his opinions, attacked Jimmy week after week. "Yes, the boy is brilliant, the best technician on stage we have," he wrote on a typical day, "but his effeminacy sickens as does his shameless mugging. If he's obliged to touch a real woman, he treats the ballerina with the disdain usually reserved for an ordure." Then shifting into a tone designed to cater to the Yanks, he added, "Come on, Jimmy, give us plain folk in the audience a break; we can't help thinking *you* are the one who'd like to be the *girl*! And doesn't the company recognize you're just too small to be a *jeune premier*?"

Jimmy dreamed of changing his sex, not because he rejected his . . . well, *boyhood*, but because he thought that if he were a woman he'd be the strongest ballerina in the world with the most startling elevation and he'd never have to totter and struggle to lift another big girl off the ground.

I moved to Rome and lost touch with him but I heard that he'd quit the company in a pique. His talent was so particular and his reputation so bad that no one else would hire him. For a while he danced at Radio City Music Hall. Audiences went into raptures over his long, floating adagios, whiplash turns and hummingbird *entrechats*, but Easter came along and the Rockettes had to break out of painted eggs wearing nun costumes, tap dancing to "Climb Every Mountain," and Jimmy was again out of work. He went to every casting call but he was too small to be a Broadway chorus boy. He produced his own one-man recital but the attendance was disappointing and he lost all his money. He swallowed his pride and tried to rejoin his old ballet company, but no one wanted him back. Life had been so much calmer without him.

Six years ago a famous American painter came to dinner at my house in Paris. Since his girlfriend was a choreographer with her own company, I asked him if he'd ever heard of Jimmy. "Of course," he said, "but surely you know?"

"Know what?"

"He was a répétiteur for Nancy's dancers but even though he was in his late thirties he wanted to perform just one more time himself. Nancy promised to create a new solo for him and she even scheduled it for last fall. But then she got so busy with *Switch Hitter*, her big new dance to a Stan Getz score, that she never got around to Jimmy's solo. Poor Jimmy, he'd invited all his friends to see his farewell performance. He couldn't bear the shame and killed himself."

I HAD SEX with so many different men, usually a new one every night, that once a month I came down with a case of gonorrhea, usually rectal, sometimes penile, once in the throat (so sore I could scarcely swallow, my only symptom). I was covered by the company's health policy and the doctor invented ever more fanciful but innocuous diagnoses to enter into the insurance forms. I'd sit in the waiting room, which played the best classical FM station, and as I waited my turn I'd read through back numbers of *Architectural Digest* or a stylish magazine called *After Dark*, in which the glossy black-and-white photos were all of new dancers, young athletes and up-and-coming male models. All the other patients were men, and since we were there for the same reason we'd smile sheepishly if we caught a friend's eye. One of us would mime exasperation, hands on hips, while the other wagged a mock-reproachful finger. We'd cruise strangers fitfully, attracted by the other man's imagined excesses, put off by his current illness, so like our own.

Once in the examining room, the usual decorum of concealing screens for disrobing and paper gowns for sheathing nudity was dispensed with. I'd dated my doctor, he'd even fisted me once on an afternoon on Fire Island when we were both stoned and bathed in a sea of grease, and he was so rich and manly that I longed to go out with him again; with a shameless alacrity I cast my clothes aside and mounted the examining table, "as naked as a jaybird," as my mother would have said, convinced that this new glimpse at my occasionally hidden charms would tempt him to invite me out to dinner again. A second later I'd pressed my chest to the table and stuck my rump in the air. With a similar efficiency he'd already entered me with a long hollow chrome bar, a surgical flashlight that permitted him to say at a glance, "Yep, that's it, but I'll take a swab just to be sure." A long, cotton-tipped wand was inserted into the speculum and a smear swabbed onto a slide, which the doctor looked at, and into a petri dish, where the bacteria would be cultivated and challenged by various antibiotics in order to verify which treatment would work best. "Okay, you can get dressed," he said with disappointing indifference.

In his adjoining private office (silk Turkish rug of the tree of life on the floor), the doctor perched briefly on a corner of his desk and said, while writing a prescription, "I've given you two massive shots of Penicillin. Drink plenty of water and take two Bactrim three times a day for a week. If you have a resistant strain that should show up in the culture, I'll let you know. And of course I've drawn blood to check for syphilis."

No shame attached to these frequent medical visits; they were Aphrodite's spoils. The only fear we felt was that one day a strain of syphilis or gonorrhea would evolve that would be resistant to all available drugs. Already the original doses had been boosted dramatically. Yet we felt we were enlightened both in science and in the arts of the flesh. We thought we had a right to express ourselves sexually wherever, whenever and with whomever we chose. A venereal disease, far from being a price to pay, was a frequent medical accident, easily remedied, which bore no moral weight. A residual and unrecognized sense of guilt might make us depressed for an hour, but a visit to the handsome doctor absolved us, especially since he had a sort of Mr. Fixit approach to our mishaps. One day he said to me, "Since you get the clap so often, maybe we should put you on a daily diet of Bactrim as a prophylactic. The only problem is that it might mask the symptoms without killing the bacteria. And you'd have to add a few things to your diet to replenish the intestinal flora and fauna it might kill off. I suppose you'd never be willing to try condoms?"

"Are you kidding?" I said. "Let's try the Bactrim. Isn't there a danger that if I take it too long it won't work anymore?"

"No. *You* don't become resistant to it, but *it*—the whole population of bacteria—can mutate and become resistant to the antibiotic, but if that happens everyone will just boost the dose again."

My only regret was that if the new regime was effective I'd be seeing my doctor less often. Armed with Bactrim, I hesitated not at all in my endless couplings and found this new license enviable, certainly an admirable freedom, an essential article in the code of our personal liberation. Just as the Pill freed women to do with their bodies what they wished, so antibiotics made us invulnerable to the puritanical menace of disease.

One day my doctor was on vacation and his weird older partner filled in for him. Despite the Bactrim I'd contracted gonorrhea in my penis. After the doctor gave me two horse shots of Penicillin, which he stuck me with as painfully as possible, he said, "Wanna fuck me now?"

"But I've got the clap!" I protested.

"I'll give myself a shot as soon as we're finished." He dropped his pants but did not remove his white doctor's smock or stethoscope. The strange setting and kinky situation excited me and I climbed onto the examining table behind his bare, lean ass. I caught a glimpse of his legendarily big penis, which had never been seen erect. It dangled, as did his stethoscope, on the table.

As I was leaving the examining room I saw him shooting up and quickly buckling his trousers. I still had to pay the full fee.

ALTOGETHER twenty-four editors or their assistants had rejected my novel. Two years later I met several of these editors, two of them gay; one of them told me he'd liked my book but had seen no way he could have defended it in a meeting without "destroying his reputation." Soon after that, I learned that he'd been fired for spending hours each day in the toilet and for being cripplingly disorganized; he hurled himself under a subway. The other said he'd found parts of the book "amazingly sophisticated" and other passages "shockingly naïve." "I mean," he asked, indignantly, "how could the protagonist not know what a *garlic press* is, for Christ's sake?" Another admired the first chapter (before the narrator meets "Sean"), but found the rest "obsessive" and "tiresome."

I didn't know how to respond to the criticism that my very life was "tiresome." If everything I'd experienced and valued and suffered over was just a big bore, then from what vantage point of scintillating cleverness could I revise my very existence? I'd read once that a philosopher had said that to discuss language with words was like trying to build a boat that was already under sail; for a bore to inject interest into his tedious book (or life) was surely every bit as impossible a task.

I suspected that the homosexual subject matter of my book was the principal problem in getting it accepted. Jamie objected that there were plenty of "weird" books being published—those by William Burroughs, Jean Genet, Hubert Selby. But I argued that they were all about hustlers or robots or thieves or transvestites and that, whereas low life and drag were actually reassuring to straight readers, my middle-class gays with their jobs and friends and bank loans were far too close for comfort.

But now I had an idea for a new book, which I resolved would be my last one. Like most other writers I saw the composition of a novel as a terrible expense of spirit, a reckless and dangerous overdraft drawn on alarmingly meager funds of energy. Or I imagined the book was a precious vase I had to carry during a rough-and-tumble obstacle course, but a vase that I was somehow molding as I ran along. I believed that I'd have a pleasant, easy-going life if I could only get the art monkey off my back. I'd seen so many of my friends accept spirit-deforming poverty and miserable living conditions in roach traps in exchange for humiliation and overwork as actors, painters or poets. I refused to be a "martyr to art." Statistically it appeared to me that the chance of being published at all was infinitesimal, and if one was published the chance of being reviewed and permitted to publish a second time was even more remote. Yet such worries were way beyond my means. I longed for the authentication of a single acceptance. Nor did I dream of being famous; I just wanted someone occasionally to whisper when I entered a room, "That one? He's a novelist. What? One book, I think, I don't remember the title." I didn't know any published writers and in my seven years in New York I'd never even seen one.

The Newspaper Guild had won us five weeks of vacation; I had accumulated three weeks from the preceding year, which gave me two months of freedom. I spent them on Fire Island in a beautiful Chinese-style house with sliding glass doors looking out on the Bay, and there I wrote most of the new novel.

On Friday evening pale, tired-looking young businessmen, my roommates, arrived in their suits and ties smelling of cigarette smoke and the beer they'd drunk on the train. I'd come down to the dock to greet their ferry. I'd load their suitcases in my red wagon. I'd be soft-spoken and tan, barefoot, in shorts with no shirt, eager to talk to them after my week of solitude though I was on an entirely different timetable. They jostled for control of the bathroom with the same nerviness they showed in pushing onto a subway car before the door shut. By midnight they'd applied their facial masks and peeled them off. They'd ironed and donned their painter's pants (the thin white cotton trousers were attached to a bib and shoulder straps, the whole supplied with several long, narrow pockets for paintbrushes). They'd gelled their hair, reshaved and applied some bronzer. Drops had whitened their eyes and a cream had erased the dark circles under them. And they'd taken such powerful drugs that they talked incessantly, fell down laughing, forgot the food burning on the stove and at midnight, when it was served, had no interest in touching its charred, gummy remains. By one in the morning we were all off in a loud wolf pack bound for the disco, where we'd dance till dawn. Everyone was frantic to cram in as much fun as possible during the forty-eight hours of freedom allotted them each weekend. The rents were so high that some of the guys could afford only a half share, which entitled them to come out only every other weekend.

By Saturday night everyone in the house had settled down a bit and dinner was more decorous, the conversation earnest and thoughtful, the food well prepared and eaten with appreciation. My roommates had strolled up and down the beach all day, checking out the new faces and bodies, running into friends and exchanging gossip and invitations. Now they were tanner, more rested, carefree adolescents rather than the careworn men they'd been the night before. Fourteen of us sat down at ten in the evening and we saw our reflections suspended in the plate-glass window, as though we were a corporation of burghers painted by Rembrandt, until someone turned on the porch light and canceled us out. Caught between the exigencies of work during the week and the laborious pleasures of disco dancing, seduction and sex that were to follow, we had just this long, quiet moment to joke, to confide, even to talk.

For me the weekends were like the splashy, passionate acts and the weeks like the nearly silent, certainly solitary intervals. So often in the city I was impatient with the smoke and drink, the coming and going, above all the defiling talk with which we so pointlessly filled every moment. But here, on the island, I rose with one perfect dawn after another, made my coffee and in the Baccarat-clear, ringing silence I sat down to write a novel nearly as mysterious to me as it would eventually be to a small cult of readers.

I had found an exhilarating if suicidal liberation in my rejection slips. Everyone said my writing was cold; now I'd become glacial, although the ice would contain a flame, the same secret passion that only those men who'd made love to me knew about. Editors had said my subject matter was too "special" to interest other people. Now I would imagine for myself an undistractible reader whose mind was limpid and composed, ready to follow me no matter where I might lead. I wanted to show the anguish of being a frightened, crafty being in a hostile world full of sensual delights.

In the book, the narrator remarks that he is playing an organ sounding in another room somewhere. He can't hear what he's playing, nor does he know how to play, but when he runs down the hall the rapt listeners assure him he's inspired and hasn't made the slightest mistake. I hoped that my novel, which I knew how to drive but had never seen on the road, would perform just as dazzlingly. When I wrote it I sometimes felt as though I were wearing a lab coat, so precise and objective were my manipulations of every elusive element. At the same time I kept repeating to myself with a smile, "I just work here," as though to excuse my incomprehension of my own book.

The hero was no longer meant to be a simulacrum of myself. No, he was a "character" to whom I attributed a fussy, pedantic voice, a logic-chopping niceness, a systematic, endlessly metastasizing paranoia; he shared my desire to please and a sexuality based on gratitude though all too sensitive to violence. He was far more snobbish than I although like me he was by turns shy and a show-off. That he was no longer a stand-in for me relieved me. I was tired of being dogged by this too-precise double who converted my soft clouds into palpable rain.

My life that summer on Fire Island was one of solitude and discipline during the day, debauchery by night. During the day I filled the big, sun-struck house with Mozart's Clarinet Concerto, ate diet food, did a hundred sit-ups on the sliver of private beach down beside the Bay. I took an hour of sun, carefully basting myself in oil and stretching and pulling my muscles through yoga exercises. If I made a sortie at all it was only to the market. Otherwise I indulged in long unnumbered hours of entranced writing. I knew that my whole being generated a distinctive hum if I found the right tone for my novel, a register unlike any I'd ever sounded before. Sometimes I felt I was traveling at the bottom of a sunless sea in a submarine and the only thing that kept me on course was that thin, sonic signal. I had no other principle of literary construction.

I'd read *The Pillow Book of Sei Shonagon*, an eleventh-century Japanese court diary full of anecdotes, lists and jottings about daily events. The writer, like my hero, was an unapologetic snob who included in her list of "hateful things" a curious item: the sight of beautiful snow on the houses of poor people. At the court, women seldom married but were free to choose lovers, even on a rapidly rotating basis. The men never actually *saw* the women until the (still obscure or at least dim) moment of erotic encounter, a moment oddly violent and brutish, although preceded by courtship poems and followed by poems of regret and longing the next day.

But in fact every moment of the day required the production of such "spontaneous poems." I remember once running up to Jamie at the office and saying brightly, "Have you ever thought what it would have been like to live at the Heian court at the time of *The Tale of Genji*?"

Haggard, he stared at me and said, "A nightmare."

Suddenly I saw Fire Island as an exact analogue to medieval Japan— an idle and gossipy court society, profoundly hierarchical if superficially egalitarian (didn't the islanders all dress alike, wear the same sawed-off jeans and ripped T-shirts, though back on the mainland one was a bank president and the next an ailing and penniless hustler?). Just as the courtiers had replaced ethics with aesthetics and worried more about matching the colors of superimposed layers of sleeves than about the fate of last year's favorite, in the same way the islanders were capable of watching a fire destroy a house in which people were dying and judge it a pity the flames weren't *bluer*. Even the contrast between decorous social life and brutal sensuality seemed to be a common denominator, as did the disposable sex partners and the unchanging terms used in speaking of them. Every night I'd bring someone different back to the house, find another hand prying open my ass, another mouth engulfing my penis, and no matter how eccentric his pillow talk or behavior, the next day I'd call to tell a friend, "He was a hunky number, well-hung, very hot to trot."

And yet, I thought, what Heian Japan hadn't known was that Fire Island specialty—the endless Saturday made up of hours and hours of walking up and down the beach cruising (even here our hedonism had its practical side, since kicking through the surf was intended to build up our calves and the burning reflection of sun on sand to hurry up and even out our tans). Stripped of clothes and yet dressed in our expensive haircuts and Speedos and gym-bought muscles, our feet pumiced smooth by trudging through miles and miles of sand, we felt the freedom of breasting water and wind, of slipping a hand around an ocean-clammy waist, of kissing a shoulder tasting of brine if smelling of coconut oil, of exchanging glances and, if the glance lingered, of detouring behind the dunes where a moment later we'd be ambling up a path redolent of sun-hot pine needles, an erection poking its sticky red head above a loosened drawstring. If we were each by chance on the same cycle of the same drug, our blue lips and twitches and paranoia at last surpassed and evened out toward universal love, we would touch each other with childish awe, we'd lie naked in the sand for hours, white loins burning pink, and we'd hold two penises in one hand, dumbstruck by this new member's heft and heat, or we'd lick the closed eyelid, fluttering like a moth caught in a hand, or lick inside each nostril, tasting its concentrated, snail-like saltiness, or explore the earlobe, surprised at its marsupial thinness and its delicate, ramifying veins transporting blood even to the most farflung periphery. . . .

Nothing in Japan, surely, ever equaled this intense, worshipful intimacy, when every sideswipe of a hand would awaken a glissando of mental music, the sweet yearning as you (or I) would hitch this big, erect man a millimeter closer, though he might already be glued to you, his nose pressed against yours, his mouth feebly sipping kisses from dry, swollen lips, the toes of your feet digging into the cold sand. As the sun began to sink and a slight chill to set in, you would walk, sad as refugees, back down the beach huddling close together for warmth, your thick-thighed, small-headed shadows becoming elongated Giacometti versions of your compact Canova bodies. "I love you," you might say, "but what's your name, anyway?"

⎯⎯⎯

JAMIE'S SINGLE REMARK ("A nightmare") had fired my imagination, as did another made by my friend Maria, who said one day, "Isn't it strange the way intellectuals always think that art, in order to be 'cerebral,' must be grey? Analytical Cubism, for instance. Whereas, truth be told, there's no reason it can't be gaudy." I didn't dare tell her that an English friend of mine had referred to one of her paintings that I owned as an expression of "gaudy pessimism." I wondered if the formula would offend her (certainly it was meant to be both affectionate and derisive). She went on to say, "Beckett's books and plays are enacted by dying men on a plot of scorched earth, but they could be just as 'philosophical,' even as harrowing, if they took place in a palace." Or at a seaside resort, I thought.

But I didn't want my new novel to be cerebral so much as a verbal equivalent to Abstract Expressionism. If in my last novel, the failed one about Sean, I'd embraced hyper-realism as an avant-garde technique, now I'd be an abstractionist. During my prep-school years I'd listened to young painters at the neighboring art academy defend this movement and so imbued was I with their principles—the canvas was not a representation of something else but an arena in which actions were perpetrated and intentions formulated only to be toppled—that I kept wondering how to adapt these principles to fiction. Gertrude Stein had been an action painter in words but for her, as she admitted, the paragraph was the "unit of meaning." She opposed one paragraph to the next, but such verbal microeconomics was fatiguing for the reader, who thought not in paragraphs but in stories, and whose attention was held by mystery and suspense, action and dialogue, rather than by the push-and-pull of syntax. In my new book I would float great shadowy panels of color and form, apparently the fragments of a coherent narrative, but in the end they wouldn't cohere, except in the paranoid schemas propounded by my narrator. It never occurred to me that the reader would be frustrated by my failure to deliver what I seemed under contract to provide.

At this time in my life I was troubled by the question of sincerity. Was it even possible to be sincere? Years of psychotherapy had made me doubt all my feelings, especially the apparently benign ones.

In looking at those writers I admired, I decided they'd all tackled subjects they were in two minds about. Only dullards knew what they thought about every subject. I could find no theme that tormented me more than sincerity, since it was a term that applied both to art and to behavior, but unequally. All other things being equal, behavior that was sincere was necessarily superior to that which was insincere, whereas as an aesthetic quality sincerity certainly counted, but not as an absolute: if you could praise a novel for being "sincere," you could just as easily admire one for its duplicity.

But back then sincerity tormented me mainly because I could never be sure I'd achieved it. I was so naïve that I imagined it must necessarily be delivered devoid of style. As I thought then, to accept the idea that a feeling could be communicated *effectively* or *indirectly* or *humorously* (the horror of those sly adverbs!) meant that a strategy was permitted to intervene between thought and act—and any strategy, any intervention, by its very nature abnegated sincerity, didn't it? Or so I imagined. What I failed to accept (until a few years later when I read Rilke's *Letters to a Young Poet*) was that a *distance* necessarily separates any two people. Separation is the most human aspect of existence and to rail against it is puerile—or rather literally infantile, since it is the infant who abhors the slightest, epidermal distance between his mother and himself, teat and lip. Once that inevitable separation is accepted, then any further uneasiness about a knowing self-presentation is pointless. As Rilke suggested, the game now becomes one of taking pleasure in *playing* with the distance between any two people or between thought and action.

But this acceptance of an irreversible exile in the world would come only later. Now I took pleasure in my seductive powers and worried about them. My novel was about an amnesiac who has forgotten quite simply who he is and how he is supposed to act; afraid to admit his loss of memory, he patterns his responses on the cues other people feed him. He becomes what they expect—an extreme dramatization of my own horrid adaptability. Only occasionally does he wonder whether his burning desire to please whoever happens to be beside him might not entail betraying his real if absent friends, even his real self-interest. His amnesia—which turns out to be self-induced or at least functional—is designed to absolve him of all responsibility for his deeds.

The book, however, wasn't really so philosophical. It was born less out of debate than out of the sober days and long drunken nights, out of the intricate interplay between all the latest gadgets and fashions floating over from the mainland and the unchanging serenity of the adjacent wildlife preserve, the sudden crash of a deer through the brush.

At nine in the evening, after a nap, I'd prepare a steak and salad for myself. By eleven I was at the bar, by one in the morning at the disco, by three I was coming home with a big man in tow.

No wonder I can't bear smoky urban clubs now; I was spoiled forever by the Sandpiper. There we'd dance under colored gels beside tables covered with white linen glowing dimly in the candlelight pulsing through cut-glass shades. The beach was so omnipresent that sand had even blown up over the steps leading into the restaurant. The floor-to-ceiling windows had been flung open and a cool briny breeze flowed across the harbor and its spotlit yachts. At one table sat men in white shirts, blue blazers, white duck trousers, silk ties, while beside them was someone who'd never made it back home from the beach this afternoon but who'd been waylaid by various cocktail parties and progressive dinners concretizing and dissolving on one deck after another. He was still barefoot, dancing in his swimsuit and a T-shirt advertising the Canal Street Hardware belonging to the most recent party-giver he'd visited before ending up here. The clear spotlights over the bar and entryway were angled to parody the inconsequence of desire, since they would illuminate only what an eager eye might fetishize—a small brown hand dwarfed by a starched white cuff, a thick neck rising out of powerful shoulders, a pair of hairy legs emerging out of well tailored pistachio-green linen shorts.

If the smell of poppers and the clamor of music became too heady, I'd hurry down to the beach and the pounding waves, for every human pleasure was contrived to appear as insubstantial as possible beside the eternal verities of sand, surf, sky. The matchstick houses posed on pylons, the slat walkways suspended over scrub brush, the evanescent voices calling out in the dark—everything evoked the impermanence of our arrangements invaded by the tides and the rolling fog. In the city, laughter, smoke, exchanged glances and music can saturate a closed space, but here every space was open and all our energy and fire were dissipated by the dull thud of waves on sand, by the august disdain of remote stars and by the constant wind, metonymy for the inexhaustibility of desire, but also its cool negation, the good currency driving out the bad.

THREE

I went to Rome because I was intimidated by Paris.

My thirtieth birthday was approaching when I decided I'd have to make a break with New York and my job. I'd finished my Japanese-Fire Island novel and typed it up and one of the most respected editors in New York, the head of a prestigious publishing house, had read it and was trying to come to a decision about it. The prospect of being published was the only thing that I could imagine would make me authentic, redeem all the small defeats and lost nights. I ached for print, in the way someone else might ache for a new roadster or true love. All of my moods—my despair as well as my elation—could be keyed to even the slightest tremor on the Richter scale of my ambition.

Sean phoned me: "Hi, I'm back."

"I'm so relieved. Where are you?"

"New Jersey. I'm enrolled as a grad student in comp. lit. at Rutgers."

"I've been so worried about you. I've never gone through such anguish." I thought, He doesn't want to hear about my suffering, which he'll perceive not as friendly concern but as amorous blackmail. Anyway, he's the one who's been put in a straitjacket and drugged and been sent home virtually under arrest—my anguish is inconsequential beside his. And besides, how presumptuous I'm being. I said: "And now it's all over." But what if it isn't? I don't want to rush him into health. "I knew you'd come out of it with flying colors."

"You did? Really?" Sean's voice, the aural equivalent of a frown, tightened; he was always so at sea about what he was feeling that he would embrace any interpretation proposed by someone else, no matter who, no matter what, although a moment later he'd be suspecting it.

"How long have you been back? When am I ever going to see you?" Instantly I didn't like the way I had asked the question, almost as though I was challenging him to disappoint me.

"Well," he said, "school's just started and I'm occupied as the devil." I'd forgotten his slightly old-fashioned, high-falutin' locutions and smiled now as I was reminded of them. "Angel—" he pronounced it in the Spanish way, *On-hell*, "Angel and I don't get into the city very often."

"Who's Angel?" I asked, disdainfully emphasizing the strange name.

"My lover. Angel Rodriguez. He's Puerto Rican. He's doing a degree in contemporary Spanish literature. And he's a very prominent Nuyorican poet."

There, I thought. That's the surprising but idiotic conclusion to the story. I'd thought if he'd ever admit he was gay, Sean would come back to me. Now I saw he needed a new, exotic lover. If Sean can even refer to another man as his *lover* he's changed completely. And when did he find time to meet him, much less seal the matrimonial bond? I'd longed for Sean for so many years now (six years) that I'd almost forgotten he was real—a real person with options, not just a tragic fate. And I'd forgotten that history, gay history, was rattling along around us like a cannon rumbling over cobbles.

"But he's giving a reading at a Nuyorican café this weekend, so we may be in town. We could all have a plate of spaghetti together." He said it less as an invitation than as a possible trap to be approached gingerly, at least feared. I'd never even heard the term *Nuyorican* before and was shocked by Sean's quick appropriation of his lover's life. Of course, I thought. Of course. These milk-fed Midwestern boys with their khakis and perfect teeth and small blue eyes, forget-me-not blue (and I won't, can't), they long to meet a Puerto Rican smelling of saffron rice and black beans who will fuck them to salsa music and make them feel it's okay to be gay if you wear a thin, lizard-skin belt around pleated, aubergine-colored trousers hitched high, a guinea T-shirt and a white porcelain medal of the Virgen del Carmen on a brown, hairless chest and grow just a little tuft of a goatee smudged under the lower lip.

"We *could*," I conceded. "But I'd love to see you alone."

"You would?" Sean seemed incredulous, almost displeased, that anyone would prefer an encounter with just him to a chance to meet the fascinating Angel. Or perhaps he was merely wary of seeing me—after all, I'd been a witness to (possibly a cause of) his crack-up. Yes, he'd cracked up, been sent home bloated and medicated to Minnesota, but here he was, back again in a new incarnation, and I felt slightly offended by this, yes, literary impropriety, since after all he was my character and the last page had been turned on him staring into a void of madness, yet here he was, back again, lively, wincing with hypersensitivity. The novel I'd written about him now seemed inconclusive, kitschily downbeat. It certainly hadn't called for a sequel, at least not a *comic* sequel, this grotesque update.

But I was too curious about my rival to resist the invitation. It was the first week of December and peculiarly warm. I took the bus from the Port Authority out through the New Jersey wasteland, looking back over my shoulder after we emerged out of the West Side Tunnel at the new twin towers of the World Trade Center, turning to golden stone in the late afternoon sun.

If I stayed in Greenwich Village month after month with forays out to Fire Island alone, I could convince myself that "everyone" was gay, at least that more and more people were living openly as homosexuals, that the person next to me in line at the bank or in the neighboring booth in a restaurant might be gay, even a friend. If I sat in a café on Waverly Place reading a paper, I could hear, without glancing up, the voices of passing gay men—voices with their over-articulation, their swooping and falling intonations, the occasional lisp or hiss, the verbal italics, the rich vocabulary. But here, on this bus, I was surrounded by grey, sagging adults, no longer on the make, their clothes a compromise between necessity and habit rather than an advertisement for the self, their conversation a desultory read-out of scattered neural impulses rather than a sharp comment on the revival of *West Side Story* or a much-rehearsed disquisition on a new lover's sexual quirks ("Just before he comes he has to take over, he'll pull it out of my mouth to jerk himself off, ever the control queen"). I'd gone from fearing in the 1950s that I was the only homosexual to believing in the late 1960s that we were everywhere, an army, the coming thing, but over Labor Day I'd visited my mother at her summer home near Lake Michigan and when I'd gone to the public beach I'd walked for miles through thousands of bathers and seen not one male couple, not one sharp eye, not one stylish swimsuit, not one starved, over-exercised or artfully tattooed body, not one person who'd ever heard of the Stonewall Uprising, which had occurred the preceding summer.

Sean was the same man he'd been when I'd first met him—the same dirty-blond hair growing low on his brow and straight and thick out of his skull, the same small grey-blue eyes wincing with complication, the same full lips, though now a half-shade less red, the same rangy, slender body stiffly maneuvered, as though manipulated by the long sticks of a Balinese shadow puppeteer. He gave me a vigorous, pumping handshake, then, seeing my disappointment, thumped me on the back with a hard hand. Angel was there, his hair already turning grey at the temples, his body unabashedly *plump*, his forearms as round and hairless as a cheerleader's legs, his smile huge under a wispy mustache.

I drank so much wine that I remember the whole evening only as blurred and grotesque. They cavorted intellectually, bantering back and forth tags from Latin and Greek, quoting bits of Cervantes or Rubén Darío, jauntily invoking Roman Jakobson.

I was aching as I saw Sean restored not to health but to an antic gaiety designed to please this chubby guru. They had a bizarre way of calling out, "*Ho-ho!*" to one another from room to room or even across the same room if one of them was busy brewing coffee or clearing dishes or was trapped into a conversation with boring, stuffy, uninitiated me. "*Ho-ho!*" they'd call out, and Sean's eyes sparkled, his vexed gaze at last clarified, his full lips wreathed in a glycerin-bright smile. I wanted to banish Angel, silence Sean, force him to sit still, undress him, make sure that his penis still crooked to the right when erect, that his chest was still Ken-doll smooth and unarticulated, that his tongue was still as fresh and perfumed as a saint's, miraculously preserved for hundreds of years in a skull turned bomb black. But my desire, always so static and intent on immobilizing the other person, as though I were a tropical female insect, was frustrated that night. Sean used me only as an audience of one, he cast me in the role of an elderly, even rural, relative, before whom he could play out this new romance, so eccentric, so pedantic, so curiously sexual. I sat there sullenly, transfixed by the shuttle of their exchanged glances, smiles, remarks, hoots. Angel touched Sean's rump, a gesture that evoked a whole chorus of "*Ho-ho*'s," as though they were gondoliers approaching each other down adjacent canals in the winter fog. We ate some white rice and black beans, which Sean explained the Puerto Ricans call "Christians and Moors" because of their contrasting colors, although the combination, he added, as given as I to over-elaborated, arthritic conceits, was more a marriage than a conflict since together they turned into the equivalent of a healthy, nourishing protein.

If your vision of love is static, then all you want to do is lie—peaceful but heart racing, ecstatically conscious of that peace—in your lover's big, tanned hands, hands with guitar-playing calluses and dry, warm, sensitive palms, hands that move ever so slightly, relaxed and taut as an unsounded musical string. You don't want to hear about metaphor versus metonymy, or *La Celestina* in comparison with *Don Quixote*, you don't want to be jostled from one course to another, the dessert spelling out your imminent departure, the brandy signaling that it's already past due, or to observe an angelic hand on your lover's rump or to note that his madness and melancholy have been redefined into an hysteria of Indian love calls.

Now there was nothing holding me in New York. Christa was no longer even my spiritual fiancée and Sean was no longer Sean. In January I would turn thirty and, though I'd written what I thought was an entirely original novel, what was unique was by definition incomparable, off the scale, and might be prized, rejected or ignored according to the world's whims. I didn't want to turn into an office drudge. Thirty sounded awfully old for me to be beginning my life.

⌒‿⌒ DURING THE TWO MONTHS before my departure I'd taken private Italian lessons from a young woman freshly arrived in New York from Palermo who'd fallen a bit in love with me. My mannerliness and unavailability made me appear to be both kind and remote, in need and inaccessible, a fatal combination, especially for a lonely girl in a new country. She'd said, as an amorous compliment, that I seemed more European than American. She'd assured me I'd have no trouble communicating with people in Rome, but when I arrived I discovered no one spoke with her accent and no one was willing to let me piece my pauper's vocabulary together into three-penny sentences. If I should happen to say something vaguely plausible, I then had the problem of a long, laughing, ironic, gesturing reply, entirely incomprehensible. When my interlocutor would see from my stunned expression that I'd understood nothing, he'd walk off with an impertinent, big-city shrug.

I never did learn what some of those gestures meant—the forefinger tugging the cheek down just below the eye, or the slow, appreciative shake of the whole hand, as though casting off drops of water in the wind.

Through a real-estate agent I found an apartment on the Vicolo del Leopardo in Trastevere, a fakely luxurious floor-through on a decidedly *popolare* street, really just an alleyway that smelled of backed-up sewage. The building itself smelled of a gluey black heating oil, referred to as *nafta*, pooling ominously on the floor of the entrance hall. The walls of the *salone* in my apartment were covered with a red and pink cut velvet in patterns of loose, floating, Louis XVI knots. The street-side wall was festooned in purple velvet hangings as though they concealed generous french doors instead of small, dingy windows looking out on lines of laundry that were eternally being fed out across the narrow street. I sat inside and dully strummed the "book furniture," as decorators refer to volumes bought for their fine bindings alone. All the titles were theological, examples of nineteenth-century casuistry. Like a child I looked in vain for illustrations.

For some reason I was morbidly afraid of offending my neighbors with my "wealth," although all I had was the seven thousand dollars I'd taken out of profit-sharing, a sum that with careful husbandry might buy me a year of freedom. I was even more fearful of seeming too American, for if Midwestern parents bray and bellow through Europe, bits of straw still clinging to their bib overalls, their neurotic children dress in black, dart like shadows around corners and order again and again the only item on the menu they can pronounce without too strong an accent.

The apartment required a considerable outlay of three months' rent as a deposit. The agent, Susie, a young Englishwoman with fat lips and sad eyes and a wonderfully cozy, confiding manner, told me she was so pleased I'd rented the flat, since I was her first "success" and without my acquiescence she would have been sacked. The proprietor, an Italian countess, showed us all the "features" of the furnished flat with a hostessy manner while speaking in a strange British English that sounded comically affected. She then went over a maniacally detailed inventory and I was made to understand I would be responsible for every broken whiskey jigger or misplaced olive oil cruet. Susie kept rolling her eyes, embarrassed by the contessa's pettiness.

A week later Susie was, in fact, let go, and I took her out for a drink in order to celebrate this melancholy rite of passage. She wept on my shoulder and said she was sure she'd find something better. She dabbed at her eyes and smiled her big, lazy smile, which seemed to expect nothing but appreciate everything.

Perhaps because she was "European," even if English, Susie was more at home here than I. In 1970 Americans were still sure of their superiority to Europeans—if not culturally, then at least in all the ways that counted: economically, hygienically, militarily. I knew that students back home were protesting the American invasion of Cambodia but I wasn't sure it was "patriotic" to join a *manifestazione* in front of the American Embassy. I'd never been active politically back home, since as a homosexual I felt certain no leftist group would knowingly accept me.

I couldn't understand the Italian press and only bought the English-language Roman paper, the *Rome Daily American*, a Republican rag imbued with the bigotry and optimism of a town booster's newsletter. It had been started by three American veterans who hadn't wanted to go home after the war ended. I picked it up once a week when I walked the two or three miles from my apartment in Trastevere to the Spanish Steps, where I collected my mail and cashed a traveler's check at American Express. I then treated myself to a hamburger at Babington's tea room while I read my paper.

Everything was a chore, an intimidating chore. I knew no one and except in Babington's, where all the customers were English spinsters, I didn't want to eat alone in a restaurant. Too conspicuous. Besides, I didn't understand what the waiter was reciting when he reeled off the daily specials. I couldn't go to a neighborhood delicatessen because I didn't know the names of the various cheeses and cold cuts nor the words for metric quantities and, if I had, I wouldn't have been sure what they represented in ounces and pounds. I did go to the butcher once, armed with a phrase for four hundred grams of hamburger, but I spoke so softly he couldn't hear me and after the third time he ordered me to speak up I fled, red-faced, into the street, pursued by the cackles of the other customers waiting their turn. At last I discovered a supermarket and a five-and-dime called Standa where I could select items by sight without knowing their names.

Initially, all the men seemed gay, with their silk shirts open to the navel, their gold religious medals buried in chest fur, their blow-dried hair, shiny shoes, tight velvet jackets and pocketless trousers that featured a large mound in front and prominent, soccer-playing buttocks behind. Because their garments left them no space for a wallet or keys, much less for their *documenti* (the police were always checking everyone's papers), they carried everything in a small, square necessary dangling from a shoulder strap. As these Guidos would slowly cross a square thronged with people, they'd twirl Maserati keys, though ninety-nine times out of a hundred they didn't even own a Cinquecento and had just arrived from the suburbs by public bus. When I looked at these men longingly, what only confused me more was that they looked back, smug in my admiration, hostile to the admirer.

The only cruising place I'd heard of was the Colosseum, and on a rainy January night I headed there for the first time. The city appeared empty as I walked toward midnight past the spot-lit churches. When I'd looked at it earlier, my guidebook had explained that every Catholic order had had to build a mother church in Rome, but that many of these orders had died out and accordingly their houses of worship were overgrown with moss, the portals off the hinge, the disaffected altars now just platforms for mice and cats to scamper across. Baroque Rome of grandiose, insincere volutes and illusionistic ceiling paintings was omnipresent, but I kept constantly coming on bits of ancient Rome—an altar to Love, an emperor's pyramid, the Mouth of Truth, yet another triumphal arch. Wedged between were slivers of the Rome I liked, medieval Rome, exemplified by my favorite church, I Quattro Santi Coronati.

In the rain I was convinced I could smell rotting bones and that all Rome was a cemetery.

I felt that once again I'd been betrayed by the movies. One couldn't just dance all night with a handsome stranger, throw three coins in the fountain, speed to the shore at dawn in an open car full of an opulent blonde in a tulle gown. No, one couldn't even speak the language nor order a plate of spaghetti. One was ignored as a poor, unknown, badly dressed foreigner. The Fountain of Trevi, when one finally found it, was an embarrassingly operatic stage set shoe-horned into a run-down little vaudeville house of a square, and at midnight on a Tuesday in January no one was there to see the soot-streaked Tritons emerging out of the pool into the rain except two boys, mudlarks fishing for tourists' coins.

Cars and sputtering Vespas circled the Colosseum as I attempted to cross the street into the shadowy old building, more a city than a building, more a tall ship than a city, a ship leaning into the watery moon and the racing ermine clouds and with most of the sailors down below in the hold, although two or three were stationed on the upper decks, signaling to one another with glowing cigarettes. A young gypsy crossed my path as I entered the stadium, and I was suddenly grateful I had so little money, just a few thousand lire and my documents. I was also pleased that my trousers had deep pockets.

Whenever I sidled up to someone he fled. I couldn't tell if he found me undesirable (but what was I in the dark except a slender silhouette of normal height, a man with a face that, if visible, still looked surprisingly young?). Or was he looking for an older man who'd pay him? Or was he—were they all—too horny to leave and too frightened to touch? I longed to touch someone, to have him decide I was desirable, to communicate without these troublesome words intervening, to establish my right to be here by giving a hard-on to just one Roman.

At last I found a young guy drenched in a curious perfume, who revealed, when he cleared his throat, that his voice had never changed, although his sexual organs were of a normal size and shape as I discovered when he pulled me between two columns into—what? The emperor's box seat?

Afterwards we spoke, each in his halting Italian, and I finally pieced together, from his high-pitched accent, that he was a Romanian refugee waiting to go to the promised land of New Jersey, where he'd been offered a marvelous job as an au pair boy and apprentice butcher with a family he felt certain would be *molto simpatica*.

I was disappointed that he wasn't Italian, although I'd initially confused the Italian words for *Romanian* and *Roman* and he'd had to clarify the distinction. I was wounded that he was so desultory in making love. As we'd wanked off he'd continued to look around, I feared, for someone better. Now that I'm fat and in my fifties I go to bed only with men I pay or men who love me or fans and all three categories are usually handsome and are ardent or obliging or at least put on a good show, whereas when I was young and handsome myself, I might occasionally awaken a profound, anonymous desire but more often than not I was treated all too casually, as just one more interchangeable insect milling around the entrance to the average hive.

He told me of the one gay bar in town, the Saint James at the top of the Via Veneto, and there I headed the next night. Instead of raucous New Yorkers in jeans swilling beers in a bar with sawdust on the floor and rock and roll in the air, here I found decorous Romans in velvet suits and satin shirts sipping Prosecco from stemware while standing under spotlights or sitting on half-hidden settees and listening to Milva crooning heart-sick ballads. Each drink cost a small fortune and everyone nursed his glass during the entire evening. I started talking to a soldier in uniform. At first he attracted me because I'd made up a fantasy that he was a *contadino* from Calabria, a "peasant" (the very word makes Americans laugh).

But soon enough I learned that if he continued to speak to me in his stilted English he did so because he wanted to practice and indulge in cultural chat at the same time. He was a *baronino* from Florence whose research into William Blake's *Songs of Innocence and Experience* had been tragically interrupted by two and a half years of national service; as he primly explained, unfortunately he'd neglected to enlist in an officers' training corps at university, more appropriate to his aristocratic status, and now he was, alas, a common soldier. I said I thought a common soldier was sexier, a remark that eluded him and, when he grasped it, miffed him.

Guglielmo was taller than I and six years younger, but thanks to my youthful looks and American Innocence as contrasted to his European Experience, we came out roughly as contemporaries.

"I'm delighted to meet you," Guglielmo said with his vagrant vowels and odd lilt, as he stared down at me through his tinted glasses, which gave his eyes a sickly, jaundiced look.

"Me, too," I whispered. "I've just been here two weeks but it's hard—"

"It is what?"

"It's difficult to start off, to *begin*, in a new city."

"Even for me. *Also* for me?"

"Even."

"Even for me. I'm from Florence. We call it Firenze. Are you art historian?"

"No."

"Journalist?"

"No," I said. "Nothing. I'm nothing. I don't work. But I'd like to be a novelist—*romanziere.*"

"You does not work? Millionaire?" There was a hint of playfulness in his question, the first sign that he might really be an aristocrat.

I smiled mysteriously.

Although Guglielmo could speak English, on our subsequent dates he insisted we communicate in Italian, but instead of complimenting me on my little achievements in threading together three or four words, he criticized me for neglecting to use the pluperfect subjunctive; soon my mental nickname for him became Fossero Fui, two of the forms I could never master. His new family name I mentally spelled as Phooey. When we went to bed he took a shower first and sprinkled talcum powder on his feet, then he mounted me as he smiled a beatific smile of Fra Angelico gentleness, a million miles away from the I'm-going-to-fuck-you-until-I-take-out-your-tonsils New York attitude I'd been conditioned to find exciting. He had lots of *manie* that I considered tiresome probably because I wasn't in love with him. For instance, he'd decided that he detested newspapers and refused even to read one. He thought that Italians wasted all their time in cafés talking politics and shuffling through several morning and afternoon papers. Like Blake he was an aesthete and a visionary above current events. (But wasn't Blake a *printer*? I wondered.) Guglielmo had also made a cult out of promptness, to distinguish himself from all these lazy southern Italians (the south begins at Rome). I felt certain that Blake had not been punctual and could see nothing visionary about so much fussiness. And I thought bitterly that only a son doted on by his family would have had the encouragement necessary to elaborate all these caprices. In my family I'd remained underdeveloped because unnoticed— a neglect, however, I'd come to like, since it permitted me to invent a simple, all-purpose personality.

He wanted to reprimand me for my boorish American manners and teach me the fine points of Italian cultural history, which he tried to make more accessible by drawing analogies with similar moments in William Blake's life, a personal trajectory I knew no more about than Leopardi's or Alfieri's. Two men together search for a style—brothers, best friends, father and son, mother and son, husband and wife, rivals—and one pairing slips over another like those successive lenses at the eye doctor's that finally bring the smallest and lowest line of print into focus. Guglielmo's choice was to be a long-suffering father with a lazy and disobedient son who was adorable simply because he was an only child. I thought he'd never have become my lover in New York, but in Rome I didn't know how to maneuver, I was lonely and no one seemed to like my looks.

Fortunately he was seldom free to spend a whole night away from the barracks, which gave me ample opportunities to cruise the Colosseum. There I met a tall blond Venetian waiter with a distinguished face and a beautiful body. His voice sounded hollow to me, as though he were calling from the other room and the other room was a big, tile-lined bathroom. Like a child, I'd touch his forehead when he spoke and it always resonated. He generated a sort of silent gusto that I found very reposeful. He had very bad breath that I started to think was erotic. It wasn't a passing embarrassment caused by sleep or garlic, say, but a permanent rot that I'd search out, something initially repulsive but finally exciting, like a very ripe cheese.

He couldn't keep his right index finger out of my asshole. If I cooked spaghetti in my tart's flat with the velvet swags, every time I approached the table with a new dish he'd pull me onto his knee and shove a hand down the back of my jeans. Later, in bed, if I'd kiss his big, veined hand it would smell of my ass, which I liked. For him my penis was just a laughable little handle he used to turn me over in bed. He didn't correct me when I flubbed the subjunctive. He probably didn't know how to use it himself.

An American college friend I'd stayed in touch with had told me to look up his Roman cousin, Tina. On the phone she had a wonderfully low, seductive voice and a schoolgirl's sudden, explosive laugh. She told me to come right over. I'd pointed out it was three o'clock on a Tuesday afternoon, which had seemed to surprise her but leave her indifferent. She'd laughed when she said, "But I don't understand nothing you say."

Her huge, nineteenth-century *palazzo* was near the Quirinale, the President's residence, and beside a Baroque fountain so ugly that when it was unveiled all Rome had mocked the sculptor, until he'd committed suicide. A sour-faced *portiere* opened the small, low door let into two big ones and growled something at me. In the dark, neglected courtyard at the bottom of a seven-story well, a thick-thighed Diana drew an arrow from a quiver on her shoulder. The tip of her cement bow had broken off and the exposed metal armature dripped rust stains down her gathered hunting skirt. The elevator clanked noisily.

Tina opened a heavily barricaded door, shook my hand manfully and led me down a dark hall with a stone floor. I experienced the tension of meeting someone new whose sex and language placed her at a considerable distance from me, which neither love nor talk would ever close. In her cold, damp sitting room with its ineffectual heater and tattered couch and chair marooned in the midst of an immense stone floor, we stood for a moment, eyeing each other. She seemed to be as much a stranger here as I and just as uncertain what to do. She lit a cigarette and sat down and murmured, "Hmmmn" on a falling note, indicating the armchair with her chin.

Stretched canvases were leaning against every wall, their backs turned modestly to the viewer. For an instant I tried to imagine Tina (short for Diamantina, a family name) as a blend of Christa, the plain-mannered European woman, and Maria, artist and intellectual, but these clues soon evaporated as I was faced with Tina's unpredictability.

"Yes, Emmanuele told me to look you up," I said, naming her American cousin. "He seems to be doing very well. Ever the dandy, of course, ordering his hats from Lock's in London with his initials stamped in gold on the sweatband."

"*Cosa?*" she asked, looking at me with huge eyes, liquid as oysters, floating between lids as black as mussel shells. Her cheap Italian cigarette burned between the yellowed fingers of a drooping hand. She shook her head silently as though to wake herself out of a bad dream.

"I'm sorry," I said. "*Mi dispiace.*"

She never let her eyes drift away from mine. Even when she lowered her head, her eyes would still be fixed on me, their whites tinted yellow. She was in a simple grey skirt and white blouse. Her hair glistened wet on the sides where she'd just slicked it back, which gave her a slightly raffish glamor. She scrutinized me so closely that I felt false, as though so much attention must automatically uncover my superficiality or hypocrisy.

The room was cold and dark, the windows shrouded in velvet curtains the color of wine dregs, curtains that had gone bald at the hem and at the height where a hand might have tugged them open or shut, day after weary day. Now they were shut. A floor lamp with a chromium hood and a flex—an old-fashioned dentist's lamp—was lit and trained expectantly on the velvet, as though the curtains might suddenly part and reveal an old *chanteuse*.

I started a sentence with the respectful form of *you* ("*Lei*") and she immediately corrected me, not, I felt certain, because we were already such friends but because any sign of formality went against her bluff style.

An hour went by as the smoke from our cigarettes floated through the lamp light trained on the velvet curtain. Every attempt I made to communicate, putting my two hundred Italian words together in various unlikely combinations, fell flat and I became nearly hysterical from frustration and the shame of boring Diamantina. She let her large, unhealthy eyes dissect me. As I became more and more hearty and despairing in the production of conversation-manual banalities, each so full of faults that I could distinctly see the big C-minus scrawled in red across my exercise sheet, Tina dropped into ever-gloomier silence. She had a two-liter bottle of red wine on the stone floor beside her chair, the cheap kind of wine bought at the corner for pennies in an unlabeled bottle sealed with a metal cap, the sort of bottle that suggested it marked a daily necessity, not an occasional festivity. Her teeth were blue from it, I noticed.

Just when I thought I'd exhausted her patience, she said I should stay to eat something. I stood in the doorway of her ancient kitchen with its marble sink and tiny modern stove installed on a site that had once been occupied by an immense iron oven, to judge from the rust scrapes and stains on the wall and floor. Tina was suddenly efficient in the dimly lit kitchen, no longer a sibyl hanging over the smoke of her cigarette and staring into the void, but now a much younger woman, slim-hipped in her grey skirt, her pale slender arms weaving the air as she spin-dried salad leaves, mixed a vinaigrette, filled a cauldron with water to cook spaghetti.

She gave me the name of Lucrezia, someone who could teach me Italian, a friend of hers—another "sad lady," she said in English with a smile. I immediately wanted to know all the details behind Lucrezia's unhappiness, since in America curiosity counts as a social grace. Tina was highly evasive in answering me, since in Europe satisfying curiosity of my sort counts as a betrayal. Americans serve themselves and their friends up as stories, laced with pathos and spiced with scandal, the dish piping hot on demand. A European *discloses* himself, if that word can be used to suggest a series of locks opening and shutting, the whole slow and cautious. For an American a confidence is an ice-breaker and we describe our grandmother's suicide with the same desire to appear amiable that a European employs in commenting on the unseasonably warm weather. We forget what we've told to whom, whereas Europeans tremble and go pale when they decide to reveal something personal. In Europe an avowal counts as a precious sign of commitment; in America it amounts to nothing more than a how-do-you-do.

MY FEAR of the bus—I didn't know which end to get on, how much to pay, how to signal my wish to descend—meant that I walked everywhere, miles and miles until my legs ached at night and I longed for someone to rub them. The next afternoon I walked along the Tiber for an hour and then found, a mile behind the Vatican, Lucrezia's address in a 1960s piazza of yellow-brick apartment blocks.

She was small, chubby, tidy, sharp, always laughing, terminally depressed. Her three-room apartment was dark and hushed as though even on a cold, rainy January day she were determined to exclude the summer heat as a form of gaiety inappropriate to her deep mourning. She loved the latest American slang and pronounced it as though in italics; she was very proud of her hoard of *argot*, which she regularly replenished by translating the latest American novels and puzzling out these novelties with her American students. Sometimes when she laughed she hissed like a snake and this sound drowned out the ends of conventional sentences.

She lifted her arms away from her body and let them fall back in place, as though she were a duck too fat to fly. Her eyes would be squeezed shut when she laughed. Somehow her laughter struck me as mirthless, even sad.

Her teaching method was clever. She invited me to gossip away in Italian as best I could, discussing what I would ordinarily discuss in English; when stumped for the next expression, I'd pause. She'd then provide the missing word. I'd write it down in a notebook I kept week after week. Somewhere no doubt that notebook still exists, a record of my frivolous chatter.

I discovered that vocabularies had their own propriety, just as did people, and that they could not be mixed any easier than could the social classes. For instance, the word for a sports fan was *tifoso*, a "typhoid" victim, since the soccer enthusiast presumably foams at the mouth and shakes all over, but when I said I was "*uno tifoso di Beethoven*" (a Beethoven fan), Lucrezia looked at me as though I was mad. Whereas rapidly shifting from one register to another was a source of liveliness in English, it seemed barbaric in Italian, or just, quite simply, wrong.

Day after day I trekked to Lucrezia's and she tore out the seams of my shoddy, ill fitting Italian and found ways to tailor it to my needs and interests. Her apartment was dustless, underfurnished, plantless; she seemed the chubby, cinched-in *soubrette* in a tragedy, the winsome maid who simpers as she opens the door to let in the Stone Guest. Slowly I filled in the story. She'd been married to an American professor of Italian and had lived with him at the University of Illinois at Champaign-Urbana; one day, quite banally, he'd divorced her to marry a slim, freckled student with granny glasses from Bloomington, but Lucrezia, unlike an American, was not willing to adapt to this change. She didn't want to work through her resentment in therapy or channel it into lesbian feminism; she vowed herself to a life of mourning, returned to Rome and closed her shutters. She suffered from headaches that made her unavailable on certain days. Tina explained that Lucrezia's "headaches" were in fact paralyzing depressions provoked by anniversaries of key dates in her marriage.

My impatience with her grief was not only that of an American optimist but also of a homosexual pessimist. The American in me was astonished, even offended, by her irrevocable decision to take grief's veil and I wanted to line her up for an exercise class, a husband-hunting Caribbean cruise or a macrobiotic diet. But the homosexual in me, that lone wolf who'd been kept away from the campfire by boys throwing stones, who considered his needs to be perversions and his love to be a variety of shame—that homosexual, isolated, thick-skinned, self-mocking, fur torn and muzzle bloody, could only sneer at the incompetence of these heterosexuals in maneuvering their way through disaster. Of *course* men betray you, of *course* love is an illusion dispelled by lust, of *course* you end up alone.

I SPENT MORE and more time with Tina, who took a sort of big sister's interest in me, as though I were a frail, naïve boy. She'd pick me up in her battered Cinquecento and speed me confidently through the narrow, clangorous streets. We'd have dinner in a dim, cheap restaurant looking out across an empty, rain-swept square at a rugged Renaissance palace. We'd eat our plate of spaghetti and nugget of veal in almost total silence. In the center of the square a wide, ancient Roman basin overflowed in the rain, its surface smooth as polished onyx.

Through Tina I started to meet young Italians from good families and they were shocked by my primitive, egotistical brand of leftism. When I told them I was a writer working on a "love story" (I said that just to shut them up, since in the States such a theme would have been unexceptionable), they laughed mockingly. "*Ooh-la-la, l'amour,*" they cackled, pretending to be mustache-twirling French rakes, as though nothing could be more idiotic, retrograde, even *menopausal*, than *love*. A young woman who defended me said she was sure there must be a translation problem.

What shocked me was their conformity. Everyone was a Marxist, albeit of a sophisticated cultural variety. I didn't yet know the writings of Gramsci, but when I discovered them ten years later I saw that these Italian kids weren't American-style New Leftists who confused rebellion with revolution or who thought vegetarianism, nudism and Buddhism were part of a progressive package deal. In America there were only two political parties, virtually interchangeable, and even to our ears talk of real political change sounded unconvincing and quixotic. But here in Italy there seemed to be half a dozen parties, each with a distinct program, newspaper, geographical stronghold, elected senators, and any ruling coalition appeared to be so fragile that the police and the army were always present, night and day, on every corner, to quell a riot should it break out.

I was warned not to talk too freely on the telephone, not even in English, since most phones were tapped.

Tina took me by to meet her father, a tiny, wizened scholar who lived in another apartment in the same family *palazzo*. I was used to the American notion that parents are dull if responsible creatures and their children wild and fascinating, but Tina's father was as hopeless and eccentric as she was. He forgot to eat and lived on cheap wine, he turned night into day and wore the same suit all the time, although every third day Tina convinced him to change his shirt. He was usually morose as he thought about the hundred-page philosophical essay on Time that he'd been writing for the past twenty years, but occasionally he'd throw a rust-colored scarf around his neck and gaily saunter forth in his old Jeep. His girlfriend was an extremely elegant lady his age who invited Tina and me to her palace for a party. Champagne and canapés were handed around by servants in white gloves, although at midnight the hostess herself put on an apron and made us a *spaghettata*—the Italian aftermath to an otherwise stiff, French-style reception. This woman—so dazzling in her diamonds and so punctilious in her politeness—took Tina's father's bohemianism in her stride. She sat placidly beside him in the Jeep, a scarf tied around her impeccable hairdo, her tiny black shoes poised on the floorboard with its gaping hole through which the pavement was visible.

One night when I was alone with Tina—the two of us under a lamp, our armchairs and scrap of carpet marooned like a cheap set hastily assembled on an immense sound stage—I was about to break the exhausting silence to say, "Look, I'll come back in a month when I know more Italian," but she spoke first and said, "I love you."

I was amazed by this declaration, which I hadn't seen coming, but if it made me important and desirable rather than an annoying pest, a tongue-tied foreigner, it also scared me. "But you know," I told her, "I like men."

She stared at me with her huge black eyes turned toward me, humbly. She did not wheedle or seduce or whine or even argue her case; she simply presented herself before me, at once Salome and the head on the platter, pure desire and the bloody sacrifice to it.

"*Sono frocio*," I said, "I'm a fag," using the worst word I knew, the most shocking.

That stung her into a response. "Don't say that. You can say whatever you want—*omosessuale*, *invertito*—but not that horrendous word. You use it only because you don't know Italian."

I tried to explain to her the strategy of adopting the enemy's worst insult, something the new Boston gay commune had done in naming its newspaper *Fag Rag*, but she merely shook her head as though awakening from a bad dream and returned to the assault: "We are *peoples*," she kept repeating in English, which I assumed meant we're individuals before we're gendered (a truism I wasn't sure I believed) and that as individuals we're as likely to fall in love with another soul as another body, with a *simpatica* woman as a dull man.

I began to think how soon I could plausibly take my leave. We were both drunk, she drunker. She let the silence collect in a big cistern ready to overrun. Her instinct was not to permit me to wriggle gracefully out of an awkward situation; does Medea let Jason off the hook, does Phaedra give Hippolytus an easy out?

I stood and she walked into my arms. We began to embrace. My hands traveled over her lean body and pressed her flanks through her skirts. I could feel myself kindling under her touch, but I instantly worried that I'd disappoint her—as a lover and as a husband, for every time I kissed a woman I feared I'd be impotent and insolvent, too flaccid to penetrate her and too poor to support her. When I looked at married men I often sympathized with their obligation to mount their wives, tirelessly, night after night—and to have to *pay* for the pleasure. In gay life, hustlers were paid to penetrate men; we assumed passivity was always the more desirable role and that the drudgery of activity naturally had to be recompensed.

But now all the wine I'd drunk calmed my fears. Nor was Tina decorous or cold. We grappled as violently as any two men might have done and somehow I found myself in the dark hallway leading to her bedroom where her bed glowed like a moonlit pond seen at the end of an alleyway of firs. Then she bit my nose, hard, and I thought, She's mad, she's dangerous, I'm getting out of here.

"Okay, that's it," I said. "I'm leaving." I said it in English, quickly, and I didn't care if she understood me or not.

Once I was outside in the hallway, groping toward the light switch and fumbling to close my trousers, a chilling certainty came over me that she really was crazy and might try to kill me.

I didn't wait for the elevator but ran down the five flights and through the rainy courtyard, my feet striking sound off the cold, mossy pavement just as I heard behind me the elevator motor groaning into action and I knew that soon Tina would be pursuing me.

I ducked through the small door set into the *portone* and found myself

on a deserted street, beside the ugly fountain that had provoked its designer's suicide. I felt seized by an intense fear: Tina was going to run me
over with her car. I started to streak down the hill past the Barberini
Palace; then I sighted a street on the other side and I ducked down it, although after I'd run another block I saw to my horror that it was a dead
end. I crept back up to the main thoroughfare, hugging the shadowy wall,
and arrived at the corner just in time to see a grim-faced Tina hurtling by
behind the wheel of her tiny, battered car.

With a bit more composure I went down to the taxi rank in the Piazza
Barberini. I told the driver to let me off beside the square at Santa Maria
in Trastevere; I'd walk the rest of the way home.

Yet as he was pulling up to our destination he said, "Do you know this
woman who's following us?"

I said to him, "Here's a bit of extra money. Could you just wait a moment while I talk to her?"

He smiled knowingly and suddenly I saw that he thought I was a rogu-
ish husband coming to see his Trastevere mistress and Tina was my jealous wife—and I realized that whereas gay life is always aberrant, there's
not a moment of straight life, no matter how bizarre or melodramatic,
that isn't cozily familiar, that can't be associated with a song lyric or a
movie or a poem. Whereas I'd have felt ashamed if my pursuer had been
a man, now there was a hint of complicity between the driver and me.
Every heterosexual occasion is an institution, every heterosexual sin a
source of pride.

I went directly up to Tina's car, ducked down and spoke to her through
the open window. She was very pale. I said, as a hypnotist might, "You're
tired and you're going to go home now and we'll speak in the morning."
She nodded slowly.

I crossed the square, which was dim and deserted in the midnight rain.
The square was closed to cars but I kept expecting to hear Tina's Cinquecento gunning its motors as she came crashing down on me. By walking
confidently away from her I felt like a *torero* who turns his back on a bull,
stunned but angry.

My mother, who was working in Germany, came to Rome to spend a
weekend with me. When she left I bought a big bottle of Chianti and
drank it all alone until I passed out. Around three in the morning I was
awakened by the smell of what seemed to be burning tar. (In fact it was
the *nafta* heating oil that had been pooling for weeks in the entryway on
the floor.) I thought I didn't care if I burned alive, I still needed a ciga-

rette. I lit up and groggily got dressed. I wondered if Tina had set fire to my building.

Then I did exactly the wrong thing. I threw open the front door and was knocked back by the billowing black smoke. I ran to the windows that gave onto the street and opened them, thereby creating a draft. Soon the whole apartment was so full of thick, smelly smoke that I couldn't even see the lights I'd turned on. The alleyway was full of noise and whirring lights. A ladder was extended up to my window and a fireman with a smoke-blackened face and brilliant blue eyes beneath a silver helmet came rushing up, smiling.

"*Non posso*," I said. I can't. I'm afraid. "*Ho paura.*"

"*Sì, sì*," he assured me. And he promised he'd be right behind me as we descended, an offer not to be refused. I remembered how as an adolescent I'd walked along the top of a high wall to please Tommy, despite my vertigo. The fireman, small but bristling with bravura, talked me down the ladder, step by step, his voice low and fatherly. Once I was down he rushed back up the ladder to put out the fire but slapped his forehead when he reached the top because he'd forgotten the hose.

Everyone had a good laugh, as though to say, "That's an Italian for you—everything is theater." There was a crowd in the street who treated me with sympathy and I was so glad to be accepted at last by my neighbours, even if as a victim, that I scarcely regretted that all my belongings were burned or covered with tar. A woman from down the street gave me a glass of warm milk, the best cure, she swore, against swallowed smoke.

For some strange reason my tall blond Venetian waiter appeared out of nowhere; why he'd been on his way to visit me at five in the morning I'll never know. Someone called the countess, my landlady. I thought of the inventory she'd made me sign, the list of every item down to the last egg cup. When she arrived she was in a state of shock to see her whole apartment—new flocked wallpaper, heavy velvet drapes and ecclesiastical library—covered with an inch of tar. My waiter, whom I'd considered so distinguished till now, tried to speak to her, but he was obviously out of his depth and just talked in a falsely elegant circle. His hollow voice now sounded pretentious, his choice of words meaningless, his manner by turns insolent and humble.

"Is this your friend?" she asked with a condescending smile and quite genuine curiosity.

"He's *a* friend," I said sheepishly, which scarcely explained what he was doing here before dawn.

The fire, in fact, was my salvation. Susie, my English real-estate agent, took me in for a couple of days until she found me a roommate, Thomas, who lived near the Pantheon. When the contessa refused to return my security deposit, the equivalent of three months' rent, Tina found me a tough woman lawyer who made her pay up the very next day. At last I could make something happen here in Rome.

I returned to my old apartment to see if anything could be salvaged. It was like visiting Pompeii if one were a Pompeiian. In the bedroom I found a very young workman in a blue uniform who was scrubbing down the walls. He told me his name was Decimo. He seemed worried that his boss (*il mio principale*) would come back and catch him idling. I stood uncomfortably close to him, smiling into his handsome young face, feeling the crazy confidence that desire sometimes conferred on me. Perhaps this all-black version of my once red and purple apartment excited me, or perhaps the smell of coal smoke awakened in me memories of melancholy Chicago winters, memories that were horny because they brought back a sharp recollection of loneliness, a lack, an emptiness I wanted to fill as soon as possible.

I reached out and touched his erection under his uniform, which was the sort of single garment that zips down the front. I pulled his zipper down. He had nothing on underneath except a hard-on. He murmured something again about his *principale* but I pulled back the bedclothes. Where the sheet had been exposed it was pitch black, but where it had been covered it was startlingly white and I pushed him gently back onto that pure surface as I knelt between his legs. I could barely fit it all into my mouth, so thick was it, so rigid and smelly with youth. He exploded with anxious alacrity and I swallowed it all down like a cat licking its bowl clean.

The next day, when I told Lucrezia about the fire and my subsequent visit to the scene of the crime, she was convinced I must be lying about my sexual encounter, except as proof to the contrary there were two bits of evidence that seemed incontrovertible, more to her than to me—the fact he was called "*Decimo*," the "tenth" child in a huge peasant family, usually the name of someone from the South; and the fact he called his boss *principale*, an elegant working-class word substituted for the more casual *capo*.

That she was so shocked proved to me what a gulf separated us, woman and man, straight and gay, Italian and American. I suppose if I'd been Italian I wouldn't have told her. Or if I hadn't been a student with a language tutor in search of a topic I might not have brought back these curious vocabulary items. Or perhaps I quite simply wanted to give Lucrezia proof that I really was a faggot, evidence she could pass on to the still brooding and unconvinced Tina.

⟶ THOMAS, the roommate Susie had found for me, had a sunny three-room apartment and terrace. From the kitchen window I could look out at a pure white marble horse, four times life size, on a tiered wedding cake, the Monument to Victor Emmanuel. In reality it was one of four horses pulling a chariot in which a goddess stood upright, but from our window only this single horse was visible. Seen as an entity from the Piazza di Venezia, the monument was no doubt frightful kitsch, but this single horse, poised against the blue sky and racing clouds, struck me as the very image of romantic audacity.

On the terrace a fountain ran night and day, although sometimes the flow was so copious and forceful it spilled over onto the flagstones and a neighborhood cat would tiptoe through the water, shaking its paw as it lifted each leg like a dancer doing a tentative *battement*. Most of the dirty cats belonged to no one and jumped from terrace to terrace; they made me think of skinny, dirty burglars, their faces pointy and triangular from hunger. They were not the sleek, haughty pets I'd known in America, who sniffed at their food with a disdain bordering on impertinence. No, if I put some uneaten spaghetti (even cold, gummy, meatless spaghetti) in a bowl on the terrace, no sooner did I pass through the doorway than a grey, smoky swirl of cats coalesced out of nowhere and began prowling at my feet, weaving rapid figure eights, growling menacingly and hissing at one another, like pressure cookers releasing steam. I'd have to put the food down and pull back in a flash or else my hand was in danger; a shriek, a slashing claw, a leap in the air, glinting teeth, convulsive necks—and it was all over, the plate licked clean, and a moment later the whole team of robbers was bounding away across the rooftops, each pair of skinny, lusterless flanks mobile as two fingers playing a trill.

I had joined a gym, the Roma, near the Piazza Barberini, and went three times a week to lift weights and take an exercise class. At regular intervals the *professore* would stop our workout and spray the air with a perfume atomizer. No one wore the smelly, ratty clothes I'd grown used to at the Sheridan Square Gym in the Village, nor did Italians prize the "good, clean smell of sweat," as we Americans had put it, always linking the words together. I can remember that the Italian word for "jumping jack" was *farfalla*, "butterfly." (I can just hear the jeers of the Village jocks.) I grew used to the idea of washing my newly acquired designer gym clothes after each use. Shorts were frowned on, as though they were less hygienic than long pants.

But now I wondered if my pumped-up body wasn't what scared off Roman gay men. Thomas had a skinny Sardinian lover who looked at me in a T-shirt and jeans and said, "*Povero ragazzo, è doppio corpato.*" ("Poor guy, he's double-bodied.") Embarrassed, Thomas later explained to me that Italians were still so close to the soil and just a generation away from poverty, that they perceived a big body as a shameful sign of peasant origins and physical toil; city dwellers had to be stylishly slim. "Anyway," Thomas said, "Emilio is a bit jealous of you since you moved in."

Thomas and I slept in twin beds in the bedroom separated by an aisle, although he often fell asleep on the couch in the living room. I never saw him naked at first. He seldom changed his Jockey shorts, which were stained yellow across the Y-front from piss. He was my age, but his life had been entirely different. His father was a baron from Bukovina, his mother an American from Virginia. He'd been raised and educated in South Africa and had given the valedictory address for his graduating class, but now, just twelve years later, he could scarcely remember a word of Afrikäans. He enjoyed speaking English, which he spoke with an unexceptionable American accent except that his *o* was too resonant, too rounded and too far back in the throat. But though he sounded like any other American, thanks to his mother, his English vocabulary was very sketchy. He'd say, "Put my shirt on the, you know, on the place where we eat."

"The table?"

"Yeah. *Table. Tavola.*"

From him I learned how to take a bus, how to make a lunch out of tiny, crustless sandwiches (*tramezzini*), how to conceal one's groceries in a suitcase (since a man out shopping for food was considered a disgrace), how to repress my big goofy American smile and regard everything with a certain disdain or *sprezzatura*.

I was fascinated by his survival skills. He had just one good jacket, close fitting, cut out of black velvet, which he was constantly brushing. His hair was wavy and reddish blond and he combed it straight back to emphasize his widow's peak. His teeth were large and yellow and when he smiled he resembled an old, friendly dog that comes padding up to you, trusting, limping slightly, expecting to be petted and babied. Except there was also something crafty and observing in his eye. With his big relaxed smile and tight, scheming eyes he gave the impression of someone basically kind, even downtrodden, who'd had to maneuver cunningly in a hostile world of poor, handsome young men on the lookout for a free meal or ten thousand lire.

He was an extra in the movies, he said, but I never saw him go for an audition or a day's shoot. He had plenty of stories to tell about the cinema, however, and his dog, a cross between a beagle and a mutt, he'd found on the set of *The Battle of Anzio*, and he'd named her Anzio, not only after the city but after the word for "anxiety." He'd awaken at nine or ten, be dressed and coiffed and brushed-down if not exactly bathed by eleven and then he'd descend the four flights with Anzio and me clattering along behind him. He'd walk, erect and proud, his Titian-blond hair resplendent where it crested over his black velvet collar, with Anzio straining at the leash. Old Italian men would stop him and ask if Anzio was an English hunting dog and instead of saying with an ironic smile, "No, she's just a mutt," Thomas would go into a long, serious and entirely fabricated explanation of her genealogy, which amounted to an invitation to a discussion of past dogs the stranger had known and his long-lost hunting days in the Abruzzi. Only after several such encounters would we finally arrive at a bar where we'd order (and I'd pay for) tall glasses of *caffelatte* and three *cornetti*, one each for Thomas and me and one for Anzio, who'd wait for it with a humble, pleading look on her pretty face with its moist, black nose and liquid eyes all black iris and brown pupil, devoid of whites; she'd swallow it in one bite and then, nonchalantly, fastidiously, lie down on the mosaic floor and lick her chops once before balancing her chin on her outstretched paw.

Slowly I saw that his day was made up of promenading his dog, window shopping, drinking a cheap grappa in the Piazza Navona, banging the piano, debating politics back home with unemployed friends who dropped by and smoked the cheap national brand of cigarettes, MS, listening to absurdly passionate pop songs sung by hoarse-voiced guys, songs that sounded shockingly out-dated to my trendy American ears but that I quickly came to adore because they expressed the vein-bursting adolescent male love that I longed to be the object of. Thomas and I went to the apartment of one of his friends who owned a television in order to watch the San Remo Festival, a pop song contest that seemed at once innocent and vulgar, the lyrics so unabashedly sentimental, inevitably ending on a wailed *"Piangerò"* ("I'll weep"), whereas the women's dresses (and hair!) struck me as more suitable to prostitutes than to entertainers, admittedly a fine distinction in that part of the world.

Tina came up to inspect Thomas and the apartment. She liked the terrace with its big stone planters and its endlessly flowing fountain, which a neighbor lady had told me was fed by an ancient Roman aqueduct. *"Almeno,"* she said, "at least no one pays for it and sometimes the water is a flood, all very mysterious, unless it's the snow melting far away in the mountains."

Tina told me that Thomas was a leech who'd suck all my blood from my veins and then cast me aside. "You don't know these boys, so charming and smiling, but lazy, they never work, they prefer sucking the blood of innocent Americans. I don't think he's even homosexual. He just wants to excite you. Pay attention!" With her forefinger she pulled her cheek down below her eye. "I'm sure he's not homosexual. He was looking at me like all these neighborhood Romeos do."

Tina must have liked the simplicity of the apartment—the plain, rugless red tile floor, the battered straight-back wood chairs, the table with its blue-and-white checked oilcloth cover, the sagging old couch, the witless bullfight posters. The only luxury was an upright piano and the only expense I ever saw Thomas go to was hiring a piano tuner who spent four hours inspecting his invalid, for he was like a doctor listening to respiration and pulses, palpating organs, inspecting cavities and hammering out reflexes.

And to what avail? Thomas simply banged out big chords relentlessly, leaned with his elbows and forearms on half the keyboard at a time and played a noisy "Chopsticks" designed to remind the neighbors that the piano is a percussive instrument. I never met a homosexual who was so violent, so indifferent to nuance, so majestically sure of himself. No wonder Tina had her doubts about him.

Nor any foreigner who'd so thoroughly Italianized himself. Living internationally as an expatriate invariably promotes a double vision, a queasy sense of the arbitrariness of all conventions, and makes one wince at the vulgarity of one's compatriots and mock the humorless provinciality of one's hosts. Thomas, uniquely, had forgotten his past, nearly even forgotten his first languages (German, Afrikäans and English) and had embraced everything Roman with a big sweaty hug. He spoke with the falling querulousness and mushy consonants of a fruit vendor on the Campo dei Fiori. He followed the soccer scores with the gimlet-eyed fanaticism of those paunchy *tifosi* whose only connection to sports is in the decibel level of their jubilation or anger.

He could start out lying, oh, about anything at all, his eyes squirming with inventions, and within five minutes he'd be staring at me, self-hypnotized and round-eyed with conviction. He'd lounge around the apartment in his stained underwear and a formerly white T-shirt, his hair on end, but by the time he went out he was impeccable, even imperious, and at the café he'd toss back his thimble-full of sugared black coffee with the requisite briskness, rather than nursing it with the mild-eyed panda-bear innocence and unfocused amiability of American tourists.

He'd talk politics for hours with the same passion if a bit more nuance than he'd devote to soccer squabbles. Like other Italians he saw conspiracies everywhere and dismissed everyone who disagreed with him as corrupted by the Mafia or the Americans—or as even more shamefully simpleminded. I paid no attention to Italian politics and dismissed the whole activity as *opera buffa* but Thomas shouted at me, red-faced, a vein popping out of his forehead, "Italy is *the* battleground. As Italy goes, so goes the West." I was never sure what he meant, but I suppose he was referring to the battle between Communism and Capitalism. Like other political cognoscenti he was so fascinated by lawmakers jockeying for position, by signs of secret deals, by evidence of shifting alliances, that he never came right out and said what he was *for* or *against*. Was he a Communist? I never found out (and perhaps he never knew); he preferred to pooh-pooh other people's gullibility and unmask Byzantine scheming than to state clearly what cause he espoused.

It struck me as odd that someone could care so intensely about Italian factionalism, someone who was an African-raised Romanian-American, much less a homosexual who, in my eyes at least, would always be disenfranchised by every party, a pariah even among outcasts. "Not so!" Thomas shouted as he explained to me about FUORI, an acronym that meant "outside" and that stood for a coalition of prostitutes, gays, anarchists, ecologists and other "marginals" who'd already elected a senator. I laughed out loud, since compromising with such a band of thieves seemed far less desirable to me than total isolation, our natural state and a splendid one (Lucifer is alone by definition). In any event, unlike me,

Thomas saw himself as "bisexual," although he never spoke of women and seemed to know only one or two; yet certainly he was nothing so disgraceful as a *frocio*.

⟶ THAT SPRING I drank so much bad white wine that I became bloated and was always tired. Thomas, Anzio and I would eat our pasta and on special days a bit of veal and peas as well, always at the same restaurant, which was across from the Pantheon. If we had cherries or peaches as dessert, the lugubrious waiter would carry the stones on a plate to the majestic cashier, enthroned behind her old bronze cash register, and she'd count these juicy remains to figure out how much we owed her. Once when it was my birthday we celebrated with an extra course and ice cream as well as fruit. When the bill was presented Thomas took violent exception to it. It was much too high.

There was never a question of challenging the addition, which was impeccable, or the prices, clearly marked on the menu. No, Thomas argued that since we were regular clients and our father was ill at home and all our money went to support him, such robbery was inhuman and even bordered on the illegal. The proprietor descended from her throne and replied that she had a sister at home who was an invalid as well, that taxes were rising and that the rent had shot up so high that soon she'd have to close her doors. Thomas responded with more heart-rending details about our poverty and the tragedies besetting our relatives one after another. He was so convincing that I studied him with genuine sympathy until I remembered his sad story was also supposed to be mine and I hung my head with aching sorrow. Finally the owner of the restaurant drew a vigorous line through our bill and gave us a twenty-percent *sconto*, which I paid as Thomas shook the hands of the waiter and his boss, a big doggy smile on his lips as he looked shyly around through his shaggy blond eyebrows.

The first few weeks I lived with him, I had one bad surprise after another—the electricity was turned off, then the phone, then we were served an eviction notice. I paid the six months' overdue back rent, which was still cheaper than a single month's rent for my Trastevere tart's flat. And I paid the phone bill, especially since in those days the waiting list for a new phone was so backed up it could take a full year before a new line could be installed. Thomas had inherited this number from the former tenants, who'd been Communists, which explained why our line was tapped. The tapping equipment was so crude that the moment an eavesdropper joined us the volume dropped and the line sizzled like a frying pan. Thomas wouldn't let me pay the electricity bill; he was convinced he could get it turned back on by invoking our invalid father, stumbling in the dark, housebound but deprived of his radio, no electric blanket in an unheated apartment to ward off a fatal chill. I went with him to the government office where he made his plea. He succeeded in having the service re-installed, although never for a moment, I'm sure, did the office clerk who heard him out believe his story. No, Thomas was simply being rewarded for his fine performance. Now, of course, everyone's *mani* are *pulite* in Italy and those bravura arias are no longer heard in public places. In fact all this talk about corruption is just the noise generated by the switch from the old feudal baksheesh system to a rational and impersonal Northern European capitalist system.

I didn't mind paying the bills. As the weather became warmer we ate outside at the Piazza Navona or in a square looking across toward the Palazzo Farnese or, around the corner, in a restaurant called La Quercia, which was also the name of the huge tree shading the small square. I'd pick up the check, even when our group grew to include six, eight or ten of Thomas's friends.

In June Italy's soccer team beat Brazil in the Coppa Mondiale. As soon as this victory was announced all Rome went wild. Thomas said that Italians became so excited after a major soccer victory that they could be easily seduced and we should head up to the Via Veneto right away.

On the street all the cars were honking and kids were poking their heads out of the open vents in car roofs and unfurling Italian flags, which streamed and fluttered behind their ecstatic faces. The swerving yellow and white headlights lit the flags from many angles. Usually the streets were so deserted after nightfall, the *palazzi* so hermetically shuttered, that the city seemed abandoned to its cats and a few night watchmen, who left chalk marks behind on doors to show they'd passed by on their inspection route. But tonight the gloomy buildings—with their massive sooty stones on ground level gouged in "wormlike" patterns or left rough and rusti-cated—came alive with noise and light. Shutters flew open and revealed behind these majestic Renaissance façades the poverty of apartments lit by a single dangling bulb. Thomas said, "And they live on nothing but spaghettis and they eat them without sauce" (he was so Italianized that even when he wanted to invent an English plural for pasta he habitually added an *s*, since he could never imagine that *spaghetti* could be a collective singular in English).

His prediction that we'd find a willing *tifoso* was spot-on. We were walking up the slow bend after the Piazza Barberini that marks the beginning of the Via Veneto when a kid all on his own, overflowing with joy, walked between us, put his hands on our shoulders and cantilevered his body up in the air. He swung like the clapper of a bell and made about as much noise.

Thomas, usually so discreet, even haughty, in public during his daily sorties with Anzio, suddenly asked, with stunning simplicity, if he'd like to come home with us to make love. The young man turned somber, which I thought meant he was going to say no, but in fact he was just coming to terms with our offer. "I've never tried homosexuality but I accept your invitation," he said at last. Perhaps he was most astonished that we had a place to go to, since unmarried men in Italy at that time were forced to live at home. Only foreign bachelors possessed their own apartments.

Enea, as he was named (*Aeneas*, I realized with a start, as I glanced at him again, hoping to discern something classical in his face) was a student of what I made out to be hydraulic engineering and he came from Lucca. The Romans he considered to be, one and all, "turds" (*stronzi*) because all they thought of was making money and showing off. "And they're all lazy, they never work; either they're making a new strike or picking their noses and taking a four-hour siesta." Enea was amused by my American accent and my plucky if hopeless attempts to communicate; he assured me that he liked Mickey Mouse and hamburgers. I might have said something cutting if I'd known how to or if he'd been less sexy.

He had red cheeks like taffy apples under a flawless permanent tan, very red lips, one clean white canine on the right side that overlapped another tooth and left a little gap, not at all hickish but rather disconcerting, so at odds was it with his quiet good manners and dignified if thrilling smiles. Perhaps because of the gap, the adjoining teeth were always sparkling with saliva as though a celebrity photographer had added highlights. He had a small, pale Adam's apple raised like a knobby dial to regulate the volume of his husky tenor voice. When his face was immobile it took on a stern *condottiere*'s expression, cold and disabused beyond his years, as though a boy, after fighting in his first battle, were to lift his visor. I forgot to mention he was tiny.

When we got home Thomas went into the bathroom for a second. In that same instant Enea was naked and I, still half-dressed, reached down to touch the hard little urgency he was presenting me out of a bush of black, glossy hair strangely pornographic because it was such a neat little plantation in an otherwise creamy-white body: flat tummy, hard loins, an ass as hard and round as a soccer ball. He exploded in my hand after a single thrust. I wiped the copious semen on one of Thomas's dirty T-shirts I found under a chair. I worried about what Thomas would do or say. Enea, perfectly composed or if embarrassed determined not to show it, put on his underpants and said, "*Insomma, era un po' banale*" ("It wasn't all that exciting after all").

Thomas, red and peeled and naked as the devil, figured out right away what had happened. He put on his grey plaid robe and poured us all a glass of white wine.

"*Adesso*," Enea said primly, "*cominciamo il dialogo*."

"What'd he say?" I asked Thomas.

"He said we must begin the *dialogue* now."

"What *dialogue*, the little wanker!" I wailed.

"A, you know, discussion about homosexuality and what it means. Now that we've had sex—"

"You mean *he's* had—"

"Anyway," Thomas interrupted, generously brushing aside my nasty precision, "he feels he's at least earned the right to a discussion—"

"—Marxist, no doubt," I grumbled. "Anyway, I'm bushed. I'm going to bed."

I shook Enea's hand rather stiffly; he looked shocked by my rudeness.

Once I was in bed I could hear their voices through the closed door rumbling on and on, punctuated by all those rhetorical markers that are always more noticeable in a language other than one's own and that in any case are strikingly efficient in Italian. "*Anzi*," Thomas kept crying, which means "On the contrary." "*Cioè*," they'd both interject ("That is to say") by way of piling up new explanations. "*Dai!*" Thomas would shout murderously, a word that means no more than "Get off it!" "*Dunque*," Enea would say from time to time, a word that may signify "therefore," but which Italians use to suggest a verbal sponging down of the blackboard and a vain aspiration toward order. "*Magari*," each of them would mumble after any hopeful remark, to mean "Would that it might be so," much as an Arab might say "*Inshallah*." Lucrezia would be proud of my knack at making sense of it all, just as sleep overcame me and nothing made sense any more.

⌐⌐⌐⌐⌐⌐◯ ONE DAY as I was waiting on a street corner a block from the Fountain of Trevi, three soldiers started chatting me up. They were *bersaglieri*, Garibaldi's crack troops, and they wore feathers in their caps. Thomas had told me that a soldier received only three feathers with his kit and if he had more that meant he'd paid for the extra plumage and might be worth pursuing. These *bersaglieri*, I noticed sadly, had only the regulation three feathers, but one of them talked to me with masterful assurance. "We're in a crack company," he said in Italian, "and we have to run several kilometers every morning. We have beautiful bodies, our bodies are wonderfully fit, unfortunately we earn only a few pennies every day, not even enough for cigarettes, so we're always on the lookout for a bit of extra change, besides we have lots of free time and nowhere to go, you'd be surprised what good shape we're in, our bodies are really beautiful." At last Thomas came up and I ducked away with him; I was afraid to invite three tough heterosexuals home (they might rob me) although to this day I wish I'd done so. By the time I'd explained the situation to Thomas the soldiers had vanished into the crowds. He was angry we'd missed what he said was a rare opportunity—"Nice Calabrese boys," he said, "with no hang-ups."

Thomas had an American friend named Bill (so often pronounced "Beal" by the Italians that to this day I can hear it in no other way). "Beal" had a lanky, boyish figure, a wonderful full head of hair that was glossy and straight, long on top and short on the sides, which made me think of Prince Hal's tonsure, a winningly lopsided smile, fine hands boned like Indian wickerwork and an intellectual seriousness that seemed unusually becoming in one so beautiful. He was very tall but always standing, as though embarrassed, in *contrapposto*, like a tall woman in flats, a beautiful hand on his hip—or in the air as he grasped after a point he'd just sighted. The Italians couldn't get enough of him. He was the slender American boy, rangy and just a bit gawky or rather coltish, and his serious, distracted way of smiling up through his glossy hair, then flicking it aside as his smile faded, conformed to their ideal of how an American should look and manage his looks. He was healthy, naïve, available and yet a bit mysterious.

Just about when I'd decided no one in Rome was really gay I met "Beal" and watched him bring them out of the woodwork. Around him every Italian man seemed to be at least bisexual. I wasn't ugly (in fact I was never cuter) but the Italians didn't like me, possibly because I was "double-bodied" or at once too serious about art and too frivolous about politics. No, that wasn't it. Their reasoned disappointment came only after knowing me a bit and merely confirmed their bad first impression, based as it was on an allergy to my earnestness—my efforts to learn Italian, catch the drift, win a place.

Nor did "Beal" like me. He made a careless little effort at first to ingratiate himself by having me listen to a record of "Switched-On Bach" he'd just received from the States, a precious harbinger of a new American trend. It was a speeded-up rendition for chipmunks of the great Toccata and Fugue played on twittering electronic instruments, excited gibberish that struck him and Thomas as terribly contemporary, yet another of the horrors that people back then were always announcing as about to replace traditional art forms.

When I said I liked my Bach switched off, he and Thomas looked at me with a mixture of pity and contempt, even dislike, and after that I felt I'd lost Thomas's friendship forever. He and "Beal" were always cooking up schemes in whispers behind my back. They'd go silent when I came into the room. "Beal" himself was a composer who lived in a maid's room and worked up new sonatas on an electric keyboard he'd plug in, play and listen to with earphones, the only sound that was audible to visitors being the click of his fingernails on the plastic keys. Thomas admired "Beal's" self-discipline and up-to-date "American" tendencies; he was half proud parent, half sponsor, though in fact he was penniless and incapable of sponsoring even Anzio with a daily *cornetto*.

If mentally I put *American* in inverted commas I did so to mark a shift in my feelings. Until that time I'd never thought of my country as having a national character. When I'd lived in it I'd experienced it as vaguely coterminous with all cultural possibilities; only now, here in Italy, could America be praised for its energy or efficiency or youthful audacity or damned for its capitalist greed or colonialism. When Thomas was with his Italian friends he'd routinely characterize America as a country that had passed directly from puritanism to decadence and that was in the thrall of the "military-industrial complex." But now with "Beal" he let on that he might admire American culture for its teenage vitality and saucy irreverence.

One night Thomas took me out cruising with him. Just as I'd given up on him he squandered a sudden if short-lived interest on me. We went to the Janiculum Hill, a very long trek by foot for us, though just a five-minute ride for all the others, the car owners. Lights advanced, bobbed and swerved, then went dead as the drivers parked in their extinct but still creaking automobiles. No one got out. All these men were eyeing each other from their parked cars—another Italian stalemate.

Thomas and I brought someone home with us, a Chilean millionaire in an English cashmere turtleneck and Gucci moccasins with gilded bits decorating the uppers. He drove us back in style in his sky-blue Mercedes. He brought a quart of gin up with him but after Thomas started humping his leg, Juan abruptly changed his mind, mumbled an apology—and left the bottle behind.

We drank it down, drank deeply right from the bottle, without a glass or an ice cube, much less a lemon slice, and we sat under our bare light bulb on the couch and then somehow the light was off and we were on the floor.

Thomas pulled my clothes off with his hot hands. There was a smile on his open lips but his eyes had lost consciousness; all he knew to do was to keep medicating himself from the bottle and tapping my anus with his right middle finger. I was just a Johnny One-Note, but that one note he wanted to play.

Whereas the gin sickened me and made me want to sleep, it excited him. He didn't talk, he just leaned his face into me, his face with its slack smile, pulsing vein in the forehead and big, nutcracker nose. His body was scrawny and appeared unhatched, but his urgency made him a real man, a lot more real than all those Greenwich Village gays with their bored indecisiveness (indecision lowers sperm counts). His cock tasted of tarama.

His face might have been dazed but his body pounded into mine, as though the gin-stunned loss of cortical control had left the big red setter with just two automatic responses, positioning and grasping with the powerful forepaws and a strong thrust with the pelvis. For two months day in and day out I'd studied Thomas across the corridor between our twin beds or across the oilcloth-covered table or across the colander of steaming spaghetti in the sink. Now I was so happy to wrap my legs around his waist and surrender to this canine excitement. I could even feel the head of his penis, dog-like, swelling inside me. He whispered dirty things in Italian into my ear.

He moved the mattress from his bed out into the living room and there we grappled with ever greater fierceness. Thomas's violent, relentless sexual style was all of a piece with his political harangues and long arguments vaunting the superiority of Verdi to Wagner or of Fellini to

Bergman. Just as he was an idle, unfocused man capable of working up unflagging enthusiasm in a dispute with the first comer over a subject neither of them knew anything about (argument as recreation), in the same way once he started fucking me, the double-bodied roommate he'd taken on only to pay the bills, he made my asshole the object of his abusive lust and convinced himself of his sincerity as he went along.

When we woke up in the morning, I was just about to smile ruefully in my middle-class way, apologize for my "zoo breath" and start bustling about setting the house in order, but Thomas reached for the half-empty quart of gin, poured more of the transparent liquid down my throat and his, and soon he was humping me again. He never touched my erection— of course not, since he considered himself heterosexual.

We drank, fucked and slept, drank, fucked and slept in a cycle that blent day into night and his body into mine. The bottle was the magic source of pleasure, its genie our delight. My mental eye widened as it glimpsed the possibility of limitless gratification. No need to wash, shave and dress the body, to go out, to work, read, discuss things. No need for the party ever to end. Anzio whined to be walked and finally, in desperation, relieved herself on the terrace. She lay above us on the couch, her paws dangling over the edge, each ear cocking successively as she watched our couplings. At one point (it was night), I awoke to see Thomas draining some cooked spaghetti, his face emerging out of a cloud of steam. He came back to the mattress and fed me with a fork that kept clanking against the metal bowl. My mouth was still warm with *penne* and butter when he started stuffing it with his cock again. He put the bowl on the floor for Anzio, who greedily gobbled down the rest; the bowl slid over the tiles like a teacup across a Ouija board. The muscles inside my thighs ached, as though I'd been riding a horse too long.

When we awakened the next time the gin was gone. We didn't speak to each other and separately we took long showers that washed us clean. While I was in the bathroom shaving, Thomas must have put his mattress back in place, straightened the furniture and left with Anzio. I stood on the terrace and looked down at the buses and cars turning around the Largo Argentina and its small, ugly Etruscan temple. When I saw him next he was hostile, as though I'd tricked him into our sex binge.

EVERY WEEK I walked to the American Express office to cash one of my dwindling number of traveler's checks, to buy the local

American newspaper and to eat my hamburger at Babington's. One day I found at American Express a rejection letter from the publisher who'd been holding onto my Japanese-Fire Island novel for the last six months. He wrote, "I like high-class junk and junky junk, but your book doesn't fall into either category. It's pure 'quality lit' and just a bit too highbrow for poor me."

The jaunty, falsely self-deprecating tone made the letter writer seem all the more inaccessible to me, drunk as he must be on his own attitudinizing: he couldn't see how cruel he was being.

I started to cry with hurt and frustration. What kind of world was it that prized "junk"? I asked myself. Had I been too much of a snob in never reading mysteries, detective novels, whodunnits or comic strips, advice books, recipes? Already cut off from the mainstream of human experience by homosexuality, I'd only compounded my isolation through snobbism.

I walked down from the Spanish Steps, past the fashionable men's and women's shops, toward the Corso. In the Piazza Colonna I imagined the triumphal column—erected by an emperor and adorned with a relief of hundreds of the vanquished—as a monument to all the defeated writers throughout the centuries, an absurdity that made me smile. But this feeble irony hatched by my brain was only a fitful distraction. Once I'd pushed through the Piazza di Spagna and its snarling Vespas and Cinquecentos and started walking past the Fori Antichi toward the Colosseum I abandoned myself to my grief.

"I . . . can't . . . *speak*," I said through my sobs, sibylline words I instantly started to interpret. Yes, I thought, they won't let me have my say. I don't want to write trash, high class or low, since it wouldn't say what only I could express. But why should the world be interested in my self-expression? I asked. Hadn't my shrink said my gay friends and I were "self-admiring and nonrelating"? Were such people suitable to literature either as subjects or narrators? Even in my new novel, from which I'd banished homosexuality as a theme, my perversion still seeped through, like a blood stain through cotton. If only I could be published I'd never ask for more or complain about anything. I knew my book was good. If it was rejected, that must mean my judgment was faulty or the world's values abominable or both; in either case I was lost.

I decided to kill myself. I'd bet everything on one number and lost. I'd quit my job thinking that such a rash act would conjure fortune and get me published. I'd bet that by becoming a writer (the spring sunlight was warm on my shoulders and all these Italians were rushing to destinations I'd never know) I'd be able to transform myself from being an exception to becoming an example. My voice would speak to readers over the barrier of years, gender and even (through translation) of language. (Down there, in the pale green spring grass, was the *miliarium*, that stone, wishbone white, from which the Romans measured all distances.) If suicide seemed philosophically inevitable, the nearly redundant plugging of a silenced mouth, nevertheless the mechanics of stopping this big, busy machine, my body, required a skill I hadn't yet worked out. Later in my life I was drawn toward suicide and that pull was literally a vertigo sucking me out toward the fifteenth-floor balcony, despair accompanying but not causing the self-destructive surrender to gravity or the vividly imagined collision of flesh and stone—a sensation utterly different from the frustration and anger I felt that day in Rome. And of course the desire to punish that editor, to lay a terrible burden of guilt on his shoulders.

I made a vulgar little deal with God that if he'd send me an angel I'd go on living. I sat down on a bench overlooking a broken, worn-down pair of Roman columns. Just as my mother had always said flashy, provocative things in elevators, hoping to appear intriguing to perfect strangers, just as she had an uncanny knack for hearing our conversation with their ears and could simultaneously respect the naturalness of our situation while imparting through hints and omissions a much more glamorous version of things to these auditors, in the same way, even in the midst of an intensely personal, isolating crisis in my life, I couldn't help but "turn out," as actors say, toward a nonexistent but potential audience, in order to make a touching effect. To God or to a stranger. To be fair, I needed to be saved.

The angel arrived. I was saved. A Danish tourist, a tall gay man in his thirties peering out through smudged glasses, came over to me, sat on the bench, watched me cry, put his arm around my shoulders, led me home, made gentle, smiling, dabbing love to me. His foreskin was so tight it couldn't roll back. He asked me if I liked his "virgin cock." I believed I'd been saved but I didn't believe in God. Nor could I decide what I'd been saved to do. My mother was always saying we'd been put on earth to "make a contribution" to others. I didn't think like that, but if I tried to, I knew what my contribution was meant to be—the problem was that no one wanted it.

THE SPRING TURNED into summer. My money was running out faster than I'd expected. A young jeweler from Spoleto who lived next door would pull me into his arms and kiss me deeply while his pregnant wife was in the other room making coffee on an electric burner. I paid their rent because I loved his muzzy, handsome face, his full, pink upper lip that had been cut and was lopsided (perhaps it was a badly repaired harelip), his way of lazily shrugging as though he understood nothing and had gotten in much too deep. (He was the long-suffering, put-upon man.) I loved the reedy timbre of his voice as he whispered in my ear. His wife smiled but treated me almost formally, as though I were a client who'd come to see her husband's jewels (family jewels, to be precise, though I never saw them).

I liked the finch they kept in a cage and the records scattered on the floor and the wet-brick smell of watered geraniums competing with the black wealth of coffee thundering up the *vesuvio*. I liked her slender legs, high instep and the nylons drying on a line stretched across the window. I liked that I could go to their apartment and take a nap on a cot by myself and no one, not even Thomas, would know where I was. I was a visitor, of course, but I was paying their rent. The jeweler would push me away, gently, as though to do so were one more weary obligation, and he'd indicate with a jerk of his adorable tousled head the adjoining room, where his wife was fussing over the bird, a bit stagily, perhaps, to kill time till I left. They seemed somewhat unhappy, very much in love, a little sleepy and confused. Of course I gave money. Wouldn't you? Since I had so few savings left I felt compelled to spend my last dollars as quickly and disastrously as possible.

Jamie, my old office mate, came to Rome with his lover, the tall, blond Gerry. The three of us went to Capri where the season was about to begin. The island was deserted except for workmen making last-minute repairs; as we walked along pathways consecrated to the memory of Augustus or the Krupps, we could hear hammers rhythmically tapping in the distance. We smoked a joint. The whole island, apparently deserted if secretly inhabited, knocked and knocked like a woods—glossy, hot, breathless—inhabited by woodpeckers. The sea glittered straight below us. Jamie sang the Nöel Coward song about life coming to Mrs. Wentworth-Brewster when two Italian sailors goosed her at the bar on the Piccola Marina. We walked past a house spilling bougainvillea from every balcony like Persian carpets being beat and aired.

Jamie, such a timid, somehow battered guy with his falsely booming voice and one slow eye, seemed so happy with Gerry, just as a reserved husband is both proud of his glittery wife and relieved she can do the talking for him. Certainly Gerry talked all the time. After six months in Rome, I found these two New Yorkers to be loud, purposeful, meticulously organized. Gerry made a huge salary in public relations and Jamie received a comfortable enough paycheck, though what they didn't have was time—just two weeks of vacation a year in Gerry's case, five in Jamie's. So they needed every moment to count. They wanted to go from thrill to thrill and an unprogrammed delay while waiting for a ferryboat or a bill tortured them both. They each had three guidebooks, knew what ruins to look for and what special dishes to order; they'd been forewarned to avoid the Blue Grotto and to insist on taking a detour to see Malaparte's house cantilevered out over the coastline. They regarded guides as cheats and hotels as rip-offs. They'd planned their wardrobes for each moment of the day and night and Jamie had brought along a portable iron and an electrical converter to give a last-moment touch-up to his linen trousers, though Gerry invariably exclaimed, "We didn't schlepp all the way to Europe to *press pants*, for Chrissake!" But that was half a joke, as was everything else they said, and if they were to have seen a comic film based on their trip to Italy they would have been the first to laugh.

They were eager to learn, quick to bicker, sullen as owls and chipper as sparrows, their faces mobile, expressive—*funny*. They were polite and asked me questions, swooned over the dullest details of my Roman adventures; I felt buffeted back into life by so much animation. Whereas for the Italians I was dull because an outsider or at best an imperfect copy of a Roman, for Jamie and Gerry I was one of them but newly exotic because I'd dared to be an explorer.

That night I heard a knock at my door in the hotel. It was Jamie and Gerry, wearing grins and towels wrapped around their waists and nothing else. I smiled and pulled them in by the hand. As soon as the door had closed I kissed Gerry full on the mouth and reached out behind me blindly to pull Jamie toward me, against my back. After all those hundreds of hours of staring at Jamie's crotch in our office I had an overpowering urge to open that package at last and to be fucked by him. He was too subtle and too gentlemanly ever to talk about what he did in bed with Gerry, but when he used to speculate about Richard Smith and describe his body in obsessive detail, I noticed that he lingered longer on his perfect buns than on any other feature except his intelligent, flickering smile and mocking, *social* eyes. And even if Jamie was reserved and aesthetic and had suffered at Groton, nevertheless he'd been forced to defend himself in boarding school, to play rugby and dominate the younger boys and swagger with the other prefects—he'd been espaliered by his whole world into an oppressor, and that was the side of him I longed to submit to now.

In a three-way with old friends the first chuckle, the least hint at an intention to enter into discussion, can evaporate the preliminary translucent drops of desire. I smiled at them but as though through a dream, as though I recognized them but through a glass darkly. What I wanted to communicate was not the surprise I felt but quickly reined in, nor my awareness of the comic possibilities, all too rich and unwelcome. Intellectuals are the best sex because to be intelligent means to skip steps and to prize the unprecedented, to know how to tune out static and beam in pure melody, how to find the depth and originality in even the humblest coupling (or tripling). But if an intellectual is proud and keen to prove he's alert to irony, then his snickers, his raised eyebrows, his running commentary undermine the theatricality of passion and make erections melt. I wasn't an intellectual but I was smart enough not to blow this scene. Two men were crossing over from the safety of friendship into the danger of sex and pushing their cocks toward me as gifts, as rods divining the well of loneliness hidden within me. I was going to make this transition as easy for them as possible.

What I discovered was that if most gay men you pick up want to get fucked because that's somehow easier on a first date or a fifth, and if to be fucked is to become the object of desire and the subject of fantasy, nevertheless after the years have passed and both men feel secure within the confines of their affair, at that point they both want to be active in bed. The simple joy of penetrating and the complex satisfaction of dominating supersede the even more sophisticated pleasure of being dominated. These tribes of two chiefs look for a solitary Indian to rule, as I was about to discover.

But if I was able to give them my hunger and an oneiric compliance, I wasn't the one to say exactly how things were supposed to go. After all, it was two against one. They'd undoubtedly done this before and had probably sketched out in advance a scenario for tonight. Nor need I have worried that something so minor as a snicker could put them off; they approached sex with the New Yorker's usual determination to *have*, to enjoy—English verbs which in New York alone need not take an object but can be conjugated in the hortatory ecstatic intransitive (as in the command, "*Enjoy!*"). Living in Rome had slowed me down to the point where I wondered how I'd ever walked the Manhattan high wire. I was in danger of falling off it now through an excess of self-consciousness; Jamie and Gerry were still speedy from New York and rushed across the wire and jumped onto the trapeze. My long afternoons of drinking wine in the sun, of taking two naps and roaring nonsense over dinner had sapped my courage to act, whereas their crowded, programmed days—eight a.m. piano lessons followed by jogging in Central Park, habitual emergencies at the office, the split-second timing of psychiatric and haircut appointments, cocktails with X and dinner with Y—had left them lean, honed, impatient.

Jamie fucked me doggie-style while I sucked Gerry, still quizzical and bird-like as he looked down into his lap to see what I was doing with his long clean cock rising up out of a blond's light cloud of brown pubic hair dusting an unusually red scrotum. Gerry, who had an exquisite, long-limbed body as assertive as his ski-jump nose, was ashamed of a deep hole in his chest just where the breast bones met or failed to meet. He unveiled this "imperfection" with a timidity I found *attendrissant* and exciting. Then I was instructed to squat down on Gerry's dick while Jamie kneeled between Gerry's legs and tried to fuck me at the same time, but a minute later Jamie had given up on that and had come around to face me; he was standing on the mattress and stuffing my mouth.

The trick, of course, was to remember that this was Jamie's cock long enough to lavish on it the keening years of pent-up desire *and* to depersonalize both men sufficiently to turn them into an ownerless congeries of arms and legs to lick, to hug, to kiss. If they remained Jamie and Gerry too concretely, each bristling with an aura of individuality, then I'd never be able to overcome the social dilemma, the etiquette problem (Am I paying too much attention to Jamie? Would Gerry like two cocks in his face? Should I absent myself to the toilet for a moment so that they can reconnoiter and re-establish their solidarity?) long enough to set myself adrift in a sea of pure, moaning pleasure. The id, in order to flourish, needs to put aside the ego's quibbling negotiations with reality. I succeeded in serving them by forgetting them until I was merely a spark ignited between something rough (Jamie) and something smooth (Gerry).

The main impression I came away with from the trip to Capri was of Gerry's ingenuous pleasure in opening up every minor mystery that experience presented him with, even if it was only my body, and of the brimming, husbandly pleasure Jamie took in Gerry. Jamie loved Gerry with a mixture of curatorial, sponsoring pride (the desire to show him off to someone else) and of continuing astonishment at his good luck in knowing this guy, so much more lively and expressive than he, even if occasionally garrulous. I hoped that someday someone would love me as much as Jamie loved Gerry.

⌐⌐⌐⌐⌐⌐⌐⌐⌐ BACK IN ROME, through Lucrezia I met a famous American movie star, a matinée idol of my adolescence, a man whose first name my sister and I would moan, pretending to swoon, parodying the real lust his long pale face and glossy lashes and bruise-dark lips would excite in us. He wasn't a Hell's Angel or a sweet boy-next-door type pawing the ground shyly but rather a grown man in a white dress shirt, with long legs and a formal dark suit he wore casually. He was good in scenes in which he pulled his long lithe body, tie fluttering like a loose tongue, onto a moving train, or when he reached gloomily for a drink and exhaled smoke from his long, straight nose. He'd had a promising career in the 1950s and then the rumors he was gay caught up with him and even seeped through to the public. My sister and I'd somehow heard, for instance, that he was likely to wear green on Thursdays, considered a sure sign of perversion. He'd suddenly had no more roles. What we hadn't known then was that he'd worked briefly and brilliantly in Italy until he'd started drinking too much. I'd seen him once on the stage in New York in a Chekhov play.

Now, apparently, he had a new lover and he was sober and he'd come back to Italy to relaunch his career. I decided I should write him a "vehicle," a screenplay tailor-made to his age, accent and abilities. Of course I was too shy to tell him about the project and too inexperienced to line up a contract from a producer. My scenario was about the affair I might have had with Tina: an American painter falls in love with an Italian woman in Rome. They can't communicate but they end up having lots of violent sex. He goes back to America on a brief trip but dies in a car crash. She has almost recovered from his death when a three-month mail strike in Italy finally ends. Every day she receives another passionate love letter from him and she finally decides to make the trip to the States in order to learn what kind of man he was. There she discovers that her lost love— and by extension most educated Americans—are not just chameleons but also masters of deceit; with a sense of relief she returns to the innocence of the Old World.

Susie, who was still unemployed after being sacked as a real-estate agent, worked for me every afternoon as my secretary. I would scribble bits of dialogue on paper, then dictate them to her and she'd type them, slowly, with lots of muttered commentary. The weather was hot, I was a bit fuzzy after midday lunch and wine consumed in a sunny café and her presence inhibited me from thinking. But I knew I'd become too lazy to work on my own. I needed the waiting taxi, meter ticking, to force me to travel mentally. Anyway, she needed the job.

And besides I liked her stories about her sexual adventures. Her lover Enzio lived with his mother and, like every single Italian man, twenty or forty, straight or gay, he had to be back home in his bed by the breakfast hour. He could slip into his room at six in the morning and his mother could hear his late arrival and nothing would be said, just so long as he was there for roll call. In return he could shower and change shirts three times a day and Mother, his laundress, his cook, would think nothing of it.

He'd pick Susie up in a car he'd especially rigged out with a passenger's seat that at the flick of a lever would flip back so that the passenger would suddenly be flat on her back, legs in the air, as though prepared for an obstetrician. His dandyism, his randiness, his easily wounded pride seemed funny to her, since she was used to British coldness and self-deprecation. I didn't dare tell her that I preferred a stiff cock to a stiff upper lip, and that Italian strutting delighted me more than English reserve. Perhaps she would have agreed with me.

When at last she'd typed up the script on stencils and mimeographed it, I sent it off to three producers Lucrezia had done translations for. Two didn't respond and the third contacted me only because he was so angry at my portrait of Italian men, for if I'd branded Americans as dissemblers, I'd shown Italians as macho brutes. In one of the most dramatic moments in the film the heroine, after learning of her American lover's death, goes stumbling out into the night. She's sobbing but around her swirl boys in cars honking and heckling and shouting obscenities and making grotesque sucking noises with their mouths. One even moons her. Because of Maria and Christa I'd thought about feminism more than any other man I knew, although as a writer I was less attracted to the substantial issue of economic equality than to the flashier question of sexual harassment.

The Italian producer, a bald tycoon in his sixties always in search of vehicles for his wife, a famous actress, spluttered with indignation that Italian men *loved* women and paid them court as knights had done for centuries, throwing them verbal bouquets. I remembered that Christa, a six-foot Brünnhilde, at least professed to enjoy the excitement she created in the streets, but I also knew that Tina had bought a car because she couldn't even walk to the corner without being hassled. I knew that Swedish women, bored with their polite but tepid compatriots, reportedly came to Italy for "the phallic cure," but I'd also heard from Susie that two of her English friends who'd married Italian men had left them after a year of alternate brutality and neglect.

What complicated my response still more was that I wanted to be treated brutally. Thomas hadn't resorted to violence only because I'd been so compliant as we'd wallowed for three days in our sty, but the posed threat had only intensified my excitement. Before I ejaculated I was capable of relishing mental images of profound abjection, pictures that repulsed me as soon as the sperm was drying. I liked the idea of being captured by a gang and raped by its members, one after another, all night long, but a minute after I'd finished masturbating I was cross if Thomas so much as asked me to walk Anzio when it wasn't my turn.

I made an effort to understand that what for me was an idle if persistent fantasy constituted a real danger for women—but the effort failed, since the minute I contemplated, soberly, disapprovingly, the idea (or the image) of rape, I immediately became aroused.

Of course I *mouthed* my sympathy to women, as I would for years to come, since the years of the New Left in the sixties, just ending, had so corrupted me that I did not measure my political opinions against my actual beliefs but rather against what I thought I should feel. As a writer I had nothing but feelings to count on, but a conviction, I thought, shouldn't be simply an amplified sensation; no, it brought together, didn't it, experience, judgment and a code of morality one had presumably picked over and, somehow, verified.

Because I wanted to get my scenario read I pushed Jamie and Gerry to introduce me to an Italian film director who'd pursued Gerry for years. I phoned the director and he was eager to see me, believing no doubt that Gerry had sent him another willowy All-American blond. When he met me he was visibly let down. I wasn't his type—a category of taste I always forgot about and was startled, each time, to rediscover, I who didn't have a type, any more than I had a set way to take my coffee. I suppose an enemy would have said anyone as sexually driven as I could not afford to have a type: obsession precludes choice. But I prided myself on my whore's ingenuity. If I found myself sucking a fat, bearded man with an inch-long cock, I convinced myself he was the pasha, I the new girl in the harem and this was my one chance to persuade him of my talent. I never stopped to wonder why I had to please everyone.

I managed to get a few "important" people to read my scenario, but no one was interested in it. I was a failure in the world but at least I had it all before me. It was withholding its acceptance, which infused me with crimson indignation, nor was I at all certain that approval would ever be granted. I couldn't even claim I'd prepared myself diligently or worked with great application (in *The Paris Review* I kept reading interviews with successful writers who maintained banker's hours, and I would imagine them typing rapidly on an old Remington, gradually building up a mountain of foolscap as they tried a scene first one way, then another, fiddling with point of view, tense and the proportion of reported to quoted dialogue). I needed a full day to summon up the courage to write a paragraph; it would never have occurred to me to strike it out. Words came to me slowly; even slower to materialize was the courage to commit them to paper.

My father had predicted my failure, and although I'd succeeded in working as a journalist for eight years, I'd failed until now to publish even a single page of fiction. When I quit my job, my boss had predicted I'd fail as a freelance writer, and now it appeared he was right. Just at the moment when New York was entering an era of gay liberation, I was off in repressed, provincial Rome. Butler, my friend from New York, wrote that my letters indicated I was not profiting from a study of "the central city of Western culture," but rather treating it as "a slightly kickier version of Scranton" (a reference to a particularly blighted and dull town in Pennsylvania).

Tina and I took the train to Naples. We had dinner there in a restaurant where solemn men toasted one another. "They're using strange nicknames for each other," Tina said. "*Bear* and *Wolf*—I think they're in the Camorra." When we wandered the streets we saw kids everywhere jumping on the backs of trolleys or swarming around us, demanding a coin with irresistible raffishness. "It's like Rome just after the war," she said. "I'm amazed this is still going on." I could see she relished the direct contact with people, the feudal dignity of those toasts, the independence of the kids, the theatricality and danger of Spacca Napoli.

We took a boat to Procida, an island where we stayed in a Swiss pension on top of a hill. Huge lemons grew on a tree just outside our window. Down by the water, arches of bare light bulbs crossed over the street, and a band from Naples played while people danced in the square. At night Tina lay beside me, an explosive waiting to be detonated. Her passion thrilled me, I who had no lover, but I didn't want it. She was willing to damp her fires in order not to scare me off, but I knew all along she was after just one thing.

BUTLER ARRIVED alone in Rome, without Lynne. He was cool, genial, perfect. He took the sun just the right amount of time on our balcony amid the pots of azaleas. The oil he applied to his chest and stomach turned his skin to a lustrous mahogany brown. His shirts were impeccably white and collarless, his forest-green trousers pleated but never creased, a silver chain slid discreetly over his dark chest. His feet looked immense but exquisitely formed in his expensive leather sandals from Greece.

He had an itinerary in Rome, things he needed to visit because he hadn't seen them the last time: the Michelangelo statue of Moses; the Borromini Church of St. Ivo with its corkscrew tower; the Raphael frescoes in the Farnesina on the other side of the Tiber. He thought Rome might serve as the backdrop for a short story in which every tenth word would rhyme with the name of a place here ("heavy" for "Trevi," "hollow semen" for "Colosseum"). He took one long look at my life in Rome, and a mercifully quick one at my body (I was at once skinnier and flabbier) and drew me aside and said, "I'm getting you out of here."

"That's a good idea," I said. "I think I could be ready in a week or ten days."

"A week! No, we'll be leaving tomorrow. I've rented a car. We can drive to Paris slowly, stopping in all the important hill towns. I have a very good guidebook. First we'll go to Assisi, the only city in Italy that does seem holy. No, frankly, you've gone to seed, I hope you don't mind my telling you so directly. Of course that happens to most Americans in Rome, just look at all these losers you've surrounded yourself with. I guess we could say *la dolce vita* has definitely turned *amara*. Isn't it funny, you've come halfway around the world to create an inferior version of what you left behind: Tina is a less talented, less refined version of Maria, just as Thomas is an uncooked copy of your old lover in college, what's his name? Lou?—the sex without the brains. And after you wrote that exquisite Fire Island novel you've cranked out this vulgar little screenplay, so listless in its language, so obvious in its ironies. You know, it's really a form of arrogance on your part, this *mauvaise fréquentation* you seek out, as though you were trying to prove your talent and intelligence are so durable they can resist even the lowering effect of idiots and drunkards. But you know you're pressing your luck."

I saw a sharply etched, despairing truth in his words where I'd intuited only vague cloud shapes of disappointment. "It's true enough, I've gone to seed," I said, not rejecting the floral imagery, "but I wouldn't say I was *escaping* New York or my friends, just my job." And yet I saw myself as a dandelion gone white, held up to his pursed lips. Trained by so many years in therapy to smile foolishly whenever someone else presumed to know my feelings better than I, I snickered in agreement.

The last night I was in Rome my English-speaking friends gave me a party. We sat very late at a table outside in the Piazza Navona. In distant streets the last *saraceni*, those linked metal gates that protect storefronts, were thundering shut. Two aggressive gypsy girls were pushing roses at us; a shy, lean Senegalese in a dashiki passed by, selling electric yo-yos that glowed briefly when set in motion.

We wandered about all night and at dawn ended up on the Capitoline Hill. The armed forces were rehearsing a huge patriotic parade. From our perch we looked down on the wide boulevard that led from the Colosseum to the Piazza di Spagna. Tanks rolled by, rank after rank of soldiers filed past, fighter planes swooped low. We were the only spectators. We were drunk. Susie's pale pink gauze skirt was tangled up in her belt, as though she were a can-can dancer clutching at her hem to reveal her legs. An English guy had tears in his eyes, although perhaps the glare of the rising sun was just making his eyes water. He told me he was sad to be going home. As an American I was used to the idea that "home" was superior to everywhere else (richer, more powerful, trend-setting), and it was with a jolt I realized that for this man Rome might be preferable to London.

Suddenly I saw that for an American travel abroad is always a form of slumming, and the city, under Butler's microscope, became distasteful to my eyes. For him, as for all New Yorkers, human action was only useful in so far as it produced results. I had to return to New York, and make my mark as a writer, but I was terrified I'd fail. Or rather, that I'd go on failing.

FOUR

I've always said I was a Buddhist, but now I know I'm no longer one. Perhaps I've never been one. Immediately after Brice's death I wanted to die, yet not out of a philosophical indifference to this illusory world. I went to church every day, the Catholic church of St.-Merri just across the street from where I live in Paris. I lit candles in front of a saccharine painting of the Virgin and Child. I imagined that the Virgin was Brice's mother, who'd committed suicide ten years earlier, and the wise, dry-eyed baby was Brice himself. I liked the way disembodied angels' heads, propelled by wings, hovered around the holy couple. I lit my candles before a modern polychrome statue of an adult Jesus pointing with unsurprised fatuity at his own heart.

I cried a lot. I said, "Why did you leave me?" I sang, over and over, the first line of an old pop song, the only line I knew, "Where are you? You went away without me, I thought you cared about me."

Brice, I was so focused on you for our five years together that when you died I felt an enormous silence descend all around me. At the time I said, "It's as though I've been in a totally absorbing play for years and then once, by chance, I wandered out to the edge of the stage, the apron, and then the asbestos fire curtain came ringing down, thud, and there I was, alone, in an immense, echoing theater, separated from everything I cared about." I suppose it was just my fancy way of saying something that a book review I was reading the other day said was the "greatest banality: we want to share our mourning with the dead."

My Catholicism has no Pope and no God and only a few, rather helpless saints (I pray to St. Anthony of Padua when I lose something and in Prague I said a prayer to St. Vitus against the shakes and excessive weeping). My Catholicism centers on the Virgin and Child, who don't do anything for anyone except themselves; their love is a wonderful example, a closed circuit, a thing of beauty to contemplate: Brice and his mother. My Catholicism is a home-made cult given over to lighting candles and making the sign of the cross and genuflecting with embarrassment, a child's animism quarried out of the grown-up Church and its ruins, a primitive superstition inferior to the solitary splendor of monotheism. There's no morality in my Catholicism and no hell except the one we're living in, this fiery posthumous existence I'm inventing.

After Brice died I discovered that all my clothes were rumpled and stained with food. I threw out some of them and took the rest off to the dry cleaner's. I'd neglected my appearance completely during the last two years of Brice's illness.

Just a month after Brice's death I went to Easter mass at St. Eustache and—while contemplating the gold and white altar under the pale clarity of the spring light pulsing in through the unstained-glass windows and transecting the incense—I listened to the intimate words of the Resurrection, all the more striking because filtered through the unfamiliar suavities of the French language. Distanced in this way, the words reached right inside me, words that said, Do not mourn me. I have come back, I am here beside you, I live. I live.

I called my friend Brad and told him I was terribly lonely but couldn't bear to be with friends, not all the time, because then all we'd do was discuss Brice. Maybe I didn't like my familiar self looked at by old friends. I wanted to discover someone new and be someone new to him. I wanted Brad to find me a nice hustler, someone who'd come in the afternoon or at midnight or whenever I needed him, someone who'd hold me in his arms and watch old movies with me or tell me the story of his life.

He found me Olivier, a disillusioned sweetheart, a thirty-something guy as disabused as a man my age but someone who just five years earlier had still probably had lots of hopes. I told him about Brice and he said he understood, he'd lost his mother, she looked so young everyone had assumed she was his sister, they went out to dance in the clubs together, and then she'd died—and suddenly he *was* Brice, my Brice who'd lived through his twenties and until his death at thirty-two in the shadow of his mother's death. Olivier was the sort of boy who shrugs a lot, whose handsome full lips are always turned down, who expects nothing more out of life, the sort who'd be hopeless as a lover since he'd have no enthusiasm to offer, but who, as a rent boy, can kiss you sadly, professionally, and make you feel good because that's his job.

For so long I'd lived a life disciplined by Brice's crises; like a mother who awakens when her baby cries, I'd fly to his side whenever he'd need me in the middle of the night. I was like one of those mothers whose milk spurts out of her breast when her baby cries in another room. Now I had vast, empty hectares of time to fill. Olivier was ideal because I could summon him whenever I needed him and send him off with a polite, "Gee, I'm awfully tired." I liked the sinfulness of drawing the curtains in the middle of the day and getting stoned.

As the days lengthened the sun became brighter and more invasive. From the sidewalk I'd look down long passageways at inner courtyards, usually so gloomy and glaucous, suddenly gaily sparkling with light dancing on the basin of the rusting water pump or with light projected across the flagstones and reflected off the warped panes of the concierge's *loge*. I felt that that light, like the sunlight that once a year follows a brass line traced into the floor of the cathedral at Bologna, was exploring a secret vein in my soul that had never been touched before. Aren't there all sorts of temples, Mayan or Egyptian, in which the holy of holies is illuminated only on the single day sacred to the local deity, eagle or alligator?

⎯⎯⎯⎯⎯○ WHEN I FLEW back from Europe in 1970 after my six months in Rome, a friend met me at the airport in New York, popped some speed laced with a hallucinogen into my mouth, and led me on a tour of the new gay discos that had sprung up like magic mushrooms since my departure. I was shocked by how much the city had changed. Where before there had been a few gay boys hanging out on a stoop along Christopher Street, now there were armies of men marching in every direction off Sheridan Square. Not just A-Trainers—the blacks and Puerto Ricans who would come down from Harlem on the express subway, men who were already bold and streetwise—but even the previously timid white boys of lower Manhattan were now out in sawed-off shorts and guinea T-shirts, shouting and waving and surging into the traffic.

"Is this a holiday or what?" I asked my Virgil.

"Not at all," he said to his wide-eyed Dante, "it's an ordinary evening in New Haven or should we say Greenwich Village."

At the foot of Christopher Street, near the docks, there was a new bar called Christopher's End where a single stripper, a bit pudgy and smiling drunkenly, danced on a dais while he wriggled out of his Jockey shorts. He threw them at a famous painter I recognized, who then got up on the stage and tried to fuck the guy right there. A bouncer snatched the painter by the collar and lifted him off the dais. When I introduced the painter to my friend and said, "Do you two know each other?" he said, "Know each other? We were crumb-girls together at the Last Supper." I then remembered that the painter collected and preserved these odd camp expressions of the past, verbal memorabilia, the verbal equivalent of drag ball tiaras or boas from the twenties.

Afterwards I went into a dark backroom and looked down a narrow chute—just a foot wide, too narrow to walk through—at two naked men who were taking turns sucking each other. It was too dark and I'd drunk too much to understand what was going on. Were the men performers or just other customers? Was it permitted to take one's clothes off in this room? What about the police? We were looking at the couple, I imagine, through the slowly rotating blades of a fan, but the effect was of an amateur porno film unwinding so slowly that the black bands separating each frame were visible and hovering queasily in the middle of the screen.

I was led to a huge disco in a warehouse in the meat-packing district. There hundreds of guys were dancing under black light, which turned their city-pale torsos tan, their white T-shirts radioactive blue, a false tooth black, a trail of eye drops snaking down a cheek light green, a shock of peroxided hair a weird white. At the old Stonewall (now a wood bowl and sheepskin rug store) the music had been pumped out of a jukebox with intervals of silence between each selection, but at the Zoo a *discaire*, important as a broadcasting engineer in a glassed-in booth, blended the music seamlessly from one turntable to a second, the transition almost unnoticeable. Back then no single song was long enough to sustain our drug-induced frenzy so the disc-jockey often went from one record to an identical cut in another copy of the same record, thereby doubling our pleasure. The disc-jockeys themselves were becoming prominent members of the gay community—known for their ability to build a mood and take it even higher.

On a dais a go-go boy in a white towel was dancing. The towel glowed in the black light as he draped it with ingenuity and provocativeness. He was a small blond who showed us his ass but never his cock, which grew larger the longer it remained invisible. I watched him for hours, entranced. He handed out his phone number and name, which he'd neatly printed out in advance, to several of us gathered around him. If guys got too grabby he pushed them back down the steps with his long legs.

During his break he said, "Wait till I'm off and I'll go home with you." I suppose I thought that meant at four in the morning, the hour when bars used to close in New York, but in fact last call was at six. All the men he encouraged, I noticed, had hair as long as mine and thick, Viva Zapata mustaches. For him we were bandits and he our bandit queen.

When he and his roommate, the obese bouncer, were at last ready to go, it was seven in the morning. Once we emerged into the daylight I saw that my dancer was a trashy bleached blond with horrible pizza-face acne and rotten teeth, but I was too polite to back out of our date. The bouncer had an old car and drove us to their apartment in a remote section of Brooklyn. My ardor turned to stone as my speed wore off and I recognized how hard it would be ever to get back home. And I picked up that the bouncer was in love with the dancer and was brooding ominously over my presence.

The apartment smelled of roach spray and bacon. Dirty dishes teetered in piles all over the kitchen. The couch opened out into a bed. The candy-striped sheets were stiff with come. Beside the bed was a life-size plaster statue of a Moor in a turban and culottes, his chest and legs bare, his eyes large and white and his lips painted a ruby red. With one arm he held up a floor lamp, its shade as big as a bustle and dripping glass bangles.

The dancer, a bronzed faunlet who'd pushed all those broad-shouldered men away from his dais last night like Marilyn Monroe toppling a line of adoring chorus boys, was now desperately whining and trying to pull me back into his lumpy couch bed with the hinged bar of metal that cut across the back. Minutes after I'd come I was so repelled that I went staggering out into the sunny empty Sunday morning streets.

I told Maria that I was impressed by how seriously New Yorkers took themselves now, how sure they were that all the world was hanging on their latest cry; of course eternal Rome, by contrast, was so unchanging and its past so indisputably central that today's Romans could afford to be trivial, shepherds in rags grazing their sheep beside toppled imperial columns. I was probably just irritated that no one in New York wanted to hear about my Roman holiday and that by the time I'd sorted out my mental slides for a thorough presentation my audience had melted away.

For eight years in New York I'd worked for a world-famous firm that employed primarily bluebloods from the best schools, and even if I'd arrived disastrously late for work every morning and sipped at two-hour-long, wet luncheons and spent the rest of the time on the phone or roaming the corridors looking for conversations, nevertheless I had the security and prestige of my job—and a good salary. I'd proved my father wrong, he who'd predicted I was too unstable and mediocre to succeed in New York.

He'd paid a lot of money to a psychiatrist hoping I'd recover from my homosexuality, marry and settle down to the humdrum, workaday world. He'd always said I coveted too much attention, that I imagined I was special, that I expected an existence of all frills, that I was incapable of creating a normal, average life for myself. To reassure him I'd patched together a simulacrum of an average life, first at the university, where I joined his fraternity and studied something useful, Chinese, later in New York, where I worked for the conservative weekly magazine he himself read. I hadn't dyed my hair or tattooed my arm and if I was unmarried at thirty that omission could still be dismissed as a minor eccentricity or an excess of choosiness soon to be rectified. Since my father had no friends he couldn't even worry about what the neighbors would think. No, his sense of propriety was purely abstract, a Karma accountable only to the gods.

But now I was falling off the edge of the world. In six months of sipping white wine in Rome I'd spent the seven thousand dollars in profit-sharing I'd accumulated over eight years. I was back in New York without a job or an apartment. When an older guy I'd tricked with a few times before my Roman holiday saw me at the gym, he said, "But you've lost your looks. What have you been doing? You're skinny *and* puffy, not such a great combination." My father was right—I was unsavory.

I was living with Maria, but I felt out of place. She was fastidious, calm, unambitious, whereas I was sloppy and driven by my twin appetites for sex and success, both of which struck me in her presence as hairy and unwashed. She spoke to her cats in German and gave them fragrant cooked chicken livers to eat but let them slip through the bars on her windows and roam free through the wild New York night, noisy with sirens and rustling with a life more exciting than one's own because of its speed. Those overexposed photographs that eliminate the substance of vehicles and render traffic as just the scrawled calligraphy of headlights seemed the surest transcription of the urban blur. Strafing lights, the rumbling of the subway, the smell and spoor of sex, the tides of pedestrians channeled by the massive seawalls of skyscrapers—these were the never-stilled dynamics of the city pulsing just outside Maria's windows.

I too wanted to slip through the bars but I also needed to prove to her and to myself that I was still capable of sitting home and "schmoozing" (our newly acquired New York Jewish word), far from the world's *michigas* and *kvetching* and *tsuris*. Maria promised cozy evenings imbued with *Gemütlichkeit* (a German word from her German youth in Iowa). Just as Yiddish was considered to be a warmer, friendlier version of German, so her spotless apartment with its violets on the windowsills, its many little lamps, the black leather and rosewood armchair, the framed family photos and the folding screen she'd painted with a scene of a moonlit balustrade and a diaphanous curtain blowing in the wind—so this New York home, half bohemian and half bourgeois, was an ideal version of Midwestern propriety.

I remember we fought over ideas as we'd done when I was a teenager and we'd first met. Back then we'd quarreled about art and politics; now we disagreed about whether women or gay men were the more oppressed.

"How can you say women are a minority when they constitute fifty-one percent of the population?" I asked.

"In South Africa blacks are ninety-five percent of the population and they're slaves."

"Yeah," I said, "but women at least don't feel guilty about just existing. Femininity isn't classified as a disease or a crime or a sin, but homosexuality is."

"Essentially all this fancy new gay liberation just involves a tiny part of a privileged male population and is a fairly trivial matter. I'm talking about half the world's population, about hundreds of millions of women who are beat and starved and overworked and underpaid if they're paid at all. Even in America most poor households are headed by single women."

Maria's political views would make her blood pressure mount dangerously; I'd convince myself I could see her veins ticking just behind the transparent skin stretched over her temples. To calm herself she'd make a German salad of sliced cucumbers marinated in white vinegar, sugar and dill. She'd gulp down a glass of white wine. She'd throw a leg over the arm of a chair and say, "Here I am, nearly forty, and I'm still hurling my-self about like a teenager. I thought I'd have acquired a certain *gravitas* by now." She leafed through magazines and poked at her potted plants in the back yard. "My aunt Carlotta visited me," she confessed, "and of course she's used to big Nebraska houses with four bedrooms upstairs and two acres of gardens. She looked around my apartment and said, 'You mean you live in these two tiny rooms?' I said the garden was the best part but when we went outside she said, 'Does this dirty little alley actually lead to a garden?' and I said, 'This dirty little alley *is* the garden.' " Maria shook all over with laughter.

For her as for me the real if vigorously rejected world was one of Mid-western suburbs in which kids with silky blond hair walked down side-walks under old elms, where the ice-cream wagon played its chimes on the street corner in order to summon forth inhabitants from shadowy, cream-colored, stucco-covered houses, where basements were filled with hun-dreds of neatly stacked cans of food, where the living-room furniture was dressed each spring in flower-sprigged slipcovers and where winter woolens were stored in cedar chests—a whole world of irreproachable ennui, styleless comfort, solid, dozing bank accounts.

The only difference between us was that I thought my New York exis-tence was a temporary form of camping out whereas Maria said, "I vis-ited my brother and his family and I can see it's a perfectly nice life crowded with tennis lessons, church socials and Sunday brunches, but if I had to live like that I'd just as soon put a bullet through my brain." I could never bring myself to buy any furniture other than Salvation Army junk, since whatever I'd be able to afford would appear pathetic beside my father's gleaming piles of blond mahogany and pale velvet. Maria was happy to piece together her own bohemian nest, her Manhattan take on Iowa, just as a florist, tilting her head from side to side, composes a bou-quet out of plants never found together in nature—a bird of paradise, two hollyhocks and a clump of buffalo grass.

Now down to my last six hundred dollars, I'd lie awake on my little cot at Maria's and calculate how long I could make it last. An old Fire Island friend offered me a job working as a stock boy in his Madison Avenue shop where he sold objects in lucite. I told him I'd get back to him in a month, if he could wait that long. He couldn't; reluctantly I let the offer slip through my hands. I auditioned to be a bartender but flubbed in mak-ing a sidecar, even though I'd stayed up all night reading a book of recipes.

I found a dirty little one-room apartment in a tenement at the foot of Horatio Street which cost only a hundred dollars a month. The fall was setting in and I could glide through the cool, blowy nights like a sailboat, the sail now drawn tight against the propelling wind, now flapping as I drifted. In Rome I'd been intimidated into dressing up before I went out, even to carry my dirty shirts to the laundress (garments I transported in a suitcase), but now I lived with a freedom I'd never known before, since I didn't need to keep any particular hours or show up at an office.

I signed up to ghostwrite a thousand-page psychology textbook for college freshmen at four hundred dollars a chapter, payable upon delivery. Publishers had discovered that academics were incapable of delivering a manuscript on time and in comprehensible prose so they paid a professor for the use of his name and outline. The in-house editors prepared a package for the ghostwriter of a cut-and-paste collage of the best passages on any given topic (perception, memory) from rival textbooks and a thick set of Xeroxes of the best and latest relevant articles ("Primacy and Recency in Rat Memory: A Review of the Literature"). I'd rise at noon, drink instant coffee, shower and shave, go to the gym, eat a late lunch of thick bread and minestrone at the Front Porch, browse at a used bookstore, then amble home, pausing to stare back at any idle man who might cruise me. I'd sit at my kitchen table and pound out two or three pages on size constancy or proprioception, proud of my powers of assimilation and synthesis. Then the phone would start ringing as friends would call shopping around for dinner dates; I kept a little appointment book in my back pocket, the only accoutrement recalling my old office days and its schedules.

I tried to write a new novel, now that the salt and sewer breezes of New York had blown the Roman cobwebs out of my head, but I felt it too was doomed never to be published and an aching feeling of hopelessness paralyzed my hand whenever I took up my pen. My heroine, Alyx, was based on Christa. I wrote from her point of view and tried to imagine her as an American heiress, resolutely heterosexual, who becomes best friends with a gay man (me) and a lesbian (Maria). Alyx was compounded of Christa and Henry James's Isabel Archer as well as a fox-hunting girl I'd known at college; she realizes when she turns thirty (my age then) that she's followed a false scent in copying the personal style of a gay man and woman who exalt independence because they're artists and a cult of friendship because marriage will never give a continuity to their lives. Alyx, in a panic, decides she must marry but chooses unwisely—the handsome, cruel, gold-digging Osmond. In *Portrait of a Lady*, James calls giving up one's friends for one's beloved "the tragic part of happiness" and for a while I toyed with the idea of calling my book *The Tragic Part*.

If my Fire Island novel was considered obscure, Baroque, overly ingenious, this book would be limpid, its effects at once melodramatic and refined. Because its inspiration was medieval and Japanese, my Fire Island novel, I decided, had failed to connect with anything American editors could recognize—it seemed almost too original, for if critics and publishers say they esteem originality, what they really mean is a small variation on a known theme, not an innovation *ex nihilo*. In *Woman Reading Pascal*, as I decided to call my work-in-progress, I would deal with homosexuality but only as observed by a sometimes uncomprehending heterosexual woman never exposed to the gross physicality and obsessive sexual covetousness of her friend "Dan," as I named myself; no, Alyx would compare herself unfavorably to Maria and Dan, ironically unaware that in most people's eyes she was a golden being and we disgusting misfits. If my Fire Island novel was mostly invented, this new book would, I hoped, seem entirely mimetic.

ONE NIGHT in a bar I was cruising two young men who were obviously hoping to put together a three-way. I kept flickering past them in a vain attempt to attract their attention. At last I gave up and went into the backroom, so dark that very little was visible. Two other men were kissing deeply, their hands ecstatically touching each other's faces while their bodies were turned away, as in a dance in which only the shoulders may touch; each man was being gone over by a whole retinue of gnomes, much as a race car is feverishly serviced at a pit stop. One gnome was licking a flank, another was sucking a cock, a third was burrowing into buttocks. The royal couple, two Oberons, kissed while their invisible cloaks were unfurled around them by attendant fairies. What was wonderful was that I, too, could touch them, kneel beside them, lick, suck—or kiss a hand as a vassal might. Dancers, cars, fairies, lords—a whole kaleidoscope of successive images was refracted around these two lovers.

The usual mating ritual, with its feints and hesitations, its coquetry and crowing, was abridged in the backroom into a nearly silent passage from desire to act. I moved easily from one man to the next, my hand sifting through long hair, my lips grazing a soft mustache, my cock engulfed by a hot mouth that like a glass-blower's would make grow and glow through its motion a shape and an urgency.

Someone pushed my blower aside and was about to go down on me when I caught a whiff of his distinctive perfume and heard him clear his high, unchanged voice—my Romanian! "*Ma come mai!*" I whispered, amazed.

He rose then and fell into my arms, we withdrew into the light, the focus of friendship replacing the blur of generalized lust, and he told me in his halting Italian of his disappointment as an au pair boy in the industrial wasteland of New Jersey, the terrible slavery the butcher and his family had imposed on him, his official complaint registered before the Romanian immigration board in Newark, his new placement as a "house boy" to a distinguished elderly Korean diplomat on Gramercy Park. . . . While he spoke the attractive young couple in search of a third partner cruised closer and closer to us. At last, when my Romanian went off to the toilet for a second, one of the handsome strangers came up and asked me, speaking slowly, eyebrows raised, "Do . . . you . . . speak . . . English?"

"Uh leetle beet," I rattled off fluently.

I went home with them, lined them up side by side, face-down, and fucked one for two strokes, then the other, then back to the first, all the while muttering things in the gruffest Italian ("*Porca madonna*" or "*Che culo!*" were two of my standbys).

Near my apartment were the docks where late at night fellows from New Jersey ("the bridge and tunnel crowd") would stand in a line between parked semis, undo their trouser buttons and let the guys crouched under the trucks suck them off. After a warm autumn day the night was cool and airy. Manhattan without a wind is like a becalmed ship festering in a Sargasso Sea of sewage and despair, but as soon as the first fresh breeze stirs, then the ship comes to life and its maritime men move smartly, shimmying down from their perches to pace the decks.

In the 1960s the homosexual population was small and I'd known most of it, at least by sight. On some November nights there had been just a few skinny queens in wheat jeans and red windbreakers darting through the rain. Now there seemed to be more and more visible gay men, thousands of them, all similarly slender and mustachioed, many of them with the same loud voices and crude way of talking ("Hey, Howie, wanna cwoffee?") as the guys who used to beat us up.

I went out for a few weeks with Joey, a gaunt six-foot-three, hundred-and-fifty-pound kid from Long Island ("Lawn Guyland," as he said it, and

I imagined a million guys set up like bowling pins on a clipped green). He drove his parents' ten-year-old Chevy and showed me snapshots of his high-school graduation (last spring). To my taste he was too romantic and not sexual enough, a spindly giraffe wanting to be consoled in my arms for everything he'd ever felt, which had suddenly coalesced around me. He drank too much and sat weeping in his car in front of the door to my building. Eventually he moved in with an Italian-American cop in Sayville, someone also named Joey, who presided over a large white house filled with all his relations.

I became thinner and thinner as I lived on a diet of cigarettes, espresso and vodka, as I dashed up and down my stairs on the way to the gym, the bar, the trucks. Sometimes to write my psychology textbook I'd swallow amphetamines, work all night and still be wide-eyed and excited at dawn. I'd race down to the trucks in dirty jeans—without underwear—ripped strategically at the knees, over the buttocks, and beside the crotch. The last pervert would already have left and a garbage truck would be slowly edging along from house to house, its maw open and swallowing. Desperate, I'd press myself against the wall and stare holes through the garbage collectors. Dawn would be twitching brighter and brighter, as though God's rheostat were too old and cheap to function imperceptibly. The first office workers, pale and yawning, their hair still wet from the shower, would be automatically hurrying down the four steps of their stoops, off to the subway entrance five blocks away. I stared at them, too, thinking I might lure one up to my eyrie for a quickie.

I was keeping up a desultory correspondence with Tina. I worked out how to say, "I miss you" (*Sento la tua mancanza*), and after receiving my letter with that expression in it she hopped on the next plane to New York. She seemed momentarily taken aback by the squalor of my apartment, but she must have been pleased that we would be lying side by side in a small bed every night, even with the two mattresses of the single bed separated and thrown on the floor. I had found so little echo in New York of what I had now expanded into a whole "year" in Rome that I was happy to have her here, with her wonderful, heady laugh, her face devoid of makeup except for the mascara tracing her huge eyes in black, her skinny flanks, clean but unpainted nails, her eternal MS cigarettes, her curiosity about everything.

Like all European Communists, she wanted to see Harlem first thing. She tried to walk the streets alone but after she discovered that wasn't such a great idea she insisted that I find a friend with a car; we drove up and down the streets and she seemed almost disappointed by what she considered the look of relative prosperity, though we told her the apartments were dangerous, overcrowded and rat-infested. She didn't believe us when we said the principal victims of black crime were other blacks. In Little Italy she was shocked to discover in a shop an ashtray bearing the portrait of Benito Mussolini. "And it looks like the past! This is Italy after the war."

"Ah, yes," I said, "America is Italy's attic where everything outmoded—including outmoded ideas—is stored in mothballs."

"*Cosa?*" she asked, puzzled. I never knew whether she went blank around me because she was studying me sorrowfully or whether she was overcome with desire and not really listening or whether I was speaking too fast in English or incorrectly in Italian. I'd never had anyone look at me so searchingly and it flattered me and made me feel guilty.

One night she wept because I never cooked her any spaghetti and she felt she couldn't get through another day without "them." I took pains to make a rich, delicious Bolognese sauce on my little stove poised on top of the waist-high fridge; as soon as the stove heated up, roaches came scuttling out of it.

When she threw herself over me again that night I exploded. I sat up, switched on the light, lit a cigarette and held it in a trembling hand. "Tina, this can't go on. I'm a homosexual. I don't want to sleep with you. We're friends."

"*Ma hai detto che hai sentito la mia mancanza.*"

"So what? In English that means nothing special. 'I miss my mother, I missed my train, last night I missed my enema.' It means absolutely nothing at all."

She was in her slip, sitting up on the mattress, her hair pushed forward on one side. She looked miserable. "In Italian it means 'I love you.' "

The next day she took a train for New Haven, where she knew a tall, skinny American graduate student who'd spent a year in Rome studying Italian social structure. Two weeks later they were married.

⟨‿‿‿‿⟩ I HAD BECOME almost entirely a Villager and I seldom ventured above Fourteenth Street, not even to see the ballet, and if I put on a coat and tie for a Midtown lunch with Jamie I felt as strange as a cowboy must feel in Paris. My "dress up" clothes were out of date, the trousers pegged and cuffed rather than bellbottoms, the jacket lapels straight and narrow rather than wide and notched, and my ties weren't as broad and floral as fashion dictated. Jamie, of course, wouldn't have noticed since he was still wearing garters and white breast-pocket handkerchiefs to go with his Brooks Brothers "sack" suits. I was a bit embarrassed to see any of my former colleagues, almost as though I'd lost the knack of playing straight, talking loud, thumping backs, and had clearly come down in the world.

Sometimes I read my work to Butler, who was also working on a novel. He had left his wife for a shaggy-browed Jewish architect who owned an immense Hoboken loft into which he'd inserted Mackintosh ladder-backed chairs and gesso panels inlaid with gems. Butler was free to stay home, perform his sit-ups while listening to a recording of Shakespeare's sonnets, which he was trying to get by heart. He kept a blank notebook from Venice constantly at his side in which he could jot down a line, a thought or even just a word that might end up some day in a story. He was at once exquisite and heavy-handed, the perfect student with very little sense of humor. At least he had none of Maria's ability to catch herself and quake with laughter at her own pomposity or absurdity.

Butler kept carbons of all his letters, which were obviously written with one eye on posterity, full of nature descriptions, lengthy impressions of historic monuments he'd visited and reflections on current social problems, all adorned with appropriate tags from Horace or Boileau. He hadn't yet published a book but he was already lamenting that his future works would probably not be printed on acid-free paper. "Microfilm! That is the only solution. We must be sure our books—" (mine were included as a courtesy)—"are microfilmed or else they'll end up as brittle, yellowing scraps scattered on the library floor." This archival quandary kept him awake at night. He returned to the problem often. His letters and manuscripts, I noticed, were confided to paper that would outlast the centuries.

Like many American intellectuals raised in small towns in modest circumstances, he'd not grown up listening to classical music, though he'd played the tuba part in his high school band's version of Sibelius' *Finlandia*; now as an adult and cultured New Yorker, he listened dutifully to records, studied scores and read program notes. There was no indication he ever closed his eyes, swept away by melancholy, longing or a sense of excruciating beauty. Right away he'd learned to sneer at Tchaikovsky, Dvorvák and, incidentally, Sibelius, and to esteem Bach (especially the unaccompanied cello sonatas), the Beethoven of the late quartets, Mozart's operas, all Monteverdi; he even sang motets in an a capella group and when we were driving from Rome to Paris after he rescued me he offered to teach me medieval part songs so we could sing together while driving and not "waste time." When I nixed that plan, he translated, whenever I was driving, from a fat guidebook in Italian published by the Automobile Touring Club, a scholarly tome of a thousand pages printed on bible paper that told me much more than I wanted to know about the history of Volterra and the iconographic eccentricities to be found in Rosso Fiorentino's strangely Manneristic *Deposition from the Cross.* I once teased Butler by saying he was like a Victorian miss who'd been required to pick up all the accomplishments (sewing, music making, canning, painting on china) since she didn't have a dowry.

The same guilt-provoking complaints (that no doubt made Butler a lover whom one could never take for granted because one could never please him) rendered him annoying as a friend. Somehow I was always "disappointing" him because I'd forgotten to phone, to wonder how his cold was progressing, to ask after his current novella. If he was severely disappointed, his dismay could send him into a terrible pout.

He told me I was basically a consumer—of words, money, men. He said he thought I had to be fueled with a high-octane version of all the world had to offer. His observation blended astonishment with distaste. Certainly he was an epicurean who could pick quizzically over a single fresh sardine during a long evening in which I would knock back two dozen oysters, an entire roast chicken, potatoes with a whole head of garlic and a half gallon of California red. He kept up with me only in his alcohol consumption, although unlike me he modulated tastefully from blond Lillet on the rocks with a twist of orange peel to a white wine with the sardine, a light Beaujolais with the four kinds of goat cheese (chalky, white and nearly tasteless—the ultimate upper-class food), an Armagnac in a giant globe snifter to toy with beside the fire, as though he'd accepted it only for its light-refracting properties.

When he was elaborately sauced he'd become genial. His accent would revert to Southern, suddenly one understood why he had laugh lines around his eyes, and he sketched an elegantly scaled-down allusion to . . . yes, it must be, to a slap on the knee. He passed around thin, expertly rolled joints. When he crossed the room he appeared to have an extra folding place above his kneecaps. In sandals his feet looked immense, as though so much willowiness above needed a big taproot below. When he danced he seemed to be treading grapes in place. In fact, closer study revealed that he never moved his size-twelve shoes at all, although his feet generated waves of motion sent up through his long legs and into his lean flanks and supple torso, down through shoulders which shone as though they'd been chamoised with an expensive, furniture-makers' beeswax. No doubt he'd practiced his movements as he perfected everything else, but he gave the illusion at least of forgetting himself entirely when he danced.

Late at night his true kindness and vulnerability would come out. Then he'd tell me in fits and starts the story of his childhood. His real mother, a sweet Southern woman, had died when he was five. His father had married two years later a woman who was good to Butler until he was nine when she started having children of her own. She went on to have three children altogether and with each birth she turned fractionally further away from Butler. He'd gone from being the center of a family and his father's cherished link to his lost wife to an unwelcome outsider, someone who ate too much, breathed too much air, occupied a bed needed by one of the legitimate children.

It was then that Butler, until that time a lazy, moody boy, decided to become irreproachable. He read with a pencil in hand, he excelled in all subjects, he even achieved as much popularity as a boy could in a Southern town if he wasn't athletic. The church replaced the playing field. He taught Sunday School, he visited sick parishioners and he memorized all the Psalms, the Song of Songs and large parts of the Gospels. His constant bedtime prayer was, "Oh, Lord, make me a preacher when I grow up."

But his high school English teacher had other ideas for him. A patrician from Nashville, she pushed him to write poetry of the obviously beguiling Sara Teasdale variety, the sort she herself wrote in the privacy of her room. He and she discussed the books she suggested, including some racy ones banned in their Georgia town such as *Catcher in the Rye* and *From Here to Eternity*.

Thanks to her encouragement he won a French contest *and* the poetry contest (prize fifty dollars) held at the public library in memory of Mrs. Wentworth Bean III. He scored in the high 700s in the College Aptitude Tests, the best mark in the state, and was admitted a year early to the University of Georgia. From there on in he always pulled in every available honor and scholarship, did his doctorate on Mallarmé at Columbia and began his succession of comfortable if not luxurious marriages (only the first one to a woman). For someone who'd emerged from such a dismal childhood he had unexpectedly few material ambitions; all he longed for was the novelist's laurel and a place on Mount Parnassus. As a consequence he was judicious to the extreme in his praise of other writers; once when I asked him to name his top ten, he couldn't get beyond five ("Stendhal wrote too rapidly although with admirable verve," he said with typical reserve, "even if he *tells* us more than he *shows*").

The strange thing was that I too had what we called in our campy way a "bluestocking side." I, too, had been an unhappy sissy boy who'd found consolation in books. Like Butler I'd confounded the arts with European refinement, which in turn I assumed must guarantee a smiling moral tolerance. I'd hated myself when I wallowed away for an evening watching TV and only Maria's early influence had made me appreciate pop music, though I felt more reassured when I listened to *The Magic Flute* or a Bartók string quartet. In the 1970s, even when I was so drunk I had to hold one eye shut in order to read, what I would read was Spinoza or the *Minima Moralia*. During those years I vigorously underlined passages in dozens of the most austere books of philosophy, yet when I page through them now I neither recognize the words nor can discover any system behind my highlighting. I had everything in common with Butler; perhaps what I despised in him was precisely what we shared. By laughing at him I could pretend I wasn't a Midwestern exquisite, a homegrown dandy, and by criticizing his finickiness I could suggest I was made of tougher stuff.

Certainly many people teased me for being an intellectual and an aesthete, although around Butler I could think of my prose as coarse, my manners democratic and my tastes promiscuous. Perhaps I liked him because beside him I felt crude and careless—an attractive contrast that excused my failure to learn foreign languages, remember opera plots or capture the devotion of a handsome man.

During the nine years I'd lived in New York I'd never met a published writer, although we were always on the alert to the possible passage of such a rare bird. I blamed my sexual interest in younger men for my paucity of interesting acquaintances, but the explanation remained theoretical since I continued to resist the approach of anyone over forty. To me it was impossible to see an older man as gifted; I was convinced that age's motley (bald spot, second chin, sagging belly) could be worn only by fools.

Butler met a famous poet and man of letters named Max Richards at a gay bar. We'd heard that Richards went to one bar, the Stud, and through frequenting it almost nightly, Butler finally met him. With extreme generosity Butler spoke to Richards mostly of my work and especially my Japanese-Fire Island novel. Richards was ubiquitous as a judge of literary contests, poetry editor of little magazines, friend to the famous and patron to the young and talented.

One morning the phone rang about eleven while I was still sitting tragically over my first cup of coffee and could barely articulate. Before I picked up I sang the scales to chase the sleep out of my voice. "Hello."

"Oh, I see I awakened you. This is Max Richards—I presume that name means something to you?"

"Hi, of course, Butler—"

"I see it does." There was a little burst of laughter, not Richards's, and I realized he must be playing to an admirer. "It appears you have something to show me?"

"Well, I have some stories, a novel, and now I've started a new novel—"

"I want to see it all. But let's start with the finished novel, not with the *œuvres complètes*. Do you have a typescript at your house?"

"Yes, Mr. Richards, I'd be delighted to stop by—"

"No need for that. I'll be heading uptown today at one to have lunch with Lee Krasner? Jackson Pollock's widow? And then to see my shrink. Do you think you could be standing at the corner of Horatio and Eighth Avenue, on the southwest corner, at precisely twelve-fifty, with the manuscript in hand?"

"Of course, Mr. Richards, I'll be there."

"I realize it's only an hour and fifty minutes away. Will that give you time to do your toilette and, as the young say, 'get your day on the road'?" Again, the appreciative chuckle in the background.

"Sure, plenty of time," I said, now more relaxed.

"Very good. Then I'll count on you."

Suddenly I was holding a buzzing receiver in my hand.

If I'd had a dog I would have waltzed it around the room, so exultant was I. I instantly called Butler. "Am I disturbing you?"

"Well, if I sound funny it's because I'm doing a full facial wrap. You take these plantain leaves—"

"Max Richards just called me. I'm going to hand him my manuscript on the corner in two hours."

"Sounds very Goldfinger. He probably wants to see what you look like before he commits himself to a full evening."

"Precisely. What should I wear?"

"Angora sweater and Dacron pedal-pushers?"

"I thought pasties and micro-skirt, perhaps the lamé? Oh, Butler, I am thrilled. Maybe my luck is about to turn and all thanks to you."

I put on sneakers and no socks, my tightest blue-jean shorts and an unironed grey T-shirt. I was reeling in a Breughel peasant dance of signifiers. At thirty was I too old to be dressed so trashily? Would I look a Village vagrant, part of the great lost tribe of actor-singer-dancer-waiters, baker by night, novelist by day? Or would I come off as a pathetic hustler, pushing the body because the work was feeble, one of the superannuated downtown sex symbols? Certainly I'd never have worn the same clothes if my manuscript drop had involved a straight man. Nor a gay man my own age. But I knew that Max Richards was a decade older than me and I, who'd had so little experience seducing older men, made the coarsest assumptions about them. And yet, as Maria had once said, "It's terrible how your most cold-hearted, cynical predictions usually turn out to be true."

I stood on the corner at the agreed-upon time near a hardware store and across from a dreary 1960s apartment block called the Van Gogh. Down the street I could see a man with a gleaming bald head rushing toward me. He seemed to have on a plaid cape—yes, it was a Sherlock Holmes Inverness cape with a panel that floated behind, so aerodynamic was he. "The young author, I presume," he called out, extending his hand while he was still ten paces away, speaking with a gusto that sounded mocking to me only because I wasn't sure I was either young or an author, although I'd been one and aspired to become the other.

I gave him my free hand, which he shook. In a theatrical way Max looked me up and down. He jerked his head in that strange gesture Greeks use to mean "yes." I imagined that what he was miming was the judgment, "Well, you're certainly a minor star, enough to conjure with, but your way of serving yourself up is rather tacky, isn't it?" If most Americans dissolved all their messages in a corrosive bath of laughter and tepid smiles, a compulsion to chatter vapidly and make feeble jokes, Richards appeared, on the contrary, as pointed as those shards of glass embedded on the tops of city garden walls to prevent pigeons from strutting along them. No aimless billing here, his personal style announced, and no sleepy cooing. Nor was he afraid of acting in a preposterously legible manner worthy of a silent film actor.

"I'm so pleased you have the time to look at my work," I said.

"One never *has* the time," he declared, with a horrible smile, "but one must *make* it. When I was starting out none of my elders would receive me. Now, fortunately, all *our* doors are open to all of *you*. Which, of course, is exactly as it should be." A frown and a little self-approving nod had replaced the smile, as though he were listening to his own words and judging them to be unexpectedly true. I had become nothing but a monument to gratitude, all long, exposed legs and humble smiles, someone as eager to offer up my spirit as my body.

Suddenly he glanced at his gold wristwatch. "I'm off!" he shouted as he seized my manuscript and headed uptown. I felt as useless as the little village girl in her Sunday best after she's handed her flowers to a general.

Three days later Richards phoned, waking me up again. "Your book has some extraordinary things in it and I'm certain it's publishable, but we must work on it. I'm not afraid of work—are *you*?"

"No," I burbled, "I long for nothing more—"

"I see I've awakened you. Very good. Are you free tomorrow at five?"

"I'm always free."

"You *are*?" He laughed wickedly, as though he'd just discovered me in a compromising position. "But the vagaries of your personal life engage me not at all; I'll be the midwife to your art."

"Midwife or progenitor?" I asked.

He laughed on a different frequency, as though to say, "Touché."

HE LIVED in a sumptuous modern building called the Trafalgar which, though it was in the Village, was guarded by a doorman and was suspended over a series of inner gardens. I walked up two steps and down three as I passed tinkling indoor fountains in the spacious lobby and headed toward the elevators.

My patron was at his open door. His study was brightly and cheerfully lit, as though against the gloom of the other rooms and the darkness gathering outside. Max offered me a white-wine spritzer; the soda water shot out of a pale blue siphon caught in a wicker net. A little bar, comprised of bottles of Scotch, vodka and gin, red and white wine as well as the siphon, was poised on a mirrored tray, which threw up a gleam onto Max's face as if from footlights.

His head was Mussolini's: the same shiny bald pate, the same full, fleshy face, the same orbits for eyes, the same carnal nose and square jaw. A sculptor would have needed a large, round, flawless piece of grey marble, the unveined kind that takes a high polish, to do a portrait bust that would have done justice to the monumentality of Max's head, for even though his face was pink and his skull nearly white, only finely chiseled grey stone frozen into a look of ironic surprise would have rendered the contradiction of a presence that was both elemental and exquisitely human and humorous. The flesh and bone reality conveyed the contradiction through the *speed* with which his expressions changed.

Max's voice, a heldentenor's, was pitched too loud, given my proximity, but I had the impression he was playing to a shadowy gallery behind me, rank upon rank of the great writers and artists of the past. Even during that first conversation I was aware that if he was tireless in his schemes to coerce the imaginations of his contemporaries, his only real witnesses were the dead. As we picked over my manuscript, which he'd annotated in his microscopic hand, he kept referring to "the Master," who I realized must be Henry James, except that he spoke of him as though he were still living and about to knock discreetly at the door. Max was full of pronouncements: the three great literary gigglers in history, he affirmed, were Proust, Kafka and Ronald Firbank, all of whom would become so convulsed with laughter when reading out loud that they couldn't go on. Most creators, he told me, were despicable people, twisted or infantile, and the only exceptions were Chekhov and Verdi—"the two most affable men who ever lived."

He clearly thought he was living after the Fall, in a bronze or brassy age far separated from the silver or golden epoch that had so fiercely captured his imagination. Even his own school years he looked back on with nostalgia (to heighten this effect he exaggerated his age, which was not yet forty). "These students today are unbearably lazy; yesterday I had to dress down that pack of barbarians I baby-sit at the Columbia Graduate School of the Arts" (I noticed he gave the full prestigious name of his department even as he disparaged its students). "When I was an undergraduate—before the Punic Wars—Lionel Trilling had but to mention an author, ancient or modern, for me to go running out to look up all his works and to devour them. But I wasn't exceptional. We took our own education in hand and sought energetically after more and more titles; today the kids try to do as little as absolutely possible. What they cannot understand is that art is a form of discipline; as Gide said, writing a novel is solving a thousand little problems. Shall *we* solve a few more?"

His corrections to my novel were all judicious and practical. At one point, well into the book, I'd added an asterisk and a footnote to the effect that the starred word was almost impossible to translate since the original term stood for an aesthetic concept that had no equivalent in our language. Max struck this. He appreciated the hint that the novel now in the reader's hands was translated from an obscure language, a further complication of what was already a cat's cradle of meaning, but he pointed out that by pinning down one definite meaning I'd actually reduced rather than increased the sense of mystery. "Besides," he said, "there's something too exuberantly sophomoric about it in what is otherwise such an austere and rigorous book. Beckett made the same sort of error of formal taste, if you will, in *Watt*, the last book he composed in English before he switched to French and the first person and the purity of the trilogy."

How thrilling, I thought, to share an error with Beckett.

On nearly every page Max also corrected a fault in "diction" I'd made. I was astonished by his knowledge of the intricacies of the language—indeed of language *tout court*, since apparently he knew so many. He explained that he'd spent many years reading dictionaries.

But in fact any explanation of his energy and brilliance seemed a form of modesty on his part, since to reduce such a floodlight of intelligence to a pinpoint of motivation actually belittled it. He knew everything, at least everything about the classics, about the Victorians and about poets of every era in every language. His contacts with music were extensive but naturally, in so literary a being, were concentrated on opera. Painting he knew as well; he ransacked the Renaissance for poetic subjects. Some of his best poems (including one that he would later dedicate to me) were either descriptions of paintings or the ongoing correspondence between a Da Vinci and a Medici.

His criticism of the great writers of the past was uniformly ecstatic. If Butler could barely get up to five authors on his list of favorites, Max wouldn't have been able to reduce his enthusiasms to five thousand. No matter whom I mentioned—Tennyson, Edmund Gosse, Cavalcanti, Lucretius, the Brownings, Bunin—his face lit up as though I'd just alluded to an old friend to whom he wished me to convey his warmest greetings. Nor was his encyclopedic knowledge a matter of bluffing. Although he constantly lectured everyone about the art of "erasure" (whatever that was), nothing he'd ever read seemed to have faded from his mind. He remembered whole passages from hundreds of novels, thousands of poems, and discussed them with a rapturous delight in their turns of phrase and narrative strategies. His study walls were nothing but books packed together so tightly that I feared if he removed one the whole room would tumble down. He was constantly lending or buying me books because he was thrilled to have another mind to form, even such a clouded mind too old to be satisfyingly impressionable. I didn't want to have opinions, not as he did, since I had a priest-like respect for my own inner chaos. It seemed to me that whatever I'd written of value had emerged out of this fermenting mess; to clarify it, I was convinced, would kill it.

Like other New York Jewish intellectuals of his generation, he was an Anglophile, more likely to have read Graham Greene and Angus Wilson than James Gould Cozzens or William Goyen. He distrusted most actual living English people, however, and warned me that they were very cheap, always cadging free meals and moving in on one and refusing to leave. "Oh, no, dear, don't pay any attention at all to what he says, not that we can decipher the least syllable given his woof-woof way of mumbling and never finishing a sentence and simply *gurgling* when he's had his fifth whiskey at one's expense," he told me after we ran into a visiting professor from Oxford. "They never wash, you know. And they're all frightfully anti-Semitic. They think of us as colonial idiots and don't realize that the balance of power, especially in the arts, changed forever after the war."

He was predisposed, nonetheless, toward the English literary milieu of the fairly recent past and referred familiarly to the emotional tangle created by Isherwood, Auden and Spender and had a firmer grasp on the intimate lives of the Bloomsbury writers than he did on those of his own friends. Virginia Woolf's *The Waves* never struck him as absurd, not even her decision to have all of her characters speak alike and the children to sound like the adult Woolf herself. He had a large tolerance for the tiresome sea descriptions.

If I hazarded the least rebuke to anyone in his pantheon his face would arrest its eager, playful mobility and freeze into a mask of disdain. He was skillful at arching just one eyebrow and turning his face into three-quarter profile, both to illustrate his recoiling from such ignorance and to render more graphic the unique, serpentine design of that solitary, disparaging line.

If his disapproval was sudden and glacial, his ways of endorsing a friend who shared his taste were manifold and warm. When I was expressing ideas to his liking he'd let our allotted time together spill over into the following hour, like the dentist-friend who pushes back the next appointment in order to worry over the familiar molar another ten minutes and indulge in some one-sided chat echoed by gurgling sounds of pain or idiotic assent.

His life away from me was never a mystery since he always gave me an exact report of where he'd been and where he planned to go. Meetings with a French editor, lunch with von Hofmannsthal's great-niece ("Such a *saftig* woman, one could hardly say *she* was *ohne Schatten*"), tea with a translator—and then there were the *young*: all those young men with manuscripts. One night we came down from Max's apartment and there, on the street, waiting by appointment, standing in the drizzle, was a young poet, collar turned up, unshaved, eyes burning, lips pale, manuscript in hand. Perhaps because I was there watching, Max was even more arrogant than usual. "No need to linger about," he said to the poor poet, "I'll give you my—oh, to such a pale, handsome face, what could I say except my *verdict*—in a week." Hearing in so much angular, rapid verbiage the highly familiar word *handsome*, *le beau ténébreux* smiled divinely and stepped back into the night.

Unlike me, Max lived mainly in a heterosexual world and he had intense, chiding relationships with women, who were usually intelligent, occasionally beautiful, always artistically talented. "Poor June," he'd say, "she's so brilliant and so lost, mainly because of her fatal attraction to fame. Have you ever heard of her falling in love with a nobody? And fame, alas, is built on obsessive work and, once achieved, promotes egotism of the most chilling sort—neither quality exactly conducive to happiness in love."

He never hid from these friends that he was homosexual; he even pointed out to them that his fifteen-year-long marriage to Keith was the only enduring union amongst their acquaintances. When he said "marriage" he was merely honoring the sense of permanence and duty and trust that reigned between them. He certainly wasn't referring to any vulgar male-female role playing. He and Keith were of the same age and they were equally assertive or at least controlling, Max as the darting dragonfly of literature and Keith as its exquisite corpse. Max gave an unending series of lectures, introductions, readings and broadcasts. He could be counted on to review or write a recommendation for virtually anyone, but his availability did not ensure a permanent ardor. No, he prided himself on what he called his "nuanced" judgments and his fellow poets responded queasily when he offered to champion them. I once heard him introduce a writer as a "*souse*—in the root sense of *source* and resource, of immersion and brine." The red-nosed Midwestern poet stumbled to the podium and muttered, "*Thanks*, Max. I *guess*."

I didn't mind when Max was nuanced at my expense, since I wasn't sure I wanted to be an intellectual, at least not of his sort. I was dazzled by his generosity—his catholic tastes, his absorptive and retentive memory, his curiosity about everything, his arch but bountiful conversation—

but unlike him I retained ideas, not names, citations and dates, nor did I want to be entirely at home in any world.

During that first work session together, however, I had not the slightest criticism of Max to make. He was the one doing the criticizing. He held my life between his hands—my book!—and as I turned the pages and he explained to me the scores of small changes he'd made, I felt the way a parent must feel toward a pediatrician: fearful, grateful. When it was all over I smiled a broad smile of relief. As the wet autumn night drew in outside, I was intensely aware of Max's office as an island of light in all that darkness. His bulldog, Ricardo, wheezed disgustingly in the corner, snuggling further into a dirty, cushioned nest. "We call him the Humidifier," Max said. I was thrilled by Max's surgical expertise and the cozy room and the sense that we were two writers working together.

My pleasure increased a day later when I began to read the volume of his poetry that he'd given me, fine verbal marquetry patterned out of all the words he'd read and remembered, for in his poems he re-created real historical men and women and put dramatic monologues into their mouths. None of the detritus of a life was eliminated or stylized; no, he gave us his heroes, wardrobes and all, nor did he spare us a single horsehair sofa or the least antimacassar dimmed by brilliantine. Here were the roll-top desks, the basement kitchens with the wood doors of their giant, cream-colored iceboxes, the patent cough pills, shoe stretchers and salves for piles. Through the stereopticon of Max's poems the nineteenth century seemed proximate and glowing, since what he was showing us were the feelings of his characters, not always exactly ours but recognizable nonetheless, the same pale human feelings breathing under the jet jewelry.

THE AUTUMN when we met was, in fact, the high point of Max's literary life, although I had no idea that the glory he was reaping was so recent nor did he know then it would never be harvested again in exactly the same golden abundance. As the witness to his triumphs, I was unworldly enough to be dazzled and old enough to share his joy. Despite his posturing, his elaborate, bookish conversation, his determination to maintain a "high level of discourse" at all times, nevertheless he had his failings and sufferings as well. I didn't like him *because* he suffered. No, I liked and admired him because he was someone who'd chosen to lavish all his vast energies and supreme intelligence on a literary style that even most other poets would have considered eccentrically *passéiste*. In those days people would have said he was busy "doing his own thing" ("pursuing my idiosyncratic enterprise" was Max's translation), but that explanation would have amounted to a good-natured dismissal.

I was embarrassed by Max's effrontery, especially in public places. He'd call out to a sleepy young waiter in a Village restaurant, "My good man, fetch us something iced and ambrosial," and would go on to give him orders at once so peremptory and so obscure that the good man would freeze in his tracks, caught in the twin headlights of anger and confusion. Nor did Max say such things unconsciously, as a grandee might, but rather in full awareness and as a dare. I couldn't roll my eyes, in collusion with the waiter, as I might have done during one of my father's public tirades, since Max was acutely aware of my responses and, in fact, was playing to them.

Where he was vulnerable was with respect to his body and sex. If I told him how striking he was he'd puff his cheeks out and exhale like a Frenchman and claw at the air with one hand, then let it fall nervelessly, as though beating off annoying cobwebs. He had two entire sets of clothes, fat and thin, so used to gaining and losing weight was he. Whether he was losing or gaining, his eyes would never stop scanning the entire table. During lunch he ceaselessly inventoried who was eating what and what remained to be consumed. If he was in his gaining mode, his hand would move delicately, rhythmically over the table, conveying nourishment to his mouth, which never stopped both talking and munching for an instant. One night I saw him break up a ring of a meringue *vacherin* in the middle of the table and slowly, methodically ingest it down to the last, snowy shard. If he was losing weight, he smiled with the anorectic's martyred pride when his friends began to complain that he was overdoing it and that he looked lined and unhealthy. "Really, Max, you're far too thin. You're going to become ill," they'd say.

He believed that he'd have more and more success romantically the thinner he became. He didn't understand that his age and baldness went better with a solid, stocky body. What was sexy (and admirable) about him was his brilliance, his conviction in delivering his opinions and his refusal to adopt an American-style masculinity, which would have been too close-mouthed and inexpressive to convey the range and subtlety of his ideas. Perhaps because he'd spent so much time in France he'd picked up a kind of masculinity composed not of silence but of intellectual domination.

He and Keith took turns reading out loud to each other three nights a week. "We're working our way through *Diana of the Crossways* and it's splendid, exhilarating stuff," Max would tell me. If I asked who'd written it, Max would simply raise that magnificent eyebrow and leave it to me to discover the answer, which he considered too rudimentary to be pronounced.

If sometimes he treated me as a slow learner, usually he flattered and frightened me by treating me as an equal. "Of course *we* know the 'Homage to Sextus Propertius' by heart," he'd say, "but that poor moron Ben didn't recognize my allusion to it at all and simply scratched his head over my inverted word order, not seeing I was echoing Pound's re-creation of Latin grammar." In such moments perhaps half the time I smiled shyly and confessed that I, too, was as ignorant as Ben or whoever, but the rest of the time I blushed, nodded and rushed home to look up and acquire the knowledge he'd so flatteringly attributed to me.

Max started dating a sweet guy who made paper flowers and dealt in Tiffany lamps, someone I'd known for the ten years I'd lived in New York. His name was Silvio and he limped slightly and had a way of holding his head to one side and smiling; I imagined he'd spent his twenties at deafening rock concerts (I'd seen him often in the old Stonewall) and had learned to smile at no matter what people were saying to him over the din. I'd introduced him casually to Max when we ran into Silvio on the street and I'd been surprised that Max was taken by him. Silvio wasn't an intellectual, nor was he beautiful, the only two objective assets that I could imagine appealing to someone so magnificent as Max. Suddenly I realized that powerful as Max might be in poetic coteries, he was just a bald middle-aged man "on the open market," as I thought of it. Max wielded an influence only over other writers, but perhaps he wasn't attracted to them. He'd said that homosexual couples were plagued by the "incest taboo," a brotherly similitude that early on tranquilized desire, and that the only way to keep things hot was to search out "the Other" (his vocabulary was inflected by his years of undergoing a Freudian psychoanalysis and reading French Existentialism). Was Silvio "the Other"?

Although Silvio seemed charmed by Max's attentions—the theater tickets, the jeroboam of champagne, the piles of paperbacks that arrived on his doorstep each morning as footnotes to Max's lecture of the previous evening—he preferred silence and smiles, was allergic to the theater, drank beer, didn't read. Max could conceive of no love that wasn't pedagogical, but unfortunately someone who was truly Other didn't want to learn.

It dawned on me that I was the guy who could make Max happy and that he liked Silvio only because I'd introduced them. Max had told me once how "beautiful" he found me. I knew he cautiously admired my talent (he was cautious because no one else shared his enthusiasm yet) and he'd promised to send my revised manuscript to a publisher. It had already been read and turned down by several more houses since I'd received that first rejection letter in Rome, the one that had made me want to kill myself. Now I was more resigned to waiting. I knew I was enough of a student to warrant Max's playing the teacher with me, the only role that made him feel useful and appreciated, and enough of an equal to raise my affection out of the category of abject adoration. If I was not yet as culturally eager as he or Butler at least I was quick to absorb whatever I felt I could use. Though outside I shook constantly and bobbed my head when I was tense, inside everything poured very, very slowly. From Maria I'd acquired a patient certainty that an artistic career must be long and slow to come to fruition, although now that she was only two years shy of forty I wondered if she'd ever begin to show. Perhaps her nearly geological sense of time would be her undoing. And mine.

Even if Max fancied me, I wasn't sure I could ever find him attractive. I loved his beautiful head, at once so sensual and intellectual, just as I could only admire—from the vantage point of my dirty little slum apartment with its camp bed and army of roaches, its heavily barred windows looking out on a pulsing, sun-struck screen of green leaves—the powerhouse Max's study represented: mirrored, gleaming, book lined, perfumed with the smell of waxed wood, invaded but not submerged by a correspondence worthy of a minister of state. This study was the hatchery of his passionate, erudite poems.

Exhilarating as every meeting with him was, as he doused me in alternating showers of praise and mockery, I wasn't ready yet to domesticate my sexuality and take him on as the useful older lover. I loved my wild white nights along the docks and in the back of parked trucks. I didn't want to buy a joint subscription to the opera (even if I could have afforded it). I didn't want to grow a little paunch and discuss Roland Barthes with the same man who was fucking me. I didn't want to trade in my come-stiff jeans for tailored slacks with a "self-belt." I didn't want the patina of my dark feelings to be rinsed clean in a liquid polish of irony, learned humor and literary allusions. I didn't want to be faithful to a hairy body, a *faux-maigre* starved thin so often that the skin hung slack on the bones like wet woolens on a wire hanger. If I were faithful it would only be by becoming faithless: until now I'd always explored the unique mystery of each man I held in my arms and during sex I'd never thought about another; but if I was forced to sleep with the same man night after night I'd have to fantasize about all the others in order to stay hard. The prospect of that kind of disloyalty violated my code of bodily sincerity.

But in other ways I was well suited to love affairs or friendships with other writers. If most writers were hostile to one another, I was so different from them that I fascinated and never threatened them and they struck me as energetic if awkward stunt ponies. For some reason I wasn't the least bit competitive, perhaps because I believed that creativity was incommensurable. Then again I probably *was* competitive but had acquired my mother's reflex of "rising above" all base feelings.

And then for other writers I had a physical glamor with my drooping mustache, shoulder-length brown hair, huge eyes, slender, muscled body that set me apart, although my looks would have counted as beauty only in a literary milieu, where the standards were so low. Since I'd published nothing I was permitted to be handsome; by the time I became a known writer, ten years later, I was conveniently beginning to lose my looks. Even when I was thirty I wouldn't have turned a single head among the serious cruisers on Greenwich Avenue, but at one of the literary discussions organized by the newly founded Gay Academic Union people nudged one another when I squeezed past them, heading for a vacant seat. In those days I had a white gauze musketeer's shirt with leg-of-mutton sleeves and white drawstring laces up the yoke neck from the chest to the clavicles. The string was never drawn tight and looked as though it could be easily yanked even wider open. My torso inhabited that pale shirt like the blue updraft at the heart of a flame.

Butler convinced me to go to a gay consciousness-raising session. Twelve guys sat around someone's living room. The topic that night was "coming out," that is, not the moment when we first made love with another man but when we first let the people around us know we were gay. According to the rules (which we were assured were both "Maoist" and "feminist"), each participant could bear witness to his personal experience as long as he liked. No one could interrupt him or offer him advice since a CR session was the opposite of group therapy. Here each story was treated as invaluable political information ("the personal is political"), not as a neurosis to be outwitted.

At the end of the session we were encouraged to draw a lesson from all these testimonies and devise a corrective political action. We decided that we'd all suffered because in secondary school our teachers had provided us with no information about homosexuality; each of us planned to write his high-school biology lecturer, including a mild reproach and a serious recommendation, that he or she take up this important topic in a scientific fashion. I never did a thing—I was as indifferent to other people as I'd always been. I belonged to that group of gay men who lost all interest in the others the minute he left the club, the trucks or the baths; it was only by pious convention that I signed a petition deploring the fire that had destroyed the Everard Baths and burned to death dozens of the homosexual clients inside.

Lou, my old lover who'd moved from Chicago to New York at the same time as I did, was much more militant, even though he was now happily married to his second wife (an eccentricity he had to conceal from the Gay Activists' Alliance). He'd tell me about "zaps" he and his friends were staging—sit-downs in front of the Suffolk County police station, for instance. Fire Island was in Suffolk County and the police thought nothing of crossing the bay at night in motorboats to raid our discos and to arrest men sucking cock down misty, lonely walkways at dawn, their eyes spiraling with acid, the only sound that of deer nosing open garbage cans, or the sharp gasp of an orgasm, or the heavy breathing of an overweight cop lurking in the underbrush. . . .

Lou's motives struck me as irreproachable, since his zaps allowed him to meet handsome, fearless younger gay men, to feel as young and rebellious as he looked (despite the fact he was over forty, married and the vice president of an advertising company) and to exercise his extraordinary gift for demagoguery. Of course I remembered when, ten years ago, we'd laughed at the idea of homosexual rights and said one might as well demand respect for safecrackers.

MAX, despite his arrogance, which came in fitful gusts that alternated with a touching insecurity, didn't believe that he alone could keep me entertained. He invariably arranged for us to drop in on someone after dinner, old people who'd known Arshile or Maxim Gorky, younger ones who'd studied with Hannah Arendt or worked for Djuna Barnes. He introduced me to a charming man with Parkinson's disease who assembled from their own writings collage-autobiographies of classic French authors. I met through Max a millionaire from Nebraska who edited a little magazine.

And one night we dropped in on Tom, the poetry editor of a famous magazine, which represented the wedding of New York glitz and sophistication to solid investigative journalism. Tom was allergic to cigarettes; since I was a chain smoker I'd have to sit on his windowsill, with the window pulled down to my knees like a transparent skirt, and smoke and talk outside (Tom had a hard time hearing me through the glass though he could see me smiling, fuming, gesticulating). In a little magazine I reviewed Tom's collected poems, which, paradoxically, were seldom discussed because Tom wielded so much influence that poets were afraid to appear to be currying his favor. He was delighted by my praise, just as I was pleased to be published.

One evening Tom read me a verse play he'd written a decade before. On another he introduced me to an amateur boxer with a lisp who'd been a paid fuck-buddy for years; the boxer's only passion was opera and he made annual pilgrimages to Bayreuth and Salzburg. He and Tom camped it up and laughed the bored, knowing laugh of the cultural consumer. But Tom wasn't happy with him. They'd become too comfortable in their joking remarks on the leading sopranos of the day to engage any longer at night in fierce sexual combat; there was no way that sex and friendship could be made compatible—Max's theory of the incest taboo. I can remember one night the boxer said, "I don't like Beverly Sills. Her name reminds me of Beverly Hills."

Tom replied without a pause, "Funny, you never had that objection to Victoria de los Angeles."

Tom longed for true love with an intellectual inferior and physical superior, preferably with someone who spoke no English (and would thereby be immune to Tom's only charm). Tom had been in Freudian analysis for twenty years and made sophisticated jokes about his treatment as about everything else (his parents, his lack-love life, his failing health). He was a famous wit, as dry as his own martinis, and I knew a joke was on its way when his eyebrows would rise above the solid black rims of his round glasses and his small body, swaddled in a tightly buttoned tan summer suit made by "the Brothers" (Brooks) and sporting a pastel rep tie, would begin to rock all over. Since his humor never overturned his preconceptions it didn't take him or his listeners by surprise; no, it was a local affair, just a snarl in his mental traffic, not an accident.

One day Tom said to me, "I'm terribly embarrassed but I don't know any of your books. Could you tell me some of your titles?"

"I could," I said, "but that wouldn't get you very far since all my books are still unpublished."

"That must be very painful for you," he said, and though I was ready to be miffed by any remark that came close to condescension, I could tell right away that he knew exactly the humiliation and frustration I was experiencing and I felt relieved, acknowledged. I was the youngest man at most of the parties I was attending now and at age thirty I was still able and eager to play the attractive student, but at the same time I was sure I'd soon lose my looks, my only entrée into this society, even if I'd written a perfect novel, as I judged it, a book at once intimate and impersonal, a closely woven web of signifiers that could be mapped onto our everyday life, though only imperfectly—"God's allegory," as Dante scholars called it, referring to those Biblical passages that can be interpreted only partially, that have only a limited correspondence to reality, passages that refuse to be completely teased out and that strenuously guard the mystery of the concrete.

My secret pride, I felt, however, was vexed and sore to the extent it was based on something shadowy, an unpublished novel, which is like a song no one has sung yet, or a set of plans for a house that has yet to be built. I'd quit my job on a wager that I'd succeed as a novelist. I'd deformed my personality just as a ballerina bloodies her feet or as a nun shaves her skull—always on the wager that one is going to become a star, a saint, an artist. My deformations were less dramatic than the dancer's or holy sister's, perhaps, but they were pursued just as fatally. Someone proposed I write for a television soap opera at a fee of a hundred thousand dollars a year, but I would have had to live on the head writer's estate on Cape Cod and turn out two hours of dialogue a week. I convinced myself that I was too pure (too artistic, idealistic) to accept, but in fact I was too addicted to sexual adventure of the sort only New York could provide.

Among all the people Max introduced me to, only one, Joshua, became a close friend. In fact he became the great friend of my life, although at first I scarcely noticed him. His charm was oblique, his humor understated, his looks appealing only to the initiate.

He wore contact lenses, but his eyes were so bad that he saw little enough by day and nothing by night, and when I'd send him off in a taxi at midnight after a drunken dinner and a nightcap or two, I had the impression I was pushing a wind-up soldier toward a precipice, for if the New York of Max, Tom and Joshua was a pinnacle of civilization, inhabited by these eclectic geniuses who knew everything and read books in every language in their calm, spacious apartments, the city outside was also as noisy as an Arab bazaar and as dangerous as a bear pit: the streets were piled high with uncollected garbage and pulsing with revolving police lights; on the fire escape beyond an open window lurked a house robber—or the shadow of laundry on a line; even the ground was just the thinnest layer of macadam poured over ten stories of hidden wires, sewers, subways, all rattling and steaming like pots on a stove. Only the lofty, raggedy roof gardens beside the forest of aerials and the slat-sheathed water tanks suggested another, tribal landscape—those roof villages or the dim inner courtyards flooded with pooling rain that pasted down layer upon layer of gingko leaves into a thickening vegetal collage of what looked like parchment, wax paper and butcher paper.

Joshua had a mind I couldn't fathom quickly. Early on I'd learned (perhaps because when I was a child we changed cities every year and I was faced each September with a new classroom of potential enemies) to characterize and seduce the people around me, but I could never figure Joshua out. Since the intellectuals I was meeting wanted to explain their work and to read it out loud, I was happy to listen (after all, most of them were at least part-time professors and used to a captive audience). My questions and welcoming silence could precipitate them into hours of glittering talk or recitation. Joshua, however, was quiet and curious. If someone like Max was always fearful that the tone might be lowered and spoke only on what he considered to be the highest plane, Joshua was delighted to gossip about friends, to speculate about the sex lives of the dancers at the New York City Ballet, to alert me to a good new restaurant reviewed in the *SoHo Weekly News*. He was deeply suspicious of ideas and liked to quote William Carlos Williams's injunction, "No ideas but in things." Whereas I was convinced by almost any idea I could grasp and passed quickly from Structuralism to semiotics by way of a Gramsci-inspired Marxist cultural analysis, Joshua smiled at my enthusiasms and yawned at my lectures. He wanted to know how to prepare *pasta alla puttanesca*. He hoped to meet the ballerina assoluta Suzanne Farrell. He wondered what Lola was up to in the soap opera *The Guiding Light*. We had a very campy way of talking together that we deleted the minute Max or anyone serious was around. We gave all of our friends, men and women alike, female names and referred to them all in the feminine gender.

Joshua had been first in his class at Harvard as an undergraduate and had written an acclaimed doctoral thesis on the migration of the Petrarchan sonnet from Italy via France to England. He was considered one of the leading experts alive on Sir Philip Sidney, but the Renaissance bored him, although he quickly scanned articles every week or two in learned journals just to keep up with what everyone in his field was doing.

No, what interested him were the poets whom he was meeting and whom he was beginning to write about. His own life had been changed by Eddie—a poet, millionaire and gay man—who'd transformed Joshua by convincing him to buy contact lenses to replace his extremely thick glasses, and silk shirts and pale, pleated slacks to wear instead of the heavy, old-fashioned wool suits his father, a small-town tailor, had outfitted him with. Joshua and Eddie visited a tailor in Venice, a certain Signor Cicogna, every summer, and Joshua would come back with sports jackets in a fabric that in English is called houndstooth but in French (and Italian) "hen's foot." Or a black wool suit lined in red silk, which would cause Joshua, as he flipped his jacket open, to say in Italian with a sly little smile, "Priest outside, cardinal inside." His new look lifted him out of the category of the dowdy academic into that of the smart man-about-town.

At first Joshua—so wry, so unemphatic, smiling quizzically because he wasn't sure he was seeing the right expression on the other person's face—seemed like a charming extra in my new life, but soon I came to love him for the intimacy that sprang up between us as well as for all of his virtues, which were precisely the ones I lacked.

I had a way of shamelessly courting and flattering people such as Max or Butler because I felt I was acting in a play, whereas Joshua took them seriously, he was at home in this New York intellectual milieu, this was his one and only life, and he wasn't about to concede an inch to someone as high-handed as Max or as slippery and self-righteous as Butler. Joshua had started out as a bookworm. He'd excelled in studies that had obliged him to learn Greek, Latin and Renaissance Italian and French. If he looked fifty when he was only twenty-five (I was shocked by his old photos) and back then had been both loveless and envious, at least he'd had the satisfaction of mastering his field and even writing an essay on Shakespeare's sonnets that everyone still quoted two decades later. Anything judged remarkable that touched on Shakespeare, no matter how peripherally, repositioned the very cornerstone of our civilization—or should I say *their* civilization, since I could speak about it so pompously only because I didn't feel part of it; I bowed my head before Shakespeare as one might stand or kneel in an unfamiliar church. I'd majored in Chinese, I'd been a Buddhist, my favorite college courses had been Buddhist Art and the Music of Bartók, I knew *The Tale of Genji* better than *Hamlet*, I'd never studied Marlowe, Sidney or Spenser (Joshua kept telling me there was no greater pleasure than reading *The Faerie Queene* but I remained unconvinced), I'd read all of Ibsen (even *Emperor and Galilean*), revered Knut Hamsun, and Colette and Nabokov were the writers I read whenever the world appeared colorless, but if I wept when I read Keats my eyes were dry when I perused Dante—dry or slowly drooping into deep sleep.

If I was a public-library intellectual, someone who read without a plan and followed only his whims, Joshua was the real thing. I went with him one day to the university where he taught. Whereas Max bullied his students and hoped above all they'd consider him intelligent, Joshua was the good shepherd who gently prodded his flock toward the paddock. Max was exhilarating because he poured so much energy into every encounter and had a vaudeville extravagance about him. But he was also absurd with his swooping intonations, dictionary words, Inverness cape and deerstalker, and no one would have wanted to be like him—or if, bizarrely, the desire to emulate him had been awakened in some undergraduate breast, no one would have known how to go about copying such a preposterous style, so angular precisely because it joined a European erudition to a Midwestern bumptiousness (he avoided these two psychic and geographical extremes in favor of New York, where no one could judge him because no one could quite place him, and where energy, a quality he bristled with, was prized more than polish).

But Joshua, during all the years and in all the different countries and contexts I knew him, was always more admirable than intimidating and esteemed more for what he was than for what he said or did. Any guy in his classroom was fitter, more agile, better looking than he and abler at seeing the world around him, but his very frailty only pointed up the strength and suppleness of his mind and the high finish of his manner. Anyone could tell right off that Max was a tyrant; he could make it disadvantageous, even perilous, to disagree with him. But his friends and students didn't fear Joshua. No, they longed to please him. Joshua's hands gently molded the air when he spoke. He sat on the edge of his desk closest to his students, which suggested without demonstrating casualness, since his performance was so highly organized that nothing about it went unpremeditated. He cocked his head to one side and listened to his students, whom he sometimes deliberately pretended were saying things more intelligent than they intended. Everything he said was designed to lead his audience to a more focused vision of Shakespeare's world, an almost pictorial apprehension; as Joshua spoke one could see golden clouds banked in Tintoretto-blue skies above Cleopatra's sun-baked walls.

For Joshua the woods in *A Midsummer Night's Dream* or *As You Like It* were a charmed precinct in which young lovers would try out new (even androgynous) roles before returning, wiser and more humanly gendered, to the city or court. Perhaps that's why Joshua loved the New York City Ballet, since it, too, showed us a utopian society in which a man and a woman wordlessly moved through the *enchaînements* of other couples under the charged regard of spectators, symbolized by the lateral lights raking them from out of the wings. Joshua admired the ballet criticism of Edwin Denby, who had a Shakespearean vision of dance as both urban and utopian.

And Joshua adored "cruising" the main lobby of the newly opened State Theater, although his prowling and looking were more social than sexual and even under the bright lights he could scarcely make out who anyone was. As I squired him about the lobby from the bar onto the vast outdoor balcony he'd make funny remarks about all the celebrities we were passing; he'd give me their pedigrees, tell me how they were related to each other—and then realize he'd conjured up the wrong person. Perhaps his blindness stimulated his imagination and permitted him to construct better plots, nobler lineages, more amusing social conjunctions.

Like so many people I'd been taught from the very beginning that society was entirely negative: a hypocritical, gossipy artifice from which sincerity was necessarily banished and intimacy absent. But Joshua taught me (though only because I wanted to imitate his example, not because he ever tried to convert me to his beliefs)—Joshua taught me that society provides the necessary amplification of our private thoughts and acts. We gay guys had gotten things exactly the wrong way—we made love in public (in trucks and baths and backrooms) but shared our thoughts only in the confessional of the tête-à-tête, preferably over the phone in which the spirit was entirely disembodied and all that remained of communication was a crackling silence or a tinny, transmitted voice. Of course even so we were better attuned to urban possibilities than heterosexuals, since at least we were always cruising the streets.

Joshua's utopian expectations of society never occluded his awareness of its more usual grotesqueries. "It's simply past belief," he'd tell me during our morning phone call, recounting some new outrage that on my own I would have accepted as normal behavior. "He's gone too far this time," he'd say, and then the suppressed laughter in Joshua's voice would bubble over or he'd start munching his rye crisp or he'd tell me what was going on in the street below—usually pure invention, since Joshua saw only what he imagined.

FIVE

My mother called me to tell me that she was going to be operated on for breast cancer. "Honey," she said, "I'm afraid this may be it."

"Really?" I asked. "But millions of women have survived a mastectomy."

"It's spread. It's in my lymph nodes all up and down my left arm. It's the left breast."

"Have you had a second opinion?"

"What for?" she asked, offended. "I can read X-rays and medical reports for myself. After all, I'm a professional woman." She had a job as a psychologist in a medical clinic for mentally retarded children and she never corrected anyone who called her "Doctor." If truth be told, she had spent so many years studying the then-new field of mental retardation that her judgment and diagnoses were usually sounder than those of any medical doctor.

My question about the "second opinion" was the only canned response I had to this emergency and I knew for sure now that I'd never have been able to write for daytime television.

My mother would have been equally ineffectual; she'd been schooled by radio soaps and didn't have the jaunty, self-deprecatory manner of television characters. She was portentous, not "cute," in talking about her worries. I could almost hear the sustained organ chord underlining her tragic utterances. I admired her style, although I found it unbearable.

"Son," she said, "I need you."

"Maybe it would be better if I came out while you're recuperating. During the operation you'll have all your friends around. Later, when you're feeling better—"

"No," she said, with a force teetering on the edge of anger, "there may not be a recovery period. I need my kids near me now. I'm not being melodramatic. I could recover and have many more productive years" (Mother always spoke of productivity not happiness), "but stastically, sta*tis*tiscally" (like Dad she always stumbled on this word and this word alone), "the statistics also suggest my life could be *much* shorter. And a mastectomy is not minor surgery."

"Okay," I said. We discussed what plane I should take. I'd arrive on Friday, the night before her operation, see her Saturday and Sunday in recovery. "Then if I'm out of the woods you can fly home. You can stay in my apartment while you're here. The doorman, George, will give you my keys. Your sister wants you to have dinner with her when you arrive." She went into all the details; I noticed how she'd planned to the last moment how long we'd visit her and when, as though she knew she couldn't otherwise be assured of our doing things properly.

On the plane to Chicago I felt a powerful anger against my mother filling me. I wrestled with her in my mind as though she were sitting beside me. "I won't let you drag me into the grave," I whispered soundlessly as New York tilted and shrank below me. I was shocked to see how almost unidentifiably small was the part of Manhattan I cared about; Greenwich Village was just a pimple on the backside of the five boroughs and the sprawl beyond—and then I came back to this inexplicable anger, so unfair. Already here on the plane the crafty faces and sinewy dark little bodies of New York had been replaced with Midwestern prize pigs—fat, pink, guileless. Years ago I'd said good-bye to the possibility of a steady job, early nights, mashed potatoes, porcine love, knee-slapping jokes.

But who was I kidding? It wasn't the Midwest I'd escaped but my mother; I'd fought free of her gravitational pull but now, like a dark lodestone, she was drawing me back to her. If I was cold and incapable of love it was because I'd given all my love to her so long ago. When I was fourteen I'd said, "If you die I'll throw myself in the grave with you—I couldn't go on living."

In Rome and New York I'd fashioned a new personality for myself. All the things I did in the holds of parked trucks and all the books I read and all the masterful men and books I discussed with Joshua, Tom, Max or

Butler—these were all the ways I had of convincing myself that I had nothing more to do with that woman, who was almost illiterate and who always said the predictable thing except when her idiocy surpassed even my predictions.

When I was a child she'd seldom held me though she'd sung to me in the dark before I went to sleep, sung "I'll be with you in apple-blossom time" in her frail voice, a plaintive war-ballad addressed by a soldier to his girl. Together we'd listen to FDR's "Fireside Chats" and the teenage Frank Sinatra singing on the radio during the war years. At our rambling Michigan summer house I remember the smell of my mother's wool swimsuit when it was wet; I'd run to her and bury my face in it. Her features, thrown into relief by the sculptural white swimming cap, frightened me with their boldness, free of mascara and makeup. I remember the wasps that haunted the artesian well and that would sting the backs of our necks until my father bagged and burned them. I remember the smell of trapped heat and dust in the empty servants' quarters over the garage, a smell that to my mind seemed to emanate from the clear glass tear-shaped sphere of red liquid (fire-extinguishing fluid) resting in a rusting metal hoop projecting from the pine board wall.

When my mother and father divorced I'd become my mother's best friend, her confidant and, somehow, her older brother. She'd say, "You're so much more mature than your father," or, "If I could find a man like you I'd marry him right away," or, "You were already wise when you were born. There's something almost . . . Christ-like about you." This sacred, consoling spirit that inhabited me when my mother was drunk or lonely had nothing to do with the whining, sniveling brat who wouldn't get up in the morning, on one of those winter mornings when it was still night outside and the world had died and gone mortuary cold under a sheet of snow. Nor did this Christ-like spirit have anything to do with the ugly, embarrassing nerd my sister despised; I had believed her when she told me I smelled. Nor did this holy spirit cohabit my body with the queer I was in danger of becoming, head ready to be shaved for some eventual lobotomy, skin potentially white and veins putatively blue because when I grew up I would never go outside or if so only by night, a monster whimpering for compassion but incapable of keeping his big, clammy hands off boys' cool thighs, so like girls' thighs except the knees were knobbier, the pores microscopically larger, the skin pierced by the first dusting of sperm-smelling fuzz.

No, what my mother loved in me was the wise child in the temple, consternating the rabbis, the compassionate listener who seemed all-knowing only because I parroted back the advice she'd already offered to herself just the day before during an inebriated monologue. She loved me when I said to her, "You're a wonderful intelligent woman who possesses a very deep, wise soul; you're pre-eminent in your field, you're surrounded by friends who idolize you, and if most men are frightened off because you're such a fine person then that is their loss. You must hold to your own high principles and never cheapen yourself." No matter that if her friends "idolized" her it was only because they were the sort of people so pitiful that they had no other friends. No matter that she made me spend my eighth, ninth and tenth birthdays in a nightclub with her while she cruised men at the bar; her principles lurched ever lower with every highball and she wondered if she had cheapened herself only on subsequent nights when her phone refused to ring. Cheapness became a vice only after it had proved to be a bad amatory move; as good Americans our morality was almost entirely pragmatic.

If God had taken away her husband and failed to give her a rich, constant new lover, at least He'd provided her with a son she could engulf entirely. With this son—her hobby, her lapdog, her portable altar—she could enter into a soothing trance induced by exchanged compliments. He was a genius, sensitive, kind, insightful; and she was a hard-working, dedicated humanitarian making a great contribution to science and the community.

We weren't alike. No, she told me, I was a dreamer, poetic, like her father Jim, an Irishman who'd died young. I would never be able to handle money, drive a car, land a job, according to her mythology. That's where she came in. She was the practical one and I was dependent on her. All that was obvious from the psychological tests she gave me—my high score on the verbal part of the Stanford-Binet, my mediocre one on the Wechsler, which was oriented toward problem-solution.

Although O'Reilly, the psychiatrist I'd had as an adolescent, was an amphetamine-popping, booze-swilling crackpot, constantly dozing off during my hours when he wasn't picking at a scab on his nose and murmuring how much he loved me (avoiding my name, which often eluded him), nevertheless his one big theory about human neuroses blamed Mom, and he'd drilled me in it until I broke my dependence on her. When I was seventeen and eighteen I'd heaped abuse on her, accusing her of having turned me into a homosexual, attacking her for spoiling my childhood by forcing me to play her husband. Even her habit of calling me a "genius" had made it impossible for me to fail at things, to experiment, to grope. If I'd learned to drive, to work, to manage my money it had been in defiance of her behavior-shaping and her pseudo-scientific test results.

Her eyes would fill with tears and her mouth would tremble as I shouted at her, but more from the anger in my voice than from the power of my argument. She was always very sure she was right. Each time after I challenged her she'd begin chanting to herself a mantra of self-justification as she turned a prayer-wheel of self-praise.

Once I moved to New York weeks would go by without my calling or writing her, but when we were in contact everything was calm and kindly. I developed a new tactic for dealing with her, a sort of Confucian filial piety. I decided to be scrupulously respectful of her, patient, attentive, laudatory. I never told her anything about myself and with some bitterness I noticed that she seldom asked me questions. The summer before going to Rome (1969—the summer of Stonewall) I'd joined her for a week in what she called her "summer cottage," although it was a sordid suburban house in a small Michigan town an hour north of Chicago.

After three days my Confucian filial piety eroded away and I became irritable again. My anger as a teenager had been inflamed by my psychiatrist, just as my later piety was more a pose than a conviction: since all my friends routinely treated their parents with hostility ("Never trust anyone over thirty" was their slogan), when I turned thirty I decided to treat my mother with elaborate deference—an aesthetic, not an ethical decision. The only genuine, unmediated way to deal with her I'd ever known had been the rapt devotion of my childhood, expressed by that cry I'd shouted, "If you die I'll throw myself in the grave with you."

Even back then, when I was a child, I'd occasionally rebelled against my desire to curl up beside her and deal out reciprocal praise, but these episodes were brief. Otherwise I was so satisfied with her that I never sought out friends; I didn't even know that people had friends other than their acquaintances in the classroom. Like a somnambulist I sleepwalked from bed to school, school to library, and there I'd slumped on the floor in the open stacks and so entirely forgotten time, and even my own existence except as an eye moving over print, that night would fall and the dinner hour creep by before the closing bell and dimming lights would shake me out of my stupor. Later, when I was fourteen and fifteen, I tasted the apple of friendship and was driven out of the paradisal garden of maternal love; once out, I never again had the self-forgetfulness necessary for the sort of reading in which the page becomes a layer of the cortex, its letters struck directly onto the neurons.

When I was ten I looked at my thirteen-year-old sister and shocked my mother by saying, "The poor girl has already become sexual and I guess she'll go on that way for a very long time. As for myself, I feel I'm on a hill-top looking down at a wide valley that I'll have to cross." The valley of desire, I was sure, would make me much less intelligent. I even wrote an essay arguing that children should be given the vote since they alone were objective, swayed neither by the looks of the candidates nor influenced by their own economic interests in evaluating the issues. They were without desire and without possessions.

I'm the sort of person who still turns off the television when the movie becomes too frightening or even tense; even then, I couldn't bear the high drama of seeing my mother ill or dying, as she might be dying now from breast cancer. I'm the sort of person who can lick a stranger's boots in a backroom, then come home, turn on all the lights, make coffee, take a thirty-minute shower, listen to *The Well-Tempered Clavier*; if someone touches my shoulder tenderly I jump and glower; I couldn't bear to look at my mother's bleeding, excised flesh because I could tolerate neither intimacy nor the sight of pain.

With my long hair, dirty jeans, buccaneer's shirt, and my clothes and fingers smelling of cigarettes, I felt unwelcome in my mother's apartment building on the Near North Side, although George the doorman (the same grinning sneak who'd tattled to my mother about my teenage affair with Lou) welcomed me with oily enthusiasm and asked me how she was doing, his face bent down in a conventional glyph of silence while his little eyes darted from the street (to see if a taxi was approaching) to the security screen above his station, which revealed that someone ominous was trying to enter the building by the alley door.

I was still angry with my mother for dragging me back to Chicago and I was muttering harsh words against her when I let myself into her apartment. The silence that greeted me was spooky, the silence of ducts feeding the exact degree of warmed air into the room. Everything was impeccable. She must have done a thorough cleaning in anticipation of my visit and her convalescence—her death, possibly. Here were the knick-knacks I'd played with as a child, the two Chinese figurines in symmetrical niches flanking the breakfront, the glass bird through whose transparent brain I'd studied the world for idle hours, the glazed oxblood vase always cool to the touch, even on the most stifling summer days.

My mother was so formidable that it was hard to remember she was just five feet tall until I looked at her dresses hanging on white satin hangers all in a row. She was a tiny dowager empress and here were her beaded and brocaded gowns, her mink, her hats on higher shelves that she needed a ladder to reach. The wall-to-wall carpet was white and thick; I pictured her snow-sledding through it in her stocking feet. There, in an armchair too large for her, she'd sit, legs dangling in the air, glasses perched on her nose, sewing something. Although she prided herself on being a professional woman, she possessed all the traditional feminine skills and could cook a succulent pot roast, crochet, polish silver until it emitted a high C, bake a cake from scratch. I can still remember the bitter chocolate she swirled into a batter of egg yolks, marbling, then blending the two, slow-pouring colors.

Over the dining room table was a chandelier I'd sent her from Rome. On the side table were black-and-white photos of my father, then of my sister and me as well as color pictures of my sister's three children. The family's decline in fortunes was obvious: my father impeccably groomed in a tailor-made suit, starched white handkerchief cresting in three stiff peaks out of his vest pocket, an affable chief executive's smile promising bonhomie and intelligence but no warmth; my sister's white-blonde hair drawn away from her face when she was just eight and still resembled a Princess Imperial; a recent snap of me stronger in mood than lighting by an arty Village lesbian who portrayed me as a backlit terrorist, eyes two anarchistic holes above the wispy surrender of a mustache; and my sister's three kids, two boys and a girl, all decked out in J.C. Penney plaids and denim, their freckles and big-toothed smiles also ordered from a mail-order catalog. At a time when most American families were climbing the ladder we were clearly descending it.

In the bookcase were the same old volumes Mother had had when I was a baby (Mary Baker Eddy's *Science and Health* and *Key to the Scriptures*, *The Victor Book of the Opera*, *Ben Hur*), as well as more recent acquisitions ("cute" books about being a besotted grandmother or about the darndest things kids are likely to say). In fact most of the newer objects in the apartment were cute gift items—magnetic cartoon characters adhering to the fridge, "Granny's" cookie box painted with a smiling old lady in an apron and glasses, a porcelain cow that poured milk from its mouth—but I dimly recognized that they were the sort of novelties nice women with droll tastes bought for themselves on trips or exchanged with other ladies, not to be confused with the still cruder kitsch poorer people picked up at filling stations with Green Stamps. But I was no one to make such observations, I who'd never owned a car, pumped my own gas, listened to pop music, visited a shopping mall, possessed a television or played miniature golf. I saw that New York was a sort of monastery where people gave up comfort and mindless distractions for the austere but thrilling excitement of making art, meeting eccentrics and enjoying constant sex.

I slept in my mother's bed, which was so difficult to make up in the morning or prepare at night that often she preferred to sleep on the couch. A decorator had designed the bed with a wrinkle-less, quilted cover rigidly outlined in dark cotton piping that was supposed to be pulled down over the mattress and that fitted a rounded cardboard bolster nailed onto a wooden frame; the pillows were squeezed up inside the bolster and then "accent" pillows in contrasting shades were scattered over the entire dressed bed like rose petals over a costumed corpse. The same decorator had installed matching curtains, so heavy they could scarcely be opened, but I pulled them to look out at the glowing city below and the beach a block away. I tried to imagine my mother living here, making and unmaking her state bed, painting her toenails, pouring milk into her coffee out of her droll porcelain cow, preparing her microscopic suppers out of the groceries she'd picked up a block away at Stop n' Shop, curling up in her nightgown to watch *60 Minutes* (she swore she never looked at mere comedy or variety shows, and indeed she preferred routine to variety and had no sense of humor).

As I smoked my cigarettes and polluted her lightly perfumed Fabergé egg of an apartment I both longed for her death and feared it. Without her I'd have no more ties to my family; I no longer spoke to my father. I'd be entirely self-sufficient, as solitary as I already felt I was. In fact her death would simply mean that the scaffolding would fall away, revealing at last the gigantic Statue of Solitude I'd been working on becoming. Without her the suspense of waiting for her death would be over. Did I want her to die because I longed for something, anything, to happen? In my poverty and impotence, my frustration at not being able to coerce someone into publishing me, did I expect the banal inescapable drama of loss and death to transform me? Sometimes I marveled at how my Texas relatives could pick over one another's woes, keen and mourn, but now I saw that theirs were the unearned tragedies, those that befall everyone. My old uncles and aunts weren't being punished for daring, hands bound to a rock for stealing fire; no, these were just bored, retired people whom custom had long ago prepared for hospitals and funerals. They were almost glad that at last they could say the lines they'd so often rehearsed. Or so I imagined.

Was I glad my mother was sick?

Not at all. I was indignant. I was like a debutante called back from the ball by her father's heart attack. I wanted to cover my face with a heavy black veil so no one would see it was flushed with petty vexation. The sort of excitement New York offered, fueled by celebrity, money and sex, could never come to an end precisely because these three rewards were unobtainable. One could never have enough of them and what one had was never a fixed sum. To be called away from New York was like forcing a broker to leave his phone and computer. Just as buying and selling were hypnotic activities, writing, cruising and social climbing were every bit as randomly reinforced and gripping.

When I was a young teenage boy I'd been invited by the lifeguard, Forrest Greene, into his tower, the changing room inside the wooden frame that narrowed as it rose and that held high his chair for surveying the swimmers in Lake Michigan. It had begun to rain and the beach was deserted and even Forrest's girlfriend had finally gone home and here at last I was with him, just an inch separating us as we stood facing each other in our swimsuits. There was already a swelling in the green pouch of his white-sided Speedo swimsuit. I had just to raise my hand to touch his chest, hard and sun-baked as a clay tablet superscribed in cursive gold hairs, a cuneiform of ringlets, commas and dashes I knew I must touch in order to decipher—but just then there was a loud banging, and Forrest unlatched the door to reveal my mother standing, hooded, in the downpour. She dragged me home to our apartment just across the street. She'd obviously been spying on us from the window. She'd saved me from the fate of being held by Forrest's big, sun-baked body. She'd saved me from having my lips smeared with his white sun-protecting liquid, which he'd also streaked down his nose and over his cheekbones like an Apache. Just as she was saving me now from another night in the trucks.

Funny. At the time it would never have occurred to me I was addicted. I didn't imagine for an instant that I was a prisoner to sex. No, I was free. After those years of my mother's vigilance, after my boarding school, where the halls had been patrolled all night and we'd slept in chaste, separate rooms, at last I was free—free to go out every night, all night, to respond to every glance, to shower between tricks before plunging back to the docks or the trucks.

My sister came by for dinner. We went to a neighborhood place she loved where the all-women staff baked their own bread and the recorded music was played by a bluegrass band. She was a big Midwestern woman with her blue plastic glasses frames, wide stance and worn-down heels, leatherette handbag and loud, nasal voice, but in an instant I was leaning forward, trying to please her. She seemed more vulnerable but also more erratic than I'd ever seen her.

Yet she was a star, always would be. When we were teenagers she'd been captain of the Blues at summer camp and had won gold stars in fencing and was always surrounded by her court of adoring girls wearing braces, their chubby, sun-browned bodies in uniforms of shorts and pressed cotton monogrammed shirts with cuffed short sleeves. She stood among and somehow above them, her jaw strong, her cap of blonde hair bleached almost white, her arms muscled, as though her will alone had burned off the baby fat and given her legs a lean, male strength.

In September her estival plumage would molt and she'd go back to being a little brown wren at high school in long, pleated skirts, thick white socks and lead-soled saddle shoes, a frightened girl who hugged her school books to her breasts as she darted, head down, from one class to another. Later, in her small Ohio college where our father had forbidden her to study pre-med and had made her take up primary education, she'd become a Theta and eventually the president of her sorority, firm and confident in glee club concerts or all-girl basketball games, though paralyzed with fear when forced to attend sock-hops. She married Dick, the first man who asked her, virtually the first man she ever dated.

Like her, Dick was training to be a teacher ("a school teacher," as my Texas father said with the faint innuendo of the shabby one-room schoolhouse). He was from a poor family living on the outskirts of a big Ohio city and was paying for his education by working summer jobs in construction and by taking out huge student loans. He had a permanently red beak for a nose and a face that never changed expressions away from an innocuous half-smile and eyes so shallow and fixed they looked painted on. His shoulders were bunched around his ears but instead of indicating tension they made him look merely beleaguered—if not decapitated, despite the constant chuckle filtering out of his mouth as if on a tape loop. No matter what we said (and in our family my sister, my mother and I never stopped talking or shifting from one register to another), Dick just laughed his little chuckle, originally intended to suggest merriment before it wound down and got softer. An Englishman, I was sure, would have found him more stylized than a Kabuki dancer, so exotic was he, but in America he counted as a "good guy." People might have said, "C'mon, you guys, lay off Dick, he's harmless. He may be a little nerdy but he's basically a good guy."

Dick wore plaid shorts and outsize button-down dress shirts, hanging out and rumpled right from the dryer. He treated everything—from wearing clothes to entering the room to breathing—as a kind of nerdy joke, which squeezed a bit of laughter out of him as though the organ grinder were turning the handle of his hurdy-gurdy one more desultory time.

But he liked me and because of him my sister came to see me in a new light. She'd always regarded me as nothing but a curse, a blatant sign that she'd never really be popular, a weirdo who proved that her own efforts to be normal were doomed. When she brought Dick home she posed my mother in an armchair with needle and thread and me before the television watching a boxing match, but as soon as we spoke, of course, all was lost. Or gained, since in spite of his idiotic laugh, which afflicted him as a low-grade fever indicates a constant but not fatal illness, Dick was an intellectual. I couldn't talk about his subjects, politics or sociology or John Dewey's educational theories, but at least I'd read a few books and heard of the thinkers whom he was studying. My sister was amazed by our compatibility, which raised me, not him, in her eyes; Dick was already at the summit of her esteem. My sister's new-found affection for me seemed false at first and I kept fearing it was just the bait in the trap. She was acting a kindly role but in her eyes burned the same old contempt.

Daddy sent my sister to Europe for a summer. "Anne," he told her, "I want you to forget that boy with his silly grin and mumbling speech. He snuffles and mumbles and giggles and will never amount to a thing. No one likes mumblers. If you spend three months in Europe and travel with an open mind you'll see that you deserve more than this chump and that the world has much more to offer." Anne burned with resentment—a third-degree burn that took the full European tour to heal. While traveling she wrote daily letters to Dick and collected postcards to show him later. Since the trip was an organized one she met only other American students and though she became extremely close with several other girls not one guy looked at her as anything more than "a great gal, real popular with the other girls," the ultimate formula of failure back then, the female counterpart to the male version, "basically a good guy."

As soon as she returned to Ohio she married Dick. Daddy didn't attend, and certainly didn't pay for, the wedding. I gave my sister away.

Once they were married Anne became a model wife, a pillar or at least pilaster of the community and soon enough the perfect mother. She had two boys and a girl. Our father came to see his first grandchild and was so appalled when he observed Anne breast-feeding the baby that he predicted she'd give up this nonsense within a week—and seven days later her breasts ran dry.

Her husband was appointed an assistant principal in a local junior high, which was considered progressive. Anne hid her natural sporty beauty under long skirts, full blouses, a man's trench coat. She plunged herself into PTA activities and soon became the local president. With a group she was authoritative and humorless, but the minute she was alone with another woman she became giggly and conspiratorial. Between such encounters, public or private, she walked about with extreme concentration like a somnambulist who half-knows she's teetering on a ledge. When she was at home she sat vacantly at a glass-topped desk and looked down into reflections of moving clouds. The minute the phone rang she was stung into amiability, but otherwise she felt so tired that her children often found her asleep when they came home from school. The tireder she became the more she ate meat for energy—not the roast beef of her childhood, which she could no longer afford, but ground beef patted into "hambies," as she and the children called them.

She'd always treated me sarcastically when we were kids and now she found herself lashing out at Dick, whom she was surprised to discover was less intelligent than she'd believed but far more passionate than she'd suspected. He loved her, loved her long, hard body and loved her restless mind. When she unleashed her harsh tongue and covered him with insults, he pretended it was a parody of an attack and he covered his head with his hands and grinned, as though he were being pummeled by his kids.

She hated sex with him but he could never leave her alone. He wasn't a rapist, certainly not a seducer, but he could never get enough of her.

Two years before our mother's cancer surgery, Anne had fallen in love with the neighbor, a woman her age, married to a much older husband who neglected her. Peg liked the attention but was afraid to sleep with Anne. They drank Bloody Marys together. In that neighborhood of turn-of-the-century wood houses with peeling paint and rusting porch swings and of quiet streets as grey as watery reflections of the sky, the sidewalks buckling over rampant tree roots and the whispering silence of rustling leaves punctuated by the distant bark of a tethered dog—in that damp, colorless suburb that at certain hours appeared abandoned, as though a siren had driven everyone into bomb shelters and a lethal ray had fried them underground, leaving above nothing but dogs and a few crying, hungry babies and a single goldfish staring out through the magnifying glass of a bowl—in this vacant world my sister would pay lightning visits to Peg, streaking across unraked, moldering lawns still in her bathrobe and nightie at eleven in the morning on a Tuesday.

Peg and Anne had come to visit me in New York before I'd gone to Rome, back when I'd still had a nice apartment and a good salary, before I'd sunk in the world. The two women had drunk Bloody Marys all morning in their robes and seldom emerged from the apartment before dusk. They had secret jokes, code words, a strained complicity that unexpectedly would break down and send my sister wailing into the bathroom.

When I was in Europe my mother phoned me to tell me my sister had attempted suicide: "I just don't know what that girl wants. She's had all the advantages. She says I neglected her, that I gave you too much attention, but if there's one thing I know it's that I always loved you both equally. Of course you were different. With you it was more a spiritual companionship, why, even when you were a little boy we were so close that I'd forget you were with me, I'd lose you at the department store—"

"*Mother*," I said, exasperated, "what happened?"

"Well, your sister, poor little thing—" and here her unstoppable narrative voice dried up and she sobbed tiny little sobs on a baby-doll frequency, so unpracticed, so unlike her usual saturated style, that I knew she'd never cried like this before and couldn't even recognize herself— "she's in a coma in the hospital, St. Luke's, and we don't even know if she'll come out of it." More crying. "She drove her car into the woods up near Zion, I don't know what she was doing way up there, and she drank a bottle of vodka, Smirnoff's I think, and took a whole bottle of sleeping pills and then she slumped into the front seat and it was cold—" Here she broke off again, perhaps crying over the image of my sister in the cold woods, *la Belle au Bois Dormant*, a Sleeping Beauty without courtiers, awaiting the kiss of a princess who, alas, liked only princes.

"Someone found her and called an ambulance, I think it was a man out walking his dog, and she was saved, they pumped her stomach but she's still lying in a coma, the kids haven't been told, Dick just said their mother is away for a long rest. I just don't know—don't—" And here she dissolved into her funny little sobs, as though a cruel child were slapping a doll on the back again and again just to hear its faint, broken mew.

After my sister recovered she was signed over by her husband to a lock-up ward in a hospital on the Near North. For weeks she lay bedridden, in a stupor, and moved only enough to avoid bedsores. Her husband, stricken, frightened, visited her every day. His nerdy grin had been dehydrated into a mere pellet of a smile. Under the watchful eye of a psychiatric nurse he knew he couldn't touch her, much less rub up against her.

After a month her old camp spirit re-emerged. She organized round-the-clock group therapy sessions in the hospital. Fueled by cigarettes and black coffee, she and other unhappy men and women talked and talked. My sister had discovered an almost uncanny ability to read other people's thoughts, explain them clearly to her "patients" and to will these broken people into healing. Everyone liked her and wanted to be near her. When she walked down the corridors it was as though she were once again a summertime sovereign going from cabin to cabin. Here where men were not allowed to touch her she became amiable, even with them.

Sometimes, however, the least frustration would make her fall apart— literally, it seemed, for the parts of her personality would separate and collapse, like the walls of a rocket silo, except the missile wouldn't rise and roar but burn itself out in place. She'd rage and sob and hug her knees to her chest and her "patients" would look in at her as fearful as children.

Her own children weren't permitted by their father to visit her and she was relieved, since she could see them only as reproaches. She'd set out to be the perfect mother and she'd ended up by lingering at Peg's for the fifth Bloody Mary of the afternoon when the kids came home from school.

If her children made her feel guilty, the thought of Peg scared her. She'd suffered so much over Peg that now she shied away even from the recollection of her face or name. Anne couldn't afford the luxury of thinking about Peg, not if she ever wanted to get better. Nor did Peg write or try to see her.

Anne, who'd always had such power to dominate other women, had been surprised that she'd been unable to talk Peg into bed. It had been a failure of will, and now Anne doubted her will altogether. Her will was broken.

Her failure was almost exactly like mine with Sean. In our different ways for a long time Anne and I had both exerted an appeal over a few people, and various men and women, whom we'd scarcely noticed, had loved us or wanted to be constantly with us. Yet despite all our stratagems we'd failed to secure Sean or Peg, our two big beauties, and the defeat had shaken our entire self-esteem. I'd always wanted a man like Sean and for a moment I'd believed I was close to marrying him. I thought that if he became my husband I'd finally have the life of sex and status, an ideal and superior life, that I'd always dreamed about. His beauty was to me what wealth and beauty were to Jay Gatsby—a dream more than a reality, an identity more than a dream. Gatz had become Gatsby the day he'd seen his first yacht; when I first slept with Sean I felt tempted to become fully human.

In the restaurant my sister and I both ordered thick, rare steaks and ate pounds of red meat with a gnawing, gulping desperation. "Why are we like this? Oh, Brulley," she said, using her childhood name for me, a version of *brother*, "these women who work here are *horrified*, look, you can tell, they're all vegetarians, granola dykes longing for a rural commune, and look at us, we're horrible carnivores." She inched closer, a smile exposing her crooked teeth. "Do you sometimes wake up in the middle of the night and cook yourself a steak? For that matter, if you have an extra steak in the fridge doesn't it call out to you like a siren until you've eaten it? You do! It does! You see, we're exactly alike. Where did we get that? Do you think it's because Mully—" (her old pronunciation of *mother*)—"never gave us enough to eat, just that awful pork tenderloin because it was the cheapest cut and she—"

She began to cry, to *leak*, and her pale nose turned red and all at once I understood how much Christa resembled my sister— to be sure a taller, nobler, blonder version, neither so mercurial nor so intelligent, but Christa was the sad, resigned resolution to what had always been so anguished about Anne, so raw.

"I'm crying, Brulley, because I'm *scared*. What if she dies? I haven't seen her in a year, since I started therapy; my shrink says I must recognize how evil she has always been. I have to shout and pummel a dummy labeled 'Mom'—"

"I did that, too," I said, "when I was with Dr. O'Reilly. . . ."

"Poor Mully," Anne said, sighing deeply. She suddenly looked much older, as though she'd taken off dark glasses to reveal ancient eyes. I didn't know whether she thought we'd desecrated Mother's memory and that's why she was "poor" or whether she suddenly remembered her cancer. "I talked to her doctor and it looks bad. It's going to be a radical mastectomy, they're going to cut out all the lymph nodes in her upper arm as well, she'll have to wear a surgical gauntlet to keep her forearm from swelling with uncirculated lymphatic fluid." As she raced on and on, the precise, technical vocabulary dried her tears. Her feeling of scientific control replaced her fear. She smiled. I smiled.

And yet, whipped kid that I was, I kept worrying that our armistice was fragile or might even be a trap and would give way in an instant to Anne's old scorn.

"You know," I said, "when you came that time to visit me in New York with Peg, I kept thinking you weren't really gay." I used the word *gay*, which united us, rather than the divisive word *lesbian* (lipstick-less mouth, cigarette behind the ear)—used it even while I was doubting that we were alike. "I thought you were just imitating me because you were unhappy."

"I don't know what I am, but don't you remember that crush I had on Jeananne back at Camp Sibelius, and I pined all winter over her?" She laughed. "That should have been our first clue. But, Brulley, it's neat but right now I'm involved with this really cool guy, early forties, big manly hands, clean as a surgeon's, but with flossy black hair on the first knuckle of each finger, and he's rich and well read, his name is Arthur."

"Where'd you meet him?"

"The madhouse." She smiled wanly.

Did she think I preferred her to be heterosexual? Did she imagine I found a straight woman to be more attractive, less weird than a lesbian (perhaps because straight women shared my taste for men)? "And what about Dick?" I asked.

She just made a face. "He's so icky." With me she reverted to our childhood vocabulary. "No, poor thing, he dotes on me, it's scary, sometimes *he's* the one who acts crazy, I never knew someone could love anyone so much, but he leaves me cold. Anyway, I've moved."

"Yeah, Mully said you had your own place near here."

"The only problem is I can't earn my living. Dick pays the rent and gives me and the kids an allowance, but we're so poor, you've never known this kind of poverty, I can't even afford a movie on Saturday nights and those steaks I was talking about are ghostly memories from the past, now it's just macaroni and cheese, even the kids are complaining."

"What would you do—what kind of work I mean—if you could choose anything, if you were a millionaire?" I asked.

She said she'd like most to be a psychologist and that she'd learned she could practice if she had a master's degree in social work, just two years of course work. I told her that I'd find the money for her tuition if she really wanted to go.

She had tears in her eyes.

For the ten years that had gone by since university days all my affinities had been elective and it was strange to be back home, responding to my sister, worrying about my mother, these women I'd inherited. With lovers I imagined an ideal life to come; with family members I remembered the tormented life of the past. With friends everything was new and renewable; with my sister everything, as Tom had written in a poem, was "old, inadequate and flourishing." A friend could please me in one or two ways; my sister and I could anger and hurt each other in myriad ways despite a firm resolve to be friendly.

"What does Mully think about your being a lesbian?" I asked.

"Well, maybe I'm not a lesbian, but when I was so nuts over Peg, Mully was horrible, she kept saying that *she* was feminine and loved men, too bad none of them was good enough for *her*, and the only time she'd ever been attracted to another woman—"

"Was that time," I interrupted, laughing, "when that woman friend of hers bent over and Mully could see her breasts and wanted to touch them?" I laughed, and Anne laughed, too, because suddenly we'd recognized that another thing our mother said was a "rap," one of her set pieces.

"Of course there's something weird about that story, anyway," Anne said, adding, "I think she was sending me a double message." We subsided into a psychoanalytic dissection of our mother, a familiar vocabulary that expressed little beyond our general irritation with her and our certainty that she was the source of all our problems.

Anne ordered a second bottle of wine. We were both smoking so heavily that the disapproving waitress, dressed like a chef in a white hat and a huge apron wrapped around her ample figure, kept exchanging empty ashtrays for full; the ashtray itself was so small and provisional that it was doubtless designed for a single after-dinner lapse, not a continued bad habit.

Fueled by red meat and nicotine, all our pain dulled by wine, we forgot our weariness and the inexorable lockstep of time. We flew high, then hovered above our mere bodies, these machines pulsing air and blood and mulching food. Our words weren't plucked from vocal cords but rather were the spontaneous condensation of thoughts precipitated out of the cloud of smoke hanging in a dense haze above our table.

"Do you remember, Brulley, how when we were kids we saw the movie of *The Glass Menagerie* and we howled with laughter because Mully was just like the mother? 'We're going to go to Bowman's Department Store and charge and charge and charge.' " She imitated a fancy Southern accent, a Tidewater exaggeration of our mother's faint Texas twang.

I didn't want to fall into all our old shared jokes, these vaudeville turns of our adolescence. We'd been the ones to torment our mother, and if our shrinks had taught us to blame her, they (and we) conveniently ignored the hours and hours every week my sister and I, as children and adolescents, had devoted to mocking the poor woman. If she said, "I need nice things in my life, I must make a nice appearance, I'm going to charge some lovely winter outfits at Neiman-Marcus," then Anne and I would howl in chorus, "I'm going to charge, charge, charge at Bowman's Department Store." If she'd talk about how cute and popular she'd been as a girl, Anne would paraphrase Tennessee Williams, "Why, when I was a girl I had so many gentleman callers one Sunday back at Belle Rive that we had to send for extra chairs."

Our satirical idea, I guess, was that Mully was self-deceiving and pathetically out of date; we ignored her gallantry. After our father had left her for another woman she'd had to go to work for the first time at age forty-five. She'd made a success of her life, although at a terrible price, one that everyone around her had to pay. She never stopped singing her own praises in her frail soprano, a voice weak exactly to the degree her will and self-absorption were relentlessly strong. One of her colleagues had drunk too much once at an office party and had told me he thought she was crazy. "With the parents and children she plays Lady Bountiful, with the doctors she plays the best and brightest student, though she's not bright, in fact she's an idiot, begging your pardon, but with the people who work under her she's suspicious, hysterical, hectoring, ungrateful, a real bitch, begging your forgiveness, a real dragon lady. Just last week she sobbed and screamed at us that we were obstructionists, *little* people who didn't appreciate how a *big* mind like hers thinks. She shook all over like a crazy woman. I mean, I think she is crazy."

I who'd heard nothing but my mother's endlessly repeated rosy version of her life as a "professional woman" was at first shocked by what he was saying, although an instant later I realized she was self-aggrandizing, fearful of failure, in need of burnt offerings which, however, failed to nourish her spirit and left her ever hungrier for praise. She knew she preened too much to encourage her collaborators. And she had such a weak grasp on reality that she couldn't head off insurrection until it was too late.

Now, with my sister I contented myself with saying, "You know, those lines about Bowman's Department Store aren't in the play, they must have been added to the movie script." I wanted to remind Anne that as a New Yorker and a writer I'd acquired a coolness, a certain sophistication; I wasn't the same old nerdy Brulley whom she'd grown up with.

"Charge, charge, charge," my sister sang on a falling tone, hoping, I suppose, to elicit from me a silly laugh, silly because it fed on repetition and was dependent on a squalid, feeble mockery.

The next morning my sister phoned me at eight (disastrously early for me, who arose only at noon). She picked me up in her battered old station wagon, full of the kids' toys, clothes, books, the ashtray overflowing with lipsticked butts. We drove to the hospital.

We were told by a nurse that our mother would be wheeled back to her room at nine-thirty. "Were there complications?" my sister asked. The nurse called the recovery room and reported to us that everything was normal and the patient was doing nicely.

In the corridor we saw the elevator doors open and two orderlies emerge with our mother on a gurney. She was greyish-white. Her mouth was sunk in on one side where she'd removed her dentures. A traveling intravenous feed was bandaged to her right arm (not the arm that had been filleted); the flabby skin was bruised a bright sulfurous yellow. Her face appeared even whiter than when she would cold-cream it down before bedtime. In fact she looked less a patient than someone who'd just emerged from a refrigerated morgue. Any pity I might have felt was held back by horror—by awe, I thought. Awful.

Anne wasn't affected by my brand of squeamishness. She was magnetized to our mother's side. She swooped down and kissed her forehead, then tucked a strand of hair back into a plastic cap they'd put on her. With my quick irony and brittle mockery I was disarmed by the moment, one that required my mother's kind of solemn heroism.

That afternoon she looked just as lifeless as she lay in her hospital bed in a room she shared with another old woman. The roommate, apparently, was deaf and her two daughters, themselves middle-aged, had to shout in her ear. My sister and I sat bleakly silent while this cheerful, alien din clattered away just on the other side of the half-drawn curtain. All I could think about was smoking a cigarette.

When we were back in Anne's car she said, "Brulley, we've got to talk about what we'd do in case of . . ." Her voice trailed off.

"In case of what?" In this part of Chicago the stores were all of brick and just one story high; half of the shopfronts were boarded shut.

"In case she . . . turns into a vegetable."

"Do you want to pull the plug?"

"We must tell them not to use any extraordinary measures to keep her alive."

"Okay."

But that night our mother was awake and the next morning she was woozily talking and smiling. Anne and I never discussed our agreement, but we knew we'd been sinfully quick to bury our mother. Was it because we hated her? Wasn't it, rather, that we wanted some leverage over this massive stone that had so long blocked the path leading to the treasure, which for us was an undetermined, indescribable future, one that surpassed our imagination because all our thoughts had always concentrated on the past and on our mother?

Or were we tired of her, just as we were tired of ourselves?

I FLEW back Sunday afternoon but only after I'd spent an hour beside my mother. She was wearing her makeup and had arranged her hair very carefully. Her bedside table was covered with flowers and cards. "My friends just won't stop calling me," she gaily complained. "Can't they see they're exhausting me? You'd think people would be more considerate. But then everyone depends on me. It makes them so anxious when they see me vulnerable. Honey," she added, "I'm tired. Why don't you read to me?"

I'd always been impressed by Italian operas or nineteenth-century English novels in which it was assumed that no love was more precious than that of a mother for a son. "You only have one mother," my aunt had said to me. "Treat her well, because she's all you've got and when she's gone . . ." But for me that love was as troubled and eternal as my own consciousness.

When I was a kid of nine or ten I'd read to my mother while she drove, a book by Will and Ariel Durant about Greek philosophy or a Romantic biography of Beethoven or a study of the child's mind by Bruno Bettelheim (whom my mother had once met and called by his last name as though he were an instrument, a "Steinway" or "Stradivarius." She'd even say, "When a Bettelheim takes a look at autism—that's childhood schizophrenia—there are no more mysteries").

We'd ride for hours on the open highway down to Texas or up to Michigan and as she drove I'd read. She'd say, "Isn't that beautiful?" or

"What wisdom! What *wis*-dom!" when struck by a passage. She'd even drum the steering wheel with her gloved hand, smile exultantly and bounce up and down with a little-girl glee that looked slightly mad.

Now I read to her from Mary Baker Eddy, whom she admired without believing, or believed without following, though such distinctions were inappropriate to Mom, since she could approve of even contradictory ideas so long as they sounded familiar, and if I asked her if she espoused the doctrine of free will or determinism, she'd say, "A little bit of both, dear."

Mary Baker Eddy's ideas about health she entirely ignored but her philosophy she endorsed, especially her belief that evil doesn't exist except as a form of ignorance. "How true," Mother whispered, and she said to me as though I'd written the passage instead of just read it, "I've always felt I was on such a high spiritual plane with you, darling." Now I was too conscious of the hard-of-hearing woman and her shouting daughters on the other side of the curtain to let myself go—and too worried about my mother to be able to bathe in the warm restorative waters of her praise. But I could remember when we'd driven hour after hour over the green, rolling countryside and I'd been so happy to provoke my mother's spiritual pleasure that I was convinced I shared it.

When I got back to Kennedy Airport, I was so spooked by my weekend with my mother and sister that I rushed into the subway system and down to the Village like a rat scurrying down its hole. It was night and cold but within a few minutes I'd changed into my dirtiest jeans and my leather bomber jacket with no shirt, not even a T-shirt, underneath. I headed for the trucks but it was too early, just nine o'clock, so I went to Julius's bar and ate a hamburger and drank some white wine.

Suddenly I remembered it was Sunday. That must be why the bar was so deserted. Tomorrow would be a work day for everyone else. I worried I wouldn't find my fix tonight.

I ran into someone I'd tricked with ten years before (I couldn't remember his name but for some reason recalled his initials, E.G.G., which he'd had monogrammed on his dress shirts). We encapsulated our last decade for each other in a few brief sentences, two upbeats to one downbeat, which gave me that bravura rush of somehow being in control of my destiny and knowing exactly where I was heading, until he said, "How's the writing going?"

"The pits," I said. "I've just added another unpublished novel to my invisible *œuvre*." From New York stand-up comics I'd learned to make a brassy joke of my plight, the opposite to Midwestern ways, which for my parents' generation dictated hiding failure and for mine providing a full, unhappy confession.

"Oh, well," he said, "keep up the good fight." His bromide was so formulaic that it constituted a dismissal; I looked into the mirror behind the bar to see that he'd caught the eye of a guy the age I'd been when he'd seduced me. The few words we'd exchanged, however painful, had repatriated me to New York. On a good day I could walk down Christopher Street and know every twentieth guy, know to nod at him, even know a scrap of personal gossip about him, but tonight I'd been desperate to exist if only for a few seconds in someone's familiar eyes, no matter whose.

I walked down Christopher to the docks, passing a few roving packs of noisy men in leathers and denims. Before, in the sixties, gay men had dressed with care in pressed trousers and pastel-colored cashmere sweaters under Burberry raincoats or, more usually, tan windbreakers cut short enough to reveal the basket and buns. Guys had street-cruised at any hour back then and sought to "turn a trick" (as both gays and prostitutes put it)—an hour or a whole night at home that began with a drink and a bit of conversation and ended between sheets. Now, since the innovation of the back room, all sex took place only very late and while still partially clothed and in public or semi-public places where no talk was required. In fact the least word broke the spell.

This vow of silence had eliminated the last link with the old, established world of man and woman, the one in which sexuality was used as a bright bait, as reward or recompense, in a game that otherwise concerned suitable pairings, the suitability determined by money, age, religion, race. Gay *couples* might still observe the familiar conventions, but for that very reason gay men looked down on marriage itself as retrograde. Perhaps that's why gay couples were usually relegated to Brooklyn Heights (if they were dully domestic) or the Upper East Side (if they were stylish) or West (if bookish)—anywhere out of sight of these bold, laughing Villagers with their mustaches, ringing voices, their clothes contrived as erotic advertisement, their warm, seasoned faces, just a bit lined and vulpine from so many nights on the hunt, their scent-free bodies molded, more and more, by black leather since the sadistic was the only look that went well with extreme pallor.

At four in the morning I discovered beside a warehouse dock, wedged between two trucks, a man-mountain being ascended by five alpinists. Here was a huge, barrel-chested man, strong all over, devoid of the sculpted definition of a gym-built body; no, he was like a turn-of-the-century wrestler, hair brilliantined and parted in the middle, mouth engulfed by a handlebar mustache flowing directly into shaggy sideburns, the shoulders like boulders in cream, the oiled chest broad and the calves encased in knee-high black stockings held up by garters. I couldn't see him very clearly but I could see my Gulliver accepting the feverish attention of these five Lilliputians.

I was taller and stronger than his admirers but Gulliver submitted to us all with the egalitarianism of passivity—anyone could get a grab of him. I tried to push the others aside but they came clawing and chewing back, like a litter of newborn pups fighting for their mother's teats.

After a cop car glided slowly past and frightened us, I said, "Why don't you guys come just around the corner to my place?" Once Gulliver agreed the others fell in behind him. They didn't trust me not to exclude them at the last moment so stuck as close to their leader as Fafner to the Rheingold.

In my tiny, dirty, neglected apartment, my studio with the barred windows and the sour smell of mildewed bathroom tiles and the sharp, chemical odor of roach spray (odor of burning rust), I pushed aside my still unpacked bag and pulled my two mattresses onto the floor. Within seconds the elves had undressed their giant, and one after another they sat on his long, thick penis. I whispered into his ear, "When they leave, stay with me and sleep over." As the dawn light entered my dark room like a Michelangelo releasing a figure from stone, it chiseled more and more detail into the David's back and buttocks, which were pounding with powerful strokes into the fourth of the five tiny guests, pile-driving this guy, too, into a moaning, swooning climax until his fist foamed over with spurts of sperm.

At last they were all smiling and sipping cups of instant coffee they had to share (I had only two cups). They were dancing on one foot and staggering as they stepped into fancy bikini underwear, the sort a Spanish mother might buy in packs of five in a Newark shopping mall. They wriggled into jeans and finger-combed raven-black hair as they took turns looking at themselves in a broken shard of mirror they passed around. At last they were gone. Now the sun had sculpted my big captive much too long and left him flawed, passing directly from the ideal lineaments of a Greek deity to the deformities of a late Roman statuette of a comic character. Even his skin no longer looked like sugar dissolving in a spoon but had taken on the grainy, tobacco-stained hue of old piano keys.

I assumed his exertions had exhausted him, but no, he mounted me, too, not with a cocksman's challenge to himself to plug every hole but rather with a rhythm that struck me as machine powered, intentionless and unstoppable. When it was over he turned into a sad, heavy man.

"When I was growing up," he said, after we'd talked a while, "everyone made fun of me. They called me the Doofus."

"What's that?" I asked.

"What do you mean, what's that? Don't you know what a doofus is? It's an idiot, a moron, a retard. You see, everyone in my family—my mother and father and my brother, they're all slow, they're retarded, and they can't work. I'm the only person in the family who can do things like read and write and add and drive a car and cash checks. I'm no genius. I never graduated high school. But I can look after the others. I work for the Automobile Association of America. I work nights. I dispatch repair trucks to accidents and breakdowns. I can't read real books—and the news on television? That's too hard for me."

"It's hard for everyone," I said suavely.

"Not for you, not for most people. But I'm just a doofus, I guess."

I kissed his oily forehead. We were still lying on a bare mattress although the sun had become as bright as it was going to get today. The doofus had put on a pair of boxer shorts covered with brown diamonds. I suppose modesty was suitable to someone who had so much to hide and whose attributes were so in demand. I wanted to write, to call my mother, to eat, to check in with my friends, but here I had beside me this sexual prodigy who'd turned into a sad, struggling human being, and if I put it to myself that way I did so because, earlier, sexual desire had blinded me to his suffering humanity.

His back was covered with boils and his teeth were etched in scum; these afflictions seemed like those of a punished Job or a half-human Caliban. Or maybe he seemed more like an erotic golem about to revert to mud and straw, having served his master by servicing him. Even these comparisons were the idle, systemic chatter of an over-educated, undisciplined mind, one that couldn't come to terms with the Doofus and what he represented.

"Did you ever date girls?" I asked.

"Nah, what goil—" he had a Brooklyn accent—"what goil is gonna wanna be seen wit' me, a guy like me? Huh? I ask you. . . . Nah, I stick with the fellas. All these little guys are real nice to me—"

"Well, sure they are," I said, "considering you're a sexual maestro!"

"A what?"

"Well, you're great sex."

"Thanks. I dunno. Anyway, there's no future with guys. They all like me till they come, then they wanna get rid of me. *You* prob'ly wanna get rid of me, right? You know, you remind me of this other guy I met, this poet guy, I think he said he was a poet, anyway a hell of a nice fella, who lives in a house with a red door on, what is that, East Eleventh Street?"

"Tenth," I said. "Is he called Tom? Is he the poetry editor of a magazine?"

"Dunno—"

"Thick black glasses, bald, bow tie, looks like Mr. Magoo in the comics?"

"Yeah, that's the guy."

"Yeah, that's Tom."

Suddenly I was delighted by this coincidence in Tom's and my taste. Just when I thought I'd surrendered to my most exaggerated predilection for a man covered with boils, an Atlas who held a world of sorrows on his shoulders, I realized I wasn't alone in appreciating his monstrous gift. His appetite hadn't won him any girls, it excited most men but didn't hold them, and yet Tom and I had singled him out, just as he'd found us or at least in my case allowed himself to end up on my sweat-soaked mattress after a troupe of perverse *amoretti* had tiptoed away, flambeaux held high, leaving behind the satyr and his willing nymph.

So many comparisons, classical or Biblical, did not prevent me from wondering if I could live with the Doofus. I knew that I was capable of jerking off for years to come thinking about him; now that the years have come and gone I can swear to the accuracy of my prediction. But if he was all I desired, or what I desired most, could I surrender everything else to him, even my long, tormented dream of Sean?

I called Sean and found out that his Nuyorican poet had dropped him. I invited him into the city and we had dinner, just in a cheap little joint, something I could afford, a coffee shop near where I lived, although it had a small glassed-in terrace giving on Hudson Street and its light foot traffic.

I didn't ask him about the end of his affair with Angel because I didn't want to become his confidant. I wanted in his eyes to remain a potential lover, in the hope that absence had regilded my aureole—although I'm sure now (and suspected even then) that things don't work that way: once friendship has demagnetized someone, he never again becomes attractive (in French the word for "magnet," *aimant*, is just one letter longer than the word for "lover").

As the silences collected around us once again, Sean punctuated them by singing in his booming baritone voice little snatches of melody, including the opening four notes of Beethoven's Fifth (is it called the "Fate theme"?). The seeming aimlessness of the evening and our assumed casualness kept being underscored by this alarming motif, the knocker hammering at the door.

He talked of school, of classes he was taking, but I felt the presence of a new decorousness in his grave turns of phrase. If I used even the slightest bit of slang he'd wince. He narrated every stage of the evening, appreciating for us our food, our conversation, our friendship. This new man I sensed inhabiting him might have been an older lover, a professor perhaps, or maybe simply a teacher he admired, possibly an author he was reading—whoever it was, the gentleman had a highly developed appreciation of ceremony.

Suddenly I interrupted myself and said, "Sean, would you marry me? It's been ten years now that I've courted you. We've both been through a lot, you especially, but you'll never find anyone as devoted to you as I am. Now that we're entering our thirties, devotion—the longevity of my devotion—should count for something, surely."

He was smiling, charmed by my proposal, which wasn't at all campy; there was no suggestion that I wanted him to be my "husband." He'd heard me often enough rail against the "bourgeois institution of marriage," which in those days we pronounced as though it were a single conglomerate German denunciation. What I was proposing, he must have recognized, was a rite to commemorate a relationship that went beyond (as I hinted) mere passion and that was more permanent than the vagaries of desire. If he was always afraid that I lusted after his body alone, now I was reminding him that no lust could endure a decade. If he was susceptible to the appeal of ceremony, I was invoking one of the oldest. If he was lonely, I was here beside him.

"May I consider your proposal for a while, kind sir, before replying?" he asked, smiling, bowing his head in polite obeisance. We talked of other things until we parted.

Everything seemed damned and I stumbled through the rest of the evening with only the greatest difficulty. Now I know that this catastrophic feeling of hopelessness falls over me whenever I fear rejection, as though I've already anticipated the worst and suffered from it. But then I did not yet know how to interpret (and discount) my despair. I let it wither and kill my sentiments; the gold that played through my fingers smelled a moment later of ash.

If I remember that one evening out of all the hundreds I've forgotten, it's because that was the night I buried my adolescence—not an easy moment for a writer to say good-bye to. Sean was the great love of my life, not because of what we shared; we shared nothing, not even an idea, never an apartment, only a few times a bed. No, he was the fulcrum where the weight of my loneliness was balanced by the weight of my hopes—or should I say their weightlessness, since neither one existed except as an absence: I was lonely because I had no one and hopeful for a life I'd not yet started living. If I hovered so nervously around him, the trembling empty pans of regret and longing seesawing in the slightest disturbance of the air, I was able to do so because I never understood him. Love is a child who wears a blindfold and shoots an arrow; I was both sightless and the target, and I was certainly childish enough, in the triple sense that I never accepted that the slightest distance should separate us; I refused to study Sean to discover his tastes, habits, limitations; and I was certain that the force of my will alone could render the impossible possible and make him mine in a frozen instant of eternity.

After that night I never phoned to find out if he'd marry me or not. I never saw him alone again and only spent one more evening with him, and that years later. I was afraid to know the truth, no doubt. But also the slightest chance he might accept my proposal spread a salve over the inflamed wound where the arrow had pierced me.

Perhaps I suspected that I'd no longer be content with—well, I won't say the love he had to offer, since I knew nothing about his love, nothing concrete about him as a functioning person, whether he winced with fear or awakened with a smile, worried about his diet or panicked about money. No, what I no longer wanted was the dream of love he represented—or rather I could no longer wear his grey habit and vow myself to a life of perpetual adoration.

When I thought of Sean I'd remember when I'd first met him. We'd walked for hours at night in what was then called the "Warehouse District," an area of Civil War buildings that presently, in the early 1970s, was becoming fashionable SoHo. Back then the Village had been quieter, simpler, poorer, although even then, ten years earlier, on a summer Saturday night, the streets could become so thronged that only the roof was lacking that would have permitted us to call the whole thing a party. I tagged along behind him. I avoided mirrors, which would have proved to me I wasn't his little brother. He'd cooked me lentil loaf, talked about the Latin language, read to me his overly serious translation of "Lesbia's Sparrow," made love to me by candlelight before a mirror I looked into, with fear and shy delight, as one might look into a dream renamed reality. Then we showered together in a tall, narrow, sentinel box of a shower stall, as narrow as Forrest Greene's lifeguard tower. The shower was in the kitchen and Sean had lit the burners to warm up the room. The blue flames glowed through the translucent shower curtain. All my memories of him can be reduced to a paragraph and I feel unsure of each element in it, especially the lentils. Did he really cook lentil loaf or was that some other guy? I never kept journals and for years I drank too much. Even unaided, time itself (thirty-five years of it) wears away at memories, like pollution eating away the detail of the Carpeaux sculptures in front of the Paris Opera House, the blackened Bacchus with his raised tambourine sinking into a soot-stained circle of dusky, high-breasted revelers. And yet if a few scratches on a wax cylinder are enough to keep alive Caruso's voice, let these words, these few, faint memories, constitute Sean.

THE NEXT MORNING I spoke to my mother long-distance for half an hour, a luxury I could scarcely afford, but I was so relieved to find her convalescing at home. "Honey, thank you for flying out here. I needed that. And your sister has been an angel. If I can be grateful for one thing it's that my operation made Anne and me get back together. You see, it was a blessing in disguise. I'll be back at work next week." She chattered on in her bubbly way. What amazed me was that she could be so self-absorbed and yet so sweet. She never asked me anything about myself and yet she seemed to care about me. My mother was in a fever of self-promotion but curiously she took in every detail about me and my sister.

As soon as I hung up Max called me to tell me that my novel had been sold to one of the best known publishing houses in New York. "At last," I thought. While I covered him with thanks in a warm babble, some determined, frantic little person in my head kept repeating, "At last. At last." I was afraid of crowing like the cock of the walk; I affected casualness. A muscle that had been holding on for so long I'd stopped noticing its existence relaxed. I sat deeper in my chair, my lungs breathed in and out, fully, smoothly. Enfranchised. Legitimate. Never once did I wonder if I'd become famous, nor did I daydream about what I should do to promote my product. I was simply relieved that I'd passed over from that vast army of those with dog-eared manuscripts to the small elite of those with printed pages between boards. I felt that after waving my arm for hours, the teacher had finally called on me.

Max and I went out that evening to celebrate. I was too poor, especially after my ruinous trip to Chicago, to invite him to a restaurant, but he took me to an "Inn" on a quiet street in the Village we liked because of its shabby gentility—its deep booths, pewter chandeliers and its clientele of old women eating hot biscuits and gravy-covered meat loaf, this battered parody of respectable, rural New England in the heart of the kicked-out, bohemian West Village.

From there we went on and on, deeper and deeper into the night, reeling from bar to bar, stopping only at eleven to look at books and at twelve to buy a few records before heading back to the gay bars to drink till four in the morning, closing time. In those days on Eighth Street there was a bookshop many stories high where one could browse for hours, ascending from the new hardcover fiction on the ground floor to the poetry mezzanine and on up to the paperbacks about sociology and political science and philosophy. Friends ran into each other there—or across the street at a record store that prided itself on stocking the oldest or most obscure recordings of early Italian oratorios or never-performed Bohemian operas or on novelties such as the only extant recording of the last genuine castrato, at the beginning of the century, who at the time had already been a very old member of the Vatican Choir.

In these stores Max was imperious. He'd recently affected a monocle, which he screwed into his eye when he wanted to size up some young man or upbraid a clerk. Tonight Max asked a college student shy to the point of surliness if they'd received the new edition of Aksakov's childhood memoirs and the kid, perched on a high stool on the dais behind the cash register and reading a book, just shrugged and waved a hand vaguely toward the gleaming stacks of books all around us. Max nudged me and lifted his monocle to his eye, as though he needed its aid to quiz such a noisome insect. "Do you realize who I am?"

"Yeah, everyone's warned me about you. Guess you're one of the most infamous cranks who haunt this store."

Max was charmed by the boy's soft, breathy voice, such an inadequate medium for his scorn, and by the deep red color that was infusing his face and neck. "*Tiens*," he said loudly, "a rude homosexual, now there's a new one for the books." Like so many of Max's insults it was flirtatious.

"*New?* I thought you'd cornered the market on that one," the boy replied.

"Our respective positions are rather different."

"Yeah," the kid interjected. "Mine is higher." And he was miming the literal truth of his statement when Clive, the middle-aged, pipe-smoking manager, intervened. "Good evening, Mr. Richards, can I help you find something?"

"A civil clerk, for instance?"

"Did I hear you mention Aksakov? Right this way."

Max explained to me, "This bookstore is as famous as a Chinese restaurant for its rude help, and their abrasiveness constitutes a considerable local sideshow that the cognoscenti like to visit in an always undisappointed anticipation of genuine unpleasantness." Clive, overhearing the remark, removed his pipe as though to defend the shop but then thought better of it and put his pipe back in place with a smile. I felt a strong conflict between my normal meekness in dealing with clerks and my secret relish of the scene, just as at my age I half-identified with the arrogant youth and half with the offended adult.

As we went through the bookshop Max, his talk enlivened by vodka, hailed various titles as though they were charming eccentrics or delicious *grandes cocottes* he'd known all his life. "Here's Tanizaki's *The Makioka Sisters*. You don't know it? Now I *am* shocked. It's the Japanese *Buddenbrooks*, but touched by the delicate perversity of its author—not always so delicate since he takes as horrible a pleasure in describing physical pain as does Tolstoy. The description of sawing off a leg in Tanizaki rivals the same scene in Tolstoy's war reportage. Here's a strange trifle by Monique Lange, *Kissing Fish*, a story of a woman's obsessional love for a homosexual. Lange's husband is Juan Goytisolo, the great Spanish avant-garde novelist (*and* homosexual, one might add). Now here's an Alexandrian love story, written just after the birth of Christ, in which a gay couple is played off against a straight couple, they're separated and, just as in *Candide*, undergo many travails before they're reunited in a double wedding— you don't know it? How can that be? Here, let me buy it for you."

At four in the morning Max and I found ourselves seated on a stoop on Charles Street. It was a strangely balmy night. The sky was still bright with rolling clouds and reflected light. A breeze, warm and briny, was blowing although we were in the first week of December; I swore I could hear gulls calling in the wind. Just down on the corner of Seventh Avenue the changing traffic signal released heat after heat of racing cars, but here, just fifty feet away, we were in a side paddock of parked automobiles.

"Oh, it's so wonderful being here, Max," I exclaimed affectionately. "I missed you so much when I was in Chicago."

"You did?" he asked, in an uncharacteristically small voice.

"Oh, yes!" I assured him, resting a hand on his shoulder. "When I'm with you I'm always so excited. You're such a stimulating man." Every time I moved my head it continued to describe a motion way out into space; I felt a lunar freedom from gravity.

Dimly I became aware of a small, vigorous activity beside me, as though Max were scrubbing diamonds and rubbing them dry. At last he said, "I'm crying because I'm so moved. Of course I longed for you, too. I dreamed, I dared not hope—oh, my darling!" He took my face between his hands, pressed his lips to mine and filled my mouth with his thin, muscular tongue—I had the impression that I'd bit into an overripe, nearly flowing persimmon and a lizard had darted out of it into my mouth. I suddenly remembered that Max had told me he was always the active partner in sexual "congress" and I wondered what being fucked by him would be like.

With a start I realized that somehow in my drunkenness I'd given poor Max a misleading signal and suggested I was in love with him.

Now I was too polite to clear up the mess I'd made. Besides, he was so delighted, so gallant, so touched that I couldn't bear to cool his ardor. And, after all, he'd been the one to sell my book.

I hoped he'd forget our drunken love vows, but the next day he called me and spoke with a new diffidence. "My darling, did you sleep well?"

"Very well. I was so drunk."

"And how's your work going?"

"I *never* work, Max. That's one thing you must understand. I can't. I must talk to ten friends a day on the phone—"

"Oh, I hope I'm not intruding."

"But I *want* to talk to them. I call them if they don't call me. It's as though I'm cold when I awaken, spiritually cold, and I must talk to everyone under the sun to convince myself I exist, even to refill my word banks. What does Madame de Staël say of the French—that, unlike the Germans, they're addicted to conversation, which may be an art of civilization but also a disease, one that keeps the French frivolous, since they can never bear the solitude necessary for serious intellectual work."

"Very witty. Quite brilliant!" Max exclaimed. "You're quite right to bring us all back to Madame de Staël whom we've been neglecting *far* too long. '*Stahl*,' dear, is how it's pronounced, in spite of that distracting useless umlaut. Remember that her husband was Swedish."

He invited me for a weekend on a farm in New Jersey that belonged to his friend the publisher who'd printed my review of Tom's poems. When we arrived I realized that Max and I had been assigned the guest cottage on the other side of a pond from the main house. The three other guests were all in their forties or fifties.

During the weekend we went to a neighboring farm to visit a famous old gay couple in their late seventies. One of them had been a brilliant writer of late-Jamesian prose in the 1920s and '30s and had lived in Paris. Although his sexually neutral if erotically charged writing had been much admired back then, it had been largely forgotten since; now the writer, Ridgefield, had become all caught up in the workings of the American Academy of Arts and Letters. There was the question of whether a higher and a lower house should continue to exist or, more democratically, whether they should be "conflated" into just one body. And then there were the committees—Ridgefield headed the Citations Committee—and the luncheons, not to mention the star-studded spring awards day, open to an invited public.

Now that I knew my novel was going to be published I no longer feared being introduced to other writers, but I still felt I was an outsider—a status I clung to.

We were sitting in Ridgefield's old stone farmhouse at the edge of a wood. His brother had married well; Ridgefield's house was on a vast estate dominated by the brother's mansion with its eighteen-column façade.

A fire was crackling on the hearth. Despite Ridgefield's twenty years in Paris, there was no trace of anything French in the room. Everything was rigorously Colonial or English, from the fox-hunting prints to the rag rug on the wide-board wood floor to the gleaming drop-leaf table and Duncan Phyfe chairs. Piles of books and literary reviews in several languages were neatly centered and graduated, largest book on the bottom, smallest on top. Tangerines from some warmer part of the world filled a blue and white Chinese bowl.

Max had shown me pictures of Ridgefield taken in the 1920s by his aristocratic Russian lover of the time, a famous fashion photographer in Paris. It was hard to acknowledge that this twittery old man in a tweed jacket with the big, red, Scotch-nourished nose and fluty voice had once been the scrubbed ephebe with the prematurely deep widow's peak and the skin that looked as though he'd swallowed a light bulb, an inseam of light rising from each corner of his mouth toward the narrow shadow cast by the sundial of his long, straight nose. In his dark suit he'd looked like a boy going to his First Communion, inconceivably young and fragile (he'd been just twenty-two), incapable of holding a pen in his hand or a plot in his head, much less of writing a book about rural life in his native Ohio (the fictionalized memoirs that had won him his small bit of celebrity). Nor in his mid-Atlantic tones could one detect any trace of his Midwestern past.

For some reason the conversation turned to Jean Genet and Ridgefield said, "Oh, I knew him. That was a nasty piece of work."

"Rough trade?" Max asked daringly.

"My dear, a bit of fluff, I would have said, in prison drag. No, seriously," and he passed his hand over his face to wipe away his faint, wicked smile, and his expression, as announced, emerged perfectly serious, "I met him several times and he was a crafty peasant—*I* know the type. After all, I'm a farm boy myself!"

Everyone mumbled well bred chuckles of protest against the far-fetched humility of this grand old man of letters who was as proud of his contact with the soil as the Duc de Guermantes yet who sported in his lapel the purple and gold braided rosette of the American Academy.

"No, what I object to most," Ridgefield continued, "was not his way of lying systematically or lifting his hostesses' antique silver demitasse spoons . . ." Again his hand effaced a tiny smile, as though he were a judge who'd forgotten the dignity of his office and its objectivity. "No, those are mere bagatelles, worthy of gossip and nothing more. What I object to most is his way of wallowing in his perversion."

"Hear, hear!"

"Even if he'd presented his . . ." and here Ridgefield paused, searching for a euphemism, "his *uranism* in an attractive light, I would have objected. After all, a writer writes for everyone, for the man, woman and child in the street and, mad as it may seem: *They. Don't. Care* what Monsieur Genet daydreams about in his cell. And then (and here I'm being merely frivolous) I think it spoils everything if our . . ." (again the problem of the euphemism, causing Ridgefield to wrinkle his nose) ". . . our *Athenian* pleasures are described to the barbarians. I think our world is amusing only so long as it remains a mystery to *them*."

Everyone chuckled warmly and repeated his words in cozy asides.

"But *why*, my dear?" Max cried, smiling hugely, playing the straight man. "Isn't the duty of literature precisely the depiction of even the most exotic and depraved corners of human experience?"

"Well, it's true that Dante *presents* Brunetto Latini," Ridgefield replied, letting his little smile alight once more on the swaying perch of his lips, "but only to identify his punishment in *Hell*, which would be exactly my way of dealing with, uh, the love that dare not speak its name—"

"And that won't shut *up* these days," Max concluded gleefully. Everyone chortled.

Max seemed so happy to be in the presence of a writer of such consequence that he didn't pause to wonder if he agreed with him or not. Max's joy was partially exemplary: he wanted to indicate to me how to chat gracefully and clubbily with the great. The urgency of his enthusiasm was also proprietary, since if Max knelt before Ridgefield he did so only after having crowned him. Whereas Max would have responded waspishly to Mailer or Miller—acknowledged and, fatally, middle-brow authors (not to mention aggressively heterosexual)—his respect for Ridgefield, this obscure exquisite, was inspired by curatorial, king-making pride.

I felt my temples throbbing and my mouth going dry as I began to speak, "But Genet is no sociologist. He's a poet and his vision is lyrical—"

"A *poet!*" Ridgefield exclaimed, indignant. "There, my dear chap, you go too far. Unless an unbridled slut is your idea of a poet."

I blushed deeply and smiled faintly.

"*Really*, darling," Max echoed, a single line creasing the gleaming smooth expanse of his brow.

That night I drank a lot knowing what lay in store for me. I wanted to perform successfully, although when we were at last alone in our cottage and Max mounted me, I was impotent, which he didn't seem to notice. I couldn't tell if he was too polite to mention my flagging attention or whether he was indifferent to it. The next day he was just as polite and attentive as ever but he'd marginally withdrawn. He no longer called me "my darling," and I saw that I was going to be let off lightly. I'd not wanted to wound his vanity; I'd wanted to be open to his ardor; but my body had failed me and him and he was enough of a realist to understand its verdict and enough of a gentleman to forgive me.

When I returned the next evening to Manhattan I headed to a leather bar. I knew that many of these leather men were artists or intellectuals, but their manner, unlike that of Ridgefield's generation, was gruff and menacing. Or rather, they maintained an on-stage silence even if in the backstage corridors (over dinner or on the phone with friends) they chirped away gaily about holidays and movies. I found a young guy with a big belly and a yellow hankie in his back pocket who took me and twelve cans of beer into an abandoned warehouse. We each swallowed a half hit of acid, smoked joints and recycled the beer back and forth into each other's mouths. We laughed and hugged each other and smeared our spit, sperm and urine over each other's bodies. The beer, filtered so rapidly through our kidneys, had almost no taste though it was warm and foaming. "I like a good session, don't you?" my partner whispered; what I liked was that gay life had become so specialized, so shamelessly fetishized. I supposed Ridgefield would assign us both to Brunetto Latini's ring in hell, but I thought eternal damnation seemed an excessive punishment for a game babies in a playpen would have found wonderfully sociable. At last I staggered home at dawn, drenched, trembling and stinking.

I KEEP THINKING of a couple of Americans we met during the year before Brice died. One of them, Neil, was a heavy, stoop-shouldered man like me and like me he had a barrel chest that descended directly into a barrel waist. Unlike me he still wore a mustache, which was grey and so thick it covered his upper lip. His hair he treated like an accessory he despised and he batted at it with his hand or slapped it impatiently away from his brow.

His lover, Giles Satsumi, was a Japanese-American lawyer in his thirties who no longer practiced. He'd been brought up in San Francisco and had met two of my friends who'd migrated there from New York in the early eighties and died in the first three years of the plague. Giles was always smiling and knew all the lyrics to Nöel Coward's and Cole Porter's songs. He kept nodding other people into agreement. He never spoke about himself and seemed more intent on understanding whatever was light and amusing about his guests than in confiding his darker secrets or eliciting theirs.

Neil was from an old New England family that had made a small but necessary item. He apparently had a large enough fortune to finance a life of decorous leisure. But since they were Americans Neil and Giles felt the need to improve themselves even if in rather disjointed and ultimately useless ways. They studied cooking at the Cordon Bleu in Paris. They'd toured gardens as far apart as Vancouver, Sissinghurst, Nara and Florence. Giles had also spent months in Japan learning the tea ceremony and buying fabulously expensive cracked and mended pots and exquisitely crude Korean cups. They'd purchased a little house in the eighth arrondissement that for them was just a bagatelle, since they rarely lived there.

"It's so funny," Giles said in his choppy, rat-a-tat way that made everyone laugh but that didn't coerce laughter, "we're so naïve, Neil and I, at least about certain things, that when we bought this house we couldn't fathom why any residence would have eight bedrooms, each with a *bidet*, and no kitchen, until our French friends, stifling their *éclats de rire*, explained to us we'd just bought a bordello!" That one French expression, with its double *r*, so tricky for American uvulas, was so perfectly produced that I remembered they'd also studied French diction with a private instructor.

In honor of this *bonbonnière* from the turn of the century with its fake Greek statues of laughing girls in shorty peplums and slipping togas, its slender Ionic columns in the tiny salon that appeared to be made of lightly licked spun sugar and its courtyard fountain of a verdigrised Pan leering over his pipes while a drunken naiad embraced his hooves, Neil and Giles had covered their windows with crackling yellow satin curtains and their Louis XVI *bergères* with a faded lemony and beige tapestry. Everything looked as though it had just been pulled out of a dress-shop band box and flung with prodigal abandon over a bed. I could imagine a *cocotte* in an ice-blue peignoir trimmed in coffee lace smoking a cigarette in the salon and listening to a wind-up Victrola playing a recording of Mistinguett. The bathroom upstairs was royal, intended more for the piquant display of pink female flesh to special customers than for routine hygiene.

We ate a "gourmet" dinner and I remembered to keep up a constant stream of *oohs* and *aahs* and compliments, which sounded so exaggerated to Brice that he raised an eyebrow and suspected me of mockery until I explained to him later, when we were alone, that Americans don't mock each other, at least not with such subtle cruelty, and that praise any less dithyrambic would have struck our American hosts as poorly concealed disappointment.

After dinner, Giles asked if we'd like to participate in a tea ceremony. Brice had just recovered from a bout of wasting brought on by a bacterium in the blood related to tuberculosis and though his cure had been miraculous he was still thin and weak.

"How long does it last?" I asked.

"About an hour."

"And we're seated cross-legged on tatami mats the whole time?"

"On tatami, but most Westerners lounge about or even lie down."

"But I want to do it," Brice said. "I'm sure it's very spiritual and beautiful." The problem with dying for an atheist is that there are no normal spiritual occasions; exotic ones—or improvised moments—are made to bear a heavy weight.

Giles nodded and left the room. Neil sniffed at us a bit like a faithful family dog. He was companionable and heart-breakingly kind but he seemed a bit lost without his brilliant companion, so decisive, so magnetic, so full of amusing ideas.

After ten minutes Neil led us into the courtyard, where we were supposed to remain silent, drink sips of water from the fountain (this absurd fountain of a lean, leering Pan and a lubricious maiden). Neil said, "We're purifying ourselves of the dust from the outside world. Our thoughts must settle." I worried that Brice, so fragile and bony, might catch cold, despite his many layers of shirts, sweaters and vests, but I could see he was concentrating and participating in everything with great seriousness.

Brice *had* become purer over the last few years, since the onset of his illness. When I'd first met him he'd been a swaggering playboy, always sporting a well-cut jacket and a silk foulard (which looks prissy to Americans, rakish to the French). He'd been unduly fascinated by the rich and the titled—especially the titled, although that taste for old names can be read not just as snobbism but also as a form of poetry; in his case he never found any advantage in his collection of aristocrats beyond a simple pleasure in associating himself with a Golden Book of history.

Recently he'd put all that behind him. After all, he'd been only twenty-seven when I'd met him. Now, five years later, he'd aged by several millennia. He'd had to accept that he wasn't going to live, that he wasn't going to have the brilliant career as an architect that everyone had foreseen, that his promise wasn't going to be fulfilled. He had every reason to complain—of the pain that racked his body, of his bitterness at all his losses—but he maintained a stoic silence. At first, before he'd become ill, he'd been the usual French hypochondriac. But now that he was nothing but a skeleton, he made no protests, certainly he said nothing general or cosmic about the unfairness of life. He had prepared his little cache of pills with which to commit suicide, but just a few days before the tea ceremony he'd admitted that he no longer had the strength (either moral or physical) to take his life. Now he was prepared to drift ever closer to death.

It would have been irrelevant, certainly impertinent, to urge him to fight back. His only fight was to draw another breath, ascend another staircase, hold down another cup of soup, especially since he'd arrived at the point where the lightest sustenance (what anyone else would have considered to be "diet food") repelled him. Every morsel was too heavy, too fatty—one would say, too substantial.

Neil led us into a narrow but high room (one of the many *chambres d'assignation*?) that was carpeted with tatami on platforms around a recessed heating element and a bubbling cauldron of hot water. Giles was outfitted in elaborate robes of many layers, the outermost of black silk. His shoulders were motionless somewhere under stiff peaks. He was wearing a glossy round black hat and a sort of brocaded apron. He seemed a cross between a Shinto priest and a Masonic Grand Master. He was easygoing and quick to explain things and laugh at passing awkwardnesses, but nevertheless the room, the costume and the singing of the kettle made him seem more subdued.

Brice was panting slightly, no doubt from the pain of sitting on his uncushioned bones, the hip bones, which looked as huge as an old nag's when he was naked, and the bulb at the base of his spine where the coccyx had worn through, red and inflamed. But his eyes were sparkling with excitement.

Neil, in stocking feet and trousers, big belly hanging over his belt, scooted about on his knees, the grave, mustachioed acolyte serving the priest and presenting us, the communicants, first with small, beautiful and nearly tasteless rice cakes and, after the elaborate brewing and whisking, the foamy, bitter green tea. Giles explained everything he was doing. He showed us all the ancient elements of the tea service. He explained the painting on the wall. He demonstrated the method for receiving the cup and turning it a hundred and eighty degrees away in order modestly to drink from the inferior side and to present the superior side, with a bow, to the next drinker. We examined the black lacquered caddy and the bright green dry tea piled high to resemble Mount Fuji. After two rounds of tea the bowls were rinsed and dried with a smart swipe of a folded towel. "Now you're allowed to handle the bowls and look at them from every angle, since often a visitor might see a particular bowl only once in his lifetime." I could see that Brice was sweating from the effort to stay seated this way but that he was charmed by such a fussy ritual combining spirituality and connoisseurship. And he was certain that this was the one time he would be seeing these bowls.

Nine months later, on New Year's, just three months before Brice was to die, we were invited back, this time with Brice's brother Laurent, a big, strapping weightlifter from Nice who, despite his bulging muscles, was every bit as much an aesthete as Brice himself. Since he was shy and in any event spoke no English, Laurent was very quiet, but he, too, marveled at the refinement of the ceremony, conducted so improbably in this Belle Epoque *maison de passe*. The elements of the tea service were all decorated with silver and gold this time, since these precious metals were considered to bring good luck, appropriate to a New Year's Tea. Giles was extremely attentive to Brice, who was now ectoplasmically thin; his cheekbones looked as though they'd burst through the translucent yellow parchment of his skin. And yet Giles seemed driven to complete this dolorous if inspiring ritual in the most exacting manner.

Brice died and I received a condolence note from Giles and Neil. Six months later, Neil sent me a black-bordered printed bristol announcing Giles' death. I called our only mutual friend, who told me that Giles had been secretly ill for years, but able to travel, cook, garden, make tea. When his health suddenly took a turn for the worse at the end of the summer he'd refused all medication and faded in two weeks. Neil, his passionately devoted lover, had vanished, inconsolable. It seemed strange to me that Giles had never spoken of his own status and that of the five participants in the New Year's Day Tea, two were already dead.

SIX

The spring came and on the hot, sunny street in front of my apartment building I met Kevin. He was riding a bicycle, the kind racers use, all sparkling, wire-strutted wheels and a gentle, expensive ratcheting sound of well-oiled gears winding down. After I met him I'd be walking along the street and suddenly I'd hear a sound, perhaps it was the sound an ant would hear if it was pursued by a dragonfly, and I'd look up uneasily to see his iridescent wings descending on me.

I fell in love with blonds but liked to have sex with dark-haired men. Kevin was as pure as the youngest, most odorless blond and as sexy as a rancid brunet. Like a dragonfly he could hover so long in one place that he would seem stationary and his whirring wings would become invisible but suddenly he'd swerve off at a dramatic angle, sunlight mica-bright on his body. Which is just Kevin's metaphorical due, words to suggest his way of sampling me, as a rap composer might sample three bars from a standard.

I don't remember our first words. All I recall is that he was a bit of an orphan or a Cinderella. He was living across the street from me and two doors up, not in a tenement like mine but in a proper Federal house with a brick façade, a grand stoop, a red door with a glowing brass knocker and mail slot, except the door was marred by extra locks and the door jamb with four buzzers, one for each floor-through apartment. Kevin lived on the top floor with Hal, a musical comedy star who'd always played the young leading man (Puerto Rican rocker or Manhattan bachelor suffering from a bad case of anomie and exceptionally nosy friends). Hal had picked Kevin up when he was just eighteen on his first trip from Ohio to New York, almost seven years earlier. Little Kevin had been thunderstruck by the attention and had fallen in love with all the force of first love, that complete union of the physical and the spiritual that we seek to duplicate the rest of our lives. A kiss is a meltdown, a fuck is the first perfect Christmas morning, a three-a.m. embrace is tantamount to a delicately engineered rendezvous of ships in darkest space.

That quickly came to an end, that bliss. Hal was a famous cocksman, easily distracted, quick to follow any kid down an alleyway. Soon he was using Kevin as bright bait to lure other boys home.

"That must have hurt," I said when Kevin told me the story. We were sitting on his stoop.

"Not at all." Kevin had a dirty laugh, low and throaty, and it came welling up now. "I was a simp, mooning over an alleycat like Hal. I learned my lesson. There was never anyone less romantic than Hal." He sat up with that perfect poise of a dancer, someone who never makes an unpremeditated move unless frightened. Now he was becoming centered in his body as though reminded of that past mastery over his aching, heart-sore spirits. In any event, he was always suddenly stretching—dropping his head forward or raising one arm, then the other like a jerked marionette, or clasping his hands and turning them palm out while he pushed them slowly away from his chest—and I learned not to read any special meaning into these abrupt exercises. They meant nothing. No more than a thoroughbred's caracoling.

Now Hal let him live rent-free in his apartment as a houseboy, chairwarmer, package-receiver. If Hal was lonely Kevin would climb onto his vast slab of a bed, although normally Kevin slept in a corner on a little cot. "Of course, if he's brought home a trick I'll find the door locked and I have to wander the streets till dawn. He's even capable of waking me and saying, 'Okay, babe, it's over and out,' and I'm supposed to get dressed and clear out in no more than ten seconds—unless, of course, the trick wants a three-way, but usually Hal's sort of boy isn't looking for another twinkie."

"Oh, Kevin, how awful."

"Let's face it, Hal's a real pig but he's a sweetie in his grotesque way."

When I'd arrived in New York ten years earlier and was young even if shapeless, the famous Hal had fucked me a few times with his small, hard cock. It had been an efficient business. Oddly enough, his natural curiosity about other people asserted itself *after* sex. Whereas lust makes most men convince themselves they want to share secrets with the person they hope to bed, Hal was very efficient about undressing and penetrating his victims—his lean, taut body, broad smile and avid sexuality made him irresistible to most guys. That he paid no attention to what I was saying and seemed more interested in how my anus rather than my mind worked only flattered me. Afterward, however, he asked me all kinds of questions about myself, not with the bell-jar concentration of the hovering lover but rather with the gum-chewing affability of a buddy staring at the ceiling.

I told Kevin that Hal had "decked" me a few times years ago.

"Of course," Kevin said, as though nothing could be more natural, although he looked at me with a new respect, as if I'd just been promoted a notch. I was a "number" suddenly and no longer a cipher. A few days later he came back and said that Hal remembered me as "hot sex" and "a real interesting guy."

That spring was hot and sunny although a breeze was always flowing, as though Manhattan were a rowboat about to tug free from its cleats and drift out to sea. The city seemed deserted; maybe on our street people were either away for the weekend or at the office during the week. Kevin crept up on me—I mean my love for him did. Like an idiot I thought he was a poor little kid because Hal treated him so badly. I wanted to take care of him—conveniently forgetting that every other man in New York would feel the same way, not a particularly noble sentiment given how handsome and young he was.

Young but not fresh. Any mention of sex would automatically release that low, sophisticated gurgle of a laugh in him. If I ascribed altruism to someone or doubted the sexual link between any two people, Kevin would say, "Oh, puh-*lease*, give me a break."

A love that was once very dangerous, even if it's in the distant past, one continues to handle with asbestos gloves; I find my love for Kevin easier to analyze than to experience anew, especially since I spent so much time talking myself out of it with a shrink. Kevin came at me from so many angles all at once, like one of those karate demons on a kiddies' TV show, at once motorized monster and ubiquitous, half-hallucinated spirit. He was a waif but his body was so well trained that he was swift and strong. He drank too much and liked to be degraded at night, but the next morning he devoted himself to aerobics and vitamins. He observed everyone with the professional eye of the actor on the lookout for novel intonations and tics, but he could also discuss books with Joshua and be as urbane as any man of the world.

He'd been wounded long ago and needed love, but only laughed at my attempts to give it to him. He rejected my body but prized my "art," as evanescent as his own. When I'd make sheep's eyes at him, he'd laugh cruelly, but a moment later he'd be beside me, small warm hand in mine, telling me that he admired me, that he knew I could be a great writer, that he was certain we could be one of those legendary artistic couples, like Stieglitz and O'Keefe, like Britten and Pears, like Esenin and Isadora. (If he chose those examples perhaps he did so because they all spent so much time apart and came together only occasionally in incendiary, spiritual encounters.)

Kevin was right about one thing—living with him was the high point of my artistic life and with him I wrote a book that some readers consider my best. No matter if that book is not as original and charged as its defenders claim or as sentimental and obscurantist as its critics allege, what was crucial for me was the experience of living with a restless young man who would sometimes, just when I'd given up hope, make love to me and who flickered into and out of the fantasy of sharing the rest of his life with me.

He kept me in a constant state of desire—desire for his boyish body and manly dick, desire for a permanent love with a committed gypsy, a desire (as Mallarmé puts it in a poem) "to introduce myself as a hero into your story."

So many of the gay men I knew, even those who went to the gym now, were such klutzes and had never really been athletic, but Kevin swam for miles with egg-beater effortlessness. Or he taped his wrists, put on shorts and dusted his palms and performed acrobatics on the rings or the sawhorse, always with a look of open-mouthed concentration, as though such grace and power were only a question of forcing thought down through a narrow hose into his muscles. Shorts revealed his strong, unexpectedly hairy legs, so at odds with his smooth, nearly luminous torso. His prowess, as well as his air of being a disabused waif, made him irresistible to me.

Kevin came into my bed easily enough the first time but he must not have liked my body or quite simply perhaps I wasn't virile or mysterious enough to excite him. We never discussed it but he must have thought he'd given it a good try but sorry, Doll, being blown by a worshipful egghead ain't my idea of a hot Saturday night date.

After that Kevin began to stutter all the time. It was the strangest thing. He couldn't get out two words in a row without a struggle. Since I knew he was an actor and performed regularly, his stutter seemed an odd liability, but in any event I'd observed him speaking perfectly normally with other people and even with me when we'd first met. Now we would sit for hours on his stoop or wander down to the docks just a few blocks away through crowds of young gay men. Huge silences would hover over us as Kevin gulped and tried to spit it out.

Was he blocked because he liked and didn't want to lose me and yet he didn't want to give in to my oppressive love? My old lover Lou had once said to me, "You show your best side to your friends and your worst to your lovers. You're funny and lively and contentious and charming and easygoing with your friends whereas your poor lovers are treated to nothing but your appalling *mooning*." I tried now to stay varied and lively with Kevin but every instant mattered too much: love, in fact, can be defined as precisely that state in which every moment matters.

On a rainy day we'd sit inside my small room and listen to Satie's piano music with its strange blend of Spartan simplicity and *brasserie* roguishness. Some of the pieces sounded like the hangover improvisations of a jazz pianist goofing off down at the empty clubhouse. Of someone playing on the other side of the lake on a rainy October afternoon. I say "rainy" because the slow, angular notes were struck with the same irregular rhythm with which the rain flowed down from the sill of the upper sash window and smeared across the lower pane.

Kevin had thick, straight, reddish-blond hair, a domed, slightly bulging forehead, dark eyebrows that grew together in a pale blond union above his straight, small-nostriled nose, and this fuzz seemed related to the down dusting his cheekbones. He had a face too strong and ironic to go with the waifish role he liked to play in his old, deformed sneakers, as eloquent as Van Gogh's peasant's shoes. His white painter's trousers were baggy and his faded T-shirts had nearly effaced letters and symbols advertising the most ordinary household products or even spark plugs (the sort of chic my mother would have pitied as a sure sign of poverty—nor would she have been far wrong).

He was very bright and twenty years later he would become a talented writer, but back then I suspect he subscribed to the notion that an intelligent actor is a bad actor. He read but often the same book over and over again and I made him laugh when I referred to his "little book" because I constantly used diminutives out of affection although he thought out of condescension.

His life—his encounters with other people, his meals, his exercise, the movies he saw, the concerts he attended—*everything* he considered part of his preparation for the stage. For a while he toted around a copy of Stanislavsky's *An Actor Prepares* and although I never read it I suspect it, too, took a global view of professional training. If Kevin looked at an old woman on the bus he'd study the movements that betrayed her age—the stiffness in her back, her difficulty in taking a step up, her way of turning her whole bust rather than rotating her arthritic neck—and a moment later he'd be able to reproduce the entire ensemble of movements.

Sexual adventures were just another theatrical experience for him. With one man (a well known performance artist he recognized without revealing he knew who he was) Kevin pretended to be a Swedish gymnast in town for an Olympics training session. He had the falling cadence down perfectly, the unsmiling Nordic brow-furrowing, the outrage at American social injustice, even the Swede's indignation about personal questions: "I do not have the need, no, to be revealing my life to you just because we have shared this hygienic moment together."

"*Hygienic!*" the performer squealed indignantly. "You're totally weird."

"Now you are becoming insulted," the handsome gymnast muttered, clenching his jaw, grimly donning his previously neatly folded clothes. When the performer was introduced to a wickedly smiling, hundred-percent American Kevin a year later he was furious, then amazed, finally amused.

Kevin's favorite character was Pete, a painfully naïve Ohio hick just arrived in New York, a boy of nineteen incapable of sustaining a thought, a sweet kid who would unexpectedly become stubborn just when he was wrong. Pete would say at the moment when someone was going down on him, "You sure this is okay to do? My pa warned me that in the Big City guys would—wow! That feels great! Don't stop, don't stop."

One day Kevin told me that he hustled through a service and made a hundred and fifty dollars for each trick he turned. "But I have to get stoned to go through with it and then the money I just throw away with both hands, it's dirty money. The worst of it is that it's almost impossible for an actor known to be gay to work—"

"Why?"

"No one wants to see the fag kiss the girl on stage."

"And if the play is gay?"

"Everyone prefers to see a genuine male breeder kiss the boy, sure-fire Academy Award or Tony, what talent, what courage."

"I'm sure you're right. . . ."

"It's one thing to suspect me of being a fag, but if they know for sure I'm a whore—"

"No one would know who hadn't hired you."

"All the more reason to despise me. Johns resent having to pay. Even if the idea of paying (and controlling) someone excites them in advance, after they come they feel insulted. That's why we make them pay in advance—" (his use of *we* congealed my blood)—"not just because they might try to welch out on us but also to spare their feelings."

"You must get some weird characters," I said, wondering if he'd let me hire him.

"I scarcely remember them, it all goes past in a drugged haze."

"Do you play Pete with them?"

"No. I tried. But Pete's too vulnerable. One guy even beat him up— *me* up."

I could see perfectly clearly that by confiding in me Kevin was trying to turn me into a big sister rather than a lover. Love thrives on mystery and if Kevin told me about his hemorrhoid ("I don't see what all the fuss is about, I just poke it back in with a finger and then get fucked with nothing but really big dicks, it's the little red jabbers that can do a woman in"), he was so open in order to repel me. What he didn't realize was that this usually sound technique only endeared him to me all the more because it strengthened the guise that had become so touching to me: beautiful boy with a sweet face whom New York had destroyed. Once I'd held his sinewy, slender waist in my hands, my hands could not forget the feel of steel sliding under silk. If I looked at him too longingly his wildcat laugh—dirty, deprecating and spontaneous—would come geysering up. "Oh, dear, look at the lovesick cow," he'd say, pointing at me. I'd have to laugh, too, that bitter, grudging laugh at one's own expense that the French call "a yellow laugh" (*un rire jaune*).

I suppose my love tapped the same sources that feed the public worship of movie stars: I was privy to (and could sympathize with) the small setbacks and passing crises of a demigod I should by all rights have envied and feared from the foot of the throne or even the back of the audience hall.

Kevin would nudge me when we passed a guy he fancied: a guy with grease on his forearm and barring his T-shirt with a bend sinister, caste marks he'd picked up by working under his car; a sweaty black teenager, all knobby knees like a yearling, who was dribbling a basketball across the open court on the corner of Sixth Avenue and Third Street, suddenly shouting to a buddy so that the veins stood out on his long neck, Adam's apple jutting out like a sharp elbow poking through black velvet; a beefy boy tongue-kissing his girl on a bench, his crotch swelling with a half erection ("a Hollywood loaf," as Kevin termed it, for some reason). Kevin's New York was full of startled black eyes, taut tummies seen in a flash when a hand brushed a T-shirt aside, a postal worker ruffling the hair of a blushing trainee, the full-lipped open mouth of a baker asleep on the subway at four in the morning as he headed for work and we headed home to bed—a whole democratic gang of lovers, all of them unaware of how Kevin was mentally snapping and cropping them.

We had our pilgrimages to make, including one to a foul pizza joint on Bleecker. Its only attraction was the guy who fed the oven with dough, whose uniform was unbuttoned enough to show he had a "perfect eagle" of black hair covering his chest. Kevin, from the waist up, was entirely hairless, his upper body marked by nothing more serious than a scattering of freckles on his shoulders. But precisely his own blond smoothness made him feel a child's vaguely longing curiosity about hairy men; his weak-kneed desire and envy he controlled by stylizing. He'd say, "I'm going to swoon. Did you get a gander of that chest hair? Oh, God, I could sleep till dawn on that fur pillow. And did you see the buns? He makes my panties wet."

I was a true believer whose faith is only confirmed when his messiah declares his apostasy, when the world doesn't end as predicted, when the priest himself defiles the temple. The more Kevin drooled over other guys the more I coveted him. The more he pointed out his own faults—his "washed-out coloring," his "pigmy size," his "seventeen cowlicks"—the more my imagination turned them into virtues. The more he violated his own dignity, calling his anus his "twat," his cock his "clit," his bleeding hemorrhoid his "period," the more he pretended we were just two Ohio housewives on a Manhattan spree, the more I saw him as my furry-flanked satyr, my archaic Arcadian, my sylvan prince.

AT THE END of June Joshua was planning to sail to Europe with Eddie. I was jealous like Janus—jealous of Eddie for spiriting

Joshua away, jealous of Joshua for his intimacy with this famous poet. For Eddie had in the last year, with the publication of his epic, become the most respected American poet of the day, although he'd long been the most notorious, since he was a millionaire whose childhood had been il-luminated by the glare of grotesque publicity—a suicide, a suspected murder and especially the twinned themes of custody and alimony, love and money. Joshua and Eddie had been friends since they'd first met ten years earlier on a train. At that time Eddie had yet to win his first national book award and Joshua was just an assistant professor at Harvard, teach-ing in a celebrated program, "Humanities 6." Joshua had managed to in-vite Eddie to give a reading at Harvard and though Eddie was too much an old-fashioned aesthete and dandy to be grateful for anything so public and transitory as an appearance in no matter how august an institution, the favor was registered if not mentioned and it lent the right tone to a friendship that quickly flourished for an altogether different reason: Joshua had a sense of fun.

He'd make the pilgrimage on a weekend once a month to Eddie's house in a New England village, a house that would have been perfectly ordinary except that every object in it had figured in an unforgettable poem. There Joshua and Eddie would cook pasta recipes Joshua had brought back from Italy, reread Elizabeth Bowen's *To the North* or Eleanor Ross Taylor's collection of poems, *Welcome, Eumenides!*, listen to a record-ing of "the boys" (the duo-pianists Smith and Watson) playing Fauré's *Dolly Suite*. The alternately jaunty and melancholy passages of this *faux*-naïve music for a sophisticated child scored the light-fingered dynamism underlying the apparent indolence of their long mornings established by the Hu Kwa tea steeping in the blue and white pot, the rustling of their silk dressing gowns, the blue smoke rising from Eddie's single Gauloise of the morning, the scattered pages of the *TLS* and by the combined smells of the cigarette, the smoky tea and the pot-pourri in the entrance hall that Eddie kept refreshing by soaking the dried flowers with drops of orange essence.

In the winter they'd go out for long walks down to the harbor, then crunch their way back home through the snow that the evening was already turning blue. They'd beat their hands to stay warm and smell the smoke from log fires, so sad because it suggested family life. They'd quote lines from Elizabeth Bishop in an antiphony made visible by the misty breath trailing from their mouths, look up to see the ruby lamp hanging above Eddie's upstairs dining room table. In the summer they'd take the sun on the highest terrace and peer down into a garden where a famously hermetic novelist could be seen pacing back and forth alone behind his agent's house ("We've seen him!" they whispered to the others, triumphant, that evening over cocktails. "That is, we've sighted his limp. He *has* a limp. I've seen him, *you* haven't. What? A black turtleneck").

If Joshua had been the usual American academic—pedantic, incurious, obsessed with departmental politics—he could never have become intimate with Ariel-Eddie. But Joshua never lectured, loved gossip, always won at charades, knew how to tease the local ladies, several of whom had already made reluctant star turns in the magic theater of Eddie's verse. Joshua had found just the right way to cite Shakespeare or Sidney, with unsounded depths of veneration that didn't paralyze one's own playfulness (in a charade Joshua acted out, none too convincingly, the line, "Ill met by moonlight . . .").

Eddie, who was almost a decade older than Joshua, liked to fuss over Joshua's fragile health ("Sit over there in the high-backed chair, there's a bit of a draft hitting the loveseat, though why I'll never know, must be the churning of angels' wings"). Eddie also upbraided him for his laziness ("At least I have some laurels to rest on," Eddie said, "whereas your mere *two* titles are rather scant foliage, though dense enough, admittedly, to seat you comfily for life in the Harriet Smith Silverstein Cushy Chair of Renaissance Studies").

"Some of us have to *work* for a living," Joshua stoutly called out, even if he was terribly hurt by Eddie's harping on his slender output and the name of his absurd professorship. "Ah, yes, whereas I merely live to work," Eddie replied.

He always had the last word. Of a new Japanese painting he said, "It's the usual swirls before pines." When he came back from a trip to Asia and his first taste of opium, one of the ladies asked him if it caused impotence and he replied, "Poppycock." The occasionally soggy puns in his conversation and his sometimes tedious adherence to all forms of parlor games were five-finger exercises for the flashy word play and formal trickiness of his long poems, in which virtuosity was always transposed up a note into wisdom. No wonder he liked French piano music, which at its best kept the same proportions of parody, parlor fun and stabbing beauty.

"How can he be so cruel?" Joshua asked me. "Teasing me about my output, when he knows I suffer terribly from writer's block. And of course I could point out that teaching is grueling work, not that he's ever had to think about work. The other day when I told him I'd received a raise and was now earning fifty thousand dollars a year, I might as well have been discussing shekels or drachmas. He blinked and said, 'Is that considered a lot?' "

Although I'd read little contemporary poetry since university days, Joshua was immersing me in it again. Most of the time I found it tedious and obscure and I thought it kept its prestige partly because of its ceremonial past and partly because it took so little time to read and to write—a perfect medium for dilettante writers and theory-spinning critics. Each page of a novel could be just as well written word by word as a poem—a novel was six hundred sonnets. For a poem's formal ingenuity, the novel could substitute a far more gripping plot.

But Eddie was a genius who corralled into the sacred paddock of poetry his irreverent social tone and his sense not only for how things look and taste and smell but also for how they wriggle and crawl and soar. On the page his puns and acrostics and palindromes, even his calculated written-out stuttering, were so freighted with feeling that I didn't know whether to smile in acknowledgment of his skill or cry because he'd passed an electrode over the neurons in which my strongest emotions were stored. For if Max was concerned primarily with dazzling readers, even if that meant chilling them, Eddie wanted to play them, striking all their notes, the virtuosity his, perhaps, but the resonance entirely theirs.

As a young poet he'd written bejeweled verse full of poetic props (swans, lutes), and his favorite poet of the recent past had been Amy Lowell. But to this overwritten, turn-of-the-century formula, which made the poet weep but left the reader dry eyed, Eddie brought a sudden new intensity generated by touching together the two least likely wires—autobiography and allegory. Everyone else of his generation, following Robert Lowell's example, was beginning to write confessionally, with a new straightforwardness that felt as exciting as sin after years of the monastic discipline of impersonality imposed on poets by Eliot and the New Critics. They were the theorists who'd believed that a poem was "objective" and could be read—or written!—in exactly the same fashion in Oshkosh or Johannesburg, in 1800 or 1950. Eddie's early poems had conformed to this austere ideal, but now he was slowly inserting his life into his work—with this difference, that he couldn't resist allegorizing even his own parents' divorce, which instantly became a quarrel between Mother Earth and Father Time, a marriage on the rocks.

Joshua was uniquely qualified to understand *this* kind of autobiography. If he would have been titillated but left speechless by shocking personal revelations, Eddie's approach, which harked back to Dante's *La Vita Nuova*, reconciled the Renaissance with the second half of the twentieth century. Dante had alternated exalted but abstract sonnets with short, straightforward prose paragraphs narrating his various meetings with the historic Beatrice in the streets of Florence. Eddie melded the poetic and the prosaic, the symbolic and the literal, the religious and the frivolous into verses that glowed as though the glassblower had just pulled them out of the furnace, puffed and twisted contrasting colors into shapes, then pinched them off and set them aside to cool.

Since I'd studied Chinese at the university I should have been used to the idea of generating endlessly proliferating commentaries on the classics, but something in me was alternately scandalized and charmed by so much of Joshua's careful, resourceful attention being focused on just a few lines of poetry. I don't want to suggest that I was a free spirit, an artist, and that Joshua was "dry" and "pedantic" just because he was employed by a university and I wasn't. On the contrary, my skepticism about Joshua's work was a bit philistine, whereas Joshua's method was anything but mechanical. No idea was driven into the earth and no theory was allowed to crowd out intuition, *his* intuition, which he began and ended with and to which he remained faithful.

Joshua and I would eat our green beans and rare steaks, our "diet food," at Duff's on Christopher Street while downing a bottle of white wine. From there we'd go to the Riv and drink two stingers each, a sweet concoction of white crème de menthe, brandy and vodka. Often I'd accompany Joshua home and in his charming floor-through in Chelsea we'd talk till dawn about poetry over "splashes" of brandy on the rocks while listening to LP records of the music Balanchine had choreographed—Stravinsky's *Agon*, Hindemith's *Four Temperaments*, Tchaikovsky's *Serenade for Strings*. Our conversation would skip lightly from a discussion of the Wordsworthian Solitary to Elizabeth Bishop's old fisherman in "At the Fishhouses" ("There are sequins on his vest and on his thumb. / He has scraped the scales, the principal beauty / From unnumbered fish with that black old knife / the blade of which is almost worn away"). Or Joshua would show me a recipe in Marcella Hazan's cookbook he wanted to try out. Or I'd tell him about my strategies for seducing Kevin. One night we fell drunkenly in bed together but I didn't want to be Joshua's boy. I guess I wanted to be his equal, his friend.

Joshua was clearly in love with me. At the door he'd cling to me a second too long and his lips would open when we'd kiss. I felt that he'd been waiting all the long, long evening just for this moment. I resented his insistence on this tribute, his "due," which in my eyes invalidated his professions of friendship whereas to his mind love was the natural overflow of so much laughter, so many shared secrets. Whereas I was willing to tell anyone everything about my sex life, I was reluctant to confide my ideas even to my closest friends, not because I was proprietary about what lawyers call "intellectual property," but because, well, I scarcely ever *had* carefully defined ideas and, as a novelist, I was more likely to form an idea in a dramatic context I'd invented, in a conflict between two characters, than in the abstract. But with Joshua I felt the need to share with him all my half-baked ideas, except those about a sexual temperament that excluded him.

He knew that often after I left him I'd hurry off to the bars, which were slowly migrating farther and farther north, from the Village up to Chelsea, and farther west, from residential areas into the meat-packing district and on over to the docks. He saw my sexual energy as a force unattached to a specific object—why not attach it to him? He must have known that I would willingly have grappled with him in the hold of a parked truck in the dark at five in the morning—why not now, here in the hallway after the most wonderful conversation?

The irony was that when Joshua pleaded with me, he used the same arguments I advanced in trying to seduce Kevin. Because I was more abject than Joshua, because I'd already suffered through six years of hopeless love with Sean, I'd already heard all the arguments—from my own mouth—and I knew just how useless they were. As a consequence I was never angry with Kevin, just wounded or humbly patient (even more tedious for him, no doubt). But Joshua was frequently exasperated with me, since we had all the elements between us to create the "affair of the century," as he said, if only I weren't so hard hearted.

Joshua was the best friend of at least six people I could name and I was aware that I could easily be replaced. As Maria had once muttered, "Practically anyone can be my lover, whereas it's very difficult to be my friend." I knew that Joshua—famous for his warmth, intelligence, sociability and refinement—was drawn to me because he loved me, not because I was especially worthy of his friendship. I complained often to Joshua of Kevin's rejection of me so that he could see that I, too, suffered in love and that Venus dealt out her cruelty capriciously. Sometimes I'd picture myself to Joshua as a neurotic incapable of reciprocating affection, which was probably truer than I believed and less a permanent defect than I feared. After a whole evening of dissecting my spiritual faults, I'd achieved the unintended effect of talking myself into feeling miserable.

I needed Joshua. I felt he was my first real ally in the world of cultured and powerful adults, these men and women who published reviews in the *New York Times* or the *New York Review of Books*, who traveled regularly to Italy and France and knew their intellectual counterparts in England. As a boy I'd said, Isn't it strange that the writers of another era—Keats and Wordsworth and Byron—all knew each other, whereas writers today are isolated one from another. Now, from Joshua's stories, I saw that I'd been wrong and that the proletarian author of a famous comic novel was no longer poor but dined at the Garrick Club with the author of a four-volume family saga, a minister of state and the head of a museum. I saw that the same names migrated from the *TLS* to the *New York Review*, that the writers all met one another in Manhattan or Nantucket or Castine or Key West, that the editor of one literary periodical was married to the editor of the largest book publishing cartel and that anyone who objected to such a co-incidence was accused of "provincial paranoia," for the great idea of all these dazzling New Yorkers and Londoners was that obscure authors and intellectuals stranded on remote American campuses or at red-brick colleges were burning with unfounded and farcical resentment.

Joshua may have been incapable of driving a car or picking up a guy in a gay bar, but he was a shrewd navigator up the treacherous rapids of intellectual life. Through him I began to write "career-building" book reviews that were designed to win me friends in high places; he also kept me from looking like a fool in print. My Marxism, which could sound absurdly heavy handed and naïve if expressed in ready-made statements, became "*sympathique*" if turned into a lightly tossed off question. Joshua would hover over my typescripts with a pen quivering in the air like a barber's shears already clicking before they come into contact with the client's hair—and *oops!* he'd snip away an awkwardness, a smug bit of over-explanation, the incorrect use of *while* to mean *whereas*, a show-off digression, an overly explicit allusion, a gratuitous insult of someone I might need later. When he read through the new novel about Christa I was writing, he cut passages of what he called "aristocratic admiration," that is, excessive hand-rubbing over Christa's jewels or her thoroughbred profile. His censorship was less strategic than temperamental, since carping of any sort irritated him, bragging made him smile pityingly and only ardor—an ardent defense, an ardent espousal—engaged him fully. For instance, he liked my portrait of Christa because she reminded him of the ardent Dorothea in *Middlemarch,* his favorite novel. Best of all, he had the experienced teacher's Socratic tic of correcting his wayward, bullheaded student by merely raising a polite question. Perhaps his awareness that I was putty in his hands everywhere except in bed only added to his chagrin.

Oddly, despite his sense of how to maneuver he had a strongly romantic, idealistic nature, a Brahmsian composure and fortitude about the inevitable ache of beauty. In fact he liked to quote Wallace Stevens's line, "Death is the mother of beauty," in acknowledgment that what makes the beautiful heart-rending is our certainty that it is transitory.

I wasn't frightened by transience but by tepidness, the feeling that God was no longer taking pains but letting things go to seed. Chipped nails, sloppy proofreading, unreplaced burnt-out bulbs, received ideas, the unexamined life—these were the sources of my fear, as was any form of whistling in the dark if the dark didn't have ears. When I was with Joshua this fear of sentence fragments, yellowing bed linen and unrenewed subscriptions was held at bay, since he insisted on taking those very pains God had recently been so carelessly neglecting.

WHEN I ARRIVED at Joshua's one evening Eddie was already sitting there. I'd been anticipating this first meeting for weeks—at last I was to be introduced to my idol's idol, the man sensitive enough to appreciate my talent and rich enough to help me. Eddie had brought along a little package of things he could snack on. "It's all *feng* and *shui,*" he murmured, "and *wu wei* and *yang* and *yin.*" Suddenly he raised his hands and shook them and said in a high-pitched voice, "Lawdy, Miz Scarlett, Ah don't knows nothing 'bout macrobiotics . . ." Eddie avoided looking at me and when Joshua wandered into the kitchen searching for ice, Eddie subsided into himself, a grumpy display of deliberately cruel unsociability that Joshua, of course, would have admiringly chalked up to "shyness."

I was intensely uncomfortable. I knew that Joshua considered Eddie to be not only the greatest living poet in English but also our sole candidate for immortality. What's more, Eddie was fabulously rich and had set up a foundation for handing out grants to deserving artists. He was meant to be witty and worldly, but with me he seemed like a snake curled into a ball, the only sign of life a flickering tongue, for he licked his lips like someone who takes amphetamines.

He and Joshua referred to a new diet they were both going to try. Then they spoke about two of Eddie's neighbors, a mother and a daughter, but there was nothing I could add.

Finally Joshua "begged" me to read the first chapter of my Japanese novel, but we'd already conspired to spring it on an unsuspecting Eddie and so I just "happened" to have the manuscript with me. I read it in the deafening silence around me. Joshua's eyes were swimming shut, although from time to time he sat forward in his chair, as though by putting himself in a state of precarious balance he could keep himself awake. Each time he lurched up out of sleep he smiled and pantomimed opening his eyes wide. From time to time I glanced over at Eddie to see his reaction, but he was nervously pressing the fingertips of one hand to those of another. When I'd finished the chapter he didn't say anything. He just lowered his head at an enigmatic angle with a soft smile but no eye contact.

"Jeepers! It's late! I must fly," I said, and within seconds I was at the door.

"Dear heart!" Joshua murmured. "Lovely reading. I'm afraid I had too much Pinot Grigio." Still seated on the couch, Eddie waved with that gesture of unfocused beneficence peculiar to royalty.

I was devastated. Just at the moment I'd imagined I was about to win a word from the greatest writer of the day he'd refused to make even a single assuaging remark. I'd heard so much from Joshua about Eddie's exquisite manners that I'd assumed that at least I could count on *them*. Faced by Joshua's drowsiness and Eddie's rudeness, I'd felt my chapter dying, as though it were a fish drying on the dock, flopping a few times, then going still.

I wanted to die. I'd wagered that my life—humiliated, obscure, frustrated—would be redeemed through art, but now I could see that my novel would be despised or ignored, even by other queers, if it were ever published. I was on the curb as a taxi came hurtling by: I wanted to step in front of it.

The writer's vanity holds that everything that happens to him is "material." He views everything from a distance and even when the cops arrest him for sucking a cock through a glory hole he smiles faintly and thinks, "Idea for Story." As he submerges himself in the bilge of everyday life, all its disorder and tedium, he holds his thumb out at arm's length and squints, as though to get a take on this patch of swarming nonsense. Each new occurrence offers a new end to the story, in the light of which everything that preceded must be revised.

Now I saw the absurdity of this whole project. If I'd never really felt poor it was because I'd been inoculated by the sense that even being in want is "colorful" and in any event, viewed under the sign of eternity, merely an annoying detail. I was engaged in a conversation with earlier and later writers; our beacons were flashing one to another through the dark centuries: no longer. Now the diplomatic immunity granted by art had been stripped away, now all the normal rules applied to me. The lighthouses had been turned off.

When I got back to my room I was so desperate for love or violence or just a transfusion of human warmth that I ordered up a hustler. In a gay paper I'd seen an ad for an escort agency. Now a deep, well smoked man's voice was on the end of the line. He said in one breath: "Good-evening-Dreamboys-this-is-Harold-how-can-I-help-you?"

"Hello. I saw your ad."

"And-you're-looking-for-one-of-our-hot-young-guys-to-get-together-with-tonight?"

"Uh, yes."

"Look, hon, give me your number and I'll call you right back."

"Oh, I can hold on."

"No, it's a security check. Just to make sure I'm not wasting my time with a crank caller."

When he called back I could hear him bathing the telephone receiver in the smoke of a filtered cigarette and I could picture his chemically streaked hair, his sterling-silver ID bracelet, his starched white shirt with the soiled collar open to expose a tuft of black hairs nestling like brambles around a pink-gold crucifix. "Now, tell me, what kind of young man are you looking for?"

"Well . . ."

"Top or bottom?"

"Top."

"Blond or brunet?"

"Blond."

"Short or tall."

"Tall."

"Okay, we've narrowed it down to a tall blond top. Kink?"

"Huh?"

"Are you into water sports, CBT or TT or VA?"

"What's that?"

"Cock and Ball Torture, Tit Torture or Verbal Abuse."

"Well . . ."

"Are we a little bit shy?" A rich laugh that ended in a cigarette cough.

"No, it's just that it's a matter of chemistry, of what the other guy wants."

"I see." I could picture Harold stagily suppressing a yawn with an outstretched hand. "Let's say we want a Severe Taskmaster—"

"Who's tender later."

"Do you want Daddy to console his little boy after punishing him?"

"Yeah, sort of. That's a possible scenario."

"Now, I've got three fellows who are available. We're talking a hundred dollars for a full hour—on an outcall?"

"Yeah, my place."

"Where's that?"

"West Village."

"How did I guess. You have such a young voice—how old are you, doll?"

"Thirty-two."

"You sound nineteen. Now, I have Jason, who's a six-foot-two blond hockey player, twenty-four years old, a hundred and seventy pounds of firm, naturally athletic manmeat, definitely a top, nine inches and thick, low heavy hangers, smooth chest, hairy butt."

"Yeah, sounds great. . . ."

"Do you want me to try Jason? He should be at home. He's on call. And he lives near you, in Chelsea, you pay the cab ride."

"Okay."

While I hung on, Harold called Jason on another line. I could hear a muffled conversation but could not make out the words. Suddenly Harold was breathing smokily into my ear again. "It's all set, doll. Jason will be over right away. He's going to phone you now and you can give him directions for getting there. Remember, no checks or credit cards, cash on arrival, have fun, kiddo!"

Seconds after I hung up Jason rang me. He sounded bored and resentful and his voice was high pitched and nasal—a turn-off. I asked him if he had any poppers. He'd said he'd look for some.

Despite his voice I became increasingly excited about his arrival as the time approached. Usually I was filled with a hopeless lethargy when I contemplated housework but now I raced about straightening things, putting fresh sheets on the bed, running the garbage down. I showered as rapidly as possible, afraid I wouldn't hear the buzzer. I dressed in a torn

T-shirt and jeans frayed at the crotch. My mind filled with pornographic fantasies that alternated with a romantic scenario. He'd said he'd be over in forty-five minutes. I kept looking at the clock.

Joshua phoned. From his voice I could tell he was already in bed. "Well, that was fun, wasn't it?"

"Yes. Lots," I lied. I couldn't afford the time needed to be sincere. I didn't want to tell him how much Eddie's silence had tortured me simply because I didn't want to be on the phone still when Jason rang the bell. I knew Joshua would be wounded if he thought I had a trick coming, especially the sort of repeat trick who'd be stopping by for a sex date at midnight; he'd be outraged if he thought I'd hired a hustler.

We chitchatted about this and that and then Joshua began to giggle, half to himself.

"What's so funny?" I asked.

"Eddie's too wicked. When I asked him what he thought you looked like, he said: 'Minou Drouet.' "

"Who's he?" I asked, suspicious.

"*She.* Oh, only Eddie would remember her. She was this ten-year-old French poet in the 1950s who had little round steel glasses like yours and bangs and the French had decided she must be a genius, the new Rimbaud, and her poems were published on the front page of *Le Monde des Livres* and Cocteau—" Joshua began to laugh again "—Eddie reminded me of this, isn't his memory extraordinary?—when they asked Cocteau what he thought of her, he said, 'All children are geniuses *except* Minou Drouet.' "

"Listen, I've got to go, that's my bell."

"Your bell? *Really!* Minou Drouet, leave it to Eddie. . . ."

"Most amusing. I have a very hot date. 'Bye." I hung up, furious. I recognized that Joshua was so enthralled by Eddie's least witticism that he could momentarily forget my feelings and become uncharacteristically cruel.

In fact, I had to wait another twenty minutes for Jason's arrival. The tension, which might have titillated someone else, to me seemed almost excruciating. "Waiting," I said out loud, "is the best part," since in fact it was the worst. I tried to immerse myself in the psychology textbook I was ghostwriting, but I'd drunk so much at Joshua's that I couldn't bring into focus the page I was typing. Eddie's scorn—comparing me to a fake genius, a child, whom only a real writer had had the wit to unmask—had stripped me of my precious second identity, the writer's.

Would Jason be surprised by how young and handsome I was? Would he fall in love with me? I'd send him back to school, we'd become lovers. No, he'd be stoned, belligerent, he'd want to hurt me—he left me behind naked, chained and bleeding. He was small and hairless, good enough to eat. No, he was tall and hairy and strapping, a farm boy who wanted to plow me. . . .

The buzzer rang and I signaled back. I stood in my open door and heard his loud, heavy steps battering their way up the flimsy staircase; everything was suffocatingly erotic, an absence about to be filled. "Jason?" I called out.

"Yo!" he said. His voice sounded deeper, rawer than on the phone and not at all petulant.

He had a big head, bristling with light brown hair (*some blond*, I mentally grumbled, even as I found him exciting). His shoulders were broad, his chest heavy, as a worker's might be, but his waist was a slender, stylish column, which only emphasized his wide hip bones. He was certainly six foot two or even three, as advertised, but he was twenty-eight, not -four, and I became dubious about those promised nine inches. Suddenly I thought how numerical desire is, all a matter of number of years, inches, dollars, and that lust, which would seem to be the most concrete science, was actually a twin to mathematics, the most abstract, and just as a tailor's flimsy pattern is all penciled numbers scribbled on paper, numbers that will someday sheathe the body of a walking, talking man crossing the Place von Fürstenberg, in the same way a lightning mental calculator quickly jots down proportions to create a dressmaker's dummy labeled "Jason"—with this difference, that a big ass (as I could now see he had after he'd turned around) is a quantity that can be redeemed by the appropriate word, "a *hockey player's* big firm ass," although I was sure Jason knew no more about hockey than I did.

"Hi," I said in a low voice, standing on tiptoe to kiss his lips, wondering if he was thinking, "Shit, a romantic little kitten, he'll probably be wearing black lace panties." I shook his hand as an afterthought, which, because it was nonsexual, came off as more genuinely welcoming and, I hoped, masculine enough to offset the girlish peck I'd just planted on his mouth.

"Would you like to smoke some grass?" I asked.

"Sure," he said. He was talking too loudly, given our proximity. Surely his volume was meant to push me away, or rather position me at the right professional distance, just as a private dancer's refusal to lock glances or to

drop a glassy smile reminds the customer of just how stylized this performance really is, no matter how close the performer and client might be.

"Sit down," I said, indicating the bed. I sat on the floor and rested an
arm on his knee. I liked that I'd bought his time and even his body. He'd
be the one to fuck me, possibly even hurt me, but I'd be the one to indicate when we would start—and at any moment I could always say, "You
can go now," or "Let me sit on you." And if he might not have found me
to his taste in a bar, now I was the one who could say, "Here's half the
money, but you're not exactly blond and twenty-four and I do insist on
truth in advertising."

I'd switched the radio from my usual classical station to a rock program. Now I lowered the lights and lit the joint. As we passed it back and
forth I caught something dangerous in his expression and so I said,
"You're great, exactly my type. I've been looking for someone regular I
could see at least once a week," because beyond the soothing power of
flattery (fatal on a first date with an unpaid equal but reassuring to a skit-
tish whore) my words were meant to plant the idea in Jason's head that
he'd better not rob me or force me to come too quickly since he had a
stake in pleasing a potential regular.

But as I looked at "Jason's" face, I sensed he was too wild and destructive to be swayed by reason or self-interest. I said, "You know, when I
make it with a guy, I love to whisper his name—don't worry, I'm not noisy
in bed—and I'm sure your real name isn't Jason. Look, I'll give you an
extra twenty bucks if you tell me your real name and kiss me from time to
time as though you really meant it."

"Yeah, talkin' about money, where the fuck is it?"

I passed him back the joint and watched the brightening end illuminate his face, as though all the blood had rushed to his head and lit him
up. I gave him the hundred.

He counted it. "So where's the extra twenty?"

"So what's your real name?"

He swallowed. I noticed for the first time that his neck was hairless, not
just shaved clean but totally smooth, and that his hair in back fell in thick
locks directly brushing the naked skin. His head was so large it must have
been heavy; I could imagine its weight. He had three moles along his jaw
line that I wanted to connect with a pencil to form an isosceles triangle.
He had a tuft of baby-fine hair under his lower lip that the razor had
missed; now I was willing to revise his age back down to the early twenties
after all. What made him look older were the big knobby shoulders and

his hard, thin mouth and the smudges under his eyes, as though he'd been eating too much sugar and sleeping too little, the sort of dark circles priests used to ascribe to masturbation.

"Elmer," he said. "Gotta beer?"

I found him one and sat back down on the floor, this time between his legs. I gave him twenty more dollars. As I turned around with the money I looked in his eyes. When he took it I could swear his crotch filled out and what had looked like a broad, loose fold in his trousers suddenly stiffened. Getting paid got him hard. He passed the joint back to me and I felt how big and rough his hand was.

Now I really was stoned and it was as though the smoke I'd inhaled had lit a bonfire inside me. I felt lust playing on my solar plexus like a drum that the instrumentalist crouches to retune softly before pounding it hard. Lust was also rudely flicking my nipples with the back of a fingernail, then injecting molten silver into my neck veins and forcing it to rise through my head and flow in a thin sheet of hot, shiny fluid behind my eyes. My hands, without receiving any instruction from my brain, were rubbing his calf muscles, which now had passed over some line to become really and truly a hockey player's. Sitting on the floor I could catch the sour, mildewy smell of his sweat socks and sneakers and after the idea that he wasn't impeccably clean repulsed me I decided to like it. Behind me, in a V-shaped enclosure I couldn't see but that I intuited through my transparent skull, his hardening cock was pressed down by his jeans at an uncomfortable angle. I knelt and turned and buried my face in his crotch and suddenly his voice, a low, country voice, was coaxing me, as though a father usually too taciturn to say anything were forced to talk his boy out of a burning window into his waiting arms.

With medical efficiency he held one of my nostrils and made me inhale poppers through the other. He cupped my face in his hands and looked at it unflinchingly, with a huge, unvarnished power of confrontation. He spit on me, then smoothed the spit over my closed eyes and open mouth with that slow, rough palm. He pressed my face back to his crotch, which smelled of piss, he'd tucked his still wet cock away after urinating and let his piss dry on his jeans day after day—and I could hate it or love it, but when his fingers found my nipples through my T-shirt I knew I loved it.

He pushed me away from him, back on my heels, fed me another hit of the poppers and as I watched he lit a big, black cigar, rotating it expertly. He reached over and turned off the light. Now all that was visible was the pulsing tip of his cigar and the thick clouds of smoke filling the room, bathing me—and I remembered how much I'd hated my father's cigars and loved and hated him and now this rich, burning odor broke something in me, as though I were one of those glass vials within which Europeans store liquid medicine. The end just snapped off, easily and cleanly, of this sealed glass vial I was carrying somewhere inside me and I wept the liquid and became all greedy mouth and unstrung, undone body as Elmer, a big dangerous presence behind clouds of cigar smoke, pushed me down, this time to his exposed cock, stewing in its own subterranean liquors. It had a circumference as many inches around as it was long, a cock so hard I couldn't imagine it had ever been or could ever be soft, for it wasn't pulsing or still inflating, no it was just as thick and hard as a bit of root a gardener digs up after he's already cut down and extirpated a tree, a hard white root so old it's become mineral.

⟋‾‾⟍ J O S H U A didn't phone me for the next twenty-four hours, long enough for me to miss him. If my life was an on-going novel, he was the only one reading the installments. I realized that Eddie was his most precious possession and Joshua imagined he'd honored me by introducing us. If I were now to complain about Eddie's rudeness Joshua would never understand. Gratitude was the only acceptable response to Eddie in Joshua's eyes.

I knew that Joshua's boat sailed the next day. "Oh. Hel. Lo," he said over the phone, sounding a bit distant, spacing the syllables as though he couldn't quite remember who I was.

"Can I see you before you sail?"

"Come by for a drink at five, if you like."

I did like. He quickly warmed up. I decided never to mention my disappointment with Eddie, since I knew it would reflect on me, not on the great writer; if I bit my tongue I could pretend I was an "Eddie groupie," as Joshua called himself.

"Dear heart," Joshua said, holding my hand, "I *am* going to miss you." The shadowy hallway behind him was full of packed bags.

"But you're the one off to glamorous Venice. You're the one who will be swimming in the Cipriani pool—"

" '*Lourdes*,' as Gore calls it."

"—and squiring Peggy exclamation point about."

"Exclamation point? I think not. More like dot, dot, dot. . . . I always call her the laziest girl in town."

"It still sounds better than New York in August, stale pizza crusts and hot subways filled with piss and psychos. Well, no matter, my novel will be out in the fall and you'll be back to help me celebrate. I hope you make lots of progress on *your* book this summer." Joshua's book was a study of five contemporary poets, one of them Eddie.

Things went so well between us that Joshua told me he had a wonderful surprise for me—a ticket for that very evening to the Tiny Troupers. We'd be going with Eddie and from there on to a party at the Central Park West apartment of the dual pianists Smith and Watson, men who'd commissioned Poulenc and Rorem and Stravinsky to write them four-hand compositions. I wondered silently whether Joshua had arranged for the ticket for me a long time ago (tickets were very scarce) but hadn't told me about it until now because he wasn't sure I would deserve the treat, or whether Eddie, one of the benefactors of the Troupers, had just made the ticket available.

Some thirty people were seated in a large living room in the West Sixties just off the park. Everyone seemed to know everyone and there were lots of anticipatory coos and exchanged winks that filled me with hate and made me want to throw a stink bomb. At one end of the room was a puppet stage. The lights dimmed and the curtain went up to reveal a Victorian family of puppets at home with a puppet maid in uniform. The family members were all seated in a middle-class drawing room of over-stuffed furniture and heavy gilt frames beside the fireplace. The lady of the house had decided she wanted to play Phaedra in an amateur theatrical. Her maid, Lucy Lump, would of course be playing the maid Aricie and the stepson would be playing Hippolytus. The father would double as Theseus and the Chorus. After a brief pause, the curtains opened again on a set of a Greek palace. The hand puppets had an extremely limited repertoire of gestures: the double take (which elicited the most laughter), the conspiratorial glance at the audience, nodding *yes*, shaking the head *no*, clapping hands together in glee, thumping the chest in despair and, when singing, a violent trembling all over.

Eddie had commissioned a ne'er-do-well Alexandrian tourist guide who spoke six languages badly to write a ballad opera, providing old tunes with new words in a macaronic Italian-English-French. The opening number, "Allo, Phaedra," was of course set to the tune of "Hello, Dolly." Eddie rushed up to tell us that when the librettist had asked him to summarize the plot of *Phaedra*, he had offered to give him a copy of Racine but the librettist had said, "Oh, no, I don't want to get into details, just give me the gist." Eddie professed to find this impertinence wonderfully droll.

At the end of the opera the audience went into ecstasies. With my outer face I, too, smiled and cooed but my inner eyes bored holes of hate through them all and my inner teeth were instantly filed to spikes. I ran into Butler, the only other person present who was under forty.

"Isn't it all disgusting?" I hissed at him.

"Oh, groan, I can't bear the idea that Eddie bankrolls this frivolous rubbish whereas we're too poor even to Xerox our work to submit it for publication. If I were a patron of the arts I'd set up a free copy shop for writers, for any and all writers, no distinctions made, all welcome."

"Where are the puppeteers?" I asked.

"See those two old eunuchs over there surrounded by admiring dowagers? This room just stinks of money—*our* tax money, I might add, since the Tiny Troupers are a tax-deductible charity and therefore what should be public money goes to support them."

"If they were avant-garde," I grumbled, "they might be tolerable— didn't the Princesse Polignac commission Colette and Ravel to write *L'Enfant et les Sortilèges* for her salon?"

"Yes, that was Singer Sewing Machine money." Butler shook his head sagely. "It's pathetic how the times have changed. Now we just have recycled showtunes and absurd lyrics that do nothing but make a mockery of *two* of the greatest works of literature, *Hippolytus* and *Phaedra*."

"Eddie's own poetry is superb," I said, "but his influence as a patron is sort of questionable. So frivolous, as though he just wants to ridicule all the great art that has come before." I suppose we were both wondering how to apply to his foundation.

At this moment Joshua brought up the puppeteers themselves to meet us. That we'd not been led over to them was, of course, an unusual honor— so unusual it must have stemmed from the sudden desire of the camp old puppeteers themselves to meet the youngest men in the room.

"What an utter delight!" I exclaimed in a fruity mid-Atlantic accent I didn't recognize. "Do you do *all* the voices?"

"Yes," one of the men replied, who incongruously seemed to have just outgrown his clothes, as though he were a senile adolescent; his trouser cuffs fell at mid-calf and his sleeves ended three inches above his wrists. "I'm afraid I wasn't in very good voice tonight—the arias Phaedra sings are just too difficult, especially the 'I love you, a scepter and a crown.' "

"That's to 'A bushel and a peck,' isn't it?" Butler asked with his warmest, most sparkly and soft-focus smile, as though he were an old-fashioned starlet shot through gauze. "It was all deliciously amusing."

"Well, we're retiring after this season," the other puppeteer said. "We have a farm in New Jersey that a writer friend has found for us."

"Oh? What discriminating Maecenas still exists in this philistine age?" I asked, beaming, burning with avidity.

"Perhaps you know him: Max Richards."

"My dearest friend," I hastened to throw in.

"Yes, yes," Butler exclaimed.

As we all streamed over to the party at the duo-pianists, Butler and I avoided looking at each other.

Only outsiders are satirical about a party; the other guests are having too much fun, even if it's a tepid, ordinary sort of fun, to notice what's going on or to work up much bile. I was intimidated by the wealth and culture of the older guests. My father and his acquaintances were rich boors, boors I could easily dismiss, but here was a famous white-haired choreographer, talking about his secret passion, cooking, to one of the duo-pianists, whose shortness and gold watch made him look like a prosperous businessman—except he instantly began to talk about an Italian Futurist cookbook which calls for waiters to spray the bald heads of diners with warmed liquid and which condemns pasta as the chief cause of Italy's stagnation. The son of a Spanish marquis and an American heiress showed up with a kilo of Beluga caviar ("I found it at the Caviarteria, where my father used to buy *his!*" he announced with that fatuous respect for the habits and practices of his own family one often remarks among the rich, as though their wealth lent an Olympian importance to even their smallest actions). In a wheelchair sat a slender woman in her fifties who'd once been a famous ballerina; she'd been one of the last people to contract polio before the Salk vaccine was developed.

Soon we were all seated at six tables of six people. Butler mumbled to me afterwards, "It's Eddie, of course, who's paying the caterers, although he's pretending to be so grateful to Smith and Watson—a bit like Ronald Firbank, who slipped some money under the table so that his guardsman could pay the bill, which prompted Firbank to clap his hands and exclaim, 'How *thrilling* to be invited!' " The Tiny Troupers were fussing over each other's health. "I *told* you not to eat strawberries," I overheard one telling the other. "You know they only cause you to have mouth ulcers."

Joshua invited me back to his place for a nightcap. We ended up drinking several brandies and talking Troupers and Eddie and poetry. Joshua surprised me by fishing a tape recorder out from under the couch. "I just bought this. It's voice activated," he explained, mentioning a feature that at that time was brand new. "I thought I might keep it beside my bed in Venice in case I get a good thought during the night about my book."

He replayed our conversation. What I'd imagined had been warm, intelligent, witty chat between two cultivated men turned out to be slurred, drunken nonsense. Our voices rose and fell in shrieks and mumbles. Laughter rang out tinnily, fakely, and our voices sounded as fruity as old dowagers'.

At the door Joshua grabbed me and filled my mouth with his tongue. Overwhelmed by anger, I stamped my foot. I said, "No! Why must *every* evening . . . Oh, nothing. Good night. Bon voyage."

SEVEN

Max and Joshua and even Butler had gone away for the summer and I felt that the city had been handed back to us, the kids. It was hotter, more violent, smellier than in the spring, but at least it was all ours.

I seldom went north of Fourteenth Street, but when I did nothing seemed as muffled and elegant as the rich neighborhoods I'd seen during my week in Paris or my six months in Rome. Here in New York everyone was a "character" and a white-uniformed black maid walking her mistress's poodle was wearing green basketball shoes, whereas her white counterpart in the Bois de Boulogne or on the Via Giulia would have scuttled along hoping to be inconspicuous. Here in Manhattan chauffeurs in waiting limousines reamed their nostrils with a dirty index finger, wealthy women shoppers spoke so loudly they endangered the sales clerk's eardrums, a chic young couple outraced an old lady for a cab, a vagrant sprawled across a subway grating on Lexington Avenue was drinking and bawling out "I want a gal just like the gal who married dear old Dad." No one whispered as they would in a Paris restaurant nor did they cover their eccentricities as Romans cover their mouths when they pick their teeth.

It's wrong to say that North Americans don't have a Latin sense of theater about street life. Our theater, however, is a farce full of crazies, not a well-made boulevard comedy.

Kevin told me that he was fed up with sex and that he was entering a chastity phase. Everything with him was a passing trend, a New Year's resolution broken at the beginning of each month, since as an out-of-work actor he had to turn his life into an experience or at least an experiment. I was happy to join him in his vow of chastity, since as long as we observed it I could convince myself he wouldn't fall in love with someone else—and he'd let me sleep beside him. We were the founding members of the Society of St. Agnes, in honor of that virginal girl who considered God to be her betrothed. As a lapsed Catholic Kevin enjoyed this sort of Papal Camp more than I did, even though he railed against "failed" Catholics. "There's always a horrid moment," he said, "when all the Catholic fags in the room start swapping Sadistic Nun stories and stories about closeted Father Dan the basketball coach. I really can't bear all that obsessive wallowing." Of course even his objections only perpetuated what he was criticizing, much like complaints about the class system—an unhealthy commentary that only further immerses the critic into the system he's attacking, since snobbism and Catholicism are superstitions that can thrive on anything but neglect.

At first that June wasn't hot—not the suffocating humid heat of the usual New York summer. Or maybe it was simply that I was so happy with Kevin. I mean to say that just as I'd awaken to a room full of light consecrating this boy beside me, in the same way a cool breeze was always blowing through the big blocs of heat bearing down on the city, the breeze like an occult joy redeeming something stale and quotidian. No day was the same as my other days. Every day with Kevin was like a day in a novel—animated by observations, economical, eventful, intended—and not like the slow ether drip of ordinary existence.

We lay beside each other like brothers and children. Kevin didn't mind if I touched him, so long as it was innocent. Of course nothing I did was innocent; not even my sleep was innocent, it was shallow and Argus eyed, ever alert to Kevin's slightest movement, especially a shift toward me in bed. As he'd fall asleep his hands and legs would pass through five minutes of jerks and twitches and I'd prop myself up on one elbow to observe this fitful pianism of the body. How I longed to be the instrument he played and once I even placed his small hot hand on my chest so that he could drum his nervous tattoo on me.

We slept naked under just one sheet in Kevin's apartment (Hal was in Chicago in a musical). One night a cold salt atmosphere advanced up the Hudson and we clung to each other in the chill. There was nothing feminine about him—he was far more assertive, independent, athletic than I— but what I felt toward him must have been something like what an ugly man feels toward a beautiful woman. First came the realization that despite such perfect skin, despite the strength and elegance shaping every step, despite the panoply of personality rustling open like a peacock's eyed glory, never- theless at rest, naked, in bed, this bewitching person was just a small body, almost a boy, merely an upward tilt of nose and chin, two baby-pale nipples, a taut stomach, just a grip on an udder of hot, streaming air. Then there was the ugly man's longing, my longing to be married to this enviable crea- ture, a desire born from a strange confidence in the binding irreversibility of marriage, a union imagined to be entirely transubstantial, for if the bride changes her name, the groom changes his nature and becomes her equal, superior to his previous, single, unbeautiful self.

My head was full of these magical words, more like lights gently ex- ploding than pronounced words. I dozed beside Kevin in the still night as though we were two loaves the baker had forgotten and left in an oven he'd switched off. Through the open windows we could hear the hard, deter- mined footsteps of someone pacing out the dimensions of the night or we could hear a throbbing air conditioner in some rich person's window. But otherwise everything was quiet, dark, still, and in the articulated emptiness of a big summer city we were more alone than we would have been in a boat at sea or on a deserted mountain top. The digital clock nervously counted illuminated hours and minutes without any of the old-fashioned clock face's suggestion of eternal return. No, here each green digit seemed anxiously conceded, another chip placed on a losing number. Two guys harangued each other drunkenly, then a bottle was smashed and the voices, suddenly calmer, trailed away. My thoughts kept sliding obsession- ally before me, those same phosphorescent numbers twitching on toward a dawn that wouldn't materialize. I'd never gone so long without sex. I didn't even masturbate, though I slept with an erection tucked between Kevin's buttocks. Everything became erotic, the timbre of his voice, the feel of gymnastics calluses on his fingers, especially the ratcheting of his expensive bicycle gears unwinding, unseen, behind me, as though the so- lution to the skeptic's familiar objections about the weight of an angel's body to the size of practicable wings was a previously unsuspected and elaborate system of *gears* catching and slowing down through a dozen little downshifts, a sound like the patter of diamond chips on glass.

Now I suppose I wouldn't even start to fall in love with someone who hadn't indicated he'd welcome my affection, but back then I loved only someone who was unavailable—or, rather, *not yet* available. Kevin didn't despise me completely, any more than had Sean; in fact, both men admired me. The French divide love into esteem (the sort Corneille promoted) and passion (the tragic vice of Racine), and what I felt for Kevin and hoped to educe from him was Racinian, although I fooled myself into imagining that *l'estime* could serve as a transition down into that darkness and despair.

There's something much simpler that needs to be said as well: I had no confidence in my looks, in my body, in my sexuality, and I longed for a demi-god to confer desirability on me. Most people who are timid or unsure of themselves probably set their sights low, but bizarrely I courted men far above me. Just as I hoped the publication of a novel would redeem all that I'd suffered and worked for and in one stroke elevate me out of ignominy, in the same way I believed that a great love, magically reciprocated against all odds, would prove to other people, even to me, that I was worthy of such distinction. The milieu I lived in of actors and writers, who were used to miraculous changes in status, only encouraged my fantastic ambitions in love and art.

JOSHUA sent me a letter:

Dear Heart,

I was so wounded and, worse, angered the night you Stamped Your Foot, that honestly I never wanted to see you again. So that's where all the subtle exchanges and only half-transfigured longings have led us: the Young Tyrant has Stamped His Foot. If I wanted all year to be your lover it was chiefly, I thought, because we already *were* lovers in every way but carnally— the only way, alas, that counts in the eyes of the world, that place where, finally, all marriages must be consummated.

Did it ever occur to you that I also wanted you to fulfill yourself—and not just as an artist (that you'll probably do in one way or another, you're that driven) but as a man, I mean someone not living at one remove? I know how much you worry about being inauthentic; that's not the fear I'm playing on. No, I mean that despite all your years of therapy you can't seem to connect with anyone (maybe that's why you drink so much). Kevin's adorable, of course, but he doesn't love you. You're afraid of me, no doubt, because I'm older, more settled—"bourgeois," to use your word, one which erases distinctions rather than making one. How many years will you go on sucking off strangers between trucks?

You're lonely, driven, poor, and I'd like to share everything with you, make you happy, help you along in the world, release you from the drudgery, the need to do so much soul-killing hackwork. But more importantly I'd like to discover the body through you (you know what an innocent I am) while through me you discover . . . the deep-dish apple pie comfort of being loved, really and truly loved by someone alert enough to know what you're feeling and bright enough to fire your imagination.

Anyway, you Stamped Your Foot, the veil trembled and fell. I was white-hot with fury on the *Queen Elizabeth* but on the third day out Eddie said to me, "Look, Joshua, that nutty boy loves you; even if it's only half a loaf it is the bread of love. There's not that much love in the world. Who are you to refuse what he's offering?"

The rest of the letter contained gossip about the English vicar, Peggy Guggenheim and her hunt for a *retired* gondolier who might man her boat at below-union wages, the party at the Duc Decazes', the arrival of Grace with Gore, plans to receive Lillian and so on. But all that was there to deflect the sweet blow of his renewed love and its declaration. What a joke: here he wants to learn about the body through me, I thought, whereas I'm tuned to Kevin like a bird dog to a pheasant.

Kevin and I decided to live together. He told me that Hal's tour was over and he wasn't really welcome at Hal's place anymore, Hal had met a great kid, a fun little slave named Tony. "He's hysterical," Kevin said with a voice that sounded almost hoarse, an "exciting" register he'd found to lend a new urgency to tired expressions. "I was talking to Tony the other day and he said Hal was such a monster. He'd heated up a soup spoon and burned Tony on the ass. Tony said, 'I just *flew* across that room in pain. But you wanna hear the weirdest thing? Next thing you know I found myself backing up to get the other cheek burned, you know, symeh-, semi- —uh, symmetrically.' "

"But what's that got to do . . . ?" I was so excited by the prospect of living with Kevin that all these details irritated me.

"Well, Tony is a typically pushy masochist and now that he's wormed his way into the apartment he's getting *me* kicked out. No, I shouldn't complain. Tony's great for Hal. At last a little stability."

"*Stability!*" I exclaimed. "What lives we lead," I said in Joshua's tone of voice. Now I was impersonating Joshua, although all I wanted to talk about was our house, Kevin's and mine, *our* stability. "I think I'm on to a fabulous place on the Upper West Side, eight rooms for just four hundred dollars," I said.

"*Just!*"

"Well, I'll pay for it. But—" and here I thought I was adding something appealing to take the curse off the neighborhood and the pricy rent—"the landlady only likes fags, she lives in the building, it's a fairy palace, and we have to *audition* for her, I mean, she has to *like* us before she'll give us the apartment. The building is full of all these middle-class queens swooning over her, she's called Daniella but she's actually Armenian, *everything* in her apartment has a price tag on it, if you admire something—ashtray, coffee cup, rug—she'll turn it over and read the tag through bifocals and say, 'You can have it for just fifty dollars.' I'm *serious*. The point is that these queens are all competing to do Daniella's *hair* or nails—"

"Or walk her apricot poodle?"

"*Wrong!* That's the Catch-22. She'll rent only to fags, but *fags-without-dogs*, and that's a contradiction in terms."

"*We* don't have a dog."

"Our sole virtue, and how good are we at being fags? We can't bake, we don't do interior decoration, we can't burn hair. Anyway, put on your best clothes and smarmiest manner."

Kevin of course liked the challenge. He would have been too shy to meet an unknown sixty-year-old landlady as himself, but as an Upper West Side Priss who spends all day looking at fabric swatches, shopping at Zabar's for some mythically lean and odorless Russian sturgeon or eating Godiva chocolates with a chin strap on, stabbing out cigarettes in a pot of cold cream while listening to Helen Morgan seventy-eights, *that* was a role he could play with utter confidence.

In the early 1970s apartments were available because everyone had given up on New York. The city itself had gone bankrupt. Crime was on the rise. The streets seemed dangerous and deserted except in Midtown, where dark-suited executives and high-heeled secretaries were piped in underground from New Jersey and extruded up into sealed skyscrapers. By six o'clock they were all sucked back home and the district was empty. Property values were plummeting uptown and down. The Lower East Side (which only white urban pioneers called, optimistically, the East Village) had lost its bloom after a hippie had been stabbed in a soured drug deal; now the old Poles and Jews and Ukrainians who'd always lived there were creeping back onto stoops and the smell of dill and cooking kielbasa had once again replaced the sweet scent of burning marijuana. The West Village was sad, even creepy; a twenty-nine-year-old gay man had been stabbed in his apartment in the Village. Two more young guys were also stabbed to death in their Varick Street apartment. And the bodies of two others were found floating in the Hudson.

When Kevin and I went up to the West Eighties and Columbus for our interview, we felt a bit like pale mice darting up out of a sewer. I was worried that something awful would come off me, something like a roach or an attack of diarrhea, and that not only would we not get the apartment but I'd be eternally humiliated.

I might more reasonably have worried that Daniella would want to see our bank statements, which would not have reassured her. Kevin didn't even have a bank. But she was, fortunately, perversely personal in her method of selection.

When she opened the door to her apartment we were almost overwhelmed by the cigarette smoke. Everything was dark (no bulb, it appeared, had more than fifteen watts), torn silk shades dangling tassels topped every turquoise-blue Chinese vase. Smoke hung visibly in the air in long strands. In this dimness the entrance hallway, with doors opening up to the right and left, looked almost mythically long. What gave me a thrill of cupidity was the realization that the apartment upstairs, *our* apartment, was exactly the same size.

Daniella led us into a small sitting room. The shutters appeared to be nailed tight against the bright summer afternoon although one thin stripe of sunlight cut surgically through the swirling clouds of smoke, the sort of leak that might penetrate into a House of Horrors at the fairground and turn its scariness silly. She seated us in a pair of slipper chairs dangling fringe and price tags and offered us whiskey neat in oily shot glasses. Her grey hair, dry and spun high in a bun, was stabbed through by what looked like chopsticks; the hair itself resembled congealed smoke and suggested a child's cotton candy found by archeologists beside Vesuvius.

We had to reassure her we did not now possess a dog nor would we ever buy one in the future. "The minute I hear the pitter-patter of little feet, you're out of here!" She fixed us with a steady stare as she screwed a fresh cigarette into her grey-lipped mouth, small but efficient. I lit up a Pall Mall, adding my faggot to the bonfire.

"So you're friends of Tom and Tom?" Daniella said, mentioning the gay boys who'd tipped us off about the apartment.

"Great guys!" I exclaimed in a thick burst of smoke, although I couldn't think what else to say about them, since they were only friends of friends.

"Tom B. does such wonderful designs—I wonder what he has in store for us this year?"

In a panic I said, "He sure keeps us guessing, doesn't he!"

As it turned out, Tom B. worked up the Christmas windows every year for Harry Winston, the jeweler, sometimes nothing more than a palm tree of emeralds and a forty-carat Star of Bethlehem. Tom L., his "pal," as Daniella referred to any homosexual lover, was, as we later discovered, a feverishly active homemaker who was singlehandedly keeping alive Victorian household practices, everything from canning fruit in the fall to lining the linen cupboard shelves every month with new scented paper. At Christmas time he would have dark circles under his eyes from cooking so many fruitcakes, gingerbread men and star cookies with silver sprinkles.

Throughout the interview I experienced the peculiar anguish of making small talk with someone who holds your fate in her hands. Kevin mentioned that his parents were English and his granny Welsh, which sounded classy or at least civilized. When asked his profession, he risked all and said he was an actor; Daniella surprised us by saying she liked actors. I realized that Kevin found our audition amusing but not crucial. He didn't much care whether we lived together or not. For me it was vital; I sweated and grinned in the dark, swirling atmosphere. I asked her about her own background out of politeness and she told me her father, an Armenian rug dealer, had bought this building for her and she'd grown up in it. I wondered if she saw the missing tiles on the floor of the entryway downstairs and heard the unoiled whining of the closing elevator gate, the tarnished brass guard gate which was shiny only where the old black elevator man, hatted, smiling and half toothless, pushed it shut day after day (at night we had to take the stairs).

"Well, can you afford to make a month's deposit?"

"Oh, yes," I said brightly.

"I'm not going to give you a lease because I—" she seemed to be smiling behind her smoked glasses—"I might not like you."

I virtually kissed her hand as we left. At that moment I was ready to buff her nails every night and with my own feet pump the iron lung she must sleep in. I convinced myself we had tons in common and would be best friends. A week later I never gave her another thought.

TOM AND TOM invited us to a cocktail party a week after we moved in. Fifteen men in coats and ties sat around in a sitting room with hunting prints on the chocolate-brown walls and ate hot prunes wrapped in bacon and drank Beefeater martinis while listening to a cast

_I_

I

---

album of *Mame*. Daniella was the only woman there. She was wearing a silk robe her father had brought back from China in the 1930s and all her white-haired, cap-toothed boys were oohing and aahing over the craftsmanship, the beadwork, the cut! Tom L. drew me aside and said, nodding toward Kevin, "You really robbed the cradle this time. What a beauty! And yet he looks vaguely familiar." I wondered if Kevin had once come up on call as a hustler and forgotten the two Toms in a drug haze.

As soon as the party was over Kevin was off on his bicycle to the Village. He didn't come back till dawn. I felt I'd made a terrible decision to move uptown. I was far from all my haunts—the docks, the trucks, the dozen gay bars I liked downtown. The empty apartment with its fourteen windows and eight rooms was half a city block long. We'd never furnish it or even carpet it. It smelled of old plumbing and mouse shit. Dust squares and rectangles on the wall indicated where the previous tenant's furniture had been, apparently for decades. "It must be a ghastly mess in there," Tom L. said. "I suppose you'll get someone in to redecorate entirely."

"Entirely," I said, knowing I had just two hundred dollars left in my checking account.

Now I tried to sleep in my lumpy little bed, which looked so forlorn here, as though vagrants were squatting an emptied, once elegant building, something like an abandoned expensive asylum. I glanced out the window and no one was on the street. People in other, lit windows looked old and poor, but not picturesquely poor as in the Village. An old lady was looking at her television, which I couldn't see, but which kept X-raying her over and over again with its scanning, shifting lights and shadows.

I rooted around for work and found an educational publisher who wanted to do a thousand-page, two-volume "managed textbook" on U.S. history which would be one of the first college texts to give a prominent place to the accomplishments of women and blacks. I'd receive twenty thousand dollars in three payments (on signing, after turning in the first volume and finally, when the whole manuscript was in). Six "authors," specialists in their field, would supply me with Xeroxed articles on each topic. The "in-house editor" would prepare a cut-and-paste outline of the best passages from all the rival textbooks.

I had to meet with the "authors" (I was merely the "writer") in order to discuss with them their concept of each section. They were flown, all expenses paid, with their wives or husbands from their remote campuses and put up at the Sheraton for three nights. From my old days of regular employment, I had my one remaining suit; I took it to be dry-cleaned so that I could meet them. One of the couples was from Montreal and though their English was perfect the more I drank the more certain I became that my French was adequate, no, fluent. Way after midnight I was burbling along, cigarette in one hand, brandy snifter in the other, when the Canadian woman (expert in America's nineteenth-century colonial expansion) frowned and said in English, "But you know you're not making any sense at all."

I could see that the other authors had lapsed into silence and were looking at me with that combination of fear and hatred people feel when they think their own profits might be compromised by a drunk. Was I the alcoholic charlatan I appeared to be, someone who'd capsize our brave, academic galleon? Or was I, as the publisher had described me, an experienced journalist and promising young novelist? During the sociable dinner, amidst references to rival textbooks being launched, I discovered that if *our* book was widely adopted we could become very rich indeed, despite our laughably small percentage points. As we stood outside at three in the morning, facing Central Park South, two of the authors, themselves reeling by now, continued to harangue me about a new statistical analysis of the Founding Fathers' wealth, which showed they'd *lost* money by voting for independence. "They were motivated by principles, not by the profit motive," one of them shouted. He was wearing a bow tie and his hair was clipped short; an overhead street lamp picked out the shiny bald spots. Across the street single gay men in jeans and ripped T-shirts were darting into the dangerous, appealing park. I was furious that I was trapped here in a coat and tie.

Christa called me the next day to say she'd heard that one of the biggest women's magazines in the country was looking for a senior editor. The salary would be between fifty and seventy-five thousand dollars a year. I thought that if I landed the job I could drop the onerous textbook project. I called Mrs. Helier's secretary for an appointment. She told me I should buy the new issue and prepare a five-page critique of it, have lunch with the man I'd be replacing and "drop in" on the people I'd be working with, finally come in a week from Tuesday at nine a.m. to see Mrs. Helier herself.

The magazine, which I'd never looked at before, took up the questions of abortion, extramarital dating, premarital sex, a woman's right to multiple orgasms, new fall colors, how to wrap prunes in bacon and how to lacquer apartment walls a chocolate brown.

With whorish facility I entered into the project and drew up a list of pros and cons, making sure that the pros far outnumbered the cons, since I knew Mrs. Helier wouldn't really enjoy being substantially criticized about an issue she'd put together in accord with her time-tested formulas.

Todd, the outgoing senior editor, though married, was obviously gay. He knew Tom and Tom in my apartment building and had even worked with Tom L. in the distant past. He kept raising one eyebrow and staring at me haggardly whenever I mentioned Mrs. Helier, although everything Todd actually *said* about her was diplomatic, even approving. After our second martini we were entirely open, even flirtatious, with each other. The next morning I feared he'd regret his candor and might even jinx my chances. Would he want someone floating around in the small world of magazine publishing who had the goods on him? The woman whose boss I'd be took an instant liking to me, even though she was ten years older than I and by all rights should have had the job herself. She knew Christa, she wanted to write fiction, I reminded her of her son. By the end of our meeting she'd told me I was her candidate for the job. Her name was Elena.

For a gay freelancer in the 1970s, nine a.m. was the equivalent of four a.m. for anyone else; I arrived at Mrs. Helier's office on the twenty-fifth floor of the Kipniss Building pale and tense, my brain puréed and molded into something resembling a brain. My stomach was growling and my outraged biological clock had stopped in protest. My old suit looked even more dowdy here in the offices of a magazine devoted to the ephemeral verities of fashion.

I held my critique—superficially brusque, profoundly flattering—in my freshly laundered hand. At nine-ten Mrs. Helier—tiny, wizened, dressed in fur-trimmed embroidery and a barbaric necklace and girdle and resembling nothing more than a Siberian dowager—darted in, squeezed herself in beside me on the loveseat, looked me in the eye and said, "How will your homosexuality affect your performance at *Eclipse*, which is all about fucking, man-woman fucking?" She winced slightly each time she said "fucking," which she pronounced with the final *g* intact as though she'd trained herself to say it fearlessly, deliberately, as a way of staying up to date, despite the squeamishness of a woman of her far more euphemistic generation.

The blood rushed to my head and finding nothing alive there immediately deserted it. In all my years of office work no boss had ever asked me a personal question, certainly nothing about my sexuality. Suddenly all the rules were changed. I felt at once violated and thrilled, since like all

Americans I was excited by the sudden promise of a higher sincerity, one that would cut through all ignoble forms of timidity. At the same time I badly needed this job in order to support Kevin and me and to turn our apartment into a real showplace with white carpets and sectional sofas, lacquered brown walls and hunting prints.

"I suppose my homosexuality, Mrs. Helier, would make me less competitive with *you*. I mean, a heterosexual man with my qualifications would have trouble taking orders from a woman, wouldn't he?"

She was shaking her small head, her antique forged-iron earrings, heavy with topaz, grazing her starved shoulders. This barbaric splendor, so incongruous in a Manhattan office, was yet another proof of the violence of her willpower, that force which had turned her from a namby-pamby single girl, a mere secretary, into a publishing phenomenon, whose lean, exercised body was regularly brought to multiple orgasms by a loving, faithful husband, himself a captain of industry or at least industriousness. If I knew her legend it was because she'd written a best-selling book about her rise to the top, a pinnacle that struck me as curiously unenviable as I smelled her bad breath from continual dieting, looked at her elaborate Kabuki makeup, which she must have begun to apply at six this morning, *after* her workout, and as I imagined a whole life trapped inside this office, reinventing again and again the same magazine. The man I hoped to replace had told me, "Mrs. Helier *is Eclipse*. It's her story. She'll stay up all night rewriting a perfectly good article, but make it a great one by injecting into it her own fears from twenty years ago, which it's her genius never to forget. She was a nobody from Indiana, a plain girl with a big tummy, no money and no eyebrows. Now, by God, she's rich, thin and she can afford the best mink implants or whatever those things are, but she'll never forget her origins, not for one second."

"No," she said, "I'm sure you're going to be disgusted. At *Eclipse* we're talking about the female body—reproduction, labial hygiene, lubrication, clitoral stimulation, orgasm, breast lifts, tummy tucks—and it's not for the faint hearted. But what we're mainly all about is fucking, man-woman fucking." She turned her huge eyes, outlined with the firm hand of a Chinese calligrapher, and smiled at me sorrowfully—for a second I thought part of her sorrow came from her conviction that I would forever be immune to her charms.

"But I think you have in mind gay men of an older generation," I said. "*Before* gay liberation homosexual men were afraid of women, and probably some of them envied women. They didn't usually *know* many women."

And those they did know, I thought guiltily, they called *fish*, and they were always going on about their smelly effluvia. "But now," I added brightly, "gay men and straight or gay women see that they share a lot—such as the oppression of patriarchal society."

"Nice try." Mrs. Helier smiled sadly, with just one corner of her small mouth a brush had painted the color of weathered pink brick. The smile was a parenthetical acknowledgment.

I didn't get the job. I called Elena and asked her what happened. "We just couldn't tell her that Todd—" the man I'd be replacing—"is gay and that she loved him and with you she was just inventing a problem. What a pity!"

I began the U.S. history book at the same time that Watergate was occurring, a chain of events that raised serious Constitutional questions about the roles and rights of the White House and Congress. Joshua came back from Venice at the end of August and he and two of his women friends, both classmates from Harvard, avidly pursued every twist and turn of the drama over the next year and a half. They phoned each other up every time a new story broke and took time off from work to follow on television the unfolding of the tale. At dinner their conversation was nothing but speculations about Gordon Liddy and E. Howard Hunt, Judge Byrne and Ellsberg, Judge John Sirica and James McCord, John Dean and the Ervin Committee, John Mitchell, Archibald Cox, Ehrlichman and Haldeman—and of course the vengeful, petty, ignorant, incompetent, immoral Nixon himself.

I never bothered with a second of it. To me it was *their* history in the making, not mine, just as it was their rights being violated, since mine had never existed. When Joshua, Rebecca and Ludmilla would express shock and dismay over the government's ethics, I considered the crimes that excited these responses laughably minor and inevitable. Just by going to Harvard and meeting professors who had advised presidents, Joshua imagined that what he thought counted. He was slow about deciding how Judge Sirica should proceed; to Ludmilla and Rebecca, the judge instantly became a hero. They needed *someone* to admire, they said. Admiration of men in public office was not a possibility for me, never, not under any circumstances. I knew that, like Nixon, I would have said or done anything to succeed and stay on top; fortunately for the sake of my morals and public ethics, my life presented me with no opportunities for serious wrongdoing.

Kevin and I went shopping at Secondhand Rose in the Village, a used furniture store with a trendy image, and there we bought 1940s wicker garden furniture. Kevin wanted bare floors, pure white walls, the frailest chairs and sofas suggesting the least substantial season, paintings leaning against the chair rail rather than raised and suspended at eye level. He wept when I bought an ugly dining room table and six heavy chairs, all of oak, at the Salvation Army. "Oh, it's so depressing," he said.

"But, darling, I want to invite people to dinner and we have a whole dining room."

"A loft. We have a big, airy loft, or *did* until you—oh, how could you?"

One night I came home at midnight and Kevin was stoned and pushing the furniture onto the landing outside our apartment door. "You'll see," he said, with a wacky grin, "it'll be much nicer without furniture."

"You're stoned." I was angry and started shoving the furniture I hadn't even paid for yet back into the apartment.

Kevin snapped, "Have it your way, doll," and left on his bike for the Village. At dawn, when he came back, his hair smelling of beer and cigarette smoke, I told him I was sorry.

"No, you were probably right," he said wearily. After that I felt he lost interest in the apartment and decided to live in it as he would have lived in a hotel.

Like me, Kevin drank a lot and was often drunk and stoned, but for him it never appeared to be habitual. When I got stoned I was so consumed by my desire for him that I assumed he must share it. Every cell in my body was magnetized by him. It was a religious frenzy that forced me to my knees before him. "You sick cow," he'd say, laughing, "stop looking at me like that."

Can it be called *lust* if it's a longing to be owned by someone, to write his initials on every chromosome of your body? I was haggard with lust, if that's what it was, idiotic with desire, certainly cretinous and repentant and humorless with longing. We'd be standing in the hallway, stoned, grinning, talking about something, and I'd suddenly sink to my knees, a vassal to love, as though I were a boyar (shaved, wigged and perfumed in the newest European fashion) who still wanted to kiss his tsar's foot.

"What are you *doing*?" Kevin would complain. "Girl, get a grip."

Perhaps as a hustler he'd known all too many men who'd longed for a bigger, crueler fantasy looming right behind him, someone Kevin was standing in for but couldn't entirely embody. What he wanted from me was something more affectionate and offhand and palsy; I should have played his Sister Eileen, and every time the subway detonated under our apartment I should have rushed into his arms for a chorus of "Why-Oh Why-Oh Why-Oh, Why did we ever leave Ohio?"

Instead he had to live with my heavy penitent's tread up and down the house and my absurd genuflections, as though he were one of the Stations of the Cross.

One night he surprised me by staging a sex scene with me—of course! Why hadn't I guessed that he could be stimulated only by sex-as-performance? He turned off all the lights, blindfolded me, left me naked with my hands handcuffed behind me in his bedroom. He fed me a joint, speaking quietly to me all the while. He led me, gently, like Antigone leading the blind Oedipus, down the hallway. There I had to kneel again. I knew that recently he'd been seeing a guy who practiced "sex magick," who, apparently, treated an orgasm as just one incidental part of a long propitiatory rite complete with chanting, incense and a record of Steve Reich's *Drumming*. When Kevin released my eyes and hands, there he was, naked, erect, lit from within like a thick altar candle in which the wick and flame have burrowed deep into the flesh of the beeswax. He ordered me to suck him as one might take Communion. Only now do I realize that the performance, far from exciting him, was designed as an offering to me.

I was social in a robust style, he in a glancing way. He'd drop in on one of my dinner parties and as Ludmilla who, for complicated reasons, had an English accent, spoke of one of her passions (Nixon, child psychology, Balanchine, documentaries), or as Joshua railed against Max or Butler, laughing at their foibles, fulminating against their effrontery, Kevin would just perch on the edge of a chair, curious, smiling, but too stoned to follow the charged vocabulary, the complex syntax, the livid reactions so at odds with his own cool detachment to everything. "Nixon?" he'd say, blinking, "the President?" asking it in a tone of disbelief, dumbfounded that anyone would bother with someone so remote. Rebecca would say, "No, *not* the President, the *man*," because she found a subtle distinction lurking behind Kevin's question, unable for a moment to imagine he was really so dopey or doped.

MY NOVEL was at last published. It struck me as strange that publication, which to me was as momentous as the canonization of a saint, took place so simply, even humbly. I suppose even the cardinals must trudge into their chilly chambers on a November morning to vote for or against that Chilean martyr who'd whipped herself in her parents' garden so many centuries ago; in the same way this book, which I'd composed on Fire Island six years earlier and which existed in my mind as a chord that took two hundred pages to get resolved, now existed in the world as a quire of flexible paper bound in harder paper.

I'd been presented with a cover design that I'd rejected (hadn't my contract said I had "cover approval"?), but it was used anyway: a seashell dripping a blue tear. Max wrote a "blurb" for the back cover that mentioned Freud and Darwin and pronounced on the saving powers of forgetting. I was thrilled and told him it reminded me of when at fourteen I'd written a few bars of music which a professional composer had played on a grand with crashing chords and rolling arpeggios: I hardly recognized my broken little tune. Max was generous if he could be proprietary, although unlike most great men he did not require that his disciples resemble him artistically. He had a grasp, a very wide grasp. Perhaps his moral study of the history of art and artists made him avoid the usual pitfalls of genius; he resented Goethe's failure to sponsor Kleist and blamed him for the young man's suicide. "Goethe liked only his imitators, the feebler the better," Max said, "not like the Master—" by whom he invariably meant Henry James "—who recognized the genius in everyone from Flaubert to H.G. Wells, the ingrate!, and if he missed Whitman the first time around at least eventually he made up handsomely for his regrettable original misprision." Max had no respect for the minor virtues (he could be shockingly rude) but he honored the one he took as major, even sublime: generosity.

The *New York Times Book Review* published a well meaning but confused review of my book on page 3; the reviewer, a novelist I'd never heard of, treated the story as a mystery and years later I'd still find the book in remote public libraries under "crime fiction" or "tales of the supernatural" or just "mystery." There were few other reviews except one I recall from a local New Jersey paper with Catholic tendencies: "Every year New York flushes its intellectual sewers and down floats another load of crap like this pretentious doozy. C'mon, guys, can't you put together a good, old-fashioned plot for once? How about an honest day's work?"

I never saw the book for sale anywhere, I never saw anyone reading it on a park bench or in the subway, and within a year the publishing house had informed me it had sold just five hundred copies of the two thousand they'd printed. They were pulping the rest. Five hundred sounded like a lot to me. I was delighted when I imagined a room full of five hundred people who'd read my book and allowed their minds to be tattooed by my needles.

Because my affair with Kevin was going so badly—in fact Kevin referred to me as his roommate—I had all my evenings free for Joshua, as many as he might want. Occasionally he looked at me with big eyes, with the very same anticipation I directed toward Kevin, but most of the time Joshua held himself in check. That first winter after I stamped my foot he was sometimes harsh and chiding with me, but only by flashes.

We went to spend a weekend with Eddie in his New England village. Eddie read to us a poem he'd written to his goddaughter, the plump one-year-old child we could hear laughing and talking to herself in her playpen on the landing below, as she batted at the fish mobile dangling above her pillow. Fifteen years ago her father had been a handsome *evzone* in a white skirt, with a narrow waist and strong, hairy legs. He and Eddie had met in Athens and every stage of their love had been celebrated in poems with titles reminiscent of Cavafy or Rilke, a blend of heart-piercing nostalgia and a throbbing angelus of narrative and allegory. Now the Greek was a portly, balding family man of thirty-five and he and his wife and daughter lived downstairs. He was the janitor and caretaker and he also worked in a nearby pizzeria Eddie had bought for him. Once a month he came upstairs, tool in hand, to give Eddie a tune-up. His wife probably didn't suspect a thing. She stayed inside, grew broader, smiled shyly, knitted baby things against the winter cold, made Eddie the lemon-rice chicken soup he loved.

Joshua and I read the new poem for Cassiopeia, worked our way through its elaborate astrological conceits and consulted with each other. Finally Joshua, despite an admiration that bordered on awe, dared to say to Eddie, "Isn't it . . . a bit . . . *cold*?" Eddie slapped his forehead and said, "Of course! I forgot to put the feeling in!" He rushed upstairs to the cupola that served him as a study and fiddled with the verses for an hour before he descended with lines that made us weep, so tender were they, so melting and exalted. That night, when we were alone, Joshua whispered, "A rather chilling vision of the creative process, I'd say. We must never tell anyone about this, since how many people would understand and forgive the heartless, manipulative craftsmanship of great art?"

The village, for Eddie, was a repository of good stories. For him the walls of the houses were transparent and inside he could picture the drunken wife beater, heir to an automobile fortune, or see the spinster sister pulling aside an inch of curtain to peek outside, or overhear the tire-less wrangling of the celebrated mother and daughter, novelists both, one a Romanian baroness by marriage. Greek Revival houses were the set-tings for Gothic passions. In such a small world, over-observed by fine minds all keeping detailed diaries, every *bon mot* was treasured. When Eddie came back from Italy with an antique clock for Gloria, the ancient novelist who talked like Mae West, she said, "I don't want a clock. I like things from Gucci. When Mary came back from Rome she brought me a lovely handbag from Gucci." Eddie murmured in mock exasperation, "Oh, Gloria, sometimes I have the feeling that for you Italy is nothing but the shores of Gimmegucci."

With me Eddie was kind in a deliberate way, as though he'd written himself a reminder. Perhaps he'd realized how wounded I'd been the night he'd said nothing after I'd read him the first chapter of my book. Eddie was a bit like a royal prince who's naturally shy, even slightly cruel, who's been trained to recall that his slightest remark or smallest gesture can crush one of his subjects. He sat with me one afternoon for a quarter of an hour in the living room while Joshua considerately went out for a walk. He told me he'd read my novel and liked it, then asked me about my plans. He suggested I apply for a grant from his foundation. "Of course I'm not the only member of the jury—there are four others—but I'll be plugging for you."

It struck me that Eddie had resolved brilliantly the problem of being an artist with inherited wealth. He worked hard, revised constantly, won all the prizes and in no way bought his celebrity. Since his other friends were all poor poets, he had set up his foundation to help them out with small sums; they couldn't ask him directly for handouts, nor need they feel beholden to him for grants given by five jury members. Money was never allowed to poison his relationships with other artists. Since Americans *ad-mire* wealth and have no ideological hostility to it, Eddie's legendary fam-ily fortune only added to his splendor. Everyone always assumed that he'd endowed his foundation. What no one knew was that every year he was bankrolling it out of his own pocket and that he was quite literally shar-ing his wealth with his friends. Perhaps because my father had been pros-perous if not rich, money held no mystery for me. Nor did I think of myself as poor. Certainly it never occurred to me to resent someone rich.

Having read every line of Eddie's considerable *œuvre* out loud with Joshua, in long, drunken evenings of appreciation, I now found myself, for a few days, living with the great man, drinking his tea, returning his smiles, listening to his quips, which only one time out of ten became airborne. I came to realize that meeting a writer, knowing him up close, in the hope of better understanding his work, was a useless, even destructive exercise. In his poetry Eddie was quicksilver, not only funny and irreverent but also compassionate and wise, and he tilted from one mood to another word by word with an unprecedented fluidity. But if he was all at once Dante (the law-giving man) and the Marschallin (the sad, civilized woman in *Der Rosenkavalier* bidding farewell to love), an Ariel of wit and a Caliban of sensuality, nevertheless this composite self, this kaleidoscope of roles, gained nothing by being experienced at first hand.

When I told Eddie that I knew a young poet who wanted to meet him as well as Elizabeth Bishop, John Ashbery, and Robert Lowell, Eddie laughed and said, "But he'd only be meeting empty shells propped up around a table." He was exaggerating. Eddie's living, breathing body was not extinct. But he was right that to the degree a writer has metamorphosed his blood into ink his is an abandoned body. Or if the writer still has a personality, it is full of sharps and flats at odds with the tuned melody emitted by his writing.

In Eddie the man I detected a perversity and snobbishness that he radiated in spite of himself, qualities he'd entirely transformed in his writing into impishness and humor. In life he had an age, a pear-shaped body, a maddening drawl; on the page he was eternally youthful, a charged field of particles, a polyphony of voices. While nothing that showed up on the page was unintended and everything was a pure product of the will, Eddie, like everyone else, sagged after lunch, generated a body heat, created an impression (of nervousness and effeminacy, in his case) that he himself was unaware of and that might not have been interpreted that way by someone who avoided appearing nervous and effeminate less strenuously than I. Or by someone less impressed than I by his mere mannerisms. Joshua, for instance, who'd gone to Harvard in an era of eccentrics and who'd also known Marianne Moore and Ezra Pound, did not take any notice of such superficial characteristics, mere caste marks, that might have made Eddie into a figure of fun in a movie meant for the masses but that signified nothing special *within* his clan of mid-Atlantic artists and that wouldn't even have been mentioned in the memoirs written by any one of his friends.

When Joshua, Eddie and I went for a walk after a dinner at the baroness's and fell into whoops of drunken laughter, I changed my mind. No, after all, Proust had been right when he'd said that great artists make the best friends, for they alone are at once sympathetic to the life around them and sufficiently detached from it to see it. They may be unworthy of their work and falsify its values, but if writers are merely distracting as exegetes, they're good value as friends. No matter how crusty or irritable a writer might be, in the right mood he or she can assume any age, remain open to everything, become at once satirical and kind. Certainly Eddie was that way with me, for if he found me by turns self-hating and pretentious and teased me for it, he also knew, as he said, that I'd been made to wait too long. "Your first novel, this so-called first novel of yours," he said, "is so good it must be your fourth or fifth?"

"Fifth."

"In another, better era you would have been encouraged and published from the very start. You were made to wait too long. Of course that means your work springs fully formed and armed from your mind—but that will only intimidate other beginners, no?"

I laughed, blushed and stammered, since I had never thought about such a thing. Eddie's praise and understanding were the first I'd received from someone I admired so intensely.

"No wonder you have that whipped-dog look," he said, "that fear of being ridiculed." He scrutinized me closely, trying to take in the full extent of the damage. "We complain," he said, "about paranoid writers, but look how we treat them!"

WHEN I RETURNED to New York I went to the Candle, a local leather bar on Amsterdam. I couldn't afford leather chaps and a matching motorcycle jacket, nor would I have wanted to make such a commitment to a scene that back then was neither as acceptable nor as potentially ludicrous as it was to become. It was still frightening.

A raunchy, smiling guy close to forty in worn black leathers with a worn, leathery face and quick, intelligent eyes came up to me and put his gloved hand down the back of my jeans. He cupped my bare ass in his hand. "Hey, you're nice."

"Thanks," I said. "You, too."

"Live near here?"

"Yeah." I liked his speed, his self-assurance, so rare in gay pick-ups, which usually advanced with the slowness of an auction between misers. "Want to come home with me?"

"Yeah, and with ten other guys. Let's get an orgy off the ground."

"Great!" I said. Because I felt confident that this guy, Herb, was sexy, I had no hesitation in going up to someone handsome and saying, "See that guy over there, the guy with short black hair and a mustache and a silver eagle on his sleeve?"

"Yeah."

"Well, him and me's tryin' to git a little group action off the ground. My place's about ten blocks away—wannus to deal you in?"

"Yeah, I guess. Sure. Why not."

"Don't leave without us, you hear. S'goin' to be *hot*. We got grass, wine, poppers, downers."

When five guys and I walked into our apartment, it was after two a.m. but Kevin was still up, painting. He was stoned and he'd placed clip-on work lights all around the living room. He was listening to Phoebe Snow, whose bluegrassy voice, with its coppery inflections and guitar-string glissandi, negotiated treacherous jazz tunes with coolness and lightness. We listened to her day after day, night and day, because we only owned half a dozen records.

I brought my boys in to meet Kevin. I asked him if we could use his room, since he had a large foam cube for a bed. He said sure. I was afraid he would be angry at this invasion, but he wore a crooked smile and looked at my squirming catch with desire.

Suddenly I was proud of my knack for rounding them up, a social magnetism I could exert at those rare times when I wasn't feeling unsure of myself, an excitement that worked a charm in gay bars, where everyone was paralyzed with fear. The best way to cruise, for me at least, was to come to a bar with two noisy friends, talk and laugh with them in the center of the room, then at the crucial moment disengage myself from them and tackle someone who'd been watching our group with a faint smile that echoed our laughter. I didn't have the sort of brooding looks that silence and mystery could enhance; I looked my best when I was the liveliest.

Now I passed joints, Quaaludes and wine around rather nervously to my five guys, worried that in the bright lights of Kevin's studio their erections would melt and they'd remember they had to get up in the morning for work. Kevin was explaining to one guy how he wrote backwards for hours and hours and, at a certain moment of inspiration, continued producing his reverse calligraphy with colored inks on expensive drawing paper. The guy, round eyed, was standing with his hands clasped at crotch level as though he were a cowboy holding his hat and respectfully listening to the rancher's wife.

"Let's go in the other room, guys," Herb said, for he and I were sending inaudible bat cries back and forth across the room about the necessity to act quickly. "Come and join us, Kevin," I said with an offhandedness that sounded convincing, at least to my ears.

I could describe the way Herb undressed the slender blond whom we mistakenly had thought would be shy. I stood behind the blond and breathed on his nape, his ears and down his spine between his shoulder blades while reaching around and tuning in Venus by turning his nipples. Within seconds he was a lion holding Herb down with a tawny paw and jabbing his mouth full of a long, straight but flexible penis. I could say how every man in that room looked to me like a package to be opened with just one soft tug at the big bow. Now that I'm in my fifties I see most men as social beings who have a pedigree and a past, a nature open or closed, someone fun or boring to talk to, remote from me or no more than six or seven acquaintances removed through snob golf, but back then, in that bedroom illuminated by a single candle on the sill, they were just wide cocks or thin, balls light and tender as seedless grapes or big and veined like walnuts, insensitive and straining in their leathery sac; they were a short-sleeved coat of black hair as closely woven as a knight's mail singlet—or just a tuft at the neck, as though the filaments were the exuberant waste siphoned off from the column of breath. A man was the surprising assertiveness triggered in the little guy with the pinched breastbone and a lowered sight line as he realized he was being given permission for once to dominate another man and accordingly he widened his stance and squared his shoulders. Or a man was this thick-thighed mesomorph who, through a trick of the will, became light, reversed the metamorphosis from tree trunk to nymph and was lifted in Herb's strong arms, lifted and screwed. The guy threw his head back dramatically and extended the line of his long neck with a flung-back arm, an Adam's apple and an elbow becoming the only knobs in such long, smooth, weeping branches. The Quaaludes relaxed our muscles, turned us into slow-motion divers plunging into one another's bodies.

Herb talked dirty, verbal kindling until we all caught fire, then he went silent and let us listen to the slap and sigh of the general slow conflagration. In the flickering candlelight and in the transitory Roman-candle highs induced by the passed poppers, our bodies may have resembled those of Laocoön and his sons but our desire writhed around us like the snakes.

Kevin came in, already naked as a child, and in the melee I was able to lick the instep of his foot and inhale the crushed-dandelion smell of the sweat under his arms, to feel the cool heft of his buttocks, at once firm and yielding, and to see the leonine blond's cock emerge taffy-apple shiny from Kevin's mouth. Hadn't I staged this whole orgy just so I could touch him in the anonymous confusion?

One man would never join in. He crouched in a corner, naked, chin in hand, despairing as Blake's Job, looking at us with huge eyes. We tried to encourage him to enter our fold, but he disapproved of us, it seemed.

When they'd all gone and the daylight was developing and printing Kevin's body, he knelt above me, his knees burning into my pinioned biceps, and with infinite peacefulness he watered my mouth and face and chest with his bitter, hot urine.

Sex was a shadow we cast wherever we went, which traveled at our speed, like the calm shadow of its wings that an airplane inevitably projects onto the fields and forests below, that assumes the shape of the changing landscape and yet remains constant. None of our friends would have said we were "obsessed." That was a word heterosexuals used, or older, envious homosexuals. We thought having sex was a positive good, the more the better. A straight guy I'd known when I was an office worker and whom I kept up with, said to me, "You fags are so fuckin' lucky, always getting laid. You know what a fuckin' pain in the ass it is for us? We gotta wine and dine the chicks and dish out all this sweet talk and they still don't always fuckin' put out, whereas you fuckin' horny bastards just grope each other in the public crapper or at the back of the fuckin' movie thee-yay-terr without so much as a 'thank you ma'am.' Not that I could fuck some hairy guy's hairy asshole, for Chrissake, I like that sweet honeypot pussy." He pronounced it "puss-*say*."

We believed that women held out in order to force guys into the servitude of marriage, that pussy was scarce so men would have to work for it, and that religion conspired to make men believe they were doing the right thing when they put on the iron collar and manacles. We thought that if women were as horny—as *disinterestedly* horny—as men, then everyone, straight or gay, would be having sex on every street corner.

We were free. We didn't fall for any morality bullshit—anyway, the Christians had already assigned us to hell just for looking at men: the thought was as bad as the deed and the offending eye had to be plucked out. Before we plucked it out, we wanted to wink with it. If we picked up a case of clap the cure was just one shot away. Courtship was a con, again part of female culture. If we loved one another it wasn't something we confused with glandular deprivation. Even "love" was a suspect word, smelling of the bidet. Guys just sort of fell in with each other, buddies rubbing shoulders. We wanted sexual friends, loving comrades, multiple husbands in a whole polyandry of desire. Exclusivity was a form of death—worse, old hat.

If love was suspect, jealousy was foul. We were intent on dismantling all the old marital values and the worst thing we could be accused of by one of our own was aping the heterosexual model.

I went to bed with a straight man, a young hippy writer who thought he should try sex with another guy and chose me because he liked my work. He treated me as he'd obviously been trained to treat women, with little fluttering kisses along my brow, a tender tracing of my erect nipple, jokes whispered in my ear. We smoked some grass laced with PCP and when he found himself fucking me brutally and slapping my ass, he was so horrified by his violence and my pleasure that he hurried into his clothes and still half-undressed, half-erect, ran away, never to be seen again.

We equated sexual freedom with freedom itself. Hadn't the Stonewall Uprising itself been the defense of a cruising place? The newer generation might speak of "gay culture," but those of us thirty or older knew the only right we wanted to protect was the right to suck as many cocks as possible. "Promiscuity" (a word we objected to, since it suggested libertinage, and that we wanted to replace with the neutral word "adventuring") was something outsiders might imagine would wear thin soon enough. We didn't agree. The fire was in our blood. The more we scratched the more we itched—except we would never have considered our desire a form of moral eczema. For us there was nothing more natural than wandering into a park, a parked truck or a backroom and plundering body after body.

There had been no radical break with the past (we'd all heard about the orgies in the navy during World War II), but at least since I'd first come on the scene in the 1950s three things had changed: in New York City the cops weren't closing down our bars any more or harassing us if we held hands on the street; we now had a slogan that said "Gay is Good," and we'd stopped seeing shrinks in order to go straight; and there were more and more, *millions* more, gay men with leather jackets and gym-built bodies and low voices and good jobs. We used to think we were rare birds; now the statistics said that one out of every four men in Manhattan was homosexual. When we marched up Fifth Avenue every June there were hundreds of thousands of gay women and men, many of them freaks, but the bulk of them the regular kind of people we liked. These were the kinds of guys I had sex with several times every week. If I had sex, say, with an average of three different partners a week from 1962 to 1982 in New York, then that means I fooled around with 3,120 men during my twenty years there. The funny thing is that I always felt deprived, as though all the other fellows must be getting laid more often. A gay shrink once told me that that was the single most common complaint he heard from his patients, even from the real satyrs: they weren't getting as much tail as the next guy. I was so incapable of fitting my behavior into any general pattern that I would exclaim, aghast, "You know Liz has been married *five* times!" If my marriages had been legal, they would have been legion.

Nor did all this sex preclude intimacy. For those who never lived through that period (and most of those who did are dead), the phrase "anonymous sex" might suggest unfeeling sex, devoid of emotion. And yet, as I can attest, to hole up in a room at the baths with a body after having opened it up and wrung it dry, to lie, head propped on a guy's stomach just where the tan line bisects it, smoke a cigarette and talk to him late into the night and early into the morning about your childhood, his unhappiness in love, your money worries, his plans for the future—well, nothing is more personal, more emotional. The best thing of all were the random, floating thoughts we shared. Just the other day a black opera singer, who's famous now, sent me one of his recordings and a note that said, "In memory of that night at the baths twenty-five years ago." The most romantic night of my life I spent with an older man on the dunes on Fire Island, kissing him until my face burned from his beard stubble, treasuring the beauty of his skin and skin warmth and every flaw as though it were an adornment. When he walked me home through the salt mist floating in off the sea and the sudden coldness of dawn, we strolled arm in arm as though we'd been lovers before the war, say, any war, and were reunited only now.

Of COURSE the sermons I preached against love and jealousy were all the more absurd because I was so besotted by Kevin. I wanted to be his wife in the most straitlaced of marriages. I wanted to cook his breakfast and bear his babies. I wanted him to be my boy-husband, my baby-master. I suppose when I say I'm an atheist and always have been I'm not being quite honest, since I've worshipped two gods in my life, Sean and Kevin.

Kevin was suddenly off every night working as a waiter in the Village and on a good night he could pull in a hundred dollars; during the days he went to gym class or dance class or an audition. I seldom went out and felt all the more becalmed in the wake of his excited entrances and exits. Once in a while when he was out I'd sneak into his room and turn the wheels of his bicycle, which was hoisted high on the wall and held there by protruding industrial clamps. I just wanted to hear the ratcheting of his gears, the sound of that month when we belonged to the Society of St. Agnes and had slept in each other's chaste, feverish arms.

The man at the orgy who'd stayed apart and looked as inconsolable as Job became Kevin's lover. His name was Dennis. He was a Catholic boy from Boston with one blue eye and one green and a faint birthmark on his forehead, as though the forceps had caused a hemorrhage when he was born, a bruise just beneath the skin, and the mark had never healed. He was tall and pale skinned, with teeth that were small, flat and tinged with blue like the teeth of Victorian dolls. One tooth was broken and he hid it with his hand when he smiled. His beard grew in a moment after he'd shaved. His biceps looked like veined gooseberries packed in snow. He was so handsome we scarcely noticed he had no conversation beyond a way of shaking his narrow head in mild amazement and exclaiming, "Jeez . . ." under his breath, eyelids lowered. At a time when most gay men were lifting weights he was doing very precise and demanding stretching exercises of his own devising. Other young gay men wore their new shoulders as though they were store-bought football padding, but he was as familiar as an animal with his own muscles. A line of black hair crept up his pale, ridged stomach like a trail of ants across tablets of white chocolate. His hands were big but refined and the knuckles were dusted with glossy hair. You pictured them playing the piano, reaching for octaves, so pale they made the ivory keys look dingy. He didn't pay much attention to what other people were telling him. Strangely, he seemed indifferent even to what he was saying. He'd just rattle on, coming up with whatever he thought would please his listeners or merely filling in the blanks as dictated by convention. Meanwhile, his thoughts, all unnoticed, would spin out of control. He'd go off in a secret, sick direction and end up hot-wiring a stolen car or shooting heroin, almost without even noticing it. Or he'd smack his fist through a window pane a moment after calling his sick grandmother to cheer her up or mailing a thank-you note to a hostess. Kevin teased him constantly, usually about sex, and though Dennis was too blue-white to blush, he lowered his eyes and complained happily in his Boston-Irish accent and laughed behind his hand.

Kevin seemed to be madly in love with Dennis. After Dennis would leave, Kevin would drum his own heart with his open hand and say, "God, that *man*, he's so wild. Those eyelashes grazing his cheeks like black wings. He's a solo version of the second act of *Swan Lake* all by himself. Those buns? Slurp, slurp."

Dennis lived with Al, a forty-year-old window designer who devised chic, scary scenes of rubber fetishism to advertise the new Magnavox or who came up with the public hanging of a skinny mannequin in a Givenchy frock for Bonwit's. Al was very possessive and Dennis was not only his lover but also his employee. From the way Dennis referred to him, Al sounded like a fat, sweaty old man; imagine our astonishment when Kevin and I dropped in at their *atelier* one afternoon and discovered a bald little he-man who'd been a champion figure skater and had the butt to prove it.

A straight man doesn't want to sleep with his rival, just kill him, but a rejected gay lover hopes to seduce his successor in order to spite his ex-partner, perhaps, but also out of curiosity, even desire. I couldn't hate Dennis, especially when I saw how headstrong he was in his self-destruction, any more than Al could hate Kevin.

I liked Dennis and when I thought of him I saw him as I'd first encountered him at the orgy—big eyes struck with horror, chin resting on his fist, body folded into itself. And yet when Kevin and Dennis would sit on the couch and smooch while I counted stitches—no, I didn't really knit, but I felt like a maiden aunt in a black dress, skinny loins on fire and a cobweb in her pussy, nervously rattling the spoon in her teacup.

I'd put an empty water glass to the wall between my room and Kevin's and listen to Dennis's sighs and Kevin's groans. I asked Kevin who "shtupped" whom and Kevin said they took turns though their favorite thing was sixty-nining for blissful, suckling hours. For some reason I thought of Melville's description of baby whales in the warm Caribbean nursing underwater, their blue eyes looking up through the water toward the sky and off to one side, as though they'd sighted an angel.

If we hadn't lived together I would have stopped seeing Kevin for a few weeks and I might have regained some dignity or at least independence. Living with him meant I became more and more abject. Joshua would go along with my plotting and scheming, probably because he'd been in on my obsession from the start. He heard every detail in our twice-daily phone calls. Also because Joshua was a true friend, someone who takes you at your own evaluation, who buys your version, the opposite of a shrink.

I began to see a psychotherapist, but a gay one this time, which made all the difference. Abe was a fat, bearded guy who walked around his big West Side apartment in stocking feet and was in love with a skinny, sexy dandy who had pursed, purple lips and, the one time I chatted with him, seemed to know everything about everything—hieroglyphics, Rasputin, Mao's Cultural Revolution—but was also in possession of the inner, esoteric meaning of every system, person or event he mentioned. He was spooky in an amusing, original way, which made me admire Abe's taste and feel that my habit of falling in love with picture-perfect athletic blonds proved how banal my character must be.

Soon Joshua and Kevin were also going to Abe. I didn't worry that they were crowding me out; on the contrary, so much Beta conformity made me feel all the more an Alpha leader.

The American Psychological Association had taken homosexuality off its list of character disorders and neuroses and reclassified it as falling somewhere within the normal range of sexual behavior. Although I suspect most psychotherapists, especially the Freudians, kept their reservations about homosexuality *in petto*, we were gratified that officially we were off the books.

With my other shrinks, paradoxically, I'd never had to talk about my real problems because for them the unique problem had been homosexuality. With Abe, because he was gay (if such a butch, bluff, overweight man could be considered gay), I had to trace out the exact topography of my unhappiness. Where did it hurt? What did I want to change? Whereas before the therapist had felt like a priest I was hoping to placate, Abe made it clear he worked for me, was providing a service and I could use him as I saw fit. There was a certain wary respect and affection between us and no love lost and no "transference," if that meant exaggerated, unearned feelings of hate and desire.

One day he made me look in the mirror and list all the things I liked and disliked about myself. Surprisingly the likes outnumbered the dislikes, even though the dislikes were deeper. Another day he focused a camera on me and later he played back ten minutes' worth of film. I said, "God, I sound like such a sissy," and he said, "All American men say that, straight and gay. It's because the real men in the movies—cowboys, criminals—make no gestures and speak in a low monotone. *Any* expressivity comes across as effeminate by that standard."

I came in with a dream about being trapped in a mummiform coffin with my father's face painted on it, which was positioned down a long processional row of statues of Anubis. Abe said that from everything I'd told him he thought that I was afraid of dying inside while going on living outside—as my father had obviously done. I no longer thought about my father nor did I have any contact with him. I hadn't exchanged a letter or phone call with him in two years. When I was a boy I'd wanted to be his lover; he'd never come through and now I hated him with a cold, denying hatred. I imagined him wondering why I never phoned and feeling too aggrieved to mention it even to his wife, despite the fact she fed his resentments whenever she could.

My mother still received her small alimony from him every month, enough to tie her to him, and my sister drove down to Cincinnati to see him occasionally, but when she asked him for money after her divorce to go to graduate school so that she could eventually earn a living, he refused. She cried at yet another proof of his indifference. He lived in his fourteen-room house with the two new Cadillacs under the car port and the chain-smoking, hillbilly maid and looked down through acres of landscaped grounds at the Ohio River, but he couldn't afford three thousand dollars a year to send her back to school (she wanted to earn a master's degree in social work so that she could be a psychotherapist). I earned only twelve thousand dollars a year, but I ended up paying for her education. Daddy had always seen Anne and me, no doubt, as nothing but a potential financial burden whom he'd contracted in the divorce agreement to help until we reached age twenty-one or graduation from college, whichever came first. When Anne had married he'd presented her with an itemized life bill, a fiendishly detailed document of every expense, no matter how minor, he'd ever incurred on her behalf; the object was not to demand reimbursement but to warn Anne of the forbidding cost of raising a child, lest she begin breeding heedlessly. Once I'd left university to come to New York, he'd never advanced me another nickel. I'd done everything myself, but my survival, rather than making me proud, caused me to feel lonely.

I wanted to define myself as my father's opposite. Where he was tight-fisted, I'd be generous. Where he was cunning, I'd be guileless. Where he was cautious, I'd be reckless. Where he was intent on preserving his reputation as an upstanding citizen and moral paragon among people to whom he was entirely indifferent, I would lay myself bare in full public view through my exhibitionistic writing.

And yet I could feel his expressionless, self-centered face hardening over mine like a plaster death mask. The humiliations I was suffering almost daily over Kevin had sapped my confidence, unmanned me. I was like a troublesome tooth that a dentist desensitizes by killing the nerve. The tooth continues to sit tranquilly in the mouth, resembling the adjacent teeth, but it is dead. Perhaps I'd suffered so much I'd died.

Abe said that everyone was always going on about cruel heterosexual fathers who reject their gay sons, but he asserted that more frequently the gay son, who wants a kind of gentle, half-romantic love that his bewildered heterosexual father isn't programmed to provide, ends up by rejecting old ineffectual Dad. I didn't know when or exactly why I'd rejected my father, but I hated him now with the cold, abiding resentment of the jilted lover.

Even though Kevin was small and boyish and looked no more than sixteen, even though I was the one who paid the rent and ran the household, with him I was once again hoping, as I'd always hoped with my father, to squeeze a bit of love out of a distant man.

At least that was the sort of thing we discussed in therapy, Abe and I, although now it all sounds both pat and unconvincing. I could just as easily have said, I now see, that I was impersonating my father and Kevin me, but with a new twist: now it was the son who was denying his father love, not the contrary. Or I could have said that no one was playing anyone and that the drama between Kevin and me wasn't a restaging of roles but rather a re-enactment of certain tensions created by crossing the themes of money and love when I was a child.

Or I could have said that I loved Kevin, as who would not, and he didn't love me, which was reasonable. The story was just that simple and any effort to extenuate that unacceptable fact was pathetic.

While writing my history textbook, I'd been polishing my novel about Christa. I'd spent five years writing it, most of that time occurring before the long-delayed publication of my Japanese-Fire Island novel. Now, having put the finishing touches to it, I submitted it to the same woman who'd published the earlier novel. She wasn't too sure about the new book. She asked for extensive revisions; by the time I'd done them she'd changed her mind and rejected the manuscript. "You tried the most difficult thing of all," she said, "to make a passive woman your heroine. Good try, but you didn't pull it off."

Kevin was so stoic in facing his own almost daily defeats during auditions that he set me a heroic example. I didn't complain, although I registered in my marrow every one of the twenty-three rejections the book subsequently garnered. Kevin and I smoked so much dope and dropped so many pills that we were in a constant confusion of creativity. He disliked my solid, bill-paying side, even though he depended on it, but he warmed to me whenever I'd tell him about a new book I was planning or whenever I'd listen as he told me about his plan to memorize *backwards* the whole first-act balcony scene in Nöel Coward's *Private Lives*.

An older poet whom I'd met through Joshua told me he'd been to see an ancient Jungian famous for curing blocked writers. "What did she tell you?" I asked eagerly. "She asked me to give her the schedule of my typical day and I said, 'Well, I wake up and get up,' and she interrupted me right away and said, 'But you must never get up. You must pee, make coffee, then go back to bed right away before you've spoken to anyone and contaminated your mind with chatter and then write for just half an hour a day. That way you're close to the unconscious and the universal language of dreams, and your defenses are still low.' "

I don't think the poet ever followed her system, but I did. I had such a crushing schedule to follow with my U.S. history textbook that I felt the only way I'd ever write fiction again was by doing a half hour in bed every morning. I hadn't reread my Fire Island novel since I'd written it five years earlier, but a few people had praised it for its "Baroque" quality so that now, in my new book, I began to write in that complex, ornate style; for me, at least, a Baroque style is one that sets every element in motion, that confuses religious sentiment with sensuality and that makes little distinction between ornament and substance. Despite the fact that those early readers of mine had been wrong and my Fire Island-Japanese book may have been surrealistic in its vision but quite chaste in its style, I was now in the process of imitating their mistaken impression of my earlier work.

But my new book wasn't altogether healthy; I confused my fantasies with reality, replaced the simple past with the past-subjunctive of wish fulfillment. I turned my boring father into a satanic playboy, my hysterical mother into an operatic madwoman. My narrator was Kevin twenty years older, who regretted that he'd rejected his patient, wise lover (an amalgam of Frank O'Hara, God and me). I feared I was beginning to lose my mind. One morning I knelt in the hallway outside my bedroom door and prayed to God, but when I opened my eyes He was standing there dressed in full saturnine leathers.

At noon my secretary would arrive. Through a friend at the gym I'd found William, a smiling, deferential, painfully thin man in his midtwenties. He was an aspiring actor who, I gathered, lived with a lover (in those days people would admit almost apologetically that they had a lover, as though it were a bad habit or the survivor of an earlier, less enlightened age). He would sit patiently while I shuffled through piles of Xeroxed historical articles and the cut-and-paste outline. Then, suddenly inspired, I'd begin to dictate pages of my textbook. I feared that if I didn't have someone sitting there whom I paid by the hour I'd never get around to writing *Changing Eras*.

Of course we ended up talking a lot about our lives. William even invited me to catch his performance at the Upstairs at the Downstairs. I went one evening and was surprised to see him in chains, alternating tap dancing and a humorous monologue in which he spoke about his childhood in New Hampshire, his desire to be dominated and his struggle with diabetes. Part of me was shocked by such candor; I still believed in Virginia Woolf's distinction between art and self-expression. But another part of me recognized that every dare William made against propriety generated a spark, and that energy I was almost certain could be called aesthetic. To me, a work of art is a performance of a certain length that generates *interest*. Hovering just over the divide between invention and reportage struck me as inherently interesting, especially when what was being reported was a whole new world of experience.

EIGHT

Kevin and I were both passionate admirers of Ross Stubbins, the avant-garde theater director, but he seemed to us as unapproachable as all other celebrated people. We were certain that he held no brief with the New York commercial theater, nor did we, although Kevin kept auditioning for it and I kept writing for it; during the preceding ten years I'd written five full-length plays, which were meant to be attractive to a Broadway producer, since they required only a single set and no more than six actors and were intended to be funny and topical, but I never had the energy or confidence in my theatrical skills to push them. Nor had I ever admired a play I'd seen on Broadway.

Stubbins didn't seem to have financial restrictions. He would put on a three-day play with a cast of two hundred at a festival in Casablanca or Aix, and in New York he had his own foundation, his own school of acting and an association with a Fifty-Seventh Street gallery, where he sold his costume sketches at high, conceptual-art prices. He had a fascination with *The Beauty and the Beast*, which he'd adapted and staged in dozens of different versions, variously mixed and crosshatched with Spanish religious processions, textbook explanations of ballet or a largely effaced script of Ibsen's *Little Eyolf*.

I'd met a man who claimed to have been his roommate in an Oklahoma madhouse twenty years ago, when they'd both been of college age.

This man had even written an article in a learned journal about Stubbins' obsessive arranging of the coffee service on a tray. Since Stubbins' staging was all based upon the elements of the set being juxtaposed to one another according to the most minute calculations and those proportions reflected in the actors' movements, the article about these arrangements provided a key to Stubbins' mysterious but apparently rigorous staging.

Kevin and I went night after night to see Stubbins' current play. Usually we smoked some marijuana, occasionally sprayed with a hallucinogen or a horse tranquilizer—we scarcely knew which—and once we ran into Brewster, one of the White Russians, with his wife covered in brilliants. Kevin and I, in our T-shirts and leather jackets and dirty, ripped jeans, clung to each other like two little kids lost in the adult world. We giggled at everything Brewster said and I was incapable of responding conventionally to Brewster's hard-edged, insincere show of seeming "interested." I laughed and laughed, certain that Brewster himself was in on the joke and playing a role just to amuse me. I could imagine what Brewster and Muffy must have thought, for even though I'd fucked Brewster years ago, before his marriage, now I'd gone from what he would have called "decadent" (i.e., stylishly, mysteriously bisexual) to "raunchy" (poor, obvious and no longer redeemable).

Stubbins was able to attract Village gays as well as Italian art dealers in their dark glasses, baggy, expensive suits and grey-striped collarless linen shirts. There was even a sprinkling of uptown millionaire collectors in search of new thrills. Ten years later in New York *le beau monde* would reject all other groups and would become as narrowly exclusive as their parents had been, but in the aftermath of the 1960s they'd momentarily lost their confidence and thought the way to be chic was to be promiscuously social and arty.

Kevin was thrilled one night when he picked up a dark, muscular, nappy-haired guy who danced in Stubbins' plays (he simply walked, in place, or backwards and forwards, for hours on end). At last Kevin had met someone who was intimate with the great Stubbins—*how* intimate Kevin learned only during the long, druggy, talky night when Maurice confided he lived with Stubbins and had been his lover for years.

Kevin gave Maurice his phone number on a scrap of paper and half-hoped he'd hear from him. After two weeks without a call, Kevin, disappointed, said, "Gee, I thought the sex was great and we sure had a lot in common, but my mistake was that I made him dork me. Have you ever noticed you only get a call-back when you've done the dorking? No, I'm serious, it's absolutely a rule." (*Call-back* was the show-biz word for a second audition.) Kevin also worried that Maurice might have looked down on him for being the type of actor who was still going to "cattle calls" (open auditions) for Broadway plays. On the other hand, Maurice had told Kevin that Stubbins didn't despise the commercial theater but had just found that everything on stage happened too fast. "Everyone was speeding around in such a brisk, artificial way, making entrances and exits like birds in an overwound cuckoo clock, and Stubbins thought any five minutes would be good if it was slowed down to five hours."

The morning after their one night together, Kevin had told Maurice over our noon breakfast things I hadn't known. We were seated around a little brown metal table painted to look like knotty pine. The double sink was from the thirties and the huge stove and the fridge, with its rounded edges and big chrome handle, from the fifties. We'd scrubbed them to a gleaming white, and just painted the walls a shiny white all over. One night on speed we'd washed the windows with vinegar and newspapers, but the bright sunlight showed the unreachable smudge where the upper and lower sash panes overlapped. Kevin was saying, "I lived in London for two years. I told everyone later that I was studying at the Royal Academy of Dramatic Arts, but actually I just clapped on a cowboy hat and hustled. The English are so weird. In England a typical john is a married bank clerk who arrives with a briefcase in which he has a wooden cucumber he's whittled and painted green for a month every evening in his basement shop and now he wants one to insert it into his not altogether clean posterior—they know nothing about douching."

"I think I'd like that," Maurice said, unsmiling, coolly exhaling smoke. "I'm into shit—*not* to eat, mind you, but . . . otherwise."

I wondered if Kevin's coldness, his degrading comebacks and snappy putdowns, might not be a remnant of his days on the street in Piccadilly. It was one thing to turn a paying trick from time to time in New York and another to hustle for a living in another country, to be exposed, day after day, to the resentment and stinginess of rogue customers.

We began to receive dirty phone calls from someone who identified himself only as "Jimmy." I would have hung up on him out of unreflecting prissiness but Kevin grabbed the receiver and shooed me out of the room, miming that I was to close the door behind me. (His miming, unlike everyone else's, was completely understandable.) Ten minutes later he strolled into my study, where I was dictating the crossing of the Delaware to my masochistic, tap-dancing secretary. "Excuse me for interrupting," he said, "but that guy on the phone had a very sick and admirable imagination. He threatened me with the most refined tortures and ended up chaining me to a tree in the Rambles and strangling me with my own knickers. Verbally, of course."

William smiled with that Mona Lisa smile variously attributed to the joys of pregnancy, the desire to conceal bad teeth or fatuous self-regard (was the Mona Lisa Leonardo's self-portrait?). In William's case (was it Mona Lisa's?), he was smiling with that mixture of slyness and shame with which a masochist recognizes a fellow sufferer. Even among otherwise sophisticated homosexuals a committed masochist must conceal his penchant. No one truly understands him, although friends are vulgarly curious or tell stupid jokes ("Beat me," said the masochist. "No," said the sadist)—jokes that reveal no understanding at all of the subtle reciprocity between master and slave.

Something about William's smile—the guilty, dawning, What-Woman-Wouldn't smile of complicity—excited me. Kevin left, I dictated a bit more and stood uncomfortably close behind William. He looked up at me with harassed, humorous eyes.

"Wanna go in the bedroom?" I said.

After that, every afternoon we'd continue our dictation in the bedroom for half an hour. William's body was thin, his skin flaky, his hair long, fine and dry, but he was also supple and seraphically obliging. His face was pointy as stiffly beaten egg whites—a point for a nose, a pointy chin, darting, funny eyes with long, stiff eyelashes. They bubbled with sparkling wit and a knowledge as sophisticated as it was perverse. I felt a complete control over him that I didn't think about very much and certainly didn't question. After I'd come in his ass (William didn't usually even touch himself or get hard), he'd smile the rueful, indulgent smile of the older woman humoring her vigorous young lover.

William had a lover he'd been with for years and I knew from a mutual friend that if with me he was awed and mostly tongue-tied, with his own crowd he was a chatterbox and hysterically funny. The thought that he had a whole life apart from me only reassured me. I didn't have to take any responsibility for him. He admitted to me that he drank too much, given that he was diabetic, and twice in the last year he'd passed out. He could rarely get it up and explained, blushing, that as a diabetic he was intermittently impotent.

Judging from our sessions, he was *always* impotent, although it occurred to me that he wanted to please me but didn't desire me and this lack of desire was the real reason he couldn't get an erection. I didn't mind. I even took a secret pleasure in the thought that the only stiff dick in the room was mine. I'd throw his legs back and hook them over my shoulders and fuck him with less performance anxiety and more genuine enjoyment than I'd ever known before. So little was at stake emotionally for me that I could relax enough to feel the sensations flowing through me. Sometimes after I'd come, while I was still in him, he'd jerk off modestly, hygienically, with a half-hard penis. If I had made the least grunt signaling impatience, I'm sure he would have waived his climax as an unnecessary luxury.

I felt a nice, simple affection for him, the sort of feeling a married man must have for an ugly mistress, one he keeps assuring is "the best pal a fellow ever had." Our mutual friend told me that William was in love with me, but I didn't want to hear too much about that. Usually I was the ironic, wounded, quick-to-forgive party (observant, mocking, grateful), a Merry Andrew of thoughts and half-thoughts, but with William I was the bluff, nice guy who just wants a hug and a squirt and who taps his partner woodenly on the back at parting and says, "See you sometime"—the very words my father would murmur, cigar clenched in his teeth, when he'd rush us at the last possible second to Union Station and put my sister and me on the train to go home to our mother.

One day I asked William if he'd told his lover we were fooling around. He blushed because I'd broken the unspoken etiquette of our relationship, the rule that we should never acknowledge what we were doing or the consequences it might have. He said, "Oh, well, you know, he and I have a New York marriage, sexless, companionable, flourishing." He looked at me with his mild smile, his narrow head cocked to one side, and added, mildly, "Alas."

A friend of mine had said, "Even if gays weren't oppressed they'd still be unhappy since ninety-five percent are bottoms and only five percent tops," or, as someone else put it, "Lot of hens around here and not enough roosters." With William I enjoyed impersonating a cock because topping someone was the role everyone admired; in the old Mediterranean world the active partner wasn't even considered to be gay. I knew, however, that I was a hen, though I'd not started out thinking that way at all. When I was a boy of twelve I'd convinced the neighbor boy that one guy could screw another (he could scarcely believe it, especially since I'd damaged my credibility by insisting that men always mounted women doggie-style, which Stuart knew for sure couldn't be true).

One night when he stayed over I convinced Stuart I was right at least about the possibilities of the male anatomy and we took turns every afternoon thereafter cornholing each other. I can still remember the feel of the tops of his big cold feet against which I'd press my hot little soles when he'd lie on top of me. His skin smelled of acne medication and his retainer of grape jelly and peanut butter, which he always ate for lunch. His buttocks were nerveless and clammy, his chest flat and blue veined. In the Midwest of the 1950s before they had learned from television to deliver snappy, rueful one-liners about themselves, Americans were nearly comatose from lack of awareness, drugged on the simple fact of existing, of constituting the *Ding an sich* of Ohio in the summer heat. This unconsciousness even gave Stuart a dreamlike intensity for once I'd gotten him used to sex, every afternoon he'd sit beside me on the piano bench while I practiced and he'd stare at me with a half-grin suffusing his face, an expression that had a nearly geological pressure, as though it would continue until all the stone had compressed into a single diamond. I could see the dark spot on his grey trousers where his twelve-year-old desire was secreting its tincture, drop by drop.

When we ended up in my bedroom, as we inevitably did, there never was the slightest hint of romance or even friendliness. He wanted to stick it in me and I wanted to stick it in him and we'd each complain with grumpy humor about the "pain in the butt" that the other guy represented. "Aren't you done yet?" he'd ask while I was screwing him. "Hold it!" I'd mutter, as he was shoving it in. "Take it out. Take it *out*, it hurts like hell, I think I'm going to poop." It never occurred to us that anyone could enjoy being penetrated or that anyone could fuck with style or bring anal pleasure to his partner. Stuart would just lay his full weight on me, not even propping himself up on his elbows, breathe his peanut-butter breath on my cheek and rock his pelvis back and forth with almost no thrust until a sigh and a spurt would escape him.

His body was the pudding-soft, unexercised body of the teacher's pet, the kid who never does anything more strenuous than reluctant jumping-jacks in gym class. He was still just a boy with knock knees and big elbows, legs skinny as stilts and huge feet, a rib cage that stood out in relief when he breathed in, a bellybutton that was an "inny" and collected lint. There wasn't a hair on his pale body except the new, black, luxurious triangle planted so prominently below his flat little blue stomach. I was already sufficiently thoughtful—and therefore gay?—to fuck him first so that he wouldn't come and then have to endure my exertions while resenting me. I preferred to make the sacrifice and be the no-longer-desiring passive victim who'd already come.

After we'd both ejaculated in the torpid Cincinnati heat, we'd get up and see a sweat-soaked, dark blue outline of a man on the pale blue bed cover, a blurred outline as though the man had moved during an X-ray.

I saw Stuart four years later at a party his parents were giving and though a whole crowd was reeling drunkenly up and down the stairs in a house that was normally dim and silent he dragged me into his room and locked the door and pulled his cock out of his fly. It had grown huge since I'd last seen it, not just long but wide, and with his geological smile he tried to make me sit on it. I whispered hoarsely and angrily, "Are you *crazy!*" No one could have been more conventional than Stuart, but now, unaccountably, he was fearless with lust and his usually stolid, silent house was alive with carnival excitement. That was the last time I ever saw him and I regretted that I held out on him. Now I hear he's a grandfather. Would he pull it out now if I saw him in his downtown office? If I went there, where he manages the family business, would he lock the door, sprawl back in his desk chair and look at me with that old, unaffectionate, nearly unconscious desire?

But what struck me then was that there was no longer a question on the night of the party of our taking turns cornholing each other while the other waited impatiently. Now Stuart just assumed I was the one who'd sit on him. Of course he was right. I can still see him wearing a lazy, confident smile, so at odds with his usual bank-clerkly earnestness. Was he exhibiting the secret coquetry of the chief accountant? He was right in assuming I no longer cared about my cock, about getting my rocks off. His cock had become immensely wide and long and mine was still as small as when we'd met. Stuart didn't reach for my crotch, as though he knew it meant nothing to anyone, least of all to me. He just gloried in his, as though he'd pulled me into a closet to show me his pet mink and we both stared at its caged lustrousness frozen and crazy in the beam of a flashlight.

KEVIN KEPT RECEIVING his dirty phone calls from "Jimmy" and eventually I grew used to closeting Kevin away with his invisible lover, even bringing him the necessary poppers from the fridge.

When Kevin's parents and grandmother came to visit us for a few days, he was soon enough wild with impatience. His granny was Welsh and sang in a choir back home. She was nearly deaf but always trotting about with a sense of purpose, even when she had nothing to do; she was like a wind-up toy that will scurry forward no matter where it's set down, even on the edge of a very high table. One evening they were all sitting around our gloomy, underlit, underfurnished apartment singing a chorus from *HMS Pinafore* when the phone rang. I answered and called out, "Kevin, you can take it in my study." I bustled off to fetch his poppers and rejoined our guests just in time to sing with them the last chorus of "For he *is* an Englishman." When Kevin staggered in fifteen minutes later, grinning lopsidedly, he was perceptibly less tense.

Soon after Kevin's parents left, "Jimmy" asked to meet him at the Eagle's Nest at midnight. Jimmy said in detail what he was going to do with Kevin. "Of course I'll never go," Kevin said. "It's one thing to serve a psychopath over the phone and another to be stripped and branded as dear Jimmy proposed tonight."

"How would he recognize you, or you him?"

"Funny. I asked him the same question but he only grunted in reply. Do you think he knows me? Ghastly thought. Is he (groan) a Fan?"

I went out to the Candle and saw a guy at the bar who was tall and rumpled and wearing his keys on the right. I'd been to bed with several men who'd turned out to be masochists and often I'd visited a real fury on them, at least verbally, but I'd never had the nerve to present myself as a bona fide sadist at a bar where a masochist was clearly advertising his desires. I felt that whereas I might thrill a secret bottom who was expecting nothing more than "vanilla sex" (as we contemptuously called peaceful, reciprocal lovemaking), a self-declared masochist who was signaling in a public place for a master could only be disappointed by me.

Nevertheless the night was a cold, quiet, rainy weeknight in early March, no one could be expecting much excitement, there were only fifteen men in the bar, most of them friends chatting to each other. The real leathermen would be off at the Eagle's Nest in West Chelsea, the very place Jimmy had named. I moved up behind my masochist and rubbed his ass, bought him a beer, soon had him up in my apartment. We smoked a joint sprayed with PCP. I had him undressed and was about to fuck him when he suddenly said, "You don't know what you're doing."

He fucked me for hours until finally I gave up. Something coiled and watchful in me relaxed, blinked off. He who'd looked so rumpled and uneasy when he was playing a bottom now became a jackhammer of pure will. Did he envy the submissive men he brought so much pleasure to? Did he want to be a top topped by a still stronger top? Not that he had a muscled or well worked body. By our rigorous standards he was flabby, although any normal person would have found him to be fit. But I didn't think about what he looked like, only about what he was doing to me. He wouldn't let me touch my own cock because he didn't want me to come and no longer be cooperative. His whole body was permeated with sweat like an unglazed clay pot filled with water. The water was seeping through. His hair, blacker now that it was wet, clung to his forehead like a whiplash. His sweat dripped onto me, drop by drop. His eyes were closed, his mouth open. He smelled of cured black olives. For once I wasn't worrying that my ass was too loose; in fact he was whispering, "Open it up. Give it to me." I was dimly aware that Kevin had come home and I could hear the murmuring of a deep male voice, someone else's. The man I was with was fucking me so hard, so constantly and for so long that finally Kevin whispered through the door that Daniella, our landlady, was in the hallway, irate because of the pounding noise. It was five in the morning. My bedroom was just above hers, apparently. Kevin said, "I told her that you were piling *books* but would stop now."

I couldn't bear for this man to be out of me even for a moment but I wriggled out from under him and led him into the living room, where he fucked me for another hour on the floor. Kevin had forbidden all curtains as old-ladyish. As the dawn twitched like the sphincter of a man who's about to hit his climax, our neighbors across the way could have looked in had they not all been blind or feeble or asleep. Kevin's guest left. I heard the bass murmur of his voice and the click of the front door. I was certain that their lovemaking had been romantic whereas ours had been bestial. Kevin's beauty made him a member of a higher species, one that lived in an airy medium of flirtation, lingering kisses, murmured vows, whereas I was just nails clawing a back or a dirty butt lowering itself onto a lapping mouth. The daylight was now bright, high enough that it no longer cast long, canyon-like shadows. At last my partner came, his body doubled back like a bow that finally releases its long, straight arrow. I'd waited so long for his climax that now I couldn't believe everything was over. My spine ached where it had been pounded, vertebra by vertebra, into the hardwood floor.

We sat on the couch—naked, dazed, stinking like horses—and I was still so stoned that I didn't know if the guy's cock was really huge or if I was incapable of judging size. We smoked cigarettes. Kevin came in, naked, childlike and friendly on drugs, and sat on the other side of the man. He smoked a cigarette, too, not inhaling but sipping at it like a schoolgirl. "You'll never guess who that was," he said. "My beau?"

"No, who?" I prompted.

"Well," he said, politely explaining to our guest, "I've been getting dirty phone calls from a stranger named Jimmy. Tonight Jimmy wanted me to meet him at the Eagle's Nest. No way, I thought, this guy sounds dangerous and crazy. But by chance I was with some friends and we ended up at the Eagle, where I saw Ross Stubbins, the famous theater director. I kept circling around him, grinning like an idiot, and finally he noticed me and I bagged him. I brought him home and as soon as we got in bed he started a dirty, violent rap and my hair stood on end and I said, '*You're* Jimmy!' but he just pressed his finger to his lips."

"How terrifying!" I said, delighted.

"Not really. He's a pussycat. He could barely get it up because he'd drunk so much vodka. After he came we talked about theater for hours."

"How did he get your phone number?" my trick asked.

"Well, I'd made it with Stubbins' lover, Maurice, a dancer. I gave Maurice my phone number and Stubbins found it and thought I was someone else, someone he'd met before on a heavy scene."

"But he ended up with you after all," I said. "What a weird coincidence."

Finally at about ten in the morning our guest showered and dressed. At the front door he said, "Don't you even want to see me again?"

And I said no. I found a small, inexplicable revenge in coolly rejecting the man who'd reduced me to a hungry hole; at the door social conventions were re-introduced, the formalities at customs even on the border of the Land of Dreams. I suppose I was so sated that I thought I'd never need to be fucked again. Although I spent hours every week looking for sex I had no interest in arranging for a regular supply of it from a steady. And I had said *no* in front of Kevin, almost as an offering on the altar of my love for him. All Kevin could say, when I told him the story of how my slave had become my master, was, "Well, of course, I saw the size of the meat."

I craved love, sex, fame, money, food and drugs, and yet I never suspected I was addicted to these things because my specialty was hopeless love; sex I'd never institutionalized in my life except with William, my secretary; money and fame I wooed only very indirectly through my postmodernist metafiction, which already in the 1970s was a disappearing art form; I concocted elaborate French meals that were so demanding that the cost and effort of preparing them outweighed any pleasure in eating them; and I'd never *bought* drugs and didn't even know a dealer. I had a puritanical horror of organized pleasure, routine lubricity, regular fêtes, and I would have agreed with that philosopher who said a habit always represents a failure.

The next day I sent Daniella a bouquet and a note: "So sorry about the noise I made last night, piling books. You'll be pleased to hear 'Books' won't be back."

MY MOTHER was happy and healthy and back at work; she reported to me (with that candor about her intimate life that I took for granted but that my friends found so peculiar) that Randy, her lover, had treated her missing breast with wonderful tenderness. At fifty, he was fourteen years younger than she: "I was so worried and anxious that he'd reject me. You wouldn't understand, dear, but men, normal men, are funny about things like that. They're not tough like women—or like you. Aesthetics is so important to them. Maybe it's because a breast takes them back to their infancy. Freud was undoubtedly right. Men need to be nourished. And then our age difference. . . .We think we've outgrown Freud what with the new thinking, the new emphasis on the physiological, I'm surprised that psychoanalysts are still in business, what can *you* be doing with a shrink, why don't you just accept yourself as you are? I'd never let anyone tinker with *my* mind."

This gust of strong-willed self-satisfaction gave way to gently ruminative self-satisfaction. "Randy just leaned over and kissed my scar—it's horrible, I'll have to show it to you, just for scientific interest—he leaned over and kissed it in the dark, he'd turned out the light, he's so diplomatic like that, he lowered the strap of my nightgown and kissed the scar, I felt so vulnerable, you can't imagine how a woman feels when she loses a breast, it's as though she has been castrated, for you, for men, it would be the equivalent of castration, so I was feeling very vulnerable when he kissed me." Mother liked Randy more than any of her earlier lovers, she said. "He's the only one who ever liked to go grocery shopping with me. We just push our cart up and down the aisles without any rush and we choose what we need. We're very cozy. And, honey, he always says the most beautiful prayers. Just today at dinner he said, 'Oh, Lord, thank you for protecting us on the I-90, especially at that dangerous intersection where the traffic comes in from Gary.' Isn't that beautiful? He's such a feeling, religious man. He's like my father. I don't think Randy has any Irish blood, but he has that deep Irish soul like my father." She remembered her original subject: "And honey, he was so sweet, he said when he was kissing my scar, 'Hello, little missing boozy, my girl's not complete any more but I don't mind,' isn't that sweet? I cried, I tell you, I wept."

I didn't think what Randy had said was very gallant, much less sweet, but I didn't say so. My mother spoke about the most delicate things in her own life with the irony-free manner, rough-and-ready vocabulary and clarion tones of a bad actress in a black-and-white film of the forties. My sister and I were always wincing. "Oh, *Mother . . .*" we'd complain.

"I don't know why you two are so sensitive. I just call a spade a spade, but you're always cringing and wincing."

Anne was miserable. She had been living in a small apartment on the Near North Side and driving up to a North Shore college where she was studying for her master's in social work, but she'd become such a drinker that her ex-husband had insisted on taking back their children. Even though he'd loved my sister so deeply and suffered so much because of her, he quickly remarried and at last turned very cold toward her.

"You can hardly blame him," my mother said during one of our weekly phone calls. "I just don't know what's wrong with Anne. Here she had a nice-looking husband—"

"*Mother*, he's not nice looking."

"Well, maybe not by New York narcissistic standards, but he was a perfectly presentable—"

"Randy boor."

"She should have been glad he was attentive, most men are unfaithful after a few years of marriage, look at your own father, when we were just a young couple living in a furnished room in Gary, Indiana, why, we had to share the bathroom with another couple, but I didn't mind, we received a book once a month from the Book of the Month Club and we read it out loud to each other, we read Will and Ariel Durant's *The Story of Philosophy* out loud, and then he dragged home a filthy disease, he gave me *gonorrhea*—"

"*Mother*, you've told me all that a thousand times."

"Well, I'm just establishing what men, most men, are like and how Anne was wrong to reject her husband, so upstanding and devoted, this is just between us, I'd never tell her—"

"*Mother*, Anne is a lesbian."

"She's not, she's just imitating you, she's always been impressionable."

One night, very late, my mother called, sobbing, to say my sister had tried to commit suicide again. "The poor little thing, we've been frantic, we didn't know where to look for her. She had another bout in the hospital, I didn't tell you, I didn't want to upset you, and when she was released she thought her shrink would be there, I guess she's in love with him, well, he wasn't and she never left the parking lot of the hospital, talk about acting out, she'd stashed some pills in the car, just in case, I guess, that girl is so unstable, though I always showered her with advantages—"

"*Mother*, tell me about Anne."

"Well, don't snap my head off" (she said "snap" instead of "bite"). "Although I can understand that you must be terribly upset. It seems that her shrink had gone on vacation. She must have felt terribly abandoned. Of course I would have been there upon discharge but she won't take my calls. I'm the villain. Her doctor—oh, brother, you've never seen such a weak-chinned, limp-wristed, weasly little shrimp as this doctor, who's not even an MD. He's only a social worker who subscribes to some sort of barmy 'contractual therapy' where you sign a contract to do certain things and not others—"

I felt threatened by my sister's breakdown, especially since I'd grown up thinking she was our hostage to normality, the only one of us three who wasn't weird. Ever since I'd been a child, my mother, my sister and I had formed a rag-tag tribe of three. We were like mice curled up inside a drawer in the attic who can recognize one another by the family smell. We fought, we complained, we had our shared jokes. Our mother kept up a perpetual litany of self-praise and some of it spilled over onto Anne and me. We were both "brilliant," of course, although Anne was "practical" and I was "in the clouds." We were the Three Musketeers. We took long car trips together, making five hundred miles a day as we drove across the Mississippi and on down to Texas to see our grandmother. We'd stop in roadside motor lodges where for five dollars our mother would rent a bungalow for the night ("Isn't this exciting, kids?"), one that would smell of backed-up sewage and where nothing was clean but the water glasses in glassine envelopes and presumably the toilet seat, which when upright retracted into a machine that treated it with germ-killing ultraviolet rays. If there was a TV, as there only sporadically was and then only after the mid-1950s, we had to feed it with quarters. Often it had glued to it a translucent plastic sheet dyed blue at the top for the sky and green at the bottom for grass. Sometimes the bed would vibrate with "magic fingers" if it was fed quarters. The motel owner would roll down the hill a metal cot on wheels for me, which opened up with all the grace of an iron lung and was as comfortable as the rack. More than once we'd be awakened by bedbugs. Tiny red dots would appear around our ankles and across our tummies.

When we'd get to Ranger, Texas, where our grandmother lived with her second husband, Anne and I felt like Yankees and city slickers. We settled down, slightly in awe of these very old country people. Our grandmother, Willie Lulu, had been one of twelve children. Her parents had been homesteaders who'd come in a covered wagon from Louisiana to Texas a couple of decades after the Civil War. We went out to their original farm, where one of my great-uncles still lived. My own mother had lived there as a girl after her real father had died and before her mother had remarried. There were pecan trees by a stream. There was a smoke-house behind the main house; the main house had started out as a log cabin that had gradually been engulfed by the rooms that were added on in every direction. My mother remembered her Grandmother Oakes, who'd sit in a leather chair reading the Bible and chewing tobacco. Her pale-eyed husband never said a word. The family picture of all twelve children and the parents on the porch looked like road kill caught in the headlights.

Our grandmother, Willie Lulu, had ended up somehow in this nearly abandoned town of Ranger, which still flew a tattered banner over the main street that proclaimed, "Oil Capital of the World," even though the wells had long since run dry. Folks had to drive fifty miles to the nearest movie theater. Willie had a little house on one level of just five rooms and a kitchen. There was the front parlor we never went into, as rarely visited as the front door that led into it. In that room were armchairs and a sofa of tufted velveteen and an empty cut-glass flower vase on a pale blue mirrored coffee table. In a bookcase, which was a separate piece of furniture covered with a doily and sheathed with clear glass doors that could be unlocked and swung open, were housed all the volumes of the Harvard Five-Foot Shelf of Classics, including the poems of John Greenleaf Whittier and James Whitcomb Riley, Charles Dana's memoirs, *Two Years Before the Mast*, Lowell's *Breakfast Chat*, a rhymed verse translation of Dante and many other treasures. They must have belonged to my step-grandfather; Willie could read only by moving her lips. Then there were two bedrooms, each heated by a gas burner. There was a family room where everyone spent the whole day and finally a dining room next to the kitchen where we ate our fried chicken, collard greens, black-eyed peas and biscuits and gravy.

She chopped all her hair way back so that it looked like a crewcut growing out. Her eyes were nearly white with cataracts and she could no longer see to sew though she could read and write letters. Willie wrote her letters in pencil and spelled phonetically. She and my mother corresponded every day they were apart. Willie was always smiling, a bit lopsidedly because her face was palsied on one side. She had three ripe, heavy wens on her face, one beside her mouth. Willie dressed up with a hat and black shoes and a store-bought dress with a belt of the same color to go around her broad waist when my mother would take her in the car to see other relatives in far-flung Texas towns, but at home she wore a short-sleeved house dress and backless slippers. Her arms were heavy and crêpey and jiggled when she moved. She babied her husband and even bought him his clothes and cut his hair, but at the same time she respected him as an educated man. If she called him "Mr. Wentworth," he called her just "Willie."

The back door was always open in the summer, night and day, though a screen door kept out the flies. A fan swept us all in its fugitive breeze. A grape arbor produced tangy, almost bitter dark blue grapes with cloudy, blue-grey skins. When Willie would call her chickens to feed them she'd produce a high wail as strange as a Bedouin's ululation.

Work was minimal when we were there. Most of the time we sat around "visiting." We'd go over every little thing, such as the weather or the mileage our car was getting or the immoral goings-on of the local high school coach, who was bedding several of the married women in town. My grandmother would stand on her porch and watch his progress from house to house, as though he were the rooster servicing all the chickens. My mother would talk a lot about her plans. I noticed she made them sound even more idealistic and humanitarian than when she was alone with us, although her tone was always somewhat exalted. If a joke was good, there was no reason it shouldn't be repeated, and hours later a silence could still be filled with a reprise of the punchline ("And *that*, son, is the difference 'tween courtesy and *tact*"), which would trigger off a new chorus of laughter that would reduce my mother and grandmother to tears.

Of course we couldn't say anything strange or negative about our life up north, because my mother was so eager to shine in Willie's eyes. I suppose we half-suspected, Anne and I, that we were deeply disturbed, and we were relieved to look like a happy, successful family for a moment in our grandmother's eyes, even if she was an old woman whose face was scored with lines, as though the person tracing out portions with a knife on the soft icing had gone mad and continued to score it senselessly into ever smaller pieces. We wanted to be approved of by our grandmother, even if she said, "Why, ain't that nice," to almost anything upbeat and would shuffle back to her kitchen the instant the talk took an "ugly" turn. If she was forced to listen to something harsh, the most she would say was, "Well, I declare."

She had a certain reserve that worked as a reproach to her garrulous, self-dramatizing children. Just when everyone else was leaning into the conversation, Willie would step outdoors, pretending to chase a neighbor's cat away. Or she'd head for the kitchen to dry her dishes and arrange them. Our mother turned to her stepfather, "Willie would never let me do chores. When I got married I didn't even know how to boil an egg. If I so much as offered to dry a dish she'd say, 'I want you to study. Anyone can do chores. You've got to make something of yourself so that you can be of service. You were put on this earth to help humanity.' " At that my mother would tear up and grab her stepfather's hand. "You two have always believed in me. When I was going through the X-A" (our code word for my parents' divorce) "it was your faith in me that kept me going."

Willie had a cat she liked but she kept it outdoors. As a farm woman she had no truck with household pets. Her favorite chicken was called Biddy. She was a good laying chicken and Willie stole Biddy's egg every morning. I asked her if she'd ever kill Biddy and eat it, but all she would say was, "Eat that stringy old thing?" Typically she concealed her real affection under feigned disdain.

Willie's first husband, Jim, had died when my mother was just twelve. I confused the stories: sometimes it was said that Jim, who worked repairing or maybe laying train track, died of malaria, which he'd contracted when the railroad was being built through miasmal Houston. Other times it seemed he'd suffered a sunstroke. All that remains of him are a few beautifully penned postcards to my mother from a hospital in Colorado where he'd gone to "rest" (could he have had tuberculosis and they were afraid to name it?) and a tintype of a handsome young man—deep-set pale eyes, sensual mouth, unreadable brow, lots of hair—sitting on a porch beside a standing Willie, round-faced, hair up, her hat and traveling suit covered with jet-black embroidery. My mother and her defiant-looking brother in plus-fours and a newspaper boy's cap are squeezed between them. What seems suggestive is that, contrary to a Victorian wedding photo, here the man is seated and the woman standing.

As a railroad employee my grandfather had been lodged in a little house beside the tracks, but after he died my grandmother and her two children were ousted. They'd gone to the homestead farm—bliss for my mother, who'd run wild and played with dozens of cousins. And with one teenage uncle. "He used to rub me down there when I was just five or six. I liked it. It felt wonderful. Everyone makes too much of sex with children. After all, children have their sexual needs, too. As long as there's no violence. . . ." Willie, however, had to work terribly hard from dawn to dusk on the farm to earn their keep, although no one would have put it like that. She was just "doing chores."

She'd been released from servitude when she unexpectedly married Mr. Wentworth, a local high school math teacher. He took my mother's education in hand and later, when she was eighteen, made sure she went to university. He went with her, since he was working on an advanced degree that would allow him to teach on the junior college level. Without him my mother would never have had a higher education.

He was a good fifteen years younger than Willie and had always been fussed over by his mother and spinster sisters. He was almost an invalid since when, as a boy, he'd tattled to the schoolmarm on the other boys and they'd rewarded him after class by beating his leg to the bone with a thick stick. It became infected, then gangrenous, and finally had to be sawed off. Now he had a heavy wooden leg that was attached to his body by an elaborate harness. He walked with a rocking gait and had to lift the leg with both hands when he went upstairs. If he was resting he'd slump down in his chair and keep it stretched out in front of him. When Anne and I went to waken him in the morning, his leg would be standing in the corner like a totem garlanded with orthopedic straps.

When I was very young—fourteen?—my grandmother put my mother and sister in one bedroom and my grandfather and me in the other. She slept on the couch. Mr. Wentworth was a randy old thing who'd hug us all to his big soft chest and belly with his surprisingly powerful arms. At such moments he cocked his head to one side and wore a big, fatuous smile as though he were transfixed by some private joke. My mother said, "Poor

Mr. Wentworth, I'm sure Willie won't—well, I'm sure he's not getting much tenderness from her. Mother is as good as good gets but she doesn't set much store by—well, I'm sure Mr. Wentworth is *starved* for affection. But he's always been a terrible hugger and grabber. Maybe it started with his infirmity, but when I was sixteen and he became my stepdad, I can remember how he'd hug and hug me and I didn't like it at all but Willie *refused* to see anything wrong, she'd just say, 'Stop your fussin', can't you see he's just being *sweet*?' "

I wasn't his favorite grandchild and I'm sure he preferred little girls to boys, but that night—in the big featherbed which smelled of the yellowing cake of tar soap that Willie kept out in the wash house next to the chicken coop—Mr. Wentworth and I squeezed each other for hours on end. I was interested in his penis but no matter how much I let my hand, seemingly innocently, trail or flop about, he kept shifting adroitly away to avoid its touch.

He would, however, squeeze me and let me squeeze him, which was like squeezing a huge bolster loosely packed with feathers, but *heavy* feathers, as though they'd been dipped in mercury.

I could scarcely sleep, but I must have drifted into and out of sleep. My grandfather seemed to be mostly awake as well, since nearly every time I looked at him he was smiling on the pillow beside me. He was dressed in big, baggy white undershorts and a loose white T-shirt. When he'd unstrapped his wooden leg he'd hopped on the other over to bed. I was fascinated by his stump and he was never shy about showing it. But I'd never touched it and now I kept trying to judge from the pressure against me whether there was a bone in it or not.

My erection, pressed by my underpants against my stomach, throbbed, unrequited, and acted as the motor to my dreams. My dreams were at least half literary. My mother had given me a rhyming dictionary for Christmas that also explained all the traditional meters and forms. All through the holidays I'd been working on a paean to the seasons in Byron's *ottava rima*. My pleasure in the writing was registered as a light strum of my whole body and as a sizzling behind the temples. Sometimes I felt as though I were in an elevator that had just fallen a foot. For the first time my life was no longer all staccato notes. The idea that I had a big ongoing project had added to the score graceful, interlocking legato marks. The coal-tar smell of the clean sheets, smooth as wilting flower petals from hundreds of washings, the outrage of the cock's strangled cry just on the other side of the window, the metronomic pulsing of my penis under the waistband of my underpants, the pillowy disarray of my grandfather and his shy, half-awake smile, the visceral certainty that I was writing a great poem—that even now, as dawn was painting layer upon thin, silvery layer of lacquer on the blinds, my poem was metastasizing somewhere inside me—these were the elements that as a young Buddhist I tried to separate out, to disentangle and card. I wanted to cut through the knot of self, but as a writer I was incurably self-centered. I mean that I watched my mind at work and tried to catch it in the act of thinking; I was like a fisherman who watches a still pool, looking for a tell-tale ripple, that second when a wave takes on the substance of a fin or tail.

At last I fell asleep. When I awakened, my grandfather was already in harness and dressed and in the adjoining back parlor. Even through the closed door I could hear him saying to my grandmother, my mother and sister, "Ooh-ee! That little boy is just as sweet as he can be. We hugged and kissed all night long. He wouldn't let me go one single minute. He just hugged and kissed me. I never did see such a sweet little boy."

"Wall, ain't that just the sweetest thang you ever did hear?" I could just picture my grandmother's faint smile, her clouded eyes and the way her palsy shook her head slightly left to right, right to left as though she were saying *no* when all she ever said was *yes*.

My mother and sister were ominously silent. They, of course, knew exactly what sort of sickness and perversion I'd been up to. I wanted to rush out and shut my grandfather up, but it was too late, he was already saying it again, "Well, he's just as sweet as sugar. I never knew he loved his granddaddy so much. He just hugged and squeezed me all night long. He's as loving as a little angel boy."

I got out of bed and knelt beside the gas burner. I turned on the gas without lighting it. I inhaled deeply. I wanted to die. Finally I lost my nerve and turned off the gas and got dressed.

A FEW WEEKS AFTER my sister's second suicide attempt my mother phoned to tell me that my sister's oldest child, Gabriel, had been put by his father and stepmother into a mental hospital because he was cutting classes and had even run away for a week after having stolen seventy dollars from his father's wallet. "The poor boy, he's become violently anti-social," my mother said, "he just lives in the basement like an animal, he won't bathe or obey his father. He sleeps by day and won't go to school. Of course it's all your sister's fault for having put him in that

Free School where the kids do nothing but read Mao's Little Red Book all day and where the students, if you please, voted math out of the curriculum as being too bourgeois and just a capitalist tool. I'm sure the Russians have many fine mathematicians. Now poor Gabriel is just fourteen and he's out at the Lakewood Facility and the doctor is a total tyrant who acts like one of those religious cult leaders, those nuts, and he lives there with them, and the kids study nothing, they just sit around in those morbid group therapy sessions all day and drink coffee and smoke cigarettes." My mother burst into tears. When she recovered herself, she said, "Willie wasn't far wrong. Remember how she'd say, 'Don't smoke or drink'?"

' "*Drank*,' " I said. "She said, 'Don't smoke or *drank*.' "

"Don't make fun of her. She was a simple country woman but a lot more on the ball than—"

"I'm not making fun of her. I loved her. And poor Gabriel. Have you seen him?"

"When I think I have a daughter and a grandson in the asylum at the same time! Honey, what is the world coming to? We need Willie's good old-fashioned values. My, she was down-to-earth. Do you know that the day she died she laid out her dress and shoes and even chose her brooch, the things she wanted to be buried in?"

When I hung up I thought there was no choice between family life with its squabbles and sordid melodramas and single life with its melancholy pleasure seeking. I knew young mothers who dreamed of a few minutes in which to write a poem; I had vast acres of free time and not much heart to fill them. I could mope around the house for hours, berating myself, wilting onto a sofa or strumming through an insipid book, lighting up for a long, juicy phone call, then sinking into a hot bath in the middle of the afternoon with a pack of cigarettes and a pot of tea on the floor beside me, my eyes unhappy with the wall paint that had been slopped over the tiles although I would never have spent the ten minutes necessary to scrape them clean.

Outside, in the great world of Manhattan, a few lesbians and gay men were fighting for our rights. I was sure that for them the conviction of working for a community spared them both the squalor of family life and the stale narcissism of artistic isolation.

Of course I filled my free time with New York friendships—exigent, hysterical, invasive. I had many friends I saw once every week or two and long parts of my day were devoted to lunches, dinners and phone calls. The calls could be rapid-fire reports ("Howard's really done it this time. I think it's all over. I'm off for an emergency session with the shrink. I'll call later") or in themselves, long therapeutic sessions ("Okay, now let's get this straight. You were talking *intimately* with your father—and your mother *dared* to pick up on an extension?""). Joshua would call up to read me the John Ashbery poem he was working on ("Don't you see the title, 'Soonest Mended,' comes from the saying, 'Least said, soonest mended'? Except here nothing's mended and the voice is endlessly self-renewing. All those loose, sloppy connections, John's 'Meanwhile, back at the ranch' sort of construction. Last night at John Myers' cocktail party, there was a kid who asked John Ashbery what was his own favorite poem and all three of us—John, Harry Mathews and I—we all said, 'Soonest Mended,' in the same breath. Isn't that somehow . . . marvelous? Not to mention reassuring, given how . . . *nutty* John's work is?").

Through Joshua I met Lillian Hellman *and*, a week later, her archenemy Mary McCarthy, over for a visit from Paris. Through Max I met Lee Krasner, Jackson Pollock's widow. Of course none of them would have remembered me half an hour later. Joshua took me to a party at George Plimpton's where I *saw* Norman Mailer, small and thuggish, grey hair curling on his neck. But most of my contacts with the celebrated were at one remove. An art critic I had worked with was one of Warhol's best friends. They'd talk on the phone to each other late at night while each, at home, was watching the same television program.

We had cool, distant artistic gods—the poet Elizabeth Bishop, the nearly silent Samuel Beckett, the painter Jasper Johns and, in France, remote, dandified thinkers such as Roland Barthes (whom I had belatedly espoused)—but as New Yorkers we also needed art that wasn't eternal, that was hot and ephemeral. We ran off to all of Warhol's movies, even now that he himself no longer made them. We saw Sondheim's musical *Follies*; Joshua and I, after yet another romantic disappointment, would sing "I'm still here!" We bought expensive, whacky, certainly tacky clothes. We grumbled about the propagation of Black English in the schools, which we feared would deny black students access to ordinary jobs. We visited an art gallery where Vito Acconci was lying under a raised boardwalk, masturbating while imagining the people walking above him; he collected the sperm and sold it under the name "Seedbed." Robert Wilson and Philip Glass had taken over the Metropolitan Opera to present *Einstein on the Beach*; Kevin and I attended, so high on acid that soon we were weeping from the flood of revelations rushing over us, and I wrote a review for *Christopher Street*, the new gay magazine, comparing the event to the premiere of *Parsifal*. We spurred each other on to exaggerate so that we could feel at home in our own era and could convince ourselves that New York was truly the center of the world. If so much was going on around us, then we, too, must be about to do something brilliant.

I W E N T to Venice in June to visit Joshua. He told me that if I could pay my way over he'd pick up all my other expenses while I was there.

I took a boat in from the airport. It threaded its way past abandoned islands and pylons bound together like asparagus held upright in a steamer so that the stems cook faster than the tender heads. I thought that if I were a painter I'd paint this vast pale blue dome—streaked with pale cirrus clouds and gently quaking with unreleased light—which fitted over and joined the dark blue scumbled sea below, and on the low horizon line I'd place all the interest, just the finest band of minuscule towers and flashing windows and thread-bright flags.

In the big water taxi I was seated staring up at a teenage boy who was a crew member: he wore the regulation dark blue trousers and T-shirt. The T-shirt was beating violently in the wind. He ran along the gunwale and then hung out over the waves, his back to the sea, holding onto nothing but a guy wire. His skinny tan arms were as long and improbable as a colt's legs. His nose was shiny, his chin slightly red and sprouting stubble, his hair tea brown with apricot highlights. His stare was as intense and puzzled as a deaf man's.

Now the horizon line was thickening and filling in with fantastic detail. We could see the pure spire of San Giorgio on the left, the lifted gold ball of the Dogana gleaming straight ahead of us and over on the right all the layered complication and panoply of the Riva degli Schiavoni, the church where Vivaldi was composer, the house where James finished *Portrait of a Lady*, the hotel where Georges Sand and Proust stayed, the Oriental filigree of the Doge's Palace, suspended over a low, columned walkway, the soaring monument topped by a saint and crocodile, behind it the green-roofed ten-story brick campanile and, just to the right and beyond, the great clock with its two Moors striking the hours, both with bare asses and big dicks. And as the drone of our motors shifted softer, the hollow roar of thousands of milling human beings flowed in on us, the tumult of voices and shoes striking stone, the muffled busyness that suggested an undressed opera stage where a director was rehearsing a crowd scene with extras in street clothes. Guides with raised, colored umbrellas were trying to keep their different groups together (Joshua called them the *pecore*). Faintly, in the distance, an out-of-tune café orchestra was playing a palm-court version of "Strangers in the Night."

As we approached the landing a dirty old lady, thin and wren-like, with famous blue eyes, wearing dirty sneakers, her hair styled by an eggbeater, cried out, "I'm lost. I can't remember a word of Italian." Panicked, she looked at us all, one after another. "I lived here years ago and now I've come back to die but even though I once spoke Italian as well as English now I'm like the girl in *Three Sisters* who can't remember how to say 'window' in Italian and I have a reservation at the Ambasciatori Hotel but I don't know how to get there, I'm utterly disorientated." She spoke in the fluty accents of an English duchess. Her voice and her scatty non sequiturs made me realize that she must be an aristocrat, but the Italians were all laughing at her and suddenly I hated them for their beastly conformism. All they took in was a crazy old woman with Luna Park intonations and eccentric, soiled clothes. *Their* duchesses, I thought sourly, are surely as well dressed as a tailor's dummy and as well behaved as prize fowl.

I offered my services as *cavaliere servente* to the old lady, got her calmed down and led her to her hotel. "You're my angel," she cried. "I prayed for an angel and here you are." The handsome adolescent crew member was laughing at us as we left and I thought he was as flawless and ignorant as the unwounded must always be.

Joshua was there at the café where we'd agreed to meet, wearing a lapis-blue shirt so tight that when he sat down it buckled between buttons to reveal little moon shapes of tanned flesh. He was bronzed as Pontiac, his hair sun-whitened, his manner so relaxed it was almost Dada goofy. He was eating a raspberry *gelato* that turned strawberry red where he licked it.

That evening I saw the handsome young sailor washing down the taxi where it was moored in front of the Salute Church. We spoke. His name was Giovanni. Now he was barefoot and wearing a sleeveless white T-shirt and shorts. He told me he admired the way I'd helped the crazy old lady; the flat, neutral way he said *pazza* and *sporca* ("crazy" and "dirty") made the words sound like colorful but not particularly judgmental adjectives.

And then I began a new life battered by channeled water and wild, unfocused sunlight. Joshua put me in a storage room converted into a bedroom on the ground floor beside the front door. In the small hours of the morning the water's rhythm slowed down so much that it seldom lapped the mossy steps; it sounded like a domestic animal so tranquil it was in danger of dying. The wind died down and an eerie stillness stepped in as though the melodramatic princess had at last been transformed into the dull girl stirring the cinders.

Comforting, acrid smoke lazily lifted away from the small burning eye of the anti-mosquito coil. I dreamed I was a slave held belowdecks in a cage; the ship was marooned in the hot horse latitudes. I was being slowly smoked, like bacon. . . .

When I awakened, children were running up and down the narrow stone walkway beside the *rio* just outside my window and two workmen were unloading tiles from a small barge. They talked to each other in the thick, blurred accents of the Veneto, voices that slowed and ran down at the ends of sentences like a record on a wind-up Victrola. I couldn't understand a word but the voices sounded childish, wheedling.

Joshua was transformed by Venice. In New York he was so blind he was always frightened crossing a street or walking through a dubious neighborhood at night (and which neighborhood wasn't dubious?). But in Venice cars were banished and the steps were bordered by little white stones. He and I wrote in the mornings, the air redolent with espresso. Joshua could never sit still more than five minutes, nor could I. He'd be out on the back balcony inspecting the indigo-blue morning glories; for Joshua, their delicate beauty was contrasted with the military vigor of the Italian word for "climbing," *rampicante*, which he loved to say. He had to hold the local Venetian paper, *Il Gazzettino*, an inch away from his eyes in order to read it. Or he'd show me the "disgusting" photo of the Pope with the count and countess, the owners of the apartment, who let it when they went away every summer to the Dolomites.

I dropped my ballpoint and it rolled downhill; the marble floor was cracked and it tilted dramatically away from the Zattere side and toward the Grand Canal. The ceiling was low but painted a greyish-white and faded pink; the vices and virtues were ensconced along the cornice above their names in Latin; interchangeable and bored maidens alternating with amusing male caricatures stuffing their mouths or dozing or lustily grabbing a wench. The lesson to be learned was that vice was active, fun and individualized, virtue impassive and impersonal.

Joshua would adjust the heavy shutters, their hinges unoiled and complaining; for a moment he'd be a dark shadow pressed against bars of light, like a cat stretched out on piano keys.

We'd eat a green salad, wedges of fontina and gorgonzola and translucent slices of prosciutto, red and thin as a hematological slide, and dark, wind-dried beef, bresaola (so hard for us to pronounce with its gentle growl of unfolding vowels). Sometimes we'd laugh ourselves sick pretending to be middle-class Italian matrons who could scarcely stand each other but elaborately feigned mutual affection (*"Carissima!"*). I think the idea was that we were fiercely competitive—and conformist—housewives, each sure that her kitchen was even more *casalinga* than the other's. It wasn't as though we were satirizing women we actually knew; we were simply performing a vaudeville routine *ad nauseam* (the nausea, too, made us laugh).

America was a country of broad streets and well sprung automobiles, of sealed elevators emitting Muzak and huge shopping carts gliding on rubber wheels up and down wide supermarket aisles, but here we were crossing the choppy Grand Canal on a *traghetto* manned by a gondolier and queuing up at the *pasticceria* to buy half a kilo of fresh *fettuccine* and, at the *drogheria*, black olives, artichoke hearts in oil, bits of pimento and a crumbling block of *grana*. American life, it seemed, was contrived to minimize contacts with other human beings, whereas here Joshua and I were in love with the delicatessen clerk, a neat family man named Giorgio, slender, with well scrubbed hands, his body wrapped in a white apron as he sliced our ham or reminded us to take a small carton of heavy cream (Josh lingered over the double *n* of *panna* as though he were munching manna itself).

In the afternoons Joshua would dash across the curved, wooden Accademia Bridge and squeeze past the *pecore* on his way heading toward what the German guides kept calling *"Sanmarkplatz."* He'd hurry along under the arches in the square toward the Piazzetta, on his right the dimly lit hand-painted rooms of a café, on his left the badly tuned orchestra sawing its way through a Viennese waltz. It was such a pleasure to live in a historic city, the most beautiful in the world, and to treat what Byron had called "the drawing room of Europe" as just another obstacle course. It was the ultimate luxury to be racing for the speedboat while the echoing voices of hundreds of people rang hollowly off stone. The Japanese gawked at the bell tower (no one had told them the original had collapsed early in the century). Storekeepers cranked egg-brown awnings out against the noonday sun, pigeons descended on a living St. Francis proffering bread crumbs who was posing for his picture, and the gilded domes of the Basilica hovered above the bejeweled mosaics in the three tympanums like the setting sun and a half-moon over sparkling waves.

Joshua was heading for the Cipriani pool, which was so expensive he could afford to invite me only two or three times a season. When I did go it was like entering a society hospital. Tanned, deep-voiced, friendly but discreet *bagnini* accompanied us like orderlies from Josh's locker to the lounge chairs he designated. The boys draped the chairs in immense downy white towels. Waiters brought us iced drinks. We'd position ourselves away from the side of the pool closest to the changing rooms, the side reserved for South American dictators, Mafia godfathers, deposed royalty and Milanese millionaires. We were out among "the young," that is, those over forty but under sixty, the well exercised woman who ran the dress shop next to Harry's Bar, the always amusing, relaxed curator of Peggy Guggenheim's museum (he was from Oklahoma) and the divorced baroness who ran the "Save Venice" committee. There, standing at the shallow end of the pool with her diamond-encrusted hands resting on the edge, was an American woman burdened by the possession of a fifteenth-century palace her family had bought a century ago; her exhaustion from maintaining so much splendor seemed well expressed by her slim, heavily freighted fingers.

But most afternoons I had free. I roamed the city and tried to imagine myself into the lives of the family whose flame-shaped window framed a noisy canary cage or the man who sold vegetables off a flatboat or the waiter who sauntered out of Florian's bearing drinks of every color and who always looked impeccable in black bow tie, white jacket and red epaulettes. At every turn there was a surprise, a walkway wide and gracious or narrow, laced through arches smelling of cat urine. Or there was a sudden explosion out into one of the few squares with trees, San Giacomo dell'Orto. The great patient herds of daytrippers plodded wearily along as their leaders barked at them through bullhorns, but I ricocheted off them into the wide, almost deserted square of Campo Santa Margherita, where I bought fruits and vegetables at several outdoor stands—blood oranges from Sicily, fennel bulbs from the Veneto (fennel, or *finocchio*, was the word for homosexual for some reason)—before I darted into a church to stare up at a huge painting on canvas glued to the ceiling, detailing in delirious perspectives the patron saint's martyrdom. Or martyrdoms, since he refused to be killed the first several times Diocletian's executioners went at him and only finally permitted his head to be cut off; his blood ran white as milk and the tree to which he was bound sprouted olives.

On one of my lonely jaunts I ran into the boy who'd been on the boat. He wasn't wearing his uniform and I asked him if he was enjoying a day off. He said that he'd been fired.

"Not enough work?" I asked.

We were standing on the half-moon bridge over the Rio di Fornaci in front of Josh's building. If I looked to my right I saw two other small bridges and beyond them a noble one that continued the wide walkway of the Zattere with its pontoons where families ate pizza and ice cream. Nearby was the house where John Ruskin had lived.

"They let me go," he said. Apparently he didn't want to explain why, but at the same time by dwelling on the mournful fact he seemed to be appealing for sympathy.

"Well, come with me to the Zattere," I said, "and I'll buy you a lemon ice."

He hesitated, and I thought he might be reluctant to be seen with a foreigner who was also a man twice his age.

"You live there, don't you?" he exclaimed, happy for a moment, pointing to the shutters covering the three windows of Josh's *salotto*. When I nodded, he said, pointing to the smaller windows under the roof on the opposite side of the *rio*, "And I live there!" An old woman scuffled past us, a net bag for groceries over her arm; I recognized her as Olga Rudge, the violinist who'd lived for years with Ezra Pound (Joshua had pointed her out to me before).

When I started to lead Giovanni across the bridge, he stopped, turned twice in place, then spat over his left shoulder. I said nothing, for though I loved to ask unsettling questions of self-assured people I at least knew enough to leave the vulnerable mercifully alone.

Giovanni and I began to spend every afternoon together. I'd wake in the morning and look across the *rio* and there his sun-burned kid's face would be, smiling over the geraniums on the windowsill. Once while we were walking along the Zattere he confided in me that he had a terrible *mania*. He couldn't say the numbers "three" or "seven" but had to resort to "two plus one" and "six plus one." He couldn't cross a bridge without turning and spitting. He was at all times vulnerable to the attacks of evil spirits unless a friend (and here he turned his huge eyes on me) would take responsibility for him, in that way becoming a sort of spiritual lightning rod.

I resolved to be Giovanni's friend and never to touch him. Sex—or so at least he claimed—was no problem for him and he regularly seduced the Swedish girls who stayed in the *pensione* next door. In every way he seemed touchingly average except for his *mania*, but it was so severe and obvious that everyone, especially the other kids, made fun of him.

Once, when we were walking along the Zattere beside the hospital for the *incurabili*, Giovanni said, "Would you like to see me swim? I'm a great swimmer," and he instantly stripped down to dark brown shorts and plunged into the water, the wide, choppy Canale della Giudecca where cruise ships sometimes anchored and where the *vaporetti* crossed back and forth to three churches that Palladio had built—San Giorgio, the Zitelle and the Redentore. I felt a touch of embarrassment as though I was this kid's uncle and I'd permitted or even encouraged him to do something dangerous. But what I mainly felt was desire for his body—he didn't even have hair under his arms, the hollows as nacreous as the lips of a nautilus shell, and when he crawled away from me the trapezoids were furled against his back like a scarab's wings.

I was determined not to touch him; he already had enough problems. Everyone in the neighborhood avoided him. I saw him only once with another person—his tiny grandmother who just smiled when Giovanni went into his obsessive-compulsive rituals. She came out for the cool of the evening and walked along the Zattere in her black lace-up shoes, each no bigger than a child's mitten.

One afternoon Giovanni wanted me to go with him to a kung-fu movie being shown in a desanctified church. If Joshua and I spent long evenings with American art historians, with the English vicar and his boyfriend or with two Venetian aristocratic families he'd somehow encountered, my afternoons were devoted to Giovanni's adolescent pursuits. When we were seated in the cinema, surrounded by boys who were bopping one another over the head and girls who were dissolving into giggles and slumping even farther down in their chairs, Giovanni looked at me very gravely and said, "If you want to protect me all you have to do is to take my hand and say, 'You are my responsibility' (*Tu sei la mia responsabilità*)." I nodded, a lump in my throat, a lump in my pants.

The film began. The room was hot and giggly and every time Bruce Lee twirled and delivered a kick to a villain the audience produced the necessary sound effects. The screen was raised high on what had once been the altar in this early Renaissance church. "Say it," Giovanni hissed in my ear.

I grabbed his hand, which was bigger than mine, and whispered, "*Sei la mia responsabilità*."

Muddy Waters (which he pronounced "Moody Vahterre") was his favorite American singer and Giovanni and three other boys practiced every afternoon his group's repertoire. I was astonished: I thought that Giovanni had no friends and no talents. He begged me to come to the storeroom on the same *fondamenta* as Joshua's house but at the other end. The boys had fixed this place up as a clubroom with out-of-date fluorescent posters of Jimi Hendrix and Jim Morrison and Paolo Conte.

With sheepish grins the boys thumped and twanged and crooned their way through a Moody Vahterre ballad. They gyrated their bodies. Their feet were too big and in the way. One T-shirt was too short and always hiking up to reveal the baby fat on the stomach of a boy with a cruel face, a boy like Donatello's *David*. Their adolescent sexuality took up so much space, was so awkward and charming, that they had to smile, as a mermaid would smile about her inconvenient tail.

When they'd finished, Giovanni, who'd been singing, said, "Did you understand the words?"

"Well, no, it sounded like English, but I couldn't make out the individual words."

"Listen to this," he said, dropping a needle on the well worn record.

After a few minutes I told him I couldn't understand the recording, either; which was incomprehensible to an Italian since their singers always articulate clearly.

"Are you sure you're not really a German?" Giovanni asked unsmilingly.

The next day I showed him my American passport but he'd already moved on to other thoughts. We were sitting near the stone cistern in the Campo San Trovaso, looking out at the people moving on the far side of the canal. In other towns people were a distraction from the architectural beauties, but here humanity was the very medium in which the city worked—the flow and direction of people, their dispersal and concentration, the game of herding them up and down steps, of doubling their white shirtwaists or a black nun's robes with diluted watery reflections, the dense clotting of walkways and then the broad human wash let loose across a vast *piazza*, the calculus of moving spots of color on the balconies of churches or palaces. People were the notes that rippled across the musical staves laid down by the city, but even the staves weren't fixed but constantly sunk in fogs or tides, obscuring rains or overpowering sunsets, and on days of *acqua alta* the old stones under our feet would be replaced by a big new mirror.

Giovanni held my hand as we sprawled on the grass. He said, "You spend every afternoon with me but I don't understand how a fine man like you, a *professore*—"

"Giovanni, I don't teach!"

"How could a *professore* be fond of someone like me, someone everyone else avoids, a *maniaco*? I love you, you are my only friend, but what can I offer you?"

"But you know, Giovanni, I have my own . . . vice."

"What do you mean?"

"I like men." I had no idea whether I hoped we'd fall into each other's arms, or whether I was simply striking a blow for personal honesty (as Maria had so many years ago when she'd told me, so straightforwardly, that she liked women), or whether I thought my candor would show him he was not alone, that the world rejected my kind even more categorically than his, but that I was surviving.

Giovanni looked puzzled. He released my hand, which was no longer a friend's. He said, "But have you never tried it with girls? You're not ugly, you could find a girl, you're just shy, I'll find you a girl. There's one I'm supposed to see at the *pensione*, a big Swede, Yulla, she's named Yulla, you can go with her in my place, she'd prefer you to me anyway, I'm sure."

"Giovanni, I've tried girls."

"*E allora?*"

"*Niente*. Nothing. I like them. I especially like big blondes. But I love men. I feel good with men."

Which wasn't true. I never felt good with men; with a gay man I always felt something indefinable was missing, whereas with a woman I *knew* what was missing: a man.

Giovanni thought about it, then said, "*Che bella coppia siamo, tu con la tua malattia, io con la mia mania*"—"What a fine pair we make, you with your sickness, me with my mania."

I was even grateful that he was generous enough to put my sickness on a par with his compulsion.

Despite his generosity I could see that something had gone out of the friendship for him. I was no longer the *simpatico* guy who was also a real man, the sort he wanted to become. Now he must have thought back to that moment in the church when he'd made me take his hand and tell him he was my responsibility; he must have replayed that moment and winced, emptied the church, blown its roof off, exiled me in one kung-fu somersault to the other side of the *rio*, even the ocean, the big one, the Atlantic, wasn't that its name?

I didn't go back to Venice the next summer, but when I visited Josh there two years later he said that Giovanni and his whole family had moved to the Cannaregio district, to a little house of their own, apparently.

And then one day I saw a new Giovanni—taller, rump rounder, black shoes heeled in steel—and he was wrapped around a cigarette under the statue of Goldoni near the Rialto. He was hanging out with two other fellows and he looked fine, unexceptional, but just to make sure, I watched as he walked up the inner steps of the Rialto Bridge and never once did he spit over his shoulder or turn and I was certain he could now say "*tre*" and "*sette*" without a hitch.

 BUT that first summer in Venice, I met one other guy, a real gay man. We picked each other up by the Molo, that strip of pavement beside the public gardens between the Piazzetta and Harry's Bar. Men cruised there, although gay Venetians in those days would have been afraid of being seen there. At midnight, people—straight couples, families, sisters, friends—were always hurrying past, arm in arm, from the closing cafés on San Marco to the *vaporetto* pontoon or to the landing for the powerboat that crossed over to the Cipriani hotel at the tip of the Giudecca. Men, foreign gay men, sat along the railing or perched on the wood backs of benches. They stared at one another. They almost never spoke and usually ended up walking home alone. But sometimes a guy would walk behind one of the shuttered and locked kiosks that sold curios and guidebooks by day. He'd stand between a kiosk and the metal fence that surrounded the public gardens. He'd pretend to piss but would jerk off. A guy doing the same thing behind the next kiosk might, if he were brave, slip over to join him.

I met Sergio in a more normal way. He just smiled at me with a big, comic smile that was out of phase with his eyes, as though he were wearing a *commedia dell'arte* half-mask. His mouth was very wide, comically wide, with lips as thick as those that women in the 1940s used to paint on. His nose was big and hooked. He had a prominent jaw and his face looked as though it were flooded with blood. Laugh lines flowed away from his eyes like the tails of colliding comets.

He had that high, childish, gently querulous voice of the Veneto, but of course he spoke to me in Tuscan, not Venetian, and he talked so slowly and with such deliberation that I suspected he must be used to dealing with foreigners.

I brought him back with me to my stifling little room next to the *rio*. It was so hot that our bodies were exuding sweat. He was strong, his hands callused, his back just a bit stooped. He fucked me and called me *"Amore,"* shamelessly, without any of an American's cheese-paring niggling over accuracy.

In those days gay men had sex first, before conversation, and only in post-coital chat discovered if they would be friends. Sergio told me that his mother was a peasant and lived in a village in the Veneto. He was a servant and cook and looked after an old bachelor who lived in Vicenza. On his days off he took the train into Venice. Right now he had three days off because his boss was away in Turin visiting his sister.

As we talked we lay beside each other in the little bed. There was something reassuring, calming, about his slow way of speaking to a foreigner. The water lapped the mossy steps five feet away. Sergio kept pressing his finger to his lips and listening, as though hoping to discover an eavesdropper; I thought of the slot in the wall under the Doge's Palace where anonymous spies and informers had dropped denunciations of their neighbors.

I said, "I've never known an Italian to be so at ease with his homosexuality."

"Many people tell me I'm like an American, although I've never traveled abroad. Perhaps because I'm a Communist and have a critical outlook on things, I seem like a foreigner." He had a huge nose, deeply recessed eyes and that wide, comic mouth—truly the face of a *commedia* mask. A ray of light cast the shadow of his big nose on the wall.

He stayed with me. Joshua liked him, I could see, but was jealous of us. The third night I said to Sergio, "Maybe you should spend tonight in the *professore*'s bed."

"Tu sei furbo—you're crafty," Sergio said, laughing, and he pressed his finger to the side of his nose.

The next morning they were a couple. Within a week, when Sergio was back for a night off, they'd become thoroughly domestic. They went shopping together. We gave dinner to Peggy Guggenheim and a few other friends and Sergio chopped up all the fruit for the dessert and put Josh's tomato sauce for the pasta through the blender, which infuriated Joshua:

"I don't want it to look like something in a restaurant. It's lost its peasant character."

Sergio never lost his. Josh forced him to sit at the table with us, but Sergio called Peggy "*Principessa*" and occupied his chair only for a second at a time, as though nervously exercising a new-won right that made him uncomfortable. Peggy, always so vague, scarcely noticed, although in her own house she was severe with the servants, gave them food to eat that was different from her own and counted the number of apples they'd taken out of the fridge.

Italian friends suspected that Sergio must be working Joshua for money, but the only thing Sergio wanted Josh to buy him were huge silk lampshades dripping fringe for his mother's house in the village, shades worthy of the Nile Hilton. Otherwise he was happy to spend his days off with Josh, to iron Josh's clothes, over-water his plants and in the evenings, to dress up in tight white trousers, a lightweight blue blazer, yellow shirt and silk ascot and saunter forth with us to one of the half dozen restaurants we frequented. He opposed expensive places, criticized a stingy *antipasto*, wanted Josh to tip generously but treated other waiters with seigneurial disdain. One evening, when Josh discovered he had no cash, Sergio said, calmly, grandly, "*Andiamo in plastico*" ("Let's go with plastic," by which he meant Josh's credit card).

At home Sergio spared his clothes from wear and tear by walking around in his underpants. His toes and fingers were stiff and swollen, as though he'd had to work for years in cold water, say, cleaning fish. Whereas Josh and I were always reading, writing or talking and generally lounging about in the pretzel shapes of thought, Sergio could never sit still and was scouring the kitchen sink or emptying the fridge of the moldy bits in clingwrap that Joshua never wanted to throw away, or dusting the cornice with a rag tied to the end of a broomstick. He seemed to have no other friends. His mother had recently put in a phone and when Sergio called her he shouted, spoke to her harshly and never stayed on the line longer than three minutes.

He showered three times a day. When he passed me wrapped in a towel I'm ashamed to say I half-expected he'd wink at me or even embrace me rapidly while Josh was out of the room, but he never flirted with me again, not once after he moved upstairs. Josh's name was hard for him to say but each time he tried it with a new, experimental pronunciation he added, "*amore mio*."

Several times Joshua said to me, "No one ever gave me such a marvelous present as you did." I envied the lovers on their weekends together although I recognized I wouldn't have known how to create the easy, chattering domesticity they had together which even their spats made more intimate.

Sergio became "the treasure"—*il tesoro*, and soon everyone referred to him that way, even Eddie, who was delighted by my matchmaking. Eddie was the one who'd convinced Joshua to buy contact lenses, style his hair differently and to be dressed by Eddie's own Venetian tailor. But only now had I found Joshua a lover who if he wasn't a scholar was at least a sexual athlete and who, if he couldn't discuss contemporary poetry, was still sufficiently exotic as an Italian servant to fascinate Joshua for years to come. Sergio had shrewd political opinions and large, naïve lapses of the most basic information. Like the peasant he was he attributed the pettiest possible motives to strangers and was entirely gullible with friends. He thought that he, too, was crafty, but his life went nowhere. Year after year Joshua thought of inviting *il tesoro* to live in New York and I, ever the romantic, urged him to do so. But Josh had read too many Henry James novels to risk the transplant.

Perhaps Josh feared his New York friends would disapprove of Sergio as an absurdly strutting Italian male *and* a kept boy. Joshua knew that Sergio was a lot more complicated than that and if he was always the aggressor in bed (which Joshua liked), everywhere else he was flexible or at least unpredictable—needle and thread in his mouth, dustcloth in hand, off in the kitchen soaking something in vinegar, polishing the *pavimenti* with a rag under his big, deformed feet. Josh may have been the adored *amore* who got screwed every night, but he was also the great *professore* who must not be disturbed while he was writing his *capolavoro*.

Sergio's age was something we speculated on endlessly. I thought he couldn't be more than twenty-two; he might *look* twenty-seven, but everyone knew Italians went off early. Joshua thought he might be as much as twenty-nine; something suggested he'd known the tail end of the 1950s. When I asked Sergio one day, he said thirty-nine, which made us gasp. He was five years older than I and not that much younger than Josh. Suddenly I felt protective and still warmer toward him because I realized he wasn't ever going to escape his life as a servant.

On my way home I flew to Rome to see Tina. She was living in a big, white, nearly empty apartment that looked down on one of the forums.

She told me she'd already divorced her tall, skinny American academic. "I married him just to spite you, anyway," she said. She held my eyes a long time whenever she said something so direct, but otherwise she seemed much more remote. She said she was in love with an Argentinian and hinted that he might be a terrorist.

Eduardo was away when I called. Tina herself slept in a windowless bedroom at the very heart of the floor-through apartment with its fifteen windows.

She asked me if I'd seen the gaily painted gypsy wagon on the gravel just outside her building. She said that the *strega*, the witch who lived in it with four of her children, had knocked at her door one evening with a sick child in her arms. "I must see a doctor," she'd railed, "or the little one will die." Gradually, using one ruse after another over a three week period, Drusa inserted herself into Tina's apartment. She needed to wash her family's clothes, cook up some white beans, bathe a little boy who'd had diarrhea and was now covered with filth. Drusa elbowed her way into the apartment without even asking, always determined, sometimes desperate. Soon the gypsies were living full time with Tina, breaking dishes, fouling the toilet, handing over to Tina a grocery list that needed filling, strewing bedding over the stone floor, playing the television till all hours at top volume. Drusa advised Tina about love and gave her a talisman designed to bind the terrorist to her forever.

In the end Tina, sentimental Marxist, was completely under Drusa's spell. She could see no reason (nor can I, even now) why she shouldn't share her inherited wealth—enough to keep her idle, drunk and unhappy in those airy, sunlit rooms all by herself—with a family of five, poor and despised gypsies. It was Eduardo, the terrorist, who finally cleared them all out one day, changed the locks, had a metal gate installed downstairs.

Tina seemed strangely indifferent to me. I knew that since I'd hurt her it was only normal that she'd protect herself. Or perhaps she was so in love with Eduardo that she had little energy left over for me. Her coolness piqued me. It wasn't my vanity that caused me to feel irritated. I just missed her love, even though it had troubled me so much.

JUST LAST SPRING I was in Rome again. Tina's American cousin (the one who'd originally introduced us) had told me her father had recently died. He gave me her phone number, and asked me to call her.

Her voice sounded even lower except when she cried out my name with a genuine enthusiasm on a high, hoarse note. She wanted to see me instantly.

Suddenly, there was Tina, still slender, back in her old *palazzo*, except now I was jowly and she seemed to be missing a few teeth. I told her, just for the pleasure of recollection, everything I could remember about her father, every last detail, and that pleased her, as though such clear and detailed memories proved her father had made an impression after all, even on a foreigner. She wanted me to repeat what I'd said about him to his elegant old girlfriend, who'd become his wife. Tina said her father had abandoned his little book about Time some ten years ago.

I asked her about Eduardo.

"He died last year, and I suffered terrible *angoscia*," Tina said, sitting forward and nursing her cup of espresso between her hands, even though the day was unusually warm for Palm Sunday, "but now I'm just angry."

"Angry?"

"Yes!" And she let her wild laugh geyser up out of her. "He told me he was an Argentine terrorist living incognito and we drank too much and never went out because we were in hiding from the enemy." She sliced the air repeatedly with a sideways karate chop, an Italian gesture that, combined with her smile and frown, meant that she was playfully threatening to punish a child—Eduardo, I suppose.

"Why are you angry?" I still wanted to know.

"Because when he died his entire family came to the funeral, they were all Romans, he wasn't Argentine, he was a Roman, for fifteen years we'd been hiding and drinking and he'd been making up stories, even his accent he'd made up."

I looked at her, amazed, then burst out laughing, and she burst out laughing, too. I told her my young French lover, Brice, who'd just died of AIDS, had pretended for the five years we were together to be a member of the "minor nobility," but after his death I'd found his mother had been a hairdresser in Nancy.

"*Cazzo*, these men!" she said. She laughed again, her huge eyes searching my face for some explanation. Now that Eduardo was dead she'd stopped drinking and was painting again. She gave me a painting and a sheaf of her poems in Italian. Tina may have been lined from so many years of drinking and hard living, but she was also miraculously vital—hardheaded in her vitality. I thought she wouldn't have killed herself, not

even if all Rome had laughed at her for making an ugly Baroque fountain. She laughed at "these men," as did I, and suddenly the intervening
years melted away. She seemed as vital as that day when she'd come gunning for me in her car, the day I had refused to put out, except that now
she said she'd never wanted to kill me, just find me, talk to me, convince
me of her love.

<table>
<tr><td>

NINE

~~~~~~~~~

</td><td>

When I returned to New York at the end of that first summer in Venice I couldn't bring myself to wear socks.

I hadn't had sex more than four times in two months but putting it like that suggests that I felt justified in going out to get laid now because I had an exact notion of how much sexual activity I needed and of how much I wanted, whereas in fact

</td></tr>
</table>

I'd never considered sex to be an appetite, certainly nothing needed on a regular basis. I could never—well, perhaps I *could*, but I wouldn't have *wanted* to—answer a questionnaire about my sexual habits. For I was convinced my erotic behavior was no more habitual than anything else I did, whereas in fact the scientists hovering over my cage could no doubt have plotted exactly my activity patterns, the number of times I could press the sex lever without receiving a pellet before becoming discouraged as well as the precise percentages of time I devoted to feeding, working, socializing and mounting.

I was a dandy, and a dandy is a moral tourist, not a habitué. One night I went to a party with Butler and when we left it, both fed up with the way the young gay lawyers and account executives (guys I knew from Fire Island) had tried to impress us with their new possessions and their costly, lightning visits to big gay weekend bashes in towns scattered across the country, I said, "These circuit queens are satisfied with so little. Say I, with fifty-seven dollars to my name. But can you imagine debating the virtues of a Corvette and an Eldorado convertible for a whole evening? One of them even said, 'I'm an Eldorado kind of guy.' And even though he had the obligatory way of snickering when he said it, in reality he'd trade his immortal soul for a new model every year."

Butler smiled as much at my indignation, I'm sure, as at the circuit queens' cupidity. "What you forget, hon, is that as a writer you think you'll be able to *use* all this years later, that this life in 1974 is just raw material for some future, eternal version of it you'll be hammering out twenty years from now. But these guys aren't going to have the last laugh. They won't have another chance to get it right. They need that fine automobile right now because, well, *this* is their one and only life."

If Butler sounded so aloof it was also because he'd moved on from his last lover, the architect, to another writer, someone much richer, more usefully connected and more conspicuously devoted. This new lover, Philip, had beautiful teeth and wavy hair. Max referred to them as King Carol and Magda Lupescu.

When I spent an evening with them I decided that Butler was always so successful in love because he was so quick to reproach and complain. He didn't let Philip's slightest burst of bad temper pass unnoticed. Butler, so fastidious—one could say so *idealistic* if a querulous perfectionism constitutes an ideal—could be content only if their own communication was complete, the decorum of their life unrelentingly grave, their pleasures refined, their superiority widely acknowledged.

Philip, a Boston Brahmin who alternately cosseted his friends and made them face the usually grating music, caused Butler often to frown with disapproval. Philip had a way of barreling right into even the most highstrung and rarefied existences and bullying everyone with his favors. He and Eddie had become best friends almost overnight. Maybe Eddie was predisposed toward Philip as a fellow poet, but the real attraction surely was Philip's astounding energy. For a dozen friends he mailed their packages, bought their opera tickets, edited their manuscripts, ferried their pets to the vet, advised on plants for the new herbaceous border and talked turkey to their ineffectual agents or bankers. Eddie was selling his house in Athens and restoring a cottage in Key West, but it was Philip who barked at the brokers or swooped down on the contractor. Philip printed up a private birthday edition of Eddie's poems for Eddie's old bridge-playing mother and her friends. Philip went with Eddie to the surgeon when he had a cataract removed. At the same time Philip was writing and publishing his own poems, which sharp tongues said rendered an almost excessive homage to Eddie's *œuvre*, and was conducting interviews of elderly bards for a book he'd been commissioned to do. And such industry couldn't be dismissed as social-climbing, since his family connections were as much Mayfair as Mayflower and Philip had already won all the prizes.

Butler became more and more languishing in the presence of such solar energy, as though he were a good Christian Southerner fatigued by the lung power of a Yankee huckster. He'd wanted Eddie to be his friend, but by that he meant he'd wanted Eddie to exclaim over him and to promote his career. Famous writers, of course, are not on the lookout for neglected talent. They're more concerned about how to ship all those Seroukis paintings back from Athens or how to fill the chipped molar, upper left. Philip's money, competence and generosity far outweighed his boisterous habit of saying unpleasant truths—a habit that, as the mood struck him, he could easily reverse. He once even said to me, "You're my favorite prose writer," the sort of lunatic compliment every struggling writer hugs to his chest even though he knows he must set it instantly aside, much as an ugly girl who's received a love letter looks at the postmark to make sure it wasn't mailed on April the first.

Philip liked everyone, or if he didn't he said so, loudly, whereas Butler was worried about being taken up by unsuitable people whom later he wouldn't be able to shake. Philip came sauntering out of a new movie shouting, "Pretty ghastly, huh?" whereas Butler was never ready to deliver a snap judgment and needed to submit the experience to what he called "the first freshets of my brooding."

Maddening as I found the priestly airs he gave himself, all I had to do was spend a long evening with him and soon he was the sort of Southerner I loved in my mother and grandmother—knee-slapping, country wise, fiercely independent. Suddenly I saw that so much of the strain and pretentiousness he embodied derived from the provincial's unease in New York, a discomfort I myself felt. My social insecurity was spurred to life when a Swedish acquaintance of mine said, "It's a shame you can't live in Europe for a while. It would give you some of the polish you need." His advice struck me as absurd—wasn't I considered almost archaically courtly by most of my friends? But the suggestion did haunt me. I thought maybe he meant my off-color remarks and saucy questions, or maybe he meant my sweaty clownishness, my determination to amuse.

My sister phoned me. "Brother, I'm doing better. I'm living in a sort of halfway house and I think I'll be able to go back to graduate school next spring and finish up."

"Oh, Anne, that's marvelous. Mother told me you're still not talking to her."

Anne suddenly flared up. "Don't put any—you can't imagine—I—" and she lowered her voice and added wearily, "I just can't hack her."

Secretly I envied her the exemption she was enjoying from our mother's own kind of madness.

"You do what's best for you," I said. "When Mother complains about your rejection I point out that at least you're alive. I say, 'Don't forget that just a few months ago she was suicidal. Wouldn't you rather have her alive and incommunicado than dying and on the line?' "

Anne laughed: "I'll bet she wouldn't, Brulley."

I laughed too. I said, "Everyone praises her for being a survivor. At least she praises herself. But I think she'd push us overboard in order to grab the last lifeboat for herself."

"Amen. How's she doing?"

"Fine. That slimy boyfriend of hers is up at her house every weekend and when they're not fucking they're praying or cooking. She loves him for his prayers." We laughed. I said, "You?"

"I can't stay sober, not even with two AA meetings a day."

"Try Antabuse. It's a pill that makes you vomit if you take a drink."

"AA doesn't approve of it."

"Fuck them."

Over the next few months I kept checking in on my sister. With Antabuse she was able to stop drinking and get a taste of sobriety. She had to report to a pharmacist every morning who made her swallow the Antabuse in his presence. After that she was safe for the day.

My own drinking worried me. I never kept any liquor in the house but when I went out, which I did every night, I inevitably got drunk. A guy I knew sent me a case of California wine and I looked at it with horror when it was delivered, because I knew I'd drink it all in a week. I'd lie in bed, holding one eye shut, and read German philosophy and reach over to uncork the second bottle of the evening. Drink is supposed to ease pain. With me it broke down all sense of time (is time pain?) and released me into a soft, floating cloud of classical music, a swimming contentment, heady reading. I'd lie in my dark, narrow room, the door open, listening for Kevin to come home. Sometimes I'd hear his voice and the laughter of other men.

One evening in winter my sister called. "Honey, I can't bear it that Gabriel is still in the mental hospital."

"Is he *still* there?"

"Yes, it's so strange. You know, all three kids have been living with their father and stepmother ever since my last attempt. The younger kids grin and bear it, but Gabriel is so rebellious. You know he always scared me, even when he was a baby. I could never bond with him. I always felt he was this adult, dangerous man, just little. He was always built like a little boxcar. For years he was fine. He was even a Little Leaguer. He and his dad were real pals. But then, after the divorce . . . Oh, I feel so guilty." She began to cry.

I'd been in therapy for so many years that I didn't rush in to comfort her. I let her "experience her pain," as we said.

"Anyway, Gabriel's just rotting in that hospital. The shrink keeps them all in a lock-up unit. They don't study, there's an elaborate token system of merits and demerits. The shrink appears once a day like Louis XIV strolling through the Hall of Mirrors. The kids vie to catch his attention, beg a favor, receive his blessing. What an ego trip for that *merde*. . . ."

"What should we do?"

"Well, Gabriel's case hasn't been presented in court because he is his father's ward and his father has put him there. But if I challenge it—you see, my lawyer says that I can get what's called a 'release order' and if no one arranges for a court hearing within five days he'll just be released to anyone who's there—me—willing to take him into custody."

"But then what?" I asked.

"I'll put him on a plane and send him to you."

"Okay. I'll raise him then?"

"Yeah."

"Okay."

"I'll be there to receive Gabriel. Then I'll rush him in a cab to the airport. I don't have a ticket. . . ."

"Don't worry. I'll have a prepaid ticket waiting at the counter as soon as you give me the details."

When I told Kevin he just laughed and said, "Great, I've always wanted to be a mom."

        I'D AGREED so glibly to taking in my nephew because I thought it was stylish and gallant to make split-second decisions, just as I thought farewells should always be cut short, and my idea of elegant haste had offended more than one person. But as I later contemplated the responsibility of supporting Gabriel I panicked. I'd set up my whole life so that I wouldn't have any responsibilities, but already my passion for Kevin had caused me to give up my hundred-dollar-a-month roach-trap for this four-hundred-dollar floor-through. I often said I wasn't rich enough to be heterosexual and that children were beyond my means. Now I feared I'd become so burdened with expense that I'd never write again.

In our family we never met each other at the airport; as our mother said, "We all travel too much to waste our time like that." The day in early January when Gabriel arrived was no exception. His mother had called to tell me that the release order had worked like a charm since her ex-husband was, as predicted, too passive to challenge it. Anne said Gabriel was in the plane and on his way. He had a twenty-dollar bill to pay for his New York taxi.

I'd bought a single bed for him and put him up in the maid's room next to the kitchen; his room had a half-sink and mirror and a little built-in closet. Whereas my own sheets I changed only every two weeks, now that I had a . . . child, I was determined to do everything properly. I wanted to run a household that was beyond reproach since I was now responsible for the welfare of a young person. I'd laid out a big towel, a little towel and a washcloth for him.

I hadn't seen Gabriel for several years. When I saw him getting out of his taxi below I rushed down to help him up with his bag. As soon as I got a good look at him across the street I said to myself, "Oh. That's it," for his face was covered with acne, the deep, red, quilted kind. I thought, No wonder he lurks in the basement and only emerges at night. He doesn't want anyone to see him.

I embraced him and brought him upstairs. He looked exhausted. His nails were black and ragged and he stank of cigarettes. Kevin was nowhere in sight. I took Gabe on a tour of the apartment. "You may notice it's seriously underfurnished," I said, smiling at him. I was glad he wasn't handsome, at least not for the moment, given his acne; I won't be attracted to him, I thought, and won't have to fight temptation.

We sat in the kitchen and drank coffee and smoked cigarettes. He didn't take off his overcoat, a heavy grey and white tweed that looked as though it had been picked up at Goodwill. His hair was dirty and matted on one side, where he must have slept on it in the plane. I decided I wouldn't fuss at him in any way. Nor would I forget that he must be intimidated by the big city, freedom, me. My plan would be to challenge him slowly and through the smallest possible increments urge him to return to life.

I gave him an omelette and salad for lunch; he barely touched the eggs and completely ignored the greens. Always afraid of gaining weight I never ate much during the day, but the day before I'd stocked the fridge and cupboards for the first time ever.

"Where's the TV?" Gabriel asked.

"We don't have one. Do you want me to get you one? I mean, do you have to have one?"

Gabriel looked at me as though I were mad or maybe teasing him. "In the bughouse all we do is look at TV. I'm sick of it. I like to read, anyway."

A remark designed to ingratiate himself with me, I thought. I noticed that he said, "In the bughouse all we *do*," not "*did*."

He said he was tired and wanted to lie down. I drew the shade (there were no curtains) in his room.

My secretary, William, arrived and I dictated the Mexican-American war. We didn't take our usual sex break; I'd told him my nephew had come to live with me and was in the house now. I was constantly aware that this kid was sleeping under my roof, a thought that elated me. Only now, looking back, do I recognize that I was patterning myself after my parents but hoping to correct their faults. I wanted to be as solid and responsible as my father but more generous and less angry. I wanted to be as matter-of-fact and brisk and basic as my mother without her hysteria and bragging. Like her, however, I believed in the importance of sleeping and eating well and performing well the most ordinary chores such as dressing and cleaning one's nails and washing up the dishes. Not for myself; when I was alone I sank down through seas of depression and self-neglect and had as sketchy a sense of time as a dozing dog. But for Gabriel. He'd gone too far, touched bottom and didn't know how to push off and swim back to the surface. He needed a strict, totally ordinary regime and I would provide it. If he detested his father and stepmother and rebelled against them, then with me, his uncle, he'd cooperate, since he knew I had no legal or conventional reason to support him. He was here because I wanted him; he couldn't rebel against me.

I was afraid that if he slept too long this afternoon he'd never be able to sleep tonight. Around four I took some tea in to him, even balanced the tray on his chest so he'd have to sit up and take charge. "Aren't I awful, waking you up?" I babbled. "I remember Nanny—" Gabriel's word for his grandmother—"would sing out on school days, when it was still cold and dark outside, 'School bells are ringing,' and I wanted to wring her neck." Yes, clearly, I saw myself as Gabe's mother, I thought sourly.

When I went back half an hour later he'd put the untasted tea and the tray on the floor and was sound asleep. I thought that he must be full of that antipsychotic medication that had so brutalized Sean.

For the first five days he was in New York I never once made him leave the apartment or even do any chores. I'd hear him in his room, door closed, strumming his guitar and singing in his high, hillbilly voice. He had to raise his eyebrows in order to sing and lift his head high; his face turned red from the effort and the veins on his neck popped out. I liked his voice.

I sent him across the street with the laundry on the sixth day. On the seventh he walked the ten blocks to the supermarket and back alone and successfully bought the list I'd given him.

On the eighth day, a Monday, I just handed him the card of a dermatologist on Park Avenue. I told him to make an appointment and get there and back on his own; I had far too much work to worry about it. I didn't mouth the word *dermatologist*. I could see that Gabriel would never be able to bear a conversation about his skin.

Soon he was boiling up sulfurous concoctions twice a day and pressing them to his skin. He took antibiotics regularly.

I went with him to my barber and at Brooks bought him a sports jacket, two pairs of slacks and four shirts.

He began to speak like me, so much so that my mother mistook him for me. And my mother and sister, despite my warning them specifically, told Gabe, every time they talked to him, that he was becoming exactly like me. Of course I hoped he would, a bit; I even had a fantasy that he might change his surname (take his mother's maiden name), but though he had nothing good to say about his father he greeted my proposal with horror, and I immediately withdrew it.

We spent hours and hours together, but I didn't want to "hang out" with my nephew. I wanted him to read, which he began to do obsessively. He said he hoped to see a therapist but I told him, briskly, that he'd had quite enough of that. "I can't afford it," I said. "Anyway, it never works until you pay for it yourself. You'll have time enough later, when you're grown up. Your problems aren't psychological so much as practical. You need to get back into school and catch up with kids your own age."

I took my nephew with me to San Juan. We stayed in a cheap hotel two blocks off Condado Beach I'd heard about, more an apartment than a hotel room since there was a kitchen where we could cook. I had only three hundred dollars but I thought the sun might be good for Gabriel's skin.

We'd lie on the sand and he'd talk shyly about which girls he liked. If I talked too crudely about big tits or the outline of a vagina seen through a swimsuit, Gabe would say, "Gross," and look at me pityingly. He had very romantic ideas about Spanish-speaking women. He told me that back in the psycho ward he'd fallen for a thirteen-year-old girl called Ana, a Mexican-American who was beautiful and royally fucked up. Her father was a drunk and violent and her mother had a heroin habit.

I was a bit in love with Gabriel. I could see through his swimsuit that he had a large penis, much bigger than mine. With him I wanted to be a buddy, another teen, even a straight one, and soon enough I was looking at girls, too.

In a way my relationship with Gabriel was a continuation of the love I'd felt for Giovanni. At night, our faces burning from the day's sun, we'd walk through Old San Juan down blue cobblestones that Spanish galleons had brought over to the new world as ballast—Spanish stone to trade for Peruvian gold. Gabriel encouraged me to go off on my own to a gay bar, but I *enjoyed* being with him. I never thought of Kevin, or even Sean. Gabe knew how little money I had. He was grateful that I was sharing what I had with him. He said, "You don't really seem like a grown up. You look so young and you know all the latest dances and pop songs, more than I do, I'm not really into pop, more folk, and you just live from hand to mouth but always seem to be having fun, drinking, getting high, getting laid, but you get your work done, too." I thought that maybe I'd taken the curse off growing up for Gabriel, but I couldn't be sure he wasn't just saying what he thought I'd like to hear. He was a bit of a con artist, the result of therapy and his Maoist school and his overly analyzed mother.

She seemed jealous when we called her from San Juan. She said, "I don't think Gabriel needs or deserves expensive vacations in the tropics. He needs to be thinking about the serious business of getting back on the straight and narrow. Life isn't all laughs."

But I thought it should be. In the weeks following our trip Gabriel picked up what he called my "aristocratic" code of never pontificating, never seeming to struggle, never complaining or speaking fearfully of the future. Now that his face was clearing up he began to dress fastidiously. I said, "Oh, God, I'm sick of always having my nails look so dirty and *urchin*-like. I've broken down and bought a manicuring set and a brush, though it makes me feel like my father, the cold, old narcissist endlessly buffing his nails." Instantly Gabe began to take care of his nails, as I'd planned. He barely knew my father, but he'd concocted a myth about him. He decided that in his nocturnal, misanthropic splendor Daddy was "cool." Perhaps I couldn't serve him as a model since I was gay; my father at least had the virtue of being heterosexual.

Of course I disliked my father even if I remained hypersensitive to the faintest signals he emitted. He told my sister that he thought it was admirable the way I was looking after my nephew. He'd even said he admired me for paying Anne's tuition. I found such "admiration" shocking. Why should I have to worry myself sick, digging into a very shallow pocket, when he was so well off? Of course I was also gratified that he recognized what I was doing. I suppose my gratitude betrayed my slave mentality.

In influencing Gabe so indirectly, I wasn't trying to manipulate him; the truth was that I wanted him to love me. To please him I introduced a chapter into my Baroque novel, one set in Spain. I even invented a character named Ana in order to titillate him. He was delighted by my literary compliment.

Every morning I'd lie in bed and write, waiting for the day to come rushing down on me—Gabriel's needs, especially his need for company, the phone calls from Josh and Max and Butler and Maria and Lou, the secretary's arrival and the necessity to shop and cook and clean. While I lay in bed, I could feel the day, just outside my door, coiling to pounce. My novel became my "little" novel, a secret journal, and if the language was overworked that was because I needed to prove to myself I could still write. And not so secret either, since I read it to Gabriel every morning.

At first Kevin kept his distance from Gabriel except if he ran into him slumped over coffee and a cigarette in the kitchen. Then Kevin would exclaim, "Yogurt! Steamed vegetables! Lots of fruit!—this is Miss Jean Brodie warning you!" Gabe would just smile feebly, sleep sand in his eyes. He didn't catch the reference but he was willing to be amused and stared at Kevin as a Siberian prisoner might stare at a Balinese dancer. Kevin looked much younger than Gabe, though he was ten years older. Gabe slept, smoked, strummed his guitar and masturbated (I could see the shadow of his thwacking hand through the crack of the bathroom door), whereas Kevin was almost never home and was usually off somewhere on his bicycle or at classes or auditions. Some nights he worked for a gay caterer who did large parties.

But one day Kevin, triumphant and a bit shaken, announced that he'd just been cast in a big Broadway play, a psychological thriller, and that he'd be playing the juvenile lead, a crazed teenager. Suddenly I noticed that Kevin was drinking my nephew in with narrowed eyes, noting his strangely mechanical walk, his mirthless laugh, his rigid neck, his way of folding up into himself when he was seated and alone. The performance that six months later earned Kevin a Tony Award was based on Gabe. Never for a moment did Gabe resent the exploitation of his pain. It certainly wasn't doing *him* any good. Besides, Gabe himself was by then writing a novel and studying both of us.

Kevin changed overnight from a bored profligate with a cutting tongue into a serious, home-loving professional. The play was a monster hit and he quickly became entirely subservient to it. The director was a vile Englishman who called women "slits" and who thought that an actor's ego had to be broken down before it could be reconstructed in the proper way. Worse, the star, one of the most famous men in the world, was recovering from a seven-year binge and couldn't remember his lines. He'd be moving easily along in one of his first-act monologues, thrilling everyone with his plangent voice, the only voice I'd ever heard that *spoke* in the minor key— when suddenly he'd be off and running in a *second*-act speech (one key word, used in both monologues, must have served as the hyperspace button). It was Kevin's job to herd old Wet Brain slowly and seamlessly back into the proper first-act lines.

The action called for Kevin to be fully nude at the end of Act One. Nine tenths of the audience was seated in the normal fashion but a symbolic few, usually students, were placed in a half-circle on the stage, perhaps to suggest that this "serious" drama appealed to earnest young minds and not just to the usual well-heeled crowd of bored expense-account executives— the "carriage trade," as it was still quaintly called.

Here and there, scattered among the couples, were a few gay men who'd come for the nudity—as well as for the hot and cold splashes of hysteria and wisdom, an invigorating bath that Tennessee Williams had first drawn for them. These older men, their conservative tailoring so at odds with hair colors never seen before in nature, would pull out opera glasses at the crucial moment when Kevin would go berserk and rip off his clothes. Then they'd be able to see if Kevin had the smallest pimple on his ass. The kids on stage, used to looking at television actors who couldn't hear their remarks, would comment audibly on a blackhead—or, just once, a love bite on his neck ("No wonder he's so neurotic if he's getting mauled by a vampire"). The director, vulgar and hateful as he was, had never asked to see any of the actors auditioning for Kevin's role nude. In fact he saw Kevin's body only during the first preview. Kevin was vexed that the tension of being on stage made his large cock shrink; "Why don't you come backstage and fluff it for me, doll," he said to one of his boyfriends. The size of Kevin's penis was the unspoken point of the first-act curtain.

There was one man in his sixties who attended the play three or four times a week, often with an attractive group of younger guys. He'd half-doze but at the moment of truth he'd sit up and focus his high-power binoculars, even though he was only in the fifth row and could see perfectly well.

His name was Tulsa and after twenty performances he started sending mountainous bouquets, fruit baskets and kilos of Belgian chocolates to Kevin's dressing room. At last he came by after a matinée and shyly introduced himself. I happened to be there and he instantly latched onto me, whom he correctly diagnosed as the high priest of the cult and much more approachable than the god himself.

I needed a job. I wanted to send Gabriel to a private school, the Rockford Academy, in which "problem" students were taught all day long, one-on-one, by tutors. Kids who'd been ill or living abroad or in a madhouse or prison or who'd just been goofing off could catch up with their age group through accelerated courses. Gabe was eager to attend. In fact he'd become almost alarmingly motivated to re-enter the middle class. The only hitch was that the school cost each semester half of what I earned in a year, even if I did bits and pieces of journalism on the side. Kevin paid all the rent now out of his Broadway salary, but I was still far from coming up with the tuition.

Tulsa offered a solution. He was a consultant for several corporations and found me a job in the publicity department of a big chemical manufacturer that had its headquarters on Madison Avenue. My salary was generous, although after deductions my paycheck looked pretty measly; I felt I could supplement it if I labored every night on the history book.

I was back at work in an office after a five-year hiatus of getting stoned, sleeping late and working long days in little snatches. Jane, my boss, the token woman on the board of directors, made it clear that I was expected to be at my desk twelve hours a day, from eight to eight.

I had to buy two new suits, which I saw as an investment in my corporate future. The job itself, like every other position in this old-fashioned company, was devoted entirely to passing the buck. If I sent round a memo asking for "input" on the corporate report, the memo would pass from office to office, always being referred on to someone else whose "expertise" coincided with just such a question. The vice presidents were twenty well fed men in their fifties who were fiercely protected by their female retainers. Everyone was white.

I had a variety of assignments. I was asked to make a twenty-page condensation of *The Coming of the Post-Industrial Age* for the chairman of the board; I received high praise from the chairman himself, which threw Jane into a panic of insecurity and resentment. The company had major investments in South Africa; I was asked to explain how such investments were in no way abetting apartheid.

It was all too clear to me that having a child cost dear—in hours, money, compromises. I recalled one of my buddies from the sixties, who'd published three novels in his twenties, had never written another word after marrying at age thirty and becoming a father. With my day job and my night job there was no chance I'd ever get back to my "little" novel, which I abandoned. Our apartment had gone from a place of casual sex, irregular hours and constant creativity to one where we kept normal hours, ate ordinary meals, remained more or less chaste, never wrote fiction or painted, drank little, did our homework.

I figured out that when Kevin had not been acting he'd needed to stage daily erotic adventures in which he'd perform for an audience of one. He'd invented new personalities for himself and tried out new sexual techniques. Most important, he'd dazzled man after man. As "Pete" the hick or "Ivan" the Latvian gymnast or "Clarence" the English runaway Etonian, he'd tried on the new roles. As a hustler he'd intuited his clients' fantasies and starred in their private dramas. He told me, "One day I was on a call and I walked into a hotel room and there was Tennessee Williams. I had a choice. Either I could gush and say, 'Oh, Mr. Williams, how you've enriched my life!' or I could march over to him and say, 'Lick my boots, dog.' I chose the latter and I could sense he was deeply grateful."

Now that Kevin was acting he was kind if vague with Gabe, as though he were a poor relation whom he wished well but scarcely knew. Sometimes he was so lost in thought that he glanced at Gabe in surprise, as though he'd forgotten who he was. Gabe and I lived our dull, routine lives beside this man who rose at noon, steamed his vegetables, did two hours of aerobics and napped before cycling down to the theater. He wouldn't be home before two or three, since he was too wired after his performance to do anything except drink and pick at a salad. Sometimes he let himself be asked out by Tulsa and his band. Gabe and I felt we were the grey, self-effacing child and governess living in the house of a *grande cocotte* whose métier was her body and who sold it at night.

Three or four nights a week Kevin spent his evening after the play with Dennis, that strange Boston Irishman he'd met at my improvised orgy. They were always playing the young lovers and Kevin, after Dennis would phone, would hang up and let his hand pound against his chest to mime his fluttering heart. I'd hear the endless litany of their romantic talk through the wall. I felt as though I belonged to the workaday world of parents and breadwinners, whereas they were youngsters who, no matter how many hours they worked, could still take the most intense pleasure in each other. I'd never had that sort of affair, or at least not for longer than a few days, but I could imagine what it must be like to melt without a transition out of an embrace into sex and then, after the second or third climax, continue whispering about all the things one loved about the other's body ("You have the smallest, *cleanest* ears and I cream whenever I see your birthmark or notice the difference in color between one eye and the other and then that dramatic black hair, so straight, and that pale Heathcliff skin"), praise that would be silenced by still more kisses. I could imagine awakening near dawn with that black hair fanned across my chest and weeping hot, hot tears of pleasure, knowing how tender and still and intimate the night was, so unlike the horror of waking up beside a snoring pick-up, this disgusting foreign body, not even clean perhaps, smelling of stale beer. . . . No, Dennis was the romantic lead in Kevin's domestic drama and they'd often appear at the door hand in hand or Kevin, who was so much smaller, would sit on Dennis's lap and they'd joke until Dennis would whisper something dirty or sweet in Kevin's ear and carry him off to the bedroom.

The only problem was that Dennis not only looked like Heathcliff but also acted like him. He'd suddenly descend into a dark, angry mood. His beautiful jaw muscles would work. He wouldn't talk at all for an hour or a week and would just keep pounding a cushion or pacing back and forth. A fleck of blood would float across his eye—or, maybe it had always been there, but it looked like a symptom of the storm raging in his head.

With me Kevin was eager to discuss his interpretation of the role late into the night. Over the years I'd dated so many actors (but never one as intelligent as Kevin) that I'd learned to talk about "actions" and "motivations," never about appearances or meanings. I knew it was useless to say,

"The boy should seem pathetic here." Rather, one had to say, "As he crosses a room he must lean his weight on one table after another because he's afraid he'll pass out otherwise." At last I could see how I might be important to Kevin. I was his confidant, his big brother, possibly his big sister, certainly his artistic adviser. I saw the play so many times that I'd memorized his lines and had to keep from mouthing them.

Gabe's father refused to release his school records so that they could be transferred to the Rockford Academy, and the academy legally couldn't admit him before it received these documents. I spent night after night seething over this problem. Finally, when I called his father in a rage, his second wife got on the line: "Do you realize what you're doing?" she asked. "You're tampering with the mind of a kid who's been diagnosed as *schizophrenic*."

"Those labels don't frighten me," I said. "When I was a boy a psychiatrist told my parents to lock me up and throw the key away."

"Well . . ."

"Don't be rude. I happen to have a dictionary right here. I can read you the three definitions it gives of *schizophrenia* and you can tell me which one applies to Gabriel."

"I didn't realize you were such an expert."

"Look, I'm not asking you to help support Gabriel. I want to send him to an expensive tutoring school and I'll pay for it. I just don't want you to be *obstructionists*. Just release the documents."

"How do we know this school is the right thing for him? We think he should be in a hospital receiving treatment."

"Treatment? Smoking cigarettes and watching TV? Struggling to catch an egomaniacal shrink's eye? Well, if that's the right *treatment* he'll have a lifetime to devote to it later. Just give us a chance now."

Reluctantly, Gabe's father released the documents.

BUT GABE had developed a new obsession. He thought all the time about Ana, the Mexican-American girl he'd met in the mental hospital. Now she'd escaped and was hitchhiking to New York with Christie, her girlfriend. She'd said she was going to come directly to New York but soon she was calling from road stops in Virginia or Mississippi, high and giggling on drugs, and when Gabe called her back at first she'd tell him how scared she was and a moment later she'd be describing how much money all these great truck drivers were giving her. She worried

that Christie was kind of in love with her, she had some definite dyke potential. But when Gabe asked her if they'd actually made love, Ana was
elusive. As a Mexican-American, she could always pretend she didn't understand the question. Anyway, Gabe knew she could always hang up on
him if he bugged her. "You and your questions, you're like a shrink,"
she'd say, taunting him.

Gabe lived for the phone to ring. He wouldn't leave the apartment, not
even for a second. If I lingered on the phone talking to Josh he'd scowl at
me with tragic eyes. He'd bound up from his bed in the maid's room and
rush in on the first ring to the wall phone in the kitchen. "Yes, operator,
I'll accept the call," he'd shout. "Ana! Where *are* you? You said you were
coming to New York last night. South Carolina? What are you doing
there. Yeah. . . . Sure. . . . *Bill.* You sleeping with him? Okay, okay, calm
down. How's Christie? Ana, you sound sort of weird. What are you on?
I'm not talking like a shrink. . . . My uncle? Yeah, he's kind of cute. He's
got a mustache and he goes to the gym and he wears black T-shirts and
jeans. Long. No, just touching the shoulders. Brown. His hair's brown,
too—but he's *gay*, I told you that. No, he does not ever get it on with
chicks, so stop talking about that. No, he's not a sissy. Okay, well, maybe
you're right, maybe his voice does sound sort of high and, yeah, like a
girl's. . . ." When he hung up, he told me gloomily that Ana thought that
he, Gabe, was also starting to sound sort of faggy.

One day Ana called at dawn from Fort Worth saying she was frightened. She was staying with a trucker who was fucked up on pills and she
didn't know how to get away from him and he'd already hit her twice and
busted her lip last night. I told her to leave the house tomorrow at dawn
and hitchhike to the center of Fort Worth. She should ask for the main
courthouse and stay there, directly in front of it. At noon Gabe would be
there to bring her back to New York on a plane.

I thought, I can't go fetch her myself, I can't leave my job and wouldn't
I be breaking the Mann Law? Even if Gabe does go, am I not creating a
situation that will cause a judge someday soon to scratch his head and
look down at me from the bench and say, "Exactly how many kinds of de-
viance are you striving to perfect?"

I decided that Ana couldn't pass a single night under my roof for legal
reasons, although now I realize that where she slept scarcely mitigated my
guilt, if guilt there was. Just across the avenue were rooms to let and I had
my nephew rent one in his own name.

We dashed off to a travel agent and bought a round-trip ticket to Fort

Worth for the next day in his name and a one-way Fort Worth–New York
ticket in hers. Purchasing the ticket I wondered whether I shouldn't be
wearing a beret and hornrims as a disguise. I spent two hundred of the
four hundred dollars I had in my account.

Gabriel could never sleep at night. I'd hear him padding about the
apartment, coughing occasionally. His old metal lighter would snap shut
with a soft *ching* and a minute later the acrid smoke, manly and somehow
Asian, would creep under my door. I felt we were on an ocean liner and
that anxiety, Gabe's and mine, was the throbbing propeller. Somewhere
belowdecks shirtless men were stoking the engines with coal. Kevin kept
away from us, as a cat picks its way fastidiously through the debris after a
party, its nose flinching and eyes narrowing in the smoke from a still smol-
dering ashtray. Kevin had The Play to worry about; otherwise he kept
everything simple.

Gabe, I think, was astonished that I was going along with his desire to
live with Ana. I could see no reason he and she shouldn't be allowed to
live as they wanted to; illogical, autocratic denial and the deprivation of
all pleasure did not strike me as beneficial child-rearing methods. I could
remember vividly all the nights as a teenager when I'd lain alone on my
bed, longing for sex and tenderness and, mainly, escape. I was terrified
that my nephew would scorn me, that he would think I was unenlight-
ened, antipathetic; my compulsion to be his best friend was both my
strength and weakness as a parent.

When Ana arrived with Gabe I liked her right away. She had skinny
flanks and big breasts, like Helen Paper, the girl I'd loved in high school,
but whereas Helen (like Christa) was a remote beauty, tuned to some ex-
traterrestrial signal more powerful than the world's static, Ana kept scanning us all. She was afraid. Her ten days on the road had made her jittery.
She'd learned she needed to orient herself instantaneously to every even-
tuality. She sat on a kitchen chair, tapping her foot and staring at us
through her hair.

Lou's old nickname for me had been "Bunny," which Kevin sometimes
called me, half-affectionately, half-teasingly. Ana decided to call me
"Sunny." She was always hidden behind her hair, tapping her foot as
though listening to a private jam session, and the noise and the hair concealed her within a protective swarm, but just as a single bee will sometimes lift off from the hive and fly away alone, armed to sting, in the same
way she'd suddenly dart a glance at me and say, "Hey, Sunny . . ." She'd

smile with all her beautiful little white teeth, perfect as the cubes in a doll's ice-cube tray.

She and I spent hours together on the weekends. In a parody of Josh's and my old game of playing Italian housewives ("*Carissima*..."), Ana and I would dust and run the sweeper and change the sheets and towels and mop the kitchen. I thought I had to build on what she already knew and respected. My nephew might aspire to a university and a profession, but Ana must be pious and feminine, a homemaker and a beauty. I sent her to a Catholic secretarial school. Maria understood my reasoning, since she'd worked with lots of kids from the ghetto and could see no signs of unusual ambition in Ana, but my other feminist friends were appalled. "*You*, a liberationist, and you want to put her in a *parochial* school!"

"Look, first of all a parochial school isn't very expensive."

"What about a public school? People like you who withdraw your children are exactly—"

"She's not my child, she's not a privileged white kid, she's a Mexican drug addict, child of same, and the only thing in the whole world she respects are nuns."

"Why do you put your nephew in a *college*-track school, whereas Ana, a mere girl—"

"If she ever finishes secretarial school and actually *becomes* a secretary it will be a triumph, a reversal of all sociological studies, psychological predictions, tea-leaf readings and actuarial tables. . . ."

The wife of an Irish poet I knew was a voluptuous beauty about thirty from Costa Rica. I kept inviting Mick and Pilar to dinner and I begged Pilar to take Ana under her wing. Again I thought that pretty clothes, makeup and feminine wiles, especially if suggested by Miss Rich Coast of 1973, would reconcile Ana to the middle class.

If my nephew had jeopardized his future so dramatically it was because he was certain he could always stage a comeback, a nice recovery, whereas I'd always made sure my life looked conventional on the outside because I'd been afraid of falling off the edge of the world. I'd always had good grades, I'd belonged to a fraternity. I'd worked for a blue chip company for eight years, whereas my nephew had already been put in a mental hospital. Even now I could observe him playing with his sanity or his destiny with the self-assurance of someone who believes he can always pull it out of the fire. Yet my reading of Proust had taught me that one can lose status far faster than one can ever make a social recovery. Was

Gabe so confident because he was heterosexual and on some level sure things would fall in his lap? Had I always been so fearful because I'd grown up feeling I belonged to a despised tribe of one?

Or was I wrong? My sister had been intimidated by Gabe when he was still just a baby (which was crazy) and I, too, just as crazily saw him as a prince who'd put on rags simply in order to have a few extra adventures, but maybe he really was as irremediably tortured as his stepmother maintained and he insisted.

Although I was half in love with him I was protective of his privacy. I didn't offer a penny or a pound for his thoughts. I never saw him nude. He was free to come and go as he liked and I gave him a good allowance, but perhaps I was so openhanded because I knew he was too fearful to stray far. When some gay friends of mine were sitting around my living room one day teasing Gabe, telling him that soon he'd be swishing about like his uncle, I scolded everyone: "You can say and do anything you like among yourselves about yourselves in front of Gabe, but I *forbid* you to make insinuations about him." Everyone tittered ("Get *her*!"), but at least I thought I'd shown Gabe I was going to protect his . . . integrity? privacy? manhood?

I suppose I saw myself in him, not as I was now but as I'd been as a teenager in boarding school. Then I'd daydreamed constantly about an older man—my gym teacher, one of the painters at the affiliated art academy—who'd take care of me, divine my thoughts, anticipate my needs (for I would never have voiced them and he, if he loved me, would be able to read my mind). I was the person who, through elaborate readings with the astrolabe of psychological second-guessing, could chart all of Gabe's fears and longings.

I reconciled myself to my desire to secure for Gabe and Ana a respectability I myself was fleeing as fast as possible. I thought of all my old Beat friends from college who were now leading their kids off to Sunday School and dance class. I told myself that they—*we!*—were giving our kids a choice. If later they wanted to reject a middle-class status they could, but ninety-five percent of the world longed for the security and comfort we affected to scorn. And membership in the bourgeoisie was easy to lose but very hard to come by. I thought of all those classes for slum kids in which they were taught to give a firm handshake after a job interview and never lose eye contact during it. They learned to joke easily, combine casualness with respect, call a potential boss by his first name but show deference in surrendering to him the conversational lead, speak clearly and act sincerely—oh, these were all the skills we'd spent a lifetime acquiring unconsciously and now wanted to shed.

I found an apartment in the Village for Gabe and Ana. It belonged to a photographer I knew who was going on a year-long trip to South America. Just two rooms in an old tenement building, the apartment was next to that of a hustler I'd once met, a kid from Houston named Beau. Gabe and Ana would listen through the wall whenever Beau was entertaining a client. "Does it hurt to take it up the ass, Beau?" Ana asked quite seriously. "Gabe wants to do it to me but his is too big."

They were just fifteen and thirteen and I'd had the bizarre idea they should live on their own. I was afraid the police would arrest me for molesting Ana and I instructed Gabe to say if ever he was interrogated that she was living there with him unbeknown to me. And I convinced Pilar to register Ana at the parochial school as her cousin whose school records had been lost in one of their revolutions. A lawyer I consulted said he thought we might just slip through the wide-mesh nets of society; only a brush with the law would create a snag (I pictured Gabe and myself silver and wriggling under the flashlight).

Despite my corporate job I was desperate for money. I asked Max for an appointment and went to his study to beg him for a loan, but he shook his head, avoided my eyes and kept sipping air with his *tsk-tsks*. "*Tu exagères, mon cher*," he said to me. "You've simply taken on more than you can manage." Recently Max had suffered a series of terrible fainting spells, for all the world like epileptic seizures, except his electroencephalogram was normal and not one of the six specialists he consulted could find anything wrong with him. I was sure it was because he was almost literally being suffocated by the sometimes month-long depressions of his lover, Keith. That's why he won't help me, I told myself. He's afraid of becoming an invalid. Or he wants to break away from his millionaire lover and fears he won't be able to maintain the same *train de vie* without him.

Then I called on Tom, my droll friend who was the poetry editor of a famous magazine. He was warm and sympathetic and gave me no lessons, though he did say, "I'm going to write the story of my friends and call it *Messy Lives*." He'd been so pleased by my review of his collected poems that I thought his gratitude could be translated into a check, but he, too, turned me down. Instantly I let him off the hook and lit a cigarette and sat on his windowsill, puffing into the cold night air. Tom told me he'd met a wonderful young lover—well, twenty years younger than Tom at least—at a poetry reading. "He's the love of my life. There will never be another. Preposterous as it sounds." I felt that I'd lost favor in his eyes by asking him for money—which had suddenly abrogated the sacred disinterestedness of friendship—but that I'd inch back into his esteem by listening to his long story of how he'd met Daniel, who was bringing groceries over in a few minutes to cook something for Tom. When Daniel came in, he was wearing a belted trench coat and, even in this least flattering of garments, managed to look slim-hipped. His face was attractively drained under his thatch of gleaming, coppery hair. I thought how lucky Tom was to have money, have Daniel.

Except I had Gabe. I might love Ana in a simple, admiring way even if I worried that all the odds were against her. With Gabe I was the one placing the bets *and* the croupier. I was determined to make him into a winner. More than ever before I had a clear vision of what had to be done, at least in his case, and though my friends might debate what effect all this—New York, a gay milieu, a kindly if guilt-inducing uncle—might have on him, in fact I stayed awake not worrying about what to do but how to do it. I needed money, lots of money. I felt like Nora in *The Doll's House* who doesn't mind devoting herself to her husband selflessly because she's certain that he'll come through the one time she must call on his aid.

Just as she was bitterly disappointed by him, so all my ardor for Max and Tom ran cold when they refused me. For them, perhaps, friendship had to be disinterested (that's what Simone Weil, the French philosopher, thought); for me it was a mutual-protection society. Not that I sized up a new friend by asking myself if he'd sustain me if and whenever I'd need him. But once he'd let me down I could no longer love him, not as an intimate, a brother.

Josh asked Eddie to give me some money through his foundation and within a month I received a check for seven thousand dollars. My only regret was that the money wasn't buying me time to write a novel. No, it was Gabe's tuition, rent, food, face medicine.

Gabe did office work for one of my friends, a stockbroker. He sent out large mailings between six and nine every evening and earned five dollars an hour. One whole summer I had done mailings for my father, and I remembered how tedious it was. I paid Ana the same amount for cleaning my house, but often as not she and I became completely silly, putting chairs upside down on our heads as visors—we were knights jousting one another and sounding trumpet blasts with our mouths. We charged up and down the apartment until Daniella downstairs complained.

I felt that my wards must understand we were all in this together. They'd delved into trouble because they'd defied their parents and other authorities. But they couldn't rebel against me. We didn't even live together. I said to them, "You can go to school or not, exactly as you please, but if you're not going to go let me know so I won't waste any more money on tuition. You can sleep all day, get drunk, do whatever you like. I'll give you a weekly allowance, half of what I earn." I showed them my checkbook. "You must both work to flesh out your allowances. You can eat 'hambies'—" (Gabe's childhood word for hamburgers)—"and canned corn every meal for all I care. I'm not going to set any rules for you or be angry with you or hurt or disappointed. I refuse to play that game. You're invited to my house once a week for dinner." I wanted them to look forward to seeing me and to consider me amusing, a treat.

Perhaps because I'd gone to a progressive grade school that didn't hand out marks and that encouraged personal study, I assumed everyone would benefit from maximum autonomy and a minimum of discipline. Certainly my nephew, who'd appeared devoid of all sense of guilt before, now became as anguished as I—never sure he was working hard enough, always fearful of drawing public attention to his faults. He suffered wretchedly from insomnia; Ana told me that he drank himself to sleep every night on Gallo wine and then set three alarm clocks every morning, afraid he'd be late to the Rockford Academy.

I thought that most teenagers were cranky because they weren't allowed to have sex regularly. Gabe and Ana, at least, were never deprived of that.

They worked and they studied. They kept house and prepared their own meals. Gabe doctored his face. I bought Ana sports clothes and a few dresses—she became head-turningly beautiful with her full, pouty mouth, dazzling teeth, her slender waist, full breasts, long legs and small, tight buttocks, with the black luster of her hair, now cropped and waved, her long neck and small chin, her way of tossing her head angrily if someone stared at her and then slowly raising her long lashes and smiling. Her beauty, like great screen acting, was all a matter of timing, the coltish impatience when she lowered her head and then the dark burnt sugar of her gaze followed by the reprieve of her smile. When she lowered her head and shook it you thought you'd angered her or hurt her. When she looked at you she no longer seemed so young or defenseless, but she still appeared indignant. But when her smile chimed in, then you were pardoned, blessed.

I realized she didn't understand English as well as she pretended, although she became petulant if I hinted at my doubts. My solution was to ask her to give me Spanish lessons. Soon we were making long lists of Spanish words and their English equivalents, presumably for my benefit.

But then things began to unravel. My friend was forced to let Gabe go from his afternoon job; he was caught making long-distance phone calls to Chicago. My nephew's only response was to dismiss his boss as a fool and a liar—I could hear him using the same vocabulary I applied to Jane, my boss. Ana told me that she and Gabe now had screaming fights.

She was bored. My nephew told me that when he tried to study at night she would get drunk and show him her pussy, hoping to distract him. After school, when he was still going to his office job, she would dally with a neighbor, who wanted her to put him in handcuffs and suck him. In return he'd give her grass and money. Ana had abandoned her secretarial course. Pilar thought she might find her some work as a model. They both read the latest issues of *Vanidades* obsessively.

I refused to lay down the law, since I knew these kids were skilled at defying it. Ana still came up to my house a few evenings a week to clean, although mostly we made our English-Spanish lists of words and acted silly. She was just turning fourteen. She said that in Mexico girls had wonderful dances given for them when they had their sixteenth birthdays. They danced with their fathers—would I dance with her?

My nephew had worked so well at the Rockford Academy that he'd caught up with his age group. I put him in a more conventional private school, one that cost less. It was just a block from my apartment. One evening, when I went to a parent-teacher meeting, a number of predatory divorcees chatted me up. I realized that they perceived me as a divorced or widowed *père de famille*. Everyone was extremely deferential to me, in a way people had never been before. I thought, Heterosexual men must be treated this way all the time. People strew rose petals in their path. My shrink told me that the biggest problem straight men had when they came out was the loss of status.

Tulsa had a huge party for Kevin. Forty guys were invited. Three waiters in blue hotpants, orange socks and work boots served cocktails, then dinner. It was the Bicentennial and Tulsa had rented the whole dining room of a motel on the Hudson. The tall ships sailed past. I brought Gabe, Ana and my mother, who happened to be in town. She became horribly drunk and flirted with Tulsa. "You're my kind of guy," she told him. She passed out before the dessert was served, a cake iced to look like the national flag.

When he was completely soused on champagne, Tulsa, who'd probably just spent ten thousand dollars on dinner, drew me aside. "You know, I love that Kevin with a love bordering on piety. He's my religion. I'd give a hundred thousand dollars just to sleep beside his naked body."

I couldn't resist telling him the truth: "Tulsa, you already had sex with him once."

"That's a lie—a blasphemy."

"No, seriously. You hired him three years ago through a hustling service, Bob Plum's Boys." Tulsa's eyes widened. I went on. "He came to your house. You knelt on the floor beside the bed and sucked him off. You never looked him in the eye. He said it was as though you were scrubbing the laundry on a washboard. When it was over you couldn't wait to get him out of there. It cost you forty dollars."

The rest of the evening Tulsa looked smaller and older.

I WAS ABLE to give up my ghastly office job. I'd been asked to write a gay sex manual that would pay very well. The big advance I received even allowed me to buy off my U.S. history textbook editors. I'd completed one volume; they'd found someone else to write the second.

I told Jane, my boss at the chemical company, that I was quitting because I'd just received a big book contract, but I didn't give any details. I suggested the project was top secret. She cried and asked, "Who's going to help me with the annual report?" I didn't feel sorry for her, since she'd done everything to divert blame onto me since I'd arrived. Anyway, she'd already hired an outside agency to create the annual report. American corporations were so arthritic they could no longer do their own work; everything was farmed out to freelancers. That's why Tulsa was such a success. In his consultant's capacity he'd invite warring vice presidents to his house, individually and then in pairs, for a whole day's fireside chat. He'd attempt in his sly, cornpone way to ease their differences, although sometimes I suspected he was really only sowing more discord in order to insure his own role as pacifier.

I'd auditioned for the sex manual along with nine other writers. We'd each been asked to prepare a sample entry on such topics as "kissing," "fisting" and "aging." We were all told that we were going to be teamed up with a psychologist, who'd already been chosen but whose name wasn't mentioned. When I was selected I found out that the shrink was my own, Abe. He said I could be his collaborator or his patient but not both. I chose collaborator, since I'd already had three years of therapy and needed the sex manual money.

I worried about what effect the sex manual would have on my reputation. At the ballet I ran into the woman who'd edited my Japanese-Fire Island novel (and refused my long novel about Christa). When I told her about the sex book, she laughed cruelly with her silent, almost unsmiling laugh, the laugh that made her whole chest shake while her old eyes peered out at me as though through the big, singed holes a shotgun bullet burns through a paper target. "Perfect," she said, still quaking, "that's perfect for you."

The woman who was writing the companion manual for lesbians was equally worried; after all, she'd published three literary novels already. When we told the sex book publisher we might use pseudonyms, he shrugged and said, "It makes absolutely no difference. Your names are unknown to ninety-nine percent of our potential readers."

But then I thought it was absurd to hide behind a pseudonym in writing a book urging gay men and lesbians to come out of the closet. Even tactically, I thought anonymity would be an error. I'd sold five hundred copies of my only published book and I couldn't get the subsequent novel into print. If my name was associated with a commercial blockbuster, that success would count more, especially in money-mad America, than any loss in a prestige that had, in any event, passed unnoticed. Moreover, as I knew, to sign my name to a gay sex manual in 1977, the *first* of its kind and one that would be sold over the counter across the country, was itself a political act.

My lesbian friend wanted the sex book money to send her daughter to an expensive university. We decided that if we were ever asked on television why we wrote gay sex manuals we'd say, "For the sake of our children."

Fortunately I was paired with my shrink. He'd come out late and didn't know much about bars, baths, cruising or exotic erotica, whereas I knew all that but had a much darker, tougher view of relationships. He counseled gentleness and tenderness and from his patients knew about the shame of impotence and delayed or premature ejaculation; I was the seasoned sex machine who'd traumatized them. He knew that beginners had to be coaxed to relax before they could be penetrated, I was the guy at the baths on Quaaludes who positioned his ass on a pillow under a spotlight and lost count how many times he was getting fucked. He suggested to our readers that role playing was passé. When I was stoned I shouted, "Fuck that beef pussy" or dressed a skinny, naked twenty-year-old in my black leather jacket and whispered in his ear, "I'm your cock-slave, sir." If my shrink thought that sex was a matter of cuddling and intimacy, I thought it was a cold, calculated rite promising transcendence but certainly not affection.

What neither of us questioned was that as much sex as possible with as many men as one could find was a good thing. Except Abe was less hostile than I to couples. For the strange, unaccountable thing was that I, who longed to marry Kevin, just as I'd once ached to wed Sean, responded in any abstract discussion to the concept of the couple with implacable hostility. I suppose my impossible loves, soaked in tears and mimicking the religiosity of a saint, were acceptable to me because they were medieval and only marginally sane, whereas domestic love—with its adulterous melodramas, cozy compromises, sexless cuddling, petty spats—offended me precisely because it *stank* of the possible, of what could be done, of what everyone did.

Of course I was also lonely and wanted to settle down. Since Kevin had become a star he seemed ever more remote to me. I took up with a man who worked in a dirty book store and I saw him at his place for dates. I needed to keep a separation between my life with Kevin—which still seemed as cold and silvery as those erotic, sexless nights when we'd first slept together chastely, back in the era of the Society of St. Agnes—and anything as mundane as good, adult lovemaking after a steak dinner, a bottle of Valpolicella and an evening of shared confidences. Kevin encouraged me in these affairs, but I was ashamed that my lovers weren't as handsome as his—or as he.

Even so, I was happy to be my own boss again. Whereas I could be a benign ruler, I was inevitably a devious, undermining little subject. I was so convinced of my superiority that I could not contain my hatred of all authority—worse than hatred, dirtier: my sneering contempt for anyone placed above me.

My father had done everything to please his boss, the owner of a chemical factory, and when someone else had been preferred over him my father, irreparably wounded, had quit and started his own business. That had been in 1940, the year I was born. I was like him, I saw, in this way, too, and the resemblance sickened me. During the war and for years afterwards my father had made lots of money, but in the 1960s chemical manufacturers had no longer needed representatives to find them new industrial customers—and to skim off a twenty-five percent commission. All the potential customers had already been located. My father, who'd been the world's leading broker of chemical equipment, saw his far-flung offices (in Akron, Cleveland, Charleston, West Virginia, Pittsburgh and Cincinnati) cut back and lose money. One of the manufacturers that dropped him had a new president who was Jewish; this convergence of factors inspired a nearly apoplectic anti-Semitism in my father. I thought back to the time when he had lost sleep over my homosexuality and had nearly died of a broken heart. Now he was filled with heart-bursting rage over what these filthy kikes were doing to him.

Cleverly he'd been building through profit-sharing a large fund for his top employees in each city (all chemical engineers). He now handed this money over to them in a lump sum and suggested they buy Industrial Sales from him. Two of the five men took the money and ran but the other three paid my father the remaining two million dollars for the company's name, reputation and client list. A bad investment, as it turned out.

My father, unfortunately, did not take well to retirement. He mounted his tractor and mowed the lawn so frequently that the grass turned brown. He ate so much that he gained a twenty pounds he could ill afford. Traveling interested him not at all, but investment did, tragically—he lost half his money in a year. The rest he invested in an industrial toilet supply firm, a sort of janitorial service for factories. He loaded up paper towels and liquid soap in the trunk of his Cadillac and wore a grey uniform with his own logo, "Cleanzessence," over his left breast pocket.

Cleanzessence went broke in a year. Now, with whatever money he had left he was living in his new, smaller house and watching record-breaking amounts of television. His wife's social life, which in his heyday he'd dismissed as an annoying time-waster, now became his main source of amusement. Although he was too lofty to beg to know all "the dirt" the minute she came back from a Queen City luncheon, nevertheless he maintained an unnatural, hopeful silence until she finally, coquettishly served up the day's dish—scraps from the table of female activity that he was able to reheat several times for his homey little solitary meals. American businessmen of his class and age had no hobbies beyond yard work, which never even ascended to the dignity of gardening.

My sister was well, out of the hospital and in her last year of graduate school (her grades were so good she was now receiving free tuition and financial aid). She'd met a girlfriend and was living with her.

After a year and a half in New York, my nephew was ready to enter his last year of high school. His grades were excellent, his appearance greatly improved. He was now afraid of failing and desperate to succeed; I'd inoculated him with middle-class anxiety and considered the minor infection as preventive. But Ana was tired of being on her own, of cooking for herself and, now that she'd dropped out of school, filling her idle hours. Thanks to Pilar, Ana was looking so beautiful I worried about her. I felt like a parent. I worried that her expertly painted lips and eyes, her pink nails and expensively coiffed hair, the silk dresses under which her full breasts and snaky hips glided like a rumor through a crowd would attract the evil eye.

Ana decided to move back to Chicago to live with her parents. She said, "Sunny, I want to be a little girl. I want my mother to take care of me." I didn't have the heart to remind her that her mother had never babied her. I thought, *I* am your mother, Ana, and your father, the one who will waltz with you on your sixteenth birthday.

My nephew decided that if Ana left he'd go with her. He and I were drinking coffee together in a Village coffee house, a rare break in our lives of drudgery. "Hey, Unk," he said, in a parody of our real relationship, a parody that expressed nothing except his awkwardness in discussing something that wasn't urbane, trivial, "delicious"—the qualities he imagined I esteemed, whereas my only reason for playing them up around him was to keep him entertained. Maybe I sensed that he thought gay men were "fun," even "cool," only so long as they appeared to be dandies aristocratically above the common struggle. I wanted him to like me. "Hey, Unk, I'm going to lam it out of this burg and head back to the Windy City."

"But why?" I asked, not joking at all. My seriousness sprang him out of his joshing.

"Because I can't live without a girlfriend."

"You'll find another."

"No, I won't. You have so many tricks—gay life is so promiscuous—"

"I do not. It is not."

"—that you don't realize how hard it is for a straight guy, especially one who's not so great looking—"

"You *are* good looking," I said, trying to make my paternal praise sound more plausible by adding as a joke, "at least good enough for straight life. Women have such bizarre values."

But it was too late. I could see he was panicked by the prospect of living alone. He left New York with Ana. In Chicago they split up. She was married two years later to a Cuban boy who'd dyed his close-cropped hair a greenish-blond. "You'll love him, Sunny," she wrote me. "He has a beautiful body and can wear *all* my clothes." They divorced three years later when Ana went back on drugs. Only fifteen years later did she join AA and go back to school and remarry.

For the entire time Gabriel had lived with me I'd felt I was hauling water in a leaking bucket up a hill to fight a brushfire that was quickly spreading. Every day had brought a new crisis—he'd lost his afternoon job or he'd slept through a crucial exam or he'd put his new suit in the washing machine—and I had automatically thrown myself into going back down for more water.

Now he was gone and I didn't think about him. I found I had too much free time at first, but the phone started ringing, there was a new disco to visit, a new crop of novels to read, new people to meet, for New York does not encourage a quiet, deepening appreciation of a small circle. I couldn't understand this sudden shift in my interest. Perhaps when Gabe was living with me I'd labored under some feudal sense of responsibility for a dependant, a primitive code of patronage or hospitality that absence dissolved.

Gabe went back to live with his mother and her new girlfriend and attended public high school for his senior year. Two weeks before he was to be graduated my sister discovered some beer cans in his closet and threw him out of the house because he was a threat to her sobriety. He moved into a big, noisy communal apartment where he stayed up all night and didn't study. He didn't get his diploma. I was angry with my sister as though she'd carelessly knocked out of my hands the brimming pail I'd been carrying for so long.

But there was nothing I could do. It wasn't that I'd washed my hands of him. No, I'd just rinsed them lightly in the waters of Lethe.

KEVIN WENT ON a national tour with his play and I'd go see him in cities that weren't too far away. We had a romantic weekend in Baltimore, but now that he wasn't under my roof I was gradually able to let him go. The entire time I'd been in therapy with Abe I'd wanted to free myself of my obsession with Kevin and find someone who loved me. But I couldn't end it on my own, this obsession, not so long as he was living with me. Because I wanted him and he didn't want me, I hated myself. I felt my heart turning to stone a bit more every day, as though Kevin were the gallant young Perseus holding aloft a gorgon's head of my own twisted, ugly passion, something he didn't look at but that petrified me.

In Baltimore we lay on twin beds at dusk and watched the thousands of starlings haunting the old stone battlements of the hotel wheeling through the sky like ashes blown off a fire in high wind. Our fire was dead, the log cold, the starlings the last scattering of my love. We lay there, very peaceful, and Kevin was exquisitely sweet with me. Maybe he felt that I needed a reward for having made the trip. Maybe he could tell I was slipping away from him and he wanted me back, not as a lover but as a brother or a friend—a landmark, really, in the shifting uncertainties of his life. Or, just possibly, when he didn't have my hangdog devotion served up to him every morning over breakfast he could remember he loved me, at least sometimes, at least a little bit.

But after his year and a half on the road he headed to Hollywood to make his fortune. He was gone and I resolved I'd never shed another tear over a man. For years afterwards I felt a bitterness towards him. Sean had been too crazy for me to blame for not loving me, but Kevin had withheld love perversely, I decided. When I'd write about him (and he kept showing up in my fiction, sometimes even as a woman), I couldn't resist picturing him as a cold careerist whose flinty heart kept him from succeeding as an artist. Or I imagined that someday he would come to regret the way he'd spurned me.

Proust's law is that you always get what you want when you no longer want it. Just the other day I had lunch with Kevin in New York, one of those Village coffee shops where you sit in deep, comfortable armchairs before a thrift-shop table originally designed to support a sewing machine. He'd asked his fine-boned, forest-creature Israeli boyfriend not to come along since he, Kevin, wanted to be alone with me. He was now deep into his forties, slender and well-built but no longer intimidatingly beautiful. He said that for fifteen years he'd had sex with the hottest numbers in New York but that now his luck had run out, except occasionally he could still score; I told him that even the real dogs went howling in the other direction when they saw me coming.

We laughed. He let me talk for an hour about Brice. "I have the worst amnesia about him, about our years together, which I suppose is a normal analgesic," I said, "although for a novelist it's scary, especially an autobiographical novelist like me. I'm supposed to remember everything." Kevin assured me that all my memories would come back when I started writing about Brice but that for the moment they were held on ice (the cryogenics of the unconscious).

I had my doubts, but I appreciated his gentleness, his sweetness. He, too, had begun to write about his past, about his coming out that first summer in New York when he was an acting student from Ohio and had met the famous Hal, star of a big Broadway musical (everything in the story was accurate, even Kevin's sniffing contempt for the musical).

Suddenly all the bitterness I'd ever felt against him vanished. I was glad I'd lived long enough to forgive him—not through any deliberate act of generosity but through the involuntary wisdom conferred on all of us by time, as though with age we all become morally as well as literally farsighted.

I REMEMBERED that back in the 1970s Ross Stubbins had kept calling our number, even though Kevin had left New York; I was now the one to talk dirty to him. Did he even notice the change of personnel? He started coming over to the apartment and having sex with me, although he drank so much he was usually impotent and just talked and talked and talked. Once we called Kevin in Los Angeles and had a telephonic three-way with him.

One night I ran into Kevin's beautiful lover Dennis at the Candle and invited him home with me. I was surprised he accepted, since I felt he must be two or three erotic classes above me, as indeed he surely was. We smoked a joint and made love by candlelight on Kevin's large foam cube of a bed. After sex he showed me how he did aerobic exercises. I felt appallingly guilty and swore Dennis to secrecy and he only told Kevin years later, just before he, Dennis, died from AIDS. Kevin said to me, "Why didn't you ever mention it? I couldn't care less, frankly."

I still looked young, my face unlined even if my eyes were ringed with dark shadows and the fingers of my right hand stained yellow with nicotine. For ten years I'd worried about getting older, too old to score easily and frequently with the hundreds of men I required annually, but age was held off, frozen, in abeyance. Was it because I didn't have to trudge through the rain while it was still dark on my way to an office? Was it because I was never bored? Or at least never used the word *boredom*? Was it because I'd suffered so little—or rather, suffered intensely but only over abstractions such as lovelessness or unfulfilled ambition, whereas my married friends worried, year in and year out, over the practical family problems I'd faced only while Gabe and Ana lived with me?

I had no wrinkles, no grey hairs, nothing sagged, my hairline was receding only slightly. I was proud of my youth, which had been extended ten years longer than I'd ever expected, but I also saw it as an empty honor, a sign that I was like wax that had not yet been sealed, that had, perhaps, become too cold and hard to take an impression.

I moved downtown, back to the Village, or rather to the Colonnades, a rickety old terrace built in the 1830s by the Astors for remote relatives who wouldn't be inheriting. The Colonnades was in the no-man's-land between the West and East Village, an area that ten years later would be teeming with boutiques, restaurants, gyms, bookstores and bars but that then, at the end of the 1970s, was tentatively being called, half as a joke, NoHo (North of Houston), and that local residents thought might someday become prosperous.

I had a beau named Leonard who'd arranged everything. It was he who moved me into the Colonnades. I'd met him at the gym. He was tall, lanky and blond and he worked out every night with Billy, his constant sidekick.

Leonard was from Florida, he had a job as a secretary for the New York State Council for the Arts, he knew no women socially and he loved the company of men. He was six foot four but slightly hunched, as though he disliked being so tall, so conspicuous. He ate enormous quantities at all times, hoping to gain weight.

He had a loping walk, a shifty glance, blue-white skin and a speaking voice he'd forced down from tenor to bass. The arts of life—conversation, food, clothes, holidays—left him indifferent; perhaps he'd never thought about them. Talk was either grunts at strangers or a halting, sincere confession to his two or three intimates. Food was just grams of nourishment to be consumed according to a schedule for maximum weight gain. Clothes were gym clothes and sweatsuits and parkas and second-hand overcoats for warmth.

But he was involved in a grand remake of his external experience and even his character. He went from being a timid, skinny kid to a loud, smiling, lordly man in the space of three years. When I first picked him up at the gym he liked to talk dirty while I sucked his big, silky dick. The rest of the evening he'd tell me about his childhood and his plans.

He'd grown up in Florida in a trailer camp. His father had been a high school football hero and, later, a drunk in his twenties, always going on a bender every weekend when he was through working as a garage mechanic. Leonard was still just a scared little kid, malnourished on margarine and sugar sandwiches, when his father had a bad car accident and lost both legs. After that his dad would just lie in bed all the time drinking. Every time he saw Leonard he'd call him a creep. Leonard shot up, played a bit of basketball badly, studied hard, played in the Gainesville band, and his father hated his kid with all his heart. "You're a fuckin' creep. Look at you, lurking around the house, fuckin' nose in a book, like a faggot creep, blowing on some shitty instrument at halftime instead of playing sports. You're a fuckin' nerd, the kind of creep I used to beat up in high school."

Leonard finished at Florida State with top grades, his father's voice in his ears. He came to New York because there he thought he could be a faggot, a nerd, a creep in solitude. But once he arrived in New York he met Billy, ten years older, an equally shy boy who played the piano, read poetry, was in arts management, drank to excess. He was the one who found Leonard his job and launched him into weightlifting.

Billy was small and passive and profoundly indifferent to women. Because of his work he'd met some of the most celebrated painters and poets and directors of the day, all gay men, and they called him in the middle of the night to go out drinking or invited Billy and Leonard up to a cottage in Vermont or to an island in the Caribbean and so their humdrum life, which consisted of work, brown-bag lunches and workouts, would suddenly be shot through with a glimpse of ermine or flamingo pink, that is, black and white Vermont or Technicolor St. Bart's. For most of the successful older men they knew were every bit as strange as they— paranoid or cruel or alcoholic or profoundly self-hating—and they liked these two Southern guys, one tall and one short, one fair and one sandy haired, both taciturn and socially awkward, both fiercely cultivated.

But Leonard benefited from a brief historical moment, the triumph of clone culture at the end of the 1970s. He became a huge man with a massive chest too hard to sleep on, shoulders as wide as a Jaguar's fenders, a back so bulked with muscle that his spine had become a very deep indentation, and a butt you could have balanced a martini on. His legs stayed skeletal and thousands of squats under a bar so loaded that it looked as though it might snap in two did nothing to beef them up. He trudged about the gym as though his shoes were made of lead and cement and he belched like an active volcano.

The landlord liked him and asked him to supervise the construction of two major gay venues. First he wanted Leonard to draw up some plans and oversee the total facelift of a sauna that had been a foul-smelling steambath for half a century. I used to visit that place with its come-slippery tile steps, its green pool growing slime, its steamroom decanting fifty years' worth of toe jam and ear wax, where saurian old clients flickered into life only once a century. In its place Leonard put speakers wailing Diana Ross, grey industrial carpet, spotlights trained on minuscule grey-green tiles in the wet area, a state-of-the-art hot tub and dozens of private rooms sheathed in solid metal walls painted black or terra cotta.

The lights were flattering and the sheets and towels impeccably white. There was no clock except at the entrance and time was banished along with any crack in the pleasure machine that might indicate whether it was day or night outside. Everyone looked tan, everyone was young—except now youth had been extended to include hot men in their forties. Hunky daddies as well as twinky kids. Beauty—facial beauty, fine bones, flawless skin, a full head of straight hair—was no longer important since a fighter's mug or a lantern jaw could be a turn-on, the latest antibiotics and sun treatments ensured good skin and a bald head had just been deemed sexy.

The other place Leonard built was a disco—a huge high-tech dance floor installed under whirling lights and booming speakers, the whole inserted into a historic theater. I didn't go often but when I did it was on acid tempered by downers and grass and I'd dance for hours, bare chested, my trousers soaked through with sweat, my body slipping against hundreds of other naked torsos. Some guys were wearing just silk shorts and whistles dangling from a cord around their necks. All week long these men would be pumping iron and swallowing vitamins so they could dance from Saturday at midnight to Sunday at noon on heavy drugs. They alternated five days of temperance with two of debauchery. The admission price was stiff since no one drank liquor—I'm not sure there was even any liquor for sale.

Around dawn I'd go up to the shadowy balcony where guys were stretching out singly or in pairs, smoking cigarettes and looking down through eyeleted metal sheathing at the domed dance floor and its orchestrated writhings. Sometimes I'd kneel between another man's legs and suck his salty, sweaty cock. After a few months I realized I could skip the drugs and dancing and just arrive fresh and cool at six or seven in the morning and go straight up to the balcony and give some head to weightlifters who were starting to crash.

Freed from my parental duties and determined to take advantage of the Indian summer of my looks, I went to the baths or the balcony three nights a week. I wasn't what I would have called a sex maniac. I had dinner with Joshua or Butler or Max or a beau every night of the week, usually in a restaurant. I never cruised by day, even though while I was writing my sex manual, working against a tight deadline, I became excited and frustrated. But late—toward two or three in the morning—I couldn't distinguish between loneliness and horniness. Well, it certainly wasn't simply loneliness, since if a friend had called after midnight seeking company I would have found it intrusive.

Leonard had built these two palaces, though I doubt he ever made much money from them. What he did obtain was the goodwill of the landlord, who became a rich man and who backed Leonard's own gym. Leonard designed and built it himself in the same sober but chic industrial style he'd used for the baths and the disco. He outfitted it with the best and newest equipment and hired hot Cuban and Italian instructors who were so macho they never smiled and were even rumored to have girlfriends. The most famous gay porno stars took out memberships and the young professionals from Chelsea joined up in the early spring to prepare for the annual summer migration to Fire Island.

In the midst of his wheeling and dealing Leonard found time to create my studio apartment. An old man had died after living there for fifty years in the most primitive, rent-controlled squalor. Leonard had the place fumigated, the linoleum ripped up and the parquet restored, the ceiling lamp concealed, the hundred-and-fifty-year-old wood shutters dug out of the walls and rehung, the white marble fireplace stripped clean, the walls painted a pale grey, a loft bed built over a walk-in closet and a new galley kitchen and toilet and shower stall wedged in behind a brand-new wall. The ceilings were fourteen feet high and the two noble casement windows looked out on a jungle of fire escapes, dirty back yards, glowing exit lights, gingko trees, twenty-story buildings and water tanks perched on distant roofs. When the East Side local headed downtown from Astor Place the whole building shook.

After years of living on the depressing Upper West Side with Kevin and then the kids, I was alone and back in the Village. Everyone in the building was gay—not the piss-elegant window-dressers in suits I'd lived next to uptown but young Village guys in jeans and bomber jackets and three days' growth of beard who sometimes got blind drunk at dawn and fell asleep with the same record playing at top blast over and over and over. My apartment was burgled right away—someone just stepped in off the fire escape outside my windows—and after that I started closing the heavy wood shutters and barring them whenever I went out.

Nothing could have been more streamlined than that life. I took my meals in coffee shops open twenty-four hours a day. I was free from the need to clean or cook or do anything but run the garbage down or take the laundry to the laundromat once a week and pick it up three hours later or cash a check every ten days. Leonard, I realized, wasn't just buddies with Billy. No, they were lovers and they'd recently moved a younger redhead in with them, an Irish kid from Brooklyn whom they introduced as "Nick, our lover." Nick worked at the gym behind the desk, sometimes going down to the shower room to break up orgies. "Okay, fellas, knock it off. One more warning and you'se outta hiyah."

I could still draw on Leonard sexually, however, if I wanted. I was dating a handsome little slave from Kentucky who was always looking for new thrills. I'd seen Leonard in black leather chaps, motorcycle boots and a chain-festooned black jacket. I stripped my slave naked and tied him up in one room and then, as prearranged, I buzzed Leonard in. In the living room he took off his shirt and jeans and put his boots, chaps and leather jacket back on. When we went into the bedroom all my slave could see in the half light was a six-foot-four sadist with a hard-on and leathers, his face cast in shadow by the bill of his motorcycle cap. The slave moaned and came before Leonard even touched him.

What he couldn't see was that this was Leonard the creep from Gainesville, the faggot who'd still blush if a woman flirted with him, who liked Thom Gunn's poetry and Robert Wilson's plays, who'd sat through the entire Ring cycle twice and liked to swing incense at "Smoky Mary's" Midtown church on Sunday mornings. This was the warm, smiling, genial Leonard who encouraged Billy to learn Schubert and Schumann, who gave dinner parties for all men at which the guests would linger till dawn, discussing life, love, art, money, morality. He wasn't competitive, he loved nurturing other people's talents, he'd learned, all on his own, the arts of life, but he didn't promote them in order to intimidate or impress other people but simply in order to communicate his curiosity and love. Billy was his partner, Nick was their lover, but Leonard was also in love with Walt, a big, soft-spoken fireman who once gave me a NYFD gold and blue T-shirt which I wore for years until it turned to shreds. By that time Leonard and the fireman were both dead. Leonard and Walt would go off on gay motorcycle rallies. Once they even went to Reno to a gay rodeo. To look at them you would have said they had nothing in common with the opera queens I'd known in the fifties; if you ran into them on a dark street you might even be scared. But they weren't afraid to show their love of the arts and Leonard could weep when Billy played the *Kinderszenen* or sang in his quavering, pale voice Schubert's *Erlkönig*.

I suppose the most distinctive thing about them was that they lived in an all-male society in which they adopted (and even exaggerated) a virile manner and an interest in sports. They took on hyper-male jobs (work in construction or the fire department). They spoke in loud, deep voices and looked like a lord and his bravos when they went out to the clubs at two in the morning in a phalanx of five or six guys in T-shirts and leather jackets, all of them over six feet tall. But they were not merely male impersonators. They were just as capable of staying in all evening around a table, nursing brandy and cigars, talking about Balanchine or Mallarmé, of Fred Halsted, the tough-guy porn-film director (*L.A. Plays Itself*), famous for his fist, or Halston, the celebrity dress designer. They were no longer creeps—or if so, then only on a bad, fearful morning. They could walk girders on a building site twenty stories up or enter a blaze in search of a "crispy" (fireman's slang for a burn victim).

They didn't starve themselves into tight jeans—Leonard developed a real gut, which was becoming. When years later he went out to dinner with me in Paris he ordered two of everything (two first courses, two entrées, two desserts), because he knew that otherwise he'd go hungry in France. They didn't worry about their tans. They didn't stand around in gay bars and cruise—the ultimate sad-sack act of self-hating narcissism. No, they met plenty of men in their work or even on the street. What Leonard, the dream top, secretly longed for was an even bigger, stronger stud who'd top him, and guys like that might go to the Mineshaft but not to an ordinary bar.

The Mineshaft was a new sex club in the meat-packing district. The whole area was badly lit except for a sudden flare of fire in an oil drum on the curb where the butchers warmed their hands before heaving a side of beef onto moving overhead hooks that lurched and dangled the carcass out of a truck and into a warehouse. The pavement was gummy with dried blood and the air thick with the rich, gamy smell of fresh blood.

The men in their blood-stained white aprons shouted orders or jokes—commands, anger, humor all sounded equally hostile.

The entrance to the club was at the top of a long flight of stairs. There a guy seated on a stool kept out the undesirables—men wearing cologne or silk shirts or sports jackets—and let in the guys who smelled of nothing but leather, sweat and beer. Once inside, the customer could check all his clothes at the door or all but his boots and jockstrap, or he could stay fully dressed, though the jeans often had the seat ripped out, exposing a bare butt, and the T-shirts were usually strategically torn. The hat-check boy also handed out paper cups full of Crisco.

In the first room men drank at a long bar and played pool.

In the second room the customers were plunged instantly into near-total darkness—a pickpocket's paradise (I kept just a few dollars inside my socks, pressed between the bottom of my boot and the sole of my foot). One wall was perforated with saucer-sized holes at waist height—glory holes. Guys would stick their cocks through these holes and get sucked off by unseen mouths on the other side. Some stood there silently at attention; others writhed and clawed the wood, as though the wall were their tipped-up mattress and they were having a bad dream.

As in Hell, the punishments became more severe the lower one descended. Upstairs men were being fisted in slings; downstairs they were naked in a tub being pissed on. As though Hell were a sideshow, most of the men were shuffling from the bearded lady to the snake charmer. One whip-wielding man kept driving his lover back into a corner, which represented the kennel; everyone rushed to see this noisy dressage. Elsewhere a man was being wrapped in sheets of transparent plastic—only a slender pipe came out of his mouth to allow him to breathe. This image of mummification frightened me so much I couldn't look at it. As in Hell, one circulated mechanically, bored. To enter excited and leave bored was infernal, as was the experience of having your body treated as a customs official treats luggage—patted quickly, dismissed as harmless, examined in depth only one time out of a hundred.

The place I liked more was ten blocks uptown, the Slot, where no drinks were served and the lights weren't too dim. Men paid an entrance fee and passed through a turnstile. Inside was nothing but a rabbit warren of booths with doors that locked. Each of the three walls in each stall had a glory hole pierced through it. I'd crouch in my room, four feet square, and turn from one cock to another, suck one while stroking another.

We felt like prisoners seeking to establish contact with one another.

Sometimes we'd hold hands or kiss through the holes. Yet if a neighbor invited me into his booth I hesitated. Would his whole body be as romantic as these frustrating glimpses, his presence as magnetic as my fantasies?

Sometimes we were all bottoms and at every hole was nothing but a gaping mouth. We'd slam a door behind us angrily, in search of a stiff one wanting to be serviced.

A guy might strip naked and squat and twist to let me run my hands over his body, while in the holes behind him and to one side large disembodied eyes, as in an Odilon Redon painting, were blinking and looking up, down, left, right.

One night an angry young man with a big cock locked himself into the innermost room, a long, narrow slot the size of a horse stall, and strode angrily back and forth, dipping his penis now into this hole, now into that. Everyone was trying to attract his attention—beckoning with a hand through the hole or flickering a tongue like a snake or making sucking and slurping sounds. He paced back and forth, half as though he were the Minotaur looking for a way out of the maze and half as though he were Theseus stabbing at everything in the labyrinth that snorted or pawed.

The kid on the door took a liking to me and asked me to stick around till six when he got off. To keep me there he gave me a joint that must have been sprayed with acid. I suppose he thought I'd become so confused I wouldn't be capable of leaving, but in fact I was suddenly so inundated by drugged desire that it turned me bold, much bolder than I'd ever been before. I saw a sexy guy with big, startling eyes, a cocaine-user's punch-drunk way of constantly sniffing and jerking his head and neck to one side, and a hairline that had receded in order to throw into still higher relief a strong brow, a penetrating gaze and a nose that was obscenely large. He also had a dancer's legs and ass. Instead of taking the booth next to his I marched right into his before he had time to drop the latch. We fell on each other ravenously while hands and tongues flickered around us through the holes. He said, "I live just a few blocks away."

"Let's go," I said.

We went to a second-story loft on Twenty-Third Street between Seventh and Eighth Avenues, the sort that seemed to be bare not only out of a taste for simplicity but also from extreme poverty. There was a double bed pushed against the wall, two hungry cats with soft fur and rasping voices, one chair and a single overhead light. Fox—that was his name—snapped the light off as soon as we came in; the room was dimly lit now by sodium-vapor street lamps through the uncurtained sash windows. He fed the cats quickly, muttering to them in an annoyed voice, not for my benefit.

Then we were naked and on his big bed. He had an old-fashioned dancer's body—inconsequential torso, biceps-less arms, the only important muscle being the one that rose out of his shoulders to support his neck and head and to pulley his arms up. No, it was his ass that was his glory. A trail of fur descended his spine toward his crack and then hair began again under his big, firm buns, but those twin globes were as hairless and pale as the moon by day.

I suppose his cock might have been big, too, but the speed he was on had shrunk it into insignificance. I remember, however, that when I fucked Fox he kept whispering commands into my ear; he was the father and I the son who was fucking another human being for the very first time, so naturally my old man had to give his timid little boy very precise instructions—or something like that. We were all obsessed with fantasies back then, which we kept exploring until they became absurd. One boy even said to me: "I do father-son, sailor-slut, older brother-younger brother, black rapist-white secretary, trucker-hitchhiker and a virgin couple on their wedding night."

But with Fox I didn't feel he was just another bored guy looking for a perverse kick. He *loved* me, even that first night, with the same loony love he would show me for three years—menacing, possessive, admiring, condescending.

After we'd come he kept sipping at me with lips swollen from too many kisses and he didn't want to release me from his bony chest. His mouth tasted slightly sour, like a mildewed washcloth. He talked to me in his Southern accent, sleepily, but his nose flexed and moved with his lips; it wasn't a frozen prow but something supple and expressive, like a hand under a sheet, a penis stirring in cotton shorts.

When we woke up at noon the next day the street outside was noisy with traffic, calling voices, horns and the ubiquitous New York sirens. Fox grabbed his camera and took photos of me with his white cat in my hands, held high; the picture was cropped just at chest height but you can see I'm naked and still sleepy. An hour later, as the next picture shows, I'm dressed, hair brushed, the cat held against my grey sweater, smoke from my out-of-sight cigarette rising in front of my face.

But before I got dressed he fucked me in that sunlight-flooded, curtainless room. He'd been frustrated the night before not being able to get an erection; now he wanted to enter me, to plant his flag on *my* moon. He had a dirty, Southern way of muttering things. If I groaned he'd say, "Feel good, sugar? That's a greedy little pussy you've got." He came and when he pulled it out he said, "Make a wish," and seeing that he and I had all the same books, I said, "Why don't you become my husband?"

	Now that my sex book had come out and my picture had been on the cover of a gay magazine, I was "bankable" again. As a result, my Baroque novel, which could have been subtitled "The Tragedy of Gay Sex," had been accepted by one of the first openly gay editors. This was the "little" novel I'd written while living with Gabe.
TEN	

Not only was I making some money from my books, but thanks to a friend I'd started to teach a house seminar in creative writing one day a week at Yale.

My students were all rich kids, most of them physically perfect; when I asked them to write something that they'd lived through the preceding year, they'd start the story, "I could hear the jingle of a harness under my bedroom window—the hunt was on!" I'd felt for years that if I'd only gone to an Ivy League school I would have risen quicker and been published sooner. Now I was living in the situation, familiar to me from Victorian novels, of teaching rich children; I was the poor governess preparing them for prospects that would never be mine.

When I was on campus no one looked at me. I didn't exist as a sexual being or even as an object of simple curiosity. But the minute I came back to New York and the train doors parted, I was strafed by glancing eyes, like those disembodied eyes at the Slot. Instead of being a benign professorial presence, neutered by age and position, in New York I was an on-going project solicitous of nervous attention—as a body, a past, a future ambition, a clothes horse (or nag, in my case). No matter how inferior a specimen I might be, I still invited evaluation or at least speculation.

Fox would never have turned a silly gay head since he didn't flatter any reigning aesthetic, and yet with his receding, sandy-blond hair, badly capped teeth, his way of shaking all over with laughter, his way of hectoring people and jabbing at the air to insist on a point until he caught himself being excessive and he dissolved into laughter, but especially with his lean, topographically crowded face with the big, active nose, heavy-lidded eyes and narrow, very high brow, indented at the temples as though he'd been pulled by forceps out of his mother, he was an original: at once the Middle European violinist suffering over a twelve-tone adagio and a rat-like New Yorker sniffing the air for a bit of cheese, a rump to mount or a giant foot to squirm out from under.

He was very sophisticated. He'd once made love, he told me, to an eighty-year-old man who'd been a dancer for the Ballets Russes. They had had sex surrounded by photos of the dancer when he'd been twenty performing *L'Après-Midi d'un Faune*—and they *both* had looked at the old photos the whole time.

He was a survivor, *just*, but he wasn't at all interested in money, though he longed for fame. I found out that he came from Mobile, where his father had been a banker, his mother a socialite. When he was a boy his family had been the embodiment of respectability. He'd spend every other Saturday with his maternal grandfather (the Episcopalian minister) and his ailing, distinguished wife; over the copious, buttery dinner they tried to interrogate him about his future. On the alternating Saturdays he spent the night with his white-trash paternal grandparents, who'd set up metal TV trays before the small, black and white screen. They'd drink iced tea out of sweating, shiny blue or red aluminum canasta glasses, eat TV dinners of turkey, peas and mashed potatoes, and watch a variety show. When the June Taylor Dancers performed, little Fox, nervously eager and already outfitted in T-shirt and basketball shorts, would join in, hysterically copying their movements with frantic agility. He'd end by doing the splits, his infatuated grandparents would applaud and his grandmother would say, "Isn't that the cutest thing?"

By the time he was twelve he was a drum major. With a testing trepidation, Fox showed me the hand-tinted black and white photos, three feet by two, that had been shot in a Mobile portrait studio of himself. "Just look what a little *sissy* I was, a real Southern sissy." He mimed horror and raised his hands slowly to his open mouth. "Look at the outfit—that was green silk with beige silk lapels. And the *hat*! Tipped on an angle! Saucy slut!" I wanted to have sex with Fox while we both looked at *these* photos, but he wasn't turned on by them.

His mother had died of cancer, his father had taken up with a twenty-year-old hippy from Gadsden and moved her in. Soon afterwards he had been arrested for giving payola to the county government in exchange for an investment of public funds. He was sent up the river to a golf-club prison, where he fraternized with other white-collar criminals. Fox's father, until then a good ol' boy, became a long-haired hippy who espoused civil rights and listened to Joni Mitchell records. Within two years after the death of Fox's mother his brother was living with his father's ex-girlfriend in the family home. Fox himself had gone first to Washington, where one of his father's cronies had obtained for him a job as a Congressional page, then to New York where he'd lived with a theatrical commune from Texas and danced in a group-written musical about the Little Prince.

When I met Fox he'd just given up his theatrical career at age thirty-two. For ten years he'd made avant-garde videos of nude women sucking their thumbs in small felt boxes or he'd been one of the people on four-hour shifts to inhabit a "living sculpture" in the window of an art gallery. He'd appeared in the chorus of an all-male musical about true love and marriage or, mainly, gone to thousands of auditions. He'd been an extra at the dinner party in Charles Ludlam's *Camille*, he'd sung in Al Carmines' *In Circles*, an opera using a Gertrude Stein text; he'd helped a German artist fill the Judson Church with lard, felt and dead meat. He'd been one of the stoned kids lounging around Bridget Berlin's room in Warhol's *Chelsea Girls*, but after Andy was shot by Valerie Solanas in 1969, and after Paul Morrissey began to direct the films coming out of the Factory, Fox was never used again. And Carmines "betrayed" him, too, by not using him in his stylish, uptown opera, the one that opened the Promenade Theater on Upper Broadway and that paid the performers Equity scale.

Somewhere along the way Fox had slept with Bob Constantine, a composer in his forties who wrote cerebral, twelve-tone music and taught at a famous university and did nothing from dawn to dusk but camp it up. Though Bob was fresh faced, red cheeked and, outside the classroom or concert hall, always in jeans designed to throw his massive farmer's rump into high relief, nevertheless his conversation, at odds with this healthy peasant look, was all drawled Mae West or snappy Bette Midler repartee. Bob Constantine introduced Fox to Homer, the ninety-year-old acerbic dean of American music, who was looking for an assistant to prepare his papers for Yale, where he expected to sell them to the Beinecke Library for half a million dollars. Homer hired Fox. They got along like an old Southern couple, for Homer was from Mississippi, though he'd lived in Paris and New York for the past seventy years.

Homer was a sly dogmatist, a slightly Dada authority on every subject who had a dry, sometimes cracked opinion about the arts, literature, France, Germany, President Carter, women's clothes, household pets, marriage and food. He would announce these opinions as though he were reading them off stone tablets. After riffling through my Japanese novel and my Baroque novel, he said to me, "You're far too fascinated by theory. You want to be an innovator. But a writer must be primarily interested in the world around him. You need to become a sidewalk artist, going for quick likenesses. A constant stimulus from outside is essential for a long, happy career. Otherwise you'll do your best work by forty and afterwards become sterile." I took his words to heart, I who was just two years shy of turning forty.

He warned Fox against me: "Charming guy, a real seducer, but his métier, after all, is writing about love, and for professional reasons he *can't* stay faithful." This warning only fed Fox's voracious jealousy.

Homer was deaf—and not just in an ordinary, cotton-wool-in-the-ear sort of way. No, the devil had devised a special torture for him as a composer: all the notes above the C over middle C were transposed down a fifth, which resulted in converting everything played by the right hand on the piano, say, into grotesque cacophony. Listening to his own music was purest torture. Like many deaf people who remain socially active, he dominated the conversation. When it turned from him for more than ten minutes he fell asleep.

Everyone put up with his bad manners and his dogmatism because he, like Balanchine, was a living link with the glorious past. Homer's past had been formed by the neo-Romantic composers of the 1930s in Paris, such as Henri Sauguet and Francis Poulenc and the members of Les Six. He'd written two operas that were still performed all over the world and were as simple as hymns, as eternal as plainsong, as chic as the latest fragrance. For the last twenty years he'd dominated the musical life of New York as a daily critic, not a composer; now his deafness had ended both careers. He had a lover, a painter, who was just seventy-five and had a full head of hair. Nicholas still rode a motorcycle cross-country and, as Homer swore proudly, "He's the only man of his generation who can still undrape becomingly." He became the world's oldest AIDS patient.

Homer knew everyone. He liked to cook, though sometimes he forgot to light his gas burners after he'd turned them on, and we all feared one day he'd go up in a major explosion. He lived in the Chelsea Hotel in a suite that had once belonged to the manager and had fine wood paneling. He introduced Fox and me to Christopher Isherwood and Don Bachardy. Isherwood instantly became an acquaintance of mine as well, though we lived on opposite coasts and saw each other rarely. He urged me to write more directly and simply and to take on gay politics as a subject. When I would begin to praise him he'd laugh uproariously. Later I saw a play he and Don had written, based on Chris's novel *A Meeting by the River*, and in that play the monks were always convulsed with the same laughter. Kevin had a small role in it.

Fox had many famous friends, including two Hollywood stars, several composers, a *Vogue* photographer who bore a celebrated name (which she'd acquired through marriage) and a whole host of novelists and poets, but he never introduced me to them. Nor did he present them to one another. He played with his cards close to his chest and if faced with an ambiguous situation that didn't automatically call either for openness or discretion, he'd always choose to be mysterious. I didn't even know how he'd acquired these friends—oh, the Hollywood stars, a couple, he met them, I suppose, during his acting days when they were all starting out. And he'd worked for the young photographer's aged husband, a composer, before he died the previous year. But the writers, all of them gay, he must have tricked with.

What he didn't like about me was my exuberance, often unfocused, and the copious compliments which I handed out to everyone and which occasionally misfired. Most of all he feared and detested my gossipiness, my embarrassing questions, my saucy sallies. I attributed his sense of proportion to his having grown up as a member of a prominent family in one small, traditional Southern city, whereas I'd been the son of a wicked divorcee who'd moved from city to city every year and I, like she, longed to make an impression even on strangers—*especially* on strangers, since waiters, taxi drivers, other passengers on the train or elevator were perceived to be judges, infinitely more powerful and promising than mere friends. These strangers weren't "the public" whose opinion one risked "offending." No, for my mother or me, they were potential biographers, benefactors, bosses, lovers;

they were people only now being initiated into the wonderful wide wild world of our personal circus. Perhaps this sharp, even painful, need to please everyone constituted our sole form of optimism, though it usually turned us into buffoons.

Because of his work for Homer, Fox had developed a passion for filing. He spoke constantly of his *archives*, and saved every scrap of paper, even the most inconsequential note, that he received from an artist or writer, no matter how young or how obscure. I can picture him bare-chested in his khaki shorts and sandals squatting beside his twelve big boxes of files; he slipped into them a photo, a sketch on a menu, a letter or drafts of his own stories or journal entries, even press clippings about a man eaten by an alligator or a mother who'd baked and served her children to her husband, items that he thought might someday generate a short story. Anyway he liked grotesque things, which made him whinny with laughter.

He was oddly unsure of himself *and* assertive: aggressively insecure, I guess you might say. He'd start to explain something he felt (about me, about theater, about Homer) and he'd get caught up in tangles, then, pushing his face right up into mine, he'd keep asking, "You understand? You see what I mean? Huh?" His nose moved with his mouth as he spoke, as though it were part of his upper lip. He was so persuasive, so charming, that he quickly convinced his interlocutor to accept everything he was saying or doing, but if certain moments had been frozen in a photo— when he stood very close, bugged his eyes, jabbed at the air, flexed his big nose—he would have looked certifiable.

He was much more the hip New Yorker than I and he knew five or six young men (none of whom, of course, he introduced to me or to one another) with whom he'd huddle over coffee or on the phone for hours on end. He was proud of his friends; they were his capital. He'd work at cultivating them, though *work* didn't convey his patience, his energetic casualness. He'd speak so softly on the phone I couldn't understand anything more than snatches, but I was impressed by the way he *crooned* into the receiver, laughed intimately, kept egging on the guy at the other end ("You did? Like how? *Details!*") or feign an encouraging astonishment ("No! She said *that*! You're exaggerating!"). Around him I felt egotistical and indifferent, *formal* in my boring indifference, for if I was good in a crisis I was nil as a habitual schmoozer. I could sing the arias but I stumbled through my recitatives. I didn't complain or have much patience with other people's *schreiing* (the Yiddish was infectious in New York). I was given more to *kvelling* (crowing with triumph) over my friends' successes, even my own. If people were cozily unhappy I instantly doused them in the cold water of a pep talk. Unfocused reports of dull daily activity I kept probing for the lesson to be drawn or at least the anecdote to be distilled. Fox could groan and sigh and revolve slowly through the tiresome, convoluted plumbing of everyday life.

Outside New York he was much less sure of himself. I got us a gig from a short-lived glossy magazine to do a profile of Peggy Guggenheim, story by me, photos by Fox. Although he criticized other photographers all the time he was far from sure of his own talents. He wanted Joshua, who was already in Venice, to pin Peggy down on a precise day and to make her commit herself to a two-hour photo session, but Josh, as a man of the world, knew that Peggy was bored, loved publicity and would do what we wanted but only if her decision was made on the spot. Fox hounded me every day in advance and was so nervous he shook all the time. But his pictures turned out well, Peggy took us out in the gondola, and the article was published, although no one we knew ever commented on it or probably saw it.

Fox could be very harsh about other gay men, whom he dismissed impatiently as "*these queens*" in a perfect spondee of irritation. He approved of older, celebrated homosexuals who'd never "made a fuss" about their sexual identity, just as he liked younger ones who were cleanshaven and career oriented. About this time the sidewalks around the East Village started to be stenciled with slogans, "Kill a Clone" or "Death to Disco." From talking to Fox I saw how younger gays identified my generation with unreflecting conformist machismo, with greed and consumerism, with white supremacy and sexism. "You guys were just pissed off you couldn't have all the same perks as your heterosexual white male friends, so you created gay liberation to make that one small adjustment and let the rest of us—dykes, niggers, drags—go to hell in a handbag."

I tried to tell him that a fight over sexuality would never be a small one in Christian America; Anita Bryant, the orange juice queen, was leading a fundamentalist crusade against gays throughout the South and Northwest and getting pro-gay city ordinances overturned. "Save Our Children" was the name of her group. She was using the sophisticated argument that precisely to the degree that gays were respectable, attractive people they could mislead impressionable youngsters into their infernal lifestyle. Since gays don't reproduce, they must recruit, was her idea. Or I could have said that the assertion of the clone look had originally been a political act, a way of signaling that gay men did not have to be sissies, arch and bitchy caricatures of middle-class women of the past, the very ones commemorated in the camp classic, Clare Boothe Luce's *The Women*. Just as a woman of my mother's generation would have thought a "hen party," a dinner with other women, an admission of "old maidishness" and social defeat, in the same way the gay bars I'd first glimpsed in the fifties had been temples to despair, where self-mocking queens danced and "rubbed pussies" with one another before they got up the courage to go out in search of the real thing, a bit of rough trade to rob and beat them. The clone look was a tribal look, a way of saying to one another, "We're brothers. We're the men we've been looking for."

But Fox would glaze over the minute I started talking politics. He was too interested in the artistic events of the city around him—the imminent visit of the Polish director Grotowski or the premiere of *Penguin Touquet*—to give much credence to my harangues.

I envied Fox's cultural confidence. Perhaps because he was cataloguing Homer's memorabilia from Paris in the 1930s he was certain that New York in the late 1970s would be just as artistically fertile and brilliant. Now, almost twenty years later, I can see Fox's hunch was a good one. New York gay life, just before AIDS, was both unprecedented and without sequel. In 1978 six or seven gay novels, including Andrew Holleran's *Dancer from the Dance*, were published on the East and West Coast, discussed on all sides and sometimes even read. The Theater of the Ridiculous, John Ashbery's poems (all about starting out all over again and crossing a gigantic plain), Robert Wilson's operas without music, Robert Mapplethorpe's photographs, Robert Joffrey's dances—all appealed to the sensibility we were fashioning.

In New York and San Francisco there were now so many gay men living openly that not only the genus but even aberrant species thrived. One could socialize, if one chose, only with other opera-loving sadists or only with cat-owning bibliophiles into urine. Straight members of the public saw the enormous gay parades of dykes in work boots and drag queens and the grinning, bespectacled parents of gays, but they never caught a glimpse of all those homosexuals who didn't want to participate: the doughy clarinetist scuttling from a lesson to lunch with a lesbian musicologist or the doctor who, since he was busted for prescribing Quaaludes too often, never emerged from his apartment, or the Asian teenage woman holding hands with her Puerto Rican girlfriend in the park late at night.

Even if New York gay life was a ghetto made up of minorities, all contradictory and severally exclusive, nevertheless Fox was surely representative of that moment. He was aware that we were making history of some sort. He saw the links with an older generation (Ned Rorem's, Frank O'Hara's) and even Homer's *much* older generation, but he could also glimpse how the present was preparing a new youth of wild, loud, totally freaky anarchic kids. Fox worshipped high culture, especially when it was wrapped like a shawl around the shoulders of men and women he knew personally (Homer's ancient friends, whom he had met on a trip to Paris that he'd taken with the old man, were as real to him as the New York boys he murmured to over the phone every night).

He and I assumed there was going to be a future and that it would get more and more extravagant. We saw gay men as a vanguard that society would inevitably follow. I thought that the couple would disappear and be replaced by new, polyvalent molecules of affection or Whitmanesque adhesiveness. I was having sex with a sleepy-eyed Native American I'd met through Kevin. He and I would make love to a blond steward from Norway—and sometimes with a hairless translator from the French who affected a crewcut and policeman's shiny shoes. At other times we were joined by a Kennedy-like gay political leader who'd rush in wearing a white shirt and rep tie and would have to keep checking his messages.

We were friends and lovers, more friends than lovers, and our long evenings of pasta, Puccini and sex felt as mellow as vintage Bordeaux held up to a flame and as exhilarating as a hit play in previews. In the warm weather we'd leave the huge windows open at my new place and listen to the sound of laughter and cutlery on plates welling up from the garden restaurant just below. We were inside, naked beside a candelabrum blazing with twelve candles, the long silver marijuana pipe from Morocco passing from one sun-tanned hand to another. The Indian was completely crazy; he had a paranoid fantasy about a cult of Hollywood actors who wanted to sacrifice him to the devil. But in our stupor, each guy's head resting on the next man's stomach, we'd sometimes start quaking with laughter in spite of ourselves when the Indian's plot became too impossibly convoluted.

When we were all shaking, the Indian, Tad, would catch himself: "Okay, fellows, believe it or not, laugh all you want, but I *swear*—" and at that point we all lost it and writhed with the pain of our laughter until Tad began to blow out the candles one by one and then, when the room was dark and the needle had lifted from the last record, he'd kiss the steward, then the translator, then the Kennedy, then me with his big warm mouth, juicy as a pear so ripe it's already turning brown, and he'd begin to murmur incoherent, fatherly reassurances in his baritone voice. He'd wrap us in his arms, the arms of a wrestler who's taken on a winter weight he's about to shed though the bulk can't hide the strength that lies just under the skin. His skin had the not-unpleasant smell of Cubans who live on black beans and saffron rice (maybe that's what he ate) and his big uncircumcised penis lolled so lazily, so majestically on his balls, like a river god on mossy rocks, that we four gathered around him with the vulnerability and clustering affection of smooth-limbed daughters. If in the dim light bouncing up from the paper lanterns strung through the trees below my window I saw Tad's dark hand on the white of my ass, I felt he was growing a beard, I breasts and, after the mad excesses of his Hollywood Satan story, he re-established his dignity through the simple authenticity of his body. We were still boys, even I at nearly forty, but Tad at thirty was so fully a man that only he among us need not fear aging. Our laughter melted into moans as we eased back into making love again.

⌒ I HAD TO HIDE my nights of Whitmanesque camaraderie from Fox because the more he loved me the more jealous he became. At first I found his jealousy reassuring, even exciting, after my years of hopeless love. Fox stared at me with his hyperthyroid eyes, which bulged out of his head in order to see more of me, even my slightest, most inadvertent and peripheral gesture.

After that first night when we'd met at the Slot and I'd fucked him, he never stopped fucking me. I'd lie on my back with him between my legs and he'd stare and stare at me as he'd fuck. If I'd groan with pleasure or pain (I could never distinguish between them) he'd redouble his efforts. He acted as though, if he shoved a little harder, inched in a bit deeper, he'd finally own me, take care of me. He was staring so hard at me not because he was melting with tenderness or because he wanted to transmit a thought but because, like an eagle carrying off a lamb, he wanted to see if there was still some life in me, something that might kindle in me a will of my own and inspire me to run off, head for safety.

I'd leave Fox's apartment to walk home and the phone would be ringing when I came in. "What took you so long?" Fox would ask. "Don't try to fool me—you usually make the trip in fifteen minutes. Today it took twenty-eight—nearly *thirty*!"

"I was window-shopping."

"Yeah, for *dick*. Huh? See some nice dick? Did you stop into that dirty movie theater on Second and—"

"Don't even tell me the address! I don't want to know. You're the one who knows all those—"

"Oh, sure," Fox said scornfully. "You're pure as the driven snow. Don't forget where I met you, sugar; that wasn't any convent."

When I'd come in the door he'd pull me into a tight embrace. If I didn't respond ardently, he'd push me away and say, "What's wrong? Have you already come twice today? Plum wore out?" He'd push a hand down the back of my jeans. "No undies? Wanna be ready for action? You Village Boys are like that, aren't you? Notorious for—And what's this? Your asshole feels loose and juicy. Didn't you even have time to clean it up before coming to see your hubby?"

The worst of it was that I'd grow self-conscious and giggly. I could feel myself blushing and becoming more and more awkward. He'd start nuzzling my neck and since he was shorter than me he'd have to stand on tiptoe to do so, but his ass and legs were so strong that I felt like a big, willowy girl beside this powerful little bully who would soon lift and guide me through a long floating dance.

Over dinner with friends he concealed his jealousy entirely. He was thoroughly up to date and always ready with a scandalous story, but if during the course of the meal I forgot myself and told a sex anecdote of my own about someone I'd known even years ago I'd see Fox cock an ear, sit up, take note. Later, when we were alone, his jaw muscles would flex and his nose would seem to dilate. He'd say, "Oh, so he played with your nipples, did he? Like this, sugar?"

He'd fuck me, fall asleep and in the middle of the night start fucking me again. He'd play with my nipples so much they'd bleed and scab over and they'd ache under my starched shirt and I'd think of him all day, half with revulsion.

I developed a case of prostatitis that no treatment seemed able to cure. It made ejaculation painful, sometimes impossible. Only when I was seeing a doctor in Seattle, where I was interviewing people for a new book, did I learn that the whole condition was imaginary. "I'm afraid there's nothing wrong with you beyond a bit of hysteria," the doctor said with a smile. The next day I was cured.

Fox was so jealous that even when I was guiltless I'd notice with horror if a buddy touched my shoulder or stroked my neck, in all innocence; I could feel Fox watching. I'd tense up, move away, but it was only a matter of time before he'd say, "We're awfully buddy-buddy, aren't we?"

"Who? Who and who?"

"You told me you and Stuart were just friends."

"We are."

"Look, I wasn't born yesterday."

If I'd come over to his apartment with groceries to prepare supper, he'd feel the milk and say, "It's not even cold. And this butter is melting. What happened? Did you get waylaid?"

If my hair was wet with sweat, he'd say, "Oh, ho! So you took a shower after your little romp—you're becoming more and more brazen, I see, you don't even *pretend* you're faithful anymore. . . ."

"I *am* faithful!" I lied, "but I detest this whole vocabulary, *innocent, faithful, guilty, brazen, sluttish.* You know I don't believe in monogamy. Neither do you. It's a dreadful trap. We're not straight—although maybe *you* are. Are you sure you're not a breeder?"

The next night, just to spite Fox, I stood him up and had dinner with Sean and his new lover, a big bear of a man who was a lumberjack. They met me at a restaurant in the West Fifties. Their clothes made them seem completely out of place in New York. Just as an object shifts from right to left as you shut first one eye, then the other, in the same way Sean seemed healthy and vigorous with his new reddish-blond beard and his checked shirt and jeans as he talked about their dude ranch in Arizona, but then, seen from another point of view, he appeared dowdy, provincial—in those days, as a convinced New Yorker, I invariably saw out-of-towners as drab and marginal. What confirmed that impression was Sean's insistence that he and his lover were accepted by their neighbors as "regular guys" and that no one suspected there might be something "illicit" in their relationship (and here Sean's eyes lit up crazily, as though we both shared the same vice, one he could mention only once every ten years, and then only to a fellow debauchee).

The stolid, willed normality of their love made my affair with Fox seem all the more neurotic. Fox would bite me hard to leave love marks on my neck, especially above the collar, so that "my other lover" (an obsessive figment he'd created) would see I belonged to him. Fox didn't say that in so many words, but I knew what he was doing and what I'd originally thought arose from an excess of passion I now realized was the fruit of careful scheming—and I started resenting his amorous violence.

Sometimes he thought he'd hook me for good by initiating me into ever

more bizarre vices. One night he kept passing the joint my way and feeding me brandy stingers until I was incapable of putting up a resistance or
even walking. Then with remarkable efficiency he undressed me, kissing
me with those kisses of his that always ended with a lingering little bite.
His hands were all over me (how I long for them now that I'm alone) and
I couldn't decide whether they were irritating or overwhelmingly delicious—and then, suddenly, he was pushing me back onto the bed. I toppled there in a naked heap. He left the room and I could hear water
running and running. The cats came to inspect me contemptuously, as
though they knew how dangerous so much spinelessness could be. They
looked at me, breathed lightly on me, and hopped away—or was what I
took for their breath really Fox's hand, passing lightly over me, banking
the fires of my nearly extinct aura? My eyes, unfocused, myopic (I'd taken
out my lenses an hour earlier), saw that Fox was hooking something up to
a tall pole he'd wheeled beside the bed.

"Whassat?" I asked drunkenly.

"An enema bag."

"I don't want that . . . that would make me ashamed . . . the smell . . .
loss of control. . . ."

Fox fed me a hit of poppers and said, "There, my little boy's a good
boy, he's going to let me do whatever I want," and before I could reply he
had a greasy finger up my ass and then the nozzle of the enema bag.

I couldn't feel the water going in at first but when I looked up I saw that
Fox was pinching the tube, then releasing it, and slowly the orange rubber
sack deflated. After two bags full of warm water had gone in, a wave of
cramps swept through me and I panicked. I was afraid I'd burst, that Fox
didn't know what he was doing, that he himself was too stoned to stop. He
massaged my taut belly soothingly and told me the "discomfort" would
soon pass. I remembered that there are no pain receptors, only cramp receptors, in the digestive tract; I could be ruptured, bleeding, and I wouldn't
even know it.

The cramps went away, only to return when he filled me up with the
third bag. Again he massaged my belly. I alternated between resenting his
interference even with my vital processes and inner organs and surrendering to him as though he were a doctor—or a *parent*, since my stepmother had been the one to give me enemas when I was a boy, an
operation that even then was half-erotic, at least for me.

It all ended with my sitting on the toilet (I who jumped sky-high if
someone walked in on me) while Fox crouched beside me, pushing more

and more of the spurting water out of me while I wept from shame and gratitude as the horrible smell of something fundamental within me rose all around us, something that Fox, too, was breathing, sharing.

I was a fundamentalist, if that meant I believed that every attribute was an intrinsic aspect of our essence. I was willing to submit manfully to the powerful spices in Indian food only because I believed that these dishes were *necessarily* hot; the day I discovered that this cuisine could be ordered milder I lost my faith in it—or rather, felt my faith severely shaken. In the same way when I learned that the color of Coke was added later, that brown sugar was just white sugar with molasses sprayed on it to give it a "natural" unprocessed look—oh, all of these discoveries troubled my primitive fundamentalism. In the same way I believed that shit was not just food passing through the body but something that had always lived within it. Fox had somehow sensed this funny faith of mine and gone right to it. He'd tapped the corruption residing in my heart, not just the waste passing through my tripes.

One evening we were eating an ordered-in pizza with friends, other young writers who belonged to a literary club we'd started where we'd take turns reading out loud to each other. I'd just read something and been praised for it (which was no surprise, since our organization was named "The All-Praise Club"). Fox's face darkened with jealousy—but suddenly I saw it was envy. And if the two words were often confused that was because folk wisdom recognized that the mad, possessive husband wants to *be*—no, the analysis was less well suited to the dynamics of heterosexuality: the fox wants to be the chicken.

I can't imagine Brice in that druggy promiscuity of love and friendship, jealousy and envy. When I first seduced him I'd get him stoned on American joints and I tried out some kinky sex on him that he'd never experienced before, but one year into our affair, after he became ill, we stopped making love, although we continued to sleep tangled up together, held hands at the movies and were in every way a couple. Perhaps with all my earlier lovers I'd felt claustrophobic, whereas with Brice I knew that we were both positive and he was seriously ill and that this closeness, this love, was not going to go on forever, that soon enough we'd be sleeping alone in our graves. I was no longer afraid of intimacy, since I knew that I'd finally arrived at the end of all feeling, all experience, and that the moments that remained to him and to me might as well be as intense as possible.

And as exclusive. I felt that Brice and I were wearing a caste mark, and that we were the caste's only two members. Others had lots of time to play around with, as though they were in a Gorky comedy about an endless summer house party, whereas we were in a terse Greek tragedy, compressed and efficient, plunging towards its dénouement. After all my years of defending promiscuity, I'd become a fierce champion of the couple.

WHILE WRITING a travel article, I went to Cincinnati, where my father still lived. He and I hadn't spoken in nearly five years nor seen each other in seven. I checked into the Netherland Plaza, a 1920s hotel skyscraper where as a boy just after the war I'd gone to eat lunch with my mother (chicken potpie and chocolate sundaes) and watched an ice show in the middle of the afternoon (big, heavy-breathing women in sequins and feathers spraying snow onto us as they suddenly braked with their blades, their painted eyes and lips round with the faked excitement that seemed so hard to relate to the placid, doughy, sexless housewives I called women).

But no sooner had I checked in to the hotel room than I called my father. My stepmother answered. She whispered: "Your father's had a very bad heart attack. Now he just sits around all day with a stopwatch measuring his heartbeat. Try not to excite him. Here, I'll call him."

"Well, why are you staying there, young fellow?" my father asked when I explained where I was. "I'll be right down to get you."

He was much, much thinner than I'd ever seen him. His ears stood away from his head and the skin hung in folds under his neck like an elephant's. In the past he'd traded in his Cadillac every other year (and his wife's on alternating years), but now the car struck me (an ignorant New Yorker who'd never owned any kind of vehicle) as at least ten years old, though it was spotlessly clean inside and recently Simonized outside. He was wearing sports clothes that seemed equally old; the trousers hung off him, flapping oddly, the waist cinched by a badly scarred black leather belt and a small, square silver buckle that was tarnished on one corner. His three initials, the same as mine, were inscribed onto the silver in a script so stylized as to be nearly illegible.

He was pale, almost blue, and his hair much thinner and very white. There were liver marks on his hands. He trembled slightly as he shook my hand. I was expecting him to make a crack about my long hair and mustache (he thought only little guys who wore platform shoes and needed to show off ever sported a mustache), but he said nothing, which made me

realize I'd moved out of the category of family retainer into that of potential customer, the only two human species he recognized. If one could
fart and belch in front of a retainer or read the paper while he or she sat
there during dinner, with a customer one had to make jokes, lay on a
spread, ask seemingly interested questions.

He was chewing so much gum, which made his cheek bulge and im-
peded his speech, that I asked him about it.

"Ever since I went on this salt-free, fat-free diet and lost so much weight
I've had all this flab to worry about, so I've worked out my own system—
I chew twenty pieces of gum half an hour twice a day."

"That's a very good idea," I said. "I'll have to try that. My face is beginning to sag some, too."

He offered to carry my bag but I wouldn't let him. As we walked to the
parking lot I fell behind him for a moment and saw how brittle his walk
had become, if that's the opposite of supple. He walked as though he
were a badly oiled machine. I thought his physical decline must depress
him, he who'd always been so competitive in sports. My nephew had told
me that when he was about twelve he'd raced against his grandfather on
a bike. He'd been appalled that the old man, already in feeble health, had
won, but only through a shocking expense of pedaling energy.

All my life he'd frightened me—his expansive, glowing flesh, his dozens
of dark, tailored suits, his resolute silences meant to convey disapproval.
He'd been someone who could sit for hours at a stretch behind his blond
mahogany desk, making his calculating machine, drawn up beside him on
its portable shelf and wheels, jump slightly each time he touched its keys.
He'd been someone who when he wasn't working changed into old clothes
(not old sports clothes but old tailor-made trousers and a frayed monogrammed shirt and sun-bleached wingtip shoes) in order to do yard work,
not because he loved living things or found gardening restful or creative.
No, for him the yard counted as just another job, another punishing duty.
If, like me, he'd been afraid of heights I never would have known it, since
he could never have admitted a weakness. His cigar was sometimes only a
wet black butt in the corner of his mouth. Everything in his house and car
was steeped in cigar smoke since he kept both permanently sealed and circulated through them either heated or cooled air. "I'm down to just ten
cigars a day," he said, as though reading my mind. "My heart, you know."

I'd never seen his new house, which was in a better neighborhood than
the previous ones even though it was considerably smaller. "This is your

father's room," my stepmother said. "He shouldn't climb the steps so I've fixed him up here." If he looked blue and balding and fragile, she was flourishing, more like his daughter, her hair dyed a brighter copper red, her nails freshly painted, her suit sober and burdened with only a single, exquisite branch of diamonds.

When my father was out of the room for a moment she whispered, "Don't worry, your father thinks you're still just a journalist. I've torn all the ads and reviews referring to your fiction out of his papers—you know, I'm always up early and censor the papers for him. So you can rest easy. He doesn't know anything about, what's the word?, that *gay* writing of yours. It seems a shame you've gone and spoiled a perfectly good word."

"Only you ever used *gay* in the old sense," I said. "Most Americans say *merry* or *happy*. Isn't it more an English word, *gay*?"

When my father came back in he had his stopwatch in hand. "I measure my heartbeat twice a day," he said neutrally, as though he were referring to nothing more personal than the barometer.

"That's a good idea," I said stupidly, but he didn't notice what I'd said. Anyway, even when I'd lived in the Midwest I'd never been able to predict what would rub my father and his wife the wrong way. Being fatuous and condescending or humorless and clumsy, in any event, were not faults they were tuned to pick up.

What surprised me was that he wanted to know in detail everything about my mother, my sister and my nephew, especially everything about their health. It irritated me that my sister had forbidden me to tell him she'd become a lesbian. He knew everything about me and bitterly disliked it, whereas she, despite her divorce and suicide attempts (which he read as moral flaws) nevertheless remained in the realm of the rectifiable. My father, had he known about my sister's lesbianism, would have been mainly troubled by what our homosexuality suggested about *his* genes, for he unquestioningly espoused the belief (in the 1970s considered retrograde but at the end of the century again taken up as progressive) that sexual preference and most other psychological characteristics are inherited.

In the past when he'd quiz me about my mother I'd thought he'd been looking for signs that she was about to remarry (or die an early death), either of which would have removed her from what he referred to as "the payroll." Now, however, he seemed more genuinely concerned about her welfare (he said, "She's a fine, intelligent woman," the highest accolade he'd ever given her to my knowledge). There was a touch of that old-person's curiosity about which of his coevals is going to live the longest—in particular, outlive him.

When I'd been growing up my father had been interested in things, not people, in engineering problems or financial operations rather than in psychological speculation or gossip. Now he had changed completely—so much so that I wondered if he'd always quizzed his wife about her friends, but in deepest privacy, lest my overly impressionable nature be encouraged still further in the wrong direction. For when I was a kid he'd thought that if I was a sexual pervert that couldn't, surely, be something fundamental (he too was a fundamentalist and he couldn't think of a single deviant on either side of the family) but rather something my mother had unintentionally bred into me by over-stimulating me. He'd written my mother that I was excessively nervous, bobbed my head rhythmically, bit my nails, had opinions on adults, couldn't pitch or bat a ball, avoided yard work and knew how to mix (and sip) cocktails (that was true: after a party my sister and I ran around collecting dirty glasses, which meant "drinking the stems," as we said, for our mother sometimes used champagne glasses with hollow stems). He'd offered paternal gruel to replace maternal curries, mowing and raking instead of cocktail chatter (and mixing). Essentially, he saw me as a thoroughbred (like himself—he often referred to his "racehorse legs") who'd been ridden badly and too hard and now had to be put out to pasture for a whole season before being broken in and trained all over again.

Now all that was in the past. I was nearly forty and no longer at a formative age. I'm sure he was glad we were eating at home—he wouldn't have wanted any of his acquaintances to see him with the long-haired weirdo that I was. In his eyes even my cigarettes and wristwatch counted as effeminate (as opposed to cigars and a manly pocket watch), and the fact I lived in New York and worked as a journalist suggested a character disorder, perhaps even Communist leanings.

But age had mellowed him. He enjoyed telling me about the neighbors, about his sister (the old maid who'd married late, her husband full of useless get-rich-quick schemes) and his brother: "Poor guy, he became bald as an egg. Everything he attempted failed, you remember that barbecue joint in Dallas?"

"Great barbecue," I said.

"Sure as hell was, but he couldn't run it worth a damn. Then he was selling crap door-to-door, poor old Hank, had loads of charm, folks liked him, but always thinking too big, soon as he made a few bucks he'd hire a replacement and start running after the women and drinking. He could knock 'em back."

"What happened to him?"

"Well, he got a screw loose and couldn't stand loud sounds. His wife and two daughters, lovely women all, well, he drove them out, or rather he got himself a trailer in a trailer park and a rifle, and if the little kids next door started hollerin', well, old Hank would come out with that gun like he was fixin' to fire it."

"Didn't anyone report him to the cops?"

"You'd think so, but no. But then I could see he was dangerous, out of control, and not even eating properly, and all the time he complained about the terrible pounding in his head, you remember that accident?"

"No."

"You don't? Well, he had run into a tree one night in his old Ford pickup, guess he was tight, that never stopped old Hank." I could see my father took comfort in this simple explanation of his brother's insanity.

But as he went on with the harrowing tale of Hank's hospitalizations, his isolation from his family and eventual suicide ("The pounding in his head just became unbearable"), my father was obviously relishing the story as a narrative. I saw that like me he was a novelist. Or he had become one when every other love (money, sex, power, especially the power to intimidate his family and employees) had given out. The story remained, the story of how Hank's life (and his, yours, mine) turned out or would turn out. He seemed to see his own life as irreproachable, and keeping his record clean, I gathered, he thought was an admirable activity. Just as certain literary critics end up by esteeming poems and novels which one can say nothing *against*, in the same way he'd applied this standard of unexceptionability, more worthy of a modern monarch than an actual living, breathing human being, to the trajectory of his own experience.

Other people's lives, however, as long as they didn't touch too closely on his, he preferred to be colorful, shameful, even tragic. He steered us away from my nephew because he must have feared any prolonged discussion would end with a plea, no matter how muted, for help, for money.

What struck me was how abstract—and how powerful—this meeting was. I hadn't seen this man in seven years and if, in the interval, I'd thought of him at all it was only as the malign magician of my childhood, the dull but often wonderfully angry source of all power, money, menace.

I certainly hadn't wondered how he was doing *now*. He wasn't, in my personal drama, someone who developed, nor did he ever act out of character in my imagination. Now I was faced with this reality—reduced, almost pathetic—that had slowly been taking shape in the forgotten alembic of time. He seemed smaller, he was certainly frailer, and he'd developed this late, utterly unexpected taste for gossip, which at the end of a life coincides with a sensitivity to history. Why should I have cared so much for this boring, isolated man in Cincinnati, Ohio, who'd not even heard of my books, much less read them?

And yet, of course, I did care. I never even stopped to wonder if or why I wanted to please him. I wanted to please him so much that tears came to my eyes, as they had done years ago whenever I'd dared to correct him—tears that then had expressed not so much my fear of enraging him as my sorrow that he wasn't infallible.

In September I rented a house and Fox and I went to Key West for several months. Next door there was someone who played the Hammond organ every afternoon at three. Fox's two cats would hide in the crawl space under the house and he'd go crazy shouting at them to come out. His Southern accent deepened. Across the street there was a Spanish-language Pentecostal church.

We no longer slept together. I'd ended that— Fox's jealousy was too much. Surprisingly, he didn't resist my decision. Perhaps I was releasing him from an obsession he, too, disliked. I never knew, since like most couples we chatted constantly about every peripheral concern but never breathed a word about what we were living through together, the clauses and riders we were constantly adding to our invisible but tangible contract.

If our sexual life with each other had ended, Fox was no less possessive of me, but now as a writer, as a personage: he was Prince Albert to my Queen Victoria. He insisted we meet all the other writers on the island (there weren't very many in those days) and used Homer as our celebrity bait; he thought such "connections" might someday help my "career."

We both went on the Scarsdale Diet and in two weeks I was thin, tan, clear headed (since the diet included no alcoholic drinks) and Fox's ears stuck out like a kid's—or my father's—and his eyes grew enormous in a face as long, thin and triangular as his white cat's.

I lay in a big double bed in the back room, bathing in the tepid slipstream coming through the window fan. I wrote and I read all the books I liked at the Key West Public Library. Eddie was down for the winter and lent me his library card. Here he was quieter, more relaxed, sweeter than I'd ever seen him before, as though in Florida we were all backstage and what we said didn't matter. Eddie and I would bicycle through the sudden cloudbursts, visit the cemetery with its eccentric epitaphs ("I *told* you I was sick"), cruise the "Dick Dock," as we called the wide pier jutting out into the algae-thick, shallow, warm water near the old bandstand. One day I told him how much he'd intimidated me the first time we'd met and he'd said nothing after my reading. "I was *drunk*," Eddie said. "I used to drink myself into a stupor."

Fox and I put the weight right back on in the following weeks because we drank more and more heavily: margaritas and beers and rum punches. The fall months were off-season and few tourists were around. The sun dazzled off the tin roofs of the old wood houses on White Street. There were gay discos and gay guest houses with their young gay staff members and older gay guests, but perhaps because I was drinking so heavily that competitive world of fit guys didn't much attract me. I preferred going to the Papillon, a gay bar in a 1960s hotel that catered to locals. There I'd drink so many rum punches that I'd be almost too drunk to ride my bicycle home. I'd weave my way through the empty streets, past a cat sleeping in the middle of the cool pavement in the faint light of the moon. I made loopy figure-eights under a banyan that kept casting its roots farther and farther afield and multiplying its trunks. Air conditioners throbbed in windows. Behind mosquito-haunted bushes pulsed the dim lights emitted by old trailers on cinderblocks.

A sudden tropical rain would soak me through but a moment later I'd be dry. When I got home Fox would be shirtless, in shorts, sandals and black, nerdy spectacles, typing furiously in the front room, tearing one sheet after another out of his portable Smith-Corona. Or he'd be crouched beside the house, hissing threats at his deeply indifferent cats.

I'd shower in the dark outside, slip into boxer shorts, make myself a dark rum on the rocks, stand in front of the open fridge, eat some rock shrimp we'd steamed in beer, the inexpensive little shrimp with finger-cutting hard shells. They went down like popcorn. I'd lie on clean white sheets, read Chateaubriand or James Merrill. At four in the morning I'd finish one volume, only to pick up another in an exquisite luxury of timelessness. One of the cats, marked like a sea trout, would pay me a sniffy sort of call, like a beneficent lady begrudgingly visiting a poor relation, but if she'd stay for a while I'd draw her on a blank page of the notebook in which I was writing a novel about my childhood.

Sometimes, late at night or even toward dawn, Fox would come into my room, very silly, and do his chicken dance. It was based on a TV commercial, I think, an ad for Campbell's chicken soup in which dancers strutted about dressed as poultry, but I didn't own a television and had never seen the commercial, nor did Fox know the words, but he still liked to fold his hands in his armpits, beat his wings and cluck and feebly sing, with the sweetest smile, "I am a little chicken . . ." The words quickly petered out, he wasn't even sure they were the right ones, but that tentative, *erased* jingle became the anthem of our new love.

If I was no longer the lightning rod for Fox's demonic power, his typewriter now drew his ire. He'd pound at it noisily for hours on end—he'd written the first page of his current short story a hundred times. I was afraid that if I ever stopped to study my writing so microscopically I, too, would become paralyzed.

When Homer came for ten days I gave him the typescript of the first chapter of my new book to read. Since I'd told him it was a "gay novel" he was expecting pornography. When he'd read it he said, in his best Mississippi accent, "A lot of wash and not much hang-out."

He'd stay in bed all day, making the most awful noises as he spat and hawked and snored and groaned, but at six sharp he'd emerge, impeccable, in a fresh shirt, bow tie, linen suit creased only to the right fashionable degree, and make us cocktails, usually daiquiris.

He was reading the memoirs of an ancient French *grande cocotte* who found God late, while gossiping with a society priest at a dinner party ("Our Lord shall be your last lover"). Despite her natural inclination toward lesbianism, she married a Romanian prince, much younger and shorter, did good works, said her rosary daily and remembered her glory days, all those delicious sins she'd so lingeringly repented of. "I never knew her—I *could* have—but I knew her crowd," Homer squeaked, "and here I am, seventy years later, finding out from *Mes Cahiers Bleus* exactly who was deceiving whom."

Over the previous summer I'd driven down to Princeton with a Russian friend and met Nina Berberova. I tried to get her to speak about her friendship in Paris in the thirties with Nabokov or of the brilliant novels she'd written then, but no, she was forward-looking, she was planning a sci-fi novel about the future. My Russian friend had explained to me how she'd emerged out of the rubble of Europe at the end of the war and arrived in New York in her fifties with nothing but a Chanel suit and Anna Tolstoy's address. Within a year she'd learned English, how to drive, how to type—and soon afterwards she was teaching Russian at Princeton. She went on to write her memoirs, *The Italics Are Mine.*

The mailman arrived with a package from the Soviet Union, bulky, badly wrapped in torn brown paper. When Berberova opened it she said something in Russian and read the letter out loud.

Only when we were alone did I ask my Russian friend, "What was all that about?"

"Well, you just witnessed a minor historic moment. Nina was married to Khodasevich, the poet Nabokov considered to be Russia's greatest of this century. When Mayakovsky committed suicide in the 1930s, Khodasevich irritated everyone by writing an article in the French émigré press denouncing Mayakovsky. Suddenly the Whites hated Khodasevich *and* the Reds hated him—everyone. Unanimous. Anyway, Nina has written all about it in her memoirs and the book has finally made its way to the USSR and Mayakovsky's ancient mistress, Lily Brik, has written Nina saying she found Nina's account fair—and sent her a bottle of Chanel No. 5, which you can find in any drugstore in the States but which must have cost Lily a small fortune, it probably had to be smuggled in from Finland. . . ."

These stories, Nina's and Homer's, gave me a sense of how history is nothing but feuds and fashionable conversations, how it remains in the memory of the last intact brain of the lone survivor, and if it is to be thought about at all afterwards it must become a monument to be deciphered or a legend to be read—not by hordes all at once but singly, occasionally, imperfectly. It occurred to me that what we'd thought and done, the people I knew, might someday be written about. Official history—elections, battles, legal reforms—didn't interest me, I who'd never voted and felt no connection with society. No, I didn't want to be a historian but rather an archeologist of gossip.

One night Fox and Homer and I got drunk at the local disco on Duval Street. We sat outside in the garden to escape for a moment from the heat and smoke and noise, and Homer, deaf and fat and in his nineties, said, "You wouldn't believe it now but when I was in my twenties I was sexy, at least I attracted lots of men who wanted to . . . *take* me; I think I rather resembled a clean little piglet, but I must have secreted a special . . . pheromone, is that the word? Anyway, a hormone perfume that drove men wild. I wasn't interested in my beauty, not like Ned Rorem. In fact I wasn't beautiful. I was simply irresistible."

We all three sat back in our bower, all three of us alienated in different ways from the lean, muscled gay men dancing inside like the parts of desiring machines in the *Anti-Oedipus*, the vogue book of the moment. We all three, I suppose, were thinking of the long since vanished power of Homer's rump to attract men—older composers in France, tramway conductors, bankers in Right Bank cafés looking up from a copy of the *Figaro*—a smooth, silky, hairless rump, always in danger of becoming decidedly plump, as incontrovertible a historical fact as the *grande cocotte*'s belated conversion or that bottle of Chanel No. 5 that Lily Brik had sent Nina Berberova.

I thought of the century plant, a cactus next door to our rented house, in the yard of the lady who played the Hammond organ every day at three. Its strangely mechanical, spiny branches, like a robot's arms covered with grommets, only rarely and then at night proffered at the very end of its prosthesis a delicate white flower; it was like *Der Rosenkavalier* performed in the age of *Anti-Oedipus*.

My mother came to spend a week with Fox and me. She was either drunk or so shaky that she couldn't walk without being helped from our house to the car we'd rented just for her. Fox didn't regress into a Southern Yes-Ma'am-No-Ma'am boy but rather called her by her first name and asked her for her opinion on world affairs, something she was always up on since she listened to the news all through the night. She kept her little portable radio under her pillow and woke if Israel invaded Lebanon or Carter lost the election. She was horrified by the way Fox shouted at his cats. She'd become so respectful of other lives that she would harm nothing, not even a fly, but rather shoo it out the window with an envelope. But she appeared extinguished. She was confused, she dozed all the time, she slurred her words and cried easily. Most maddeningly, she became tearful many times because she'd misunderstood a simple, factual sentence and interpreted it as a sentimental reference.

She'd retired or rather she had been forced into retirement by her clinic, which was no longer functioning. She had no pension and no savings. Her cancer had reappeared and she'd had her lower intestine removed and been outfitted with a colostomy bag. Her lover, Randy, managed to be transferred to the West Coast and he was never heard from again.

After she left Fox and me, Mother went up to her Michigan house, which she had to sell if she was going to have some capital to live on (though after paying off the mortgage she'd probably receive only thirty thousand dollars, which wouldn't take her far). One night while eating alone at a steak house she started flirting with two men who kept buying her drinks. By the time she got home she was so drunk she couldn't navigate her car into the garage and had to leave it out on the driveway.

Inside she fell in the bathroom and cracked two ribs. She couldn't move and her peristalsis seemed to have frozen. Even when she irrigated "Rosie," as she'd named her stoma, it refused to respond. And she was incapable of leaving the bathroom. She heard the phone ring occasionally, but she couldn't move to answer it.

Three days later, still immobilized, she made a bargain with God that if he'd save her life she'd never have another drink. "It was like a miracle," she told me over the phone. "Suddenly the shit—excuse the word, but it's the only one that will do—the shit came exploding out of my body."

She'd been saved, but only for new horrors. She was selling her Michigan house and moving her things to storage or to her new Chicago apartment on Lake Shore Drive or to a maid's room she'd rented in the same building and dubbed "the crow's nest." Standing beside the van when it arrived and directing the movers became a task that rendered her hysterical. She became impossibly entangled and the workers, frustrated, simply dumped most of her furniture in her new living room. She wept and shouted and the building management called me and alerted me to "a possible problem."

The next thing I knew my mother was trying to give away most of her money to "that pitiful Dot," a secretary she'd once had, a pale, skinny complainer who, nevertheless, earned a decent salary and in any event appeared to be better off than my mother. Dot called me, upset, assuring me that she'd refused the check but that my mother had become so vehement that she didn't know how to react. I told her to accept the check and tear it up when the dust had settled.

Then my mother had flown to Texas and was staying with my Baptist cousins. One of them phoned to say, "Honey, I just don't know what to do with her. She never stops talking, she's either excited as a flea or she's desperate and scared, bless her heart. She won't eat, the weight is just dripping off her, she's giving her money away to everyone she meets, why, she gave the waitress a ten-dollar tip yesterday and all she'd had was a dollar cup of coffee. Then last night, oh, it must have been four or five in the morning, she woke me up and said her room was invaded by thousands and thousands of bugs swirling around her. Well, honey, you remember how we get these little millers down here in Texas, I think you Yankees call them no-see-ums, anyway, there were just three or four millers flying around the ceiling light, but she said, '*See!* There are thousands! They're from outer space and they're going to destroy us.' Now, you know I keep a nice house, don't you? I just can't go on. My husband's been real sweet to her because he respects all the good she's done throughout her life although we're both sad that she hasn't found Jesus as her savior. She keeps saying He's a good wise man . . . like the *Buddha*, I declare! And she says she's going right to the top, to God, she likes the big guy, the chief executive, no Mr. In-Between for her, but I reminded her that Jesus said, 'I am the Way.' "

I hopped on the next plane out of Miami for Dallas and Amarillo. When I arrived in the terminal my mother was in a short pleated skirt and she had a pom-pom shaker she'd made out of clipped crêpe paper. "She thinks she's a cheerleader," my cousin said with a rueful smile. "She's cheering your arrival."

My mother and I left on the very next plane for Chicago. During the flight my mother chattered constantly. She stroked the stewardess's hand and told her, "You're a lovely woman and a very fine person. I can tell. I'm a psychologist. This is my son, a famous author, who's a chip off the old block, because I'm no slouch, I was the executive director of a medical clinic for mental retardation at Cook County Hospital, a pioneer in my field." Like an excited little girl she whispered to me, "Do you see this sad, sad old lady behind us?" I looked back and saw a nice tranquil farm woman in a flowered dress she'd probably run up herself. Her forearms and face were sunburned. She was leafing through a *Woman's Day* with the stagy off-handedness of an extra; she must have known we were discussing her. She was clearly at least ten years younger than my mother.

"Do you think I should offer her some money? Just a few thousand dollars? That way she could buy some stylish new outfits at Neiman-Marcus, have that old grey washed out of her hair, have a complete make-over— and feel like a million dollars! I'm sure she's a fine woman. . . ." Tears stung my mother's eyes. "She reminds me of my mother!"

When we arrived in Chicago I took my mother directly to St. Luke's Hospital, where her doctor had arranged for her to be admitted to the psychiatric floor. I'd assured my mother that her doctor just wanted to check her heart medicine and make sure she wasn't being over-stimulated, given how excited she was.

But when she realized my perfidy (her doctor wasn't even there and she recognized the psychiatric floor), she let out a sob and crawled across the floor to me: "Darling, I beg you, I'm your mother, you can't do this. . . ."

And she clutched at my trousers and gripped my calf through the fabric with her surprisingly strong hands.

"Mother," I said, "it's just for a few days. You have delusions, you're losing weight, you're in a manic phase."

She said nothing but lay on the floor, sobbing.

I was appalled by what was happening. My mother was no longer a kindly little grandmother but a weeping madwoman abject at my feet. I'd tricked her into accompanying me to the hospital and now I was locking her up against her will—in the very hospital where she had many colleagues and had worked over the years. She had staked her whole life on being a psychologist, a diagnostician of other people's ills, and now I'd turned the tables on her. As her child and her friend I had no right to say that I knew she'd gone too far, that she was now a danger to herself. My nephew, I felt, had been harmed the day he'd been classified as mentally ill, a definition like the crack in a bell that would mute its timbre for the rest of his life. Now I was the one declaring my mother mad and committing her. Had I no conscience?

A day later she'd checked herself out of the hospital and simply disappeared. I was icily angry with her doctor who said, "Look, that's the law. Unless we have a psychiatric hearing before a judge with several expert witnesses and a whole dossier of evaluations, our hands are tied. She's smart, your mother, she knows the law, she's used it often enough in committing crazy kids she was working with."

A week later my mother phoned. She was calmer, she said, but pleased because she was writing her memoirs day and night. "I'm in a hotel, dear, but I won't tell you where. I can't trust you now. But don't worry. I've found the very best cure for insanity: room service. I'm very worried about your smoking. It will kill you sure as rain."

I encouraged her to write. "That will help you to integrate all the traumas you've sustained recently. Writing is a way of re-asserting the mastery of the ego." We actually talked to each other that way, in psychological jargon, though we scarcely knew what we were saying. It was our funny way of saying very tender things to each other while sounding scientific.

She finished her book and, as she said, discovered in room service the exact degree of social contact and above all one-way control essential to mental recovery. She moved home. In the meantime she'd managed to give away most of her money. I began to send her five hundred dollars a month and eventually a thousand, which, with her Social Security, allowed her to live decently. Although my sister was in AA and now that she'd finished graduate school was working as a psychotherapist with drunks, neither she nor I had figured out that since our mother had so abruptly stopped drinking she was having DT's of the pink-elephant variety.

Now she calmed down and, at last, in her seventies, said farewell to love and sexual adventure, which had brought her nothing but suffering all her life, although her chapter about Randy was titled "Love at Last."

I paid for her book to be published by a small vanity press and Mother sold *A Life in Progress* to her lady friends at the church, who must have been surprised by the passages about my father giving her the clap soon after their marriage in the 1930s, or about my mother's last lover kissing with resigned acceptance the place where she'd lost her breast through the mastectomy, not to mention the parts about the binge drinking, the stalled stoma "Rosie" and the miracle of the flowing shit.

      MY SISTER, who was now living with a new lover, a woman teacher, came with her to Key West for the New Year. Eddie had the first of his many annual parties and we were invited, along with many famous writers. Tennessee Williams came, so did James Kirkwood, but in those days there were not so many writers living in Key West as there would be later. Peter Taylor was visiting with an old school friend of his from Nashville, a fine old Southern lawyer, white haired, dressed in a blue and white seersucker suit.

My sister seemed happy, but I knew she was as restless as I, that she craved intimacy and couldn't endure it and that despite feminine sentimentality (the exchange of vows beside the campfire when, as an adolescent, she had been Captain of the Blues, and now the exchange of friendship rings with her partner), nevertheless she was as disabused and suspicious as I, quick to spot the ludicrous, never surprised when things didn't work out.

Since Gabriel had flunked his final exams in high school, he'd left his teenage commune and gone to live with my mother. Now he was staying in "the crow's nest," my mother's "office," where she stored all those thousands of diagnostic tests she'd administered over thirty years to sad, squalling children. Gabriel and my mother were thick. They had an intensely active mutual-admiration club. He was preparing for university amidst all these records of retardation.

I seldom thought about my family, but it kept encroaching on me. My stepmother called me when I got back to New York and told me my father was dead. He'd been sitting watching TV and, as he was lighting his cigar, he'd suddenly stood up and said, "I can't feel anything in my feet. My God, it's moving up my legs. It's all over me." She said he should sit down. He did and he was dead, the lit match falling from his hand.

It seemed wrong that he should die before me. He was the law-giver, I the criminal, and it was as though the warden had gone and the prisoners were now allowed to creep away, one after another, without reprisals. Yet his absence made me nervous, as though he'd always been the lowering cloud cover above me and now a cold winter wind had blown it away and there was nothing between me and the stars except space. The closed, snivelling, resentful world of childhood had at last ended, the smouldering sense of rebellion against authority, the petty urge to wound, the cringing fear of reprisals. It had been replaced by—well, by space. Empty, untenanted night. I felt grown up now and experienced the gain in maturity as a loss.

My sister and I agreed to meet two days later at a certain time in Toledo; she'd be flying in from Chicago, I from New York. There we'd rent a car and drive to Findlay, Ohio, where the service would be held.

I was staying with Fox. He held me all night and got me up at six a.m., plenty of time to catch my nine o'clock flight from Kennedy Airport. I hailed the first taxi (it was still dark outside) and only when we were beyond the city limits did I notice that the driver was a Haitian who didn't know the route—didn't, indeed, know where we were or who he was, since he was completely incoherent on drugs or drink and incapable of driving. Nor did he speak English. I kept looking for another taxi I could hail, but the dawn streets were deserted. I couldn't believe my bad luck— on the day of my father's funeral I was in the hands of a drug addict who didn't know how to find Kennedy Airport. He seemed to me like one of those symbols of death in a movie by Cocteau.

At last we stumbled by chance on La Guardia, not the airport I wanted but good enough. At least here I would find other taxis.

But I missed my plane. I called my sister from the airport and told her that I'd be on the next flight. She was understanding, as was the airline, which even had a special bereavement fare. I was so used to having all the occasions of my life ignored by society that I was astonished to have my grief shared, as it were, by a company.

As soon as my sister and I arrived at the funeral home and walked into the viewing room I realized that the coffin was open and that my father's head—small, waxen, painted—was propped up on a pillow in order to be visible to everyone. I was horrified by the sight and turned my back on it. No matter where I walked in the room for the next hour and a half I kept that horrible little spoiled fruit out of sight. I was sure that he was rotting in his box—it smelled of meat that had gone off. I understood why there were so many flowers needed, in order to disguise the shocking odor.

My stepmother's family came from a little town near Findlay and a few of her friends and relatives dropped in to offer their condolences. When my stepmother introduced me to them I could see their eyes going from my face to my father's effigy behind me to verify whether there was a re-semblance. Since no one except my stepmother's brother and his wife had actually known my father they were deprived of anything to say beyond, "I've heard he was a fine man. I know your stepmother is going to miss him." They patted my hand and hers. I glittered with a huge smile as though I were at a wedding, not a funeral.

And then my sister went up to the coffin. My stepmother whispered in my ear, "Oh, God, she's taking his hand. Now she's sobbing and kissing him on the lips and saying things to him."

I didn't dare look, since that would entail seeing the head, that waxed thing. Later I sidled over to my sister, put an arm around her and gave her a cup of coffee. She said, "I told him that I thought he was a bastard. He'd never given me what I wanted. He'd always preferred other girls to me—remember that Miss Toledo he met and liked so much?—he always threw her up to me, especially when I was so roly-poly at fourteen or fif-teen. He used to walk around nude when we were alone and once he touched my breasts and told me seductive things and I cried and said, 'No, Daddy, it's wrong, you know it's wrong,' but of course I liked the at-tention and felt guilty that I liked it and I was half-attracted to him. After all, he was the only man who'd ever shown any interest in me."

"I always wanted to have sex with him," I said.

"You say that because you know it was impossible. But incest, real in-cest, especially between members of the opposite sex, is very upsetting. I think it's why I was frigid with Dick and I still have trouble getting close to women."

"Did you take his hand?"

My sister blushed and started to cry. "Yes. I put a ring on his finger. I wanted him to be buried with something of mine."

"Which finger?"

"The wedding-ring finger."

I hugged her. I had to sign my name as a chief pallbearer under my father's name. We had the same name, separated only by a Roman numeral.

On the plane back to New York the next day I kept smelling the odor of rotting human flesh. I looked at the rowdy businessmen around me who were drinking and laughing and showing their bare fleshy calves when they crossed their legs (how my father would have disapproved of their short, ankle-length socks, he who wore garters just below the knee). I thought they were dying, they smelled of the rot, it was in their clothes, all this dead or dying meat was propped up in chairs and twitching with galvanic energy, but their conversation was profanely petty, full of joking greed and jockeying for position that showed they weren't aware of death. They kept marinating their meat in beer. I thought of the meat-packing district in New York where the carcasses—peeled, legless, branded with a purple mark—swung out of the trucks into refrigerated rooms.

ELEVEN

Somebody at my gym became ill. He'd been a big guy, always snapping towels at buttocks in the dressing room, and he'd had a real mouth on him, but then he came down with something the doctors couldn't diagnose. Slightly raised brownish-purple spots appeared on his skin. One doctor said they resembled a disease that only old Italian and Jewish men got. The poor guy at the gym just seemed to deflate in front of our eyes. All the steroids and food that had made his body so immense melted away, as though a butcher were rendering fat from a prize pig. He stopped joking, then he stopped talking, then he stopped coming. Someone said he had "gay-related immunodeficiency" (GRID). That was in 1981. It seemed too horrible to be true, a disease aimed specifically at gay men and contracted through gay sex.

As a gay writer I had received my share of hate mail, including an anonymous letter that had told me I would end up wearing a sack on my side since I was putting my anus to unnatural uses condemned by God. This new disease seemed all of a piece with the hate promulgated by know-nothing American fundamentalists.

I didn't know anyone other than the guy at the gym who had the new disease but I'd heard of a whole household on Fire Island coming down with it, five guys who'd shared the same cottage for several summers.

They weren't friends of mine but friends of friends and, in the spirit of scientific skepticism, I kept asking, "What else have they shared? Needles? Polluted well water? A bad shipment of poppers?"

A writer I'd known for five or six years invited eighty or so gay men to hear Dr. Friedman-Kien, a doctor at New York University, discuss the new disease. Then, a few months later, the same writer asked me and a handful of other gay men over to his luxurious apartment at the foot of Fifth Avenue to set up an organization to fight gay cancer. I felt flattered to be included at such a statesman-like event but I was frightened by it, as though thinking too much about it might lead to my becoming infected.

We decided we should have three goals—to raise money for research; to visit the ill and perform chores for them; and to pamphlet the bars with safe-sex information. Unfortunately, our biggest idea for raising money was to give a dance at the Paradise Garage. No one thought of approaching the Secretary of Health, Education and Welfare. We'd spent so many years huddling in the ghetto that it never occurred to us to turn to the federal government. And as for safe sex, all we could advise was, "Know the names of your partners" and "Limit their numbers." In moralistic America we thought that promiscuity and anonymity must somehow be to blame. No one was prepared to believe that gay cancer could be contracted through a single exposure. Anyway, could you be "exposed" to cancer and contract it like the measles?

I had long had my doubts about our goals and values. In an article I'd written, which had come out one year before the first rumors about AIDS, I'd aired my problems about reconciling my "socialism" (which amounted to little more than a belief in sharing wealth and providing social services to the needy) with the well heeled hedonism of the urban gay men I was studying. I'd also predicted that gay men, who were now perceived as the most promiscuous element in society, would someday go "beyond" sexuality to find newer, richer forms of association.

I had just begun to read Michel Foucault and I interpreted his writing to mean that since we had a word, *homosexuality* (or, for that matter, the word *sexuality* itself), we assumed that those words must refer to real things, to a unified and constant phenomenon, whereas in fact this very act of nomination was only an arbitrary way of creating entities by naming them.

But if I had my doubts about gay clone sexuality and consumerism (which seemed to be two systems for creating an elite hierarchy that excluded me and most other gay men—those who weren't white as well as the old, the poor, the ugly), I was equally afraid of seeming puritanical. I thought that if I was unhappy on Fire Island it was because I was past forty. Certainly in preceding years I'd relished my romantic sexual encounters with strangers under the moon in the pine forest—the most poetic moments of my life—and if they'd brought me no happiness I felt, as an artist, that my only concern should be beauty, so often twinned with melancholy. And to the extent I thought about politics at all I believed in campaigning for life and liberty but not the pursuit of happiness, too elusive, surely, ever to serve as the basis for policy.

As for the new disease, I thought that it would never attain epidemic proportions. By 1983, two years into its history, there were still fewer than two thousand cases. And no one knew what caused it. Some people said that "viral overload" must be the cause, yet I knew that since the mid-1960s (almost twenty years) I'd gone to the doctor with hundreds of cases of gonorrhea—mostly rectal, occasionally penile, once in the throat—one case of syphilis, dozens of cases of amoebas, one case of hepatitis, and yet I was flourishing.

Other people said the disease was caused by poppers, those sudden blasts of amyl nitrate we inhaled on the dance floor or during sex, but again I'd been sniffing them for twenty years with no apparent damage done (I'd first been given poppers in 1964 by a black heterosexual woman friend who sniffed them just before orgasm), nor could I imagine that a chemical inhalant which caused the blood to rush to the heart would also spread a fatal disease. And what about all those people who used poppers to stimulate their hearts—had they contracted cancer?

Could the disease be contained in sperm itself? If so, then we were all lost, since we were bathed, daily, in a sea of sperm.

My own conviction was that it wouldn't touch me or the people I loved. I certainly was opposed to the idea of limiting my sexual encounters or knowing my partners' names—what good would that do? True, when people came down with a venereal disease they were supposed to call up their partners, but I was from an older generation devoid of community spirit and once a month I threw out my trick chits (on which I'd marked names and phone numbers). Anyway, we were all big boys used to dosing ourselves and mopping up our own problems.

Of course we'd never played for such high stakes before—death.

Dr. Friedman-Kien thought we should all stop having sex for a while, until the exact nature of the disease and its transmission became clear, but everyone laughed at him. Obviously the good doctor knew nothing about gay life. We'd fought hard for sexual freedom, which was virtually the beginning and end of our idea of freedom itself. Hadn't gay liberation begun with the defense of a gay bar? A cruising spot? And hadn't our progress been measured by the number of bars and bathhouses and sex clubs that had sprung up in the last decade? We felt that straights hated us because we were getting so much, because among gays sex was easy to come by and seldom used just as a reward for work, fidelity, responsibility. Should two thousand cases of gay cancer convince us to exchange our freedom for chastity? Straight doctors, straight politicians, straight cops were all too ready to order us to give up our pleasures, that sticky semen-glue that bound us together, but we weren't going to be dispersed by scare tactics.

When a German news magazine called me and asked me to comment on the disease, I said, "It's caused by mustaches. If every gay man shaved, it would be cured tomorrow."

After I hung up, my new lover, Ned, said, "Don't make a fool of yourself. You have no business making pronouncements, especially not frivolous ones, when people are dying."

I'd met Ned through one of Max's acolytes, Angus, a Boston poet who wrote about his childhood and his friends in Max's characteristic syllabic verse and with his riddling, punning insolence. Angus was good looking, well educated, rich, but he was consumed by indecision—whether to work or not, whether to settle down with a lover or play the field, whether to move to New York or remain in Boston. In the meanwhile he wrote his poems.

Angus had called me up at Christmas time in 1981 and said, "Have I got a boy for you!" He'd already told me twice about this guy, who'd moved from Boston to New York to study design, who was "pretty as an angel" and from the "ultimate High WASP family," though his parents had rejected him and thrown him out of the house.

Now he was working as a houseboy for a rich older man who had a duplex in Chelsea. We went over there, Angus and I, for a drink before heading off to see *Torch Song Trilogy*. Ned's boss was on a Caribbean cruise, as it turned out, and Ned was cooking dinner for two friends who were about to arrive. I suppose it was appropriate that the first time I saw Ned he was preparing dinner for friends.

He asked me if I knew how long a leg of lamb should cook and I said something confused—I was dazzled by this young man beside me. He had a very high-pitched voice, not a girl's voice but a boy's, a choir boy's, as though this startling characteristic should be taken as a pledge that he would never age, a statement instantly contradicted by his hair, which was already white, although he could not have been more than twenty-six or twenty-seven years old at the time. Since his hair was both blond and white, not at all receding, densely planted and standing up here and there in spiky cowlicks, I kept doing a double take to make sure that what I took to be white wasn't actually platinum.

He wasn't sensual; in fact, he was tall and gangly, but his air of innocence called for defilement, which after all is a form of sensuality (even if rather specialized).

But that came later, if at all, my thoughts about sex with him. For now, all I could think about was marriage, linking my name to his, this angelic boy with the refined accent, the choir boy's voice, the slightly goofy look, as though he were a comic-book character who'd just had a flower pot drop on his head and was now seeing stars, lurching around and humming a slowed-down love waltz before collapsing in pottery shards—to be instantly mended in the very next frame.

When we left the cozy apartment with the lit fire and odorless hothouse flowers in every vase, Angus said, "So?"

"So what?" I said, almost irritated. "So I like him, so what's the big deal, since he's much too good for me?"

"I'll call him. We'll see," Angus said with his air of the sly boots who's just licked up all the cream. "I think he liked you. But remember, a boy like that will cost you about fifteen thousand dollars a year."

"That doesn't sound like very much," I laughed. "He should raise his rates."

I had broken up with Fox six months earlier at the Riviera Café. I'd carefully explained why it was best for him, for our friendship, for our development as writers—and suddenly he'd drenched me with a glass of water and stormed off, leaving me in a puddle, dripping. The smiling waiter brought me a hand towel and I, too, smiled, glad that it was all over, the petty squabbling and endless jealous interrogations.

Except I hadn't much liked the grand silence that had followed. Now there was no one to grill me, watch me, call me, attempt to trip me up. There was no one to collate my present remarks with some long ago but carefully preserved comment I'd once made on the same subject. Now if

I came home early or late, slept alone or with two other men, there was no Fox to trot around the barnyard by the light of the moon.

Worse, he'd found another lover right away, a young curator of a fashionable new museum, and everyone spoke of them as a smart couple about town. Fox began to rise in the world. He worked for a couple of years as an assistant to my new editor and then moved on to a paperback house where he edited his own line of new fiction.

To add to a retrospective sense of chagrin, one day I ran into Glen, a dark poet with a scarred face and beautiful hands who had written a thesis on a Byzantine saint. We had a sandwich together and Glen said, "How could you ever break up with that sexy Fox?"

"I didn't know you knew him?"

"*Know* him? Why, I used to hire him as a master. Wasn't his ad sexy?"

I didn't know he had an ad or worked as a prostitute but I vamped for time. "Yeah, it sure was. . . ."

"I'd call him up all the time on his special phone and if you weren't there he'd let me come over and lick his toilet bowl clean. Or he'd stuff my mouth with his dirty socks and put me in the bathtub with a dildo and some poppers and piss on me. Once he even gave me an enema."

"Yeah, he was great at that. How much did he charge?"

"Just fifty bucks. After all, his ad said, '*Cheap*: A Bargain Top!' Later, when I found out how literary and funny he was, we became friends. But I still hire him from time to time. I think I'm his only customer now—and of course William, that old man he shits on. Once Fox called me up—I think you were out of town—" here he went into a fit of giggles "—and asked me if I'd shit on William with him. We took acid that must have had a lot of speed in it, we couldn't get it up, but we necked and necked on the bed while William ate out our asses. Later we stood over him—he was in the bathtub and we were standing, our feet balancing on the sides of the tub, and Fox actually produced one, small but creditable *étron*—"

"What does that mean?"

"It's French for *turd*. William came, of course, and I thought that now he'd regained his senses he'd be horrified by all this evidence of his twisted mind so I rapidly hosed away the dirty little clue, but he said to me, in an angry snit, 'That's *my* job,' as though I'd greedily deprived him of the best part, as though I were a rival shit eater."

Once I saw Fox and his new lover drinking at Julius's. They didn't see me and from my dark corner I watched Fox haranguing the curator. I couldn't hear them but I could easily imagine what Fox was saying. Although I was pleased I was no longer living with the Grand Inquisitor I also felt oddly weightless. Now no one cared about the exact degree of treachery in my soul, the exact shade of perfidy in my heart.

⌐────⌐ MY DOCTOR, who'd gained thirty pounds since he'd stopped smoking, seemed grouchily malevolent. He barked at me, "You have chronic bronchitis and it's never going to get better as long as you're still smoking—how many packs do you smoke?"

"Three. Sometimes four if I'm feeling ambitious."

"Well, you stink from it. Your face is grey, your fingers yellow. Here's the number for an eight-week behavioral conditioning program. Go to it or you'll be dead from lung cancer in five years."

"Oh well," I joked, "what about this new gay cancer? It will get me first."

"*Amoebas!*" he shouted. "It's all caused by amoebas." Indeed, my doctor had become obsessed by amoebas. When I showed him what was obviously a syphilitic chancre on the head of my penis he wanted to treat it with Flagyl, a highly toxic amoeba medicine that had the additional disadvantage of making the patient ill if he drank alcohol. Finally I convinced the doctor to test and treat me for syphilis; I spent the night shivering and sweating, the usual reaction of primary syphilis to antibiotics.

I stopped smoking and I, too, gained twenty-five pounds. I now looked like my father; I didn't have his final blue, skeletal mask but the flushed, fleshy face he'd presented throughout my childhood and adolescence. I trimmed my hair and shaved off my mustache, the better to own up to the full horror of this big pudding I'd become.

I fell gently, domestically in love with Ned. He wasn't jealous as Fox had been. In fact I don't think he even fancied me, though he loved being with me. Nor was he jealous of my new-found success. He had no desire to be a writer. He talked vaguely of being an architect or interior designer some day, but in the meanwhile he was happy to let me support him, to go out to the bars every night, usually on his own, to seduce the handsome men the city was filled with. He watched too much television for my taste, dressed too young to look convincing, argued with his family too peevishly, but when he was "lit," that is, drunk, he really did appear to be illuminated with a crazy happiness. He had a great capacity for joy, and it was my pleasure to bring it to him as often as possible.

He was well brought up and had gone to an expensive school for rich dumbbells. There he'd met two girls with whom he'd while away the afternoon eating unbuttered, unsalted popcorn (their diet food) while watching the soaps and discussing relatives or men. Ned would complain about his former employers and the girls would grumble about their dates.

Ned didn't mind that I'd gained so much weight. He apparently liked men for their money and power and I was beginning to have a bit of both. He'd even read one of my books at university in his "Gay Lit" class (his parents thought he was studying Gaelic). His erotic interest, when it wasn't distracted by power, was almost exclusively invested in black men, but he'd turn red with anger if I'd say that in so many words. "That's so demeaning to put it that way," he'd shout.

"Why? Face it. Everything else being equal, you're more attracted to blacks than whites."

"Nothing ever *is* equal. It's a question of individuals, not groups. You make me sound like a . . . fetishist." In fact, his "type" eventually stabilized. He was attracted to black preppies, who brought together the twin themes of success and color. He was also heavily invested in the idea of playing the *puer aeternus* and more black men than white were willing to treat him as Huck, Honey.

From the very beginning Ned and I were more friends than lovers but our friendship was a serious business. We didn't much mind if one or the other of us slept around as long as the object of attraction was constantly changing. We slept in the same bed two or three nights a week and we called each other constantly.

After we'd known each other six months I asked him to move in. I was horrified when I came home and discovered my little apartment entirely filled with twenty big blue garment bags.

"Ned, what's in all these bags?"

"Clothes."

"Are you *wearing* all those clothes currently?"

"What do you mean?" he squeaked in his high voice, driven higher by anxiety and irritation.

"We're going to go through your clothes, one by one. I'm going to hold up each item and you're going to swear to me on a stack of Bibles that you've worn it at least once in the preceding year."

"No, no, I won't work like that," he said, as though I were offering him a job. "You go away and I'll . . . *consolidate* things."

"Remember," I said, heading out the door, "everything must fit into that closet."

⟳ THE NOVEL I'd written about my boyhood was published in 1982. Ned and I were staying on Martha's Vineyard when the first copy arrived. We'd rented a room and a rickety balcony in a big, underfurnished house in West Chop, or was it East Egg? Certainly the golden-haired tennis players who lived all around us were worthy of Gatsby. Ned had gone to prep school with Jennifer, the young woman who had inherited this fabulous ruin from her parents. They couldn't pay the taxes or upkeep on this twenty-room pile, which had been built by their grandparents, so they handed it over to the kids, who rented out rooms to their friends. Anyway, the parents were divorced and feckless; the father hired out his sailboat and services in the Bahamas, the mother sold popcorn-making machines in Catalonia.

In the double drawing room downstairs only one chair stood like a crippled sentinel, a stack of books replacing a missing leg. A row of coat hooks by the front door reminded us that the house had been run, unsuccessfully, as a girls' school in the 1950s. The grim, institutional kitchen and the giant pots and kettles were other reminders, although the roomers now never ate together. Each had a half or a quarter shelf in the fridge, clearly labeled by name, and not even the most basic things—sugar, flour, salt—were bought in common, and the refrigerator stank from all the half pints of spoiling coffee milk.

Since our fellow lodgers were all New England aristocrats, their parents thought they should work every summer. In Europe kids of this class would have island-hopped in Greece or lounged around the pool at the family *bastide* near Nîmes, but here they mowed lawns for five dollars an hour or worked at the local dress shop and drank themselves into a stupor every night (just as their parents were doing over on Nantucket). At night we'd find them beached halfway up the steps, often in a pool of vomit. They kept a tank of oxygen beside their beds and came to breakfast in dark glasses. They were nice enough to us as a gay couple; alcoholism is a leveler. We'd sit on our rickety balcony, look down at the abandoned Volkswagen on the lawn; a pine tree was sprouting up through it. At dusk we'd watch the cold fog roll in from the ocean. We'd drink our boilermakers and invite other kids to join us. They were all young, blond, lithe; drink had not yet made their faces puffy.

The son of the *nouveau pauvre* family of proprietors lived up under the eaves with a Brazilian girlfriend. We'd go up there and smoke opium, lie back on overstuffed cushions and look out the dormer windows at clouds. We'd confide without much urgency thoughts that collected like condensation and formed, slowly, irregularly, into one drop of language after another.

Ned and I would go jogging. Neither of us was in very good shape and every two hundred yards or so we'd have to walk for a few minutes before falling back into a trot. We'd run past old summer cottages in need of a paint job that made me think of my father's house on a small, cold, deep Michigan lake. My father's mother, isolated back in Merkle, Texas, had read an article about Christian Science and converted to it, partly out of snobbism, since like the Scientists she believed there was something inherently tacky about evil, as though the best families would be spared its incursions, and partly out of wishful thinking, since she longed to triumph over her worsening bouts of mental illness through the will alone.

In the first enthusiasm of her new-found faith she convinced my father to drive her to the Mother Church in Boston. Afterwards through a Scientist they gained entrance into an exclusive New England resort for a week-long holiday. No one spoke to them for the first five days, until at last an old Brahmin approached the Texans and said, "I told everyone I wanted to meet you even though you shout while playing tennis."

This was that kind of resort. The grandfather of the *nouveau pauvre* hosts received us in his drafty house with the threadbare Persian rugs and terra-cotta Tang horses dipped into green and white glazes. He said, "You teach? I taught at Columbia but retired when the school became overrun with—well, you know."

"No. I don't."

"Those small, dark, avid people." When I looked blank he added, "Jews."

As a boy I'd always wanted to win acceptance from these very people, but my mother was a divorcee, my father a hermit and misanthrope. Whereas I'd wanted to attend Groton and Princeton I'd ended up staying in the Midwest among the children of the automobility. Now, here at last I'd penetrated, thanks to Ned, into the inner sanctum of these Brahmin families and I saw their conversation was as pointless and drifting, their prejudices as deep dyed, their values as fundamentally mercantile as those of people anywhere else in America.

Whereas I'd once imagined I'd chosen a world of artists and homosexuals by default, I now saw I didn't want to belong to the mandarinate even if I could. We paid a weekly visit to a famous old writer who lived close to the harbor. His eternally youthful wife went off to play tennis or retreated into her office to manage a surprisingly effective watchdog organization designed to protect the rights—and the lives—of endangered writers all over the world, while the great man himself, as heavy a drinker as I, slowly became genteely incoherent as the day wore on.

When we returned to New York I stopped drinking forever one day after a night when I'd become so drunk I couldn't climb the ladder to my loft bed. Ned was shocked and angry at my decision. "How dare you make a unilateral decision about something that obviously affects us both! Some of our best times together have been drinking."

"I know, but it's something I just can't moderate. You can live next to six half-empty bottles of booze and offer your guests a choice from your bar, but you saw how nervous it made me to have those bottles brought into the house. Butler is right—I'm a consumer of booze, food, money, men. I live off the fat of the land."

Ned asked me if I was going to join AA and I said only if I couldn't stay sober on my own. My AA friends chided me for not joining up; they said I was on a "dry drunk." But my mother had stopped on her own—or, as she would say, because she'd promised God. Even if I didn't go to AA, I was armed with its principles. I decided to start living one day at a time.

⟞⟶ NED AND I moved to Paris, we thought for just a year; that move only dramatized the slow withdrawal I was undergoing. Since I no longer smoked or drank I never went to bars in France. Because Ned and I shared the same bed, even if chastely, I would never have dreamed of entertaining a boyfriend at our apartment; our sexless love, so sustaining to us, was brittle and easily cracked. Back in the 1970s along with the rest of my generation in New York I had hated couples; Butler and Philip even talked half-jokingly about starting a support group for the promiscuously challenged. The couple was deemed dowdy, mid-American, middle-class, mittel-stupid, and people apologized for their fidelity to a lover as though it were a reprehensible eccentricity. Gay couples, we decided, were shamelessly imitating heterosexual marriage, which itself seemed a primitive institution based on the exchange of cows for cowrie shells and clitoridectomies. Butler claimed it was difficult to socialize in the gay world if one was half of a couple.

Now most of the people who'd promulgated such ideas were dead or dying and they'd been replaced by a new gay generation that blamed their threatened health on the randiness of their elders. Gay guys now dated several times before going to bed, and that's just where they went— back rooms and baths had been shut down. Now people took workshops in safe sex. Couples had themselves tested repeatedly and even so took no risks.

Not in France. In Paris AIDS was dismissed as an American phobia until French people started dying; then everyone said, "Well, you have to die someway or another." If Americans were hysterical and pragmatic, the French were fatalistic, depressed but determined to keep the party going.

I met a few people at the Alliance Française or at the gym, but no writers and few gays. The novel about my boyhood had been published to considerable acclaim and that success had even won me a couple of prizes, which improved my finances slightly while isolating me still further, even from my own ambition, for it turned out that now that I'd earned my modicum of celebrity I'd lost interest in my career, if not in my vocation. I still wanted to write novels but now out of a mild curiosity about what I'd invent rather than from a desperate need to impose myself on the world. Maria had always teased me for whoring after fame, but now I saw that I'd simply wanted to be on the map, not as Texas but as Rhode Island.

Paris with its drizzle, as cool, grey and luxurious as chinchilla, comforted me. It was a middle-aged town, devoid of youth culture, youthful fashions and young people's amusements, but ideally suited to someone "of a certain age," as the French said with all the imprecision of good manners. (Sometimes, when they were even more gracious, they called the forties and fifties "the flower of age," *la fleur de l'âge*.) It was a city of good restaurants, tolerable concerts and tradespeople who were polite but brisk. One out of every two Parisians lived alone; the city respected solitude. Friendships weren't the searing, convulsive intimacies of New York; they were more decorous, sometimes even static, and they passed slowly from *vous* to *tu*. Or perhaps I was just getting older. My father had told me one didn't make close friends after twenty; for me, thirty had been the equivalent of twenty for a heterosexual man of his generation, and even so I'd gone on calling up Josh or Maria or Butler at three in the morning if I was panicking. Now I wasn't looking for that sort of violent love; now

I was zoning out in the Paris fog, which was lit up around the newly illuminated Eiffel Tower or transected by the spots trained on the Gothic churches.

The bookstores in Paris were wonderfully specialized, American literature or Catalan, historical, travel, African. There were even two bookstores devoted just to Jules Verne's works. Baudelaire had praised the *flâneur* as the embodiment of the contemporary spirit; I did so much aimless wandering that he would have considered me thoroughly modern.

Whereas Rome had been crowded with visual and social incident, an ancient forum cheek-to-jowl with a Baroque church and a Mussolini-era office building, Paris was remarkable only for its uniformity—its long vistas of leafless plane trees, vigorously pollarded, and the unbroken façades of its Haussmannian apartment blocks. The same few elements kept being rejuggled by a clever deceiver as the unsuspecting ruler made her way through the Potemkin city—the same round metal grilles at the bases of trees, the same cafés with their dark green awnings, the same Morris columns covered with posters, the same Wallace fountains with their maidens in cast iron, the same Art Nouveau subway entrances by Guimard, even the same repeated decorative details in all those miles and miles of bourgeois Second Republic apartment interiors. Even the parquet floors creaked in the same way no matter where I went.

As an expatriate I lost touch with the news and advertising jingles and catchwords back home and when a visitor asked, "Where's the beef?" I couldn't pick up his allusion, though his knowing grin suggested I was in the presence of one. Without mastering French culture I was losing touch with American. The Americans I ran into seemed less and less concerned with what was happening "abroad." Despite being an expatriate, I remained as American as *tarte aux pommes*.

Max assumed I must be hobnobbing with all those intimidating Parisian intellectuals, and indeed I was invited everywhere by everyone— *once*. If I'd been paranoid I might have said that they found me dull, but I had the impression (which time and subsequent observation bore out) that the Parisians, those devotees of whatever is modish, like to be introduced to whoever is new and foreign but then, like people everywhere, settle back into their slovenly habits and see the same six friends.

The one exception was Michel Foucault, whom I'd met in the United States and who'd even come to a reading I'd given at the old Three Lives Bookshop off Sheridan Square, where he'd sat on the floor upstairs with the kids and listened to pages from my novel about my boyhood. Afterwards he'd said—with his modesty that was as pure and demanded as much concentration as a flame held between hands on a windy night— that I was "a real writer," unlike him.

In Paris I saw him a few times at his big modern apartment on the rue de Vaugirard. Once or twice he gave me a rich dinner—without vegetables—that he scarcely touched. When I teased him about not eating enough vegetables, he said that the greengrocer was too far away whereas the pastry shop and caterer were just next door. Usually he had a whole band of young men around him, mostly the sort of elegant, intelligent ephebes he enjoyed as friends if not as sex partners. Inspired by the ancient Greeks, whom he was studying, he'd developed a cult of friendship. He thought that we had nothing else to value now; the death of God had resulted in the birth of friendship. If we could no longer enjoy an afterlife earned by our good deeds, we could at least leave behind a sense of our achievement, measured aesthetically, and the most beautiful art we could practice would be the art of self-realization through friendship. He became highly irritated when people tried to push the resemblances too far between the pagan world and ours; he was careful not to compare any two historical epochs, but if no emphasis at all was placed on the juxtaposition, he was willing to let the classical ideal of friendship dangle before our imagination, a glittering example that we might invent a way to emulate.

But perhaps I misunderstood him. I read his last two books and reviewed them, but it was in his conversation, as reported to me by Gilles Barbedette, that he developed these notions about friendship, left deliberately vague, and I'm far from sure that at two removes I understood what he was getting at.

Ned didn't like long evenings around a dinner table, especially not with French-speaking people. He said he just wasn't on their wavelength, and in fact couldn't tolerate people who weren't "sparkly" (one of his favorite if nearly unfathomable words). For Ned, "sparkly" didn't, for instance, mean a brilliant conversationalist. I had one friend, an English writer, who was a dazzling, non-stop raconteur, but Ned found his monologues about Czech porcelain collectors or Nazi novelists tiresome. No, Ned liked people who made a real, sustained effort to draw him out and include him in the conversation and who were big drinkers and would become at the end of the evening either silly or sexual. It wasn't easy for English or American academics to talk to him. They were used to the lecture hall or the common room and their conversation included lots of intellectual allusions and campus namedropping, both of which left Ned arctically cold. He looked like such a well brought-up New Englander that no one suspected what a rage he could get into if he had to sit through a meal where he was ignored or chided or during which people had the bad taste to speak French.

Ned had learned only a horrible pidgin French that he picked up at the gay bars where he went almost every night ostensibly to cruise but actually to get drunk; I was even slower to master French conversation. What I did do was lie on my daybed and read the latest French novels and look up all the words. After I'd located a word in the dictionary on five separate occasions I was finally able to memorize it, though usually I was still incapable of recognizing it when someone else said it.

Attitudes were as unrecognizable as words. For the Parisians, determined to appear unflappable, everything, no matter how grotesque or perverse, was declared "*normale*." The only thing not "*normale*" was an unfair quality-price ratio, even though the French were willing to pay lots more than Americans for genuinely desirable things, which they could recognize in microscopic gradations more readily than we could; after all, the French had invented the idea of luxury.

Ned was studying interior design at the Paris branch of an American university. Our apartment, which was just two overheated rooms on the Ile St.-Louis, was often crowded with his models of a Summer House by the Sea for a Retired Couple or a Manhattan Penthouse for a Fashionable Bachelor. Ned was dyslexic and looked at a book as though it were someone's grandmother he respected but worried might trap him into a boring evening; he was quick to cast it aside and dash out to the bars, especially those where older men would buy him drinks and attempt to chat him up in English as broken as Ned's French.

Ned had a sidekick, Arturo, who came from Venezuela but had been educated in Florida; at least he spoke English and was always available even at the last moment to go bar-hopping. One could either believe his version, that he was from a rich family who gave him a big allowance to stay in Paris to avoid kidnappers and study, that the small but very bourgeois apartment near the Arc de Triomphe was his and he just happened to be lodging there a French lover twice his age because he liked older, chubby men but that he was contemplating moving to the vast family apartment overlooking Central Park West. Or, alternatively, one could say he was an ugly kid with a big dick from a poor family, that the Paris apartment belonged to the man who kept him and that the New York apartment was a figment that didn't even exist.

At first we never suspected him of lying but soon Ned discovered that half the men he was meeting were *mythomanes* claiming their mother was a countess whereas she was actually a concierge or haughtily asserting they were from a long line of scholars instead of, more truthfully, a short line of shepherds. I suppose we were easily fooled because, as Americans, we thought that everyone was on his own and could rise as high as his drive and abilities would carry him; as I kept trying to explain to French friends, *arriviste* didn't exist as a word or concept in America and if it did it would be a compliment, since we admired people who'd arrived somewhere out of nowhere. We were even guilty of reverse snobbism; I loved to tell people my mother had been so poor she'd never worn shoes until she was sixteen, whereas the truth, I seem to recall, was that until her mother married Mr. Wentworth she never wore two shoes that matched (they were both the right size but, since they were hand-me-downs or pass-alongs, they were seldom two halves of the same pair).

Although I was writing a novel and doing bits of journalism, it seemed to me I'd never had so much leisure. I'd go to the gym, dine with new friends from Paris or old friends from the States and, during the day, cross paths with Ned—cross and recross. Aside from Arturo he had few friends. He would have considered them to be impediments to his cruising and drinking. Until the previous year I would have seen those activities as proof of his independence but now I regarded them (privately) as signs of his addictions.

I was on a French television show discussing my writing, and Arturo's boyfriend—a mustachioed, fifty-year-old software salesman—became so excited by my fleeting celebrity that he arranged for a dinner at his (or, depending on which version we believed, Arturo's) apartment; there he pretended to be the host of the literary chat show and interviewed me with a fake microphone. I was intensely embarrassed by this tomfoolery but went along with it because I knew how much Ned had suffered through evenings with my tedious friends.

Ned's real reason for disliking the French, I think, was that they wouldn't listen to his long stories about how mistreated he'd been as a child, or if they did listen they didn't say, "You poor kid," but rather, "*Et alors?* Isn't childhood always miserable?" Friendship for the French wasn't the same exchange of horror stories as it was for Americans, those highly public "secrets" that had to be traded in the States as expensive bottles of Scotch have to be exchanged in Japan.

Once in a while I'd say to Ned, "Please be careful about sex. We've got to be more careful."

"About what?"

"AIDS—isn't that what they're calling it now?"

"I *am* careful, Petes." (We called each other "Petes.") "I'm always very careful and clean."

I don't think either of us realized how idiotic these reassurances were.

One evening I told Michel Foucault and the writer Gilles Barbedette about AIDS and Foucault laughed at me and said, "Don't you realize how puritanical you're being? You've invented a disease aimed just at gays to punish them for having unnatural sex."

"Yes," Gilles chimed in, "that's a very American idea."

The French loved to discuss American "puritanism," by which they meant a phobia about pleasure, a hatred of the body and a fanatical prudishness. I became hot under the collar explaining that the actual Puritans had been the best thing that ever happened to America, responsible for abolitionism, prison reform and universal, free and compulsory education, and that America's religious life, unfortunately, was dominated not by the somber, fatalistic, intellectual Puritans but by born-again nitwits who joined their small-minded bigotry to a convulsive but mercifully short-lived revivalism.

Ironically, it was in Europe that I became puritanical or at least bourgeois. People who'd read my books assumed I must be a real bounder, always ready for a romp; I greeted their familiarity with a profound hauteur, if height can have depth. Old friends assumed I must be as ready for a good chin-wag as ever but I was now reserved, prudent, and the French had taught me if not to stop gossiping at least to deny my interest in it with icy hypocrisy. I'd always have scuffed shoes and a shirt-tail hanging out, but now I wore a coat and tie, not a T-shirt; cashmere, not denim. When I came back to visit Leonard in my old New York apartment building, on the stairs I passed one of my scruffy, sexy former neighbors and though we'd never really been on speaking terms he felt moved to say, "Ugh! Cologne! You never wore that sissy crap before. You stink like a French whore. Time to come home." I looked at him impassively and thought that now he was past forty he'd do well to follow my example.

Leonard was dying. He shed the massive body he'd earned through years of lifting weights and became once again the skinny blond boy I'd first met. All the easygoing warmth and relaxed generosity also melted away. Now he was once again the despised creep he'd been as a boy when he'd been tormented by his alcoholic, bedridden father. Leonard hated himself and shouted angrily at his lover Billy and was always furious at something Billy had done or forgotten to do—he'd become both the tormentor and the tormented, the two halves of his childhood drama.

He'd also reverted to Catholicism, but one that wasn't the mystical, incense-swinging camp to be found at "Smoky Mary's," but rather the pinched, shabby, willfully ugly Catholicism of his Florida youth, the church of glow-in-the-dark dashboard Madonnas and plastic flowers, of sin management and grace accountancy, of confession in a booth with Father Mike, the smell of dirty feet and unwashed bodies. This was the church of an angry deity, the neighborhood bully who sent fags and unwed mothers straight to Hell for eternity, who kept minor sinners in Purgatory for dreary centuries but who sped bigots and old, holy-water frogs straight to a Heaven that smelled of chalk dust and wet blackboards and that rang out with the excited voices of constant bingo winners.

Leonard saw me reluctantly and when I stood hesitantly in the sickroom doorway he mumbled while saying his black rosary and he kissed the silver crucifix that dangled from it. He didn't look up at me. I was broken-hearted and angry to see my big, brave boy reduced to this cranky, creaking prayer wheel. I was sorry that he had lost his confidence, his belief in everything he'd so beautifully achieved.

ONE YEAR in France led to a second, third, fifth. The longer I stayed the more difficult it appeared to jump back on the Manhattan merry-go-round, whirling ever faster past me. France seemed a bit dim and dreary, almost as though I'd already died. My first psychiatrist, Dr. O'Reilly, had said that the unconscious does not distinguish between leaving and being left, and that the child who goes off on a trip from home feels abandoned by his parents; by that reasoning I felt rejected by the States. I was in a pout that America had let me go so easily.

When I did go back to New York, it was shockingly noisy but it no longer seemed the dingy, dowdy city I'd known, as comfortable and smelly and graceless as old loafers. Even the writers were becoming younger and younger, their advances bigger and bigger. But when I looked at the few aging leathermen of my generation still alive and creaking around, stiff-jointed in their supple pelts, I thought that in New York the charming eccentricity of someone in his twenties can become a grotesque deformity when he enters his fifties, since this is a city where no one conforms to a general, civilized code of behavior, which in any event exists only as one "look" or another, to be taken up as a form of travesty—the "executive look," the "broker look," the "pimp look," or the "rapper look." In a 1992 documentary about Harlem drag shows, the skinny black gays not only got all dolled up in *Vogue* fashions but also did a turn as young Wall Street lawyers in three-piece suits and button-down shirts and briefcases.

In the past New York had been a city where even rather respectably dressed old men were always rooting through the garbage in search of food or newspapers with that supercilious, suspicious look on their faces of idlers picking up books in a bookstore just to kill time. Now new buildings were springing up everywhere. The women looked chicer than Parisiennes although their voices and especially their laughter remained as raucous and nasal as ever. Money poured out of every doorway with the surging crowds or swept uptown in every stretch limo.

My friend Tom, the poet, died, bitter and angry. He'd discovered that Daniel, his handsome young lover, had for years been seeing someone his own age on the side. Instead of being understanding about a young man's needs and tastes and grateful for his love, no matter how partial, Tom had broken off with Daniel in a fit of wounded pique—and died six months later of self-pity and an early heart attack. I thought no Frenchman "of a certain age" would have made such a blunder. France instructed its men and women early and thoroughly in the cold, unblinking art of realism.

At first Paris seemed untouched by AIDS. Another American told us to pretend to be English, since presumably the French were afraid of having sex with Americans, but that warning proved to be irrelevant. If Parisians had rather despised us when I'd first come to Paris in the sixties, that was because everyone then was a Communist; now, with the suddenness and thoroughness that characterizes a French about-face, no one was a Communist and not a single qualified candidate, for instance, could be found for a chair in Marxist history at a state university. People believed Americans were funny, cheerful people, "harmless" or *très bon enfant*, which was far from being a compliment, since Parisians preferred those who were nasty, or *méchant*, to those who were uniformly nice, or *gentil*. At the very least one should strive to be *malin*, or "sly." Of course, as I pointed out to French friends, Americans had to be ceaselessly nice in order to avoid promoting murderous rages in the people around them. Every argument in America could end in a knife fight.

Michel Foucault was in the hospital one winter. When he came out he seemed much thinner and weaker and racked by a constant cough, but he was determined to give a dinner party for William Burroughs and twelve of the band of young Parisian men who were always gathered around the philosopher. Foucault could speak English wonderfully well, but his success with the language was a sustained performance demanding complete concentration, the sort of intensity that made his seminars in the States so exhilarating (and exhausting). I'd attended a seminar at New York University in 1982 and I remembered how much Foucault had had to rely on written notes and words precisely produced by a mouth glittering with silver fillings, as though the metal helped him to chew out the difficult foreign words. What he wasn't equipped to do was chat idly or understand mumbling; as the evening wore on Burroughs began to slip into slangy, stoned incoherence and I had to "translate" Burroughs's English into Foucault's.

Two months later Foucault was dead. An article on the front page of *Libération* denied that he'd died of AIDS, as though it would be a calumny against France's leading philosopher to suggest he'd succumb to such an ignominious disease. Only very slowly did the truth emerge; all I could think of was his patience, trudging back and forth from the kitchen to the salon to serve the dinner without vegetables he'd bought at the caterer's downstairs. I remembered his patient smile and cocked head as he listened to Burroughs's stoned murmurs; he was trying unsuccessfully to understand what this American writer whom we all admired so much was saying. His humility in serving dinner to friends was in complete contrast to his fiery temper, bordering on madness, when he thought he was being criticized by a member of an enemy conspiracy of intellectuals.

In Venice I stayed with Joshua in the new apartment he'd rented, the top floor of a historic palace. My bedroom, which gave onto the Grand Canal, was pink; the bed had a pink baldacchino held up by chubby cupids. We fell back into our old habits, working in the mornings, at noon eating cheeses and cold cuts that came from the delicatessen manned by the handsome clerk, swimming in the afternoons, usually at the Cipriani. We had our little routine, our way of standing steadily in the *traghetto* as it was oared from one bank of the Grand Canal to the other, our habit of saying *andemmo*, in Venetian, instead of *andiamo*, our conformity to the

European practice of ordering cut flowers only in odd numbers (no dozen red roses for Italians), and of slipping into our places at the opera while facing the people already seated rather than turning our backs on them as we might do in America.

Joshua was happy with Sergio, *il tesoro*, who invited us to his village to meet his mother, a toothless old crone in black who told us she'd stopped going to church since the cardinals had elected a *Polish* pope, of all things. We saw in the mother's house the big silk lampshades Joshua had bought as well as countless little cast-off things, as though this high, roomy peasant house in the Veneto were the Sargasso Sea that preserved all the flotsam that floated down from Venetian palace life.

In Venice I met a German film producer and fell in love with him. When Hajo would come to Paris, we'd stay in an apartment one of his friends would lend us; I didn't want to wound Ned. Most often I'd go to Berlin, but there a reciprocal situation existed, since Hajo's ex, a prosperous art dealer, was still the center of Hajo's life. This art dealer, Gerhardt, had left Hajo for a handsome young Italian who was studying law in New York, but since Italo was seldom in Europe and Gerhardt got to New York only once a month, there were a lot of cold nights when Hajo and Gerhardt still shared a bed, though now their love was chaste. They both came from the mountains in Bavaria and spoke the same dialect. They despised the Mercedes-mink-coat style of German prosperity and preferred to spend their considerable wealth on new art, French furniture from the thirties and forties and clothes made for them by the King of Spain's tailor.

I eventually realized that there wasn't much room left over in Hajo's heart for me. He was embarrassed that I was overweight and greying and invited me to a clinic in the mountains where we fasted for two weeks. We ate nothing at all, ingested nothing but tea made from apple peels, and every morning we were awakened by a nun who gave us enemas. We were forbidden to use deodorant or cologne, since our starving bodies would have seized on these powerful chemicals. Anyway, we didn't smell.

After a week at the clinic a dirty-haired, cigar-smoking German film director insisted we accompany him to a restaurant where he ate fried sausages and sauerkraut in front of us. We were nauseated—and of course wanly covetous of the rich, dripping food.

Hajo became so skinny that he looked like the survivor of a camp; I dropped twenty pounds and three years and looked as thin and pensive as writers are supposed to look. The whole time I dreamed of pizzas running with hot cheese.

One night, feeling amorous, I said, "You know, the night before I met you in Venice I'd picked up a Spanish kid and we'd had sex all night long. But after I met you I exchanged a few letters with him and then tore up his name and address. I never did that before, I guess I was never so in love before. . . ."

An ominous silence was building up. At last Hajo exploded, "Now I remember. The night I met you your nipples were too raw to touch. I guess that Spaniard had been . . . *chewing* on them. Really, you said you were a gay leader and never took risks."

He was angry. When he calmed down he insisted we have the AIDS test, which had just become available. As it turned out, he was negative and I positive, which at least proved we'd mastered safe-sex techniques, though no one really knew what they were. Most of the smart gay money lay on the idea that getting come up your ass was fatal and sucking was safe; in Australia a gay group had even printed up a poster that said, "Suck, don't fuck," but the government pulled it, because there were a few cases, it seemed, of people who'd contracted AIDS from oral sex.

Until I actually learned the results of the test I kept thinking I'd somehow squeak by; I knew perfectly well that I'd been getting fucked by strangers several times a week for years, never with condoms, and that I'd been most active in New York during what turned out to be the particularly dangerous years just before the disease began to manifest itself and was at last identified.

I'd always counted myself lucky, as a privileged white man born into a century that had defeated syphilis and tuberculosis, as the son of a mother who'd encouraged him, fervently if sometimes blindly, to follow a career in the arts, as a New Yorker who now lived in Paris, as a writer who not only finally got published but also lived by his pen. I'd somehow thought that this luck would hold out—but it hadn't. My natural Texan robustness, or some mysterious antibody that I alone possessed, or some unnamed sensory device that teleprompted me, despite my drugged stupor night after night, to select only healthy partners—I'd half believed in all these fanciful talismans and systems until the day when I heard the long-denied but long-anticipated truth.

I went to bed for a month. I just pulled the covers over my head and prepared myself for dying. Other writers I knew who'd been diagnosed flung themselves into feverish activity, determined to write in the two or three years that remained to them all the books they would have written had they been allowed to live to eighty ("Even if I have to write them badly," said the dying Hervé Guibert). But my ambition had been not only to express myself and create ingenious artefacts but also to pay my admission into a club that, now I was ill, had caught fire and dissolved into ashes.

Suddenly I was very alone. Hajo and I were still technically lovers but I saw that he was reluctant to admit it, especially when there were attractive people around whom he hoped to impress. I was venerable, famous, but old. Although he was just five years younger, he had not yet stopped wanting to be "young." He worked out every day, danced at the discos, swam off the Isle of Silt or sunned nude in the English gardens in Munich; his elegant, conservative suits gave way to extravagant outfits by Jean Paul Gaultier and Paul Smith. But if he was pulling away from me it wasn't because he was ashamed of me; no, he was afraid. There seemed to be fewer and fewer sexual practices he was willing to indulge in. We made the trip between Berlin and Paris less and less often.

At the same time I published a bitter novel that satirized some of the people I'd known in New York. Max decided he was one of my principal targets, although the character he thought was based on him actually had been meant as a self-portrait. He and the other injured parties turned against me. Perhaps out of respect for them, journalists were silent about my book, although the blackout may have been just an expression of general confusion, since I'd become identified as a gay novelist and this book had no gay characters. When the eighty-year-old French-American poet Edouard Roditi read it he said, "It's a very fine novel and if you publish another one like it your career will be over." My editor gave a masked ball in New York to launch the book and one of the offended people I'd based a character on came to it with a bullwhip to beat me; fortunately he was turned away by two guards.

My editor, Marston Higgs, was ten years younger than I. He was from a good Southern family, and had the manners to show for it, but he also had a New Yorker's impatience. He was always swearing under his breath, but his spells of vexation, during which his face would turn dangerously red, were deflated by the sudden pinprick of his laugh. "God, I'm getting to be so Type B, or is it Type A?" he'd say. He had been struck in the left eye when he was a kid, I think; anyway it was white and motionless, which made his cute grin, muscular little body, charming laugh all the more appealingly ambiguous, as though he'd once seen something tragic and been half-blinded by it. He was fascinated by his writers and regarded them as nearly mythical beings, whereas at the same time he could take a fully human interest in their declining health, the vagaries of reputation, the misfortunes of love. He was so much the image of the popular swimming star whom most of us geeky writers had lusted after in high school that the realization he liked us, even admired us, seemed—delightfully—like the world upside-down.

Marston would come to Paris and invite me to all the best restaurants on his expense account. He took a year off and traveled around North Africa and up through Italy and France in a luxurious trailer. He tried to write a novel, but abandoned it after fifty pages; this failed effort made him admire his authors all the more. His lover of many years, a handsome older man who worked as a model on ads for life insurance in which he'd pose with his "wife" and high-school age "children," dropped him for a still younger man, an opera singer. Marston, who was naturally secretive, made a deliberate effort to confide his unhappiness to me, almost as though his shrink (if he had a shrink) had told him to open up to his friends. What he didn't tell me was that he was seropositive and that his numbers were rapidly declining, which accounted perhaps for many of the changes in his life—his trip, his writing, his break-up. He'd always had a wild sex life; he burned with a simmering sensuality and I'd catch him sizing up even the most ungainly men and women. He brought a wispy, small-boned blond kid to Paris, but soon he was in love with a famous ballet dancer his age with whom he'd had a brief affair twenty years earlier.

Then suddenly Marston lost his job and was hired elsewhere, but soon afterwards became too ill to work. I hired him freelance to edit a new novel I was working on; he appeared to be surprised that I wasn't able to offer him more money for the job. I gave him the going rate, yet now he found everything disappointing. I visited him in the hospital; it puzzled him that I was still in such obscenely good health.

After he died I remembered I'd told him that I was sure he was going to beat this disease. My reputation as a writer, even my age, now lent my words a weight they hadn't had in the past. I realized that reluctantly, hopefully, Marston had believed me.

He shouldn't have. I was wrong. He did die, as did the writers from my literary club, the guys in advertising I knew, the lawyers, the fellows at the gym, the men I'd shared houses with on Fire Island—they were all dying, even though they'd all been told they wouldn't. I heard stories of a friend leaving his loft to his surviving lover, who was then ousted by the dead man's parents. I heard of a group of friends who decided to help their buddy die. He was blind and incontinent, weighed just seventy pounds and had nothing to look forward to except dementia. But at the last moment one of the angels of mercy cracked, called an ambulance. The dying man was resuscitated, only to die a month later in howling pain. Even so, whenever Dick, the one who'd cracked, saw the others on the street or at a nightclub, he started shouting, "Murderers." Perhaps Dick himself was already succumbing to dementia; in any event he died six months later. I heard of men who spent all their money having their "chakras" tuned by a charlatan with a flute, of those who ate apricot pits in Mexico, cucumbers in China, macrobiotic food in Japan. They all died.

◯ NED WAS GRADUATED from his design school and returned to the States to look for a job as a decorator. An American could never get work papers in France. Besides, he was determined to plunge back into watching American soap operas on television, listening to the latest American pop music, enjoying American humor and sex. I put him in my old studio apartment, which I'd been subletting to someone else (the Norwegian steward) all these years.

I developed a strange case of shingles that didn't produce many bumps or cause me much pain; in fact I would scarcely have noticed it if I hadn't become so tired. My doctor gave me a treatment and said shingles wasn't necessarily linked to AIDS, though it could be a "tracer illness." I slept night and day, as I'd slept so many years ago when I'd come down with hepatitis in Paris. A play of mine was being given a staged reading in London; I pulled myself together and flew over to see it, but I realized they'd got hold of the wrong version, an early draft I'd since extensively revised. I sat there stunned, indifferent, hundreds of years old.

The next night I was on a street corner in the West End, trying to find a taxi. A group of drunk young people in evening clothes swirled around, laughing wildly, speaking English, which suddenly sounded so *foreign*. I hated them because I thought they weren't going to die. They didn't have AIDS and their bodies were smug with health. They weren't sneering at me and I suppose if I'd accosted them one by one at a party with my sad story, the women, at least, would have screwed up their eyes and let their mouths open slightly, serious and unsmiling, and they might even have risked squeezing my hand before backing away, thoughtfully; girls like that will take their father figures where they can find them.

But tonight I hated them, I suppose, because I thought they'd won. They would never, under any circumstances, have thought about my kind very much, yet in the 1970s we might just have seemed if not enviable at least plausible, with our dancing, our music, our haircuts, our gym-built bodies, but now we were dismissed with a shrug of a pretty bare shoulder rising up out of a calyx of ivory silk, as though to say, "Oh, *no*, not now, when we're having such fun. Haven't we done enough for charity?" After gay liberation we'd dared to believe that we might be blazing a new trail; now we saw that our trail had run out, swallowed up by a forest of indifference.

I listened to one record over and over again back in Paris, one of Mahler's Rückert songs, "*Ich bin der Welt abhanden gekommen*" ("I have lost track of the world"). When I'd be taking the train somewhere, watching the fields opening up before me and a little French village gliding past with its squat Romanesque tower and its few dull stone houses, I'd sing this song with its words at once resigned and joyful: "I am dead to the hurly-burly of the world / And repose in a place of quietness!" ("*Ich bin gestorben dem Weltgetümmel, / Und ruh'in einem stillen Gebiet!*"). For an English speaker who'd been speaking French for so long, that *Ich bin gestorben* was so much more pungent than *Je suis mort* and that *einem stillen Gebiet* so much calmer than the sleek, glib *un lieu tranquille*. I'd fall asleep, dreaming of a lover who would smell of something burned, of old smoke in heavy green curtains . . .

Joshua asked me to come to Venice for the last two weeks of August. When I arrived he told me he was positive and had fewer than a hundred T cells, but his announcement struck me as utterly implausible. Joshua? He who'd made love to no more than twelve men in his whole life? Who'd always been too blind to cruise, too prematurely elderly ever to bed a fast-lane gay man? Of course I was only exposing my ignorant assumptions. AIDS wasn't cumulative and it didn't just strike the promiscuous scene-makers.

"Have you lost a bit of weight?" I asked.

"Alas," he laughed, "not enough."

He was always dieting and though his skin now was waxy and white and stretched across his cheekbones in that tell-tale way, his lower body was still plump. The changes wrought by AIDS came ten times faster than those imposed by age (five decades' worth of aging could be squeezed into five years) but still slowly enough that only someone like me who'd lived apart from Joshua and not seen him for a year could notice how his teeth had become more prominent, as though they'd slid forward a fraction, and his eyes had become hollower, as though they'd retreated, and the skin on his arms hung looser, as though it had already died.

Joshua had come from New York with a new lover, a tall, slender guy between jobs who, like Josh, had gone to Harvard, and, like us, talked opera, food, friends. Although he was twenty years younger than I (and I was ten years younger than Josh) Lionel seemed eager to decode our references and know everything about us. I'd hear Joshua and Lionel discussing that evening's dinner, not with the sing-song, almost weary dailiness of Sergio, *il tesoro,* but with an edge of social hysteria. "Do you think we should *really* mix Peggy with Nica? The unreal with merely real estate?" (Nica rented out apartments in the palace her family had owned for six centuries.) Lionel, too, laughed with us about how Peggy, despairing of ever finding a summer gondolier who didn't charge the union minimum, had finally engaged a retired funeral gondolier. If given his head, the gondolier would start rowing for San Michele, the island cemetery, and begin to sing dirges in a big bass voice full of wobble.

Joshua was keeping two different mental sets of books about the disease. He'd say, "This disease is a dreadful thing. I've decided to devote the next few years to raising money to fight it," but at the same time I could see he was feverishly working to finish his "study of poetic friendship." He'd always read to me every word he'd written but now he lingered less over alternative versions and seemed determined to press on, despite his natural reticence, so closely allied to his innate elegance. He'd always been slow to commit an idea to paper, just as in conversation he preferred it if one finished his sentence for him, as if in that way it was one's own fault, not his, if any utterance constituted a slide into vulgarity or error.

Since so much of his work was based on a close reading of his poets (and of their letters—in some cases he'd been the first person allowed to consult them) he was always happy to read them again out loud. His head (and to a much lesser extent his computer) was full of notes, quotations, projects, comparisons, often followed by a question mark. I think he knew perfectly well that most cases of AIDS involved some dementia, and he must have been terrified that all his knowledge, so painfully acquired after thousands of hours of research in libraries and reading at home, would be lost over the course of a weekend, as though hundreds of pages of metal type, not yet printed, would melt in a big fire. If his favorite novel was *Middlemarch* and the two or three women he loved he considered to be as "ardent" as Dorothea, by the same token he'd always feared most that he'd turn out to be Casaubon, the scholar unable to lead his research to completion. Already, on certain days, his mind, famous for its total recall, felt like nothing more than a blur, waves of heat rising and warping the view.

Joshua had never been able to decide whether Sergio was a lover or a servant and in a greedy way he'd wanted him to be both. He'd wanted Sergio to cook for him and tuck him in, then slide in beside him, but disappear when there was work to be done or a princess to be received. Of course I'd always hoped Joshua would elevate Sergio's status—I believed in fairy-tale endings—but now Lionel had taken that place, accomplishing in six months what "the treasure" had failed to do in six years. I suppose Joshua had wanted to protect his right to go to the ballet, night after night, with one of his Dorotheas, since in his heart the need for friendship was a more powerful appetite than the longing after love, although he complained a lot about the empty-bed syndrome. For years I'd told Joshua that he was "immoral" in the way he was playing with Sergio, "leading him on," filling him with unfounded expectations, but Joshua answered my sermons with lots of dithering and a cultivated vagueness. Besides, he hadn't really led Sergio to expect anything.

Perhaps because he'd lived so long among books and devoted his whole life to literature, all of his friends compared him to characters in classics— to Casaubon, perhaps, but more often to Emma's lovable yet hypochondriacal father, to Proust's aunts, so tentative as to be incoherent, too polite to communicate properly, even to Oblomov (Eddie's devilish contribution, since he constantly teased Joshua for being so lazy).

Now he wasn't lazy. I'd find him late at night, when I returned from a party or cruising the Molo, alone in front of his green, glowing screen. He'd look up and say, "If only there'd been laptops back then. I always found typing so noisy, such a physical effort, so user-hostile, whereas now I can't wait to come back to my green, glowing Rheingold." As though his new haste, even desperation, were just a minor matter of technology.

Because Joshua had never wanted to formalize things with Sergio, he thought nothing of introducing him to Lionel. They even had a three-way and when I saw Sergio next on the beach he said in his high-pitched, slow, almost whiny Venetian accent, "*O, come il suo cazzo è grande!*" and he held out his hands at river-trout length to indicate the full twenty centimeters, but I could see he was sad and bitter to be superseded by someone who could speak to *il professore* in his own language, who came from his own so-cial class and was younger and just as well endowed (Joshua and I always came out with the rather sinister *"bien pendu,"* even though we knew the French actually said, *"bien monté"* for "well hung").

Then suddenly everything went bad. Sergio stopped the owner of the *palazzo* and said to her, "Principessa, the *professore* is very ill with AIDS" (which the Italians pronounce as though it were the "ides" of March). "You must get the maids to fumigate everything when he leaves. The Ides is highly contagious."

Ordinarily, if the matter had been less serious, the princess might have slipped a note into his mailbox or accosted Joshua at the Cipriani pool, but he'd stopped swimming this summer, which only confirmed her sus-picions, and she was too upset to wait for his letter—nor did her stock of polite written formulas include a way of tackling this subject. Her solution was to phone him very early, to assure him in a tiny, shaken voice how much she'd always respected him—and finally to blurt out Sergio's accu-sation. She ended by sobbing and saying that she had a "historic palace to consider," as though that concern were of any relevance.

Joshua hotly denied what Sergio had said: "He's just a peasant, *cara*, and gets everything mixed up. I'm afraid he found himself less welcome here than he used to be and he simply lashed out with a paranoid mish-mash of all these horror stories on television. I'm *mortified* that he sub-jected you to these stories; naturally you're upset. But please don't believe a word of it—you know how these boys from the Veneto can't put two thoughts together and always get everything wrong." The princess was from Turin and had nothing but contempt for the locals, which Joshua was shrewdly counting on.

The confrontation rattled Joshua. Because he was so brilliant he'd never felt discriminated against, neither as a Jew nor as a gay man. Once, in the early 1970s, when we were thoroughly drunk, I'd asked him if, be-cause he was Jewish, he felt superior to me and he'd admitted he did—a remark that had so shocked me that it revealed to me that I myself nursed a faint sense of racial superiority invisible until then even to me. Twenty-five years ago he'd moved from Harvard, where he'd come out unevent-fully, to New Jersey, where he taught in a department headed by another gay man, a doting classmate from Harvard, and on to New York. Most of his life had been divided between the downtown New York world of cu-rators, professors, agents, critics and fawning students and a Venice of ex-patriates and aristocrats; in New York his Jewishness and homosexuality were assumed, in Venice never perceived or if detected not mentioned. Aristocrats, at least on the Continent, liked artists and intellectuals if they wore decent clothes and had good manners and acted crazy enough to be "amusing." The constant aristocratic need for amusement could take on the proportions of bulimia. Other people's bloodlines or morals would have been questioned only if they'd attempted to marry into the family— and even then money outweighed birth and birth was more important than morals.

The principessa's panic over a mysterious question of hygiene, how- ever, revealed that her ten years' friendship for Joshua had all along been extended only provisionally. After all, he'd never been an intimate, neither a relative nor a childhood friend, the only two categories to whom one owed lasting loyalty.

Venice was both stone and water, permanence and transience, the fluid element shaping but never wholly dissolving the solid, and this very am- biguity had always vouchsafed that no matter how much Joshua submit- ted to time's corrosives he would endure. One of his favorite books—and one of the crucial texts for his poets—was Ovid's *Metamorphoses*, and from it he'd learned to see life as both mutable and miraculous, but now every change that was happening to his body was frightening, monstrous. Now he rethought everything and realized that when Daphne had turned into a laurel tree, her fingers ramifying, her thighs becoming cortical, the transformation couldn't have been altogether comfortable.

As the summer came to a stormy, suddenly chilly end, Joshua began to hand over most of his possessions to the two maids, mother and daughter, who cleaned the acres of marble floors twice a week and who spoke in their gentle, caressing tones to each other. He gave one of his two fans to the maids as an offering to the cruel god of realism, then stored some summer clothes in order to propitiate the smiling, infant god of hope, for hope is the youngest of the deities, the one who has all his life before him.

We never took speedboats, which could easily cost a hundred dollars a ride, but at the end of every summer Joshua indulged himself, and the same sunburned, middle-aged man, dressed in a short-sleeved white shirt with dark blue epaulettes and pleated white trousers, backed his speed- boat-taxi into the little *rio* beside the palace. Given the narrowness of the *rio* and the backwash from the passing *vaporetti*, the maneuver was tricky, but the captain never looked the least ruffled. He was just another Vene- tian, these calm, incurious, handsome people who spoke to one another in their unintelligible dialect, who criticized their compatriots for the smallest eccentricity but simply shrugged at the shenanigans of foreigners. The Venetians never read a book (never had) but they knew they inhabited the most beautiful city in the world. They crammed their small apartments with the latest furniture from Milan, made of smoked glass and chrome, of molded Plexiglas and aubergine-colored leather, but outside everything looked and smelled as it had for centuries and nothing could be changed or improved; even the wood bridge built across the Grand Canal for the Feast of the Redeemer had to be entirely dismantled every year after the holiday. We were these foreign impostors who came from our new countries, spent all our money in order to inhabit their palaces for a summer or two, then we vanished, never to return, whereas they, the Venetians, complained of their rheumatism, the incursions of *acqua alta*, the influx of non-paying German backpackers, but they remained, the prosaic machinery rumbling under and animating these poetic illusions.

This year we loaded Josh's things into the taxi and checked our air tickets once more. Joshua talked bravely about next summer. He said he wanted to go to Istanbul for two weeks in August on the boat the Orient Express operated out of Venice. But obviously he was looking around for the last time at these many-storied palaces with their green and burgundy rosettes and their stone balconies. "Oh, look, the Duc Decazes must be in residence," Joshua declared bravely, "since there's a book on the stone lectern, look, there, on the *piano nobile*, that's how you know—that's the palace where Mr. Tissot lived, that dear man who designed avant-garde glass, the one who told Henry McIlhenny he should go ahead and rent Count Volpe's place for a thousand dollars a day since, as Mr. Tissot put it, "There are no pockets in the shroud.' Now they're both dead. Henry had to sell a Cézanne to pay the rent, but he never got to live there."

As Joshua's words come echoing across the water and down the years to me, I can't help thinking that his life was not just his finest thoughts about poetry and friendship, expressed in a style that rejected forcefulness in favor of sympathy, but it was also comprised of his long mornings in his dressing gown with the telephone, newspapers, the Hu Kwa smoked tea and the little sterling-silver strainer that sat in its drip cup when it wasn't straddled across a cup catching leaves. His life was made up of his pleasure in the morning glories as well as his hilarity when he learned that one could be friends with the Franchin or the Franchetti family, not both, and his relief when he realized the choice was easily made since Christina Franchetti was the most interesting woman in Venice, she who read everything from Hume to *Hedda Gabler* to Calvino till dawn, slept late into the afternoon, ate lunch at five at Harry's before rushing over to the Cipriani, hoping to catch a glimpse of a few friends still dozing or chatting by the pool. She sent her laundry to London every week. She talked late into the night about her childhood in Cuba and her girlhood in Spain. She spoke French, Spanish, English and Italian with equal headlong rapidity and if, after a long Italian dinner, one begged her to switch back to more restful English, she'd look startled and ask in her low, gravelly voice, "But *aren't* we speaking English? Oh . . ."

I RETURNED to Paris, Joshua to New York. As the autumn came on and every newspaper was crowded with news about Rock Hudson's celebrity AIDS, Joshua told me over the phone he was sickened by the subject, disgusted by the media blaze lighting up Hudson's sickbed, then his panicky flight from America to Paris in a private plane in search of a miracle treatment. Joshua was just as tired of seeing the before and after photos of the once handsome movie star.

I seldom went out. I lived at home on the Ile St.-Louis in my small apartment looking out on the stone volutes that supported the church roof as giant snails pry up the earth. It seemed to be raining every day and I darted out only long enough to buy food and mail letters.

I spent hours and hours on the gay party line, a number I'd dial (it was usually busy) until I'd be connected with seven or eight other men, all shouting out their home numbers or their dimensions or sexual tastes or just listening, breathing heavily. I called out my own number; everyone on the line laughed at my American accent. One man phoned me and talked me through to an orgasm.

After that he'd phone me every night at midnight and he became my demon lover, my secret sharer, a heartbeat in my ear, the drying liquid in my fist. He'd tell me how much he loved me, and I told him the same: it was the purest affair of my life, nothing but love, desire and fantasy. No face was there to mock, no body to find too gross, no demands to resent, no sex to make sure was safe. I never knew his number, but he called me every night at twelve. If, as happened only once or twice, someone else was there, I simply raised an eyebrow, let it ring and sighed, proudly, complainingly, "Men . . ." But usually I was in bed, reading French and looking up words and listening to the radio, dreading the moment when the Catholic music station—remote, classical, consoling—would come to an end and be replaced by the ghastly Protestant program with its guitar music, its pious folk songs and peppy homilies.

"*Chéri, j'ai pensé à toi toute la journée. . . .*" He was there, a reedy, throbbing voice, unashamedly romantic in the Gallic manner, urging me to do something, anything, to put his desire at ease, which now was standing rigidly at attention. "Sit on it . . . put it in your mouth . . . it needs you, it can't live alone like this, it's a fish out of water."

After a month of calls during which he told me all about his life, a recital that always shaded into phone sex with its incantatory repetitions and its vigorous, slapping silences, my lover decided we should meet. With Jamesian modesty I told him that I would only disappoint him. "My voice may be young," I said, "but I am not. I'm overweight, my hair is grey, even the hair on my chest is grey, I wear glasses, if you saw me you'd say I was a professor nearing retirement age, not the kid you want to hurt and cherish and live with forever."

"No, no!" he cried. "I love you, my love has gone beyond details like looks."

When I thought of the diplomatic negotiations a real, working, live-in love affair requires I felt tired and hopeless—would he like my friends? I his? Who would cook? Was he a vegetarian? Did he have a steady job? No, no, I thought.

He suggested that we meet at a tawdry hotel (the tawdriness was an essential ingredient). He'd already be there when I arrived, undressed and in bed, the lights off. He'd leave the door open. I could enter in the darkness if I was afraid to reveal my looks to him, undress and join him. If I liked, he'd cover his body and face with a sheet and just leave his sex exposed, which I'd be sure to like, he said, it was big, the skin much darker than on his body.

I never agreed to go and we passed over from that moment when a fantasy is still exciting because it might be realized to that later eternity when it dies from lack of nourishment.

Every time I spoke to someone in New York I heard of another death. "Beal," or Bill, the American composer I'd met in Rome, had become well known for a musical he'd written that Joe Papp had produced; I read in the *Herald-Tribune* that he'd died at age thirty-eight of complications resulting from AIDS. My old New York office mate Jamie was alive, but his lover, Gerry, the blond he'd carried up the stairs the night I'd met the White Russians—Gerry had died. They were the same Gerry and Jamie I'd slept with so many years ago on Capri. When I gave a reading in New York, Jamie, handsome although for some reason he'd dyed his hair white, came up to me, smiling, shy, encouraging; his wooden, head-prefect's manner had become supple, fluid, young with age. He seemed angry with Gerry for dying, as though if he'd only stopped smoking everything would have been all right.

None of these men had I seen in years, but they had continued to exist in my imagination, not only as real and potential stories, heavily specific, but also as allies that I'd always dreamed I could call on in a pinch. Most of the people I knew thought the world would continue in the future as it had been in the past, but I was always foreseeing disaster and vaguely preparing for it. I knew one society beauty and clothes horse who'd had two thirds of her stomach removed so that she could eat as much as she liked and remain slim, but her new condition required enormous quantities of food to maintain even a minimal weight, since everything passed through her so quickly; I was astonished that she could be so certain that she'd always be rich enough—or the world bountiful enough—to secure all the nourishment she needed. I had a war mentality and could easily imagine ending up penniless, for if I lived extravagantly, at the same time I had no savings and no possessions and my way of life required that I be constantly at work. What would happen if I became too ill to work, if I lost my mind? I'd always vaguely counted on my dozens of friends in France, America and England, although the one time I'd asked Max and Tom for a loan they'd refused me. And now, as I numbered my dead, I felt that I'd spent my whole life social climbing and someone had sawed the ladder out from under me.

I learned that my old secretary, William, had died, the brave little masochist who'd danced in leather and made jokes about his suffering and diabetes. I found out that my shrink, Abe, had lost his lover, but only after the lover had become a crack addict and carried their television and stereo out of the apartment to sell on the street. "He became demented at the very end," Abe said, "and reverted, mercifully, to his old sweetness. He'd lie with his head on my lap and smile at me. And to think how much he knew! Everything about Egypt, China, Louis XIV . . ."

Hajo's ex-lover Gerhardt died, as did Gerhardt's new lover, Italo. Ned's friend Arturo died; I ran into Arturo's middle-aged French lover, the one who'd pretended he was interviewing me on a television chat show, and he said that he'd gone on a trip alone after Arturo's death to Tangier and there he'd met an adorable Arab boy who was able to wear all of Arturo's clothes, a perfect fit, surely a sign from Heaven that Arturo had sent Ahmed to console him.

Kevin told me that his old lover Dennis, the boy with the beautiful birthmark on his temple, had married a rich, powerful Washington hostess. Dennis announced to all his old friends that he now despised homosexuality and had never "really" been gay, anyway. He said he was happy to have left "gay life" now that it had become "grim death." But soon he was ill, he was traveling to Switzerland to have his blood scrubbed, and he was on TNF, an Italian miracle drug, the "thymus-factor" as he kept saying. He became bitter and maniacally angry. He ridiculed waiters and denounced his "dumb-as-shit" Irish family, beat his wife and squandered her fortune on boats and houses and trips that brought him no relief. One by one everyone he'd ever known abandoned him. In the past his flare-ups had made his pale, birthmarked face flush under the wave of cave-black hair. When Kevin would tease him for his sexy Black-Irish temper, he'd laugh so that he'd reveal his broken tooth, which he'd suddenly remember and attempt to conceal by straining his lips back into a straight line—a remedy that would only provoke Kevin into new fits of teasing and Dennis into new fits of chagrined laughter. Now he was dead and his wife had written an inspirational Christian book about her handsome young husband who'd died because he'd been infected during a blood transfusion. Of course she never mentioned (did she even know about it?) his homosexuality.

WHEN MY FATHER DIED he'd left my mother five thousand dollars and my sister and me fifteen thousand each; the rest of his money had gone to his second wife. Now she died and willed my sister and me just five thousand dollars each; we had no idea to whom she'd given the rest, probably one of her relatives, possibly her cat. When I thought how Anne and I'd always cringed around our father, terrified we might be disinherited, I had to laugh. He and the power of his money had frightened everyone, but now he was almost entirely forgotten, no one visited his grave, and if he'd sacrificed everything to the almighty dollar, the dollar had not kept faith with him, nor with his vassals. Our biggest fear, being disinherited, had come to pass and it meant nothing to us, even the manner in which it happened was quiet, incidental.

My stepmother's death left me alone with their stories and mine, alone with my father, his cigar, his towering rages and his Cadillac. I remembered that when I'd descended once a month by train to see him for a weekend, after the exhausting seven-hour trip, after the anxiety of daily life with our mother (who was penny pinching, then hysterically extravagant, drunk, desiring, frightened), suddenly I'd been caught up in the solid, dull, Republican luxury of my father's car and big, air-conditioned mansion. The Cadillac door would slam shut with the solidity of a space shuttle hatch. Our mother resented wasting money on food and many meals were just caught on the wing, but in my father's basement a restaurant-size freezer was full of dead birds and animals, dozens of cans of frozen orange juice and quarts of chocolate, peach and cherry-vanilla ice cream, while the double-door fridge itself groaned under the weight of cooked hams and turkeys, quarts of milk and vats of cole slaw, dozens of eggs as well as pounds of bacon and of unsalted Land-o-Lakes butter divided into foil-wrapped sticks. Now the larder was empty, the house torn down, the diners dead.

I called my mother every Sunday from Paris and relaxed into the sweetness she exuded. She no longer drank or pursued men and since she'd retired she was no longer running after professional prestige and now had enough leisure to enjoy her grandchildren—the first batch and the second. My sister's three children were grown up and living far from her. But she'd adopted four biracial babies even though she was already nearly fifty years old. She'd become a therapist, working with large groups, often alcoholic lesbians and gay men. Nothing was settled—nothing would ever be settled—with someone so volatile and troubled, but at least she was living a rich, complex, productive life. Whereas I became lazier and lazier, as though I were dreaming, not writing, the big book of my life, my sister slept little and when she wasn't playing with her babies or seeing dozens of patients she went barreling off to her country house in Wisconsin or to campsites in Michigan.

Family life binds strangers together. I would never have *chosen* a retired child psychologist in her eighties living in Chicago to be my closest confidante. Left to her own devices my mother, who disliked fiction and was embarrassed by my confessions, would never have read my books, but because she loved me she puzzled over them and told me, in a vocabulary more suited to her own values and achievements than to mine, that she admired "the service I'd rendered my people," for she saw me as a political spokesman for homosexuals and praised me as she might have lauded Booker T. Washington or Gandhi. By the same token I listened as she told me of her worries and hopes and of the joy she took in planning her visits to France. I was determined to show her the châteaux of the Loire and Ned and I hired a Mercedes and a wheelchair and shuttled her through Azay-le-Rideau, Chambord and Chenonceau. I found us rooms in other châteaux-hotels. She propped her big glasses on her small nose and read the descriptions of the castles with the same breathless absorption she'd once devoted to reports on Mongolism. She feared losing her memory and exercised it daily by repeating long lists of names and facts, appropriate to a woman who'd been trained as a child back in Texas to learn by heart the names of all the states and their capitals.

She worried constantly that she might have to live in an old-age home, but I could see she was happy in her high-rise apartment looking out over Lake Michigan and downtown Chicago and encouraged her, every two years, to renew her lease "one more time." She died, five years ago, at age eighty-seven. My sister said she was angry; she'd done everything her Indian doctor had told her to, she'd followed his smallest suggestions, and now, unfairly, she was having to die, she, a professional woman, who'd always worked with doctors, who'd run a medical clinic. Now she was dying just like a lay person.

She had, as she would put it, the "inner resources" to live alone, stick to a schedule, nourish herself adequately, read, receive visits, attend her Sunday School and church every week. I bought her a subscription to the opera and to museum events. She praised me constantly for my generosity and even if I thought her praise was wide of the mark I basked in it. I'd always feared that the love of a woman, a woman my own age, would have a weakening effect on my character, but my mother's love, as uncomprehending as it was absolute, was an affection I could accept with humility and a smile.

She and I flew to Dallas and were driven all over Texas by my beautiful cousin and if we avoided certain subjects—my homosexuality, my sister's black babies, my mother's refusal to believe in the divinity of Jesus—all went well. None of my relatives even knew I was a writer, since my books were not distributed in their Texas towns.

We saw the old homestead with its smokehouse. We visited a great-aunt in an old folks' home where women with Alzheimer's were clawing at their genitals through the sweatpants they were wearing or drooling their food on their chests. We visited a museum of Texas houses in Lubbock that traced the development from dug-outs to two-room home-
˜eaders' shacks to big comfortable Victorian two-story houses—the very

trajectory my family had followed in just three generations. My mother was buried in the Texas village of one hundred and five people where she'd been born. Her grave is next to her father's; he was a Woodsman of the World and his tombstone is a tree trunk in stone, broken off at a slant where the tree of life was felled.

Gabriel, my nephew, was married to a Japanese stockbroker and living in Tokyo, where he was teaching English, eating raw fish and *miso* soup bought out of a machine on the corner and sitting in the bathtub and writing a novel at night while his wife slept.

EVERY FEW DAYS I talked long distance to Ned in New York. He'd worked as a model builder for an interior designer but now his health was deteriorating and he'd lost his job. He was living in my old studio apartment, where he gave little dinners, usually for just one other person, a man he was courting. Eventually he began to receive some money and free meals from public and private agencies designed to help people with AIDS, but I paid his rent and gave him an allowance.

It seemed to me strange that I was living in Paris, eating lotuses, while my mother and Ned, whom I supported, also lived alone, counted their pennies but managed to derive a quiet pleasure from their solitude, their friends, even just the fact of dressing well and keeping a tidy, handsome house. I invited Ned to Venice with me and some other friends one spring. I took a photo of him against a pale blue painting and though he was thin, his hair nearly white, he still had the same physical elegance I'd first loved in him ten years before. The painting was tall and wide and Ned was posed against it as though he were already an angel mounting to heaven. The sunlight must have been too bright (he was having trouble with his vision), for in the picture he is squinting slightly, but then again he always looked both friendly and slightly confused, as though he were a prince visiting a possession whose language he didn't understand; he smiled and squinted.

I remember that when in Venice I bought him a sleek raincoat and two new sports jackets, made of silk and the lightest wool, tears came to his eyes: "I'm sorry I'm getting so emotional, but I never buy myself new clothes since I keep thinking . . ." He cried, then blew his nose. "It shows you don't think I'm going to die right away."

"I wouldn't let you," I said, taking him in my arms.

We'd always agreed that if one of us became ill, the other one would take care of him. But I wasn't in New York looking after him. I'd let down my side of the bargain. Once I'd told Ned that I was so afraid of becoming ill and dying a long, painful, humiliating death that I wished I had the pills and courage to do myself in right now, but Ned, calling me by our old pet name, said, "Don't worry, Petes, we'll take care of each other and you'll see, we'll have fun, just as we always have." His sweetness and simplicity took my breath away; he'd said, "We'll have fun dying," which if I felt cynical I could dismiss as another example of his frivolity, but if I was less critical I could say was his promise that nothing was going to be too frightening to endure. We could live out our dying, step by cozy step, together.

Except we weren't together. He didn't want to come back to Paris because he was still searching for the perfect black preppie lover. In the meanwhile he liked having fifty channels in English, including non-stop cooking shows and soap operas. He would go to Joshua's apartment as often as he was feeling up to it, open the mail for him, shop, clean, cook, but mainly they'd watch TV together and, snobbishness aside, the soap operas and game shows and cooking programs and news channels were proof that life was still flowing vigorously through the wires: put your cold, withered hand on the wires and feel the hum and warmth.

Kevin and his Israeli lover, in turn, began to look after Ned. He was in such pain that his doctor had given him patches that secreted a morphine analogue, but Ned, alone and delirious, applied several patches instead of the single one required. He went half-crazy, lost track of time, forgot to eat and attempted suicide. After that I made sure that Kevin had a key to his apartment and checked up on him every day. Kevin's old heartlessness had been replaced by a sweetness that may have been tempered by humor but was nonetheless deep and genuine.

I heard that Fox was dying and I flew into New York to see him. He had a private room at St. Vincent's Hospital in the Village. Although a mutual friend had told me Fox was unconscious, when I arrived he'd had a sudden surcease and was sitting up in bed, laughing and entertaining two of "his" authors, straight guys who wrote mystery novels that he'd edited. Fox was attached to a transparent tube and a glucose bag hung high on a pole that rolled around with him when he walked—"My dance partner," he said.

Rumors were circulating in the little world of New York gay writers that Fox had written a nasty, obsessional novel about how I'd abandoned him and cruelly broken his heart and that it was scheduled to be published after his death, but I wasn't afraid of his posthumous revenge. I knew that after I'd left him he and his curator had had a passionate, quarrelsome affair and been inseparable until the curator's death (at thirty-four). I could never have given Fox that sort of belligerent intimacy.

Today he wasn't the least bit cool to me. He didn't want to talk about anything serious; in fact, he spent most of the two hours I was with him joshing heavily with his authors, who fed him tidbits of publishing gossip and kept assuring him how great he looked.

Then I left and three weeks later Fox was dead. I resented my passivity: why hadn't I insisted his visitors leave us alone for a moment? Why hadn't I wrung a bit of truth, even pain, out of the situation? Oh, I never knew what to do or how to behave. Part of me said I should let the dying man set the tone. If he wanted diversion and reassurance, he should have them. If he wanted honesty (but he never did), then he could have that too. Though usually tempted to let things dribble away in inconsequence, this time I felt cheated.

I talked to Ned almost daily on the phone. He told me that one night, at midnight, he'd received a phone call from Fox who was back home from the hospital. "He wanted me to get him some cocaine. I didn't know what I should do since he was so sick, but then I thought that as a friend it wasn't up to me to question him now. I called a dealer, scored quickly and was over there within an hour. The apartment was a mess, the cat was screeching, everything stank. I fed the cat and changed its box while Fox, who could scarcely hold himself upright, was shoveling the coke up his nose."

Ned paused. "The next morning he was dead."

"Don't feel bad," I said. "You weren't going to reform him. He was going to die anyway."

Fox had made all the arrangements for his own memorial ceremony with his usual efficiency. He had chosen the place, made up the guest list, named the speakers and established the order in which they'd address the public. His secretary from his publishing firm had only to follow his detailed instructions. After the eulogies he'd prepared a slide show of the key moments in his life; he'd included the photo of himself as a baton twirler and even a picture of us. The whole event concluded with a recording of The Nylons singing "Up on the Roof" a cappella ("And all my cares drift into space . . .").

This ceremony was his final *coup de théâtre* since Fox, who'd always been so secretive, had at last brought all his friends together—his two movie stars, his straight writers, the actors he'd directed in avant-garde video pieces, the slaves who'd paid him, his long-haired hippy, ex-con father, his respectable grandparents, one of the Washington pages he'd worked with, people from the New York art world he'd met through his curator, his boss. . . . Oddly enough, we all hung around at the Ethical Culture Center after the event because we were so curious about one another and even more fascinated by all the facets of Fox's complex personality that this heterogeneous crowd represented.

Josh, too, was failing. And when Ned couldn't be with him, Butler and Philip were there. Butler was becoming increasingly religious. He brought a pious air to the sickroom, which only annoyed Josh; and Josh worried that Butler would write a story about him. Butler had a full supply of beautiful literary citations with which to mark each stage of Josh's decline. He pillaged his "commonplace book," in which he'd stored up all these apt and quaint quotations, in order to feed his journal, in which he scrupulously recorded the *memento mori* meditations that Joshua's dying had prompted. In a fit of funereal social climbing he wrote many solemn letters (soaked in grief as women used to dab their letters in perfume) to Eddie, who was only enraged by them.

But Butler's lover Philip was efficient, confidence-inspiring. Beneath his tough-talking exterior he deployed an inexhaustible energy focused on Joshua's real needs. Whereas we all felt inept and shy in dealing with doctors, lawyers and heterosexual family members, Philip summoned Josh's brother to New York and reviewed the will, making sure everyone agreed on (or at least accepted) its terms. And Philip had found a clever graduate student to piece together Joshua's last book, to pluck it like a divination out of the entrails of the abandoned computer.

I stopped calling Joshua, nor did he phone me any more. The last time I'd spoken to him he'd seemed so confused, if gentle and kind, that I thought he must be close to the end.

He wasn't. Butler and Philip were disgusted with Lionel, who they insisted neglected Joshua entirely when he was left in charge over the weekend. "When Butler and I drop in on Monday morning it's obvious that Lionel hasn't been feeding Joshua. Of course Josh is just blissed out, always smiling, but you can see he's dehydrated, Lionel hasn't changed his diaper, and he's left Joshua alone for long periods during which he's gone out clubbing. It's criminal behavior—and disgusting that he's going to inherit fifty thousand dollars in cash, which he already knows about. He'd probably like to see Joshua die as soon as possible."

"Surely you're exaggerating?"

"Oh, well," Philip said, lowering his voice for a moment, "he liked Joshua well enough as long as he could meet famous people and go on exciting trips, but now that we're in for the long haul he's lost interest. I'm not saying he's satanic, unless a self-absorbed ninny is Satan. He insists on his right to look after Joshua over the weekend and has become annoyingly pettish with me, but now I've engaged a very sweet black nurse named Ernie who is wonderfully competent. Joshua obviously likes Ernie and if I let two or three days go by with Joshua in Ernie's care—and the care of a night nurse—then he looks clean and well fed, his hair brushed, freesias in the silver vase, just as he always liked them."

I was silently horrified that things had gone so far and that, in the few weeks since I'd stopped phoning, Joshua had become blissed out and demented, bedridden and diapered, and that his preference for freesias was now referred to in the past tense. I kept thinking of Haydn's *The Farewell Symphony*. In the last movement more and more of the musicians get up to leave the stage, blowing out their candles as they go. In the end just one violinist is still playing.

⸺◯ I WAS WRITING a short novel, as punchy as I could make it, about the 1960s, ending with the Stonewall Uprising in 1969 and the beginning of gay liberation. I thought that never had a group been placed on such a rapid cycle—oppressed in the fifties, freed in the sixties, exalted in the seventies and wiped out in the eighties. Although I didn't mention AIDS, which would have been anachronistic, I hoped the book would remind gay readers of the need to fight lest we fall back into the self-hating, gay-bashing past. The Christian Right—my very relatives in Texas!—were now attacking gays, since the gradual collapse of the Evil Empire of Communism left nothing to unite the rich few and the numerous poor on the right into the semblance of unity except a factitious agitation over "family values."

In the past I'd written for an imaginary European heterosexual woman who knew English but didn't live in America, because she functioned for me as a filter, a corrective. I was afraid of preaching to the converted, of establishing character through brand names, of nudging ribs exactly like my own to provoke predictable laughter, of playfully alluding to shared moments of recent history and of ruing attitudes I could count on other gay men to condemn just as readily as I did.

Now, the sadness and isolation I felt—as an expatriate, as the survivor of a dead generation, as someone middle-aged in a gay youth culture—made me turn to other gay men, young and old, as my readers. I wanted to belong to a movement that I scarcely understood, for Larry Kramer had called for anger and activism, but I had nothing to offer but grief and helplessness. More exactly, I wanted to see if the old ambition of fiction, to say the most private, uncoded, previously unformulated things, might still work, might once again collar a stranger, look him in the eye, might demand sympathy from this unknown person but also give him sympathy in return. These secret meetings—unpredictable, subversive—of reader and writer were all I lived for.

The project seemed hopeless. Gay men of my generation, especially those who'd shared my experiences, were dead or dying. The younger ones, with their shaved skulls, pierced noses, tattoos and combat boots, appeared to belong to another race, militant, even military, too brusque and strident to be receptive to my elegies. Whereas pioneer gay novels—Gore Vidal's *The City and the Pillar,* James Baldwin's *Another Country*, John Rechy's *City of Night*—had attracted curious heterosexual readers, now gay fiction was a commodity assigned its two shelves in a few stores, and no heterosexual would venture to browse there, just as no man would leaf through a book shelved under "Feminism." The heterosexual browser or the curious male might have even felt he was trespassing. The category of general literary fiction was vanishing, and its disappearance showed that the new multiculturalism was less a general conversation than rival monologues.

In an American leather magazine I read a personal ad written by someone looking for "a slave, looks indifferent, attitude everything." I felt I answered that description and mailed a groveling response. A month láter I received a letter. The recto side of the letter gave me cruel orders in the same growling, half-literate prose of the original ad. The verso side said, "Surprise! And now for the good news. I'm the very screenwriter who phoned you in June and whom you were unable to see, due to your pressing engagements. Isn't it exciting to think we've found each other 'in the rag-and-bone shop of the human heart'? (Yeats) I know we're going to be a great team, in bed and out! There are so many ways you could help my career—and perhaps I could help yours, too, who knows?

"I'm enclosing all my numbers, but please be cautious since I do live with a lover and, though he's a slave, no reason to hurt him *unnecessarily*.

"Actually, we met years ago at a staged reading of a very camp little musical I wrote the book for, an adaptation of *Gone with the Wind* for an all-male cast, whites played by blacks and vice versa. Do you remember it? We could never get the rights, sadly."

Absurd as the letter was, I started telephoning this guy, Ward, all the time. I'd be in Leeds on a book tour or in Berlin with Hajo, unable to sleep, and I'd phone Ward. Once I might have picked up men who attended my readings, but now most of them trembled when they came up to get their books signed (so venerable had I become in just a few . . . well, it seemed like a few minutes, but it must have been several years). I'd also given dozens of interviews about my HIV status and people, even those who believed in safe sex, were turned off by someone they *knew* was positive. In the past I'd received fan letters asking me for sex; now the letters asked me for advice on how to find a young lover. If I mentioned to a seemingly sympathetic straight friend or younger gay friend how sexually frustrated I was, I could see a look of disgust crossing his or her features, as though to say, "Haven't you created enough havoc with your beastly desires? Couldn't you just . . . *tuck it away* for the duration? Retire?"

Ward told me he was going to be writing a screenplay and working with a producer in San Francisco. I said I was going to New York to say good-bye to Joshua and would hop on a plane out to the West Coast to meet him at last and spend a few days with him.

He said, "I've got to tell you I don't really look as . . . fit as I did in that photo I sent you. That was during my physical high point as a runner—that picture was taken four years ago, *five*!—during the New York Marathon."

"Oh, well, 'looks indifferent, attitude everything,' as the ad says. You know, I should have suspected you were an educated person right there, inserting that fancy phrase into your four-letter obscenities. Anyway, I have a confession, too, although it's probably old news. I've already alluded to it in interviews and you probably know all about it. I'm positive, which I discovered just a year ago when the test became available, but I've probably been positive since the late seventies, or whenever it all started. You know, they're unfreezing the blood samples of people who participated in a hepatitis study in the late seventies and they're finding that many of them were *already* positive back then." But I could hear an unexpected, prim silence accumulating on the other end of the line. "That doesn't make any difference to you, does it, my being positive?"

"Of course not."

"Are you positive?"

"No. My lover and I are both negative."

"Yeah, I guess S&M is mainly a head trip, no need for genital contact. Luckily." I laughed feebly.

"Actually," Ward said with an unforgivable degree of self-righteousness, "my lover and I have been *relatively* faithful and we work too hard to waste much time on sex."

But still I didn't get it. After all, Ward had become famous for an AIDS movie of extraordinary sophistication and compassion and, leaving that aside, he was a middle-aged gay man who'd lived in New York all his life. We arranged that I'd come directly to his San Francisco hotel room when my plane arrived at midnight and slip in beside him if he was already asleep. I was in such a fever of sexual anticipation that I couldn't imagine his being asleep; Ward's dirty, perverse, precise fantasy, as stated in his ad, was the only combination of fifty words that had made me masturbate with hot-faced excitement hundreds of times.

When I rang the bell to Joshua's apartment, Philip—lustrously bearded, boisterously gloomy—let me in. "Well, I'm afraid you waited too long," he called out, heartless and gentle, "there's not much left. If you talk to him you might get a smile, that's about all there's left of cortical response, God knows what it means, probably just a reflex—typical of Josh that his last automatic response should be a smile."

In the front bedroom Joshua lay on his back in the blue and white pajamas I'd sent from Lanvin in Paris. His face was so white, covered with still whiter patches on the temples, that he seemed carved out of a mushroom, a big pale shelf of mushroom growing out of the roots of a tree in wet ground. And yet, when I touched his hand, it was dry, each finger dry as a new, cool stick of blackboard chalk. Even with his lenses in he'd always had trouble seeing, but now, lensless, he could have perceived nothing but light and shadow and movement. Except his eyes looked fixed, glazed over. His nose had grown an inch longer. He was terribly thin ("At last!" I could imagine him exclaiming with a laugh) and looked as though, like Kafka's hunger artist, he could be mistaken for a bit of dust or straw and quickly swept up into a dustpan by an energetic hand.

I said, "Josh?" He smiled, faintly, lifted his eyebrows, blinked encouragingly. His lips pursed slightly, as they always had, as though he wanted to meet the world halfway, not just hear its messages but also sip them, taste them.

I thought, The Egyptians had the right idea, devoting their whole lives to building tombs as big and luxurious as their palaces, mammoth launching pads for eternity, whereas even our richest men and women, who live in twenty rooms, or a hundred, are willing to be slid into a tomb no longer or wider than their lowest servant's cot—which only shows no one really believes in a life after death.

I wanted to build a monument of words for Joshua, big and solid, something that would last a century, although I doubted I had the ability.

I wanted other people to know about his intelligence, which was sympathetic, even diagnostic, but never analytic: he could learn a poet's language in just a few tries, as though he were one of those ethnolinguists who can entirely map out an unknown tongue in just twenty days in the Bush. He could also tell what were that poet's preconceptions, preoccupations, points of unresolved discord, governing metaphors and link all that to his (usually *her*) most intimate experience without gossiping about the details of her or his life. He loved Shakespeare's comedies for the same reason he loved Balanchine's ballets (there on Joshua's wall was a get-well card from Suzanne Farrell, the prima ballerina who was *assoluta* in his heart): both Shakespeare and Balanchine devised new combinations of men and women, of courtship and union, of assertion and accommodation, but transposed into a higher, purer key.

I flew out to San Francisco to see Ward, but he was asleep when I arrived and never touched me once while I was there. He barely looked at me. He was a short, pudgy man with a denture and bad breath. He had meetings with his producer during the day; the hotel he'd chosen was across the street from Golden Gate Park and I went jogging in it for long hours, weeping and running, weeping and running, sitting in the Japanese Tea Garden (with its pagoda, bridges, stream, carp and refreshment pavilion) and drinking hot tea and composing a long poem to Josh, the first I'd written since I'd been a student. I remembered how Josh would say something someone had done (usually Butler, whom he'd nicknamed "Missy") was "grotesque" or "past belief." Now my life seemed to be both.

When Joshua died, Eddie called me to tell me he'd communicated with him already via the Ouija board and that he was fine, on his first day he'd been given a lovely tea party by Wystan Auden and Chopin, and he sent me his love. Josh was very excited since he was scheduled to be reborn soon as a little brown baby girl in Calcutta.

I laughed and hurried to get off the line, so offended was I. Soon afterwards I looked through all the letters I'd ever received from Joshua and

I realized I'd been unworthy of him then, that he'd been sending them through time to me as I would become years later.

⟨⎯⎯⎯⟩ BRICE DIED almost ten years after Joshua, and it was only then that I understood this need to believe the dead go on living, somewhere, at least for a while. In medieval churches the lord and his lady are represented by tomb sculptures that show them as they were at age thirty, no matter how old they were when they died. Thirty was considered the ideal age and the resurrection was supposed to find their bodies perfect. Brice was only thirty-three when he died, but a very, very old thirty-three—three times older: ninety-nine.

He died on March 21st, 1994. On August 11th I wrote: "My day began with tears because I picked up a tarnished silver ball that Brice once gave me (it had rolled behind the radio). I used to walk around with it in my pocket; some delicate inner mechanism makes it chime when you shake it. I suppose by awakening with Tinkerbell I thought Brice could hear it if I rang it. And yet I find something tawdry, seedy, about all this Blavatsky-like cant about communicating with the dead. No, the dead are dead, which is our tragedy and their grandeur."

Those words sound colder, more decided, than what I felt then or even now, two years later, as I approach the end of this book. For a year I went to church every day and lit a candle for Brice; I lit them also in the cloisters beside the cathedral in Barcelona, in the Baroque Swiss church in Einsiedeln, in a church in Lucca, in Montreal and Sydney, wherever I traveled, almost as though I thought that on his distant star he'd like to see these faint pinpricks of light pulsing all over the globe in his honor.

It was also a way of serving him without thinking of him, for now that he was dead he seemed dark, even black, and bigger, certainly crueler. He frightened me and I didn't want to think too much about him, nor about our life together, it had taken too much out of me, cost too much.

Perhaps the price I'd paid was in what I'd lost. Brice had been the first man I'd loved at the same time he loved me. After our first six months together I learned he was, or soon would be, seriously ill. Maybe because I knew he was dying I could love him, for I'd always been more afraid of being overwhelmed by what I possessed than of being abandoned by someone who'd never belonged to me.

He died in Morocco. The day before he died we were in an oasis town. We'd been driving through mile after mile of baked mud and straw cities,

humble citadels that bordered a river in the desert that sometimes became
nothing more than a brook or even a damp line through the sand. The
structures were tall, squared off, often polished, crazy congeries of balconies and turrets and tiny, lopsided doorways. Date palms flourished beside the river; we saw a woman collecting dates in what looked like a bath
towel. Little boys were selling dates in small cages made of palm fronds;
bees were hovering around the rich, oozing fruit.

Brice had stretched out in the backseat, although sometimes he'd sit up
and say, looking at the mud houses, "*C'est superbe . . . superbe . . .*" He spoke
only in a whisper now. His face was covered with a week's growth of beard.
He was so skinny that it hurt him to wear jeans (the seams cut into his flesh-
less nerves and bones); he'd put on a long, flowing blue robe. With his
darkened skin, his beard, his cadaverous face, his skeletal hands, his feeble
walk (I had to hold him up whenever he left the car), he looked Biblical,
like an ancient prophet about to die before we entered the Promised Land.

I was in a panic, determined to drive as fast as possible with the fewest
possible stops back to Marrakesh, where I'd arranged for a private plane
to fly us back to Paris and a good hospital and Brice's own doctor, a celebrated specialist. But now, in this oasis town, he'd lost control of his body,
he was covered with shit. I tried to mop him up as best I could and put
him in clean clothes, long enough to get him into the luxury hotel where
I'd found us an air-conditioned room. We'd rest up, we'd order food from
room service, I'd place calls to Paris, lining up his doctor for an appointment—but as I was helping Brice towards the hotel entrance he fainted
and fell on the hotel lawn. A passing Frenchman said, "Good God, let's
call an ambulance," and I couldn't object, though I knew perfectly well
that an ambulance would take him only to an Arab hospital where there
would be no food, dirty beds, no medicine, lots of flies, doctors who'd
never seen a case of AIDS before. . . .

I can't go on. I can't tell this story, neither its happy beginning nor its
tragic end, the all-night ride through the snowy Atlas mountains in a
freezing ambulance, Brice's angry hateful words to me, the look of his
face, dead, when I awakened at dawn, his mouth open, his eyes startled,
as though he'd seen something dreadful and I'd not been there, conscious,
to share it with him—

◯ I LEARNED that Sean had died. His lover wrote me to say
he'd lived long enough to read what I'd written about him in my

Stonewall novel. I'd always thought that I'd get back to Sean, as though he were a letter, an important letter, I'd failed to answer. Now my correspondent was dead, someone who, because I hadn't watched him age, remained eternally young in my mind. Once, in the 1990s, when I'd given a reading in New York, I saw someone who resembled an old fuck-buddy from the sixties. I rushed up to this guy in his twenties, relieved to see he was alive—but of course it wasn't the same person, how could thirty years have gone by, leaving him untouched? In the same way, if I'd seen Sean at fifty—or seventy, since AIDS would have added twenty more years—I could never have recognized him. When I wrote back to his lover, asking for more details, he didn't respond. As a result, Sean remains for me a booming voice, wincing blue eyes, a long, smooth swimmer's body, courtly manners, a love of literature in every language, a cock that twisted to one side when erect, a Midwesterner's guileless confidence in authority, a desire to laugh and have fun not matched by any genuine merriment. . . .

I'd once told him that I thought in a masterpiece the whole network of impulses could be isolated in any paragraph throughout the book, a monad containing all the important features in miniature; Sean developed this notion into a dissertation. Ironically, for me *he* was the monad, the person whom I'd loved the most intensely and who awakened in me if not the widest, then the deepest feelings. I told him that in a medieval shield when the whole coat of arms was repeated in a miniature inset, this device was said to be placed there *en abîme*; Sean was the abyss into which all of me had fallen.

Now I understood why Eddie had invented his dress-up party version of the afterlife with its amusing social introductions across the centuries and its continuing revelations. It was a normal way of keeping the dead alive. I remember that a graduate student researching a thesis interviewed Eddie about Auden and finally asked, rather peevishly, "Did Mr. Auden say that *before* or *after* he died?" But even for Eddie the Ouija board became a drawing room game that turned sour. Before his own death from AIDS just last year, a depressed, emaciated Eddie told me that he'd followed the board's instructions to go to a certain café in Athens where he'd be sure to meet the fat Indian girl who was Joshua's reincarnation, but the child didn't come. Eddie waited until two in the morning, when the café closed, but the child never showed up.

Nevertheless, a death without rituals is intolerable. Most people would do well to stick with church ceremonies, which are noble and full-throated in the right well tested places and even dull and distracting elsewhere in just the desired degree, but Eddie had a solemn, awed, fluent way of celebrating the great, hard moments. He swirled Joshua's ashes from a gondola into the Grand Canal while reciting a poem he'd written for the occasion.

I went back to the *palazzo* where Joshua had lived. The principessa had asked me to stop by. She led me up to the attic, which looked like the reversed hull of a war ship, all ancient, rough-hewn beams. There, in that maritime desolation, stood a little pile of Joshua's things—dirty white trousers, sunscreen, the typewriter his computer had replaced, an old copy of a *Beaux-Arts* magazine, an extra fan. The principessa behaved as though it was, well, even legally necessary that I do something with these pathetic possessions, Joshua's half-hearted pledge that he'd come back if not the next summer then the one after.

I shrugged, even laughed a bit rudely, took the things away (did she think they were infected with the "Ides" virus?), and dumped them in the trash just outside the door. Joshua's spirit was no more in these things than was our virus; his spirit was lodged in Eddie's pages, in his own, even, I hoped, in mine.

BOOKS BY EDMUND WHITE

"White is a true literary pioneer. . . . He has made
the lives and culture of gay men over the past few decades
not just accessible but inviting."
—*Detroit Free Press*

CARACOLE

In French caracole means "prancing"; in English, "caper." In
Caracole, Edmund White invents an entire world where country
gentry languish in decaying mansions and foppish intellectuals
exchange lovers and gossip in an occupied city that resembles
both Paris under the Nazis and 1980s New York.

Fiction/Literature/0-679-76416-X

THE BEAUTIFUL ROOM IS EMPTY

When the narrator of Edmund White's poised yet scalding autobiographical novel first embarks on his sexual odyssey, it is in the
1950s, and America is "a big gray country of families on drowsy
holiday." That country has no room for a scholarly teenager with
guilty but insatiable stirrings toward other men. Yet even as he
launches himself into an arena of homosexual eros, White's protagonist is also finding his way into the larger world.

Fiction/Literature/0-679-75540-3

THE BURNING LIBRARY

In this collection of essays, twenty-five years of White's nonfiction
writings have been collected in a volume of exhilarating wit, acu-
ity, and candor—a book that is at once a living record of the
author's intellectual development and a chronicle of gay politics,
sexuality, literature, and culture from Stonewall to the age of
AIDS.

Gay Studies/Essays/0-679-75474-1

FORGETTING ELENA

Edmund White's first novel suggests a hilarious apotheosis of the comedy of manners—for, on the privileged island community where *Forgetting Elena* is set, manners are *everything*. Or so it seems to White's excruciatingly self-conscious young narrator, who desperately wants to be accepted in this world where everything from one's bathroom habits to the composition of "spontaneous" poetry is subject to rigid conventions.

Fiction/Literature/0-679-75573-X

GENET
A Biography

Bastard, thief, prostitute, jailbird, Jean Genet was one of French literature's sacred monsters. His career was a series of calculated shocks marked by feuds, rootlessness, and the embrace of unpopular causes and outcast peoples. This most enigmatic of writers has found his ideal biographer in Edmund White, whose eloquent chronicle does justice to the unruly narrative of Genet's life.

Winner of the National Book Critics Circle Award
Biography/0-679-75479-2

SKINNED ALIVE

In *Skinned Alive*, our most influential chronicler of gay life invents a new vocabulary of difference. It is not only the difference between gay and straight, although Edmund White defines that difference better than almost any writer now at work. Here, White measures the distance between an expatriate American and the Frenchman who tutors him in table manners and "hard" sex, or the gulf that separates a young man dying of AIDS from his uncomprehending Texas relatives.

Fiction/Literature/0-679-75475-X

VINTAGE INTERNATIONAL
Available at your local bookstore, or call toll-free to order:
1-800-793-2665 (credit cards only).